Fiona Walker .... partner and two children plus an assortment of horses and dogs. Visit Fiona's website at www.fionawalker.com.

KISS AND TELL

Fiona Walker

sphere

SPHERE

First published in Great Britain as a paperback original in 2011 by Sphere
Reprinted 2011 (three times)

A CIP catalogue record for this book
is available from the British Library.

ISBN 978-0-7515-4409-1

Typeset in Plantin by M Rules
Printed and bound in Great Britain by
Clays Ltd, St Ives plc

Papers used by Sphere are from well-managed forests
and other responsible sources.

MIX
Paper from
responsible sources
FSC® C104740

Sphere
An imprint of
Little, Brown Book Group
100 Victoria Embankment
London EC4Y 0DY

An Hachette UK Company
www.hachette.co.uk

www.littlebrown.co.uk

*For the Horseman with whom I ride night and day;
with all my love.*

Introduction

Eventful Lives – and Dirty Weekends

You have to be an optimist to want to gallop half a ton of super-fit horse over fences shaped like saw-mills, shotgun cartridges, boats, animals and houses. Brave, tough and incredibly upbeat, the event rider is a breed apart and quite the sexiest of all horsemen and women which, in a very sexy pastime indeed, makes them irresistible . . .

Eventing is an equestrian sport originating from the cavalry *Militaire*, and is now hugely popular worldwide. Comprising three disciplines – dressage, cross-country and show-jumping – eventing is the definitive test of both horse and rider, requiring immense stamina, skill, versatility, finesse, dedication and, above all, guts. On a competitive level, riding across country is one of the greatest adrenalin fixes known to man, woman and horse; on a social level, it's like attending a country house party every weekend with your closest chums all around you, gaining access to the most stunning estates in the country and partying in the park every night.

By day, combinations are set three tasks to show their supremacy, like knights and their steeds at a medieval tournament. First they must perform a courtly dance, gymnastic floor exercises set out in a precise pattern, leaping and twirling exactly on the allotted marks and lines while judges all around narrow their eyes and look for faults; this is dressage. Then they must run a gruelling assault course within a given time, leaping huge obstacles, crossing gullies and risking life and limb; that's the cross-country phase. Finally, exhausted now, they enter a gladiatorial arena filled with flimsy jumps to vault over accurately while the clock ticks down – the show-jumping phase. The prize money in eventing may vary dramatically – at some competitions winning barely covering fuel costs, at others the victor gets many tens of thousands – but glory is always magnificent, and the perks are sublime.

Governed by British Eventing in the UK and the FEI (Fédération Equestre Internationale) internationally, affiliated horse trials are graded in difficulty from entry level (BE90 and BE100), through novice and intermediate to advanced. A CIC (Concours International Combiné) is a one- or two-day event ranging from one star (novice) to three star (advanced), and the stages are run as dressage, show-jumping and then finally cross-country. A CCI (Concours Complet International) is a three day event also of one, two and three stars, with the exclusive additional four-star level being the most difficult; the phases are run on successive days in the order of dressage, then cross-country, with show-jumping last. In actual fact, dressage often runs over two days, thus making it a four-day event, but that's typical of eventers, who always give that little bit extra.

Despite a reputation for upper-class elitism, it's a refreshingly egalitarian sport in which men and women of all ages compete equally on horses of unique bravery and talent, in which princes and paupers ride side by side, where intense rivalries are matched by life-long friendships, camaraderie and old-fashioned sportsmanship that's rare in the modern world. Set against idyllic backdrops of grand country houses, ancient parkland and rich farmland, sunshine and mud, tight breeches and loose morals, dogs and wellies, toffs, farmers and tradesmen, silver spoons and shoestrings, horsepower and four-wheel drives, it's the ultimate countryside fix at home and abroad with competitions held all over Europe, the States, Canada, Australasia and beyond.

Here, it's as British as a Range Rover full of black Labradors, a Pimm's picnic on a checked blanket and sunshine and rain in June, with gung-ho galore and plenty of naughtiness behind the scenes . . .

The UK horse trials season runs from March until October, with some international trials and special events taking place year round. Many event riders and their grooms spend much of the competitive season on the road, with their horseboxes acting as second homes, some luxuriously complete with wet rooms, flat-screen televisions, king-sized beds in slide-out pods and even wine coolers. Others offer little more than a sleeping bag on straw bales. Horses are often stalled at events in temporary stabling, much like a military encampment, harking back to the sport's beginnings, although with up-to-date security and state-of-the-art care.

Despite its traditional roots, eventing is a thoroughly modern sport, employing a vast array of groundbreaking expertise, research and ever-more stringent rules. As in any high-risk sport, like skiing or motor racing, fatalities are regrettably inevitable, and much has been changed by the governing bodies to increase safety, from breakable cross-country fences to the introduction of inflatable body protectors for riders. Everything possible is done to make it safe, but nothing can take away from the sheer thrill of riding at speed across solid timber on a super-fit horse that can also perform a balletic dressage test and jump an obedient round over coloured poles.

Event riders have a reputation for living fast, partying hard and making merry, along with their owners, supporters and trials organisers. The horses can be pretty badly behaved too – but what else can one expect from a sport that demands that extra red-blooded sparkle of genius?

Cast List

Hugo and Tash Beauchamp – the eventing world's premier couple, based at Haydown in West Berkshire with their young family
Alicia Beauchamp – Hugo's mother, living on gin and Rothmans in the Dower House

Beccy Sergeant – Tash's stepsister, an inveterate drifter, just back from finding herself
James and Henrietta French – Tash's golf and gardening mad father and stepmother, enjoying retirement in Surrey
Em and Tim – Henrietta's older daughter and her husband, living with many young children and much stress in South London

Faith Brakespear – a talented young dressage rider
Anke and Graham Brakespear – Faith's mother, a former Olympic rider turned bookshop owner and her haulier husband, living in the pretty Cotswolds village of Oddlode
Magnus and Dilly – Faith's brother and his girlfriend, rising musicians now living in Hackney
Chad – Faith's little brother, going through a permanent difficult phase
Kurt and Graeme – Faith's 'gayfathers', the dressage world's premier couple, living in Essex
Fearghal Moore – Faith's birth father, an Irish horse dealer based in County Mayo
Ingmar Olensen – Faith's batty maternal grandfather

Rory Midwinter – pewter-eyed young event rider and hell-raiser, proprietor of Overlodes Equestrian Centre
Truffle Dacre-Hopkinson – his dilettante mother, currently between husbands
Diana and Amos Gates – Rory's sister and her husband, custodians of the Gunning Estate

Spurs and Ellen Belling – Rory's cousin and his wife, busy making babies

Nell Cottrell – scourge of the young Lodes set, mother to baby Gigi, now dating Dillon Rafferty

Milo – Nell's long-term lover, impossibly married to his wife and career in Amsterdam

Pete and Indigo Rafferty – the music industry's legendary Rockfather and his young model wife, who is addicted to adopting orphans

Dillon Rafferty – Pete's son, a singer-songwriter turned Cotswolds organic farmer, currently enjoying a hugely successful comeback. Owns several event horses

Pom and Berry – Dillon's daughters, who live with ex-wife Fawn Johnston in the States

Jules – a long-standing music industry friend, Sapphic muse and horse lover

Sylva Frost – self-publicising pop-singing WAG turned Britain's favourite single mum, constantly reinventing her fame

Koloman and Hain – her two young sons

Mama Szubiak – Sylva's super-ambitious Slovak mother

Hana and Zuzi – Sylva's halfsister and her daughter

Rodney Dunnet – long-suffering producer of Sylva's reality TV show

Lough Strachan – sexy New Zealand event rider, known as the Devil on Horseback

Lemon – his head groom, a jokey failed jockey

Alexandra and Pascal d'Eblouir, Polly – Tash's mother, her French husband and their daughter, living in bohemian decrepitude between Paris and the Loire Valley

Sophia and Ben Meredith, Lottie, Josh and Henry – Tash's ex-model sister and her husband, the Earl of Malvern, and their family

Matty and Sally French, Tom, Tor and Linus – Tash's older brother, an earnest documentary maker, his bubbly wife and their children

The Vs – The Beauchamps' uncommunicative Czech au pairs, Vasilly and Veruschka
Jenny – the Beauchamps' cheerful head girl
Franny – Hugo's irascible former groom
The Bells and the Carrolls – the Haydown tenant farmers
Alf Vanner – Haydown's woodland manager
The Seatons and the Bucklands – owners of some of the Haydown event horses

Penny and Gus Moncrieff – old eventing cronies of the Beauchamps, based in nearby Lime Tree Farm, perennially bickering and broke
Angelo and Denise – landlords of The Olive Branch in Fosbourne Ducis
Niall and Zoe O'Shaughnessy – Penny's sister and her actor husband, parents of young twins
India and Rufus Goldsmith – Zoe's children from her first marriage

Marie-Clair 'MC' Tucson – France's first lady of eventing, living part-time in the States with her wealthy husband
Stefan and Kirsty Johanssen – Swedish event rider and his Scottish wife, based in the States
Lucy Field – the UK's top-ranking female event rider, a flirty blonde
Brian Sedgewick – Team GB's three day event chef d'équipe
Julia Ditton – ex event rider turned BBC commentator
Venetia Gundry – Haydown's most lascivious livery
Gin and Tony Seaton – keen event followers and erstwhile owners

The Bitches of Eastwick – the Beauchamps' lazy Labradors
The Rat Pack – Hugo's terriers
The Roadies – the Haydown guard dogs
Beetroot – Tash's ancient, eccentric mongrel

Event horses Sir Galahad and gutsy Oil Tanker, plus home-bred siblings The Fox, Cub and Vixen, Tash's kind-hearted mare Deep River, fearless Cœur d'Or, beautiful stallion Rio, faithful old White Lies, the brilliant Humpty, and far too many others to mention . . .

Prologue

Melbourne Three Day Event, five years earlier

The mare was not the easiest of rides. She pulled hard, skewed left over fences and spooked away from the crowds. It was like riding a small, charging rhinoceros.

In Melbourne as part of a whistle-stop tour to promote their training manual, *Be Champions the Beauchamp Way*, Tash and her husband Hugo had taken up Australian rider Sandy Hunter's offer of rides at Victoria's legendary three day event, the second oldest in the world. Sandy had been sidelined by injury at the last minute and her horses, fit and ready to run, were at the Beauchamps' disposal. It was an irresistible offer; a top-ten result would be great for publicity. Hugo loved the challenge of chance rides, but Tash far preferred piloting her own horses, whom she knew and trusted after years working together.

Snort, snort, snort, thump, thumpety, thump – jump! The little mare was a rubber ball that bounced around before take-off and never landed the same way twice, but boy could she jump. She ballooned a fairly inconsequential ditch and wheeled left, leaving Tash dangling for a moment, all her weight off centre before those famously long, grippy lower legs and those iron-girder stomach muscles set her right and she kicked on towards the big crowds around the water.

Riding high on adrenalin and positive energy was familiar territory to Tash. She and Hugo had been on the crest of a wave all year, and today was no exception. As soon as she had finished riding across country they were booked for radio interviews, a lecture demonstration and then a sponsors' dinner, at which they would speak. Tomorrow morning they would sign copies of their book before the final show-jumping stage of the competition. As soon as that was over they were flying out to Perth to continue their book tour on the west coast. Garnering publicity was still an alien concept to Tash. This was what she knew best.

Snort, snort, snort. Snatch snatch snatch. Head flying up, duck, dart, crouch.

Utterly focused, contained between leg and hand, the mare prepared to take off at the big log in front of the water. Then, at the last minute, she spotted the wet expanse beyond and seemed to hang in the air, momentum dropping away from her, reluctant to get her feet wet.

With an almighty combination of willpower, voice and inner prayers, Tash propelled the black mare far enough forwards to tip her athletic body into the drink and through it in several sloshing strides until they were out the other side, skewing over a narrow log that would have unseated a lesser rider.

The spectators gave an appreciative roar and whooped applause at the sight of such good horsemanship.

Tash, who loved the Australian eventing crowd – so raucous yet knowledgeable – patted the mare on the neck and then held up her hand in gratitude to the banks of cheering faces just a few feet away, flying past as she galloped away.

A girl ran out of the crowd, the press later reported. A pretty girl: blonde, dressed in a vest, skirt and flip-flops, not the normal hardy spectator on a brisk June day. She ran straight in front of the mare.

All Tash could remember was a blur of blonde hair and pale skin in her path. She heard her own cries of warning, the crowd gasping and shouting, and felt the wrench of the rein in one hand as she pulled the mare sharply left and the contradictory twist of half a ton of muscle, momentum and power beneath her as the mare swerved right. The girl was almost underneath them, so close that she must have felt the heat of the horse's skin and breath. The mare stumbled, flailed on her knees and struggled to stay upright.

A man in an All Blacks hoodie hurled himself from the crowd just in time to grapple the blonde girl to the ground and pull her away from the mare's dancing legs, the two of them rolling across the muddy turf to safety.

Thrown off balance, Tash was only stopped from falling over the horse's left shoulder by her solid black neck swinging suddenly upwards and smacking her firmly on the crown, knocking her back into the saddle as the mare scrambled to her feet. Disoriented, yet still moving forwards in a lurching canter, they carried on towards the next fence while the girl and her dark saviour disappeared into the throng as quickly as they had appeared. Soon another competitor was splashing through the water to distract the crowd.

Somehow Tash managed to get the mare around the rest of the course, but she had no memory of it. Amazingly she finished within the time and retained her top-ten position on the overnight leader board.

Her head injury wasn't spotted for almost twenty-four hours. She could walk, talk and function fairly normally, and insisted she was okay despite a screaming headache and increasing nausea, both of which she put down to the stress of their schedule and the early days of pregnancy. She didn't complain because she didn't want to let anybody down.

The radio interviews had passed in a blur, the demo even more so, but Hugo naturally took control and helped her out when she was tongue-tied, which was often the case in public, despite her private gregariousness.

He had also carried her through their after-dinner speech; he had always been the raconteur, his audience in stitches as he regaled them with scurrilous tales from ten years at the top of the sport. Nevertheless, immediately afterwards he took his wife to one side, blue eyes anxious, and said they must call a doctor. He'd never seen her so grey.

'No!' Tash was adamant, great yawns racking through her. 'I just need to go to bed.'

The next morning she felt as though she'd been drugged. Her contact lenses wobbled in her eyes and she couldn't see straight. There was a foul taste in her mouth. Her swollen breasts ached in sympathy with her pounding, pounding skull.

Schooling the little black mare before breakfast, she had to get off to throw up three times. She felt increasingly spaced out and couldn't purely blame it on morning sickness and nerves. She disliked being the focus of so much attention, not all of it positive. Talk at Werribee Park was all of the 'Melbourne Martyr' and who she might be, a blurred photo of the man in the hoodie pulling the blonde from under the mare's hooves was on the front of every newspaper sports section, his identity as mysterious as the girl whose life he had saved. The media were hasty to draw comparisons with suffragette Emily Wilding Davison, who had run out in front of a Derby field, yet nobody knew what, if anything, this girl had been protesting about. In the gossip-loving lorry park, malicious tongues had already started wagging, suggesting that the blonde might be a spurned mistress of Hugo's.

Any rumours certainly didn't put off the crowds that flocked to the trade stands later that morning, eager to meet the sport's golden couple, the legendary 'Beauchampions'.

'I'm such a dolt, I can't even spell my own name right,' Tash joked as she battled nausea throughout the book signing, painful cramps starting to claw at her belly.

'Remember me?' one buyer asked as he thrust his book towards her.

His face swam in front of Tash's eyes. Lovely face. Big, dark eyes – very honest and appealing, like a young Robert Downey Junior, she thought vaguely as she took the book and wielded her pen.

'Who shall I sign this to?' Her own voice was getting smaller and smaller in her head.

She couldn't hear his reply at all.

'I'm sorry? Who did you say?'

'Like the Scottish loch, only spelt the Irish way.'

'The Scottish loch . . . how lovely . . .' She smiled up at him, pen twirling and eyes crossing.

Then she uncrossed her eyes with great effort. 'I know you.'

He nodded, the beautiful brown eyes so molten they could be fresh from a Lavazza machine.

The espresso eyes and Scottish lochs started swirling again.

She remembered nothing beyond that.

A few hours later the medical team broke it to Hugo that, as well as mild concussion, his wife had suffered a miscarriage.

Tash would dream of lochs quite a lot in coming weeks. In her childhood, when her parents had still been together, the French family had taken a house on the banks of Loch Fyne every August, where they had walked, talked, guzzled oysters and entertained vast groups of friends. Years later she and Niall – her ex – had once had a disastrous attempt at rapprochement on the edge of a loch. Most recently Hugo had taken her salmon fishing near Loch Lomond, and she had loved it with an unexpected passion – from the long walks along river banks, to delicious picnics, to the tweeds and kinky rubber waders, to the endless lovemaking during long evenings in the croft. Their baby had been conceived there.

She coped with the loss with what others took to be characteristic common sense, but in fact hid great well of sadness and self-blame.

She said all the right things if asked. She knew that almost all miscarriages were nature's way of preventing a wretched life. She knew that it was probably always going to happen with this particular pregnancy; it was nothing to do with carrying on competing and maintaining a hectic work schedule, it was just fate taking control. Yet still Tash secretly felt that it was her fault.

She lost a great deal of weight, became listless and withdrawn, stopped phoning friends or painting, and her riding became so unfocused and slapdash that Hugo banned her from top competitions for the rest of the season after a succession of three crashing falls at advanced events.

'We lost the first life we created.' He took her in his arms six weeks after Melbourne, as he did night after night, and enfolded her beneath the angle of his jaw. 'I loved that little shared bit of us, just as I love every bit of you. And I will fight for all of us more now, for you and for our children. We *will* have children, Tash.'

Tash wanted to believe him so badly, and his words did help enormously, but some scales had fallen irretrievably from her eyes with that lost child and, with each barren month that passed after Melbourne, she mourned motherhood a little more.

The stray girl from the crowd and that moment of chance, of near-fatality, haunted her for years to come. She played what very little of it she remembered over and over again in her head but she could never remember enough to paint a full picture. As pregnancy continued to elude her she felt she was being punished for not stopping that day. She threw herself back into her riding, reaching the top-ten in the FEI world rankings for the first time and joining Hugo on the national squad. Her top horse and prolific stallion, The Foxy Snob, became the highest point-scoring horse in history and, to Hugo's mild pique, got more fan mail than any of them. Yet her lost chance at motherhood was never far from her mind, however momentous the highs, affectionate the support and prolific the accolades.

Almost three years later she received an anonymous letter, post-marked the Solomon Islands. Written on woven, hand-made paper, in a beautiful indigo script, it simply read:

A heart was lost in Melbourne; it will always be lost. So many locks and not enough keys; it's easier to be lost than found. But I will make amends. Pax nobiscum.

When he read it Hugo was all for calling in a private detective, believing his wife to be stalked. Tash told him not to be so silly and tucked the letter among her keepsakes in a shell-studded box she kept at the bottom of her wardrobe.

Just days after receiving it she conceived Cora.

Chapter 1

When a small puddle suddenly appeared beneath her in the Waitrose queue, Tash Beauchamp thought that her waters had broken a fortnight before her due date.

It was only after her checkout lane had been closed, the in-store janitor and duty manager called, and half the neighbouring staff and customers alerted to the prospect of a live birth in aisle five, that the true cause of the ever-expanding pool beneath Tash's trolley was discovered.

Her fresh deli pork and sage kebab sticks had broken through their wrapping and speared a carton of pineapple juice, which was splashing everywhere. The smell was unmistakeable.

'Shame,' the manager lamented as Tash, eighteen-month-old Cora and their shopping were relocated to another till. 'We've never had a birth here – a couple of deaths, several proposals and a nasty case of ABH in the freezer section just last month, but no babies. You could have called it Rose if it was a girl. Imagine the ambulance arriving while you're in the last stages of labour, desperate to get to hospital – "Not yet, baby Rose. Wait. Wait, Rose!"; Waitrose. Getit?'

Tash flashed a weak smile. 'Actually, it's a boy.'

'Oh, lovely,' the manager beamed at little Cora, who had a finger rammed in each nostril, her tongue poking out between pudgy thumbs. 'One of each. When's he due?'

Tash started heaving her canvas shopping bags in to the trolley, longing to sit down. 'First week of August.'

'Here – let me,' the manager took over. 'So he'll be an Olympic baby. You could name him after a gold medallist.'

'His father would certainly like that.'

'We've got a local hopeful here – lives up on the downs. Hugo something . . . Beaumont or Butcher? Comes in here quite a lot. Everyone says he'll bring back gold this year. Rides horses, I gather – not really my thing. I'm allergic, and I always think the poor horse does most of the work, don't you? They should get the medals! This bloke's a right toff and a bit of an arrogant sod, to be honest, but you forget that when national pride's at stake, don't you?'

'You certainly try.'

'So do you have any names lined up?'

'His father wants to call him Hugo.'

'Does he? What a coincidence!'

'I've steered him towards Amery.'

'What?'

'Amery – it's a Beauchamp family name.'

'Beauchamp, you say?' The manager started to grow pale.

'Cora's daddy is Hugo Beauchamp, isn't he darling?' Tash smiled at her little girl and then laughed as she excitedly lisped: 'Daddy winth gold! Daddy winth gold!' as Hugo had taught her, although she didn't understand what it meant. Along with 'star', 'pig', 'hug' and 'dog', these were the only words she could say. To Tash's continual concern she had yet to say anything close to 'Mummy'.

The store manager was still blustering with embarrassment as she lifted the last of the shopping into the trolley. 'I'm sure he's not at all arrogant at home – busy man like him hasn't much time for pleasantries in a supermarket.'

'He's supremely arrogant at home.' Tash sighed fondly, eyeing the green bag that was spilling with ingredients for the intimate Olympic send-off meal she was planning for that evening.

'But romantic.' The manager was eyeing the groceries too – the clichéd champagne, truffles, smoked salmon and strawberries. 'You're a lucky couple. Once we had kids, the husband and I were lucky if we managed half an hour together to sit down in front of *EastEnders*, let alone fresh flowers every week and romantic candlelit meals.'

Tash removed the candles from Cora's sticky grip, as she was using them to smack the manager on the bottom. 'What flowers?'

'The ones your husband buys here every week,' she beamed cheerfully.

Tash swallowed, trying very hard to beam back.

Hugo never bought her flowers.

'His father was *just* the same,' Alicia sniffed disparagingly when Tash called in to drop off her fags and gin. 'He started taking mistresses as soon as I had the boys.'

Tash gaped at her mother-in-law, who was already pouring two vast gin and Its, even though it was barely midday.

'I'll stick to tea, thanks.' She headed for the kettle, waving away Alicia's offer of a Rothmans.

'You girls today!' She sparked up, but in a conciliatory gesture reached behind her to open a window. 'I smoked all the way through both my pregnancies and look at Hugo and Charles. Both marvellous specimens.'

'Hmm.' Tash topped up Cora's beaker of juice with water from the tap and handed it down to her, where she was playing with Granny Lish's elderly pug, Beefeater. Unlike his predecessor, Gordons – known universally as 'Thug the pug' – Beefy was as long-suffering and gentle as he was sad-eyed, creased and curly-tailed. He and Cora adored one another.

'The secret to stopping him straying is to get your figure back as soon as you've had the baby,' Alicia commanded grandly, draining the first gin and It and starting on the second.

'Really?' Tash looked over her shoulder worriedly as she put a teabag into a chipped bone-china cup.

'Absolutely!' Alicia avowed, Spode-blue eyes briefly appearing through their curtains of pale, crepey skin as they stretched wide in Tash's direction and then cast their critical way down to her bottom. 'Men can't stand the great fat Hausfraus most women become after childbirth. I existed on gin, cigarettes and sultanas for six months after Charles.'

'You still do,' Tash muttered, having as usual filled her mother-in-law's fridge with ready meals that she knew would get thrown out by the char at the end of the week, when they had passed their sell-by dates. In the short time that she had been shopping for Alicia the week's list never altered – a litre of Bombay Sapphire, a litre of Martini, two hundred Rothmans, two lemons, two packets of Ritz crackers, soft cheese and a biscuit assortment box.

'Can't manage sultanas nowadays – not with these teeth,' Alicia veiled her clever blue eyes behind their creases once more and bared her teeth instead – very expensive but ill-fitting bridgework in pale cream marbled with old gold nicotine stains, like antique ivory.

Tash made her tea and then settled at the kitchen table to watch Cora play, her back aching.

'When do your new couple arrive?' Alicia had noticed how much

Tash was struggling in late pregnancy, although she hadn't offered to help at all. Since writing off her car when flying rather high on gin and winnings on the way back from a bridge night at Busty de Meeth's Wiltshire pile, Alicia had been in no hurry to replace it. Having relied upon a personal driver up until the age of fifty-three, she had loathed taking the wheel in recent years and was enjoying the return to delivered groceries, chauffeured transport and more visitors, even if that did put rather a lot of pressure on her already over-stretched and heavily pregnant daughter-in-law. Nor was Alicia keen to help out with childcare; having relied entirely upon nurses, nannies, housekeepers and cooks when bringing up her own sons, she had no real working knowledge of babies whatsoever, although she was pretty useful with foundling lambs, whelping dogs and foaling mares.

'The Czechs can't start until the end of August,' Tash sighed. 'The agency couldn't come up with anybody sooner. Radka and Todor really left us in the lurch.' The Bulgarian couple that had been working for Tash as au pairs for almost a year had done a moonlight flit a fortnight earlier, to go vegetable packing in Lincolnshire for three times the money.

'I thought they were called Ratty and Toad?' Alicia flicked her fag ash into the sink.

'That's what Hugo called them. No wonder they left. They came here to improve their English, poor things, and as soon as they learned enough to find out what we were calling them they buggered off.'

Tash felt absurdly hurt by the defection, having thought herself very close to Radka, who adored Cora and who shared a very giggly sense of humour with Tash. She and the easy-going but money-obsessed Todor had become like family, and now Tash felt as though a younger sister had run away from home. Added to which, she was really struggling to manage the house and riotous garden at Haydown with just the family's pensionable retainers Gwenda and Ron for help.

Totally wrapped up in the Olympic build-up, Hugo barely registered the Bulgarians' absence, whereas Tash mourned them like missing limbs.

'Isn't your mother supposed to be staying with you for the Olympics?'

'She cried off. Something came up and she can't get away – to do with Polly, I think.'

Tash's mother Alexandra lived in France with her second husband, Pascal, and their eighteen-year-old daughter Polly, who had deferred her place to study fashion at a Parisian college and was currently causing her parents a great many sleepless nights as she spent the year backpacking with a group of friends.

'Beautiful child.' Alicia was a great admirer of aesthetics and Polly was very aesthetic indeed, if completely untamed. 'Bound to be kidnapped by slave traders or suchlike.'

'God, don't say that!' Tash gulped, stooping awkwardly to gather Cora protectively to her bump. 'After what Daddy and Henrietta went through over Beccy, Mummy is fretting all the time.'

'Your stepsister? Wasn't she banged up for drug smuggling?'

'It was awful. Daddy had to fly out to Singapore four or five times. Poor Henrietta had sworn she'd never go there again – her first husband died out there, you see. She must think the place is cursed.'

'Rubbish. I adored Singapore. Henry and I were regulars. So much more evolved than Hong Kong, I found. The Martini bar at Raffles mixes a very game gin sling.' She reached for her drink with a nostalgic sigh.

The conversation had triggered a vague memory that Tash was grasping to retrieve. On cue her mobile phone rang in her bag. It was Hugo, the personalised ringtone set to galloping hooves, which he found hugely embarrassing.

Cora immediately started screeching excitedly, a trick she had recently developed to distract her mother during calls and draw attention back to herself.

'Hello . . . Hi . . . What? Sorry – I can't hear a thing; Cora's shouting and it sounds as though you're sitting on a tractor.'

'I *am* sit . . . on a tract . . . or!' he bellowed, though to Tash his voice was barely audible. 'The bloo . . . muck . . . eap needed emptying and . . . know what Jenny's . . . ike about revers . . . this . . . ing.' Their head girl was terrified of the old yard tractor. 'Your . . . mother's here.'

'My mother?' She gasped in delight. Perhaps Alexandra had changed her mind about coming after all.

Hugo sounded far from delighted. 'And your sister. They . . . to lunch, appar . . . tly.'

'But Polly's in Vietnam— shh, Cora.' Tash lifted her chin up as the little girl tried to grab at the phone. Denied her target, she shrieked at the top of her voice.

'Not . . . olly. Th . . . sh . . . Jailbird . . . bloody inconvenient . . . lympic . . . bloody . . . uck off.'

'What? I really can't hear anything, Hugo.'

Realising Tash needed help with Cora, Alicia lunged forwards and started to try to distract her granddaughter by waving her cigarette around in pretty patterns and clinking the ice in her glass, blowing kisses and humming 'Ain't Misbehavin''. Cora, enchanted, fell silent and stared. Tash, appalled, couldn't concentrate on what Hugo was saying at all.

'Just get back here!' he ordered and rang off.

It was a beautifully bright, blustery morning as Tash drove the short distance across Haydown land from Alicia's cottage, which her mother-in-law grandly insisted upon calling The Dower House, but was in fact the old gamekeeper's lodge. The avenue of beeches that led out of the woods was rustling feverishly overhead and casting dappled shadows through the open sunroof.

'. . . and on that farm he had a cow, ee eye ee eye oh!' Tash sang along to the nursery rhymes CD on the stereo. Behind her Cora was making 'moo' sounds from her car seat and pointing at a field of sheep through the window.

The land surrounding them was farmed by the same two tenant families that had maintained it when Henry Beauchamp had been alive. The fourth generations of the Bell and the Caroll families (the Ding Dongs and the Singalongs as they were affectionately known to the Beauchamps) were respectively custodians of a small mixed dairy, beef and sheep herd run on the sheltered and lush meadows of Lower Farm, and five hundred acres of arable on the fertile, open hills of Upper Farm. The rest of the estate was divided into huge tracts of dark, serried woodland and flinty, windswept downland that was variously leased out for shoots, timber production and grazing, plus the long tree-skirted valley of neglected parkland closer to the house, and the huge equestrian operation that Tash and Hugo ran from the main house and yard.

And Haydown House never failed to lift Tash's heart when she saw it. A brick-and-flint William and Mary country house with the show-stoppingly perfect symmetrical face of a great classical beauty and the broad shoulders of a paternal hug, it was an amazing place to call home. Perched high on the Berkshire Downs, on the edge of the pretty village of Maccombe, surrounded by protective high pink-brick walls, beautiful gardens and its courtyards of old stables, coach house, cottages and barns, it was a daydream of a place to live.

Even though it was getting very ragged around the edges, cost a fortune to run and was impossible to keep remotely clean and ordered, Tash adored it with a passion second only to that for her family and animals.

As she drove along the farm track that led past the orchards and then beneath the clock-tower archway into the old coaching yard she could see Hugo's pack of dogs sunning themselves on the flagstones outside his office, but the door was wide open and the place deserted. Glancing left towards the biggest and oldest of the three stable yards she spotted Jenny, sporting a Team GB baseball cap, hosing one of the youngsters' legs. Waving, she drove on past the big open barn that housed straw and hay and along the back drive to the house itself, passing the overgrown grass tennis court and croquet lawn, and the lichen-flecked walls of the kitchen gardens. Behind the house, by the peeling black-gloss back door to the boot room that absolutely every-body used when calling at the house, apart from Jehovah's witnesses and travelling salesmen, a smart navy blue Golf was parked beside Hugo's dusty Discovery.

Tash let out a groan of recognition. It wasn't her mother that had arrived unexpectedly to lunch. It was her *step*mother, Henrietta.

On cue, she appeared at Tash's own back door, the perfect host-ess as opposed to a forgotten guest, all welcoming smiles and creamy blonde neatness in Berketex and pearls. Then a younger, pinker face topped with purple and green beaded dreadlocks appeared around the door behind her, and Tash realised that prodigal daughter and drug smuggler Beccy had come for lunch too.

'Oh Christ,' she covered her mouth in horrified recall.

She had issued the invitation weeks ago, without thinking how close to the Olympic and baby countdowns it would be. It hadn't been long after Beccy had finally made it back to the UK amid a spattering of press coverage and a huge wave of family relief. Tash had been so excited and pleased that all her father's hard work to exonerate Beccy and ensure her pardon from her fifteen-year sen-tence had paid off that she had picked a date at random. She must have forgotten to write it in the diary. Henrietta meanwhile – as organised a wife, mother and stepmother as she had been a PA to James all those years ago – had stuck faithfully to it, bringing Beccy, a basket of home-made jam and biscuits, a lift-the-flap book for Cora and a clutch of Babygros for the bump. She had even brought a lamb bone for Tash's dog, Beetroot.

'I never know what to do with them now that we don't have the Labs any more,' Henrietta apologised as she proffered the leg-bone wrapped in a Marks and Spencer bag, like a blood-encrusted caveman's club. 'It seems such a waste to throw them out.'

'I've told her she should get another dog' – Beccy resumed her position sitting at the kitchen table, poring over *Horse & Hound* – 'but she says James won't let her.'

'Your father says dogs tie us to the house,' Henrietta explained to Tash. 'He no longer shoots, after all – it plays havoc with his tinnitus. Now that he's retired and the girls have left home we do love to get away.' James had taken to whisking Henrietta away for lengthy golfing holidays in South Africa in the years since the last of their long line of Labradors had passed away.

'I'm back to house-sit now,' Beccy pointed out idly as she flipped to the classified section to look at Dogs for Sale. 'How about a Labradoodle?'

'You know it's not up for discussion, darling,' Henrietta smiled stiffly as she continued waving the lamb bone around, suddenly looking sad. Tash knew that her stepmother desperately missed having dogs, her many generations of yellow Labrador 'golden girls'. They had been her children, and even having her youngest daughter back was no match for the unconditional love of her Labs.

'I'll give this to Beetroot when the rest of the pack's backs are turned,' Tash promised, taking the bone before handing Cora to 'Granny Hen' for a cuddle. She then mixed them all Buck's Fizzes from the champagne and freshly squeezed orange juice she'd just bought for her romantic evening with Hugo, before setting about transforming the rest of the ingredients lined up for that good-luck supper into a girls' lunch instead.

Watching her, Beccy vowed that she would never, ever get pregnant. Tash had once been really quite stunning – Beccy had certainly envied her height and athleticism over the years. With a fine-boned, striking face set on a long, elegant neck, she had always possessed head-turning looks, made all the more stunning by her mismatched eyes, one amber and one green. Admittedly, she'd never learned to tame that mop of rather bushy, wavy brown hair which every riding hat moulded into a different, rebellious shape, and her dress sense had always been very hit and miss, but Beccy – who had struggled to do anything with her limp blonde tresses and extensive range of pastel fleeces and pale jeans before discovering dreadlocks, hats and Indian silk kaftans – was not particularly critical on that front. What appalled her was the bulge.

It stuck out like the huge bonnet of an ugly American car, a great snarling radiator grille of checked maternity top leering over Tash's wrinkly navy leggings, emphasising her long, bandy legs and – horrors – a bottom that had spread far and wide since forfeiting the saddle for the birthing ball.

Rendered red in the face from just the simplest of exertions, like chopping salad or loading plates on a tray, Tash panted her way around the kitchen on swollen ankles. Beccy was too busy observing in appalled wonder to offer to help and Henrietta, chattering nonsensically with a giggling Cora, didn't seem to notice.

Tash's skin looked dry. She had bags under her eyes and her usually high, hollow cheeks were puffy and blotchy. She even has a bit of a double chin, Beccy realised. And aren't those upper arms just beginning to get a hint of dinner-lady bingo wing? Oh. My. God. I am *never* having a baby.

Oblivious to the scrutiny, Tash had loaded two trays and was rubbing her wrists which were numb in parts and stinging with pain in others.

'We'll eat outside on the terrace,' she announced, unable to face clearing the huge scrubbed-pine table in the kitchen that was so overloaded with detritus these days that it had taken on the shape of a rhino. Nor could she face the dusty formality of the dining room proper. The house had really begun to go to pot since Radka's departure. She felt ashamed, doubly so because Henrietta always kept Benedict House so immaculate.

But Henrietta was far more concerned about safeguarding her expensively styled hair than encountering a little house dust. She had promised to look in on an old school-friend near Marlborough for tea and didn't want to arrive looking like Boris Johnson after a boozy lunch.

'Isn't it a bit breezy?' she worried.

'Nonsense. It's bracing!'

They ate lunch with their windswept hair and flapping clothing sticking to their food, forced to shout to make conversation above the sound of the groaning trees, flapping parasol and madly rustling leaves.

Only Cora was spared the elements. Hastily stuffed with an organic pouch meal and a satsuma, she now napped peacefully upstairs with the black-out blind lowered, a lullaby CD on auto-repeat.

Tash battled to keep her rocket and watercress salad on her plate as she alternately made small talk and apologised for Hugo's absence.

'The build up to the Olympics is always absolutely frantic,' she explained. 'He's hardly here, and when he is there's a mountain to do. Normally I can take the slack, but with this so huge' – she patted her unborn boy – 'I'm next to useless around the yard – I can't ride, I can hardly muck out and groom, he won't let me turn out or lunge.'

'Well that's one of the reasons we're here—' Henrietta started, but her daughter interrupted.

'It must be crap being sidelined after all the excitement of both going last time.'

Four years earlier, Tash was one of the Olympic team that had flown their horses half way around the world, hotly tipped for gold. It had been a thrilling time. The media had gone into overdrive following the glamorous husband and wife duo on the road to what was seen as almost guaranteed glory. They had been invincible for the two years beforehand, winning every principal event, rivalling one another for top slot and taking the sport into a new realm of popularity. Together they had endorsed endless products with lucrative sponsorship deals, written two best-selling training books and a double-headed autobiography, held sell-out lecture-demonstration tours on both sides of the Atlantic, featured in their own TV series on a specialist countryside channel, sold countless DVDs on the back of it and become universally known as the Beauchampions.

Then, amid all this furore, they had gone to the Olympics and returned empty-handed. It was a crashing blow to mutual and national pride. Tash's superstar stallion The Foxy Snob, veteran of World and European Championship teams, had boiled over in the dressage, unable to handle the atmosphere and floodlights, which meant that she was too far from the top ten to make her score competitive, despite the double clear that followed. And Hugo, far more humiliatingly, had fallen off at one of the smallest fences on the course on cross-country day, live on worldwide satellite television streaming, catapulted from the saddle when his horse left a knee and pitched over, a fluke accident that could have happened to anyone. The resulting elimination – and the fact that his horse had then buggered off at speed back to the stables to leave him with a very long walk home to his team-mates – obsessed him to this day. Selected to represent Great Britain again at the upcoming Games, he was determined to defend the family's honour as well as that of his country.

'It's a nice sort of sideline, being pregnant,' Tash told her stepsister carefully. 'I only wish I could be there to support the Brits and Hugo this time, but he insists I am far too close to giving birth and I'd only make him nervous.'

'Too right.' Beccy gave the monster bump another horror-filled glance across the table, noticing that Tash had to sit with her knees apart like an old man, vast belly thrust out between her and the table.

'Besides, I'm needed here.' Tash sighed, distractedly watching a piece of French bread fly off her plate in a gust of wind and land in Beccy's hair. Given all the other beads, ribbons and clips adorning the colourful dreads, it blended in quite nicely.

'I thought you just said you couldn't do anything around the yard?' Henrietta helped herself to more smoked salmon, which whipped around on the end of her fork like a jaunty orange flag.

'I can't physically do much, but I can oversee things. Jenny is going to be with Hugo and we're really short-staffed right now so we've got a couple of agency people along with the part-timers from the local villages and I'll have to muddle along as best I can.'

'That's exactly what we wanted to talk to you about—' Henrietta tried again, but again Beccy interrupted her.

'I'm glad your baby's going to be a Leo,' she told Tash, fingering the talismans around her neck. 'They're so positive and determined. Cora's an Aquarian like me, isn't she? We have a terrible time deciding what we want from life. I wanted to be a dog groomer for years, didn't I, Mum? James could never understand it.'

'And then a vet,' Henrietta concurred, 'then a riding instructor and an event rider, which is what we were going to—'

'I remember that!' Tash laughed. 'You did a stint with the Stantons as a working pupil, didn't you?'

Beccy nodded, eyes flashing.

'They're a lovely family.' Tash was hugely fond of the big local clan that had competed for several generations and were as synonymous with dressage and event riding as the Whitakers were with show-jumping.

'I didn't stay long enough to find out,' Beccy said quietly.

'Why ever not?' Tash had forgotten most of the details of her stepsister's attempt at a competitive career, which had been going on at about the time she and Hugo had first got together, almost ten years earlier, although she did recall her father buying Beccy a very expensive horse. And Beccy had definitely possessed a lot of talent as a jockey, she recalled, but as with most things she'd quickly lost interest once the going got tough.

'James and I had a falling out,' Beccy muttered now.

'Yes, well, he's always felt rather guilty about that.' Henrietta cleared her throat, hair whipping up from her face to reveal deep worry lines embossed on her brow.

'He sold my horse,' she gulped.

'That sounds familiar.' Tash sympathised, having fallen foul of her father's rather brutal brand of paternal vengeance several times in her early years.

'To Hugo,' Beccy was close to tears now.

'Which one was it?'

'Butternut Squash.'

'But he—'

'Was sold straight on to America for twice the money,' Beccy nodded forlornly. 'Hugo promised James that we would always have first refusal if he sold him.'

'Oh dear.' Tash watched as another piece of bread flew off her plate, this time wedging itself in the foliage of the golden hop climbing an upright of the pergola behind Beccy. 'It was a long time ago. Hugo has mellowed a lot since then. And the horse did really well, didn't he? Kirsty Johanssen bought him when she and Stefan moved out to Virginia, I remember. He was placed at Kentucky one year.'

'*I* could have gone four-star with him,' Beccy lamented, conveniently forgetting that the chances of herself at seventeen producing the horse to international level had been nil, whereas Hugo had spotted his potential and moved him on to a top-flight career path.

'Instead you went backpacking for a year and ended up staying away for almost a decade,' Henrietta muttered under her breath, 'half of it incarcerated in a potty bloody cult and then in prison.'

'Do not pass go, do not collect five hundred pounds,' Beccy sniffed, shooting her mother a dirty look.

'It cost your stepfather considerably more than that to secure your liberty,' her mother whispered, now holding her hair down with one hand and eating with the other.

Tash swallowed awkwardly. She was never sure whether the subject of her stepsister's jail sentence was off limits or not. It seemed impolite to casually drop it in to conversation – 'Now you're back from Changi Women's Prison, you must relish these cool summer days?' – yet to ignore it was ridiculous. Similarly, for several years before fatefully moving on to South-East Asia as a part of her travels, Beccy had sequestered herself in an ashram with a mystical guru who took all her money, but that long episode was also never mentioned, despite the many trips Henrietta had made at the time to try to talk her daughter into coming home. Back then Beccy had taken the clothes, the money and the Marmite on offer and stubbornly stayed put, claiming that she had seen the light. Thus her 'year out' had slowly become almost a decade's sabbatical of expensive self-denial, self-discovery, self-satisfaction and self, self, self. She hadn't won many allies among the Frenches.

It was common knowledge in the family that, at Henrietta's behest, James had continually fed funds into his stepdaughter's account to safeguard her travels and enable her quick passage home whenever the need arose. Unfortunately that need had only presented itself when Beccy – finally leaving the safety of the ashram because the mystic suddenly closed it down to relocate to Epping Forest and buy himself a premier-league football team – travelled on to Singapore and found herself behind bars, her charmed travels coming to an abrupt end. As a result, that passage home had been very hard won and very, very expensive. Ten months in a Singapore women's prison had finally knocked the glitter off Beccy's globe-trotting life. Now home amid mother comforts, she had re-dyed her dreadlocks, been to a few summer music festivals and tied fresh dream catchers up above her bed in the family home on the Surrey borders, as though she hadn't been away and the gap between seventeen and twenty-seven was non-existent.

Now Tash regarded her in wonder, memories creeping back of Beccy's teenage desire to be a professional rider, bankrolled by her reluctant stepfather as she joined the hundreds of hopeful young things who thought eventing could be a career. Surely James's bull-headed sale of her horse hadn't been the reason that she'd bulk-bought tie-dye, renewed her passport and taken her prolonged hippy trip? If so, it was a gross overreaction. But Beccy had always been as impetuous as she was ingenuous.

She certainly looked much the same, to Tash's surprise – fresh faced and pink cheeked, with those big, pale-lashed grey-blue eyes, an upturned nose and a dusting of freckles. It was a little-girl face, and seemed at odds with the hippy paraphernalia. Tash had envisaged her gaunt and weathered from her life on the road, her many adventures in far-flung climes. Much of the time that she had been travelling, especially those first years, remained unaccounted for, months having passed when she hadn't called, emailed or sent so much as a postcard, and when she had apparently crossed several time zones without explaining how or with whom. Yet Beccy's face still looked as innocent as a bisque doll that has been dressed in Bratz clothes and then covered with pen marks by the rebellious child playing with it.

'So what are you planning to do with yourself now?' she asked her.

'Come and work here.' Beccy laughed, her eyes sliding toward her mother. 'I thought it had all been arranged.'

'Yes, well I did mention something, but Tash has been very busy lately . . .'

Tash briefly closed her eyes as another lost memory popped up to mortify her.

Not long after Beccy had returned home Henrietta had called Haydown to talk through the possibility of Tash and Hugo helping Beccy back on to the road towards a 'normal' life. Terrified of losing her daughter to the high seas again, Henrietta thought it would be good for her to return to one of the passions she'd held before the travelling bug had bitten. She had even persuaded James that it might be worth buying her a horse again. She had put him on the phone to Tash, who in turn had handed her father to Hugo to talk through options. Then she'd wandered off to go to the loo, got distracted and forgotten all about the call until now. She had no idea how Hugo had left it at all.

'He offered Beccy a job,' Henrietta explained, still frantically trying to keep her hair from blowing in her eyes. 'Said to leave the arrangements to you, but that she could start as soon as she felt ready.'

'He did?' Tash gulped. It sounded very unlike Hugo.

'He did,' Henrietta assured her. 'James was very clear on the detail.'

'Gosh.' Tash tried not to look too appalled. They could really do with an extra pair of hands around the yard, after all. 'And do I take it you're ready now?'

Shrugging, Beccy stared back, looking far from ready. She just looked cornered, fed up and willing to do anything to get away from her over-fussing mother and her stepfather's badgering.

'I want to bring a dog with me,' she said, sounding just like her seventeen-year-old self.

'You'd be better off bringing a horse if you want to compete again,' Tash pointed out.

'Hugo said I could ride yours while you're off the circuit.'

'He *did*?' She was staggered.

Beccy looked rather dreamy, clearly having not lost her teenage crush on her stepsister's husband.

'I think I'd better start with something easier than Snob, though,' she told Tash. 'I'm a bit rusty; I'll build up to him gradually.'

Tash looked away, the sudden lump in her throat choking her. 'You'll have to dig him up first.'

'Huh?'

'He died, Beccy. Three months ago. Colic.' It was still so raw, she felt winded with pain by the loss of her greatest campaigner and most loyal servant.

'I didn't know!' Beccy was mouthing stupidly.

'You were in—' about to say 'jail', Tash hastily changed it to 'Singapore at the time; you can't be expected to know.'

Looking across the table she saw huge tears in Beccy's eyes and suddenly realised that it *could* work out. Beccy understood what made them all tick; it had made her tick once too. She loved and understood horses and the sport. If she really had taken off around the world because her dreams of a riding career had been scuppered, she deserved a second chance.

'I have other horses that you might remember,' she told her. 'Hunk's retired now, but Mickey's still going strong, you'll like him. And a couple of the novices I was competing last year are really good, straightforward sorts to get your feel back.'

'So when does she start?' Henrietta asked, her hair now a lopsided beehive. 'Only James and I are going to the Algarve next week and were rather hoping she could be here by then.' She made it sound as though she was trying to offload a particularly troublesome pony that needed schooling on. They clearly didn't want Beccy left alone in the family house in their absence.

'It's the Olympics next week,' Tash said weakly, trying not to feel affronted that her father was leaving the country just as his son-in-law was riding for gold.

'Oh, yes – so you said. Well that's brilliant, isn't it? You can watch all the live coverage together.' Hair on end, Henrietta helped herself to another glass of champagne – totally unheard of when she was driving; she normally restricted herself to a thimble. 'This calls for a toast, I think, don't you?'

Tash and Beccy eyed one another with suspicion.

Chapter 2

'I agreed to no such thing!' Hugo raged later. 'They can forget it. That girl is completely unreliable. Look at her disappearing act in the Far East, followed by all that drug nonsense.' He pushed his still-full plate away from him and lit a cigarette, tipping back in his chair and leaning against the balustrade so that the smoke wouldn't go near Tash.

Their romantic Olympic send-off meal was not going according to plan, even though the weather had come on side and was draping the terrace in the fire-glow warmth of evening sunshine, the wind having dropped to a seductive whisper, the birds roosting melodically in the beech wood beyond Flat Pad, the dusty old pony paddock, a huge moon already suspended overhead like a paper ceiling lamp waiting to be switched on.

Despite being forced to defrost an inappropriately unseasonal venison casserole, Tash had tried to recapture some of her intended seductive atmosphere with lemon-scented outdoor candles, lanterns and fire-torches to keep away the bugs, velvet throws on the chairs and the chimera burning away with sweet-scented apple smoke, clashing beautifully with the big bunches of sweet peas that tumbled informally from painted jam-jars on the table. She had washed her shoulder-length brown waves so that they gleamed like wet snakes and put on make-up for once – not too much because Hugo disliked anything obvious – and was wearing a pretty peacock-blue silk tunic dress that minimised the bump and showed off her long, fake-tanned legs that were only very slightly streaky. She felt attractive for the first time in weeks. But now she had blown it all by letting herself wander off topic into the dangerous territory of Beccy and the 'job'. What was worse, she found she simply couldn't let the matter drop. Her step-family had always been a sensitive subject and accepting them had taken Tash until adulthood – it was very easy to undermine the status quo.

'Henrietta seems pretty convinced that you agreed to Beccy coming to work here.'

'Definitely not!'

'How could they be so mistaken?'

He narrowed his eyes, glaring up at his cigarette smoke as he thought back to the conversation with James. Watching him, Tash's heart flipped over as it always did when she had an opportunity to study him, even when he was moody and tempestuous as now – perhaps more so because that was when his beauty was all the more like a force of nature. The way that amazing bone structure worked was sublime – she had painted and sketched it a hundred times and never bored of the high cheekbones, the sharp line of his jaw, perfect symmetry of his wide, bow-like lips, the straight Grecian-hero nose, the wide, arched wingspan of his brows and those blue, blue eyes beneath the wild mane of tortoiseshell hair that badly needed a cut before he took off to represent his country. He never had time and Tash, who secretly adored it dishevelled, sun-streaked and flopping into his eyes, had done nothing to remedy the situation. She had always loved running her fingers through his hair.

But now it was Hugo who was raking a suntanned hand through it, his fingernails still tipped with dark crescents despite ten minutes scrubbing them with a brush when he came in from the yard.

'I remember advising your father not to buy the girl a horse just yet,' he muttered, 'and something about Beccy needing a boot camp not new König boots – ah!' His eyebrows shot up in sudden enlightenment. 'I think he may have misinterpreted my words there.'

'Are you saying that Daddy thinks that we are going to provide some sort of teenage boot camp for Beccy?' Tash gasped. 'She's twenty-seven, not fourteen.'

'She hardly behaved like a responsible adult on her travels though, did she?'

Tash said nothing. Having seen for herself how immature her stepsister was earlier that day, she agreed. It amazed her that all those years on the road – or in the cult – had done nothing to wise up Beccy's outlook. She seemed more childlike than ever.

'I really can't deal with this right now.' Hugo sprang from his seat and began pacing the corners of the terrace, staring moodily out across his overgrown gardens towards the beech woods. 'You know what it's like. I have to stay focused.'

'I know,' Tash said hollowly, wishing she could stay focused on anything for more than five minutes, but that was the lot of the heavily pregnant multi-tasker with hormones in overdrive and family in increasing disarray. She had until recently been looking forward to the Games, comforted by the idea of being happy and pregnant, curled up at home with her mother, the television and a vast box of chocolates, ready to cheer on Hugo. That was when it was all a daydream, and now she was faced with the reality of Hugo going away, of the yard being under-staffed, of her mother being unable to come and help, Alicia needing her help, the baby truly imminent and Cora toddling about in almost constant peril from loose electrical sockets, stone steps, horses, dogs and water features.

Trying not to worry about her mother, who was still not returning her calls, she cheered herself up by admiring Hugo's bottom in tight-fitting chinos, creased perfectly around the long muscular legs that were as hard as carved mahogany trunks.

'You can sort it out, can't you darling?' he was saying, still dwelling on the Beccy dilemma. 'Put her off? The Moncrieffs might take her – they're always looking for working pupils willing to do the long winter slog.'

'I don't think Beccy does "slogging".'

'Which is why she can't come here. We need really hard workers, not hangers-on. I hope these bloody Czechoslovakians know how hard they're going to have to work for their euro dollar.'

'They are from the Czech Republic,' Tash corrected. 'Czechoslovakia doesn't exist any more.'

'Cumberland doesn't exist any more but they haven't changed the name of the sausage,' Hugo pointed out. 'Same bloody difference.'

'Not to the Jelineks,' she said, struggling with the pronunciation.

'And what sort of name's Jellyneck?'

'The "j" is pronounced "y" and the "k" is "tch", I think – "*yelli-netch*",' she over-emphasised the word, sounding like Moira Stuart reporting on an Eastern European skirmish. 'He's called Vasilly and she's Veruschka.'

Hugo let out a bark of laughter, momentarily lifted from his dark, pre-competition brooding. 'Silly and Verruca Jellyneck.'

'Don't start that again,' Tash warned.

He held up an apologetic hand, although he was still fighting laughter. 'Well, whatever they call themselves, they'll have to pull their fingers out and graft. Have they worked with horses at all?'

'They're domestic au pairs.'

'Bound to know about horses. Racing yards are full of Eastern Europeans these days – Nicky Heaton's got at least a dozen of them. And Indians.'

'Veruschka will do childcare and housework, and Vasilly will do general maintenance and look after the garden.'

Hugo lit another cigarette, the domestic running of the house only a fleeting distraction when he had to worry about the huge contest ahead, along with juggling horses and schedules. 'We'll need them to put some hours in on the yard. They can do night Czech for a start.' He hated night-check, the final patrol around the yard, changing rugs and filling up nets and water drinkers last thing at night.

'Perhaps we do need Beccy after all,' Tash led gently, knowing that backing out of the agreement now would be impossible if she ever wanted to speak to her father again.

'Absolutely not.' He flicked his lighter closed.

'What harm can she do?'

'Plenty. I'd rather hire in half a dozen of your finest illegals from the Calcutta slums than that girl.'

'Even they wouldn't work for the peanuts we pay working pupils.'

'Pay peanuts, get monkeys,' he sighed, glancing across at her. 'I miss having you working alongside me.'

'I miss it too,' she overstated, although right now the thought of going anywhere near a horse was anathema. She knew it would return very quickly after the birth – with Cora she'd been riding again within weeks. And she did miss the close daily companionship with Hugo. She felt a sudden happy glow from the mutual affection bubbling between them as they studied one another with lingering enjoyment and appreciation, a rare treat afforded by having the time to do so. The evening was finally getting on track, so she wasn't about to risk losing the mood by being pedantically truthful.

But, typically, Hugo failed to respect the intimacy of the moment.

'I can't believe you're about to have a baby now, of all times,' he grumbled, pacing around again, cigarette puffing. 'Bloody Olympic month!'

'You were there at the conception,' she parried. 'Shoot seed, get babies.'

'*You* told me breast-feeding was the best form of contraception.'

'You were the one who thought it was funny to start feeding Cora spoonfuls of your breakfast.' She had been too busy frying up huge feasts for Hugo and the staff at the time to spot that Cora was gummily snorkelling up great quantities of porridge dripping in milk and Demerara sugar and so weaning herself.

'So let's sue Quaker.'

He was impossible when he was as tetchy as this. Tash knew that it was pre-competition tension, plus he was picking on her because she couldn't be there with him, but it didn't make him any easier to handle.

She decided to shelve telling him that Beccy was definitely coming to Haydown until after the Olympics, by which time her stepsister would already be ensconced and pulling her weight. It wasn't as though they were short of space, and they needed more help. With Tash laid off they lacked riding talent as well as spare hands around the yard.

'Perhaps you could look around for a new work rider next week? Someone like Stefan?' Now based in the US, the Swedish event rider and their great friend Stefan Johanssen had once been based at Haydown, bringing in an essential income as well as providing physical back-up on the yard.

'Next week,' Hugo said darkly, still looking out across his acres, 'all I am going to be thinking about is beating every bastard out there to gold, and making up for last time.'

Smiling supportively across at him, Tash decided that she would also wait until after the Olympics to tackle him about the flowers that he had been buying in Waitrose.

Oblivious to her scrutiny, Hugo carried on glaring out past the overgrown garden towards the equally neglected parkland, his face a beautiful, still mask hiding a raging torrent of pre-match adrenalin and bad memories.

On the Surrey borders, Beccy was also looking broodily across several acres, although this was a well-manicured garden lovingly maintained by her mother, with rose walks, rhododendron hedges and vast tracts of herbaceous border stretching down past the potting sheds to the pony paddocks at the far end.

Like Tash and her older sister Sophia a decade before them, Beccy and her sister Emily had kept ponies there as teenagers. Now, ten years further on still, the stables were used for storage and the paddocks had been turned into a driving range for James, complete with a putting green where Beccy had once erected show jumps from oil cans, now fastidiously mown by James, week in week out, on the sit-on mower.

Beccy could hear her stepfather now, haw-hawing to Henrietta across the landing in their dressing room as they prepared to go out to dinner with some of his old banking cronies.

Beccy had never had as tempestuous a relationship with James as her sister. But whereas Emily, having loathed James with a passion throughout her teens and early twenties, was now completely reconciled to and hugely fond of the man that her children called Grampa Goffa because of his passion for nine irons and plus fours, Beccy still felt a strangely frozen ambivalence towards her mother's second husband.

Emily made James enormously proud, just like his own daughter, Sophia, who had married into the aristocracy after a successful modelling career. Em was now taking a baby break from her career in broadcast financing. Married to high-flying executive producer, Tim, with three children under five, a house in London and cottage in Dorset, and more power-party invitations on her mantelpiece than Elisabeth Murdoch, she was a stepdaughter par excellence.

Beccy was yet to attain the first rung on the ladder of James's approbation. In fact, in this particular game of snakes and ladders she was off the bottom rung, down the lift shaft and deep within the mines of his contempt.

And now that she was back where she started, sitting in Tash's old bedroom, staring across the view that teenage Tash had gazed upon, about to go and work with Tash and Hugo at Haydown, she couldn't help but feel aggrieved to be once again cast in her step-sister's ever-lengthening shadow.

'I am *not* Tash,' she muttered to herself now, fiddling with a dreadlock.

She still had a great love and passion for horses, although she wasn't sure if she wanted to ride competitively any more, remembering only too well how much it had meant to her once and how painful it had been to lose. She liked to think that her life on the global road had taken the competitive edge from her, making her far more spiritually aware.

The reason for agreeing to her mother's suggestion that she resurrect her apprentice career with horses (of which Henrietta had deeply disapproved at the time, trying to steer her towards secretarial college instead) was simple. She needed her mother off her back. She needed James off her back. She needed somewhere to live.

And she was in love with Hugo Beauchamp. She had been since the day she first met him, when she was fifteen, long before he became a member of the family.

Tash used to joke that she'd had a fierce crush on Hugo as a teenager and had gone on to marry him. Beccy wanted to go one better.

Just as her mother had taken James from Tash's mother, Beccy had every intention of taking Hugo from Tash. That would ensure that Beccy was out of her stepsister's shadow and into the sunset all of her own making once and for all.

Far to the west, high on the Berkshire downs, Tash's romantic meal was back on track.

Having moved the feast inside while Hugo was taking a call from Team GB's three day event chef d'equipe, Brian Sedgewick, Tash's pudding of improvised and expanded Eton Mess was far more successful than the rich venison that had preceded it. Combining the last of the lunch strawberries with a smashed up Pavlova base from the larder, a vat of whipping cream, gooseberries and wild strawberries from the garden and a splattering of chopped mint, drizzled honey and a squeeze of lime was inspired. Hugo lapped it up.

His mood had been completely transformed by Brian's call, which had refocused him on the competition ahead and reminded him that Tash was providing essential back-up and expertise on the ground, not just domestic distractions.

'I think you're right,' he told her as he helped himself to thirds and then started spooning it into her mouth as well as his own, 'I *will* keep an eye out for a rider to be based here. There's a couple of Brazilians I really rated at the World Games, plus new members of the Italian squad that have been taking the European CCIs by storm this year. And there's always Lough Strachan.'

'You'll never get Lough Strachan to come here.'

'Wanna bet?'

'Look what happened when you tried before.' She headed to the stereo to put on the new Dillon Rafferty CD that she'd bought while shopping, skipping the tracks forward to find 'Two Souls'. 'He turned you down flat.'

'So? I'll try again.'

Lough Strachan, current World Champion and the man universally hailed as the best rider across country since Mark Todd, was a notoriously reclusive bugger. Still based in New Zealand, he would undoubtedly be Hugo's greatest rival if he were to relocate to Europe, a move that seemed increasingly inevitable given the sport's predominance there. If he were to be based at Haydown and competing alongside the Beauchamps he would be a huge asset, creating a formidable team.

'He hardly ever leaves New Zealand or the Southern Hemisphere,' Tash pointed out, having read a long feature about Lough in *Eventing* only last month. 'He says it's the Maori in him.'

'He's very far from home now,' he cocked his head and listened as the familiar track got into its swing. The song – number one for over fifteen weeks and heading towards the record books – was a tour de force of gut-clawing, chest-pumping emotion. It never failed to grab listeners by the heart and head, even cynics like Hugo.

'Only because his country needs him to bring back a gold medal,' Tash was saying. 'They'd have thrown him off the North Island if he'd refused to compete at these Games – he's leagues ahead of all his team-mates on the points tables, and those are some of the best UK-based riders in the world.'

Home-loving Lough's reluctance to compete in Europe was well documented. Still practising as a vet until very recently, he had a reputation for bloody-mindedness as well as a preference for his own and equine company. Self-made, self-taught, hugely independent and someone who nurtured his home-bred horses and rarely sold them on, he was a man whom Hugo longed to work alongside and learn from. He would be a perfect resident rider at Haydown, renting a part of the yard and working and training with Hugo while they competed on the European circuit, pooling knowledge and resources. But every time Hugo had made an approach Lough had turned him down without explanation.

'I'll get him this time,' he promised as he kissed meringue crumbs from her lip. 'I'll take on the world, Tash my darling, and bring you back gold and the Kiwi.' He sounded like a knight about to go on a crusade.

'You do that,' she laughed, kissing cream from his lips.

The haunting Dillon Rafferty song was still filling the room, sweeping Tash and Hugo up in its sexy slipstream.

Nine months pregnant, with swollen ankles, numb fingers, a weak bladder and backache, Tash wasn't feeling at her most seductive these days, but she felt surprisingly horny tonight. She felt ravishing, in fact. And Hugo found her immensely desirable. With breasts as vast and buoyant as two hot air balloons rising from her jaunty turquoise maternity bra, her long legs wrapped around his hips and her face pink with exertion and naughtiness, she pleasured him on the small button-back chair in the corner of the oak-panelled snug room, lit only by the dim picture light that was always illuminated over the grandiose Millais portrait of Hugo's great-uncle Horace, and watched by a pack of interested dogs lined up obediently on the mud rug by the door.

Later that evening, while Hugo was out doing his routine and much-loathed night-check around the stable yards, Tash picked up the phone on a whim. Physically exhausted yet still curiously charged from a day of childcare, relatives, late pregnancy, domesticity and lovemaking, she needed to assuage the flood of post-coital affection that was raging through her. She longed to share, to radiate tenderness and to hear a soothing, cheering voice in return for a quick-fix catch up.

But her mother, top of her wish list, was still firmly incommunicado, the answer phones switched on both at her Parisian apartment and the Loire Valley house, her mobile switched off. So Tash called the next best thing. Zoe.

'Tash! At last! I was giving up hope.' That voice – as reassuring as comfort-eating Nutella on hot buttered muffins – was bliss. 'Darling one, we were just talking about you!' There was a babble of conversation in the background. 'Don't say it's happening already?'

'No, not yet.' Tash could hear laughter and music. At least she needn't have worried about disturbing the O'Shaughnessys in bed. 'If I'm interrupting I'll call back.'

'No, no, just some house guests.' Zoe's dulcet tones contorted as she clearly reached to close a door. The next moment her voice was clearer and captured in glorious isolation. 'They can wait – a few old and new friends of Niall's.'

She made them sound very unimportant, whereas Tash would happily lay a bet that at least two of them would be A-list Hollywood, much as Niall himself was nowadays. The O'Shaughnessys lived variously between London, LA and Ireland, where they were now, spending every summer *en famille* with their six-year-old twins, Cian and Maeve. Rufus and India, Zoe's grown-up children from her first marriage, were usually there for at least a part of the time. The O'Shaughnessys' Irish base was a gloriously laid-back retreat, counterbalancing a picture-postcard stone house with acres of overgrown meadows and woodland to the front and a backdrop of cliffs and ocean to the rear, plus a hidden tunnel straight from the cellars down to the beach.

Tash had spent a hugely enjoyable week there with baby Cora the previous summer, although Hugo had ducked out of the majority of their long-promised stay and dashed around Ireland looking at horses. He had only spent one night at Ballyhoon, and that was somewhat under duress. He complained that the presence of Tash's brother Matty and his quarrelsome, free-range family set his teeth on edge, but the truth was more sensitive. Although he adored Zoe, and got on like a house on fire with Niall, especially when drunk, he found it difficult reconciling himself to the fact that Niall and Tash had once been lovers.

This issue – and the time differences that increasingly yawned between them – had badly affected Tash's great friendship with Zoe. Although the latter was fourteen years older, the two women had a natural affinity and were instinctive, deep-set friends.

Tash called Zoe less often these days, but when she did, as now, the two fell immediately into an affectionate, intimate chat that required no small talk.

'I am *so* glad you called,' Zoe's voice spoke of smiles and warmth – and rather a lot of good red wine. 'You must be so fed up hauling that little passenger around, and desperate to meet him. I bet you're still working far too hard and putting your feet up too little.'

'I'm not working at all, and I can't see my feet any more,' Tash pointed out.

Zoe tutted fondly. 'I remember how fed up and uncomfortable I got, especially the second time around. India was terribly late – then as now. Tell Hugo I insist that he pampers you like mad in these last weeks.'

'He hasn't time with the Games coming up.'

'Do I take it that he's horribly distracted?'

'I wish I could be there for him more.'

'Don't you mean you wish he could be there for you more?'

Tash was grateful that Zoe knew her so well. 'Maybe a bit of both.'

'You need his support now, Tash.'

'He can't help it. Running the yard and competing every week is all-consuming; I should know. It's hard for him to understand that I'm up to my eyes in hormones.'

'Some men find it very hard to engage with pregnancy. It's such an alien process for them.'

'Niall spent every day telling you how your babies were developing,' Tash remembered, 'when they could hear and see and had begun to grow nails and hair.'

'That was Niall's way of connecting, of feeling a part of the action.'

Tash found herself blurting: 'And Hugo's is to sneak into Waitrose each week to buy expensive flowers.'

'Well that's very romantic.' Zoe's voice was joined again by babbling talk and laughter as someone opened the door behind her.

'The flowers aren't for me.'

But Tash had lost her audience.

'What? Is he? Okay,' Zoe was talking away from the handset. Her voice came hurriedly back. 'I have to go for a moment, darling. Cian is awake and needs settling. He's been having bad dreams. Here, talk to Niall. Tash was just saying how romantic Hugo's being . . .'

Within seconds Tash found the melodic and world-famous deep tones of her ex, Niall, purring in her ear.

'How are you, angel? Bountiful as a ripe pear, I'll wonder. I remember Zoe was so amazingly beautiful at nine months that I just couldn't keep my hands off her. No wonder Hugo is so loved up now. I'd never have had him down as a romantic, but there you go! What fatherhood does to a man, eh?'

'Yes. Quite.' Tash tried not to dwell on the early, sulky stages of her romantic dinner, followed by the rampant seduction that was entirely of her own making, although Hugo had been a willing participant. She was equally reluctant to admit just how much her horniness was down to hormones, Dillon Rafferty's song and – alarmingly – table talk of Lough Strachan, and how little the result of anything Hugo had actually said or done himself. 'Of course, the baby could be better timed given it's Olympics month.'

'Why's that?'

'Hugo's on the British team, Niall.'

'Is he now? Ah, that's great. Say good luck from us.'

Tash laughed with incredulous delight. The thing around which her entire life was revolving – more than having a second child, trying to keep the house running, worrying about their livelihood – was barely of passing interest to Niall.

'In that case we must watch him on TV,' he was saying vaguely. 'India is here next week; she'll be keen to see it. Still has horses in her blood after all those years grooming for Penny and Gus. Now, are you going for a home birth?' he asked cluckily, more fascinated by delivery suites than medal podiums.

'Not after last time – it's not encouraged.'

'Of course, you had an emergency C-section just like Zoe. A

malpresentation, was it not? Always makes me think of perfume girls demonstrating beauty ranges in shopping centres.'

She giggled. Niall was incredibly clued up about childbirth, having taken an active interest in that of his twins, whereas Hugo equated it all to horses and would have been more comfortable if Tash could be confined in a foaling box for the final weeks with a deep straw bed, CCTV and a sweat-activated alarm.

'Little Cora didn't want to come out, and who can blame her?' Niall was saying now, his voice laced with that hypnotic laugh. 'I remember feeling much the same way with you once.' His delighted laughter rang out.

He had obviously had even more wine than his wife. A recovering alcoholic who fell off the wagon more often than a faulty cart wheel, Niall considered his summers in Ireland to be time out from AA, pointing out that his hard-drinking Irish family would disown him if he stuck to orange juice.

'Yes, well, I really ought to—' Tash started.

But once he was on a roll Niall was unstoppable. Unbeknown to Tash, when Zoe had handed him the phone a few moments earlier she had mouthed *Cheer her up*, and that was what Niall intended to do in the best way he knew: full-throttle flirtation.

'You are a gorgeous girl, Tash French,' he crooned, using her maiden name as he had so often in the past, 'and I'm glad to hear that Beauchamp fellow appreciates what he's got in you.'

'Mmm. Quite.' Tash's eyes flashed as she heard Hugo come loudly in through the back door accompanied by his dogs.

Niall was thoroughly enjoying himself, revisiting a favourite old haunt. Zoe, who was accustomed to his wild flirtations and the fact that he remained quite hopelessly in love with every woman he had ever wooed, thankfully none more so than his wife, was quoted as saying that being married to a dedicated method actor and renowned playboy was like being in love with a dozen different men, at least a few of which would always be in love with somebody else.

'Sure I know I was a fool to let you go,' he was purring now. 'You have such an exquisite soul. Not to mention those magnificent legs. Best set of legs I've ever set eyes on. I'll bet that gorgeous arse of yours is just as shapely and firm as it ever was, pregnancy or no.'

Only half listening because Hugo had marched up behind her

and was demanding to know who was on the phone 'at this bloody hour', Tash felt her haemorrhoids throb.

'It's – um – Niall,' she managed to mutter over her shoulder, so flustered that she accidentally pressed speakerphone.

'. . . loved staring at your pins, angel . . .' Niall was still reminiscing, his voice now booming around the room at top volume. 'Sure, I remember making you walk around in nothing but frilly knickers when we shared that chilly fleapit – d'you not recall? I wanted to kiss each and every one of your goose bumps . . .'

Behind her, Hugo's eyebrows shot up and he hissed, 'What the fuck does he want?'

Tash fumbled to mute the call. 'I called him.'

Hugo cocked his head at this.

Not realising that her explanation was open to interpretation, she pressed a few more buttons but only succeeded in turning up the speaker volume even more, while now also digitally recording Niall's words.

'. . . remember when I had you all to myself to play the naughtiest games . . .' He was recounting with an enchanted laugh, his warm brogue so familiar that he could be on the battered little work-top television telling Jonathan Ross one of his hilarious anecdotes about filming on location. Instead he was on the kitchen phone remembering making love with Tash '. . . that day the heavens opened so hard that the ceiling fell in and we just carried on fornicating in the plaster dust and rainwater, watching the forked lightning overhead . . .'

Eyebrows cranking higher, Hugo stalked off to feed the dogs.

Tash finally pressed a button that cut off Niall's voice and treated them both to a tinny version of 'Eine kleine Nachtmusik'.

She turned to watch Hugo, always struck by the way that the dogs lined up in von Trapp order as they awaited their food – apart from rebellious Beetroot the mongrel who, in her dotage, liked to lie down belly-up in her checked bed when awaiting food.

The Haydown pack was large but incredibly well-mannered and disciplined, with all its members given a specific job to do. Beetroot was the genteel and ageing lady's companion, the only dog allowed up the stairs, on the sofas or the bed. The Bitches of Eastwick were three Labradors that Hugo had trained to the gun. The Roadies were two big Rhodesian ridgeback brothers who guarded the yard and helpfully rounded up stray livestock and children as required. Finally, the Rat Pack were three snappy little hunt-terrier bitches that kept the Haydown rat and rabbit population down and were named variously after Hugo's ex girlfriends and/or female adversaries.

They all adored him because he treated them fairly but firmly and was top dog. By contrast they walked all over Tash, who bribed them, spoiled them and alternately hugged them all close or shooed them away from Cora. Only Beetroot remained her ally, although the pretty little biscuit-coloured bitch with her black envelope-flap ears and long, feathered lash of a tail joined the rest in sucking up to the pack leader at mealtimes.

Tash watched the food bowls clatter down on the quarry tiles in the boot room in specific order and listened to the appreciative chomps of a large pack eating dried dog food as competitively as hounds thrown a haunch.

'I didn't call Niall,' she explained, still holding the phone as it tinkled out Mozart. 'I called Zoe but she had to go to one of the twins and—'

'Forget it.' Hugo flashed a tired on-off smile as he emerged from the boot room and crossed through the kitchen past her, heading for the rear lobby that led to the main house. 'I'm whacked. I'm going to bed. Lock up once you've chucked the Roadies out, will you?'

'But . . .'

He was already gone. Always the first to finish eating, Beetroot scuttled after him, claws slithering on the flagstones in her haste to join him in bed.

Tash remembered feeling much the same way when they were first married; she had suffered from almost continual indigestion.

Wearily she pressed the phone's green button. Niall was still reminiscing, apparently unbothered by the artificial hold music that had briefly featured at the other end of the line:

'. . . that day that you made me walk up onto the downs to make love behind the gorse bushes on Wayfarer's Walk and some spotty teenager flying a kite literally stepped back on top of us. I've never laughed so much . . .'

Tash smiled into the phone as she, too, couldn't help remembering that sunny day over a decade ago when she'd hardly had a care in the world compared to now. Laughter was a rare commodity now, as was fun, silly, adventurous sex.

'It was a man with a hang-glider,' she recalled.

'It was?'

'He was taking a run higher up the ridge and lost his footing – he passed over us so low that he kicked you on the bottom.'

'So he did now,' Niall chortled, sucking in a deep, contented breath that was no doubt accompanied by a puff on a rare Cuban cigar. 'Did the spotty kid with the kite fall over us after that?'

'He didn't.'

'He did so. I remember because he was wearing a T-shirt promoting one of my films. *Celt*, wasn't it?'

Tash suddenly found the conversation less entertaining. Face cold and heart pounding as she guessed what Hugo must be thinking of her right now. 'The kite kid must have been with somebody else.'

'Was it?' Niall was unapologetic. 'I admit I got rather fond of that spot hidden among the gorse bushes, so I did . . .'

With a rueful pang, Tash realised that not long after pleasuring her amid the gorse bushes Niall had been pleasuring another in the same spot. He had never been particularly faithful and was notorious for transferring his affections from one woman to another with shameful speed. In Tash's case, the other woman had been Zoe.

As the baby let out a series of kicks Tash touched her bump for comfort and felt a shudder of fear course through her, her cold face even clammier and her clanking heart raking indigestion up from her belly now. Any thoughts of infidelity and affairs made her very jumpy and afraid indeed.

Niall had moved on from reminiscing about nefarious activities behind West Berkshire gorse bushes and was contemplating matters at hand: 'Have you got a name for the little fellow yet?'

'Waitrose,' Tash muttered, still thinking uncomfortably about betrayal.

On cue Zoe's soothing tones came back on the phone.

'Sorry about that – Cian is out like a light again, bless him. I hope Niall's been keeping you entertained.'

'Highly.'

'Good. Now what were you saying before I had to break off – something about Hugo buying you flowers? That's so tender and thoughtful. He *must* have turned over a new leaf. Fatherhood has obviously reformed his rakish ways.'

Tash could hear Hugo upstairs, ordering Beetroot out of the bedroom so loudly that Cora was bound to wake up.

'Yes, he's quite the new man these days. He's promised to bring me a lovely present back from the Olympics if he wins gold.'

'Oh, what's that?'

Tash thought about handsome Lough Strachan with his Maori tattoos and fiery reputation, and smiled as she anxiously stroked her belly, which unborn Amery was now using as a bouncy castle. Things would get better after the Games, she was certain of it. With new staff starting they'd have lots more help on the yard and in the house; having Beccy in situ would help reconcile the increasing rift between Tash and her father. And Hugo would stop sneaking into Waitrose to buy flowers for whatever – probably perfectly innocent – reason. Yes, it would all get better after the Games, especially if he won a medal.

'Undivided attention,' she sighed. 'He's bringing me back his undivided attention.'

Zoe laughed throatily. 'In that case we'll definitely be cheering him on this end.'

Chapter 3

As a special reward for completing her A levels so diligently, Faith Brakespear was treated to a home-cooked spread of all her favourite things – her mother's *leverpostej* pâté on rye bread, then roast lamb with all the minted and caramelised trimmings, and finished with treacle tart with toffee ice cream, all washed down with lashings of kir royale – during which she was toasted with an announcement that threw all her life plans into disarray.

'I have arranged the best job for your gap year, *kæreste*,' her mother Anke revealed with the delight of a magician pulling a solid gold rabbit from a satin topper. 'You will be the working pupil at Kurt's dressage yard in Essex.'

'Essex?' Faith croaked stupidly, thinking how far away it was from Oddlode and her beloved riding coach, Rory Midwinter.

'Big county near London,' her stepfather Graham mocked kindly.

'Unusually high consumption of hair bleach and Turtle Wax. We used to live there, love.'

'You will have to start at the bottom, of course,' Anke was saying pragmatically, although her eyes sparkled with pride at achieving such a coup, 'but Kurt knows how talented you are and how much you want to be a professional dressage rider, and you *are* his daughter, so he will make it happen for you, and Rio of course. Imagine what this will do for your chances, being his protégée?'

Long heralded as Britain's best-ever dressage rider, Kurt Willis was a dashing blond cavalier who looked like a Ralph Lauren model and oozed pure, natural riding talent from every pore. Married to Anke for almost twenty years, much of it platonically, he had acknowledged and raised Faith and her older brother Magnus as his own children until the marriage finally foundered when, unable to live the lie any longer, he came out of the closet in public as well as private. Now known affectionately to his children as the Gayfather, he still lived in Essex with his long-term partner Graeme Fredericks, a fellow dressage rider – both men enjoying a famously open relationship involving a luxury gin palace, several million-pound horses, two poodles and a lot of strapping young grooms brought over from the continent each year. Anke, meanwhile, had gone on to marry a golden Graham herself, Lancashire-born haulier turned Essex freight millionaire Graham Brakespear. And after almost a decade as companionable near-neighbours to Kurt in Essex, the couple had moved to the Cotswolds with Magnus, Faith and their own son Chad two years earlier. All four collective parents and step-parents, Gayfathers and Graham/Graeme fathers remained gratifyingly close and friendly, and had recently been joined in this curious family tree by Magnus's biological father, Stig Jorgen, a Swedish dressage trainer with whom he had recently become acquainted. Only Faith's own birth father, an Irish horse trader whom she refused to acknowledge despite her mother's various attempts to forge a relationship between them, remained out of the loop. She had spent her childhood craving a conventional family; in her early teens she'd taken Graham's surname and was happy to let new acquaintances believe that she'd inherited her stubborn loyalty and broad shoulders from him.

Faith had no interest in acquiring more fathers. She simply wanted competitive glory and Rory. Now she was torn in two by her mother's proposal.

'You will go to Essex after your birthday party. You might as well start work straight away because, of course, Kurt and Graeme are not at the Olympics this year.' The duo had controversially been left off the British dressage team for the first time in twenty years in favour of an all-female squad, all of whom were under twenty-five. 'Kurt thinks the future is in a protégée, darling, and he wants that protégée to be you!' Anke finished rapturously.

Faith's mouth opened and closed, hot words burning themselves out on her tongue as she thought of every argument to refuse to go. She couldn't leave Rory behind at such a critical time, nor deprive him of the chance to compete her horse Baron Areion, who had now changed disciplines from dressage to eventing and was flying through the ranks. In the end all she could splutter was: 'Rio is staying here!' and run to her room to ring her best friend, Carly. When there was no answer, she texted: *PICK UP – URGENT!!!*

She rang the number again on redial, but again the call went straight through to voicemail.

Had it been anybody else, Faith would charitably assume that their phone was out of charge, or that they were out of range, in a tunnel, in the theatre or in hospital – possibly dead. But Carly never, ever allowed her precious pink Motorola to be out of connection.

Carly had been avoiding Faith all week. The on-off best friend status, having been firmly on in recent weeks, now appeared to be off just when Faith badly needed advice.

When the Brakespear family had moved from Essex to the Cotswolds, separating the two teenage friends by almost two hundred miles, Faith's tenacity and loyalty, matched with Carly's need for a sounding board outside her immediate social group, had kept the friendship alive. For over two years they had emailed, texted and often spoken daily.

At first glance unlikely allies, the girls had become friends at school when bonding through their mutual passion for horses. Then, as now, Faith was gangly, gingery, frizzy-haired, flat-chested and socially inept, but she had one great asset that made pony-mad Carly court her adoringly. She was a naturally gifted rider, her wealth of horsemanship gleaned from growing up with two dressage Olympians as parents. The girls became great foils, and the trade-off was simple. Streetwise Carly had the glamour, feminine wiles and know-how with boys, and Faith had the riding expertise.

As well as adapting to long-distance separation, their friendship had this year even survived the ultimate betrayal when Carly had got a boyfriend. Hugely sensible, bright and straight-talking, Faith made a perfect sounding board through the ups and downs of first love.

Recently, in the wake of the monumental split between these two lovebirds – at least as traumatic and calamitous as Brad and Jen, according to Carly – the friendship had been experiencing a purple patch. Through the weeks of A level exams and then celebratory holidays combined with anxious waits for results, Faith had drawn surprising satisfaction from helping her friend through the break-up. In exchange, Carly had galvanised Faith's determination to change her own life for ever.

Faith's mother Anke might have been concerned that all the late-night chats and emails were distracting her from her revision, but in fact they'd had the opposite effect, focusing her on the importance of academic credentials when faced with the sketchiness of Carly in a crisis and the fact that her friend was blowing all her chances of scraping the two Cs and a D required to get into the University of Essex.

'How can I concentrate on media studies when my heart is broken?' she had lamented to Faith.

Faith, whose own heart had long been hammered hard by its fruitless love for charming, womanising Rory, sympathised, although Carly failed to see the parallels at first.

'Your crush on that posh bungalow is nothing to my love for Grant!' she had raged.

Faith agreed wholeheartedly. 'That's why I need your help getting the posh bungalow to raise his shutters and see me blossom as soon as exams are over.'

With A levels behind them, it was time for Carly to assist Faith's plans to make Rory see her as more than just a tomboy cross-patch.

Carly was six months older than Faith, an age advantage she liked to point out with the sort of pride that insinuated the age gap was the equivalent of light years socially – and in many ways it was. Pretty, busty, petite and as blonde one month as she was raven-haired the next, Carly kept up with the latest trends in fashion, music, TV and language with an insatiable appetite for weekly gossip magazines. Her heroines were Posh Spice, Paris Hilton and

Sylva Frost. She had even gained that ultimate credential – cosmetic surgery (admittedly it was just having her ears pinned back on the NHS, but it still counted). She had always led the way with the opposite sex while Faith trotted around in circles, but now it was time for Faith to gallop alongside her.

In recent weeks the friends had a worked out a seduction strategy to make Rory fall in love with Faith at long last; she would acquire a whiter than white smile, buoyant 32EE Hollywood ice cream scoop boobs, a pert bottom and a tiny button nose to wow him and become his inseparable other half, living, riding and competing side by side like Tash and Hugo Beauchamp or her mother's friends the Moncrieffs.

Having won a small cash fortune in a local competition the previous year – wisely gathering interest in a savings account thus far – Faith was, on Carly's advice, now planning to blow the lot on a makeover of industrial proportions. She had already made contact with a top London dentist and a cosmetic surgeon, although couldn't actually book the veneers, boob job, nose job, lipo and chin implant until after her eighteenth birthday because she would need her mother's permission before then.

But now that she had almost come of age and could at last greenlight the offensive, she'd suddenly come up against a serious obstacle and urgently needed Carly's help.

Again she texted *PICK UP!!!*. Again her subsequent call was redirected to voicemail.

Faith howled with frustration.

The following Saturday was her eighteenth birthday. Having anticipated it eagerly for weeks, she now doubted that her best friend was even planning to come to the party her family were foisting upon her. It was vital that Carly was there to help her get ready and to discuss the way forward.

But Anke had just scuppered all her daughter's well-laid plans to lay Rory and share his life. Ironically, she had done this by using links with her own horsy ex-husband, the other half of the legendary über-pairing, the most talked about equestrian duo for over a decade, who had simply been known as 'Anke and Kurt'.

At last her phone burst into life with the ringtone that she had assigned only to her most intimate loved ones. 'Two Souls' by Dillon Rafferty rang out to pull at her heartstrings and lift her spirits.

But it wasn't Carly, or Rory; it was her brother Magnus, calling to congratulate her on finishing her A levels and ask if he could bring a couple of extra guests to her party.

'Depends who,' she hedged.

'Nell . . .'

Faith groaned. Magnus's ex Nell, with whom he had a one-year-old daughter Giselle, was always horribly conceited and pointedly ignored her whenever they met.

'. . . and her new boyfriend, now that it's official.' The crowd noise in the background was almost drowning him out. 'I've just spoken to them in New York. He sends his love, by the way.'

'His what?'

'His love!' Magnus repeated loudly. 'The guy adores you. He's never got over the day you legged up his lead guitarist on to one of Rory's horses so powerfully that he flew clean over it. I think he wants to offer you a job as his personal bodyguard.'

'Might be better than a year in Essex.' Faith sighed, wondering how much her brother knew about the Kurt offer.

But someone was calling Magnus off the phone now. 'So I can bring them, yeah?'

'Okay.' She agreed as casually as she could, heart skipping.

Tellingly, when Faith texted Carly yet again, this time to let her know of the VIP additions to the guest list, she got a call straight back from her friend, 'Two Souls' trilling out from the little Samsung on her bedside table. She listened to the whole of the refrain before answering.

'You are *joking* me, right?' Carly demanded breathlessly. 'Dillon Rafferty is *so* not coming to your party.'

'He is. I told you. He's a mate of Magnus's, after all.'

'Ohmygod, I can't believe Magnus is your brother. He's *so* cool.'

'He's okay.' Faith found it impossible to see her brother as anything other than a trendy dork who played guitar with admirable talent – and who wrote very catchy songs with lyrics she didn't quite understand.

With his girlfriend Dilly, he had now recorded an album that was enjoying modest success on the back of the music festivals they'd been playing. The duo had developed a local fan base and increasing word-of-mouth popularity. It barely registered on the celeb scale compared to Dillon Rafferty's stratospheric fame, but Faith was still growing increasingly proud of her lofty, blond brother and his undoubted talent.

'I can't believe I let Magnus slip through my fingers.' Carly sighed, having once snogged Faith's brother at a barbecue when he was a spotty teenager. 'He's really made the big time if he mixes with Dillon Rafferty.'

'*I* know Dillon personally,' Faith reminded her hotly. 'He owns some event horses at Rory's yard, remember. We go way back. That's why he wants to come to my party.'

'T'yeah!' Carly scoffed disbelievingly. 'And I have a hot date with R-Pattz next weekend, so I'm going to have to blow you out.'

'You are coming, aren't you?' Faith checked in a panic. She hated parties and was only really going along with this one to keep her mother happy, and because it enabled her to have an essential confab with Carly about her makeover, or Double-D Day as Carly had dubbed it.

'Course.'

'So why haven't you been answering my calls?'

'Dad's confiscated my mobile because the last bill he got for it was over three hundred. He is *so* mean. I'm only allowed one call and two texts a day.'

'I *am* privileged.'

'Too right you are. I got a text from Grant today asking me to call him. He wants us to get back together.'

'And you called me instead?' Faith was wildly gratified.

'Yeah. Well, I think I'll make Grant stew until after your party. Who knows – I might get lucky. Not that Cotswolds guys are a patch on Essex lads.'

'They're much better!' Faith said hotly, thinking of Rory. 'Yours are all footballers, boy bands and reality TV stars.'

'At least they're under fifty. Yours are all wrinkly has-been actors and ancient rock grandfathers. Talking of which, isn't *the* Rockfather moving in up the road from you? Are you sure you're not getting Daddy muddled up with son and Pete's the one coming to your party – I hear he likes young girls. You might be in there . . .'

'Don't be disgusting! He's *so* old!' Faith squealed with laughter.

For months it had been common local knowledge that Dillon Rafferty's even more famous rock-legend father, Pete 'the Rockfather' Rafferty, had bought magnificent Fox Oddfield Abbey, just a couple of miles from his son's more modest working-farm country retreat, and after lengthy renovation work that had kept all the locals agog was poised to move in with his young model wife. The press were on tenterhooks for moving day – and out in force in the locality – in the hope of capturing any reconciliation between Pete and Dillon. The father–son relationship was famously fiery, and the two had now been estranged for several years. It was rumoured that the Rockfather's move to the Lodes Valley was a big gesture towards rapprochement.

'My mum is really excited,' Faith told Carly now. 'Can you believe she used to have all Mask's albums when she was my age? She swears he was as big as Dillon then, and just as good looking, although I can't see it. Pete Rafferty is such an old raisin.'

'Maybe he's your real dad!' Carly suddenly shrieked. 'He lived in Ireland for ages, didn't he?'

'Pete Rafferty is not my biological father,' Faith said through gritted teeth, wishing Carly didn't always see her unconventional parentage like the plot of *Mamma Mia*. 'And he is *not* coming to my party, Dillon is. You don't have to believe me until you see for yourself, but you *do* have to promise me that you won't go all silly when he's near or flirt with him, because he's off limits. Like Rory's off limits. Dillon's bringing Nell Cottrell. It's all over the papers – you must have seen it.'

A fortnight earlier a tabloid had photographed trust-fund babe Nell coming out of Dillon's London townhouse one Sunday afternoon, wearing the same clothes that she had been wearing when the couple had been snapped leaving Bungalow 8 in the early hours of Saturday morning. 'Raff's Lost Weekend with Single Mum' the headline had shouted, much to Nell's disgust. The media had been after the story for weeks: Dillon Rafferty, the heartthrob superstar whose comeback single had been at the top of the charts all summer, had a new love interest.

'Ohmygod, it *is* her!' Carly clearly believed that, at least. 'I read about it in *Closer* this week and thought I recognised the name. It's that poisonous cow who tried to trap Magnus, isn't it? What do men *see* in her?'

'She's very beautiful.'

'If you like the boyish Carla Bruni look,' Carly sniffed.

'Some men do,' Faith mused, fleetingly wondering whether she really needed to endure the pain of a boob op. Rory had also once been in love with Nell, after all – a girl in possession of a chest as flat as her own. But that was years ago and Rory's cleavage tastes had evolved, besides which, whereas Nell had the sexily androgynous look of a tall Milanese street urchin, Faith had the wide-shouldered heavy features of a rugby forward.

'Only closet gays, in my experience,' Carly was pondering androgyny and sex appeal.

'Dillon Rafferty is *not* a closet gay.'

'If you say so. You obviously know him *so well* . . .' Carly said then, realising that cutting off her nose to spite her face was not wise when she desperately wanted to come and advise Faith on how to have her nose redesigned to suit her face, she hastily added, 'I promise I won't flirt with him or swoon in his starry presence if he actually turns up, which I somehow doubt. Please tell me you have *some* decent single lads coming, that don't have number-one albums all over the globe and a leech girlfriend parking her Kelly bag on their Porsche dashboard. I *have* to make Grant jealous. I called you instead of him today, remember? Don't let me down, Faith.'

'Not a problem – there are loads of sexy guys coming,' Faith promised, quickly changing the subject before Carly could demand the finer details. 'But Mum has just sprung something that *seriously* threatens Double-D Day.'

However, when she told her friend about gayfather Kurt's offer of a year's training in Essex, Carly's reaction was one of delight.

'This makes it so much easier!' she shrieked. 'You'll be based just up the road from here. I can cover for you better when you have your ops. My parents always spend September at the villa so you can recuperate at my house.'

'But I can't possibly leave Rory for a whole year,' Faith said in a small voice.

'You have to, don't you see? The surgery is just the beginning. You must wait for the scars to heal, for a start, and then I'll to teach you how to dress, walk, talk and shake that tush, Beyoncé. You'll need sexual mileage to seduce him – you've told me enough times he always falls for incredibly predatory women. I'll get you out clubbing, introduce you to some Colchester lads for a few flings.'

It sounded like Faith's idea of hell.

'The thing is,' she voiced one last worry. 'I can't ever be a top dressage rider with massive fake boobs.'

'Of course you can: look at Jordan.' Before Faith could protest, Carly said that her dad was coming to take the phone away, reminded Faith to line up those sexy men for her and hung up.

All afternoon Faith dwelled on the rather pitiable array of single men she had invited to her party. She had none, apart from Rory – who was strictly off limits to Carly on pain of death – and a few deadbeat computer geeks and emo types from college whom Faith had befriended by virtue of the fact that they, like her, were oddball loners.

Seeing a brilliant excuse for speaking to her beloved Rory for the third time that day – her previous calls being to ask whether she had left her crop behind after her lesson that morning (she knew she hadn't), and to remind him that the farrier was coming to Rio that afternoon – she pressed her most-pressed speed dial on her mobile.

'Yup?' Rory answered groggily, making her suspect that he'd been napping in his office again.

She came straight to the point: 'Do you have any dishy friends that you can invite along to my eighteenth?'

He laughed. 'Well, Spurs and Flipper both adore you and your mother, as you know, so I'm sure one or both could be persuaded to leave the pregnant wives sucking coal in front of old *ER* repeats for an evening.'

'*Single* friends.'

'I suppose I could sound out Hamish and Trist,' he offered reluctantly, knowing that his twentysomething hell-raising cronies were hardly likely to relish the idea of a teenager's birthday party unless the totty was seriously tasty.

'I have *several* friends coming from Essex,' she exaggerated. 'Really stunning girls – think Jodie Marsh meets Caprice.' She hoped that he'd question her definition of stunning.

But predictably Rory – an out-and-out boob man – was delighted by the description. 'Damn! I wish I was coming now.'

The colour drained from Faith's face as she held on to the wall beside her to stop herself swaying.

'You what?'

'I wish I was coming. I'll be at the Scottish Championships.

Typical of my best bloody owner to demand that I compete at the opposite end of the country that weekend.'

'But I'm your best owner,' she bleated desperately, trying to sound jokey but in fact sounding as though she had just seen Bambi's mother die, 'and I demand that you come to my party – or I'll take Rio back.'

'Don't joke, he's my only sound advanced horse,' Rory groaned, not picking up on the desperation in her voice. 'I have high hopes for him at Bloneigh Castle.'

'You're taking Rio to Scotland on my birthday?' She was practically sobbing at the injustice of it all.

'Dillon called me the day entries closed and insisted on Snake Charmer being fielded at the championships – some idea Nell's got into her head, I should think. But as you know, the horse has gone hopping lame this week. The organisers have been great and are letting me swap around and take Rio into the three-star now. And Dillon is still covering all the costs because we can take his intermediates to make up numbers.'

Rory now competed several horses for Dillon, but lameness and injury had plagued these expensive investments during their time with Rory, and Faith derived little pleasure from the fact that her own stallion was out-performing the rest, particularly if that meant he was going to Scotland without her.

'Why didn't you ask me?' she demanded now, furious that Dillon – and Nell – were unwittingly wrecking her love life.

'I'm sure I mentioned it,' he said, knowing that he hadn't. Like most event riders, Rory developed tunnel vision when it came to planning his competition calendar, the desire to field his horses to their best advantage superseding family, friends and, at times, even the owner's wishes. 'Bloneigh is a seriously good track to get Rio's four-star qualification. If he does well we might think about Badminton next year.' He was dangling a huge carrot in front of Faith's nose, but she was too upset by his desertion to care.

'But . . . but . . . you'll miss my party.'

'And the busty Essex babes, I know,' he sighed regretfully. 'Still, you should be pleased that Rio's going.' Accustomed to following his competitive progress like an acolyte and hanging on his every word, he now launched into a long, rambling monologue outlining his strategy for the coming seasons, completely unaware that, at the other end of the line, she was incredibly upset. '. . . and if all goes well there, I'll get short-listed for Aachen.' He had always dreamed of being on the British team.

Faith closed her eyes, thinking of her birthday without him – the star guest, the only reason for going ahead with this hellish, man-free unwanted party. Rare tears slid through her lashes.

'. . . if you'd told me a year ago that I might stand a chance of getting a Union Jack on my hat silk or be in a position to chase the Rolex Grand Slam, I'd have died laughing . . .'

'Bully for you,' Faith muttered, hanging up because she was starting to cry and didn't want him to realise. She was now more determined than ever to wow him with her all-new body, even if it took a year to overhaul.

Mopping her face and splashing it with cold water, she thundered downstairs to the vast Wyck Farm kitchen, where Anke was ladling homemade vichyssoise into a thermos to take around to her father, who was in a care home in nearby Lower Oddford, and complained endlessly about the food.

'I will go to work for Kurt after all.'

'Of course.' Anke, who had an iron will, had never doubted it. 'And will you be taking Rio?' She disapproved enormously of Faith's decision to let her dressage horse take part in a dangerous new three day eventing career.

'No. He can stay with Rory.'

Faith had already decided that Rio would be her hairy, four-legged spy in the Midwinter camp, keeping links with Rory alive while she focused on implants and half-passes in Essex.

'I see,' Anke said carefully, hoping that she wasn't expected to fork out for a new dressage schoolmaster.

'I'll ride whatever Kurt has free,' Faith insisted. 'You always told me that it's best to ride as many different horses as possible when you're learning the ropes.'

Anke was impressed. It was the way she herself had improved from national to international grand prix level over thirty years earlier, selling her top horses to fund a trip to the UK to be based for six months with top judge and trainer Peggy Rees-Eddison and her then working pupil Kurt Willis. The rest was dressage history.

'I'll call Kurt straight away,' she told her daughter delightedly.

'He'll be thrilled. He and Graeme are coming to your birthday party on Saturday.'

Perhaps it wasn't such a bad thing that Rory wouldn't be there, Faith consoled herself. He was *just* Kurt's type.

Later that afternoon, having cycled up to Upper Springlode to pay the farrier, Faith found Rory asleep on the sofa in his ramshackle cottage. Twitch the terrier was curled up on his chest, and both were oblivious to the television blaring in the corner of the room.

With his dark blond hair falling over his face, tangling with those long, sooty lashes and flopping over his wide cheeks to tickle his half-smiling mouth, he was so beautiful he made her heart burn with longing. His languid, greyhound-lean body was dressed in threadbare breeches, mis-matched loud stripy socks with his toes poking out and an ancient British Eventing polo shirt. He looked like a ragamuffin but, just like his horses that wore ancient, holey rugs and moth-eaten bandages, the body beneath the rags was glossy, muscled and unfairly super-fit given how much he abused it.

Quietly and efficiently, Faith tidied the worst of the mess away from the floor and surfaces – the place was a tip, as usual – and made Rory a cup of strong black coffee because he had run out of milk, although she did find a big box of chocolates in the cupboard, no doubt a gift from another admiring client. It was the only food in the house.

He awoke groggily, muttering about a broken stopwatch.

'What?' Faith thrust the coffee at him.

'Nothing – a dream. What are you doing here?'

'Looks like I'm going to finish off the yard work for you and turn horses out, as you're in no fit state.'

'I was just catching forty winks after watching the Ebor.' He nodded towards the television.

'Channel Four Racing finished over an hour ago – that's some crummy old movie.'

Rory squinted tiredly to the screen, where two people were riding on horseback across a spectacular landscape.

'This isn't a crummy old movie, Faith. It's *The Man from Snowy River*. Man, I love this film! You wait – the best movie kiss ever is about to happen. The girl in this film is gorgeous.'

Immediately interested, Faith squashed in beside him, only to leap up again a moment later as a set of teeth as sharp as a piranha's sank into her thigh. 'What the . . .?'

Rory barely glanced round. 'Oh, that's just Milo, Nell's dog. I'm looking after him while she's in the States.'

Emerging from beneath a very flat tapestry cushion, the poppy-eyed Chihuahua gave Faith a dirty look and slunk on to the arm of the sofa to lick his miniature paws.

'Is Dillon serious about her, d'you think?' Faith sneered, certain that any control Nell had over the Rafferty eventing string would be a decidedly bad thing.

But Rory shushed her as a couple appeared on screen sharing the same saddle, and Faith watched agog, now sitting on a pair of spurs.

When it happened, the kiss was curiously charming and old-fashioned. The couple rode up to the top of the mountain ridge and, as a storm gathered force in the distance, they had a long, delicious-looking kiss on horseback interspersed with fabulous sweeping shots of craggy valleys and sunset gallops.

To her amazement, Rory had tears in his eyes as he watched. 'How perfect is that, huh? And isn't she beautiful?'

'She's okay.' The girl was, Faith realised excitedly, quite unlike Rory's usual taste in ageing glamourpuss pin-ups. She had frizzy hair, for one, and quite a flat chest and her features – while they bore a passing reference to those of Sophia Loren – were not exceptionally pretty. Best of all, she wasn't over fifty.

'My sister had this on video when we were kids – she watched it to death. It's about a ranch hand who falls in love with the boss's daughter, Jessica. She's a serious crosspatch. Like you.'

Better and better.

'Later, there's just the best scene ever when Jim proves himself a man not a boy by galloping down a mountain side – you wait and see.'

Faith didn't need asking twice, although she knew guiltily in the back of her mind that the horses required feeding and turning out for the night.

Fetching the chocolates and snuggling back among the cushions, trying to ignore the fact that Twitch was licking her ear (if only it was Rory), she watched the movie unfold to its exciting denouement with what was indeed one of the most spectacular – and terrifying – bits of horsemanship she had ever seen as the heroic Jim jumped his horse straight over the edge of a cliff and chased the herd of brumbies down what looked like a sheer mountain face. To her shame, Faith found hot tears on her own face when he finally earned the respect of his boss and the men.

Rory, having whooped all the way through, sat up gleefully for the closing scene as Kirk Douglas, the boss, said, 'You have a long way to go yet, lad.' He then loudly chorused the reply from another ranch hand: 'He's not a lad, brother, he's a man. He's a MAN!'

'Is that it?' Faith was seriously disappointed that there was no more kissing, and instead Jim rode off into the sunset leaving Jessica waving from her father's gate. 'He just doffs his hat to her?'

'Not ready to settle down.'

'Hmph.'

Yet Faith was left in no doubt that she had just gained a valuable insight into the mind of the man she loved, for all his sins, and it was a surprisingly conventional, romantic one. Indoctrinated by Carly to think that all men wanted was tits and arse and attitude, she found herself absolutely swimming in love and gratitude. She almost believed her mother, who maintained that Rory was a lost sheep whose solitary life and love of classical music indicated a poet's soul, although Faith knew with absolute certainty that he'd be a poet who loved big breasts, like John Donne.

As she helped him finish off the yard, spraying horses with citronella-scented repellent to ward off the flies before turning them out into a spectacular Cotswolds sunset dancing with midges, topping up hay and water for all those left in the stables overnight and sweeping hay and straw from the aisle in the American barn, she whistled along to Vivaldi on the radio and fantasised that she and Rory were galloping around together, kissing on mountain tops. Out of habit she stopped at White Lies's box and pressed her nose to his warm, whiskery muzzle, smelling of the Polos his master had just sneaked to him as he passed. Rory claimed to have no favourites, but Whitey was special, a battle horse whose career as both a point-to-pointer and eventing star had been fearless and noble, and whose escape from death just a year earlier had been miraculous, not least because it marked a turnaround in Rory's fortunes. Faith adored the big grey horse with his laid-back attitude, knowing he was as devoted to Rory as she was. Like his master, he could be undisciplined and lazy, but he was equally lion-hearted and easily bored.

When Rory had tried to retire him to the field in the spring he'd taken to leaping the hedges to accompany the rest of the yard's horses out on hacks, so they'd brought him back into ridden work as a nanny to the youngsters, and he was now thriving in old age.

'You're the best of the lot,' Faith whispered now, planting a kiss in the sweetness of that velvet muzzle before moving on to finish clearing up, feeling only slightly disloyal to her own beloved Rio, who was far more spectacular but less cuddly.

Finding that she was sweeping her brush over two dusty riding boots, she looked up to find that Rory was standing in his office doorway watching her, pewter eyes filled with rare affection.

'Sorry I won't be at your birthday party.'

'S'okay,' she shrugged, staring at the head of her broom, anxious not to give away her acute disappointment. 'Bloneigh's more important.'

'I'll bring you back a present. You deserve something lovely.'

'Thanks.' The phone in her pocket let out a series of angry pips. 'I'd better go. That's Mum. She's got one of her literary evenings at the shop and I promised to hand round wine.'

'Good girl,' he grinned as he took her brush and she headed for her bike. 'Hey, Faith!'

She turned back and stared at him as he sauntered from the aisle into the light. Illuminated in a low ray of sunlight so golden red that his skin looked like copper, he doffed his baseball cap to her.

Faith was so loopy with love that she freewheeled down the hill towards Oddlode with her feet out at right angles, hollering happily.

Chapter 4

Sylva Frost tapped her long, perfectly manicured nails on the face of Nell Cottrell, who was all over the weekly gossip magazines and tabloids spread out on the smoked glass table in front of her. It was a pretty face, olive-skinned and green-eyed with passable bone structure and a neat bob of black hair framing it, but it was no great shakes. Dillon Rafferty could do better. Certainly his first wife – Hollywood aristocracy and Oscar-winner Fawn Johnston, daughter of the heavyweight director George – had been pure class. This single-mum Sloane Ranger looked like a little scrubber by comparison, albeit a well-bred one. Dillon obviously liked mixing with the gentry.

Sylva, whose Slovakian origins couldn't have been more humble, tapped harder and then flicked through the pages to search for shots of herself.

In order to maintain her profile it was essential that Sylva made the weeklies, and she rated her success by what she called the IFOJ and IFOP scales. If she was IFOJ (In Front of Jordan), she was doing well; if she was IFOP (In Front of Posh), she was truly on song. If she was BKK (Behind Kerry Katona) then she needed proactive PR, and fast.

This week she had done poorly, her best position being five pages into *Heat*. She didn't appear in *OK!*, *Cheers!*, *Closer* or *Reveal* until almost half way through, captured on the red carpet at an awards ceremony the previous week, despite accompanying a hotly tipped young British actor and wearing a dress that barely covered her pale bikini line and dark areolas. Unfortunately it was a dress that had also been wrapped around a young WAG fresh from the celebrity jungle and, in a readers' poll as to who looked better, the WAG had gained sixty-five per cent of the votes.

Sylva smarted and peered more closely at herself.

'*Mačička!*' Her mother, Mama Szubiak, who was also her manager, called out from the kitchen, using the Slovak word for kitten. 'Rodney wants to start shooting now.'

'Tell him to wait!' Sylva yelled.

As usual they spoke in English, an affectation they had first struck up in Sylva's childhood home, a small apartment in Bratislava that she had shared with her seven siblings and her ever-arguing parents. Back then, Mama had chosen Sylva to share her private language. Having taught herself English with the aid of an old dictionary and endless American movies shown on TV after the fall of communism, Mama had imparted her secret 'code' to her youngest and favourite daughter as a way of excluding the rest of the family, especially her second husband. She had married Sylva's father as a young widow, thinking him safe and secure, but he had turned out to be lazy and unfaithful. Deeply anglophile and very ambitious, Mrs Szubiak had been instrumental in propelling her pretty daughter to stardom, first in Slovakia and latterly in the UK. Sylva's beauty and talent was Mama's ticket to freedom, but it was not easy to control her; even as a young modern pentathlon star in her native country she had been so wilful that she had almost ruined all of Mama's dreams. Years later, and now one of Britain's biggest celebrities, her daughter could still be just as obstinate and wayward.

Now Mama turned back to the television documentary crew whose fly-on-the-wall series charting the day to day life of the Slovakian glamourpuss and mother of two, *Sylva's Shadow*, had been a huge hit on satellite and freeview since its first episode eighteen months earlier.

'Give her a little more time,' she told Rodney, the long-suffering producer, who was holding his palms up in despair at having been kept waiting for over three hours. It was his daughter's seventh birthday and he was missing her party for this.

He would have told mother and daughter to get stuffed long ago were he not so madly in love with Sylva, not to mention terrified of Mrs Szubiak, who might be under five foot tall but was over eighteen stone with strange werewolf eyes and a helmet of dyed golden hair shaped like the tip of a bullet.

He flashed a tired smile and reached for his phone to text his wife and let her know it was going to be another long day and that he wouldn't make Pippa's pool party. He hadn't been home in time to read his children a bedtime story for weeks because he was too busy documenting the life of the nation's favourite superstar single mum. Then again, nor had Sylva been around at *her* children's bedtime, not since the episode in which his team had shot her in the nursery, reading lovingly from her own children's book *Sylva Linings*, based on her take on Slovakian folk stories, curled up in a vast squishy sofa wearing fluffy slippers and cream cashmere PJs, a small boy under each arm. A perfect tableau of devoted young motherhood, it had warmed hearts across the nation. However, when not enacting such scenes for her film crew, as far as Rodney could tell, she left childcare to one of her army of Slovakian nannies – all relatives – who brought the children zipped into designer bed bags, still warm and scented from their baths, to be kissed by their mother at seven o'clock before whisking them away again.

Rodney prided himself on his easygoing metrosexual liberalism and felt that children – especially those with absent fathers like Sylva's kids – needed lots of hands-on parenting and one-to-one bonding. His wife thought Sylva was appalling, but despite his moral disapproval in principle, Rodney could never bring himself to criticise the woman who made his loins feel on fire with just a flick of her pretty head and a wiggle of her pert backside. She was the ultimate pocket plaything. Standing in her handmade baby blue kitchen, he sent his wife a text message and then stared out through the deep-set latticed window at the beautiful garden, lavishly tended by two strapping male Slovak cousins of Sylva and filled with baby blue, lilac and mauve flowers. Sylva loved blues. The first time that Rodney had seen her – sitting on the blue gingham cushions of the antique cast-iron swing chair that he could see through the window now, beneath the willow arch woven with blue clematis, her blonde hair spilling across her exquisite tanned face from which the bluest of eyes sparkled, those magnificent silicone breasts jutting improbably and fantastically from an absurdly tight, plunging periwinkle T-shirt, all his blood had rushed to his groin. Now he only had to see a certain shade of powder blue – on a magazine advert, a breakfast cereal packet, a curtain pattern – and he found himself semi-erect.

Meanwhile, amid the magazines in her dining room, Sylva banged her small fist on Kerry Katona's cleavage and called for her mother.

'Order the Complan and the Ben & Jerry's, Mama. I am going to have to put on weight again.'

'Please, no!' Mama Szubiak gasped.

Her daughter nodded with a resigned sigh. 'There is no other way.'

'You could fast. Lose weight instead.'

'I did that last time, remember? I have to stick to the rules.'

Sylva was a brand name, a new breed of celebrity who was most famous for being famous and consequently knew that she had to keep her name in the headlines to maintain her status. In addition to dating stars, wearing a path in launch party red carpets, bearing beautiful babies, merchandising endless products and living her life in the full glare of non-stop publicity, Sylva had discovered a route to guaranteed front-cover stardom which was quicker (and less messy) than marrying a Premiership star. The media was obsessed with size, equally damning of fat and skinny yet unable to stop itself salivating over the slightest hint of weight change. As a result, dramatic shifts in any celebrity's dress size were always a headline-grabber. Every six to eight months, faced with a headline drought, Sylva piled on about twenty pounds, taking her from her size six petite perfection to a size ten tabloid-dubbed 'porker', or on one memorable occasion when she'd overdone the milkshakes, a size twelve 'super-porker'. The glossy weeklies loved it, printing gruesome and unflattering shots of her thickening waist, hefty thighs and double chins, daubed with day-glo shout-lines like 'Sylva Cellulite Shocker!' Then, while the box-out editorials were still sympathetically and hypocritically speculating as to the reasons for all this 'misery eating', she would just as swiftly drop the weight again, guaranteeing yet more media coverage as her new fabulous figure was admired while her 'drastic weight loss' was now contemplated. Then, the next time she felt her IFOJ and IFOP ratings drop towards BKK, she would go the other way, fasting her way to a dangerously gaunt size four, which would launch another paparazzi feeding frenzy as shots of her 'dangerously thin' body were plastered over the front facing pages opposite the beauty ads and the editorial commentaries sympathetically speculated why devoted mum of two 'Super-skinny Sylva' was 'starving herself'. After a few weeks of conjecture she could let her body weight return to its meticulously maintained norm. Thus her status as tabloid headliner was continually reinvigorated in a cyclical pattern of feast and famine. It was an admittedly drastic way to stay famous; such extreme yo-yo dieting was hard work – the drastic weight changes played havoc with her body, and she had not had a period in almost six months – but it was highly effective.

Mrs Szubiak was a hugely ambitious woman who loved nothing more than to see her daughter on the front covers of all the magazines piled up in the Amersham hairdressers where she went to get her blonde bullet hairdo welded into shape each week, but even she could see that the regime was not healthy. Every time Sylva piled on the pounds she was also terrified that, this time, she wouldn't be able to lose it and would lose her fame and fortune completely. A star getting fat was a great story; a star staying fat was old news.

'I think we must find another way,' she said now.

'It is the best way, Mama. We know that.'

'A new lover, perhaps?'

'I *have* a new lover,' Sylva pointed out. The hotly tipped young British actor was both gay and living in LA, but their 'relationship' was holding up in front of the camera lenses thus far.

'He is not famous enough,' Mama said with a dismissive sniff.

'He was nominated for an Oscar this year, which is more than Jonte ever has been.' Sylva's short-lived second marriage, which had recently ended in a quickie divorce, had been to dashing Brit actor and serial co-star shagger Jonte Frost. As well as procuring her younger son, Hain, marriage to Jonte had lent Sylva much-needed credibility and propelled her into an entirely new celebrity super league, one in which she was desperate to stay after years as a disposable WAG. With her parallel careers of glamour modelling, writing, acting and singing; her perfume, cosmetics and underwear lines to promote; her television series and her fitness DVDs, it was essential to keep her brand constantly in the press. Dating one of Jonte's younger, hunkier screen rivals was a good tactic.

'He is not famous enough,' Mama repeated, making her way to the large reproduction Regency bureau, which she unlocked with a small key kept on a chain around her neck. 'We must find you a better man, *mačička*, a man who will put a ring on your finger again.'

'We could try a woman this time?' Sylva suggested. The trend for glamour girls to have a Sapphic phase was admittedly getting rather well-worn and sleazy – fed up with years of men wanting them only for their bodies, blah blah, get together with another woman, blah blah, media-fuelled talk of bisexuality adds to the cool factor, blah: Lindsay Lohan, Megan Fox, Jodie Marsh, Angelina Jolie, blah blah – but Sylva thought it still had mileage if handled delicately. Hadn't a publicity-hungry supermodel once let loose a rather saucy rumour about a glamorous drag queen that had worked well? Sylva envisaged something on a rather more classy scale: perhaps an androgynous aristo in tailored tweed, or a gorgeous raven-haired rock chick.

But Mama pretended not to hear. She would never entertain the idea of Sylva having a relationship with a woman, however artfully staged. Like Queen Victoria, she refused to believe lesbianism even existed.

In the bureau were her files – tens of neat pink ring binders in which she kept many acres of Sylva's cuttings (though only the most recent ones: all of the others having been archived into many large boxes in an attic room because they took up so much space). Beside these recent cuttings, so meticulously filed, was a baby blue ring binder that she now drew out and opened.

Sylva sighed. 'No, Mama, I don't think we can make that work. Not yet. It's too soon after Jonte.'

'Of course we can make it work.' Mrs Szubiak placed the file on top of the magazines in front of her daughter, obscuring Nell Cottrell's beautiful face, although her famous escort still peered out above it, looking very handsome and self-satisfied. 'It is time for my little girl to star in another fairytale.'

Ironically, as Sylva's mother opened the file, Dillon Rafferty's name was at the top of the index list in her neat, curling handwriting, along with a dozen other potential targets, all of which Mrs Szubiak had studied carefully, compiling very detailed biographies full of information and photographs to help her and her daughter in their quest. Among them was at least one dotcom billionaire, two Oscar-winning actors, several rock stars, an oligarch and a red-blooded Royal prince within a couple of croaks of the throne.

On the spine of the blue file, also in Mrs Szubiak's neat copper-plate capitals, was one word: HUSBANDS.

'It is time,' she told her daughter grandly. 'To select Number Three.'

'Must we?'

'Yes,' she covered Sylva's delicate hand with her own, gnarled and hardened from a tough life before their escape to England. She would never allow her daughter to know such a life again.

Long ago, Mama had decided that marriage for Sylva was as much a career move as launching a new clothing range or promoting her latest ghost-written book.

'Third time lucky, as they say in this country,' she said determinedly.

'Third time lucky,' Sylva echoed, sliding the file towards her mother so that she could once again study the magazine shot of Dillon Rafferty and his new girlfriend. 'Who do you have in mind?'

As if she needed to ask . . .

The knotty forefinger with its long, nicotine-yellow nail landed on Dillon's nose. 'Let's start at the top of the list and work our way down, as before.'

'Nothing like aiming high.' Sylva felt a shiver of excitement course through her. On cue, 'Two Souls' started playing on the distant kitchen radio, which Mama kept permanently tuned to Radio Two. 'Tell Rodney I'm ready for him to start shooting now, Mama.'

Mrs Szubiak gasped, clutching the file to her chest. 'You are surely not going to let him see our plans?'

'Of course not,' Sylva stood up and, turning to the huge Venetian mirror above the ornate fireplace, ruffled her thick blonde hair – a metre long including extensions. 'I am going to do some gardening with the kids. Plant veggies. Dillon's got an organic farm shop, hasn't he? He'll approve. It seems the perfect start to our masterplan.'

Mama regarded her daughter slyly. Sometimes she couldn't be quite sure whether Sylva was being serious or not.

'The children are not here,' she reminded her.

'Aren't they?' Sylva asked, vaguely recalling that her small boys and their doting entourage of nannies were currently splashing around in the pool of Lissom Hall, the nearby private spa that had made her an honorary member after so many photo shoots staged there. 'In that case, I'll plant veggies on my own. Tell Rodney that I'm going to the garden centre in five minutes. They can start shooting me there. I'll take the Cayenne.'

She raced upstairs to change into denim hot-pant dungarees with nothing but a lacy cream and blue camisole underneath, matched with patterned baby blue wellies and topped with a floppy straw hat that cast a bewitching dappled shadow on her high-cheekboned face.

Sylva knew how to set a scene.

Chapter 5

Dillon and Nell were fast-tracked through customs at Heathrow and, accompanied by his record label PR, Tania, and the super-efficient airport's VIP liaison executive, pushed their overloaded luggage trolleys past the banks of photographers intent on getting a shot of the global chart-topper and his new squeeze.

Having spent the final hour of the flight locked in a First Class wash room, changing and applying make-up, Nell was now hiding her perfectly painted eyes behind oversized dark glasses, a Hermès scarf tied over her beautifully styled hair and a long summer mackintosh buckled over the floral playsuit she'd bought in Saks the previous day.

'Where's your little girl, Nell?' one of the hacks called out.

'With her grandmother,' Nell said smoothly, despite Tania frantically signalling for her to say nothing while trying to bat all the press away with the aid of her vast Mulberry handbag. 'I can't wait to see her.'

But when they were finally ensconced behind the tinted glass of the vast car sent to pick them up, the Louis Vuitton luggage and tens of designer shopping bags crammed in the boot and Tania dispatched in a humble black cab, Nell suggested that they take a suite at Cliveden for the night. 'The label will pay.'

'Why should they?' Dillon laughed incredulously. 'They've already put us up in five-star luxury in New York just so that you could shop all week. I have houses in London and Oxfordshire; I hardly need to stay in a hotel near Henley. Besides, I want to get back for my kids.'

'They're still in LA with Fawn, packing their little suitcases,' she pointed out sourly, having found herself stranded at the Four Seasons for several dull sunbathing and shopping afternoons a fortnight earlier while he spent time with his children and ex-wife at his former in-laws' Malibu beach house.

'Yes, and when they land tomorrow the kids will come straight to West Oddford,' he reminded her.

'So I can have you all to myself for a night? At the London house?'

'That's all ready for Fawn,' he sighed.

Since their divorce, Dillon and Fawn had maintained a close transatlantic relationship for the sake of their two daughters, Pomegranate and Blueberry. When in the UK, Fawn always based herself in the couple's former marital home. The Nash-designed Regent's Park terrace was now officially Dillon's property, but they remained wholly cordial about it and anglophile Fawn regularly stayed there for weeks at a time, much to Nell's discomfort. Six-year-old Pom and four-year-old Berry, already wholly accustomed to life spread between several sites, were more than happy to rattle straight off the LA flight into a car chauffeuring them to the Cotswolds while their mother headed towards North London alone.

Nell, by contrast, felt profoundly disorientated and ill at ease after just three weeks in the States.

Coming back to find the UK in the grip of Olympic fever didn't help. It was just days away from the opening ceremony and the whole country had gone Olympics mad. On reflection, she guessed it was safest to stay at home. But Dillon's beloved West Oddford Farm felt more like a love rival than home, and he was clearly still a long way off asking her to share it with him for more than a night at a time.

Ever the rolling stone, who now had her own pet rock star, Nell was much happier living in hotel rooms and well-staffed holiday houses, where there was room service on tap and one could just as equally hang the Do Not Disturb sign on the door as walk out, slamming that door and driving away at the drop of a hat to let somebody else pick up the mess.

'The farm will be full of people,' she curled up to him. 'I want you to myself just for one night.'

'You've had me in the States for three weeks.'

'I've hardly seen you!'

'We've been together most nights.' He didn't want to get into the argument about Fawn again. Nell wouldn't leave it alone, like an itchy rash. Asking her along to the States after the story about their relationship had gone public had been a last-minute, hot-headed decision that Dillon had regretted in hindsight. He'd wanted to protect her from all the press attention in the UK, but instead he had almost suffocated her with his own commitments in America, a schedule of work, plus delicate family politics, that had been planned for many months and took no account of a girlfriend accustomed to long walks together, lost weekends and lazy lovemaking that sometimes stretched over several hours.

'I had to work, Nell. You knew that was the deal when I asked you along.'

'You didn't exactly spell out that the only private time we'd get was a few lousy hours each night sharing a bed in a strange hotel with the air-con switched off, a wake-up call booked for six and your BlackBerry vibrating every ten minutes. And now we've got your kids coming, then you're off to Italy in less than a week. I think I deserve *one* night of your undivided attention, don't you?' She licked her lips playfully.

Dillon stifled a yawn and wrapped his arm tightly around her, knowing that she was attention seeking because she had been neglected and was totally unaccustomed to it. He couldn't deny it; his schedule was so punishing that he was neglecting everything.

'Two Souls', the song that had relaunched his career, had been Number One in the UK for over three months now, as well as topping charts all over Europe and the Far East. It was now also Number One in the States and, with maximum airplay and downloads, the album had already gone platinum and promoters were howling for a stadium tour.

Dillon was exhausted and strangely depressed, hating himself for his lack of gratitude but unable to stop the resentment crawling all over him. His comeback had been a huge success, exceeding all expectations in every possible way except one – his own euphoria had not returned. He had no sense of that giddy, grateful, boy-in-a-magical-toyshop feeling that he'd once relished when out-selling every recording artist in the world, including his father. He simply felt strained, homesick and appalled at the apple-polishing, toadying and freeloading he encountered everywhere he went.

He found himself continually questioning why exactly had he staged a comeback when the place that he had escaped to was so good?

Despite having lived in some of the most prestigious addresses in the world, West Oddford Farm, a lopsided pile hidden at the end of half a mile of drive, tucked in a discreet fold between two hills as plump and soft as matronly breasts untouched by silicone, was the only home in which he truly felt content. A working farm, managed by a great team in his absence, it had become Dillon's major project and *raison d'être* after the simultaneous collapse of his marriage, career and mental health. It had helped him through a prolonged breakdown and crippling writer's block. He had bought the farm on a whim, more because he needed a bolthole away from the media glare than because he wanted to roll up his sleeves and get his hands dirty, but his interest in food had soon sparked an interest in farming. Once a dairy farm, West Oddford boasted three hundred acres of wood-skirted land with no rights of way crossing it, ensuring complete privacy. It also came with vast tracts of outbuildings that Dillon had soon bored of wandering around with a shotgun picking off crows and rats and started to want to bring back to life. Rare sheep, cattle and pigs were soon installed, initially for decoration but then for produce. He became interested in butchery and husbandry, in meats and cheeses, in nurturing the kitchen gardens that sheltered a burgeoning vegetable plot, filling the glass houses and soft-fruit frames, in maximising yield in his ancient orchards and nuttery, all of which were brought back to life by endless tranfusions from his dwindling savings. Gaining organic status became an obsessive mission, later transcended by setting up a farm shop and, more recently, the marketing of a whole range that sold in exclusive food halls and delicatessens across the world.

It had taken time, but gradually West Oddford Organics had become a byword for good quality, a favourite of the wealthy Cotswold Boden wives brigade. As its dashing figurehead, Dillon had rather unexpectedly become a spokesman for all things foodie, organic, seasonal and British, with a regular column in a Sunday supplement and radio and television shows often clamouring for quotes.

Dillon was at last taken seriously by those erstwhile harsh critics – his neighbours, particularly neighbouring farmers and nimbys. His passion and zeal were acknowledged as great things. His farm shop, which had quickly outgrown its modest quarters in a converted milk parlour and relocated from the farm itself to retail premises in picturesque Morrell on the Moor, incorporating a café and deli, was a mecca for foodies and star-spotters alike. Everyone assumed Dillon was cashing in. But the process, with its vast set-up costs and very narrow margins, had in fact almost bankrupted him and he was faced with a very real dilemma of selling the London house – something he felt he couldn't do to Fawn and the kids – or make some real money at last. He had even contemplated such horrors as the *Strictly* dancefloor to score a quick, much-needed cash injection.

It was at that point that he'd first heard 'Two Souls', in the most unlikely of settings – a local auction house where its writer and composer, nineties pop icon Trudy Dew, had played it on a grand piano that was up for sale and Dillon, like everyone there that day, had been bewitched. He'd persuaded his record label to buy the rights to it. Now the world was enjoying the haunting, uplifting, unforgettable song. Rather too much. It was currently playing in every shop and mall, was aired hourly on radio stations, was being used as lead-in music on TV and downloaded on to every iPod the world over.

Although he still rated the ballad as the best he'd ever come across, Dillon would quite gratefully not hear, play or sing it again for several years. He was fed up to the back teeth of it.

Today, a hot summer's day, it was playing out of the open windows of a hundred cars crawling along the sticky tarmac of the motorway.

Normally insistent upon leaving the air-con switched off and fresh air allowed in as a vague gesture towards shrinking his carbon footprint, Dillon irritably told the driver to close all the windows.

Nell had fallen silent now, moving away from him to snuggle up to a big leather armrest and stare sulkily out of the window at newly planted fir trees sliding by, her fingers tappity-tapping on the glass. With her slim, tanned limbs, hollow cheeks and great, black over-sized glasses, she suddenly reminded him of a fly. She'd certainly been buzzing around like a maddened bluebottle in the past few days, but he supposed he had kept her shut away in hotel rooms day after day while he worked. This was her first long trip away without Giselle and it must be trying for her, however much she denied it.

'I'm sorry,' he sighed, reaching out to take her narrow, long-fingered hand, stopping the nails from tapping. 'I meant for you to have a better time.'

'I had a great time,' she lied gallantly, 'I just don't want it to end.'

He squeezed her hand, wondering if he could explain to her why West Oddford was so important to him, to his sanity and why he so badly needed to get back there – with her, whom he so adored and with whom he longed to have a relaxed, family relationship as opposed to the show-stopping media love affair they appeared to have tripped into. He had fallen for a local girl, after all. She'd seemed made-to-measure for him from the start; like him, Nell was a city–country hybrid who combined partying with London's fash-ionistas with the shooting, tweed and mud splatters of time out country life. She understood the seasons, both the social one and the farming and bloodsports calendar. She knew the valley and the ridgeway better than anyone he had yet met. Her family were an Oddlode dynasty. On top of which, she was a mother struggling to keep her child's life as normal as possible despite separated parents. If anyone could understand him, she could.

It also helped that she looked so good, easily out-classing the leggy girls rented from model agencies by the ton to fill music indus-try parties, and who were consequently very thick on the ground in more than one sense. Nell was beautiful, bright, sharp-tongued and self-aware. She was also more adventurous than any lover he'd had, certainly any lover he could remember which, given that a lot of his past sex life, including the conception of his children, had been conducted while he was too stoned and pissed to remember a thing, wasn't perhaps as great an accolade as it first appeared. But she *was* his first long-term lover since cleaning up, and she was amazing. She could turn him on in an instant; she had him hooked. He just needed the time to appreciate her more.

'I'm better at home,' was all he could lamely muster. 'I'm a nicer person at West Oddford.'

'You're a wonderful person,' she reached down to lower the zip of his flies, a naughty smile dancing on her lips, impatient to be the ultimate groupie with an Access All Areas pass.

Dillon immediately felt his groin tighten as his band member leapt in response.

Sometimes he might struggle to get to a place with Nell mentally that was as good as their relationship on paper, but that was never the case physically, whether they were in London, LA, the Cotswolds, the Caribbean, New York or somewhere on the M25.

Much later, having nodded off soon after the Stokenchurch Gap, Dillon woke with a start to find that the car's engine had been switched off and it was parked on a familiar, weed-strewn square of gravel in front of the large American barn at Overlodes Equestrian Centre. It certainly wasn't West Oddford Farm. His driver was lurking about fifty yards away, smoking a sly cigarette behind a large rainwater butt. Nell had disappeared.

He stretched and tumbled groggily from the car to go in search of his errant girlfriend.

She wasn't hard to track down, sitting coquettishly on Rory Midwinter's desk in the yard office having just staged a very emotional reunion with her Chihuahua, Milo.

'You'd rather come here to collect your dog before seeing Giselle?' he balked.

'Gigi will be in the middle of her afternoon nap,' she pointed out pragmatically. Her mother Dibs, with whom Giselle was staying, was an old-fashioned Irish stickler when it came to strictly enforced regime.

'Besides which, Nell knew you'd want to check on your best-ever investment,' drawled a lazy voice as Rory came through from the tack room carrying chipped mugs of tea, that unique, cloud-partingly sunny smile on his face. 'Not to mention the fact that you are both no doubt gagging for your first proper brew since touching down. It must be weeks – here!' He thrust a steaming, grubby-rimmed mug of stewed tea at Dillon, who tried not to think too longingly of his big, homely kitchen with its Earl Grey and comforting earthenware mugs.

Feeling ungrateful, he took a hefty swig and burned his tongue.

'So how *are* the horses going?' he asked tiredly, wishing he felt more interested. He struggled to remember their names and only returned Rory's calls or checked how he was doing when Nell reminded him to, which was usually when she wanted to pick a fight with him or manipulate his diary for her own ends.

'The horses are not going that great,' Rory grimaced apologetically. 'We have a technical hitch in the wham-bam-Grand-Slam masterplan.'

'To what plan?' He had totally forgotten that one of the challenges he had set Rory, upon investing in him, was to win the famous Rolex Grand Slam. This consisted of taking the title in the top three international three day events in succession.

'Burghley's probably a non-starter. Sid looks like he's back in the locker room early this year. He's lame again.'

'Rory must go to Burghley!' Nell protested over Milo's head, 'You must go to Burghley, Rory. Mustn't he, Dillon?'

'Must he?' Dillon sighed, gazing solemnly at the photographs that crazy-paved the walls, almost all of them Rory hurtling across country on a horse, most of them photographer's proofs. It looked much more fun than sitting in hot studios under too much pan-stick and powder, telling a caring daytime television anchor about your nervous breakdown and addictions, and the beauty of organic brie. He was feeling increasingly jet-lagged. 'Why is Burghley important?'

'He owns a four-star horse and has never heard of Burghley,' Nell teased, threading her arm through his.

Dillon in fact knew Burghley Horse Trials was one of the 'big three', a top-ranking autumn three day event akin to playing Reading Festival in musician terms, but he couldn't be bothered to protest. There were so many horse trials at so many country houses he lost track. Like rock festivals.

'It's a beautiful place,' Nell insisted. 'We must go. Is the horse really not up to it, Rory?' She keyed him with her eyes.

Rory could be bullied on most things, but not his horse's welfare. 'The vet scanned his front legs yesterday. Might never compete again, if I'm honest.'

Dillon tutted under his breath, seeing fifty thousand pounds going up in smoke, or more accurately, retiring into a field.

He'd first encountered Rory not long after he bought West Oddlode Farm, when country life was a hobby and every weekend was a house party. Determined to learn to ride, he'd block-booked lessons with Rory and later brought along gangs of friends to ride out around the valley, falling off regularly. One such tumble had smashed Dillon's leg so badly that he was still lame, and had no desire to ride again. But Rory and his talent remained an inspiration, as did the wonderful horses he produced. When Rory's only top horse had been injured so badly that his career was thought to be over, everybody surrounding Rory thought that meant his competitive dreams were washed up too. His most loyal fan, Faith, had even given him her own horse to ride, but it was never going to be enough. Then, as Dillon's fortunes were revived through a new album deal and his career looked set to rocket, he'd stepped in as benefactor. He'd always adored shopping for beautiful things, a trait inherited from his father, and so it had been no great trial to buy a string of event horses, particularly as one of his oldest friends was well-connected and had led him straight to the veteran four-star campaigner Snake Charmer, known as Sid, and the younger, three-star Egley's Opposition, aka Humpty, who was popularly believed to be a superstar in the making. He'd also funded a clutch of cheaper novice horses, bought by Rory off the racetrack at bargain prices and schooled on to event. Some were successful, but most failed, either too untrainable or too unsound to get close to the big league.

Eventing was a very hit and miss affair, as Dillon was learning. The big gatherings at grand country houses weren't the only parallel with the music industry. For every successful rider there were tens of eager young wannabes waiting in the wings, along with groupies and teenage fans. Being a professional event rider meant a life lived on the road, a horsebox in place of a tour bus, setting up camp and performing at different venues week in, week out. Only the very lucky few ever made it to the big time. When they did, they spent even more time away from home, far from the acres of familiar turf they loved.

As with so many of his financial decisions, Dillon had sponsored Rory on a whim – and after rather a lot of bargaining and arm-twisting from one particular quarter – but his interest in eventing had dwindled dramatically in the light of his own punishing workload and prolonged absences from the Lodes Valley. Eventing seemed a very toffee-nosed, elitist sport, and Dillon had recently begun to suspect that Rory was too spoilt and self-indulgent to really make a success of it, however much cash he put in to bankroll him. True, he was a genuinely amiable character and was reputedly in possession of a tremendous riding talent, but Dillon had yet to see much evidence of it. His horses were always lame or sick. And Rory was always drunk.

Illogically, Dillon suddenly found himself envying Rory his booze-laden failure.

Dillon missed drinking. Every day of his life he missed drinking. He didn't feel the same way about the drugs, the same sense of loss or the triggers that made his hands and throat twitch for the weight of a full glass, the slake of scotch or red wine against his throat. Even cigarettes no longer haunted his dreams in the way that alcohol did. Sometimes he still craved a drink so badly that it blotted out reason – and there was only one place where he was truly safe from the craving.

His heart felt as though it was trying to beat its way out of his chest and bounce down the three miles of criss-crossing bridleways and footpaths that separated Overlodes Stables high on the escarpment from West Oddford Farm deep in the lush valley.

Burning his mouth even more, he drank his tea in record time while Rory and Nell gossiped about mutual acquaintances.

'Aunt Bell made me give pony rides at the Oddlode village fête – can you imagine the shame? I had to miss Stockland Lovell trials to do it. Poor Spurs had it even worse because she forced him to oversee the cow-pat grid . . .'

Suddenly unable to bear it any longer, Dillon let out an infuriated bellow, slammed down his mug and stormed out to the car.

Rory jumped back in alarm. 'What on earth was that all about?'

Nell took it all in her stride. 'He gets like that sometimes. He says he finds it hard to express himself.'

'He should try saying a polite "goodbye".' Rory kissed Nell

farewell on both cheeks and Milo on the top of his head and walked them to the car.

'What does this little chap's namesake make of your moody rock star?' he asked in an undertone, nodding at the dog.

Nell pulled a face. Her on-off married lover, also called Milo, had been very much off lately. She didn't like to admit how much she missed his company, his wisdom, his devotion to her and their simpatico humour. Casting around for a change of topic, she saw all Rory's tack trunks piled up by the horsebox ready to be loaded and, remembering that he was setting off for Scotland the next day, wished him good luck for Bloneigh Castle.

'Thanks.' He grinned, crossing his fingers and his eyes at the same time. 'I wish you were coming. You're my mascot now. I can't believe you've made this happen for me, N, honestly. I know it's not Dillon's horse in the big class, but I'll still ride it for my guardian angel.' He dropped another grateful kiss on her cheek.

Nell tilted her head modestly.

'You taking ever-faithful Faith as a groom?' she asked, already knowing the answer. She was very protective of Rory who, as well as being a lifelong family friend and her first boyfriend many years ago, was something of a personal pet that she guarded as jealously as little Milo. It was clear that Faith Brakespear was besotted with him, and bossy enough to influence him. Nell found the girl particularly abrasive and was livid that Dillon had accepted an invitation on both their behalves to go to her eighteenth birthday party with Magnus. Faith must have begged her brother shamelessly. Sending Rory to Scotland was Nell's retaliation.

Rory was shaking his head. 'I could use old Faith right now, but she's got her birthday party next weekend, dammit. Diana and Mummy are coming instead.'

'You have to be joking!' Nell hooted, trying to imagine Rory's blowsy sister and their gin-addled mother, Truffle, wielding sweat scrapers and stud spanners.

'They're all for it, and Aunt Til has promised to look in on the trials. She moved to Scotland a couple of years ago, remember? None of us have seen her since.'

'A family reunion then?' Nell could well imagine the three female Constantines with their feet up in the members' tent, reminiscing while poor Rory was run ragged. She hugged him again as they reached the car, surprised by her sudden reluctance to get back inside with Dillon and his black mood.

'I bloody well hope I bring back some ribbons,' Rory muttered in an undertone. 'Dillon will pull the plug on the lolly if I keep losing.'

'Oh, he'll never do that,' Nell assured him brightly. 'He'll just buy you more toys to play with to cheer you up. He does that with us all: lover, children, ex-wife, even his farm staff. It's like an agricultural equipment showroom down there. He's bought me two identical cars already this year. He quite forgot that he bought me the first one, you see, so he ordered another by mistake.'

'Lucky you,' Rory sighed, glancing at his ancient horsebox and hoping that it would make it to Scotland.

'Lucky me,' she nodded, all expression hidden behind the huge black glasses as she dropped another pouting kiss on Milo's head and climbed into the car.

They had barely travelled out of the village when she turned to Dillon.

'I think Rory needs your support in Scotland next weekend. We'll go up there and cheer him on.'

'I think I'm in Milan.' He checked his BlackBerry, which confirmed that his daughters' short visit was to be followed by a lucrative personal appearance at an AC *v* Inter match.

'No you're not. You're flying back on Saturday afternoon.'

He checked the BlackBerry again and groaned. 'Of course. Magnus's little sister is having a party.'

'We can get out of that easily enough,' she waved a dismissive hand. 'I'll book us a lovely hotel near Bloneigh, shall I? The Borders are stunning at this time of year.'

'We can't possibly do that to Faith. She's your family.'

'Hardly!'

'She's Giselle's aunt.'

She had to concede the point, but disliked the sanctimonious tone and couldn't believe that he wasn't as desperate as she was for an excuse to get out of this dreadful teen party. He could be very pious and moralising at times, like a fusty old vicar banging on about family and children. Well, he wasn't the only one who could put family first.

Her own clan, recently scattered when her parents had downsized from the vast Abbey to a barn conversion in which she and Gigi now reluctantly occupied the modest guest suite, still had a loudly beating heart that called her back to her mother's lemon cake at times of need.

'Take me to Chandler's Barn,' she announced suddenly. 'I want to see my mo— my daughter.'

The toddling explosion of joy that burst from the barn's vast double doors, blonde pigtails at wonky angles and toothy smile wide in those perfect pink, chubby cheeks lifted both Nell and Dillon's spirits immeasurably.

'Come home with me,' he urged her as she finally slowed from spinning Gigi around and around in her arms.

There was no lemon drizzle cake on offer and Nell's mother was keen to listen to a new recording of Stravinsky's 'The Nightingale' on Radio 3 so she acquiesced, her mood lifting all the while.

An hour later, creased designer travelling clothes swapped for practical country casuals, they wandered around Dillon's beloved farm and gardens in the balmy evening sunlight, dodging clouds of midges as they checked up on what had been happening in their absence. Gigi sat high on Dillon's shoulders, giggling delightedly as he jogged in and out of the fruit trees in the orchards, ducking high and low and pretending to be an aeroplane.

Dillon was right, Nell decided. He was a better person at West Oddlode, for all its dreariness. He was truly relaxed here, and she was grateful to be a part of it, not making a sulky stand for neglecting her. If that meant playing second fiddle to a herd of rare-breed sheep and several organic crops she would have to learn to live with it, for now at least. He could be a fantastic father for Gigi and a good, kind man to look after her. The urge to be cared for almost overwhelmed Nell at times. She was the moving compass needle that needed a fixed point. She had always been attracted to gentle, soulful men who saw through her tantrums and demands to the underlying vulnerability. Now, with Gigi to protect and care for, Nell wanted more than ever to find a man prepared to dedicate himself to her. Ironically, Milo, the man who understood her better than anyone, was married and determined to stay that way. His loyalty to his wife, however infuriating, meant that he had exactly what Nell loved most. He was totally steadfast. And he was rich and successful too.

Despite his chequered career, Dillon was very rich and successful, with celebrity status to boot, and although he had two young daughters and a rather annoying allegiance to his ex-wife and her family, they were at least all in the States. Here in the UK he was really more dedicated to his farm than anything else, which had to be less of a threat.

'I love you,' she turned to him suddenly as he swooped past with Gigi, who was banging cherries grabbed from passing trees on his head, so he looked like he was wearing a bobbly red crown.

He stopped suddenly and stared at her, blue eyes blazing from beneath the fruity wreath.

'Both of you,' she added, gathering them in her arms and stretching up to bite off a cherry from its stalk and share it with Dillon in a kiss. At the very peak of ripeness, the cherry burst on their tongues, its sweet flesh brimming with juice.

Left with the stone in his mouth, Dillon sucked it thoughtfully, squinting into the setting sun as he carried Gigi back towards the house on his shoulders, Nell leaning into his side. He loved being home at last, where it felt like he had the true beginnings of a family life again. For an absurd moment, when Nell had kissed him, the image of Adam and Eve eating the forbidden fruit had flashed up. He had never been religious, yet the sense of foreboding was, for that moment, as acute as pain. Now he dismissed it and smiled up at the tawny walls of his farmhouse, eager to fill it with laughter and noise. Tomorrow his daughters would arrive. He couldn't wait for them all to be together like one happy family.

'I love you too,' he told Nell as they stood on his back doorstep, breathing in the heady scent of the jasmine growing over the porch above them.

Chapter 6

'Yes! . . . Yes . . . Yes . . . Yes! Yes!'

Tash gasped with delight at every heroic thrust from her husband. His stamina was without question: he was performing for the second time that night, and barely breaking a sweat.

'Yes! Oh, yes . . . oh, darling yes!'

'Will you calm down?' Beccy laughed, her fingers being crushed white as Tash gripped them. 'You'll go into labour.'

'Over my dead body!' growled Alicia, covering Beefy's ears.

'She's talking about childbirth, not politics,' pointed out family friend Penny Moncrieff, who was holding on to Tash's other hand. 'Now shh – this is the last line.'

On the flat screen in front of them, in a huge floodlit stadium surrounded by stands packed with tens of thousands, Hugo cantered his horse past a vast flower arrangement on a pillar topped with the Olympic rings and eyed up the final four jumps.

The Fox's chestnut coat gleamed flame-bright, as golden, precious and rare as the medal he was chasing. He was a class apart from any other horse that had entered the arena that night. Wiry, short-coupled and as athletic as a Derby winner, he was purpose-built for the job. Just like his legendary sire, The Foxy Snob, he was brave and brilliant, defending the family honour for both his father and his rider at the ultimate global competition. On his back, Hugo was utterly focused on the fences ahead of them.

'Come on, my darling.' Tash could hardly bring herself to watch.

Beside her, Beccy's crushed hand ached and her heart crashed huge and proud in her chest. For one brief, disloyal moment she'd found herself rooting for New Zealander Lough Strachan, currently in the silver medal position just a point behind Hugo. He had ridden his tricky, tantrum-throwing horse with such breathtaking skill to go clear he deserved victory. But one look at Hugo and she'd changed allegiance again. This wasn't just about the best rider, this was about their horses, the trust, the training and the teamwork they shared. This was about a combination, and no horse was better produced than Fox, nor any man better at getting the most from him as Hugo. They were as cool as the cucumbers in iced Hendrick's gin.

'Yes!' Tash cried as they cleared the first jump in the line.

'Yes!' whooped Penny as the middle part of the combination stayed up.

'Yes!' Beccy hollered as Fox's white heels flicked up inches clear over the blue and white stripes of the penultimate parallel.

Then, a moment later, Tash let out an ear-splitting scream. '*YES! He's done it! Ohmygod, he's done it!*' She jumped up and down, bump and all.

Crying, whooping and bansheeing in glee along with Alicia, Beccy, the Moncrieffs and the half-dozen other friends invited over to watch the event at Haydown, Tash hugged and high-fived and danced around the snug for the second time that evening.

In Olympic three day eventing the team medals are decided at the show-jumping phase like any other CCI, but for individual glory all competitors must jump again. When Team GB had won gold the assembled Haydown supporters had gone wild. Now, with Hugo's individual gold, they went ballistic. They were making so much noise that nobody heard the phone ring.

It was only when Gus Moncrieff spotted Hugo on screen, still sitting on the horse in the collecting ring with a mobile pressed to his ear, looking suddenly anxious, that he realised what was going on and picked up the handset to pass to Tash.

But Tash was so overwhelmed with emotion she couldn't speak at all, and just made eager panting squeaks.

'What is it? Is it the baby?' Hugo demanded, the crowd still cheering in the background behind him.

'You won gold!' she managed to bleat eventually. 'I love you. I'm so proud of you.'

Now she realised that she could see him talking to her on the television screen, looking terribly dashing and brave and strangely normal despite all the lights and cameras and razzmatazz. His words and their conversation were out of synch with the pictures because of the broadcast delay.

'We did it,' he told her. Someone was demanding his attention in the background. 'I must go. I love you. I'll call you later.'

On screen he was still talking to her. There were tears in his eyes. She had only ever seen him look like that once before, when Cora was born.

While the others were popping open champagne she crept upstairs, forced to stop every few steps to catch her breath. Her pregnancy bump felt like lead now that the baby's head was dropping ever lower, making her pelvis ache non-stop.

Cora was asleep in her cot bed, clutching her comfort blanket and Elmer Elephant, one arm flung above her head and her blankets kicked off.

'Daddy done good,' Tash whispered, straightening her cover and pressing a kiss to her fingertips to transfer to her daughter's face because her bump was far too enormous to let her lean over the cot.

Downstairs they were shouting for her. The medal ceremonies were about to be broadcast.

★

Clutching their posies of flowers like two bridesmaids, individual three day event silver medallist Lough Strachan and the lanky German rider in bronze flanked Hugo as he bowed down from the top of the podium to receive his gold.

'Congratulations.' Lough turned to shake the Brit's hand straight afterwards.

'Could have easily gone the other way,' he patted him on the back magnanimously. 'Lucky my chap is so level-headed.'

They both knew that the positions would have been reversed had the over-wired New Zealand horse not required so long to settle in the first show-jumping round that he'd clocked up time penalties and dropped just one point off the individual top slot, a fact still being disputed by Lough's groom who claimed the start beam had somehow been broken early. It was a miracle of good riding that the horse had jumped at all. Lough had to concede defeat; individual silver and team bronze were spoils enough.

As Hugo turned to shake the German's hand, Lough glanced over his shoulder, to where his groom was fighting to hold his nervy grey. The horse, now black-sided with sweat, hated the atmosphere of the stadium. Both he and his groom looked livid, and quite ready to charge straight into the podiums to kick merry hell out of the medal ceremony. Beside them, The Fox appeared to be falling asleep while Hugo's freckle-faced groom Jenny leant against him, discreetly blowing kisses at the German bronze medallist and giving her boss a big thumbs-up.

Facing forward again, Hugo studied the flags about to be hoisted, the Witney stripe of Germany's tricolour clashing alongside the Union Flag and its smaller version in one canton of the New Zealand ensign.

'Let's talk before you fly home,' he muttered quickly to the man on his right as the national anthem struck up. 'Somewhere quiet. Tomorrow?'

'Sure,' Lough said vaguely, his eye caught by a disturbance in a crowd directly in front of them. Then his dark eyebrows shot up as a nubile, bare-bottomed blonde made a beeline for the gold medallist.

It was universally agreed that Hugo Beauchamp stepping on to the podium to receive his individual medal at that summer's Olympics –

his second medal of the Games – was one of the most memorable moments in equestrian sporting history. This was not just because he was among the best looking sportsman at the Games by far, not just because the man they named Hu*gold*'s battle to that top step for queen and country had been Herculean in the extreme, and not because he had just won a brace of gold medals for Team GB.

Indeed, the medal ceremony for the individual three day event was most famously marked by a magnificent, naked female body leaping from the stands and racing across the arena. Deborah Gillespie-Grant, a rampant self-publicist, had literally struck gold in her campaign to become a household name, using Daddy's front row seats, a quick-release bra top and sprinting skills honed on the Millfield lacrosse team to out-manoeuvre officials and maximise her exposure. Thought to be the first equestrian streaker at a Games, and destined to become as famous as Erica Roe thanks to her hour-glass figure and sumptuously round breasts, the tabloid-dubbed 'Debbie Double-G' raced up to Hugo to plant a kiss on his mouth before dancing around the podium, avoiding security staff until she was finally apprehended by a red-faced official who covered what he could with the aid of a panama hat and a clipboard.

Hu-gold Prefers Debbie Double-G to his Gee Gees! one headline shouted; *What a Lovely Pair!* and *Horsing Around!* others predictably cried, all displaying a very unflattering shot of Hugo with two gold medals and a nipple-flashing blonde around his neck. He was even reported to have quipped to the dignitary presenting the medal, 'I'm mounting that later.'

The moment, captured by the hundreds of ranked photographers for perpetuity, guaranteed maximum publicity for Debbie and pro-pelled the sport into mainstream consciousness, regardless of Hugo's complaints that it belittled his team's efforts and smirched his character.

However, there was no denying one tabloid's 'exclusive' photos of him sharing champagne in a hotel foyer with Debbie Double-G straight after the formal press conference that same night, salacious close-ups that conveniently disregarded the fact that the entire Great Britain three day event team was there at the time, just out of shot. They had been ordered to assemble in order to allow Debbie to 'apol-ogise'. As one of the wealthiest sponsors in equestrian sports, Colin Gillespie-Grant had three day event chef d'equipe Brian Sedgewick totally under his control. With sports council funding set to tighten now that the Olympic campaign was at an end, poor Brian would have happily streaked alongside Debbie at every remaining medal ceremony if it meant keeping her father's money in the sport. The hotel drinks fiasco, which he hastily orchestrated, was a misjudgement. Hugo was the only one whose reputation suffered when the following morning's tabloid scoop made it look like a very intimate gathering.

That report hinted that this was more than just a random piece of crowd participation. Their names were linked through various encounters, most recently a charity polo match at which Hugo had played on Colin G-G's team. It was insinuated that young, rich and pretty Debbie had performed her streak not just to get fame and adulation but also to redirect her married lover's attention back from sporting glory and fatherhood to her precocious charms.

Debbie and her new publicity agent, legendary PR guru Clive Maxwell, couldn't have hoped for a better result, having tipped off the paper about the hotel drinks. The same paper was soon pitching big money for an exclusive with Debbie, talking about her relationship with Hugo.

By the time Hugo straightened his official tie for the formal celebration lunch the day after his gold-medal triumph, Clive had negotiated the interview for Debbie. As he fixed in his cufflinks, Clive was fixing up Debbie's photoshoot. As Hugo tied the laces of his brogues, Clive explained to Debbie how to intimate intimacy even though there had been nothing more than a family friendship and a wild moment of sporting enthusiasm. She could be a big name if she played it right, he told her. The rope to every VIP area would be unhooked for her, guaranteeing many more months fame via personal appearances, chatshows and the reality treadmill. She just had to use her association with handsome, golden hero Hugo as a leg-up to celebrity. Clive thought it was no great sacrifice if Beauchamp lost some of his glory in the process. The man was an arrogant toff in an elitist sport; Debbie was the real star.

Unaware that his neck was still so firmly on the opportunism block, Hugo phoned his wife from the room in the Olympic village that he was sharing with two members of the show-jumping team.

'Any sign?' He asked the same question he'd opened with on the previous five occasions he'd rung her that day.

'Just twinges – Braxton Hicks again,' she assured him. 'He's bound to be as overdue as Cora.'

'Have you seen this bloody story yet?'

'Yes, Beccy showed it to me online; it's such rubbish. You won gold. Why do they want to tarnish that?'

'The team's mortified. Thank God it's almost over. We've got the formal lunch now, then Lough Strachan's agreed to meet me for a drink.'

'Any chance you'll persuade him to be based here, d'you think?'

'Not sure – he's hardly easy company, but I've heard a couple of rumours this week that might mean he's keen to get away from New Zealand for a bit if they're true.'

'Such as?'

'I'll tell you when I see you tomorrow.'

'You're coming home?' She gasped happily. 'I'd better let everyone in the village know. They want to give you and Fox a hero's welcome.'

'You were a big part of it.' Hugo was immensely grateful that she understood what this was really about, and was far too sensible to believe the bad press.

'I just wish I could have been there yesterday to elbow GG out of the way and take a running jump into your arms.'

'Could have been tricky with the bump in the way.'

'Might help induce labour.' She sighed wistfully, now utterly fed up with being pregnant.

'Let's try it when I get home. Hang on till then.' He laughed, ending the call and dropping the phone on the narrow dormitory bed that reminded him of boarding school.

His roommates staggered in while he was in the bathroom, cleaning his teeth. The younger of the two lay down on the first available bed while the other sprawled on the floor.

'You are not going to bel*ieve* the bar we went to last night!' The younger man, clearly quite drunk, told him when he emerged. 'It's enough to turn your head, mate. There was a glass ceiling with naked birds rolling around on it.' With his strong, down-to-earth Lancashire accent he could have been talking about racing pigeons, but Hugo doubted it.

'We were celebrating your win, mate.' The other groaned from the floor.

Hugo had noticed they were both missing the previous night, but that wasn't unusual. The show-jumping competitions were still over a week away, so these riders had more free time at the start of the Games than the eventers, who were more or less first off.

'Bloody fantastic place,' the younger man was eulogising again. 'You should go, Ooogo mate.'

'I'd get a crick in my neck,' he laughed.

'Here.' The man on the floor reached into his leather jacket and pulled out a battered card. 'Don't tell them we sent you, though – our lad there paid them with a bunch of fake notes he got given for a horse he sold last week. Isn't that right, laddo?'

But the one on Hugo's bed was already asleep.

Hugo studied the card. The place wasn't his style at all, but he guessed Lough Strachan might appreciate it. He was an urban badboy who'd punched his way into the moneyed world of event riding through a combination of guile and brawn, but had never lost his streetwise edge. He had tattoos and piercings, and his groom had a Mohican. He was bound to feel at home in a bar with naked women rolling around overhead. It was a scene Hugo couldn't help wanting to take it in too. One should always sightsee when one was in a world-famous city, after all . . .

Pocketing the card, he headed for the door.

'Congratulations, by the way.' The show-jumper propped himself on one elbow. 'That was bloody impressive riding last night. I thought that Kiwi had you beat for the individual – he rides like a machine; never seen the like. But you pulled it out. We're proud of you.'

'Thanks,' Hugo smiled, knowing the Kiwi was definitely worth having on side.

Later the younger man opened one droopy eye when a mobile phone started ringing and vibrating directly beneath his buttocks. He dragged it out from under him and answered it sleepily. 'No, love, he's not here. You are? That's grand, that is. Yeah, I'll make sure he knows.' Yawning, he rang off and turned to watch his teammate clamber stiffly on to his own narrow bed.

'Anything important?' he asked groggily.

'Just Hugo's wife saying the baby's coming.'

Chapter 7

The tabloid journalist was still writing up her interview with Debbie Double-G and the photographer retouching his shots on his laptop when Tash's waters broke. Copy had been filed by the time Beccy took her stepsister to hospital, panicking that she might give birth at any moment, but they were sent back home and told to await regular contractions. Meanwhile, the story was typeset and a laser soon danced across an aluminium plate to recreate photos of Debbie posing on hay bales in lacy underwear and long riding boots, waving a riding crop about.

Oblivious to the tabloid sensation Tash tried Hugo's mobile again, but it went through to voicemail every time. In desperation, she called Brian Sedgewick, who was partying loudly with team sponsors and too drunk to be tactful. 'He buggered off with Lough Strachan straight after the team meal, Tash, love. I think they're having a night in a strip club. Boys will be boys, eh?'

Tash ran a bath loaded with lavender oil and sat in it, trying not to panic.

Hugo regarded Lough levelly, far more interested in the story unfolding in front of him than the legs uncrossing above him. 'So you're telling me those doping rumours are *true*?'

Lough shrugged, glaring across the table, dark eyes as intent as jet arrow tips beneath their sharply angled brows. 'They can't prove anything.'

'From what I hear, there's a lot of dirt circulating back home,' Hugo said carefully. 'You could soon be in very hot water indeed.'

'I'm part Maori. We love hot mud springs,' he said edgily.

'It'll end your competitive career, Lough.'

'Is that a threat?'

'It's a fact.'

A topless waitress arrived with two garish red cocktails.

'Complements of the management,' she lisped, lowering glasses and nipple tassels between the two men.

'Thank you,' Hugo flashed a quick, dismissive smile. 'Now clear off, darling, we're talking.'

She lingered. 'You boys are athletes from the Games, aren't you?'

'Yeah – rowers.' Lough eyed her body much as he assessed a top horse he knew he could never afford. The girls in this bar were quite sensational, a world apart from the pole dancers and strippers he'd encountered on raucous stag nights. The women here were straight from the pages of *Penthouse*, had classy accents and quick minds to match their flawless looks. This waitress resembled a computer-generated fusion of Angelina Jolie and Alessandra Ambrosio.

'That's an unusual accent,' she was purring to Lough, her plump lips parted to reveal a seductive white smile biting down on a tongue so perfect and pink it could have been a new lozenge of Hubba Bubba.

'South African,' Lough said quickly. He could see the way she was clocking their table's value with the same critical interest that he was admiring her body, her painted eyes cataloguing Hugo's Rolex and signet ring with its family crest, eyeing up the Savile Row suit and Thomas Pink shirt, British team tie and private club cufflinks while quickly dismissing Lough as worthless, being neither in possession of a Black Amex nor a wedding ring. She was on a scouting mission, yet Hugo was oblivious, far more concerned with his companion's lies past and present.

'As I said, we're talking.' He waved her away to the bar.

'The girl was just offering the hand of friendship.' Lough watched her retreating backside with a sigh.

'The hand-job of friendship more like.' Hugo fixed him with an intent look again. 'Why lie to her about who we are?'

'Why d'you think?'

'You're the one with something to hide.'

In the absence of horns, their eyes locked across the sward of polished oak, two stags reluctant to give ground.

Lough looked away first. Hugo was an arrogant bastard, but at least he got to the point and demanded the truth. He envied that directness, having always been a great deal more circumspect. 'You come here often?' he asked now, watching another hostess waft past in a cloud of sweet scent.

'Are you propositioning me?'

'They don't know you here, right?'

'Never been here before.' Taking a swig of his cocktail, Hugo glanced around at the damask-lined walls, the dim lighting and discreet cushioned booths with curtains for privacy. Despite an entrance so inconspicuous it could have been mistaken for one of the many exclusive restaurants and clubs in the area, there was no mistaking the bar's function once one stepped inside. It was decked out like a cross between a femme fatale's boudoir, a First Class airport lounge and a jazz club. As well as the notorious glass ceiling, there was a stage with glass poles to either end, beyond which was a door marked 'Private', through which pretty girls led the male clientele at regular intervals. The drinks cost a fortune, the hostesses were clearly happy to earn their tips after hours, and the management no doubt watched everything that was going on via CCTV and two-way mirrors. Hugo was surprised by the showjumpers' idea of fun. He'd thought the bar would be seedy, gaudy and laughable, somewhere to loosen up Lough before moving on to a late-night espresso bar to talk business in more detail. Instead it was a high-end knocking shop, and clearly made the tight-lipped Lough even more ill at ease.

'This place stinks,' the Kiwi said, pushing his free cocktail aside. 'They want to fleece us, and I wouldn't touch that,' he nodded his head towards the glass that Hugo was lifting to his lips again.

He laughed, draining half its contents. 'Surely you don't think they've used a bad vintage in these?' He pulled a face. 'You do have a point, though. Definitely not Krug.'

'On your head be it.' Lough leaned across the table, dropping his voice. 'I lied about who we are because they want to know how much they can take us for. You might have brought me here to tell me you're going to shop me, Hugo, but believe me, these guys will strip your wallet bare of credit before you can get to the till. They know you're a one-off, and your wedding ring is hard currency here.'

'The bar came highly recommended.' Hugo looked momentarily affronted before laughing uproariously. 'You're right. It's bloody awful. I must apologise. But I assure you that I'm not going to shop you. I loathe shopping – just ask my wife.'

Lough's eyes flashed. 'Does your wife know you come to bars like this?'

'She's the reason we're here.'

'*Tash* recommended this place?'

'She wants me to bring you back to Haydown.' Hugo raised his glass. His eyes crossed for a moment.

'Isn't she about to have a baby?'

'That's not why she wants you in Berkshire. We have a midwife for that,' he ran a hand through his hair as he often habitually did. 'Nor do we need you to dope any horses.' He tried to fix Lough with a serious look, but his eyes crossed again and he blinked hard.

Lough said nothing, watching Hugo sit back in his chair, blue gaze increasingly unfocused as he squinted at the burlesque dancer who had got up on the stage and was doing extraordinary things with a top hat and opera cane. Then his eyes lifted to the ceiling and his jaw fell open. 'Call me sexist, but in this particular case I seriously hope those women don't break through the glass ceiling.'

Lough didn't laugh. 'Your wife must be a very forgiving woman.'

'She'd see the funny side.' Hugo looked down, pressing his hands on the table edge to steady himself as blood rushed to his brain. 'She's very level-headed, Tash – unlike me – phew.' He shook his head. 'This cocktail is bloody strong.' He laughed, glancing at Lough again. 'She wants you at Haydown because you're a sensational rider and we could all benefit. God knows when she'll be back in the saddle. Babies do strange things to women.'

'I wouldn't know,' Lough said carefully.

'Don't you be in any hurry to find that out.' Hugo's voice was slurring as he fought to make sense. 'The British event scene is fantastic for high-end totty, with the only strings attached being the horses.'

'That a fact?' Lough gave nothing away.

'You'll have a different girl in your box every weekend.'

'I'm not like that, Hugo.'

'All event riders are like that.' Hugo insisted.

'I guess you should know.'

'Face it, Lough, my wife's right: you would be much better off based in Europe.' Hugo was struggling to follow the thread of the conversation now, and feeling more and more light-headed, as though he was floating out of his body and up towards the naked bodies spreadeagled above his head.

'I like New Zealand,' Lough muttered.

'Ah, but will the motherland forgive you when she finds out what her sporting hero's been up to behind her back?' Hugo closed one eye at the tongue-twisting effort of saying this.

Lough glared at him. 'Rather like a wife forgiving a husband when he drinks in bars like this. I guess it's worthwhile if she gets what she wants out of it, too.'

'Got to give the wife what she wants,' he rambled. 'Keep her sweet.'

'And she wants me?' Lough asked idly, testing how wired Hugo was. 'More fool her.'

Hugo didn't appear to be listening, talking in staccato bursts as he fought to hold together unravelling thoughts. 'Tash *is* sweet. Puts up with my shit, for a start. Not sure she'll ever ride the way she did, though. More into kids now. Dreadful shame.'

'She's very beautiful.' Lough had seen her compete many times on the international circuit.

'Fuck off. She's mine.' Hugo's brain was too addled to say much more. He closed his eyes and took a deep breath. 'Christ I feel odd.'

Lough watched him with fascination. Whatever they had spiked his drink with was fast-acting and potent, morphing the Brit's usual sarcastic wit into belligerent confusion. Winding him up was all too easy. 'So it's okay for you to buy a high-class hostess for the night, but Tash can't look at another man?'

'She can look all she likes, but she can't touch. Jesus!' Hugo opened and closed his crossing eyes. 'Besides which, I'm not going to "buy" a hostess.'

'There's a Maori saying, "Only the foolish visit the land of the cannibals".'

'Don't worry, I should think most of the girls in here are on strict diets.'

'Maori men treat their wives pretty badly too.'

'Maori in haste, repent at leisure,' Hugo joked in a slurred voice. 'I do *not* treat Tash badly.'

Lough glared at him. For a great horseman he rode over people too easily; Tash had been a much-missed face among the event riders at the Games.

'If I had a wife as beautiful as yours maybe I'd keep her safely under lock and key at home.'

'Lough and key,' Hugo started to laugh at the pun. 'A lock is better than suspicion, nanny used to say, but I have no reason to suspect darling Tash. And anyway, she has free will like me. If she falls for another man and wants to bugger off, she's welcome.'

Lough had seen the effects of drugs often enough to know that he shouldn't necessarily mistake the arrogant bravado for Hugo talking from the heart, but his sense of indignation still flared.

'So you'd be happy for her to spend a night with a gigolo in a bar like this then?'

'Gigolo.' Hugo laughed at the old-fashioned word. 'Had a horse named that once. Bloody misnomer if ever I knew one; we were convinced he was gay.' He swayed in his chair before righting himself and staring groggily at Lough. 'Are you offering your services?'

Lough shrugged.

'She wouldn't have you.' Hugo let out a derisive snort.

'Want to bet?'

Lough knew men who would throw a punch for less than that, but Hugo was looking really spaced out, his eyelids heavy and movements cumbersome. When he tried to run his fingers through his hair it took several attempts for his hand to find its target, so that he looked like he was waving his arm around in a strange country dance. His voice was increasingly slow and slurred, but what he said next took Lough completely by surprise: 'If she'd be willing to spend a night with you, you're welcome to her.'

Lough stared at him. 'You don't mean that?'

'I'd like to see you try. I know my own wife.' He shrugged, hair on end now, looking away, eyes half focusing as two sensational-looking women approached their table, the Angelina Jolie lookalike waitress bringing backup in the form of a curvaceous, cloud-haired Beyoncé.

Lough drummed the table irritably as the hostesses closed in like sexual big-game hunters, now certain their medal-winning prey had been suitably tranquillised.

'I'm sure I've seen you somewhere before,' Angelina purred at Hugo, not realising that his handsome face was the one all over the tabloids that day, but scenting rich pickings nonetheless.

Laughing at the absurdity of the situation so much he almost fell off his chair, Hugo put up no resistance as the hostesses joined the table, his sense of reality now totally abstract, his need for entertainment and sexual gratification stripped down as his brain slowed to basic instincts. He offered to buy them champagne. 'We're celebrating gold and silver, you know. Never thought I'd be in a place like this to do that, but when in Rome . . .'

'The Rome Olympics were in nineteen-sixty, Hugo,' Lough stood up and walked around the table to pull him to his feet, nodding curtly to the women. 'Excuse my friend here, he has amnesia. Always forgets what a dick he is. I'll take him outside for some air.' But as he headed for the entrance, he heard the women squawk something about not paying their bill and saw his way blocked by a couple of heavies. At the same time, Hugo started to sag into his arms and he realised the man was about to pass out.

Doing an about turn, Lough dragged Hugo's dead weight through the door marked Private and along a wide corridor that resembled that of a five-star hotel, complete with potted ferns in urns and reproduction Chippendale chairs positioned to either side of console tables with copies of *Mayfair* fanned along their tops.

The third door along was open and Lough could see the room was empty. He dragged Hugo inside and dropped him on a vast bed draped with fake fur before quickly removing the key from the inside of the door and locking him in.

'A lock is better than suspicion, as nanny used to say,' he muttered. He was back through the door to the club before the heavies could even register what was happening. Moments later, they and the hostesses were distracted by an influx of Russian businessmen and Hugo forgotten.

Lough settled at the bar with a beer, yawns ripping at his jaws. He knew he could just leave the Brit there, sleeping it off – God knows he probably deserved it – but a curious sense of loyalty kept him on guard. He couldn't help thinking about Hugo's beautiful wife waiting pregnant at home while her husband cavorted about with all the responsibility of Tiger Woods celebrating another Masters win. She didn't deserve this.

In the early hours the bar staff changed shifts and one of the new workers brought in the early edition newspapers to hang from wooden poles at the end of the bar. A tabloid headline caught Lough's eye.

'Jesus!' He leaned forward to read the article. Hugo needed to be taught a serious lesson.

The printing presses had started to roll while Tash walked around Haydown, willing the contractions to settle into a rhythm; the first editions were being arranged on the newsstands as she had another bath; and the tabloid containing Debbie's exclusive interview was on sale in the hospital newsagents by the time Beccy took Tash again.

The contractions still weren't regular but the pain was getting impossible to bear, Tash told the midwife team almost apologetically.

'I rode round Badminton with a broken collarbone once – that was nothing compared to this,' she gasped.

'Welcome to childbirth,' laughed a cheery midwife, sharing a knowing glance with her assistant.

'I've had one already,' Tash reminded them anxiously. 'She was a malpresentation. The same thing won't happen again will it?'

'Very unlikely,' they patted her arms reassuringly.

After they had put Tash on a slow drip to accelerate dilation, with gas and air at the ready, Beccy left her and went to buy chocolate. The streaker pictures were, yet again, in most of the day's redtops, who knew Debbie Double-G was good for sales, but one had the story splashed all over its front page, with more 'exclusive' shots of the hotel foyer drink and an interview with GG inside. *'Hugold Love Rat!'* shouted the headline. *'It's all a Cunning (Publicity) Stunt.'*

Beccy read it quickly in the corridor outside the delivery room, in which Tash was intermittently groaning and screaming. Even though they'd got half the details wrong – they called Hugo a show-jumper and said that he was the son of a Baron – Beccy couldn't help believing there had to be some truth in Debbie's hints that her streak was pre-planned with Hugo's blessing. To her shame, she found the description of him flirting with Debbie at a polo match (*'he fixed me with those gorgeous blue eyes and said "I want to see a LOT more of you"'*) made her jealous. The reporter insinuated that Hugo was well known on the eventing circuit for living dangerously, both in his riding and his marriage. Beccy couldn't help hoping that was true. The thought of seeing him again made her light-headed.

She forced herself to bin the paper, buying another bar of choco-late, her cheeks burning with discomfort. It was just too surreal to be reading of Hugo's bad behaviour while, yards away, Tash strug-gled to bring his son into the world.

'Any news of that husband of mine?' Tash asked when she wan-dered back in. She looked ghastly, her face pale and sweaty, with dark rings beneath her eyes.

Beccy's red cheeks flamed even brighter. She shook her head.

'He's got plenty of time,' the midwife assured them as she

checked the print-out on the monitor. 'This baby's in no hurry. You might as well go home for a few hours and get some sleep,' she told Beccy.

Hugo woke up completely disoriented, half-dreaming that he'd slept with a dead man's corpse on top of him. Then he realised his own arm was slung across his face, totally numb and suffocating him. His body ached all over, his head pounded and his throat and mouth were bone dry. He had no idea where he was.

He fumbled around the strange room in search of a light switch, knocking into furniture and blinking blindly as he crashed into walls. The only dim light source seemed to come from a red light winking in one high corner. At last he almost fell over a lamp and groped around for the switch.

'Jesus.'

It certainly wasn't the Olympic village. He sat heavily on the bed and pressed his head in his hands, shaking it this way and that, trying to fill it with some facts and details, but it was a blank.

'Fuck, fuck, fuck.' He stood up unsteadily and headed towards what looked to be a bathroom, desperate for a drink of water. He glanced up as he passed the corner where the red light had been flashing and froze. There was a camera up there, discreetly tucked behind a curve of antique cornicing.

Hugo spun round, taking in the fake-fur counterpanes, the mirrors and props. He felt for his pockets and realised that his wallet had gone.

He was in a brothel. And he'd been caught on camera. Somebody out there knew what he'd been up to, even if he had no memory of it whatsoever.

At that moment he heard a key in the door and closed his eyes briefly, praying for salvation. To his amazement, it came in the form of Lough Strachan, throwing open the door and hissing at him to hurry up.

'There's a back way out.' He beckoned for Hugo to follow.

'There's a camera in here. They've taken my wallet.'

'Nobody here knows who you are, I'm sure if it. And I took your wallet,' Lough held it up, already moving away from the door. 'They didn't get to look at your ID or copy your cards. I've had it all along. It's cool.'

'I don't understand . . .' Hugo staggered out into the corridor, still disoriented and ricocheting off walls.

Lough was at the far end, heading for a fire door. 'We have to get out before they come after you.'

Following almost blindly, Hugo felt a blast of fresh, early morning air in his face before he found himself being hustled along narrow back streets towards an intersection with a bigger thoroughfare, where they hailed a solitary cab.

He pressed his face to the cool of the window, fighting the urge to vomit. Dawn was breaking. The city looked drab and monochrome, its streets gleaming metallically, zig-zagging urban snakes of stone and steel totally alien to him. He felt like he'd woken up in another man's life.

'What possessed me?' he breathed. 'Whatever possessed me?'

Beside him Lough said nothing, staring straight ahead.

'I can't thank you enough,' Hugo turned to him. 'I know I deserve no loyalty, but you got me out of there. I can never thank you enough for that.'

'It was nothing,' Lough said with feeling, eyes unblinking.

'I swear I have never done anything like that in my life.'

'They drugged you. That's what happens. They wanted your cash. Your wedding ring was a giveaway.'

Hugo looked at his ring and groaned, closing his eyes. 'What if Tash ever finds out?'

'Why should she?'

He opened his eyes and studied Lough's profile groggily, unable to work him out at all. 'They had a camera.'

'They thought we were South African rowers,' Lough reminded him.

'Did they?' Hugo rubbed his head painfully.

'Well we "rode" in the Games,' Lough joked drily, but Hugo didn't smile. 'I won't say anything, trust me.'

'I must do something to thank you. You name it. Money, a horse, the job . . .'

'I thought I told you I can't be bought – or shopped.'

Hugo winced, unable to remember. There was an awkward pause and he cleared his throat before trying to return to his default setting of flippancy. 'So I take it the answer to the work rider offer is no?'

'I'll think about it.'

'And I really can't offer you anything else by way of thanks?'

Lough pressed his lips together. 'I'll stick to our bet, thanks.'

'What bet?'

'That Tash will turn me down.'

'What are you talking about, Lough?'

'Last night, you offered me a night with your wife.'

'For Christ's sake, Lough! She's about to have a baby.' He glanced at his watch, trying to fathom out what day it was and how long it must have been since he and Tash had spoken.

'I know what you said, Hugo.'

Hugo gaped at him in utter disbelief. Meanwhile, Lough fished in his pocket and pulled out a page ripped from a newspaper. 'You'd better look at this.'

Hugo scanned it before screwing it up. 'Total pile of lies.'

His arrogance stirred up more hot springs of anger in Lough.

'Get this straight, Hugo,' he said. 'I didn't help you because I think you're a great bloke. I helped you because your wife deserves better.'

'Don't push it,' Hugo muttered, fingers raking his hair as he fought yet again to remember what he had said and done the previous night.

Lough turned to him at last, dark eyes glittering with intent. 'I take it the job offer still stands?'

'Try not to push, Tash!'

'I need Hugo. Where's Hugo?'

'The surgeon won't be long. He's performing another emergency caesarean, but he'll be with you as soon as he can. Please stop pushing, love.'

Another contraction ripped through her, a high-speed train crash scraping and tearing inside her body, pulling her along with it.

Tash gripped onto the midwife's hand and, gritting her teeth in an effort to deny nature and not push, she felt the engine scream through her, carriage after carriage buckling and roaring. When nature briefly won out and she strained to push she heard the regular little beeps from the foetal heart monitor beside her slow down.

It was exactly the same scenario she'd had with Cora eighteen months earlier. Her baby boy had twisted around inside her during a long false labour until he was in an impossible position to deliver, despite the powerful contractions and full dilation that now told her exhausted body to work its hardest to get the head through the birth canal.

As each contraction brought an ever greater urge to push, she felt unutterably terrified and desperately alone. Listening to those electronic beats drop again and again, she was isolated in a clean, scrubbed bubble of fear along with her tiny baby and his straining heart that was being weakened with every move that she made to try to bring him into the world and have him in her arms.

At last the surgeon appeared and the delivery team went into an urgent huddle. Tash could hear snatches of sentences that frightened her more '. . . foetal distress . . .' '. . . heart under strain . . .' '. . . blood pressure dropping . . .' An unfamiliar face appeared at her knees, chin hammocked in a surgical mask. She obediently opened her legs for her tenth internal examination in as many hours, now no longer caring if the entire hospital staff trooped by to take a look just so long as she could have her baby safely.

Within minutes an anaesthetist had given her an epidural and she was being wheeled to the operating theatre, unable to hold back the tears. This wasn't how it was supposed to be.

Then somehow, from somewhere, Hugo appeared beside her in the hospital corridor, blue eyes blazing with love and fear. Tash had never been more relieved to see anybody in her life.

'Where were you?' she asked shakily, the epidural having made her teeth chatter like maddened castanets.

'I got lost,' was all he would say as he took her hand tightly in his and kissed the gold band on her ring finger. 'Hopelessly, hopelessly lost, but I'm here now.'

Quickly scrubbed, robed and masked, he sat at her head and took hold of her hand again. Her belly was hidden behind tented green cotton. She was already open, the surgeon delving around inside her as though she was a lucky dip.

Then he extracted a very healthy, red-faced baby.

While Tash wept with joy, Hugo blinked back rare tears and took his newborn son in his arms.

Within half an hour Amery had been wiped, measured, weighed, placed skin-to-skin, fed his first toot of colostrum and was contentedly asleep on Tash's chest.

★

When Beccy brought Cora in to hospital to meet her new brother later that day, she encountered Hugo marching along the ward towards her and it almost winded her with joy. He was her dream, from the true blue eyes to the long stride that turned all the female heads in the maternity ward. Never had the force of her self-destructive love for him felt greater, and never had it seemed more ill-fitting as he joined his young family. She wanted him to be the roguish rake who flirted away from home in the three day event lorry parks, not this tableau of doting fatherhood. She wanted to run away.

'We'd given you up for dead,' she managed to croak her first words to him in ten years, nothing like the long monologues she'd so often rehearsed in her travels. She couldn't even look him in the face.

His reaction was nothing like her rehearsals either as he hissed, 'I got delayed. Now drop it.'

Beccy quailed, glancing at Tash.

But with Cora squeaking ecstatically at this strange new creature on her mother's chest, and Amery starting to wake up again, Tash was too distracted to care where Hugo had been the previous night. It was irrelevant. There was another gorgeous, blue-eyed male distraction in her life now.

'I never did get to do that running jump into your arms,' she looked from Amery to Hugo, tearful with hormones and happiness. 'And the village will miss welcoming home the Maccombe heroes.'

'This is all the welcome I need.' Hugo sat on the bed at her hip and kissed her, then dropped kisses on Cora's tortoiseshell curls and Amery's tiny bald pate. As he kept his head lowered, breathing in the perfection of his beautiful family, Tash lifted a hand still spiked with a cannula, its wrist encircled with a pale blue hospital ID tag, and ran her fingers through his hair.

Beccy had to look away, jealousy and loneliness burning holes in her chest.

Hugo left Tash with Beccy and went home to shower and change, finding it odd the return to Haydown after so many monumental events in short succession, and for the yard to be so utterly unaffected. His mother was barracking the temporary yard staff; Jenny was supervising and settling Fox back into his familiar surroundings and the dogs crowded around him as he climbed from his car. In the circumstances, there had been no grand welcome home, and Hugo was grateful.

He was equally grateful that it seemed the gutter press was already losing interest him. The phone messages waiting for him were from local papers and the equestrian press interested in his win, or just friends, owners and sponsors calling to congratulate him.

'You beat that bloody Kiwi!' his oldest friend Ben Meredith chortled patriotically on an answering-machine message.

Hugo wasn't so sure as he wandered around his empty house, gathering together things to take to Tash, not noticing the mess or the tea mugs on every surface; just noticing Tash's absence and hating it. The house felt incomplete, indelibly altered; as though life had changed. It echoed his memory of the previous night.

The contents of those lost hours were shared by just Hugo, Lough Strachan and the shadowy, exotic figures that inhabited a late-night bar in a gloomy little back street far beyond the safe environs of the Olympic village, a place they could never hope to find again even if they wanted to, where their medals meant far less than their hard cash. It was a night of which he remembered little, but what little he remembered thoroughly ashamed him, a blight on his character that was not only deeply dishonourable and aberrant but could also wreck his marriage if it ever got out. Hugo was immensely grateful that their identities had remained secret. In a tight-knit, rumour-mongering sport like eventing, where a whiff of gossip usually spread like kennel cough through a hound pack, this story could ruin him.

When he went back into the hospital for the last visiting hour of the evening Tash was much more together. She even remembered to ask whether Hugo had persuaded Lough Strachan to come to Haydown. He didn't like to confess that he was striving to remember exactly how he had left the situation, just as he was struggling to piece together the events of the previous night.

'I have no idea,' he said honestly, and then added with more ferocity than he intended, 'but I bloody well hope not.'

Chapter 8

On the same day in August that Amery Beauchamp fought his way into the world in West Berkshire, Faith Brakespear was in the Cotswolds, celebrating the anniversary of her own arrival eighteen years earlier.

With perfect timing, she had received her pre-operative appointment with her chosen cosmetic surgeon through the post that morning; two weeks hence, and by then she would conveniently be based in Essex commuterland. That long-awaited day she would show Farouk Ali Khan her boob and nose scrapbook – over thirty pages of carefully selected faces and breasts ripped from everything from *Elle*, *Cheers!* and the *Observer* magazine to old copies of *Playboy* and *Loaded* she had discovered under her brother's bed.

In a similar fashion, her mother had discovered the boob scrapbook under Faith's bed and suddenly appeared to be labouring under the misconception that her daughter was secretly gay and poised to come out of the closet that night as she celebrated coming of age.

Being very open-minded about sexuality – she had, after all, been married to a gay man for many years – Anke was infuriatingly eager to embrace this development, however hard Faith tried to refute it.

'I am *not* a lesbian! I am in love with Rory and I am going to marry him.'

'Yes, *kæreste*, but that is just a daydream, isn't it? This is real life . . . and if you have been having these feelings, perhaps—'

'I haven't been having "feelings"!' she howled. 'I know for a fact that I love Rory and that he is the only man, woman or animal for me, okay?'

'If you say so,' Anke nodded, unconvinced.

But Faith had far more pressing concerns, such as the need to fulfil her boast to Carly about the number of single studmuffins on the guest list. So far, her RSVPs were almost exclusively female, the only confirmed male guests being attached, gay or under fifteen.

In desperation, with her friend already on her way, Faith put out a call on her much-neglected Bebo page, forgetting to log off afterwards so that her ten-year-old brother Chad read her pathetic plea when he took over the family PC to go on the Cartoon Network site. Clicking his fingers over the keyboard he set to work. As the most computer-savvy member of the Brakespear household, it took him just moments to spread the word through chat rooms and social forums with the opener 'My fit older sister is having a party and has no friends . . .' The response was gratifying and Chad felt proud. It was the ultimate gift from brother to sister, far better than Magnus bringing along some cheesy old pop star.

At lunchtime Carly made a very stylish arrival through the Wyck Farm gates at the wheel of her pink Mini Cooper – a gift from her indulgent parents for her own eighteenth birthday – in a flurry of spitting gravel, exhausted and overexcited from her longest drive since passing her test the previous month.

'Motorways are, like, such fun!' she exclaimed, leaping out to air-kiss Faith and in no way giving away the fact that she had spent most of her time on the M25 in tears, cursing boy racers and white van men, constantly finding herself on the slip roads about to be funnelled on to other motorways or racketing along in a stream of traffic at a speed far faster than she felt comfortable with.

Faith helped her hawk out the three huge suitcases that she had brought with her, one of which was taking up the whole of the back seat.

'What have you brought? Your entire wardrobe?'

'More or less.' Carly dragged an ultra-trendy pink Hideo case up the stairs to her friend's room while Faith lugged the other two. 'I couldn't decide what to wear, and I need to lend you something too because your clothes are *so* dire. I brought a bottle of vod and a load of Red Bull because I know your 'rents can be a bit sanctimonious about anything more alcoholic than a white wine spritzer, even though you *are* eighteen. Which reminds me . . .' She heaved her case on to the bed, sprang it open and pulled out a very squashed package wrapped in glittery paper. 'Happy birthday!'

Inside was a set of racy red Agent Provocateur underwear, complete with the latest line in silicone chicken fillets.

'Just while you're waiting for your boob op,' Carly explained. 'To make you feel sensational tonight and remind you what you have in store. There's a tube of Lip Plump there, too, and bum-firming cream. I can't do anything about the nose on a temporary basis, but I'm very good with shading foundation. And there's even a fix for your chronically low self-esteem.'

Beneath the strange, rubbery boob enhancers was a small, colourful box marked 'Brain Candy'.

'Legal highs,' Carly explained, 'from New Zealand. Like Ecstasy only totally, like, safe and legal. I tried one last week. Amazing!'

'Really?' Faith was fascinated, although she had never really been tempted by drugs, or indeed even alcohol, having seen the ravages it wrought on darling Rory. Once or twice she had tried to drink alongside him to 'bond', but had inevitably ended up throwing up before he had even warmed up.

'So what do you think?' Carly held up a padded, scented coat hanger in each hand, putting one dress in front of her and then another. 'The pink Moschino Cheap and Chic or the yellow Kate Moss at Topshop?'

'Not sure,' Faith screwed up her face in thought. 'Do you have anything with a bit more . . .' she searched for the word.

'Bling? Urban chic? LA cool? Folklore funk? Heritage vintage? What?'

'Er . . . more fabric?'

Faith's guest list now contained a great many single men, several tens of thousands in fact. In just a few hours Chad's message had spread through almost every social networking site on the ether to all thirty-four counties in England, to Scotland and Wales, to twenty-seven European countries, to all fifty-two states and to five continents. Faith's eighteenth birthday party was global. The invitation had been forwarded around the world more swiftly than a chain letter offering fame and fortune when copied to seven friends.

From early evening, dubious-looking festival types began to descend on Wyck Farm from as far as Bath, Worcester, Coventry and even London. Some had heard that that the band Faithless was having a party in this famously rockstar-heavy corner of the Cotswolds. Others believed Faith No More had regrouped for a one-off private gig. A few were labouring under the misconception that Faith was the name of a underground rave club which took place in broad-span barns and disused aircraft hangers in obscure corners of rural England. And then there were the born-again Christians in search of a prayer rally . . .

Unaware that the fast-flowing influx of guests did not in fact know Faith at all, the Brakespears were stunned to find their daughter so popular.

'Most of these people seem to think they can pitch tents here for the night,' Anke announced in alarm to Graham, who had briefly dashed inside while frantically trying to orchestrate the car parking.

'They'll have to use the paddock,' he said, his normally creamy Yorkshire accent blunt. 'We'll bring the horses in.'

Anke watched worriedly as he shouldered a huge Maglite torch. 'What on earth do you need that for? It's broad daylight.'

'I figure I could use some clout,' Graham said darkly. 'There's all sorts turning up out there. I had no idea Faith knew so many people. Where is she, by the way? This is her party.'

'Still getting dressed with Carly,' Anke glanced up the stairs and wondered why Faith had invited so many people when she was normally so conservative. It seemed she really was coming out of her shell at long last.

Faith might not usually need drugs or alcohol to enhance her social life but, as she reminded herself when rearranging her chicken fillet fillers for the twentieth time in the privacy of her en suite, that was because she had no social life to enhance. Certainly not one that involved wearing rubber breasts, Magic Knickers, a hairpiece and a foundation so amazingly uniform it was purported to cover everything from birthmarks to stubble. She felt alarmingly like a male transvestite after Carly's ministrations.

Styled by Carly, Faith looked undeniably grown-up and sophisticated, but perhaps not dressed to her best advantage. Lots of big hair, frills and bling no doubt suited petite, curvy Carly, but with Faith's extra height, more square frame, broad back and wide hips it was an unforgiving look. Her long, athletic legs were usually her strongest feature, but encased in lime green fishnets and poking out from the crotch-height hem of a coral pink dress that was part baby doll nighty, part seventies lampshade, they looked like snot dangling from a nose.

'Give me that vodka,' she demanded weakly, grateful for the first time that Rory wouldn't be around to see her.

'Here.' Carly, a vision of playful sex kitten in her unravelled yellow string arrangement, handed her a can of Red Bull that was half filled with Smirnoff, plus a Brain Candy pill.

'I'm not sure . . .' Faith wavered with the pill on the end of her tongue and the can poised.

'Oh, live a little.' Carly elbowed her sharply in the back so that she gulped the little tablet back like a reluctant cat being wormed.

'Aren't you taking the other one?' Faith coughed and spluttered as Carly wiggled out to the bedroom to fetch her body shimmer puff and apply another layer to her chest and shoulders.

'No, I'm your co-pilot tonight.' She looked back over her shoulder, puff dabbing about madly, so that from where Faith was standing it looked as though her throat was being savaged by a chinchilla kitten.

Faith followed her into the bedroom. 'Co-pilot?'

'It's a drug buddy thing. I stay clear-headed while you get wired – just in case something goes wrong and you lose it big time.'

'But you've had three vodka Red Bulls already,' Faith pointed out worriedly. 'And anyway, you said these are harmless, legal mood enhancers.'

'They so are.' Carly turned back and started buffing her friend's wide, pearly white shoulders. 'They really are. Like I said, live a little. Now make sure you drink plenty of fluid and chew gum.'

'Why?' Faith loathed gum.

'To stop yourself swallowing your tongue, I think,' Carly said vaguely, pulling Faith's dress forward and buffing her chest, which made her chicken fillets plop out of her bra and bounce off the toes of her patent leather ballet pumps. 'We need tit tape to keep those babies in place.' She turned to search in one of her suitcases.

Picking up the errant pieces of silicone, Faith swigged vodka from the bottle then headed back into her bathroom to reinsert them.

Studying her reflection she changed her mind, suddenly wishing that Rory was here. He'd make her see the funny side, tease her about her stupid outfit, seeing past the lampshade dress and snot tights to the Faith he knew so well. She missed him, missed him, missed him.

Her unfamiliar eye make-up was running already. The big, pouty lips were starting to smear. She looked like a clown. She didn't want to go to her own party at all. Her social skills needed enhancing even more than her cleavage.

Slamming the Smirnoff bottle down by the basin she picked up the box of Brain Candy and popped out a second pill, knocking it back without a by your leave.

In the bedroom, Carly was too busy hanging out of the window to notice.

'There are so many people arriving!'

'Great.' Faith felt terrified.

Then Carly let out a shriek.

'He's here!' she gasped over her shoulder. 'Dillon Rafferty. He's bloody well here!'

'Told you.' Faith nodded at her own reflection, raising the vodka bottle. 'Would I lie?'

She turned on the radio that was propped up on the shelf beside her. Classic FM. Rory listened to it on the yard, claiming it soothed the horses (although he had recently staged a brief defection to a digital jazz channel when Classic FM ran an advert for wart removal cream at fifteen-minute intervals, which he said upset Rio).

Tonight they were playing Satie's *Gymnopédies*. Faith listened, her head cocked. So soothing.

Smiling, she pushed the bathroom door quietly closed and leant against it, sliding the lock and pressing her cheek against the soft, fluffy towelling of the robe hanging on the hook above her.

'Locked herself in the bathroom!' Carly reported to Anke excitedly two minutes later, eyes darting left and right in search of Dillon Rafferty. 'I can't get her to come out.'

'Oh this is ridiculous – I must know how many of these people are her friends. If indeed *any* of them are.' Anke swept up the stairs, leaving Carly alone in the hallway as unwitting welcoming party, just as Dillon Rafferty stepped in through the front door.

It was her cue, and she didn't miss a beat.

'Hi, I'm Carly!' she greeted brightly, flashing her five-grand veneers.

'Hi,' he flashed his ten-grand ones in return.

Carly almost passed out on the spot. Dillon Rafferty, in the flesh, was a pure, giddy fix of testosterone-packed, rock 'n' roll sex appeal. If, instead of 'hi', he'd said 'you – me – downstairs loo – now' she'd have led the way.

Instead he nodded politely and walked on past, leaving Magnus grinning in his wake, lofty, dishevelled and gorgeous, clutching a pretty blue-eyed toddler in a pink tutu and Gap New York T-shirt. Alongside him was an arrogant-looking, leggy brunette whom Carly recognised from the gossip mags, clutching a Chihuahua and holding the hand of Magnus's bubbly blonde girlfriend Dilly.

Carly hid a snarl. How horribly fake and boho. *No* best friends ever held hands any more, not even Victoria Beckham and Gwen Stefani. It was *so* last year.

'Hi Mags, hi Dilly . . . and you must be Nell,' she greeted with proprietorial ease as she took it upon herself to assume Anke's hostessing role. 'Drinks to the left, food to the right, recreational drugs in the marquee, birthday girl locked in the bathroom. Enjoy.'

Upstairs, Faith would not budge. The Brain Candy was starting to kick in, making her heart race and her mood lift. She was *loving* her birthday. The music was fantastic, the vibe was perfect and the warm, scented setting was unexpected but both comforting and invigorating. She wasn't coming out for anybody. She refused to open the door for her mother, her beloved gayfather and even her elder brother when he joined them.

'What's the problem?' Magnus asked Kurt worriedly.

Kurt – an athletic slice of late-forties sex appeal with artful blond highlights and unfeasibly long eyelashes, who had never quite surrendered the New Romantic look – shrugged. 'From what I gather, the guest of honour isn't here.'

'Who?' Magnus mouthed at his mother, who immediately mouthed 'Rory' in reply.

Rolling his eyes, he rapped on the door. 'Faith, come out.'

'Bugger off!'

Behind her came the distinctive strains of Tchaikovsky. There was also a strange clumping, thumping noise.

'What *is* she doing in there?' Magnus turned to his mother.

'Ballet dancing, I think,' Anke said fretfully. 'Oh God, this is my fault. She's at a pressure point in her life, a great shift from child to adult, from carefree dependant to free spirited self-seeker. She needs to get to grips with who she is and what she is, with her roots, her homosexuality.'

'Her what?' Kurt and Magnus asked in unison.

Anke waved the question away guiltily. 'She is in such desperate need of her birth father to approve of her, acknowledge her.'

'Bollocks,' Magnus scoffed. 'She just wants Rory.'

'And where might he be?' Kurt asked acidly, irritated to find his stepdaughter still enamoured of that scruffy event rider when she'd been born into such a dressage dynasty.

'No idea. But I know somebody who will.' Magnus loped off.

When Dillon Rafferty knocked on the bathroom door and announced himself in that familiar cocky, gruff voice, Faith buried her face in her hands and groaned, her artificially enhanced mind spinning and accelerated heartbeat pounding. Her lifetime shame moment had come after just eighteen years on the planet. The country's number-one recording artist, voted the man most women would like to wake up in bed beside, was standing just a few feet away in her rosette-decked bedroom, surrounded by the detritus of two teenage girls tarting themselves up for a party.

'Go away! This is *all* your fault,' she wailed, rendered even more confrontational than usual by two legal pep pills and *Carmina Burana* on Classic FM.

'My fault?' The muffled voice of a legend came through the door.

'You sent Rory away to Scotland.' She marched around the tiny room in time to Orff. 'Then Magnus said you were going to come here tonight – like Prince William visiting a bloody orphanage – and my best friend thought I was lying about it and anyway I know you're completely crap and unreliable, being a rock star and all that, so I went on the internet to make sure I had lots of lovely men here for her to get off with, only too many have come – and lots of bloody girls – and my parents will be mad at me now and you have come after all, and what does it all matter because Rory's not here. Rory. Isn't. *Here.*'

'I'm sorry, Faith.' On the other side of the door, Dillon was clearly trying not to laugh at her.

'Oh bugger off to an awards ceremony or a tropical island or something.'

'Stop acting like a spoilt brat.'

'I am so *not* a spoilt brat.'

'Tell that to your family who've worked their butts off organising this for you, only to find you'd rather spend it admiring your sanitaryware.'

'They're the ones who kept banging on about me having a party. I wanted to go to see the Kür at the Olympics this week instead.'

'The what?'

She ceased marching as Classic FM went to a break – the wart removal advert was back on, she noticed – and addressed the bathroom door: 'The *Kür* – the freestyle dressage to music. It's quite breathtaking and beautiful. My mother won her gold medal for it a *long* time ago, only now she's refusing to go because Kurt got left off the team this time.'

She could hear whispering beyond the door and realised her brother was still there. Faith secretly hoped they'd go away. But then, just as a jolly piece of Vivaldi struck up, Dillon spoke again. 'I've got a birthday present for you.'

'Give whatever it is to my poor, long-suffering mother.'

'I thought you just said she wouldn't appreciate tickets to the Kür?'

The door flew open.

'You liar!' Faith wailed when Dillon darted inside empty-handed.

He immediately clocked the bottle of vodka, the wild eyes and the disturbingly high hemline. He'd never realised she had such cracking legs, not that he had the time or inclination to linger upon them right now.

'What have you taken?' he demanded, brows locked together as he marched up to her and stared into her eyes. In his time Dillon had taken pretty much every narcotic known to man – and had the broken marriage, lost friends, stop-start career and rehab bills to prove it. He knew the signs in an instant. There was no denial.

'The box is on the side,' Faith muttered.

'Tampons?'

'No, not *that* box. The one by the mirror.'

Dillon picked up the garish empty Brain Candy packaging. 'These things can be bloody dangerous, you know. They're not sweets.'

'Duh? I'm not *stupid*. I know. I'm a responsible adult. I feel fine.'

'Could have fooled me. Have you been drinking plenty of fluids?'

She nodded at the vodka bottle and started to giggle.

'Little idiot.' He filled her tooth glass with water from the tap and handed it to her, before starting to empty the vodka into the basin.

'Oi – that's perfectly good Smirnoff.'

'You may want to jump into Rory's pants, but believe me this isn't the way.'

'Have to be a jolly good bloody long jumper to get into his pants tonight. He's in Scotland thanks to *you*.'

He glanced across at her. 'He is there trying to redeem himself for failing to make anything of the horses I bought him,' he reminded her lightly. 'He's already broken the two best ones, I hear.'

'He didn't break them,' she said scornfully. 'They were broken already. You were the one that bought an ageing dud on the recommendation of a friend who wouldn't know a top-class horse from a camel.'

'Jules is a bloody good mate.'

'Magnus says she's a washed-up record producer with a coke habit.'

'Does he now?'

There was a groan beyond the bathroom door.

Realising she had just dropped her brother right in it Faith blustered on. 'No disrespect, but she obviously knows nothing about the sport. Sid was over-competed and ridden into the ground by a ham-fisted amateur last year. No vet worth his salt would pass him sound to compete at four-star again.'

'Rory seems to think he's great.'

She marched up to him. 'Can't you see he's so desperate to please you and your little clique of friends he'd have agreed to ride a seaside donkey for you? All Rory wants to do is impress you, his biggest owner, this mega superstar who he thinks spotted his talent from afar.' She started pacing around again now, on hot coals.

Dillon sighed, regarding Faith with guarded affection, seeing the tough, tomboyish loner in the garish raver outfit, as much fancy dress as a toddler in a fairy princess suit. 'We both know that up until a year ago I thought an event rider was some sort of stuntman hired for corporate parties.'

'You know differently now,' she insisted, picking up speed. 'Rory could be the best in the world.'

He held up his hands. 'I don't doubt his talent. Nell tells me often enough that he has something special.'

An involuntary sneer curled at her lips at the mention of Nell. 'And she should stop interfering in Rory's competition schedule.'

'I suppose that's your job?'

'I never interfere.'

'Oh no?' He laughed incredulously, remembering only too well how he had got to know Faith better. She'd been the teenage stablehand who'd always looked so disapproving when he and his friends had come to ride at Rory's yard, treating Dillon with the same spiky, no-nonsense attitude she did Magnus and even Rory at times. Yet, of all of them, it was Faith who had the longest-standing friendship with Dillon, a fact both played down. It was the reason he was here tonight. Part little sister, part pet project, Faith had a special place in his conscience that in truth inspired a great deal more loyalty from Dillon than her boss.

'Rory knows what's best for his horses,' she said now, marching so briskly around the room that she swept the loo roll off its holder in her wake. 'He just needs a more supportive owner.'

Dillon sighed. 'In that case, you should be pleased Nell knows more about eventing than me. I have had a busy year, as you might have noticed. I'm almost never in the country.'

Stomping around by her basin, Faith let out a huff of frustration, all self-control starting to fray as the Brain Candy and Dillon's presence in her bathroom combined to make her feel like she was in a strange waking dream. 'It's obvious Nell just wants Rory to compete wherever's closest to a boutique hotel.'

For a moment it seemed she'd gone too far as Dillon headed towards the door, but he just stooped to pick up a fallen towel before turning back to watch as she lapped the tiny room as speed.

'Lucky Rory's got you to fight his corner for him, huh?' he ragged.

'Not any more.' Her lip began to wobble and she paced faster to stop herself crying. 'I start work in Essex next week.'

'For long?'

'A year. So you'd better look after him while I'm gone.' Faith suddenly realised that she was standing in the shower, and had no idea how she'd got there. She hastily stepped out, hoping that Dillon hadn't noticed.

He had, but tactfully said nothing. There was a smile tickling his lips and lighting up those blue eyes. 'I'll try my best,' he promised, starting to laugh. 'I can't believe I've flown in from fucking Italy to see you on your birthday, brat, and all you can do is shout at me.'

'What *are* they doing up there?' Nell handed Gigi to Magnus when he'd picked his way down past the partygoers gathered on the stairs.

'Talking about horses, from what I could hear.'

'Oh for God's sake! Dillon doesn't need this.' She made to go upstairs, but Magnus put a hand on her arm.

'Leave them be, huh?'

'That's my boyfriend trapped in there.'

'Faith won't hurt him, I promise.'

'Says who? Dillon flew back from Milan to come to this ghastly party as a favour to me. Now your sister has him locked in a bathroom and none of your barking mad family seems to care. She's probably stripped him naked and tied him to the shower rail.'

Suddenly she realised that Anke was standing right behind her, waiting to get past with a huge tray of sausages. Nell had the grace to look abashed.

'You have nothing to worry about on that front, I can assure you,' Anke said smoothly. 'Faith is not interested in men sexually, I believe. Besides, there's no shower rail in there. It's built in.'

Feeling surprisingly at home in the cosy en suite, Dillon had flipped down the loo seat and was sitting on it watching Faith in fascination, knowing the chemical reaction was contained, at least. She was quite bizarre under artificial stimulation; she was driven enough without it, after all. He still remembered his first-ever encounter with her on Rory's yard. He'd arrived with a house party for a group ride, only to find Rory had forgotten to write it in the diary. Faith, no older than fifteen or sixteen at the time, had calmly brought in half a dozen horses from the fields, riding one bareback and leading two at a time before grooming and tacking up the lot in twenty minutes, by which time Rory had emerged sleepily from his cottage to lead them off and charm them all.

Then months later, when he'd found himself standing beside her in an auction house that extraordinary day that he had heard 'Two Souls' for the first time, Faith's uncompromising loyalty and determination had taken over his life too.

Looking at her now, at that fierce little face painted so gaudily, he worried about his motivation in coming along tonight, especially hanging around in the girl's bathroom. It was a situation that could easily be misread, and yet Faith was one of the few people in Dillon's life who made him feel genuinely relaxed, who saw him simply as the lucky local farmer who strummed twelve-bar blues on a guitar. Being with her made him wish he was eighteen again too, a shy perfectionist who lived in his father's shadow and craved friendship. They'd have been mates, he liked to think. He'd have stayed up all night making her mix tapes and writing songs for her. They might have even dated, but she would have always loved another more and he would have been far too polite to fight for her, especially when his own fame had kicked in and the pretty girls started to crowd around.

But he was a long way past eighteen now, Dillon reminded himself. He was a father of two, and he was here to look out for her.

'Stop marching around like a demented drum majorette and drink your water,' he told her.

She cooperated, realising as she did so that the radio was still on and playing the last few refrains of the duet from *The Pearl Fishers*. Cocking her head to listen, she swayed along, water dribbling unnoticed down her chin and on to her dress.

'You like Bizet?' Dillon regarded her with amusement.

She nodded, hugging herself and then flinging out her arms and executing a few ballet *élèves* with surprising grace, using the towel rail as a barre. 'Sure beats the crap in the charts these days.'

'Touché,' he laughed. 'I've asked the record label to withdraw "Two Souls" from sale, but they refuse. The revenue's massive.'

She suddenly set him with a beady look, although her eyes were unnaturally bright, the Brain Candy still hard at work.

'You once said that if you ever got to number one again you'd buy Rory an international horse,' she reminded him

'So I did,' Dillon sighed wearily, having rather hoped the conversation had moved away from Rory, however briefly.

'"Two Souls" has been number one for weeks and weeks.'

'So it has.'

'A deal's a deal.'

He laughed, not taking her seriously. 'Does that mean you want a horse for your birthday, brat?'

'This is for Rory. You made a promise.'

He sucked his expensive white teeth and then flashed them non-committedly.

He didn't suppose that, once she'd gone to Essex, Rory would survive more than a month before bedlam overtook him; he was equally worried that Faith would be hopelessly corrupted by friends like Carly as soon as she cast off her Cotswold anchors.

'He mustn't know, of course,' Faith danced away. 'Nor must Nell.'
'Nell?'

'She'd only interfere. Trust me, you have to go to the very top to find what you want.' Faith had started to dance to Verdi's anvil chorus now, arms flipping about, hips zig-zagging and feet tapping to the clanking, masculine refrain. Watching her camping it up with legally high abandon, Dillon found it disturbingly erotic.

He loved Faith's utter determination in life. She really cheered him up. She had a straightforward, angry honesty he respected totally, and which reminded him of his sister Kat. Faith's love for Rory might be childlike, but she bore it with so much more certainty than his feelings about anybody. He envied that drive.

'It's not exactly difficult to identify the best four-star horse by a country mile at the moment,' she was saying, grooving into the shower cubicle once again.

'And that is?'

'The Fox. Won two Olympic gold medals this week. Finished on his dressage score. You should have seen him in the individual jump-off. Didn't so much as touch a pole.'

'You're in the shower again,' he pointed out kindly.

'So I am,' she jigged out, dripping wet from the leaky tap, the flimsy dress now clinging to her body, her wet hair in tendrils. 'The Fox is *definitely* your horse.'

She spun around to face him, arms aloft to emphasise her point, and Dillon watched as she tripped over a bath mat and tipped backwards over the end of the small slipper bath, legs akimbo, with a flash of wholly unexpected and deliciously lacy underwear through her fishnets. He had to exercise a great deal of self-control in order to keep his thoughts big-brotherly.

Somehow he managed to keep talking. 'He's for sale, is he, The Fox?'

Faith scrabbled upright and stared at him over the rim of the bath.

'Of *course* he's for sale!' She had no real idea if that was true, but she was suddenly aware that she had Dillon's undivided attention and she had to cash in. 'So will you buy him?'

'I'll think about it.' He stood up, suddenly finding the en suite far too hot. 'Now would you like to come to a party?'

'Can I just get changed first?'

★

114

When Dillon rejoined the party, Nell cornered him on the stair turn, livid that the birthday girl had humiliated her by hogging her rock-star boyfriend in a bathroom for an hour, quite possibly to create her own Paris Hilton sex tape filmed on her mobile.

'You bastard!' she hissed. 'Where is she?'

'Fixing her face and putting some clothes on,' he explained, which didn't help his case.

Five minutes later, Graham coaxed Faith outside to stand in front of the double doors of the barn that he had been guarding from gatecrashers all night. Now dressed in familiar jeans and a British Eventing polo shirt, she gaped in guilty astonishment at the huge crowds.

Trailing behind them, infuriated by her friend's ungrateful atten-tion seeking, Carly came to a sulky halt between the gayfathers and Magnus, and watched as Graham unlatched the big doors.

'We meant to show you this earlier,' he pulled open one side, 'but you've been otherwise engaged.'

The second door opened to reveal a small bright yellow Volkswagen hatchback parked inside the barn and covered with rib-bons.

'Happy birthday!'

Faith burst into noisy, happy tears.

'Ohmygoditsacar!' she said stupidly. 'I really don't deserve this.'

'Telling me,' Carly muttered in an undertone.

Faith was ecstatic. Kissing and hugging her parents, she danced inside to take a closer look. Having her own car meant only one thing to her right now: she could drive back from Essex to see Rory as often as she liked.

'Don't even think about driving it until you're sober,' Graham warned as she leaped into the driver's seat to get a feel, reminding him of Susan Sarandon in *Thelma and Louise* as she prepares to drive over the edge of the canyon.

'Do you think she likes it?' Anke asked Carly anxiously, deeply concerned by her daughter's behaviour that night.

'It's okay,' Carly conceded resentfully, knowing that the one-upmanship of having a car had now been lost.

'It's a lovely colour, I think,' Anke smiled. 'Like your swimming costume. You do know that we haven't got a pool?'

'It's a dress,' Carly muttered, noting in alarm that Graham had customised the sides of Faith's new car with silhouetted dressage decals and hung furry horseshoes from the rear-view mirror. She made a mental note never, ever to ask for a lift in it.

Anke leaned closer, dropping her voice. 'Carly, I must ask you, do you think Faith is happy with life right now?'

'How d'you mean?' she asked blankly. 'She's friends with Dillon Rafferty. What girl wouldn't be happy?' There were chips of ice in her voice.

'Sometimes she puts on a brave face, but a mother knows.'

'She's cool, Mrs B, honest.' There was a noisy jangle of bracelets as she reached up to pat Anke's arm. 'She'll have a ball in Essex. That brave face will come back quite different, just you wait and see. She'll be all smiles.'

'I hope so.' Anke sighed, watching as Faith tuned the car radio to Classic FM and cranked some Wagner up to full blast. 'I do hope so.'

Anke was left feeling ragged after the party and vowed that Chad would have all his landmark celebrations in purpose-built venues. The huge clearing-up operation took two days, unassisted by Faith who headed straight to Overlodes Equestrian Centre in her new car to welcome a victorious Rory home from his Scottish trip. She stayed there from dawn to dusk, making the most of what little time she had left before leaving for Essex.

'Why is my daughter so ungrateful?' Anke lamented to best friends Ophelia and Pixie. 'She is just so obsessed with poor Rory.'

'She's in love,' Pixie said simply.

'Dilly was just the same at her age,' Ophelia reminded her, 'and look at her now – she and Magnus are like a pair of solid bookends.'

'But Rory hasn't got the backbone to be a bookend,' Anke fretted. 'I'm not sure he could take the weight of her clever mind, and anyway he doesn't want to.'

'He's pretty special underneath that laid-back bluff,' insisted Pixie, who had always had a soft spot for Rory. 'Remember, his father died when he was terribly young. He's really had to fend for himself.'

Anke felt a sharp pang of recognition. Now more convinced than ever that Faith's problems lay with a lack of a paternal anchor, she redoubled her efforts to tell her more about her birth father, but

Faith – eventually coming down from her Brain Candy high with tremors, a dry mouth and nausea – blocked her ears to any mention of flame-haired horse dealer Fearghal.

'How many times? I *don't* want to meet my father. Much as I know it's a disappointment to you, I am not father-fixated or a lesbian or anything else remotely interesting. I am just an anti-social, flat-chested girl who wants to ride horses and who made a complete mess of her birthday party by locking herself in the loo when lots of strangers turned up.'

Which was, Anke supposed, an apology of sorts.

In her defensive but honest way, Faith in fact apologised to everybody who had put themselves out to make her party happen only to find her behaving like an imbecile, from Carly whose dreams of finding Grant's successor had come to nothing, to her gayfathers, to Graham and Magnus. To Faith's tremendous relief, they all forgave her good-spiritedly.

Finally she begged Dillon Rafferty's number from Magnus and sent him a text asking him to ignore everything she had said or done that night. The Brain Candy had turned her into a monster, and she was mortified when she thought back to how she had harangued him about Rory.

To her amazement, he replied within minutes. *I enjoyed it, brat. You are unique. Tell me more about this wonder horse. Is he really for sale?*

Faith texted excitedly back, thumb on fast-forward. *Definitely. Times are hard. Old money's suffering more than ever, and event riders are always broke. Hugo Beauchamp would probably sell his own mother if the price was right.*

Chapter 9

Alicia Beauchamp, despite her aura of fading, tissue-wrapped glamour, of Chanel, gin and pearls, was a dyed-in-the-wool thermals and thermos eventing mother.

For years she had stood in rain-lashed, muddy fields cheering on her charges, although Charles had long ago bowed out of competitive riding in favour of the odd day's hunting or polo, leaving the path clear for Hugo. From those early years of rusty pony trailers and lowly rankings, through national championships, countless three day events, British teams and medal ceremonies, Alicia had been a stalwart supporter.

When Hugo married and settled down she was happy to take a back seat and pursue other interests, friendships and loves – at least one of them deliciously illicit and involving a very dashing, very married local magistrate Master of Foxhounds. But now that Tash was so busy with family youngstock, Alicia had dug her impenetrable wet weather gear out of retirement and – despite two hip replacements and a spot of rheumatism in one knee – was nobly checking score boards, rolling up bandages and brewing coffee in the horsebox between phases, keeping the dogs under control and barracking stewards and her son.

'Hurry *up*, Hugo' – 'no, not those boots, *these* boots' – 'don't leave that bloody thing there' – 'cigarette?' – 'hup!' were her standard rallying cries.

This morning was no exception. 'We should have left half an hour ago!' she shouted from the horsebox cab, cigarette dangling between her lips and Beefy yapping excitedly on her knee.

'Are you sure you'll be all right?' Hugo asked Tash for the tenth time, reluctant to leave.

'Absolutely! We're grand.' She waved sleeping Amery's little fist at him. 'Now you heard your mother. Get going. Bring back pots. We'll be waiting here for you.'

Blue eyes glittering, he kissed her on the mouth and belted off to take the wheel, leaving Tash to turn tiredly towards the house and carry Amery inside, wondering where Beccy had got to with Cora. There were still half a dozen horses left to muck out, but Beccy had spirited the toddler into the house ten minutes earlier, muttering something about fetching a drink.

They were in the snug, Cora emptying bookshelves unheeded while, swigging on a Diet Coke and lying back on the drop-arm tapestry sofa, Beccy used the Beauchamps' phone. 'You're going to have to ask James to increase my allowance, Mummy,' she was saying. 'Tash and Hugo pay next to nothing and are *really* mean. They say I'm nowhere near ready to start competing yet, and they make me do all the most boring jobs.'

Still cradling Amery, Tash cleared her throat and Beccy leaped upright, inadvertently elbowing her new puppy, Karma. It let out an indignant shriek, scrabbled off the arm and landed on Cora's pile of books, which slithered underfoot and made the puppy do the splits.

Eyeing her sister at the door, Beccy had the grace to blush. 'I have to go Mummy – I'll call you later okay? When you've spoken with James?' She hung up, not looking Tash in the face. 'My phone's out of charge so I used your landline.'

'Fine,' Tash was hurt by the 'mean' comment and too wracked with physical discomfort to be forgiving. 'But please don't leave the yard unattended with jobs half done. It's selfish and unprofessional. If you want to ride more and earn more, you have to start by improving your basic stable care.'

She personally thought Beccy had a better standard of living than her employers. Heavily subsidised by her trust fund in addition to her wages and rent-free life at Haydown, she shopped for groceries exclusively at M&S, ran a racy little Audi that was far better than Tash's own ancient Shogun, had an iPhone constantly loaded with the latest tracks, a Mac laptop bursting with movies and pop videos, and Egyptian bedlinen and Molton Brown bath products in the stable flat. As soon as she'd arrived she'd bought herself the sooty grey Labradoodle puppy that now sported a diamante-encrusted collar and ate nothing but steamed chicken. For a self-styled global hippy who had purportedly survived on rice and lentils in India, Beccy liked life's little luxuries.

'Cora was thirsty.' She glared down at her feet, encased in pink and orange Joules socks, this season's must-have colours among image-conscious young event riders.

'So I see.' A beaker of sticky apple juice had been upended in a first edition of a Montgomery biography. Tash sighed, her anger evaporating. 'You'd better get back out there now. Jenny's taking the hunting box to deliver a horse to Leicestershire this morning so you're in charge. If you can come in and help me with Cora at lunchtime, I'll make you something to eat.'

'Sure.'

Tash suddenly felt incredibly sorry for her stepsister, who had been forced to start at the bottom like a teenager despite being in her late twenties. 'It will get easier, Beccy. You're already a million times faster and fitter than when you started.'

This wasn't strictly true. Despite a natural affinity with horses, Beccy was not a particularly hard worker, she was vague and a poor timekeeper, she overslept, got the feeds muddled up and she had a memory like a sieve, but simply having another body around the place was a godsend. She could generally be relied upon to wait on the yard for the farrier or the vet or the feed merchant, or could sit with Cora while Tash dealt with something in Hugo's absence. And when Tash had gone into labour she had been the only person on site. Without her, Tash had no idea how she would have coped. Beccy had been marvellous. For that Tash was eternally grateful, and even Hugo – who had not been best pleased to find his sister-in-law in situ when he returned from the Olympics – had tacitly accepted the situation. In fact he'd been strangely muted about it, as he had about everything since the Games. Tash put it down to the inevitable post-competition anticlimax, to worrying about money and most of all to adjusting to a new baby.

Amery was a bald, wrinkled wonder with his father's blue eyes, his mother's cleft chin and a very odd-shaped head from battering away at her pelvis for hours trying to get out. Far more passive than Cora had been, at less than a week old he was already proving happy to be hawked about in a Moses basket or car seat and plonked anywhere to gaze short-sightedly at the new world around him, occasionally thrusting a little starfish hand out to test the air. Mostly he slept with snuffly, trusting contentment, as he was now.

Beccy reached out to cup his sleeping cheek as she passed by, her face softening with indulgence, and at that moment Tash could forgive her any number of mistakes.

'Thank you for being here,' she blurted suddenly.

'I'll get better, I promise,' Beccy mumbled as she disappeared along the back lobby.

Tash sat down. The truth was that they did need Beccy at Haydown very badly indeed, even if they couldn't afford to pay her well and she was pretty unreliable. They were so desperately short-staffed that she often doubled the workforce when not AWOL, which was admittedly rather a lot.

Half an hour later, when one of the local part-timers came to the back door and asked Tash what she was supposed to be doing because there was nobody on the yard, no feeds had been mixed up or haynets filled and the tack-room door was wide open, she realised Beccy must have gone missing again.

'You *rally* must make an effort to control the estate better,' Alicia barked through stiffly smiling lips as she and her son waited between summer downpours in the collecting ring at Ampney Franchart, a small one day event near Cirencester.

Hugo found her presence at horse trials something of a hindrance these days. On a practical level, he was already perfectly well supported at events by head girl Jenny or his team of volunteer grooms, hands-on owners and friends, but he was far too well-mannered a son to tell Alicia to bugger off.

'The Haydown tenants are having a terrible time,' Alicia carried on, tucking Beefy the pug into her coat's poacher's pocket as the heavens opened again. 'I think you might have to waive the rent for the rest of the year.'

'Can't afford to,' Hugo replied, pulling up his collar against the lashing rain, a thunderclap giving a timely roll overhead that made his young horse dance, back bunched nervously.

'Your father always waived the rent when the harvest was this bad, or livestock prices this low.' Despite the hot late summer, a record-breakingly cold spring had blighted crop and fodder production, resulting in low yields and poor quality.

'Father had a private income running at about three times the estate overheads. I currently have an income of approximately half those overheads.'

'So earn more.'

If only it was that simple, Hugo thought bitterly as he was beckoned into the muddy, hoof-poached ring to coax his mount through the showjumping phase of the battle for a cash prize of less than the cost of his diesel and entry fees that day.

There was to be no glamorous Olympic medal-winners' parade along the Mall in an open-topped bus for Hugo. Just a week after standing on the podium in front of a global television audience of millions, lowering his head for a brace of golds, he was competing between thunderstorms in a humble little Cotswolds event with dressage and fence judges lurking behind their swishing windscreen wipers in ageing hatch-backs, muddy-breeched amateurs falling off under-schooled horses in the minor sections, a windswept blue plastic loo cabin and a rain-lashed burger van totalling the 'facili-ties'. It's what earned him his real money. All three youngsters were leading their sections. Two were up for sale. If they went well across country today's successes might just secure buyers in an increas-ingly sticky market.

The team gold and his individual glory was no doubt set to give the sport a great boost as such successes inevitably did, particularly at the lower levels with novice riders inspired to start taking part, but that couldn't detract from the fact that event horses were proving very tough to sell right now, and when they did they commanded far lower prices than a year ago.

Hugo needed to sell several big-money horses to bring in much-needed revenue and save on hiring more staff. But the negative publicity surrounding silly, streaking Debbie Double-G still lingered like a bad smell as she did the celebrity circuit, determined to make a career from her endeavours, and certainly didn't help Hugo as he tried to get back to the day job. Far from giving him the Midas touch, his gold medals appeared to come with an Inca curse.

Blinded by sideways rain, Hugo's horse crashed through the first fence, which hardly improved their chances.

Watching from the sidelines, Alicia was joined by her crony Gin Seaton, a grey-haired battleaxe who had been following the sport for as long as anyone could remember and had owned several horses with Hugo over the years. 'I gather congratulations are in order, Alicia.'

'Hardly,' she winced at the clattering of poles. 'He'll never win from this score.'

'I was referring to your new grandson.'

Before she could reply, Alicia let out a wail of alarm as something started buzzing and chiming in her pocket, making Beefy growl.

'That's your mobile phone,' Gin pointed out kindly.

When Hugo trotted out with a disappointing twenty penalties, glaring at a big bald event photographer who clearly fancied himself as a paparazzo and had been following him around all day, his mother thrust his mobile up at him.

'Someone on the phone about buying a horse,' she barked, taking his reins.

'Yup?' he muttered into the handset, jumping off and starting to walk to his horsebox to fetch out his next ride. 'Yup . . . yup . . .'

Not noticing that the headstrong ex-hurdler he'd handed to Alicia was tanking past him to the lorry park, trailing his mother like string, Hugo turned his back to the wind and rain and listened very carefully indeed.

'I'm all ears,' he suddenly smiled, flicking two fingers at the snap-happy photographer who was now loitering behind the blue loo, his huge lens poking around it like a marksman's rifle.

At Haydown, far from the early autumn storms that were rattling around the Cotswolds, Tash tried both Beccy's mobile number and the yard line, wondering where on earth her stepsister was. She'd promised to be around to help with Cora's lunch, and it was now after one-thirty.

Physically very limited after her surgery, and trapped in the office by endless phone-calls and paperwork, Tash resorted to feeding the little girl a carpet picnic of finger food on plastic plates. She hoped that Beccy was back on the yard and that nothing was wrong. She gazed through the open window to the bright sunlit stables in the distance, but all was still, a heat haze dancing above the long stretch of lawn that needed mowing. She'd take the children out to see what was going on after the next feed, she decided.

Checking that Amery was still asleep in his Moses basket and Cora happily banging plastic blocks together on the hearthrug, Tash waded through a few more bills, plucking out the truly urgent and the final reminders.

Beside her was a list of her own clients to ring – portrait commissions that she had taken on shortly after finding out that she was pregnant, believing that she could complete them all before the birth and put some much-needed cash in the family coffers. Painting and sketching horses, dogs and quite often people had been a very profitable sideline for Tash over the years, particularly during the winter 'closed season' months, and her lively, accurate depictions were always in demand. But she'd developed severe carpal tunnel syndrome, an uncomfortable side-effect of pregnancy, and all painting and sketching had ground to a halt as her fingers rapidly became numb and her wrists shot through with pain. Holding a paintbrush had been impossible for months now. She had a long waiting list and her subjects were all still patiently waiting to be captured in oil or watercolour, but although the feeling in her hands and wrists was returning to normal her timetable – especially now with two children in tow – was set to be more chaotic and stretched than ever.

Tash was home alone four days after a caesarean with a toddler and a newborn to look after, and a stepsister who had vanished yet again.

'Beccy?' she called out now. But there was no answer, and Tash suddenly worried her short temper earlier had made her pack it in for good. She could be notoriously hair-triggered.

Feeling suddenly overwhelmed, she covered the seemingly impenetrable pile of bills with the latest issue of *Horse & Hound* and, admiring Hugo's standing-in-stirrups Olympic victory salute captured on the front cover, answered the ever-ringing phone.

'What are you doing there, Fangs?' demanded the bossy but kind voice of her older sister Sophia. 'You should be in hospital.'

'They let us out early for good behaviour.'

'I hope you're in bed with your feet up.'

'I'm not allowed upstairs till Hugo gets home,' she sighed. She also wasn't allowed to drive, to lift weights – not even Cora – nor to make sudden moves or wear pants smaller than a galleon sail. She was exhausted and overwrought with sudden crying fits from ever-changing hormones. The house was filthy and a bombsite. The stable staff, a merry but ever-changing gaggle of freelancers and part-timers borrowed from friends' yards, kept appearing at the door asking questions. The phone rang non-stop. She missed the orderliness of hospital, the regular meals, the lack of responsibility, the regime.

But she was still delighted to be back. If it weren't for the stitches, discomfort and wrinkling surgical stockings, she'd have danced around Haydown with her children in her arms.

'Where is Hugo?' Sophia was demanding

'Oh – he just popped out,' she lied.

He would be away until late afternoon. Tash would never have been discharged had the maternity ward staff known what awaited her, but such was the force of her desire to be at Haydown – and the practical need – she'd convinced them to let her go. So when Hugo had collected her first thing that morning, sending the maternity ward hearts fluttering, neither he nor Tash let on that he would be driving off in the horsebox as soon as he posted his family home. On the way home, worried by her obvious discomfort, he'd offered to forfeit the Ampney trials and stay with her, but Tash wouldn't hear of it, knowing that horses entered there needed to be sold. She had Beccy around to help, and she deliberately ignored Hugo's aside that this was like having a well-meaning but very senile relative in situ.

'How are you feeling?' Sophia was asking. 'Still agony?'

'Not bad,' Tash assured her. 'They've given me lots of painkillers and I can get about pretty well.'

'You shouldn't be home at all, Fangs!' The older the sisters got, the more Tash saw their father in Sophia, with his sharp temper, perfectionism, superhuman organisational skills and reluctant yet assured social charm.

As children the sisters had adopted the nicknames Enid and Fanny because of their habit of chattering away like two little old ladies, and Sophia still called her sibling 'Fangs' now. She'd always been the leader. Three years older, exquisitely pretty and precociously charming, Sophia's path through life had always seemed gilded, whereas Tash's was boggy and random. Yet both had ended up at a very similar point – country mothers married to two old school friends, although their routes there couldn't have been more different, Sophia starting out as a model in an era when rich and powerful rock stars, aristocrats and media moguls chose their wives from the pages of *Vogue*, calling up the modelling agency to arrange a date. Matched up with the dashing, highly eligible Ben Meredith, Viscount Guarlford, Sophia had gone on to excel as a society hostess, charity fundraiser and country set power player, turning around the fortunes of Holdham Hall in an era when many similar family estates were being sold off as corporate headquarters or boutique spas. A decade later, with three stunning children and an address book that was the envy of all, Sophia had been promoted. Last year Ben had inherited the title upon the death of his father and she'd become the Countess of Malvern, wife of the twelfth Earl. The dowager countess, Beatrice, had then graciously vacated the family rooms in the east wing to make way for her successors. In moving from Home Farm to the main house it seemed that Sophia had also taken on her mother-in-law's legendary fierce manner. Combined with their father's short fuse, it made for an irascible mix.

Sophia regularly checked for fault lines in Tash's marriage, much as she customarily checked her own reflection for any tiny wrinkles or crow's feet indicating that she needed to get her Botox topped up.

'Who's there to look after you?' she demanded now, with steely insight.

'Oh, just the staff.' Tash was deliberately vague.

'What about Mummy?'

'She can't come.'

'What do you mean "*can't* come"? Is there a complete travel embargo across the English Channel that I haven't heard about? Or is she being tied to a chair?'

'Something to do with Polly, I think.'

'Typical!'

Tash had unwittingly trodden on her first Sophia landmine, their mother's reluctance to travel from France to see any of her ever-expanding clutch of grandchildren in Great Britain. Alexandra lived between a trio of bases in Paris, Marseilles and the Loire Valley; older age had lent her an increasing excuse for eccentricity, and yet conversely a desire to stay young that infuriated Sophia as Alexandra took up yoga, visited salt spas, hiked up mountains and went clubbing with her youngest daughter, while doggedly refusing to have the Botox her eldest swore by.

'I spoke to her from Hugo's mobile when I was in hospital,' Tash said placatingly. 'She's terribly excited about Amery.'

'But I thought she volunteered to stay at Haydown throughout?' Sophia raged. 'And now that you've had another C-section you'll need somebody there to help with the baby and Cora and the house. Believe me, you won't cope alone. It's *much* harder second time around.' She'd had all three of her children by Caesarean – elective rather than emergency – in an exclusive private London unit. Sophia had also employed a small army of nursery staff to see her through those first few weeks each time.

'I wasn't due to come out of hospital until the end of the week,' she reminded her, 'but Marlbury General said we were doing so well that they've let me go early.'

'Needed the bed, more likely. I told you that you should have gone private. Even Sally forsook the NHS to have hers in a paddling pool in the kitchen.' Sophia took a quick snipe at their sister-in-law, whose hands-on approach to parenting always made her feel inadequate. 'You should hire in a maternity nanny. Norland's are very good . . .'

Tash was only half listening. Behind her, Cora had tired of her plastic blocks and was starting to roam from shelves to cupboards in search of entertainment, wreaking havoc.

'I have Beccy.' She distractedly searched the desktop for the DVD that she'd brought in with her earlier.

'Beccy is with *you*?' Sophia shrieked, making Tash jump so much she knocked over several teetering piles of paperwork.

Sophia thoroughly disapproved of their younger stepsister. As children, she and Tash had often been presented with almost identical gifts: two teddy bears, one brown and one cream; one dark-haired doll and one blonde doll, a pair of kittens with slightly different markings. Pulling rank as older sibling, Sophia had always taken first pick and Tash soon developed a way of coping, which was to feel sorry for the 'unwanted' bear, doll or kitten and to adopt it gratefully and lovingly as her own.

In a curious way, a similar thing had happened when, after the ghastliness of their parents' divorce, James had finally married his long-time secretary and sometime mistress Henrietta, a blonde widow with two young daughters. Prone to favouritism, Sophia had immediately chosen the older, prettier and more glamorous stepsister to be her special pet. Appalled by both Sophia's and their father's obvious preference for Em, Tash had briefly tried to befriend the strange, introverted and very ungrateful Beccy – an unsuccessful adoption that had just come back to haunt her. She was no closer to understanding what made Beccy tick now than she had been as a teenager. Even today, when she really needed some help and had trusted Beccy to be there, she'd wandered off without a word.

'What on *earth* are you *doing* giving her houseroom?' Sophia was barracking.

Tash had just edged her way to the antique drinks cabinet housing the old combi television that Hugo used to play back footage of lessons and competitions. Hearing her sister's furious tone she dropped the Maisy Mouse DVD in among the bottles of malt whisky.

'Sorry?'

'She is totally unstable and, from what I hear, on *drugs*.'

'She's fine.' Tash fished around for the disc and knocked over a bottle of rare old Mortlach, which cannoned into the others with a series of wine-bar chinks.

'Are you pouring a drink?' Sophia had a keen ear.

'No.' She located Maisy and slotted her in, just as Cora rolled up to get involved. A moment later, Neil Morrissey was loudly hailing Charlie and Tallulah.

'Who's that? Not one of Beccy's awful friends? He sounds terribly Black Country.'

Tash moved away from the television, leaving Cora standing entranced, watching Maisy set out with her friends to feed the farm animals.

'Beccy doesn't have awful friends,' Tash told her sister. 'She doesn't have many friends at all any more, I think.'

There was a step outside the room.

Tash looked up as a very pink face appeared around the door, dreadlocks swinging, big pale eyes blinking. Realising that Beccy must have overheard her last comment, she felt herself turn a matching shade of pink. They looked like the cartoon piglets Maisy was feeding on screen.

Waving a silent greeting, Beccy mouthed 'Everything okay?'

Tash nodded. 'Just talking to Sophia. She sends her love.'

At the other end of the line Sophia let out a sarcastic little 'pah!' From the Moses basket, Amery concurred with a strangely sarcastic-sounding yowl.

'Do you want me to take him for a bit while you carry on talking?' Beccy offered.

Tash nodded again, telling Sophia firmly, 'Beccy's proving a great help.'

'Don't tell me you're letting her anywhere near the children?'

'Why shouldn't I?'

'You know she dropped Linus once? He was only six months old. Sally was hysterical.'

'Most of us make awful blunders like that.' Tash watched Beccy gather up the waking Amery, so tiny and vulnerable, and carry him out to look at the heraldic tapestries in the galleried hall, which intrigued the little newborn's semi-focused eyes with their geometric shapes. 'I accidentally let Cora roll off the sofa at twelve weeks.'

'Yes, but you weren't holding her over a stone-flagged floor at the time, shouting that nobody loved you.'

Tash felt a chill scuttle up her back like a huge, frosty insect. 'What?'

'Surely you remember? It was very dramatic – at my Boxing Day lunch. Or weren't you there? Of course, that was the year you and Niall went to Ireland for Christmas. Beccy got blootered on sherry and started screaming that our family had never accepted or loved her and Em like siblings. Then she dropped Linus, threw him down really. Thankfully he landed on one of Bea's gundogs, which cushioned the blow. Little chap was fine.'

Tash said nothing, too shocked to speak. Her eyes automatically sought out her newborn child, cradled in a warm bosom, listening to soft whispers, enchanted by his aunt's little tour of ancient arms and pennants.

Was Beccy about to hold Amery up over the antique fire irons and threaten to drop him because Tash had accused her of being 'selfish and unprofessional' earlier?

She hardly took in a word as Sophia rattled on. 'Before you go, we must discuss Hugo's fortieth. My spring diary really is filling up and I need to know whether you want me to help organise this surprise party or not. I know you were all for it when Ben mooted the idea, but that was a long time ago.'

Tash was still watching Beccy carry Amery around; now quiet and swaddled deeply in her arms, he seemed thoroughly content. She was suddenly groggy with tiredness.

'Can we talk about this another time? I haven't got my spring diary to hand.' It was an attempt at a joke, but it came across rather more sarcastically than she'd intended.

Her sister immediately became defensive, uncannily like their father once again. 'Very well, I'll leave it with you to let me know whether you want me to do it, but I can't promise I'll be able to spare the time if you wait much longer. Now get off the phone and get some rest, Fangs. You've just had a baby, for goodness's sake.'

As soon as she hung up, the phone began ringing again.

Beyond the door, Beccy and Amery had drifted out of sight. Already bored of Maisy, Cora had started to pull bottles of whisky from the cabinet. Tash picked up the call absent-mindedly as she lumbered across the room to stop the toddler attack.

'No! Stop it! Cora!'

'Hello? Is that Tash Beauchamp?'

Tash was barely listening. The line was terrible and there were far too many distractions at hand.

'This is—'

'Cora, no!'

Denied her game, the little girl started screaming furiously.

'This is Di—'

In the hallway, Amery suddenly burst into equally desperate mewls.

'This is Dillon Rafferty,' the caller repeated for the third time.

Tash let out a startled squeak and sat down in shock, just as Beccy reappeared with Amery, now bellowing for his feed, and plopped him on her lap.

'Can you hear me okay?' Dillon's voice crackled.

'Yes! Loud and clear!' Now acutely aware that she had the nation's favourite popstar on the phone, Tash hurriedly unhooked her nursing bra and let Amery latch on.

'Good.' He sounded as though he was in a tumble drier. 'You have a horse called The Fox?'

'That's right.'

'I want to buy him.'

Despite the background din, the flippancy in his voice was unmistakeable; as though their once-in-a-lifetime Olympic horse was a copy of *GQ* he wanted to pick up on the way home from work.

Tash balked, totally nonplussed. It wasn't every day a rock star phoned up wanting to buy your prize possession and greatest lifetime achievement, a horse just welcomed back from glory with such laurels he had even received a bundle of organic carrots sent by courier from Highgrove. She wondered what Hugo would say.

Beside her, Beccy and Cora were loudly identifying Eddie the elephant and Cyril the squirrel on screen. Suckling greedily inside the folds of her top, Amery gazed up at her with limpid eyes, a tiny wrinkled hand reaching up to her face.

'You still there?' his voice warbled on the crackling line.

'He's not for sale,' she said eventually, half wondering whether it *was* Hugo she was talking to, and that this was all some sort of elaborate wind-up to test her, but pranks like that weren't really his style, especially given today's already exhausting circumstances.

'Forgive me,' his words were accompanied by a crescendo like a long drumroll, 'I was quoted a figure to buy him outright. One—' The drumroll increased to drown out the voice.

'How much?'

When he repeated the sum to her she suddenly found she couldn't breathe.

On her lap, Amery slurped less frantically, his cheeks turning a contented pink.

'You still there?' Dillon shouted again above the background din.

'Sort of.'

There was a loud thudding noise from outside as somebody flew past in a helicopter, very low overhead. A local landowner no doubt; it drove Hugo mad if they piloted themselves back from business meetings while he was trying to school a nervous young horse in the manège. Tash reached for the window to close it so that she could hear better.

'Can I . . . and . . . him?'

'What?' With Amery still pressed to her chest she reached to turn down the volume on Maisy, but the helicopter was still close.

'Can I come and see him?'

'When did you have in mind?'

'Now.'

Tash looked across at Beccy in alarm, wondering who they could call upon for extra help. Hugo wasn't due back for hours and as far as she knew there was nobody at all on the yard right now.

'Are you nearby then?' she managed to croak.

'Yes – I'm directly overhead. Your swimming pool needs cleaning.'

Looking out of the window, Tash realised the helicopter was hovering above Flat Pad, ready to land.

As soon as she hung up she burped Amery and gestured Beccy urgently towards the kitchen as she went in search of some boots that would cover her surgical stockings, so that she could go and greet the visitor. The phone immediately rang again. This time, it was Hugo.

'At last!' he barked breathlessly. 'I was giving up bloody hope. You've been engaged for hours. *Woah – steady!* Have you lost your mobile again? *Good lad!*'

Tash realised he was riding. The competition must be still underway. 'Ages ago.'

'The number still works. I've left a stack of bloody voicemail messages. Hang on.' Although the sound of the helicopter landing was still resonating outside, Tash could distinctly hear hooves thundering in the background of Hugo's call. Then they stopped briefly, as though he was going over a fence, before thundering on again.

'Are you warming up for the cross-country?'

'I *am* riding across country. Can't chat. Tricky combination coming up. Got a man coming to Haydown to see The Fox this afternoon.'

'Dillon Raffer—'

'That's the chap. Can you handle it? *Woah – steady up, lad.* There's nobody on the yard until four.'

'Hugo, I've just—'

'Thanks!' The call ended with a clunk as he saw a stride and kicked for it.

'—had a baby,' Tash finished lamely, cradling the receiver to her chin and turning to Beccy, who had followed her through to the kitchen and was settling Amery into his basket by the clothes airer, Cora at her heels chewing on the ear of her fluffy Elmer elephant and asking to be picked up with a series of muffled 'bup bup bup' noises.

'That was Hugo,' Tash said in a frozen voice.

'Oh yes?' Beccy began swinging a giggling Cora around like an aeroplane, the little girl's cheeks curving towards her sparkling eyes, her hair on end.

Tash felt another great tide of weariness wash over her as she headed towards the back lobby again. Hormones bubbling up and tears threatening, she cursed under her breath as she found one of the terriers' balls in a boot. What did Dillon Rafferty want with a top event horse, she wondered, having been too preoccupied by multi-tasking months of pregnancy to register the pop star's recent understated connection with the sport. Wasn't organic cheese his pastime? She did vaguely recall reading that he was dating a classy Jemima Khan sort who was very horsy. Tash now wished she'd paid more attention to celebrity gossip while waiting for her pregnancy scans; she had worked her way through the antenatal department's entire supply of six-month-old women's magazines, but she had always leafed straight past the acres of paparazzi shots to get to the wordsearches, hoping nobody had got there before her.

Hurling the ball angrily over her shoulder she gritted her teeth and reminded herself how fickle their income was and how hard they needed to chase it. If it flew down from the sky and landed on Flat Pad, she'd be mad not to try to catch it.

'Could you look after the children for about twenty minutes while I field Dillon Rafferty?' She turned around to find Beccy beaming at her in a very unexpected fashion, Cora hoist high overhead letting out delighted little shrieks.

'It's not *really* him, is it?'

Tash returned the smile cautiously, hormonal irritation dissipating. 'So it seems.'

'Ohmygodicantbelievehesactuallyhere!'

Tash stepped forward with alarm as Beccy was momentarily so transported with delight that she looked as though she was going to drop Cora.

But she and Cora swung off quite safely to fly over one of the dog sofas, leaving Tash lurching into thin air, stitches straining.

'Will you bring him inside?' Beccy asked excitedly, between vrooming aeroplane noises.

Finally pulling on some matching boots that almost covered her surgical stockings, Tash grimaced at the tip around her, which had been worsened as a result of her recent footwear forage. 'I hope not.'

Landing her precious, giggling little aeroplane in the high chair, Beccy hid a small snarl as she realised Tash was going to keep Dillon Rafferty all to herself while she, Beccy, was left as unpaid nanny to the children.

'Well you'd better not let on you've just had a baby then,' she told her.

'Why ever not?'

'It would be selfish and unprofessional,' she said pettily. 'You've got to think of the business, and Hugo.'

'God, I suppose you're right,' Tash looked at her anxiously.

'I could go if you like?' Beccy volunteered.

'No, no, I'll go. I bred the horse. But you're right, I'll play down the baby thing. He'll never know.'

The house phone was ringing once more with its insistent, echoing clang.

'Oh, not again!' Tash grumbled as she looked around for something to cover her bulging post-partum midriff which was hanging out of her T-shirt above the unbuttoned fly of her softest old shorts.

She eventually pulled on one of Hugo's filthy old night-check sweaters – his graveyard for unwanted Christmas presents.

The phone rang on.

'Could you get that, Beccy?' she demanded as she waddled outside into the sunshine, cramming one of their veterinary supply sponsor's baseball caps on her head.

Beccy flicked two fingers at the door.

'Can you get that, Beccy?' she parroted with a sneer, stooping to make farty raspberries on Cora's sweet-smelling head to make her laugh again.

It was exactly a quarter past two in the afternoon, Beccy noted from a quick glance at the old Smith clock on the wall. Her mother usually rang at this time for a progress report, immediately after the Archers repeat that she listened to while clearing away her and James's lunch of cold meats and freshly baked petits pain. Beccy hoped that her mother had spoken to her stepfather about increasing her allowance, however reluctantly.

She braced herself to repeat her daily statement that all was well and that no drugs, prison cells, strange men or cult religions had featured in everyday life in rural West Berkshire. It was temptingly easy to wind up her mother. Today Beccy could casually mention that she had taken her car into Marlbury and watched a matinee of the latest Johnny Depp movie in the multiplex, sitting alone with a few saddos in the near-empty auditorium with a vast carton of popcorn on her knee, and that Tash hadn't even *noticed* she was gone. But she didn't want to push her luck. James was getting very twitchy about money, and she needed to appear to be earning her keep rather than bunking off to navel-gaze.

Ring . . . ring . . . ring . . .

Sighing, Beccy turned to fetch the phone from the wall, looking down at the Bitches of Eastwick who had lazily remained inside on the dog sofa when Tash went out, all crammed into one patch of sunlight spilling from the window at the far end.

'You're not the only dogsbodies around here, girls,' she muttered, pressing the green button and greeting the caller with a fake Mummerset accent: 'Haydown House. Kitchen maid Rebecca at your service. Please speak slowly because I am not educated and am slightly deaf from being cuffed around the ears.'

There was a pause.

'Can I help you?' she repeated, no longer quite so certain that it was her mother at the other end of the line.

'Is that Tash?'

Male. Not English. Very deep voice. Unbelievably sexy. Very slightly slurred.

Beccy rocked back on her heels, wondering if she might be speaking to Niall O'Shaughnessy. Oh. Lord. *Above*. Dillon Rafferty and then Niall O'Shaughnessy calling Haydown within an hour of one another. A double whammy of A-listers. She knew that Tash and her ex-boyfriend Niall were still good friends and apparently spoke often. He was a notoriously heavy drinker, so she supposed he could easily have mistaken her for Tash in a Bushmills stupor. Oh, to be Tash talking to Niall. Envy and excitement curdled in her belly.

'I'm sorry – the line's awful. Hello?' She tried to imitate Tash's husky, rather lazy Sloane voice just to continue the fantasy a moment longer.

'Hello!' the voice shouted to be heard, meaning Beccy had to hold the phone away from her ear because the line was in fact crystal clear. 'I'm calling from New Zealand, Tash. Is it an okay time? It's the middle of the bloody night here.'

The way he said it – '*Noo Zay*land'. . . 'noight' – told Beccy that this definitely wasn't a melodic, Irish actor. This was a throaty, incredibly sexy Kiwi. But he *did* think that she was Tash.

She glanced out at the helicopter that had just landed on the Beauchamps' dusty old pony paddock and wondered why her dreams never came true. Despite all her travels and her long, solitary quest for answers, Beccy was left unsatisfied and unfulfilled and back where she started, drifting through her lonely little life monitored by her overbearing mother and bankrolled by a reluctant, but rich, stepfather she loathed. Yet a decade earlier Tash, at about the same age as Beccy and in a similarly useless place in her life, had just gone on one family holiday to France to end up with both Niall *and* Hugo in love with her – and now entertained rock stars who arrived by helicopter at her country estate.

'It's a fine time,' she told the sexy caller, deepening her voice to her best husky purr. Beccy was always a million times more confident on the phone than she was face to face. Her stepfather liked to joke that she should work in telesales. 'It's a *perfect* time.'

'Is that so?' He sounded amused. 'That's great to hear.' Great was pronounced 'grite'.

He also, Beccy realised rather dreamily, sounded deliciously drunk. Whoever he was deserved a little sweet talk.

'Hugo's at a competition,' she said in her best smoky Nigella Lawson purr. 'I am *all* alone.'

'Are you?'

Beccy glanced over her shoulder at Cora dozing in her high chair with her elephant's ear in her mouth and her beaker cuddled to her cheek, and then at Amery so small and new and sound asleep in his Moses basket, and she smiled.

'Yesss – poor old me in this great big house. All alone.' She wondered if she was pushing it a bit far.

But her phone friend was too caned to censor or censure either end of the conversation. 'Well that's why I'm calling.'

'How thrilling!' She giggled, even weakening her 'r' with girlish, sex-kitten aplomb.

'I hope you've still got room for me and my head lad and half a dozen horses.'

'Er . . . of course we have! Yes! Always.'

'I know I left it pretty up in the air with Hugo, but I've been thinking about it since I flew home and I reckon it's a great offer. Shit, I really need out of here.' He sounded fantastically drunk now. 'I want out. As soon as. Most of the stuff's still packed from the Olympic trip. I don't need a lot, apart from Lemon and *ngā hōiho*.'

'What?'

'The horses. I'll get visas and horse transportation sorted, then I can give you an arrival date.'

'Can't wait.'

He laughed, a gorgeous hot fountain of noise.

'We'll welcome you with *open* arms,' Beccy purred again, still wondering who the hell he was.

He laughed afresh, a gruff, delicious rumble as exciting as a longed-for train finally rattling down the tracks.

'I probably shouldn't say this but you have a beautiful voice, Tash.'

'Thank you,' she replied happily, the beautiful voice dropping another octave.

'I can't wait to meet you.'

'Likewise,' she breathed.

Suddenly the pause took on such an electrical charge that Beccy could feel every centimetre of her knicker elastic tighten and every hair enclosed beneath them charge up with sexual friction, a small rustling forest surrounding a bubbling spring.

She was so turned on, so suddenly and unexpectedly horny, she wanted to hang up with fear.

The pause ached on and on. She was about to say something horribly naff like 'hello' to check the caller was there, when he finally spoke again. He sounded far more sober and dark-spirited.

'How's the baby?'

She closed one eye irritably, but then looked at sleeping Amery – and Cora who had awoken and was now happily chatting to her elephant – and she sighed.

'Which one?'

'Hel*lo*?' His drawl still made her pelvis dissolve, despite the shift in emphasis. 'I thought it was due any minute?'

Smiling at his divine voice Beccy dared herself. Go on, go on, say it, say it . . .

'One baby arrived last week,' she said with a Joanna Lumley deadpan that made her quiver with achievement and want to apply for drama school all over again, despite the twenty-three straight rejections that had cost James over a grand in audition fees and train fares. 'The other's not due back for hours – he's out competing. But I'll tell him you called.'

'You do that,' the laugh rumbled away down the tracks. 'You do that.'

'Let me give you a better number,' she breathed, hardly believing her own daring as she dictated her own mobile number. 'Call any time.'

Beccy hung up and, much to Cora's amusement, danced around the kitchen singing 'Two Souls' at the top of her voice.

Beccy had returned from her world travels with one burning ambition. In covering almost all four corners of the globe she had lost practically everything at some point: all her possessions including her signet ring, her passport, half her body weight from dysentery, her credit cards, even her hair (mysteriously cut off while she was sleeping on a train in the Indian subcontinent) and often her dignity. But amazingly she had never lost her virginity. Throughout some very close calls and some fairly tempting, and not to mention scary, scenarios it had never quite come off, and here she was at twenty-seven, still virgo intacta.

Sometimes, like today, she felt like she was carrying around an unexploded bomb primed to go off at any minute. She wanted to make love very badly indeed. But Beccy wanted the love part of that glorious undertaking to be real, and that was a very tough call – because Beccy had been in love with the same man for over a decade and he was hopelessly beyond her reach. She'd run away for years without ridding herself of that single-minded devotion. Now that he was so close at hand she felt it even more acutely, and she was more than happy to abandon herself to the freefall hope of loving another, even if it was just for a few giddy hours or days of daydreaming.

'This one is mine,' she told the sleeping Amery, dropping a kiss on his creased little head while Cora waved her elephant and cup around in support.

Chapter 10

When Dillon ducked beneath the slowing helicopter rotors and ran crouching across the dusty paddock towards the gate, he saw the longest, shapeliest pair of legs waiting for him between the wooden slats. Sporting faded, frayed shorts with long brown Dubarry boots and rather kinky white over-the-knee socks underneath, they were tanned, appealingly bruised and very classy. Above them, the baggy, oversized sweatshirt with cartoon mating reindeer on it was an odd choice on a hot August afternoon, but he could forgive those legs anything.

As he straightened up, grinning, and thrust out his hand, he encountered an exquisite tanned face with cheeks tinged with pink, a big nervous smile and the most unusual eyes – one amber, one green and flecked like an autumn wood.

'Dillon, I'm Tash.' She took his hand. 'Welcome.'

'It's so good of you to see me at such short notice.'

'No worries,' she said easily. 'I'm confined to barracks right now anyway, so visitors are a real treat.'

As they moved away from the noise of the rotors slowing, he could see that she was walking very stiffly.

'Have you had a fall then?'

'No, nothing like that,' she said brightly, almost limping as she shuffled in the direction of the stable yard, her face contorted with pain despite the cheery tone. 'You'll have to forgive me if I take you straight to meet The Fox. Hugo's not here and my children are in the house, so I have to be quick.'

'Sure,' he said vaguely, distracted by the amazing courtyards ahead.

The house and its outbuildings looked as though they had been carved out of strawberry shortcake, the brickwork was a wonderful mellow shade of pink and cream, the flint panels like hand-beaten pewter gleaming in the sunlight. Since his passion for artisan architecture and farming had blossomed, Dillon had become something of an aficionado of outbuildings. These stable yards were amongst the loveliest he had seen, with their sagging but serviceable Welsh slate roofs, their wood-framed casement windows reflecting the pretty Queen Anne gables and dormers of the main house, their multicoloured stoles and wraps of wisteria, ivy, honeysuckle and Virginia creeper. The yards were largely made up of cobbled walkways running between well-kept geometric grass beds; there were fountains and historic-looking topiary, a beautiful big coach house straight out of an early chapter of *Black Beauty*, and dominating everything was that outrageous copper-domed clock tower. It would once have been a very rich man's country seat, staffed by hundreds. It must cost a fortune in upkeep.

'This place is fantastic,' he enthused to Tash. 'Have you had it long?'

'Hugo's family have been here about three hundred years.' She was catching her breath now, moving so slowly that he had to keep pausing to stop himself falling over her.

'Are you okay?'

'Fine!' she said over-quickly, then turned in alarm as dogs barked loudly nearby. 'Oh hell, I thought they were in their run!' Two vast Rhodesian ridgebacks chose that moment to bound up and pick their targets; one rushed up to Tash and danced around her, tail gyrating, the other snarled and barked furiously at Dillon, making him step backwards until he was pressed against the gate he'd just come through.

'Cecil, stop that! He's a friend!' Tash ordered the dog away as the vanguard made way for several ranks of small terriers that yapped furiously and tugged at Dillon's laces and the hem of his jeans. Finally, bringing up the rear was a very odd-looking dog with huge biscuit-coloured ears, a tatty black coat the texture of an old, over-shampooed shagpile carpet, and white-edged eyes like an old cartoon golliwog. Dispensing with preambles like barking, yapping or snarling, she sank her teeth into Dillon's jeans leg and ripped out a neat strip which she proudly put down by his toes, looking up at him beseechingly.

'Christ alive!' He jumped back up on the gate, frightened she'd go for flesh next time.

'I'm sorry.' Tash crouched protectively and painfully to pat the little creature. 'She normally only does that to my ex. Were those jeans terribly expensive?'

'Only about three hundred dollars.'

'Oh God. I'm sure I can patch them for you. This is Beetroot. She's totally harmless really.'

'Could have fooled me.'

'It's okay. She hasn't bitten anyone for years. She only ever goes for clothes or car tyres.'

Beetroot glared at Dillon, her white-edged eyes deranged and threatening despite her grinning mouth and wagging tail. They clearly said 'one false move and your bollocks will have my teeth-marks permanently etched into them'.

'Just keep her away from me.'

'I really am sor-agh!' With a sharp gasp of discomfort, Tash tried and failed to pick up the little dog. Crouching by the cobbles at Dillon's feet she took a moment to recover. She was whiter than ever and looked as though she was about to faint. Beetroot licked her face worriedly and lifted a paw to her arm as Tash made to stand up again, teeth gritted with pain. 'I'll fetch a lead.'

'Don't worry about it,' Dillon insisted tetchily.

But Tash stayed kneeling at his feet, not entirely sure she could stand up.

'Are you only interested in Fox?' she quizzed breathlessly, at close quarters with his ankles.

'I need a truly international horse,' he said, sounding as though he was quoting somebody else. 'And I want it to go to Burghley.'

'Fox isn't going to Burghley this year.'

'Why not?' He was looking down at the top of her head as Tash played for time, admiring his Converse trainers, which had trendy cartoons on them.

'Too soon after the Olympics,' she explained, making a couple of abortive efforts to stand up.

'My girlfriend wants us to be at Burghley.'

'She could buy a four-day car pass like everybody else,' she muttered, pain starting to fray her temper. Tears were welling at the thought of selling her beautiful, clever Fox, who she had cradled as a foal. Her hormones were rising like sap now. She had to get up, she realised. She must have looked as though she was about to clean his shoes, or perform a sex act, neither of which was very professional.

This time she had truly lost the fight to keep the baby tears in check. She was now too choked to even speak. If she tried to explain to Dillon Rafferty that she had given birth earlier that week, the weeping dam would burst totally and she'd be inconsolable for hours. Beccy was right, it was best to simply say nothing. The man was a rock superstar willing to pay seven figures for a horse. She owed it to the yard's reputation to treat him like a VIP and show him their star horse as requested, even if he did fly off in his helicopter afterwards to buy his girlfriend a diamond-encrusted polo helmet instead.

It took Tash a long time to stand up again.

Dillon reached out to help but she waved him away and Beetroot snarled in agreement, making him step back hastily.

Despite the fantastic legs she was very thick around the middle, Dillon realised, the baggy reindeer sweatshirt artlessly draped over a big bulge.

'When's the baby due?'

'I'm not pregnant,' she insisted, in too much pain to be polite about it as she led the way at a snail's pace again.

Following behind her along lines of immaculate stables, Dillon had plenty of time to marvel at the baking sun on his face and the heady smell from the rambling roses tangled across the roofs of the main yard.

'Here he is,' Tash managed to croak, pointing at a friendly face looking over a half door.

The Fox was a wiry chestnut with a white stripe running from halfway down his nose and widening over his muzzle to cover his freckled pink lips, as though he'd dipped his mouth in strawberry ripple milkshake.

Her face now flaming from the lurching walk that had left blood pumping too fast around her body, Tash busied herself pulling off his summer sheet and checking him over.

'You okay?' Dillon called over the door as she picked out the horse's hooves with a lot of involuntary gasping and groaning noises reminiscent of her early contractions.

'Fine!' Tash squeaked. She wished he wouldn't keep asking that just as she thought she'd got herself under control. It wasn't fair. She *had* to stop these soppy tears coming like a tsunami. She took a deep, shuddering breath and hung on to Fox's leg, trying not to think what she was losing, and focus hard on the money instead.

It would patch up the house, cover the estate and yard expenses for a year, pay off the overdraft and buy them some breathing space in a sport notorious for costing a king's ransom. The Beauchamps were living entirely hand to mouth, and with so many human and animal mouths to feed that was a dangerous state of play. They were asset rich and cash poor to an almost ridiculous extreme. Selling Fox could really stave off the long-dreaded decision that they both knew they would have to make sooner or later: pack in eventing or sell Haydown?

Tash knew it was partly her fault. Her pregnancies and the consequent loss of so much core Beauchampions sponsorship had come at a very unfortunate time, not long after the crash in the square mile that had quickly robbed Hugo of most of the small army of investment banks, venture capitalists, private equity funds and hedge fund managers who had traditionally sponsored him and owned most of his own top horses. Last year the yard had lost no less than six advanced horses to new owners, half of them going overseas. It was a devastating blow. Family and loyal friends had rallied, doing what they could. But it was an uphill struggle and there was no doubt that Tash had disappeared from the scene at exactly the wrong time. The dream team couple didn't function as profitably as single players. Hugo's recent Olympic title was a great fillip, but the gold medals were no real draw in comparison to the original golden couple of eventing. Hugo's main sponsor, the country clothing label Mogo, had been loyal for many years, but they were now looking increasingly fickle as the brand long associated with equestrianism sought new markets in other sports.

The Fox was worth ten times as much as any other horse on the yard. Wise, robust, cocky and graceful, he was the biggest, oldest and most successful of three chestnut full siblings, and he was the ultimate equine athlete, reaching the pinnacle of the sport by just nine years old, a whippersnapper compared to most horses at the top level. He still had an amazing future ahead of him and, perhaps what marked him out as the most desirable horse competing at his level, he was a doddle to ride. Tash had hoped he would be the one to get her confidence back on the big tracks once she returned to riding again. The only European four-star he hadn't yet tackled was Badminton. He was the best event horse in the world, with the price tag to match.

Dillon said nothing as he looked at the seven-figure investment bite Tash's bottom while she took off his stable bandages. He might be a lamb under saddle, but The Fox still displayed a streak of his obstinate, bad-tempered father at times; Snob had been extremely tricky to handle. His son equalled his talent, and could be just as standoffish in the stable.

She led him out, grimacing at the tugs from the lead rope that seemed to pull directly at her stitches as he danced about, fed up with a day of box rest and eager to be out and about.

The horse in the neighbouring stable spun around in his box, kicking furiously and making the usually laid-back Fox even more skittish.

'Do you want to see him trotted up?' Tash asked, feeling sick at the prospect, then added hopefully. 'Or loose schooled?'

Dillon shook his head, glancing around. 'You the only one here?'

She nodded. This was ridiculous, Tash realised. She was about to cry again. She had to explain why she was such a mess and why it had just taken her ten minutes to remove four stable bandages. 'The thing is – shit!'

With a great clatter, the horse in the box beside Fox's jumped clean over its stable door, his body missing Dillon by a fraction of an inch as it hurled itself into the yard and swerved excitedly off to the left to trot around with its tail in the air, snorting loudly and shaking its head.

Tash thrust The Fox's lead rope at Dillon and, lumbering painfully, managed to corner the loose horse by the hay-soaker, grateful that all the gates were shut.

Dillon watched her lead the snorting, spooking rebel back towards his quarters.

'It's his party trick,' she apologised breathlessly. 'He normally has a grille above his door but Beccy must have forgotten to close it.' So much for professionalism, she chastised herself silently. Not content with letting her dog bite him, she'd now allowed Rocco Naylor's unruly thug to almost land on top of him. Hugo would weep. She definitely had to keep her trap shut about the baby tears.

Thankfully, Dillon seemed more fascinated by the escapee.

'Amazing white marking on his face.'

Tash stopped, looking across at the tall horse beside her. 'Yes, that star certainly gets him noticed.'

The big bright bay, who had eyes as wild as a crystal-meth addict, had a large white star on his forehead that was shaped like a perfect heart.

'It's how he gets his name – Cœur d'Or.'

'Corridor?' he misheard her.

'No. Cœur d'Or – heart of gold. But that's a misnomer if ever there was. He was bred by a friend of ours, Marie-Clair Tucson, as an Olympic prospect, but he's way too strong and galloping for that format. It's not his fault. He was conceived at a time the sport was far more daring,' she explained. 'By the time he came of age, the FEI had ruled for shorter distances and more technical fences, so he only suits the biggest and boldest old-fashioned courses. Now, this one *is* entered for Burghley. And he's up for sale or lease.' She suddenly fixed him with a meaningful look.

Cœur d'Or currently belonged to legendary hedge fund maverick Rocco Naylor and his fifth wife, who'd once been among Hugo's biggest owners. But Rocco's recent downsizing departure had left a huge hole in their working capital and several empty stables, with his top horse's future still hanging in the balance and a cause of a great many arguments at Haydown. Hugo rated Cœur d'Or as the most talented horse on the yard and loved riding him; Tash thought he was downright dangerous.

The horse was altogether flashier than Fox – at least a hand taller with a coat the colour of palest polished walnut, that distinctive heart on his face matched with four white socks which contrasted beautifully with his glossy black knees and ears, and his satin-shiny black mane and tail. In simple aesthetics, he made Fox look minor league.

Nell would love this horse, Dillon realised. He was a complete show-stopper. Beside him, Fox let out a loud fart, sighed deeply and rested a hind hoof on its rim.

Meanwhile Cœur d'Or reared up, whinnied and finally settled back down on all four feet to stamp furiously and fix them all with an arrogant look.

'How much?'

Tash added twenty per cent on to the price Rocco Naylor had been asking for all year with no takers. She knew the commission for selling was a drop in the ocean compared to the pure profit from Fox, but if it meant the rock star got to go to Burghley and she got to keep Snob's son, she would at least pitch it.

'He's not an amateur's horse,' she said carefully, not wanting to mislead him.

Cœur d'Or, known at home as Heart, was a notoriously difficult ride and had been through half a dozen yards before ending up at Haydown at a bargain price. At least one previous rider had almost been killed going across country with him, but he and Hugo had formed a partnership that was going from strength to strength, only missing out on a Badminton win earlier that year by the narrowest of margins. Hugo badly wanted to keep the ride, but for a moment Tash didn't care.

'He's fantastic looking.' Dillon edged behind laid-back Fox as the big bright bay continued rearing up and cavorting around for attention, neck arched, tail aloft, looking like a true star.

Fox, meanwhile, had his eyelids at half mast and his ears back, grumpily swatting flies with his tail and regarding his neighbour with huge disdain. He knew his true value.

'He's only in today because he jumps out of all the fields,' Tash explained, shaking the lead rope and growling to get the horse's attention and stop him dancing. 'Even Snob's old stallion paddock. He's notorious.'

Dillon knew without doubt that he wanted to buy the bay, but he could hear a voice of reason – a voice of Faith – in the back of his head, telling him that he had come to see the rather dull, bad-tempered one that had won the Olympics.

On cue, Fox's big head suddenly swing around, teeth bared, coming straight at him.

'Agh!' Dillon dropped the rope and leaped away.

'He was after a horse fly, not you,' Tash pointed out kindly, shuffling forwards to claim yet another loose horse.

Dillon felt foolish. She must think he was such a city gump, still dressed for a Paris television studio not a stable yard. He wanted to point out that he was a farmer too, that he could shear a sheep and lay a hedge, but she was busy putting horses back in their stables, walking more oddly than ever.

When she reappeared she was dripping with sweat and still looking horribly uncomfortable. There were sweat marks under the arms of her reindeer sweatshirt and, strangely, two dark, damp circles on her chest.

Unaware that she had started leaking breast milk, Tash closed the grille over Heart's door and lent her forehead briefly on the cool bars.

She didn't want to sell any of the horses, she realised suddenly, turning to face Dillon and noticing that his eyebrow was pierced with a barbell like Beccy's. Instead of having balls at each end, his were capped with a tiny gold hand and a diamond-crowned heart like a Claddagh ring.

She stared at it gormlessly, a country bumpkin who no longer even had time to find matching earrings looking at a megastar sporting designer piercings. All she could think was how expensive it must have been, how pointless it was and how painful it would be to take a fall from a horse on to it. He really was from another world.

Then, to her surprise, Dillon suddenly smiled his big wattage smile. 'I'd like to see them ridden.'

'What?' Tash felt the sweat on her face turn ice cold.

'I can't really part with this sort of money without seeing the horses work.'

Tash gaped at him again, at the familiar album-sleeve face, the designer hairdo and stubble, the silly piercing, whiter than white teeth and bluer than blue eyes. The man was on a serious shopping trip, however hard she tried to put him off.

'Fox has just won Olympic gold. Surely his track record stands for itself?'

'I never buy a car without a test drive.'

'This isn't a car,' Tash gasped, worried by his attitude. Perhaps he wanted to ride the horse? Was he going to hop on wearing trainers and ripped jeans and gallop around for fun?

She suddenly wondered why he'd come alone – no trainer, no rider, no expert adviser, not even a camcorder. It was unheard of in her experience, especially for a relative newcomer to eventing. Most deals like this took weeks if not months of delicate negotiations, usually brokered by at least one agent. She was reminded of the premiership striker who had famously bought two of the country's top dressage horses for his young wife as a wedding present and driven them home to her in a custom-built horsebox painted with his club's colours. The highly strung, highly trained horses, accustomed only to expert professional riding, had soon frightened their novice owner and themselves so much that she lost interest. When she fell pregnant the horses were thrown out in a field where they had stayed for three years before being sent to some backwater auction, a million pounds' worth of horseflesh and talent sold on as unwarranted hacks to the highest cash bidder.

'Hugo's the only one who rides Heart.'

'Then we'll start with the other one.'

Tash felt nausea rise as she looked up at Fox's clever red head and high sloping shoulder and knew she couldn't hope to ride him. He might be easy, but she'd had a baby four days ago and was incapable of mounting stairs easily, let alone a horse. Her boobs were throbbing as her let-down reflex went into overdrive; her scar had been stretched and strained by all this activity and her painkillers were wearing off, making her feel sicker by the second. She could feel the blood seeping between her legs and her support stockings were itching so madly beneath her leather boots that she wanted to plunge them in the nearest water trough.

Instead, she forced a smile to match his, sales girl to awkward customer.

'I'll go and rustle up a jockey,' she said politely, making it sound as though she was going to fling together Frankie Dettori as a light snack. 'I promise I won't be long. Would you like a drink while you wait? There's a kettle in the office there, and a fridge with cold drinks if they haven't all been snaffled. I'm sorry, it's self-service.'

'I can handle it.' He waved her away, already pulling a phone from his pocket. 'Thanks.'

She turned to lumber back to the house, tears of pain in her eyes, tempted to just lock the doors and hide until he went away.

★

The trademark smile dropped away when Tash went out of view and Dillon turned to look at The Fox once more, but the horse had returned to his haynet and was presenting his bum to his potential purchaser.

'Bloody idiot,' Dillon cursed himself under his breath.

He'd only diverted to Berkshire today to avoid the gathering storm clouds back home, figuratively and literally. Whisked to Paris the previous night to perform in a studio with talk-of-the-town French singer Lola Lèvres on a live link to the MTV Video Music Awards in Hollywood, Dillon was not feeling his best. He and Nell had been having a text row for almost twenty-four hours now, sparked by the fact that he refused to take her with him to Paris, knowing she'd be bored and would jealously snub poor little Lola, who might look like a horny porn star and had already been dubbed the new Amy Winehouse, but was in fact rather sweet and innocent, and guarded by alarmingly over-protective parents. Having insisted that the PR, Tania, and all the other record label hand-holders stay away, Dillon had been overridden continually by la famille Lèvres to the point that he'd practically become a backing singer to the pouty princess in the live link – not great billing for a man still in the number-one slot in thirteen countries. It had been a wearying trip. Dillon hadn't slept in thirty hours, had eaten outside his body clock, had longed for a drink more than ever and had spent far too long with the sound of his own backing track, studio talkback, rapid-fire French and helicopter rotors shuddering through him.

Now he tilted his head up to the flawless sky and let the sun bake his face for a moment. The roses clambering around the eaves of the buildings smelled incredible. It was a beautiful spot. If he knew about it, his father would no doubt try to snap it up to add to his country-house collection. Pete had once famously boasted that he wanted to buy a stately pile in every English county: 'I want to be a rich country gent, and these days any rich cunt can be gentry.' It was a very Pete Rafferty epigram.

Dillon winced at the memory. His father and family were due to move to his newly refurbished Cotswolds house any day now, and he regularly found himself wishing that the three-quarters of an acre of retiled Abbey roof was being struck by lightning that very minute.

When crossing the Channel earlier, his pilot had received reports that storms were making flying conditions hazardous north of the

M4 and had asked Dillon if there was anywhere he'd like to make an unscheduled stop. At which point Dillon had finally bothered to start reading the thirty-five texts he had received from Faith in the past two days, and which contained details of the Beauchamps' wonder horse. Faith, being better organised than his own PA, had naturally attached every contact number available for the Beauchamps, plus email, a postcode reference and even GPS coordinates. She was unbeatable, a ray of sunshine poking from the stormy Lodes valley sky. He wished she wasn't going away to Essex.

He thought about calling her now to cheer himself up, but settled for picture-texting instead.

'Oi – you,' he held his phone over the stable door.

Lifting his tail slightly, The Fox let out a drum-rolling fart and carried on munching his hay.

Dillon made kissing noises to attract his attention until, with a deep sigh, the horse consented to pose, turning around and thrusting his head obligingly from the door, dropping hay all over Dillon's hair which was still sticky from the heavy wax coating it had received from the Paris stylist.

Reaching up to remove a piece that had fallen on to his brow, he realised that he was still wearing the barbell Nell had given him before he set out for Paris, specially designed by Chopard at great expense to her specific instructions. He secretly hated it. 'They make beautiful rings, too,' Nell had said so leadingly that he couldn't help but laugh.

But that laughter, and his continued refusal to take her to Paris, had sparked the ongoing storm, the eye of which he was languishing in now. Poor, darling, beautiful Nell. She so wanted a whirlwind romance and a Vegas wedding, but he just wanted to go steady with the girl next door.

Sending the picture of The Fox to Faith, his fingers hovered over the keys before he quickly typed a message to Nell. *Life's too short. No more arguing. Paris hell without you. I love you. Riding out the storm and counting the minutes until I see you. Will bring present. xxx*

After the message had winged itself away, he cursed himself for that final sentence. He was always promising the same to his daughters and Fawn constantly gave him a hard time for it, pointing out that they loved him without bribery and corruption. Now he'd need another unscheduled stop. He didn't have a present – Nell was hardly likely to appreciate the white label first pressing of Lola Lèvres's collaboration with legendary rap producer Marley X, or the clutch of studio freebies he'd grabbed for the girls in the farm office.

He looked at The Fox and blew out through his lips, unscrewing the brow barbell. 'Know where I can buy a bunch of flowers round here?'

The horse turned away.

His neighbour with the heart-shaped star was bobbing his handsome head up and down furiously behind the grille, mad eyes boggling. He was liked a caged tiger.

'You and me both, mate,' Dillon sighed, walking forwards to scratch the horse's black muzzle through the bars. 'You should like it here – this place is great. I love it. I could live here.' The centre of attention at last, Cœur d'Or relaxed and looked almost mellow, lifting his big nose to sniff Dillon's hair. '"Heart of Gold" was a great track.' He started singing a few bars.

The horse dropped his nose, eyes wide again.

'Yeah, maybe I'll transpose the key if I ever do a cover,' Dillon agreed, turning to gaze enviously around him again. Haydown was a great find, a secret rapture. Dillon felt like a kid slotting a new platform game into a console, knowing that there could be hours of new excitements to explore here, wanting to see them all at once. He couldn't remember feeling like this since first arriving at his Lower Oddford farm.

Apart from the telephone bell ringing out unheeded and unanswered every few minutes, the only sound he'd heard since he'd arrived on the yard were horses snorting, insects buzzing and birdsong.

He thought about Tash Beauchamp and her peculiarly gentle but abrupt manner, her strange eyes and her hidden tears. He felt bad that he'd snapped his fingers to make her show him two horses when really he was just idling away an afternoon, but she was infuriatingly odd, obviously in pain yet killingly secretive and upper class about it. It was red rag to a bull. Dillon was still in green-room mode, tired and tetchy from being sideswept by the Lèvres family in Paris. Buying power was an easy fix now that he had so few addictions left.

On cue, Faith texted back. *BUY HIM BUY HIM BUY HIM!!!!*

The message from Nell was queuing behind it: *What present?*

He took another photograph, this time of the horse with the

heart-shaped star lifting his soft black lip in a distinctly Elvis fashion, and he almost sent it to her, but something made him stop and regroup. Gift horses weren't great ideas, especially ones at this high a price. His father had once bought a mistress a rare black Falabella stallion the size of a Labrador, only to discover that the lease on her Chelsea garden flat didn't allow her to keep it there and London livery was over a grand a month, regardless of the incumbent's size. The poor mistress had died of an overdose just a few weeks after the Rockfather had dispensed with her services. The stallion had then been given to a very ungrateful ten-year-old Dillon, who'd fed it variety of his father's drugs before losing interest when it failed to die, explode or do anything much, other than eat. Amazingly, Black Sabbath was still going strong at twenty-eight, in a small paddock in the grounds of his father's castle in Ireland. The mistresses were still as plentiful as the houses his father owned, and all were lavished with regular presents. If Dillon wasn't careful he would find himself going the same way and he knew it. In the modern world a rich man could buy favour far more quickly than he could earn it but, as he knew from his own childhood, buying a child's love was less straightforward if one hadn't the time to back up the extravagance. His father had sold out on that front years ago.

Buying a horse was similarly fraught with difficulties because they had no notion of their own value and no gratitude for anything beyond food and shelter. To a horse, ownership was a non sequitur. They were obedient, brave and noble servants to their riders because their trust had been earned, slowly and patiently.

Until recently, the only other horse Dillon had owned had lamed him for life. He wasn't about to buy another gift horse without looking in its mouth very carefully indeed.

And so, instead of sending Nell the photograph of Cœur d'Or he sent her a blurry shot of something pink, firm and slightly hairy with a distinctive pink pip at its centre.

What in hell's that? she texted back with obvious alarm.

My heart he wrote simply, having held the phone up inside his T-shirt and snapped his chest where he imagined his heart to be. *It's yours.*

He looked at his phone for a long time waiting for her response.

The silence spoke volumes.

Chapter 11

'Who's that on Fox?' Gus Moncrieff asked his wife as they rattled through the outer courtyard and under the clock tower on their ancient Land Rover. 'Bloody awful leg position.'

Penny automatically reached out to take the steering wheel from her husband as he lifted both hands to his face and struggled to light one of his endless successions of cigarettes. Pulling the wheel sharply left to avoid a free-range terrier, she didn't take her eyes off the rider in the ménage to their right.

'Tash's sister, I think.'

'Sophia doesn't ride, does she?'

'No, the younger one, the horsy stepsister. Rebecca, isn't it?'

'I thought she ran away to become a Tibetan monk?'

'She came home via a rather hefty jail sentence for drug trafficking. But we don't. Talk. About. It. Tash and Hugo have taken her on as a working pupil.'

Gus whistled, succeeding in lighting the cigarette this time.

'Put that out,' Penny ordered, relinquishing the wheel. 'We are here to visit a newborn child, remember?'

'You can go into the house to reconnoitre. Tash is bound to have a boob out or something. And I want to check this out first.' Gus parked the Land Rover beside the arena, where a solitary figure was leaning over the rails. He jumped out, proffering an arm. 'Hello! Gus Moncrieff.'

Sighing, Penny clambered out too, not catching the name of the man by the rails as he introduced himself to Gus.

'And this is the wife,' Gus waved his cigarette arm in her direction, still squinting critically at the horse and rider on show.

Flashing a quick smile Penny also turned to regard Beccy on Fox.

Gus was right, her lower leg was atrocious and judging by the colour of her face and the heavy breathing, she was monumentally unfit. Her shoulders were tense and she had a rather hollow back. But there was a lot to like. Her hands were lovely and soft, her chin nice and high and her seat deep and well connected. She could go a long way with a seat like that. The Fox certainly seemed to appreciate her and was going very sweetly indeed.

'Super horse.' She sighed jealously. 'Super, super horse.'

Gus nodded. 'D'you know some American offered Hugo a hundred grand to use the beast's DNA to clone him?'

Penny snorted at the thought. 'He turned him down. Said they'd have to clone Tash too because this horse had the best possible start in life thanks to her and that's why he's so perfect.' She sighed enviously again, shooting Gus a resentful look because he would never dream of acknowledging her help like that. 'There'll be no clones of this amazing creature.'

They all watched in silence as The Fox cruised around the space in his energetic, springy trot, as smooth and powerful as a train on rails.

The Moncrieffs had just been for a surprisingly jolly meal at The Terrier in Maccombe to celebrate their wedding anniversary. It was practically unheard of for either of the couple to go out to lunch, even rarer to do so together, so the uncommon treat had loosened them both up. Penny was feeling especially emotional.

'Lovely, lovely horse.' She sighed again – she had a tendency to repeat herself after more than a thimble of wine. 'Best in the world right now.'

'He's already a freak of nature,' Gus tutted. 'No horse should be that talented *and* that nicely put together *and* that well-mannered. There's got to be a catch.'

Dillon laughed, looking from one Moncrieff to the other. 'Has Hugo sent you along here to influence me?'

Now they both looked from him to the horse and back in equal bemusement.

'Don't tell me you're here to try to *buy* Fox?' asked Penny, making it sound as though he might intend to enact nefarious Wicca rituals on the horse and should be arrested.

'Hugo wouldn't part with that animal for under a million,' Gus spluttered in disbelief.

'Of course he wouldn't,' Dillon agreed.

'Exactly,' Penny smiled, turning to look at Fox again as Gus clambered through the rails into the arena to give poor Beccy some unwanted instruction.

'You're lower leg is bloody *awful* – needs to go back at least six inches to stop you hollowing your back and collapsing forward like that . . .'

Beccy's face tightened miserably. Since arriving at Haydown, she'd barely ridden at all. Her one and only lesson with Hugo, staged yesterday on an old schoolmaster that she couldn't get on the bit, or even to go forwards, had been a disaster. He had walked off in a huff, saying she was unteachable. It was many years since she'd ridden at all, apart from the odd camel and mule trek, and it certainly wasn't like riding a bike. Just hacking out left her massively saddle sore. Being asked to ride the yard's top horse was like being asked to take a Formula One car for a spin around Brands Hatch after a decade spent on car-free Sark and just a few refresher lessons in a Nissan Micra. Yet she'd thought she was doing a pretty good job up until now.

'Boy, do you need my help!' Gus marched towards her to grab her knee and reposition it.

Eyeing him warily Beccy quashed the urge to throw herself off the horse and run back to the house. Sitting on The Fox was a once-in-a-lifetime opportunity, and she couldn't bring herself to pop the bubble just yet, especially if she was going to get some much-needed tips that might mean Hugo could see past her rustiness.

Turning away, Penny picked up Gus's smouldering cigarette butt, which he had abandoned in the dirt underfoot, and carefully extinguished it before putting it in her pocket. He was always blunt to the point of rudeness, although he meant well enough. It was just his way. A decade earlier he had shouted at Tash in a similar fashion every day – when she wasn't hacking up to Haydown to let Hugo shout at her – and she had gone on to the country's senior elite squad before giving it all up to have babies.

Glancing across at the house, its windows glowing in the sunshine, Penny braced herself to meet the second of those babies. It was a tough call.

After seven years of expensive private fertility treatments that had put their marriage and finances under almost impossible strain, Penny and Gus had recently admitted defeat on their own hopes of children.

If only conceiving babies was as easy as foals, she reflected. Boozy Floozy, Penny's own favourite mare, was still competing with Gus while breeding like wildfire through embryo transfer.

And then there was dear Tash, as fecund as a rabbit. Penny, meanwhile, appeared to be as barren as the Gobi.

A voice broke into her consciousness, the accent reminding her rather thrillingly of Pierce Brosnan. 'You ride much?'

She turned to see the man with the very white teeth and very blue eyes regarding her thoughtfully.

With his silly, scruffy clothes, which were probably the height of fashion, he looked faintly ludicrous, but experience had taught her that, generally, the more messily a man dressed the more money and class he had.

'I ride a bit,' she said stiffly. 'You?'

He shook his head, creasing his eyes and glancing thoughtfully into the distance. 'I was never much good – had a crashing fall a couple of years ago and decided I was safer on the ground. I own a couple of event horses now.'

'Good for you,' she said in the clipped, chipper voice she used when talking to the wilder boys in the Pony Club. She turned to look at Fox, who was standing patiently with Tash's stepsister on board while Gus stalked around her like Basil Fawlty, waving his arms around and telling her how to completely redress her position. 'Who do you keep your horses with?'

'Rory Midwinter. He just won the Scottish Open at Baloney Palace.' The man was staring at her face closely for reaction.

'Bloneigh Castle,' she corrected kindly. 'I heard Rory did a super job there. That augurs well. This chestnut chap of Hugo's won there a couple of years ago, and look at him now – although quite frankly I think a gold-medal horse doesn't deserve to find himself being treated like a riding-school plod. What was Hugo thinking, putting Beccy up? She's pretty basic, which means Gus can't resist interfering.' She squinted through the sunlight to Fox, who was nodding off, while Gus slapped his own thighs and buttocks and gave his terminally dull spiel on seatbones. He looked rather like an excitable Bavarian dancer without the music or Lederhosen.

Dillon followed her gaze. 'He's just fabulous.'

'He's pretty special,' she agreed.

'Have you been married long?'

Realising that he was talking about Gus not the horse, she laughed. 'Twenty years to the day. I was barely out of my teens; the first of my friends to marry and now one of the few not divorced.'

'It's your anniversary?'

'Yah.'

'Congratulations. Wow. Twenty years.'

'A score, as they say.'

'Wow.' He whistled, as though it was some sort of record. Perhaps it was in his line of business; Penny assumed he had to be in show-biz or the Euro jetset.

'Is Rory your boyfriend?' she inquired politely.

It was his turn to laugh. 'You obviously don't know him *that* well.'

'Oh, I've taught plenty of dishy young eventing chaps like him that squire every female on the yard before coming out of the closet as spectacularly as a stallion charging down a lorry ramp. Most end up turning to dressage.' She shuddered. 'Such a loss to the sport, not to mention the gals.'

'Lucky you bagged yourself a straight one.'

'You think so?' She creased her crow's feet into the sun in a cross between a smile and a grimace, not looking at him. 'Yah.'

Dillon cocked a brow, amazed to find somebody in this day and age who still spoke like one of the Mitford sisters.

Not taking her eyes from the horse that was framed in front of them in sunlight so bright and luminous that his coat looked like molten caramel, she added, 'He's having an affair, of course.'

A tiny smile flicked on and off her lips, like a punctuation mark.

Dillon had no idea how to react. The country set baffled him. They were acutely, pathologically secretive about the oddest things, like whether they had a paid job, and yet they thought nothing of discussing adultery with absolute strangers.

'Bad luck,' he said eventually.

'Yes, isn't it? I bet he dresses better for her; he didn't even change for lunch. Said his one suit smells so badly of mothballs it would have put us both off our grub.'

They watched Gus for a few moments as he continued stalking around Fox on long, skinny legs, sending up puffs of arena sand and barking about 'stickability'. He was wearing faded grey breeches, blue and green striped knee-high socks, battered paddock boots and an England rugby shirt with a large mud stain on the front. His creased, weathered face with its sharp, broken nose and hooded, faded green eyes was handsome in a craggy way, and he had won-derfully wild, leonine head of hair that was a bit thin on top. He was more Richard Harris in *A Man Called Horse* than Robert Redford in *The Horse Whisperer*, but nonetheless dashing.

'Anyone you know?' Dillon enquired politely.

'Not yet.'

Her acceptance baffled him, making him think of a mother standing on a touchline during a school rugby match and saying of her son, 'Of course, he has attention deficit disorder, you know. Ransacks the house on a regular basis and shot the family cat last week. But we love him.' These people were extraordinary. When Fawn had discovered that he'd slept with their nanny while she was away filming – a deeply regrettable one-off, and a clichéd cry for help brought about by booze, cocaine, loneliness and sheer lazy stupidity on his part – she had taken the kids straight to the States to live with her parents, not telling a soul what had happened. The press still hadn't found out to this day. Only Dillon, Fawn and the nanny knew, the latter having been paid for her silence with a very big cheque from Fawn's personal fortune. The girl had walked away from the marriage with almost as much as Dillon.

Mannerly, well-spoken Penny, however, seemed to find it perfectly acceptable to talk about it.

She tilted her head as Gus finally told the girl to start moving again and she kicked Fox into the most fabulous lengthened trot. 'GOOD! THAT'S THE TICKET!' she shouted at them suddenly, making Dillon step back in surprise, before she immediately turned back to address him again in her flat drawl. 'My dressage trainer – also one of your lot – says he's just attention-seeking. You gay chaps are far more up front about these things, aren't you?' She nodded at Gus, who was still performing his strange dance, now bending forwards and patting his own bottom, repeatedly shouting 'Sit on *this*' as Beccy cantered around him. 'What d'you think?'

Dillon swallowed. 'I'm really not qualified to say, I'm afraid. I'm not usually upfront about anything, nor am I gay, although I don't mind admitting that I think he's a fool. You're a very beautiful woman.' It was a throwaway Rafferty line, but he meant it. In her cool, clipped way she reminded him so acutely of Fawn that he wanted to curl up at her feet. And it worked a magic spell on Penny Moncrieff.

'Oh God.' She went very pink. Then, to his surprise, she started to laugh. She covered her mouth and hooted and guffawed and finally howled with laughter until there were tears in her eyes.

'Oh you have cheered me up,' she said when she had recovered enough to speak. 'I'm so sorry I made assumptions. That was unforgiveable,' she snorted as another titter gripped her. 'Thank God you're not here to buy a horse.'

'I am,' he smiled.

'Oh fuck,' she laughed more hysterically now, making him think of his father again: posh women swearing was a complete aphrodisiac to Pete.

'I want the one with the heart-shaped star,' he said without thinking.

'Oh marvellous – Tash has been terrified that one will kill Hugo. Do take him away.'

Suddenly Dillon found himself laughing too, knowing his father would just love this world, imagining him let loose in it like an oversexed wolf in a parade of foxhounds, trying to mount everything except the horses. But Dillon had found it first, quite by chance. For once he was ahead of his father, whose love of horses meant he owned chasers, hurdlers, sprinters and stayers, but had almost certainly never been to a three day event in his life. The wolf would devour it all greedily, but Dillon was upwind with the fastest horse at his fingertips.

'At least you're not thinking of buying Fox.' Penny had stopped laughing with great effort. 'Hugo would never forgive me. That horse is better than anything out there by a league. But as you said yourself, he'd never sell him.'

'He's just this minute sold him,' Dillon grinned, holding out his hand to shake hers. 'You made up my mind. Thank you.'

Penny gaped at him incredulously. She took his palm in hers reluctantly, feeling his big silver rings press into her finger pads, hoping to God that Tash would be all right about it. Fox was *her* baby. But, then again, she supposed Tash had a new baby to occupy her now.

'Congratulations,' she said, not certain whether to be pleased or concerned. 'You're buying a piece of solid gold.'

'But not the heart of gold,' he sighed.

'Oh, I'm sure Hugo will come up with a deal if you want to buy both,' she urged as he stepped forward to plant a deal-making kiss on each cheek, which made her feel both rather weak at the knees and horribly Judas-like. He smelled of expensive aftershave and clean skin, she realised, a rare treat compared to Gus's usual working rider pong. Surely, he couldn't be this sexy *and* straight?

Had she not consumed half a bottle of wine at lunch Penny might been inclined to be cynical, but she was feeling more emotional than usual. If this attractive, charming, sweet-smelling man was prepared to pay the Beauchamps that much money, she wished them all luck. She just hoped it wouldn't compromise the best horse the sport had seen in years, possibly ever. Rory Midwinter was inexperienced but talented and, from what little Penny had seen of him, frighteningly capable of beating Hugo – and Gus – at their own game if mounted well.

As Dillon put a call through to Hugo from his jazzy little mobile phone she diplomatically turned away and watched Gus, who was still talking non-stop while Beccy and Fox stood to attention again, swatting flies with crop and tail respectively. He had hold of her thigh now, she noted, and was showing her how to roll it outwards to relax the knee and maximise the effect of the lower leg. Penny's own lower leg twitched with the urge to sprint into the arena and raise her knee to his crotch. She wished he'd been within earshot to hear that sweet-smelling boy call her beautiful. It was something Gus hadn't called her in a long time.

Hugo phoned the house just as Tash was loading the children in the buggy.

'The pop star wants to buy The Fox, as long as you agree.'

Even though Tash longed to disagree as loudly as possible she managed to bite her tongue, partly because Hugo sounded so impossibly excited and partly because at that moment Cora pushed the loose harness clip up her nose and got it stuck.

'He'll really pay all that money?' she asked as she tried to extract the plastic prong from the screaming toddler's nostril.

'And he wants to lease Heart so Rory has a Burghley run.'

Clip removed, Cora looked thoroughly put out and tried to ram it in again.

'No!' Tash wailed on both accounts.

'It's okay,' Hugo said cheerfully. 'There's a condition to the sale which might solve our work-rider crisis.'

Five minutes later Dillon turned as a jolly voice halloed from beneath the courtyard archway and Tash rolled into view, pushing a vast three-wheeler double buggy with tyres like a Range Rover, swathed in insect nets and sunshades. She was still sporting the baseball cap and kinky surgical stockings with Dubarrys, but had ditched the bonking reindeer sweatshirt for a pretty smock in shades of turquoise and cinnamon, the diaphanous layers of which couldn't quite hide the fact that she had failed to correctly re-clip her nursing bra and one breast was swinging inches lower than the other.

Unaware, Tash hailed everyone cheerfully. In the front seat of the buggy Cora was making choo choo train noises, waving a pheasant feather and kicking her feet around while behind her the satiated, contented newborn slept beneath his protective canopies.

'Congratulations – you have just bought a superstar!' She kissed Dillon on the cheek, hoping that he wouldn't spot that she'd been crying. She turned hurriedly to her friend. 'I had no idea you were here, Pen! You two have met, I see.'

'And we're getting along famously.' Penny gave the buggy a wide berth and kissed Tash on the cheek. 'You look bloody amazing for a woman who had a ten-pounder cut out through the emergency exit a few days ago.'

'You've had a baby this *week*?' Dillon gasped. 'Why didn't you say so? I made you run around after all those horses.'

But Tash waved away his apologies. The man had just agreed to spend a fortune on a Haydown horse. It was the easiest sale they've ever made, and by far the biggest. Hugo insisted it was the only way to keep the house and business alive and she was forced to agree. It was a lifeline and it had come in the nick of time. She'd do a hand-stand, backflip and roly-poly for Dillon now if he asked, although it might take several hours and a lot of painkillers.

When she had walked away earlier, wishing she'd never see him again, a million pounds had seemed an abstract concept, beyond anything she could readily conceive. Now that it was real she could see her own hypocrisy at work as she felt suddenly devoted to him, her trust for all their futures – Hugo, her children, Haydown and Fox – lying firmly on his shoulders. Such was the power of money, she guessed. Yet there was really something incredibly likeable about Dillon Rafferty, for all his razzmatazz and unconventional impulse purchases. He fitted in here.

He was now greeting the children like an indulgent uncle, admiring Amery before stooping to entertain Cora with silly faces and noises. The little girl shrieked with appreciation, giving him her feather and reaching out to be picked up. Dillon taught her how to high five until she laughed with little huck-huck titters every time his hand hove into view.

He was the least starry rock star Tash could imagine. Hugo's ghastly army of horse-owning City hedge funders and investment bankers had been far more spoilt and demanding. Dillon had just bought a horse for a million pounds and nobody had even offered him a cup of coffee, but he was mucking along like an old chum.

'Would you like your new horse put away now?' she asked, embarrassed that Beccy was still riding his million-pound asset and apparently getting some free coaching from Gus into the bargain.

'No, let them finish whatever they're doing,' he said vaguely, still entertaining Cora and not at all interested in the The Fox. 'I remember when my girls were this age. It's so special.'

'You must miss them when you're apart.'

'Like my arms and legs have been severed.'

Leaving him and Cora bonding gleefully over a game of peekaboo, she turned back to Penny again. 'Happy anniversary. We bought you a present, but it's in the house. It's a teapot.'

'Thanks. All this china. You'd think they'd celebrate twenty years with something less breakable, wouldn't you? After two decades one hurls dinner settings at one's spouse as a matter of course. You wait and see. You and Hugo are practically still on honeymoon.' There was a bitter edge to her voice. 'Bronze this year isn't it? Eighth? I always remember that one because our eighth anniversary was the World Championships and Gus and I won team bronze together. Seemed very fitting.'

Tash struggled to remember. 'That's next year. It'll be seven years in November.'

'Ah! Wool. That's why they call it the seven-year itch. That, and all the knitting for those ankle biters you keep producing. Talking of which, congratulations yourself.' Her eyes ran from Amery to Dillon and then back to the newborn, resplendent in the merino wrap that made him look like Yoda. 'He's . . . sweet.' Penny gave her a stiff pat on the back. Then she winked. 'Baby's quite cute too.'

'Shhh.' Tash stretched her eyes.

'I can't believe you're selling Fox,' she whispered, far happier talking horses than marriage or babies.

Tash shrugged, unwilling to say anything about her real feelings in case she cried.

'The team selectors will go ape-shit, especially with Snob gone too.'

Tash was suddenly even closer to breaking down.

'Come here.' Penny gestured her into a hug, as rare a gift as a kiss from the Pope. 'You're all full of baby tears and nonsense and I'm so glad to see you. You look superb.'

'I still look fat and pregnant.'

'A much underrated state of beauty, I've always thought,' Penny squeezed her tight.

Tash smiled into her friend's sweet-smelling, greying hair. 'I'm so glad you're here. It seems for ever since I've seen you. I've missed you.'

Before Penny could answer, Gus had vaulted the arena gate and was bounding between them. 'Tash, old thing. At *last!*'

Thinking that he was about to bestow the requisite congratulatory kiss, Tash offered up her cheek with her big smile still spread like happy bunting across her face and her arm gesturing automatically towards Amery. Gus remained one of the men she most longed to please in life, along with Hugo, her father and her old art teacher Prof Long. But he had already turned back towards the arena to point at Beccy. 'Tell me, is that or is that not a one hundred per cent improvement?'

Beccy, puce in the face, was riding for her life, aware that she had an audience that would never be repeated – a four-star international rider, two former four-star riders and a rock star . . . not to mention her niece, sleeping nephew, Beetroot and a fascinated collie with one wall eye.

'That looks good,' Tash agreed. 'Really bloody good. BLOODY GOOD!' she yelled at Beccy, making Dillon almost fall over the buggy. What was it with these horsy people? He had played stadiums night after night and had nothing close to their lung capacity. All that bellowing across the fields made for amazing voice projection. They should train as town criers.

On the far side of the rails Beccy went an even deeper shade of pink with delight. This was turning out to be one of the best days she could remember.

162

Chapter 12

Gus downed most of the two bottles of vintage champagne Tash brought up from the cellars for an impromptu celebration. Penny, who hardly ever drank except when hunting and had already had her fill over lunch, kept Dillon company sipping orange juice.

Watching the 1986 Taittinger slide down Gus's appreciative throat, Dillon mourned the loss of a beautiful vintage on an unworthy recipient. He could imagine its taste, the texture of briny little bubbles popping on the tongue, the blast of rising surf in the nose and throat, and the glorious aftertaste. The thought, and desire, made him almost deaf to Gus holding court about horses, training and the season's results thus far.

Dillon could have read the signs of adultery even if it hadn't been for Penny's tip-off. The man had made three trips to the loo already. He was either in possession of a very weak bladder or – judging from the beeps emanating from the downstairs cloakroom when Dillon passed the door en route to answer his own phone – he was having a predictable, predictive, adulterous text chat.

Dillon's call was from Faith, desperate to know how things were going.

'So? Did you buy him?' she asked excitedly.

'I think so,' he said listlessly, the head-rush of his enormous purchasing power already dissipating.

'Ohmygodthatisocool!' she blurted, hardly inspiring confidence that he'd been wisely advised.

'I bought another one,' he told her because he knew her reaction would cheer him up again.

'Tell me!' she panted eagerly.

He smiled into his handset. 'Called Corridor.'

'Cœur d'Or?' She knew instantly. 'Hugo almost won Badminton on him this year. No good. Rory won't be able to ride him.'

He paused for a moment to make sure he'd heard that right. 'He's a stunning horse.'

'Stunning,' she agreed. 'Mad brain. Pulls like a charging rhino, jumps like a stag. Seriously scopey.'

'That's the one. They call him Heart here. He's entered in Burghley. Nell really wants Rory to go there, and Hissing Sid's lame.'

'Snake Charmer,' she corrected. 'His stable name's Sid.'

'Rory can ride Heart at Burghley. I want to treat Nell. Get more involved, like you said, yes?'

Waiting for her to answer, he watched a white stripe forming across the very blue sky overhead as a jet made its way towards the horizon.

But to his surprise, Faith said, 'I think Rory's more precious than your girlfriend's dirty weekends.'

He didn't realise that she'd hung up on him until his phone, still pressed to his ear, suddenly started ringing again. 'Hello. Faith? Did you get cut o—'

'It's Nell, not your little teeny-bopper.' Her voice was tight with anger. 'I take it *she's* the reason your phone has been going straight to voicemail for the past ten minutes? Are you still in Paris?'

'No, I'm in Berkshire, buying a horse.' He sighed, rubbing his face with his hands and feeling a twinge of pain where the barbell had scratched his eyebrow.

Nell was incandescent with rage. 'Talk about keeping the Faith! You'll be setting her up in her own flat soon.'

'It's for her boyfriend.' He closed his eyes, wondering why all they did was fight these days.

'Rory is no more Faith's boyfriend than you are mine!'

'Meaning?'

'Oh get lost.'

'Nell, don't be like this . . . Nell? Nell, are you there?' There was a chime in his ear. Yet again he had been hung up on. A text had winged its way from Faith. *I am ungrateful cow. Rory lucky to have you. Nell too. You have a good Heart. Fxx*

Feeling bucked up, he reread the message several times.

'Oh, sorry – you're about to make a call,' a voice said cheerfully behind him.

He turned to see Tash with the jug of orange juice, clearly on a scout to check where he had got to.

'No, I've finished.' He smiled at her, holding up his glass for a refill. 'Thanks.'

'God, it's getting punishingly hot – true bikini weather.' She straightened the jug and looked out at the swimming pool blue sky, then glanced sideways as he pocketed his phone. 'I keep losing mine. One minute I've got it, the next it's gone.'

'Sorry?'

'Mobile phone. I'm quite hopeless. I was getting through at least one a month so I've stopped bothering with them. It drives Hugo mad. He conducts half his life via hands-free; I can't even send an email or a text.'

'You're not the unfaithful sort, then?' he said, admiring her breasts through the smock, remembered how Fawn's small cleavage, a silicone-free anomaly in her native Hollywood, had been quite amazing when she was breastfeeding the girls.

'How d'you mean?' Tash was secretly rather cheered to be getting a boob-leer from a handsome man so soon after giving birth.

'Technology is the secret envoy of the twenty-first century,' he proclaimed in his cockney-Irish accent, that familiar voice rendering everything he said poetic. 'Where illicit lovers once wrote love letters on parchment and tucked them into chinks in walls to be collected, we now use email and text as tools of adultery. Perfect for arranging trysts.'

'I think Hugo would prefer me to just text him his start times, or the business card pin number if he's forgotten them,' she pointed out.

'Of course.' He flashed the trademark smile.

Suddenly Tash lifted her head like a hound, able to hear the diesel grind of the engine long before it became audible to Dillon.

'That's Hugo!' Her face lit up, mismatched eyes luminescent, making Dillon realise how incredible it would be to be loved like that. 'I'll fetch more champagne from the cellar. He won two of his sections today with horses I broke in, so I'm almost as excited as I was by his gold medals last week.'

Dillon's first impression of Hugo Beauchamp was that he was very tall, very handsome and very, very posh. He was also furiously angry, blue eyes blazing as he marched into the house wearing a Mogo T-shirt, dusty white breeches and knee-length socks even more garish than Gus's.

'What fucking idiot landed that chopper on Flat Pad?'

'The same fucking idiot that just bought your best horse,' Dillon held out his hand to introduce himself.

Hugo shook it, handsome face unapologetic. 'Could you get it moved? It's parked on the boys' graves.'

Thinking 'the boys' had to be close relatives – possibly even younger siblings or, God forbid, the couple's own children lost in infancy – Dillon was about to fall on his sword of apology when he caught sight of Beccy waving an arm at him.

'It's all right,' she told him in a tipsy stage whisper, her face now damson, 'Bod and Snob were just horses.'

'Not *just* bloody horses!' Hugo turned on her with such a quick, white-hot flash of rage that she shrank back as though physically burnt. 'Bod had the heart of a lion, and that chestnut bugger was the quickest over timber I ever knew. Your sister adored him. Tash and I want to be buried out there with them when we go, so that we can gallop around this place once again, haunting merry hell out of it. *No*body has permission to land on their graves – not a wood pigeon or a rock star.'

Such was his bloody-mindedness that he was willing to risk a million-pound deal for the memory of a favourite horse, Dillon realised.

He knew he shouldn't approve of Hugo at all; he had that assured arrogance brought about by a privileged upbringing, and yet he liked him on instinct.

He phoned through to his pilot to get him to start the engine.

'So The Fox isn't as good as they were?' Dillon asked as they walked outside together.

Hugo shook his head with a big, easy smile that lit up his eyes like flares. 'He's *far* better, I can assure you. Both those horses were incredibly difficult, opinionated and sometimes downright danger-ous to be on. But I've always found white-knuckle rides much more fun than chauffeur-driven luxury. How about you?'

'I'll take the chauffeur-driven luxury,' Dillon admitted, feeling his old leg break throb at the very thought of mad, bad, dangerous horses. 'And Heart?'

'Pure white-knuckle,' Hugo laughed. 'Want to change your mind?'

He shook his head, 'As long as you agree to safeguard Rory.'

'I've seen Rory ride across country,' Hugo reminded him. 'He's like I was ten years ago. You can't safeguard that. You just light it and stand well back.' He paused by the gate to Flat Pad, turning to shake Dillon's hand again. 'But I can provide the controlled environment and guarantee that the right people will see the fireworks.'

★

Dillon rang Rory as soon as his pilot was cruising over the Berkshire Downs en route to Oddlode.

'You are going to be based with Hugo Beauchamp for a year.'

'Thanks, but I have a permanent base here,' Rory laughed sleepily.

'I'm bringing in a caretaker-manager to run your place,' Dillon gazed down at the flinty, rippling dowland with its amazing undulations, crevices, sheer drops and stripes of dark woodland. A huge chalk horse was carved in the land below him like a tattoo on a green shoulder. It was great playing God, he realised, wondering why he hadn't tried before. Running flocks of rare-breed sheep was nothing compared to having a team of horses in training. 'You'll get to compete The Fox. I own him now.'

Rory laughed even louder, totally disbelieving. 'As of when?'

'Today. Phone Hugo Beauchamp. He's agreed to take you on and he thinks he can swing you a ride at Burghley if you're quick.'

'Not on The Fox, surely?'

'No, another horse. You'll like him.' Dillon's heart lifted at the thought of the handsome bay. 'Talk to Hugo about it. Call me back afterwards.'

While Rory was off the line Dillon called his friend Jules, who was yet again in rehab. 'When you come out, how would you like to run a sleepy little stable yard in the Cotswolds for a year, to help you stay out of trouble?'

'It's almost ten years since I worked with horses. My counsellors say I need to *avoid* stress, Dillon. And I'm broke.'

'So rent out that big duplex of yours, take a sabbatical and come play with ponies. There's a very pretty cottage thrown in and I can vouch for the neighbours.'

'Well I've always said that where there's mucking out there's brass . . .' Her throaty laugh rang out above the din of the blades.

By the time Rory called Dillon back, muted with awe that his on-off, hot-cold patron really *had* just bought him the best horse in the world, arranged a ride at Burghley and negotiated an apprenticeship with one of the best riders in the world, Jules had agreed to yard-sit in Upper Springlode. Dillon marvelled at the simplicity of it all. Playing God rocked.

'Just what do you get out of this?' Rory asked him unguardedly.

Now flying over the edge of the Cotswolds, Dillon looked down at a little village nestled in a valley like a perfect golden toy on a green baize play table, waiting for his model railway track to be laid through it. He'd had a whole attic devoted to a model railway as a child – it was one of the few things about his son that Pete had taken an interest in, lavishing him with every Fleischmann and Hornby extra to span the vast room until it would rival Sodor for track, trains, signals, villages, trees, hills, little static people and farm animals.

'I get to be the daddy,' he said, ringing off.

Dillon looked out at the ridiculously ornate rectangle of Fox Oddfield Abbey set amid its formal renaissance gardens, the geometric box-lined beds, walkways and terraces looking like Celtic engravings set around the black opal rectangle of its huge sunken koi pond – as wide as a tennis court and twice as long – nestling in its centre, the plush velvet folds of parkland spreading outward from it. Nell and her twin brother had set little paper boats adrift across those lily-strewn waters as children; now it was one of his father's many play pads.

He squinted down as they passed directly overhead, imagining his model N-gauge track criss-crossing those manicured hectares. He wondered whether his father had moved in yet. It was hard to spot signs of occupation from high above but there were no obvious clues, although the scores of builders and workmen's cars and vans still parked to the rear hinted at ongoing preparations for rock legend habitation.

He settled back to watch his own beloved fields come into view, every hill and hedgerow as familiar as a lover's body. Only it was sporting a new and very racy tattoo.

Knowing full well that he was coming home by helicopter, Nell had found just enough time to let her feelings be known. Having appropriated the ride-on mower from the machinery shed, she had carved a giant, swirly FUCK YOU into the wild flower meadow, with the second u in the adjoining sheep field because she had run out of space.

Laughing so much it hurt his ribs, he called her from his mobile as soon as they landed.

'I'd rather fuck you,' he told her the moment she answered.

'This is Nell's mother,' a stiff Irish voice replied. 'Nell is bathing Giselle. Will you call back later, please.'

When he did, Nell was unrepentant. 'You bloody well deserved it. You're such a wayward bastard. Not taking me to Paris is bad enough, but why'd you buy a horse without me there? I might not know much, but I *do* know horses. My family have dealt in horses for years, remember?'

'It's a good horse.'

'Is he my present?' she gasped.

Dillon had no intention of giving her The Fox. Earlier, Tash had mentioned a horror story about the late, great Snob once being part of a divorce settlement and almost being sold from under her as a result. He had no immediate plans to part from Nell, but he boxed carefully these days and this horse was too big an asset to risk. His lawyers were already talking about co-habitation agreements, should he ask her to live with him.

But he'd agreed to lease Cœur d'Or for a year for her to play at being an owner, which she obviously loved. He was planning to surprise her with it at Burghley. He thought they were a perfect match, two tempestuous souls in need of taming, and a dark corner of his mind had set a challenge. For a year he would make her custodian of this beautiful, talented horse to give her a focus, to prove her heart of gold. If it worked out as he hoped they would all stop playing and he would give her his Cœur d'Or as a wedding present.

'The Fox is not your present,' he told her carefully.

'Oh yes, of course, it's your *heart*,' she sneered.

'Don't you want it then?'

She let out a gorgeously naughty giggle that tightened his groin even before she said, 'I'd rather have your cock.'

'Where?'

'In my mouth.'

Something about Nell always got to him. Despite the constant arguments, her attention seeking and her craving for commitment, she was already deep under his skin. Her fieriness and anger fuelled and invigorated him in direct contrast to his ex-wife's level-headed cool. Right now he needed fire, not ice.

'Come here at once,' he told her. 'I love you, you crazy bird, and I want you so badly I can't walk.'

Chapter 13

Tash was nodding off in a salty bath when Hugo barged into the room, still wearing his white competition breeches, scotch in hand and hair on end.

'Beccy's driving me nuts down there. Everywhere I turn she's there, singing some bloody awful Indian hippy chant to Amery. Poor lad's going cross-eyed.'

'He's newborn; they're all cross-eyed until they can focus.'

He perched on the rim of the bath and reached for the sponge to rub her back. 'When does the maternity nurse arrive?'

'We don't need one, Hugo. It's such silly money.'

'We can pay. We just made a million.'

Neither of them could quite take it in yet.

'I'll be fine looking after the children,' Tash insisted. 'I have Beccy here to help, and we've got the Czech couple coming in a couple of weeks.'

'Yes, but we have another baby on the way, remember?' he replied, dropping a kiss on her silky, soapy shoulder.

She looked up at him in alarm.

'Rory Midwinter.' He sighed. 'Our new work rider. Not quite Lough Strachan's league, but perhaps that's no bad thing.'

'Oh, he called earlier,' she remembered suddenly.

'Rory? I know, I spoke with him.'

'No, Lough.'

Hugo almost fell in the bath with her. 'Why didn't you say?'

'Beccy only told me half an hour ago. She took the call while I was outside at lunchtime, apparently. She's not absolutely sure it *was* him but I can't think who else it could have been. She's very vague.'

'Did she say what he wanted?' he demanded, his voice like rapid-fire gunshot.

Tash was surprised by how furious he looked. 'Seems he *does* plan to be based here.'

'Why didn't he call me?'

'He just did.'

He pulled his battered mobile phone from his pocket and started scrolling through missed calls. 'No record of a call here.' He then looked up Lough's numbers and dialled each one in turn, each time being sent straight to voicemail. 'Well he's left it too late. We've got Rory on board now, and I've just spoken with Mike Seith about including him in Team Mogo for the remainder of the season.'

'We have room for both Rory and Lough to be based here,' Tash pointed out, trying and failing to lean forwards enough to soap between her toes. Her stitches were really hurting now.

'That's a lot of ego on one yard.' Hugo was shaking his head determinedly. 'Too many chiefs and not enough Indians. I'll put him off.'

Tash rubbed her face with foamy, bath-wrinkled fingers. 'You're the only big chief around here,' she yawned. 'They won't be Apache on you.'

'Too right.' Kneeling by the bath he cast his phone on to the chair with clothes and towels strewn across it and sank his hands beneath the bubbles to rub her feet. 'This is my bloody tepee and you're my squaw.'

'I am an equal in this relationship, I'll have you know,' she grumbled. 'I'm *Ms* Chief.'

'I thought you'd been behaving yourself lately.'

'Oh bliss.' Tash let out a contented moan as she felt his fingers rub away the aches. 'Well Lough could arrive any day to lay claim to your appaloosas and pintos. According to Beccy, he's booking flights as we speak.'

'That soon?'

'Ow!' He had her toe in his grip like a piranha. 'So Beccy says. She seems very taken with him after the call. Is he a bit of a flirt?'

'He's bloody-minded and ruthless.' Hugo sprang upright, water splashing everywhere. 'And she told him coming here was okay?'

'Ask her.'

'That's just bloody ridiculous,' he said as he stomped off, his voice trailing away. 'He can't roll up in the middle of the autumn season without talking to me first.'

Listening as he marched through the bedroom, tripping over the lamp flex as he always did, Tash closed her eyes and sank back into the soothing warmth, knowing it could be her only me time for a long, long stretch.

A series of cheerful beeps greeted her when she resurfaced.

Hugo's mobile was flashing on the chair beside her.

Normally she would ignore it in the same way she ignored his small pack of Jack Russells when they yapped at her.

But, guessing it might be Lough Strachan, she leaned out from the bath and picked up the phone in her slippery hand, studying it over the ledge.

New Text Message, it announced across a photograph of Cora being held up on one of her Meredith cousins' ancient Shetland ponies at Holdham Hall earlier in the year. *Read?*

Why not? Tash thought to herself.

The message was from a sender listed as just V: *How did you do, darling? Xxx*

'Hmmph.' Tash threw the phone back on the towels.

She wasn't immediately alarmed, although she strongly suspected V was Venetia Gundry, Haydown's most lascivious livery – a thirtysomething childless divorcée who claimed to have forsaken men for horses and was always hanging around the yard in skinny jeans and tight little fur-collared gilets, chatting up Hugo. Tash was quite certain that she had designs on him. Whip thin, slinky and doe-eyed, if a little weathered, she had a flat voice and a saggy bum but a very determined streak – and judging from the fearless and suicidal way that she rode across country she would stop at nothing to get what she wanted. Hugo admired determination and courage in women, and Ven teamchased, point-to-pointed, evented and was a volunteer fire-fighter.

But was she worthy of Waitrose floristry, Tash wondered.

For some reason she suddenly couldn't shake off the memory of Dillon Rafferty talking about technology. What was it he had said about predictive texts being the tools of adultery? 'Perfect for arranging trysts.'

Slopping water, Tash gave into jealous, itchy temptation and leaned out of the bath again to grab the phone and re-read the message. She then looked at his other messages. There were no less than six others from V still stored on his phone, all from earlier that day. They variously read: *'Will be coming to Ampney Franchart ODE especially to see you, darling.' 'Will we be alone?' 'Where shall we meet up?' 'Can't wait to see you, darling.' 'Where ARE you?' 'Sorry had to go – thought I'd been spotted by you know who.'*

Reading them, Tash was so shocked she dropped Hugo's mobile in the bath.

Downstairs, Beccy had her laptop open on the kitchen table, logged on to the Haydown broadband. She quickly Googled Lough

Strachan while baby Amery slept in her arms. What she saw made her heart prance. Gorgeous voice, gorgeous *man*. She remembered his brave and brilliant riding at the Olympics, and now as she studied him again in the light of their phone chat her heart tripped over itself as it raced ever faster.

He was beyond sexy – that black hair, those turbulent eyes and the bad-boy reputation. *And* he was from the wrong side of the tracks, a poor boy made good – she loved a sob story. On top of all that, he was a vet who saved horses' lives. Result: hero worship.

Hugo had a love rival for her long-running crush, although with the warm solidity of his baby pressed against her chest it was a mismatched contest.

Looking at a photo of Lough receiving his silver medal alongside Hugo waiting for his gold, Beccy knew her heart was still firmly with the winner, not the runner-up. She'd carried around her feelings for her brother-in-law for a very long time, like a keepsake; this stranger was a secondary daydream. Beccy's habit of forming fantasy attachments to the men around her dated back to childhood, but her connection to Hugo was by far the most longstanding and unshakeable. For a brief moment she pressed her lips to Amery's head, breathed in his sweet, yeasty smell and fantasised that he was her baby, that Hugo was her husband and that this was her house.

'You spoke with Lough Strachan earlier?' he snapped from the doorway, making her jump.

'Y-yes.'

'What did he say?'

'That he'll come here as soon as he can.'

'Shit!' Hugo stalked out again.

She could hear his footsteps thundering back upstairs and a moment later he let out an enraged howl. Beccy tilted her head up and listened, managing to catch enough to realise that Tash had obviously done something to his phone and he was giving her hell about it.

Beccy looked at Lough Strachan's handsome face on the computer screen and thought about his sexy, gravelly voice with its strange flat vowels telling her that he couldn't wait to meet her. That was far better than Hugo's scorn; he hadn't even thanked her for helping sell The Fox. Yet he still made her so weak with longing she felt as though her shoelaces were tied together every time she walked past him.

The footsteps thundered back down, taking the back stairs this time.

'Did Lough Strachan leave a number?' Hugo demanded, marching in from the rear lobby.

Beccy shook her head guiltily. 'He said he'd call with flight dates. Is there a problem?'

Hugo's blue eyes fixed hers for a thrillingly long time. Beccy felt her face redden more and more. Then suddenly he shook his head.

'Fuck it, let him come!' he barked, stalking to the fridge and finding the last of the champagne. To Beccy's delight he poured glasses for both of them. 'What is it they say: "Keep your friends close, but your enemies closer"?' He handed her a brimming flute.

She nodded, not understanding exactly what he meant but thrilled that he was telling her.

'To enemies.' He raised his glass.

Beccy touched her glass to his. Lough Strachan was getting more and more interesting. She couldn't wait to hear from him again.

In Buckinghamshire, Sylva Frost was also on the internet that night. Now that she and her mother were keeping track of Dillon's every move as they prepared to stake a claim, she already knew that he owned horses competed by an event rider named Rory Midwinter.

Sylva was munching on comfortingly stodgy lard crackling biscuits kindly sent over from Slovakia by her sister Hana to assist in her current headlining weight flux. Dropping crumbs on her keyboard, she admired a very dashing photograph of Rory clearing a huge red jump fashioned to resemble a shotgun cartridge. It looked like fun, and Rory was very handsome indeed, looking far taller and more athletic than his pop-star patron.

'Mama!' she called over her shoulder. 'Tell Rodney I am going to go riding next week. He and the team can come along too.'

'And the children?' Mama asked hopefully from the kitchen door, wringing a Slovak-flag tea towel in her hands, knowing that there hadn't been enough footage of Sylva as a caring mum during this series.

'No, just me,' she called back, already planning her wardrobe. The weight gain wasn't helpful, but her team knew how to capture her best angle. 'I'll go to my new weekend house. Dillon's horses are very close by, I think.'

'Yes, *mačička!*' Mama announced, pressing the tea towel to her brow to mop sweaty beads of relief. 'The agent has sent the keys to the Petit Château.' Renting a base close to Dillon Rafferty's farm had been Mama's top priority.

A warm breeze carried sweet autumn scents from Sylva's garden through her open windows, which danced with leaf-stencilled sunlight, smells of mulching and bonfires. Sylva loved her pretty faux Arts and Crafts modern mansion near Amersham with its two-acre garden complete with rose walk and vegetable patch, its army of workers, its Jacuzzi, indoor pool and mini-gym. But she knew that she could not afford to get complacent when her career was at stake.

The Cotswolds were alluringly English and enticingly elitist, with their film-set-perfect villages and unique cocktail of olde worlde charm, celebrity chic and Chelsea penthouse price tag. The rented house, which according to the brochure was a fabulous fake French fantasy of crenellations, turrets and moat, was just a couple of miles from Dillon's farm in the heart of the horsy Lodes Valley.

'I will stay there next week,' Sylva decided. 'Tell Rodney that too, Mama.'

In unseen silent rapture at the kitchen door, Mama unfolded the tea towel and waved it above her head just as she had a larger Slovak flag when Sylva had triumphed in tough sporting competitions as a child. She knew her daughter would soon shed pounds, get fit, get her man and achieve a crescendo of publicity hitherto only dreamed of. Her masterplan was underway.

Sylva was equally delighted when she checked on Google Earth that her newly rented weekend house – a stone's throw from Dillon's farm – was a mere pebble flick from his protégé's yard. She picked up her little mobile.

'Is that Rory Midwinter? Hi, this is Sylva Frost. I have just rented a house in your area and I'd like to book a riding lesson please.'

'Fuck off, Faith, that isn't funny.'

It wasn't the first time she'd had this reaction when phoning strangers. 'Hello? Is this a bad time?'

There was a long, doubtful pause for thought in Upper Springlode. '*Are* you Sylva Frost?'

'I am Sylva.'

The line went silent for a while again. Then she heard laughter, rapturous and infectious.

'This really, *really* is my lucky day,' Rory told her joyfully. 'When would you like to come? I'm all yours – in every sense of the word.'

Chapter 14

Rory wasn't sure coming of age suited Faith. Immediately after her eighteenth birthday party, in her last few days before departing for Essex, she developed some strange habits – like his terrier Twitch illogically ripping up his favourite socks and cocking his leg on his riding boots whenever Rory brought home a new lover.

For one, she removed the ageing posters of Sophia Loren, Lucinda Green and Honor Blackman as Pussy Galore from the yard loo. They were his muses, and he wasn't at all happy. She did, he noticed, leave up the poster of her mother.

Then she started pouring away his secret hipflask stashes from his office. 'You're drinking away your one chance at breaking through to the big time.'

'I just won the Scottish Championships!'

Rory was left smarting and baffled.

He had never taken the time to try to understand Faith, whose unconditional love for him and his horses he took utterly for granted, much as he did Twitch, an equally loyal and fierce beast with similarly antisocial tendencies. He had no idea that she was now desperately trying to leave her mark, but as always she was trying too hard.

'Dillon has just bought you The Fox,' she said repeatedly, as though he was in danger of forgetting the fact. 'You haven't given me my birthday present yet,' she also kept reminding him.

Rory personally felt she didn't deserve one.

They rode out together on her last day in the Cotswolds, swatting horseflies and midges as they trotted hastily from the broiling sunshine into Gunning Woods to breathe the pine needles and cool shadowed air.

Faith was riding White Lies, who was now back in work and relishing the chance to show he still had plenty of mileage left. He bucked, fly-kicked and napped all the way. Jockeying a recently backed baby who was as flighty as a springbok and saw lions behind every bush, Rory didn't appreciate Faith's delight in his old campaigner's high spirits.

'Ride him better,' he grumbled as his filly almost decapitated him with every passing branch trying to keep up with Whitey.

'Come over here and show me how,' she urged.

In the distance they heard an ominous rumble of thunder.

'I can't get on there *with* you.'

'Why not? That filly is used to being led from Whitey; I've been trawling her around the lanes for weeks behind this rump. Get over here.'

'Fuck off, Faith.'

They rode on in silence, Rory swatting flies irritably and Faith trying to swallow back the lump in her throat and chest.

Yet again she had goofed up, too anxious, rushed and defensive to time this right.

Ever since watching *The Man From Snowy River* with Rory (and then secretly watching clips from it many, many more times at home on YouTube), she had imagined them enacting the Jess and Jim horseback kiss. But it wasn't going to happen today, and she knew it.

The thunder rumbled closer, making Whitey throw up his head and the filly skitter sideways.

'We'd better turn back.' Rory peered around for some sign of the sky but the wood's canopy was so thick that it was hard to tell how far away the storm was or in what direction.

They soon found out. Turning for home, they rode just a couple of minutes before they seemed to walk into near pitch darkness and the wind whistled through the trunks around them, lifting old leaves from the ground and snapping twigs. Moments later they heard rain pounding down, but it was still held off by the trees. By the time they had trotted to the derelict sawmill on the edge of the pine plantations it had penetrated the canopy and was hammering down on them.

They jumped off and led the horses under cover.

'It'll pass soon.' Rory peered out at the sheets of rain that were lashing down, accompanied by booming thunder. 'God knows, the ground could use the drink. It's as thirsty as I am. Why'd you have to empty my hipflask? I'm gasping.'

'Because you drink too much,' she said simply. 'You'll never win Burghley that way.'

'That new horse Dillon's leased could win Burghley blindfold. It's mega scopey.'

'But you can't win it blind drunk. I've been watching its clips online. That horse almost killed Clissy Dixon at Saumur a couple of years ago. Hugo's got a rare thing going on with him; you'll need a while to get to know him.'

'I'll talk to the owner about that, thanks,' he said pompously.

'Nell hasn't a clue,' she laughed. 'At least Dillon admits he knows nothing. She pretends she's knowledgeable, which is far more dangerous.'

He lapsed into sulky silence for a moment, tempted to tell her that Hugo Beauchamp himself was going to be coaching him on all the horses soon, just as Kurt was going to be coaching her, but he couldn't bring himself to say it out loud yet. He hadn't even told his own mother he was leaving, although he doubted she would notice one way or another. He wasn't sure he'd cope on a big professional yard like Haydown. He had lived alone throughout his twenties with just his horses, Twitch and the occasional girlfriend for company. He'd also heard the rumours about Cœur d'Or. He was driving out to try him in a few days time and already the thought made him sweat with trepidation. He suddenly found himself wishing Faith would be around to come with him.

But she soon irritated him again: 'I found some old footage of Whitey competing on YouTube. He looked great. I think you should bring him out of retirement.'

'No way.'

'He could still teach you a thing or two.'

'I taught *him* everything he knows!'

'You rode better then.'

'Remind me, when are you leaving?'

'Tomorrow.'

'Not a moment too soon.'

'You'll miss me.'

'No I won't.'

They both jumped as a clatter of thunder as loud as a bomb detonated overhead. The rain battering the wooden roof sounded like gunfire.

'It'll help you grow up, being away from here.' He raised his voice to be heard.

'I'm exceptionally mature for my age.'

'Could have fooled me.'

'You're the immature one.'

'I don't deny that. I come from a long line of childish men.'

'What was your Dad like?'

'Very childish indeed. It drove my mother mad. He had no sense of responsibility.'

'Neither does your mother.'

He laughed. 'True. Darling Truffle is quite the most capricious, wayward bird I know. You can't help but love her for it.'

The youngest and most attractive of the three Constantine sisters who had once been the toast of the debutante scene, curvaceous Truffle Dacre-Hopkison was still a formidably glamorous local figure, racketing around the Oddlode valley in a Mini Moke, Hermès headscarves flying and champagne picnic rattling.

Faith could picture Truffle alongside Honor Blackman and Sophia Loren. 'They say all men are secretly looking to marry their mothers.'

'Who says?'

'Psychologists.'

'Well, they're wrong.'

'So who are you looking to marry?'

'I have no desire to get married yet, thanks.'

'I mean, who is your dream date?'

He tapped the metal head of his riding crop against his smiling lips. 'Right now, I'm pretty excited about meeting Sylva Frost.'

'Do you mind that her boobs are fake?'

'What?' he looked at her askance.

'They *are* fake,' she spelled out clearly. 'They were done by Farouk Ali Khan and she has them insured for millions.'

'Well I hope he's recommended a bloody good sports bra. I don't want to get sued if she knocks herself out doing sitting trot.' He pondered this for a moment and then laughed. 'Actually, maybe it would be worth running the risk.'

Faith sulked, listening to the storm raging, thunderclaps ripping the air. She inevitably hurt herself when she asked Rory these questions; it was like self-flagellation.

Whitey and the mare remained surprisingly unbothered by the weather, having heard it hammering around their own stables in recent days. Happy to take a rest out of the rain they jangled their bits and rubbed their noses on their knees.

'There's a lot to be said for playing the field,' Rory sighed.

'Not when the rest of your team are in the dressing room sharing a bath and victory champagne. You've played the field so much it looks like the Somme.'

'Hardly. I'm not yet thirty, remember? Besides, it's better to have loved and lost and all that. You should take a leaf out of my book now you're practically grown up. Live a little. Break some hearts.'

'No thanks.'

'So, tell me . . .' Rory was pondering psychology with difficulty. '. . . if all men secretly want to marry their mothers, do all women want to marry their fathers?'

'I guess so.'

'Puts you in an awkward position.'

She glared at him. 'What do you mean?'

'Well, you could understandably become fixated on gay boys.'

'Hardly!'

'Lots of horsy girls do.'

'Not me.'

'So you like a macho man, like Graham?'

'Ugh! Get real!'

'What's your real dad like?'

Faith examined her gloves. 'Dunno. Mum wants me to meet him, but I'm not interested.'

'Why not?'

'Because he never wanted to know me. Why should he start now?'

'Might help your love life.'

'How come?'

'You'll know what you're looking for in a man.'

'A boozy, crooked Irish horse trader? I think not. Besides, I already know what I'm looking for in a man.'

'What's that then?'

The rain had started to abate, the thunder rolling further away.

Faith stared at the gloomy woods ahead of them, the darkest emerald grotto dripping with crystal light from the rain. Locals believed the woods were enchanted, that they turned enemies into lovers and married souls. Some were too frightened to walk there.

She could say it now. She could admit her feelings. On the eve of her departure, perfect timing to leave him in the shocked realisation that his little sidekick loved him and not his horses all along.

But she knew she didn't have the nerve to admit the true depth of her feelings, couldn't face his amused rejection. She secretly suspected that they both chose to ignore it. Better say nothing until she had transformed into a butterfly and returned to claim him.

'I want somebody reliable, who remembers my birthday,' she muttered instead, pulling down the stirrups on Whitey's saddle ready to mount. 'And is a good kisser.'

'Sounds fair enough.'

They rode back in silence, Faith castigating herself all the while for being so cowardly and letting the opportunity slip past. She was about to go away for months and months without telling him the truth.

At the yard Rory, as usual, left her washing off the horses and disappeared into his office. She could hear him banging around in there for ages, presumably looking for scotch.

But when he re-emerged, he was holding a beautiful bronze of an event horse.

'Happy birthday.' He thrust it towards her. 'And good luck with Kurt and Graeme. They'll teach you a lot more than I can.'

Faith cradled the horse in disbelief, feeling its smooth weight in her hands.

'It's the most beautiful thing I've ever been given. Thank you!'

Before Rory knew what was happening, she had planted a thank-you kiss on him; not the usual shy peck on the cheek but something far fuller and firmer that landed on his lips with a sweet but assertive juiciness which surprised him so much that a great whoosh of blood rushed unexpectedly from his head to his groin.

After she had left Rory put the kiss to the back of his mind and instead wondered whatever had possessed him to give Faith the trophy he had just won for being the top British rider at Bloneigh Castle. He had to hand it back to the event committee after eleven months. But eleven months was a long time, he reminded himself cheerfully as he licked his lips and headed back to his office for the bottle of Famous Grouse he had spotted while ransacking trunks for the trophy.

Anke was delighted when, the evening before her departure to Essex, Faith suddenly asked more about her biological father. 'What was he like? As a person, I mean.'

'Very funny, charming and easy to like.' Anke thought back, choosing her words carefully. 'He could be a little arrogant and irresponsible at times, but he has such wit and charisma that everyone forgives him. And as for riding, he is just so gifted. They called him fearless Fearghal on the hunting field because he was so brave and skilful across country.'

'Why did he never compete?'

'I doubt he could afford to – he had a big family to keep, a business to run, then he was a widower. And I think he was rather too fond of the liquor in the early days.'

'Did he like big boobs?'

'What?'

'Big boobs. I know you haven't got any, but would you describe him as a boob man, generally speaking?'

Perturbed by her daughter's new-found breast fixation, Anke regarded her suspiciously. 'Faith, where is this leading?'

'Nowhere. But I definitely don't want to meet Fearghal,' she said firmly. 'I already know all I need to know, thanks.'

She marched up to her room and, unpacking several sets of thermal underwear that her mother had crammed into a corner of one suitcase, replaced them with a bronze horse as heavy as her heart.

If she closed her eyes she could taste Rory's lips, their salty sweetness, the plump yield of silken lip and the scuff of stubble, the scent of horse, leather and field on his skin, the warm breath from his nostrils. She could remember the instinctive way his hand had risen up to her cheek, warm and protective, and the surprised intake of breath.

Her core shuddered with the pleasure of it, cut so short, taken from her by her own stubbornness and fear. The thought of leaving him physically hurt.

She traced her fingers along the hard, flat bronze and then up to her flat, bony chest.

She was right to go, she told herself. It was time for the caterpillar to disappear into its chrysalis.

Chapter 15

For three days, Beccy leaped on her iPhone every time it rang, but it was never her sexy Kiwi. She knew it was silly to imagine that he would call again, especially given that he had mistaken her for Tash in the first place. What man in their right mind would make secret calls from half way across the world to a married woman with a toddler and a newborn?

Yet in her Cyrano de Bergerac, Roxanne fantasy world, she'd already conducted endless conversations with him to the point of his frenzied confessions of love amid her tearful revelations of her true identity.

Then, out of the blue, he texted.

Flights booked.

There followed a list of flight times and numbers, transporter details and bedding and feed requirements. No flirtation. No confessions. Not even an *x* at the end.

Beccy had a dilemma. If she gave Tash and Hugo the information they would inevitably want to know why he had texted her and not called or emailed them. Hugo was irascible enough about it as it was. She supposed she could make up a fairly plausible excuse – she had taken his call in the first place, after all – but the more she stalled the more indecisive she became and, in her customary fashion, she ended up saying nothing at all. Instead, that evening, she texted back.

Hurry.

It seemed suitably ambiguous yet hinted at longing.

It took him almost a day to come up with: *Things bad there?*

Unspeakable.

More excruciatingly long hours passed before: *Hang in there.*

Satisfied that she had told no lies, Beccy allowed herself some more Cyrano de Bergerac fantasies before suddenly panicking that she might have put him off coming and so hurriedly banged out another message. *UK riders are quaking in their boots knowing you are coming here at last.*

Another agonising wait proceeded before she eventually read: *And you?*

Quacking with anticipation.

It was only after she'd pressed send that Beccy realised her mistake. He'd think of her as some demented duck now. She burned with mortification.

But this time his reply was almost instant: *That makes us birds of a feather.*

Beccy kissed the little glowing phone screen, wishing him goodnight – her time – with a hasty *I'm tucking my head under my wing now* before taking a victory waddle and quack around her room, then lying wide awake in bed thinking about him.

Sweet dreams arrived moments later.

Racked by insomnia and delight, Beccy could only daydream – his time – imagining him checking his phone as he dismounted after a gallop through his lush New Zealand pastures.

Sleeplessness has never felt so sweet, she told him truthfully.

Late at night and in the early hours, exchanging these intermittent, intimate bon mots that felt so bad yet so irresistibly thrilling, Beccy refused to succumb to guilt. The way she saw it, Lough's arrival could only benefit Haydown, where it was all work and no play. If he was as bad tempered and horrible as was commonly rumoured, she was happy to let him think he'd been texting Tash and to stand back to watch the storm break. That might even give Beccy a clear route to Hugo at last. And if Lough Strachan was, as she was starting to think, a misunderstood, passionate hero, then she might just be tempted to reveal her true colours. Either way, she couldn't lose.

He bowled some curveballs, however, like his next text: *How did you know that I'd know?*

Beccy had no idea what he meant and it took her ages to decide upon a reply, anxious that she was missing something and that texting back *Know what?* would expose her as an imposter. Then, listening to the radio late that night, she heard the answer sung out: *There's nothing you can know that isn't known.* Thank heavens for John Lennon.

His comeback was excitingly double-edged: *All You Need Is Love?*

Love is all you need, she picked the letters carefully across the number keys.

This time Lough's response kicked her after-hours daydreams back into check. *You don't know me, Tash.*

Beccy took her phone under the duvet, texting blindly *You don't know me either.* The irony sat so heavily in her chest that she lay awake that night, feeling weighed down with stones.

Seconds before her alarm clock rang out, her phone beeped, vibrated and lit up. *Quack.*

Quack, she echoed back, SMS flying half way around the world in less time than it took her to brush her teeth, her reflection pink-faced with joy, knowing she was already late for morning feeds and that Hugo would shout at her, and for once not caring.

From that moment on the ice broke between Lough and Beccy as they ducked and dived eagerly, quacking across a hemisphere of oceans and ponds. Every time Beccy's phone chirruped she felt her heart thrum. She lay awake staring at her phone on the bedside table, waiting for it to light up like a firefly. She asked him endless questions, longing to know more about the dark-eyed rebel who rode like Xenophon. Most of the things she quizzed him on were embarrassingly juvenile – his favourite films, music, literature – but his answers still provided her with pieces that she could put together to make a picture of a bright loner, a man hewn from two clashing cultures with a rich imagination and a great desire to educate him-self and to understand the world around him. His taste in movies ranged from old classics to art house films she'd never heard of; when asked if he liked *The Piano* he replied dryly that it was okay, but he preferred guitar music. As well as The Beatles, he loved Jeff Buckley and a band called Straitjacket Fits that Beccy had to Google. He read *mostly horse stuff, but I studied French literature as a kid and love Camus, so my bookcase scares visitors. You?*

Beccy didn't think it was a moment to share the fact she was cur-rently half way through the latest Marian Keyes, taking occasional breaks to flick through *OK!* magazine. *French literature does it for me too,* she replied happily. It wasn't a lie. She'd loved reading Zola and Flaubert for her French A level; *Madame Bovary* had been a favourite, with the dashing, adulterous landowner Rodolphe Boulanger making her think of Hugo.

Read to me sometime, Tash. I want to hear your voice again.

Beccy shuddered, thinking about that first magical call. He had heard *her* voice, not Tash's. So what if she'd softened and Sloanified it a bit to sound like her stepsister; it was still Beccy who had spoken to him, who had flirted with him and heard that amazing gruff, sexy voice in return.

Inspired, she headed to Marlbury library on her afternoon off and borrowed a translation of *Cyrano de Bergerac*, but found it highly disappointing because she'd forgotten that stupid, noble Cyrano dies still denying his lifetime's love.

She texted New Zealand afterwards: *x*

A kiss?

A rosy circle drawn around the verb 'to love'.

That blew it; she should never have quoted Rostand, least of all using the L word again. He didn't reply for two days. Beccy started to panic, taking long, unscheduled breaks from yard work to drive up to the ridge beside the telephone mast where there was maximum reception and wait in vain for a response.

Then, to her eternal relief, he texted: *Tell me you love good food.*

Beccy, whose appetite had never deserted her despite faddiness that had taken her from vegetarian to vegan to fruitarian at various points, texted back with a triumphant affirmative.

I can't wait to cook for you. What's your favourite food?

Better and better. For all her greed, Beccy was hopelessly basic in the kitchen. *Thai, North Indian, Lebanese, tapas* she replied ecstatically. *And best of all, stew with dumplings.*

I will cook you stew he promised. *That's total ambrosia for a Kiwi.*

She laughed, daring herself to suggest *And rolypoly to follow?*

Haven't got a sweet tooth, he revealed, not getting the innuendo. *Can't stand jam. My dad's favourite. Sticks in my throat.*

It was a silly detail, but Beccy's heart soared. She had always hated jam intensely. It reminded her of those first years after her mother remarried, when Henrietta went into country-wife overdrive and made endless pots of conserves from every fruit in James's vast garden. The smell of jam-making still made Beccy feel sick, associated as it was with the wretched misery of becoming a reluctant and unwanted stepdaughter.

Hate jam too. My stepfather's favourite. Sticks in my throat. But I love stew.

I love stew too.

x

x

Those two kisses criss-crossed the world as the birds of a feather finally lay down to roost, knowing they had crossed another invisible boundary.

Can I call you? he wrote the next time.

Any time, she replied eagerly before remembering that she was Tash and 'any time' wasn't an option for a married mother of two with a business to run.

When he did call she was lolling in bed just before midnight, *The Truth about Cats and Dogs* playing on her laptop, which she was finding considerably more cheering than Rostand.

'Tash?'

'Yes,' she managed to splutter vaguely, heart hyper-charged.

'Now, in this blessed darkness, I feel I am speaking to you for the first time.'

That sexy Kiwi drawl was unbelievably potent. Beccy reeled, her heart on fire. It was a quote from *Cyrano de Bergerac*, when he speaks to Roxane in the darkness beneath her balcony, pretending to be her suitor Christian but in reality confessing his own love.

He'd read the book!

'I know Hugo's in Holland tonight,' he said.

'Yes,' she managed another strangled affirmative. Hugo had indeed disappeared to the Netherlands first thing that morning to compete at Breda CIC, the one-day equivalent of the three-day CCI, catching a lift in an owner's private plane so that he could ride and return home within just two days and not interrupt preparations for Burghley.

'So you're all alone?'

'Yes.'

'Talk to me.'

For a moment, Beccy wanted to hang up so badly she couldn't breathe. She suddenly thought about Tash and her children in the house a few hundred yards away, probably breastfeeding little Amery and listening to Radio Four in bed. Disgrace and embarrassment threatened to asphyxiate her.

'I c-can't talk,' she managed to whisper.

'Sorry. Dumb of me to call. Forget it.'

'No. Please don't go.'

She clung on to the phone for what seemed like for ever, hand shaking, heart battering her ribs, watching blindly as a muted

Uma Thurman and Ben Chaplin moved about on her laptop screen.

'Okay, I have a question for you,' he said eventually. 'It's nothing personal – well, not directly. It's about my father.'

'Yes.'

'We haven't spoken for a long time. Years, you know. We fell out.'

'Go on.'

'Now he knows I'm leaving he wants to meet up.'

'That's good.'

'No it's not. He's a shit, I want nothing to do with him. He just wants money. He always does. But he's used my mum to get at me.'

'Oh.'

'I can't leave her here like this with him around.'

'So you might not come here after all?' she bleated, torn between relief and regret.

'That's what I'm asking, Tash.'

She almost wished he was talking to Tash right now. She was always good at advice and sympathy. Beccy just wanted to get back to *Cyrano de Bergerac* and flirting.

'If you meet your dad and pay him off, will he leave your mum alone?'

'I guess.'

'So there's your answer.'

There was a long pause and Beccy sensed that perhaps she'd said the wrong thing. In her head she could hear Tash's soft husky voice urging 'Bring your mum here with you, Lough' or 'Stay there and sort it out'. But Beccy, spoilt little rich girl, came up with 'pay him off'. Nice one. She needed to rescue this fast.

'I have a question for you,' she said, grateful to have found her voice, that soft Tash voice she aped so well.

'Okay.'

'Are you really as ruthless as they say?'

'Depends what they say.'

'Don't they call you the Devil on Horseback in New Zealand?'

'Some do.'

She took a deep breath and crossed her fingers. 'So why can't the Devil on Horseback stand up to his own father and tell him to leave his mother alone?'

That was more like it, Beccy reasoned, feisty and direct with a smoky touch of sensuality to her voice. She was back in business.

There was another long pause. On screen, Abby and Brian were having phone sex. Beccy sighed jealously.

'You don't know my *pāpā*,' he said eventually. 'He talks with his fists.'

'Afraid of getting beaten up?' she teased.

'Yeah, quite frankly.'

'Then perhaps you *should* think twice about coming here after all.'

'You planning to beat me up, then?' That amazing voice deepened with amusement and flirtation.

A slow smile spread across Beccy's face as she realised she was back in the game and on familiar, flirty turf.

'Not me. But there are a lot of jealous types around here, you know.'

'Don't I just. Reckon I'll have to watch my back out there.'

'Just your own?'

'I'll watch every part of you if you like.'

She was shivering with excitement now. Forget Abby and Brian, this was a million times more thrilling. Her nerve endings were so charged, she expected her duvet to combust. She couldn't resist sliding her hand down between her legs.

'I'll hold you to that.'

'I'll just hold you.'

Oh. My. God. Beccy's fingers encountered a warm geyser bubbling over a pip-hard little rock and as soon as she touched it she climaxed, shuddering quietly and shamefully into her pillow.

'Still there?' he asked after several seconds. 'Afraid I might start a fight out there?'

Beccy suddenly didn't want to flirt any more. 'This is serious, Lough. Don't you dare give me away here.'

'I was under the impression your husband had already done that?'

It was a few moments before she could take in what he had said. 'I'm sorry?'

'Nothing. Forget I said it.'

'What are you talking about here?' Her voice had risen from her breathy Tash impersonation towards her normal pitch. She didn't care whether she was pretending to be Tash or not. She wanted to know.

'Ask Hugo.'

Beccy carefully closed the lid of her laptop and balanced it on her bedside table, pulling her duvet up to her chin, causing Karma, who was asleep on the end of the bed, to fall off with a thud as she was rolled from her twelve-tog nest.

'Still there?' he asked again.

'Yup.'

'*A kiss is a message too intimate for the ear,*' he began to quote, '*infinity captured in the bee's brief visit to a flower, secular communication with an aftertaste of heaven, the pulse rising from the heart to utter its name on a lover's lip:* "Forever".'

Beccy closed her eyes, feeling the weighty lurches as Karma climbed aboard the bed to make herself comfortable once again.

'I wanted to kiss you the first time I ever saw you competing in Melbourne.'

Beccy's eyes snapped open again.

'What was that?'

'Melbourne three day event. I saw you compete.'

'When?'

'Six years ago. My first time there. The horse got a knock flying over and we didn't declare. I was in the crowd on cross-country day. You were riding one of Sandy Hunter's advanced horses. I watched you through the water – the mare was a famous hydrophobic, but you pretty much carried her through it. It was great riding. Then some nutty girl tried to throw herself in front of your horse, remember?'

Beccy closed her eyes. How could she forget?

'Somebody stopped her,' she remembered, the dizzying frenzy of that day more blurred in her mind than ever. Days on end with no food, living in a hostel in St Kilda with a Norwegian girl called Mjoll who she'd met on the Gold Coast, and who shared big blocks of crumbly brown dope and fed Beccy's paranoia about her stepfamily. Knowing Tash was going to be in Melbourne with Hugo, longing to punish her for having what Beccy wanted, for driving her out into the wilderness in search of purpose.

'I stopped her,' Lough's deep, gruff voice said simply.

'You?'

'Yeah. Small world, huh?'

'Ohmygod.'

'I came to meet you in person the next day – you were signing books. But you didn't recognise me and I got tongue-tied. You were feeling crook and Hugo was being mean, I remember that. I was a nobody then, just a small-town Kiwi vet with big ambitions. I've still got the book – you spelled my name wrong when I said "Lough as in Scottish loch."'

Beccy was barely breathing. 'And the girl?'

'What girl?'

'The girl who ran out in front of Ta—' She corrected herself, panic rising. 'In front of my horse. You saved her life. What happened to her?'

'No idea – she ran off before security could get at her. Looked pretty spaced-out to me.'

'Would you recognise her again?'

'Yeah, sure. Scary eyes. And she had a pretty distinctive tattoo of a mermaid on her shoulder.'

Beccy fingered her shoulder and wriggled lower under the duvet.

'I don't think you should come after all.'

'What?'

'Sort things out with your father first.' She rang off and switched off her phone, pulling the covers right over her head.

Chapter 16

As soon as Hugo returned from the Netherlands he was on a quick turnaround to prepare for Burghley. He had barely a couple of hours spare to spend with his family, let alone oversee Rory trying out his new rides. The following day Cœur d'Or would travel to Lincolnshire with the veteran Duck Soup, now Hugo's only Burghley ride, who was due to retire from international three day eventing after the trials. A television crew had come to shoot a feature on the famous old horse for the local news round-up. When Rory finally turned up in his battered car to sit on the horse he would ride at one of the world's toughest events in less than a week, Hugo was mid interview. He broke off to greet his new work rider with a face like thunder, which wasn't quite the start Rory had hoped for.

'You're late,' he snapped as Duck was led out across his cobbled yard for his close up.

'The car overheated,' Rory explained, awe-struck by his surroundings. 'I'll get straight on. I need to get back to teach this afternoon. You'll never guess who I've—'

'You can't ride Heart until after they've finished filming,' Hugo interrupted, walking away to talk to the television reporter again.

In the end Tash was coaxed out of the house to enable Rory to at least try out The Fox while he was waiting.

'Your husband doesn't trust that I can ride,' he told her, only mildly offended.

'He promised Dillon we'd oversee the handover,' she explained with an apologetic smile before rubbing her face with paint-flecked hands. She looked very tired.

Rory noticed that her eyes were red and wondered if she'd been crying. He knew that she'd bred The Fox herself, so she must be upset to let the ride go, however huge the financial reward. As he took a leg-up into the saddle he doubled his resolve not to screw this up, for everybody's sake. The Beauchampions were among his sporting idols and he still had their books in his office at Overlodes.

Tash's eyes were in fact bloodshot and puffy because her new Czech au pairs had arrived that week and were bleaching every inch of the kitchen, convinced that Haydown was crawling with germs. She was quietly grateful to get some fresh air, despite the fact she was madly trying to finish a portrait commission that day.

And she truly caught her breath when she watched Rory on a top-class horse for the first time. Perhaps Dillon Rafferty wasn't such a misguided patron after all. The boy rode quite brilliantly. He was going to be a definite asset.

Rory and Fox really suited one another, and the gutsy little chestnut, who could be lazy on the flat at home, lit up and sparkled. They looked like an established partnership from the off. It was a long time since Tash had felt this breathless, buzzing with excitement, and she wanted to drag Hugo out of the camera glare and jump up and down for joy. He would register the match straight away. Just for this moment, a million pounds paled into insignificance as she marvelled at Rory in the saddle. They were soon sailing over a few of the obstacles in the arena, from single oil barrels to poles set at the top of the jump wings. Fox tucking his knees up to his chin, Rory in perfect balance. The horse was loving every minute.

'Where on earth have you been for the past few years?' she laughed when he eventually jumped off. 'You should be in the elite training squad.'

His high cheeks were shot through with damson streaks of pleasure. Hearing Tash Beauchamp say that was almost better than a four-star win. For Rory, riding had never been the issue – it came as naturally as breathing – but organising his life and finances to get close to the major league had proved impossible until now.

'Without Dillon I'd never ever sit on a horse this good,' he admitted, patting Fox's red neck with the greatest of respect. 'He's in a whole new league. Mine always cost peanuts and I have to sell the good ones to make a living.'

'Who's your dressage trainer?'

'Anke Brakespear.'

'You lucky thing.' Tash's eyebrows shot up. 'It certainly shows. Don't let Hugo try to change a thing on the flat,' she insisted as they handed Fox over to Jenny, who already had Cœur d'Or tacked up. 'In fact, maybe Anke can coach you here once you're based with us full time.'

Thanking Jenny, Rory realised that the thought of coming to Haydown no longer made him feel bulldozed. He was genuinely excited at the prospect. The set-up was quite amazing and Tash was as lovely as everybody always said she was, even if Hugo was clearly just as arrogant. The thought of riding a horse like The Fox daily absolutely thrilled Rory. He was also tickled to have one horse taken away from him to be untacked and hosed while another was handed over ready to go, although he guessed that wouldn't last.

Faith had always done that for him at Overlodes, but she was no longer there and his own yard was already descending into chaos, with lessons forgotten or horses going unexercised.

Suddenly he felt an unfamiliar ache in his chest.

I need to be somewhere like this, he realised. I need to pull my act together. Faith was right, it was make or break time.

'Hugo will need to give you some guidance with this horse,' Tash told him as he headed for the mounting block to get on Heart, who was a good hand taller than Fox and dancing around agitatedly. 'You warm up, I'll go and fetch him. Best leave his mouth alone to begin with – he's a bit sensitive about it when he starts out.'

Accustomed to riding very difficult horses as a necessary evil to make a living, Rory wasn't unduly bothered as Heart jogged sideways into the arena and immediately started bunny-hopping and crabbing towards the far end. He knew a big, fit horse like this needed to settle, and that would at the very least take a few minutes' stretching work. He pulled his phone from his pocket to send a text to Faith, unable to shake a sudden urge to check how she was doing. She'd sent him about twenty texts since arriving in Essex, but the last few had been distinctly weird and preoccupied with breast size.

But he only got as far as the *H* of *How r u?*, when the over-tight horse beneath him took sudden exception to one corner of the arena and whipped round before haring off towards the gate with a series of bucks and twists.

Rory didn't move in the saddle. By the time he'd gathered the horse and set him off in a big, fluid trot he was pressing send on his text. Cooing and chatting soothingly to Heart, he pocketed the phone and rode the big, powerful horse forwards, hands barely touching his mouth through the reins, all his concentration now devoted to the task in hand.

Hugo exchanged a surprised look with Tash as they leaned against the rails to watch. She was right. He was a damned good jockey. He'd seen Heart pull that trick regularly at the start of a session, and the succession of prospective buyers who had come to try him that year had never coped so well. Most grabbed at the reins, which sent him straight up in the air, or got so thrown off balance that he started bucking like a bronco at a rodeo. Several had fallen off, despite being high-ranking riders.

But Rory seemed to have his measure.

'I still think we're mad taking them to Burghley,' Hugo tutted. 'I've told Dillon as much.'

'It's his decision,' Tash pointed out.

'Technically it's his girlfriend's decision,' he reminded her.

They both watched as Rory gradually began to take up contact and the big horse responded well.

'They might just make a decent partnership,' Hugo admitted grudgingly, having really not wanted to relinquish the ride. 'He's certainly better on the flat than I'd imagined. There's a lot to work with there.'

'You wait till you see him on Fox.'

'I still think this one's going test him,' Hugo muttered jealously. 'I've seen Rory ride across country and he has fantastic technique, but he's used to riding nippy little blood horses like Fox. He doesn't set them up enough in front of the fences. Heart's too bold for that.'

Realising his ego was in danger of taking a battering, Tash threaded her arm through his. They watched as Heart beautifully but rather resentfully came into an outline and really started to work over his back, showing off his flashy trot at its best. Rory tried out some of the movements from the dressage test they'd be performing in two days' time, and which he'd had as bedside reading all week.

'Low forties,' Tash predicted the first phase score.

'Fifties,' Hugo countered. 'The horse will react to the atmosphere even if the rider stays this cool. Christ, he's good. Where did Dillon Rafferty find him?'

'Teaching beginners at a local stables.'

'What a waste. He's just what we need here. Reminds me of Stefan.'

Tash looked at him in delight. From Hugo, that was praise indeed.

But Rory's magic spell was broken when a shrill beep rang out of his pocket, announcing a text message. It was all the excuse Heart was looking for. His white-rimmed eyes flashed as he whipped back, half a ton of horseflesh intent on sudden flight. Again Rory sat the 180-degree spin, but he wasn't quite quick enough to ease the contact and the horse was up on his hind legs. Rory tilted forwards as the withers went higher, gripping that golden neck, waiting for the horse to drop down again. But a moment later Heart had tipped back, past his balance point.

'Jump off!' Hugo yelled, hurdling the gate.

Rory only just leaped clear as the big horse crashed backwards onto the sand arena.

Nell was topless in the paddling pool with Giselle, cooling off from the scorching sunshine that bounced around the Cotswold stone of her parents' courtyard garden. She took a call on her mobile, only half listening as Hugo Beauchamp started banging on about horses.

Taking control of Dillon's eventing interests only suited her when she had something to gain, and since he flatly refused to run the new million-pound horse at Burghley she'd lost interest in it all.

'You really need to talk to Dillon,' she said, although she knew perfectly well he would be away in Greenland recording his Christmas video until mid-week. He'd promised to take her for a weekend away when he got back, which was why she was topping up her tan.

'It can't wait that long. *You* own this horse, Nell. You have the final decision.'

Not for a moment did Nell belie her surprise. Suddenly she was very interested in the problem indeed.

'And he's had a bad fall?'

'He's fine. We legged Rory back up and he took him over a few poles and gave him a pipe-opener on the Downs. They pulled together again pretty well, but the horse is unsettled. It's not the rider, it's the partnership. If it was The Fox going to Burghley I'd be right behind Rory. He's a great pilot, and he has more than enough competitive experience, but this horse is more sensitive. He can't take a last-minute jockey swap and still perform reliably.'

'You're saying Dillon's bought me a dud?' Nell flicked water at Gigi to make her laugh.

'He's one of the best horses in training,' Hugo said impatiently, 'but he's not a machine. We all agree it's better to wait and aim him at Pau, where The Fox is headed. Forget Burghley this year.'

Nell's mind was racing and her heart swelling as she realised what Dillon must be planning.

'It's bound to be a big blow,' Hugo was saying. 'We appreciate how much you want to run a horse there, and I know Dillon's pulled a lot of strings to rent that cottage on the estate for the week, but you can still both go. We can always field the horse and withdraw him after the dressage.'

'Is that what Rory wants to do?'

'He says it's up to you, but I strongly advise you to back me up here.'

Which meant that Rory was willing to ride the full three days, Nell was certain. 'Would you put him on the phone?'

'He's had to leave – he's teaching at his yard now. He's happy to come back here first thing tomorrow morning to ride Heart again before he travels, but there's no point if you agree to pull him out. That's why I wanted to speak to you personally.'

Heart. Nell registered the name. Dillon had said he was giving her his heart. She'd been so ungrateful. Now she had the opportunity to be at his side in a glorious stately setting far from his boring farm, in the full public glare, with their own love nest to escape to every night. That was his surprise weekend away; she wasn't about to give it up in a hurry.

'I will agree to no such thing until I've spoken to my rider,' she told Hugo, hanging up.

Infuriatingly, her rider wasn't answering his phone. Undeterred, Nell fished Gigi from the pool and hurriedly handed her to her mother. Pulling a T-shirt dress on over her bikini bottoms she jumped in her car to drive the short distance to Rory's yard, cramming in her hands-free earpiece as she reversed.

In Sisimiut, Dillon's Christmas video shoot was overrunning. The film crew were being hampered by a lack of snow in Greenland and continual delays, not least of which was the star's girlfriend phoning him every five minutes.

The storyboard featured Dillon on a dogsled, singing wistfully of failed love while six huskies pulled him at speed across the snow. It was bitterly cold. Between takes – of which there were many because the dogs were uncooperative and the musher so enthusiastic that Dillon kept falling off the sled – Nell phoned endlessly to complain about his schedule, his ex-wife and his staff.

Now she phoned breathlessly as she drove between her parents' barn and Rory's yard.

'I love you!'

A big smile spread across Dillon's face, cracking the ice on his designer stubble.

'You bought me a horse!'

His smile dropped away almost instantly.

'How did you find out?' As if he couldn't guess. Rory was hopeless at keeping secrets – a typical event rider from what Dillon could tell.

'He sounds great,' she told him down the crackling line. 'He's already dumped Rory so we have something in common. Hugo thinks it's too risky for Rory to try Burghley, but I think I can talk him round.'

'Well, Hugo's the boss.'

'He's my horse!'

'For a year, yes.'

'A *year*?' She was singularly unimpressed by the time limit.

Dillon cleared his throat and kicked the powdery snow that barely covered the stubbly grass. 'A year.'

'I don't want a horse for a year. What's the point of that?'

'You need to make the most of him,' he said with feeling.

'In that case we're definitely going to Burghley.'

'Thing is, I'm not sure I'll be able to make it back—'

But the line had broken off.

Heart hammering painfully, like an old-fashioned alarm clock ringing out, Dillon switched off his phone so he'd have peace, although that still meant listening to the endless playback of his Christmas single, a retro cover he was starting to hate. He'd wanted to change plans and record a cover of 'Heart of Gold', but his management insisted on sticking to something more festive.

'And why should the world take notice of one more love that's failed?' His voice sang out to him now.

'Oh shuddup,' he muttered under his breath.

The trouble was that the world would take a great deal of interest if his love failed. Journalists were already revving up their laptops to write commentaries on why Dillon Rafferty couldn't make his relationships stick despite singing and writing so eloquently about love. He knew it had to be his fault. Nell was at least making an effort, trying to share his interests and support him. He should be grateful, not dreaming of running away all the time.

Yet when the director took him to one side to warn him that the shoot was now likely to overrun by as much as a week he wanted to give him a high five.

'There's not enough snow here. We have to go higher. It means camping out a few nights with no hotel comforts.'

'I'm cool with that,' Dillon said, rather too eagerly.

'There'll be no phone reception there.'

'I'm cool with that too.' He headed happily for his sled.

When Sylva had booked her first session with Rory Midwinter she'd hoped that it would bring her a step closer to future husband Dillon Rafferty's inner circle. What she hadn't imagined was that Dillon's current girlfriend would turn up half way through, looking like a contestant in a Miss Wet T-Shirt competition. Rodney and his crew, who had got rather bored of watching Sylva trotting around in circles despite the gratuitous footage of her boobs bouncing, were refocusing with glee as Nell hurried from her car, pert nipples poking enticingly from the wet cotton stretched around her slender frame.

'Cut!' Sylva shouted, riding between the camera and the new arrival as Rory apologetically hurried to find out what Nell wanted.

Sylva was secretly relieved to have a breather. It was a long time since she'd ridden and she'd forgotten what hard work it could be, especially given the extra weight she was currently building up to get publicity. She also had an opportunity to study the opposition at first hand. Nice face, she conceded, although the attitude was very prima donna. Nell was wagging a finger at Rory now, clearly giving him some sort of lecture, while he looked cornered and desperate to be rid of her. Two minutes later and she'd driven away.

'So sorry about that,' he rushed back.

Sylva waved off the apology. 'Nothing wrong, I hope?'

'No, just a change of plans. Looks like I am riding at Burghley after all.'

'How thrilling,' Sylva giggled, checking that her crew were filming this. 'I *love* three day eventing.'

'You do?' Rory seemed surprised that she had even heard of it.

'Oh *yes*,' she nodded. 'I plan to take a very active interest. It is why I have come to you to ride your horses. You are a great event rider.'

Rory looked thrilled. 'Well in that case we'd better get you trotting again. You really have a fantastic position already, you know.'

'I have lots of fantastic positions – I'll show you some time.' She winked at him, loving the way his cheeks suddenly streaked with two red patches like blackberry cordial poured into water. He really was very sweet.

Chapter 17

How r u?

Faith re-read Rory's text, as she had many times that day to cheer herself along. Those three little words that meant he was thinking about her.

She scrolled to the next text down, from Carly, which made her feel less cheerful: *New tits soon!*

She was booked in to a consultation with Mr Ali Khan on Saturday afternoon and Carly, who had never missed an episode of *Extreme Makeover*, couldn't wait.

Through the thin ply walls of the static caravan that she shared with two jolly Dutch working pupils she could hear them play-fighting in their yodelly voices as they heated baked beans to go on their toast. It was their staple diet and they had offered her some, but Faith had no appetite.

Faith looked down at her flat chest, that boyish body that she had convinced herself stood between her and love ever after. Her mother was so immensely proud of her middle child's mind that she never seemed to notice Faith's shortfalls in other departments. Growing up naturally beautiful, Anke had never questioned her own looks. Faith had spent her entire adolescence craving that perfect geometry and blondeness, that effortless ability to attract which her mother shared with golden-boy Magnus. For years now, given a pact with the devil she would have willingly traded her intellect for beauty.

But now that she was on the eve of carving her body into a new incarnation, she suddenly doubted it was her biggest handicap after all.

The Dutch boys, who had been so friendly at first, were rapidly going off her. In her heart she knew this wasn't because she looked like a young John McEnroe. It was because of her sharp tongue and her aggression, the very defence mechanism she had built up in a lifetime of protecting herself from the bullies who had always mocked her for her physical ordinariness, especially in the light of her mother's extraordinariness.

Faith read Rory's text again. *How r u?*

She pressed 'reply' – her fifth so far – but this time, instead of telling him about the amazing set-up Kurt had in Essex, she typed: *R U going 2 Burghley?*

This time, she got the reply she had been waiting for within minutes.

Fell off horse. Scary bugger. Hugo wants 2 withdraw me. Also scary bugger. But Nell says go. She is the best. Can't believe she has made all this happen for me with Dillon. What a mate!

Faith felt her heart burning. She started to send a reply straight away but her fingers were shaking too much. She rang him instead. For once, he answered.

'Man, am I glad to hear from you!' he sounded predictably half cut, but that husky, smoky voice was still the sweetest thing Faith had heard all day, particularly when it was so clear he was pleased to hear from her. 'I need you here with me right now. Nobody pep talks me like you do. Tell me I can do it, Faith.'

'Do what?' Her heart was looping the loop.

'Ride that nutty French horse round Burghley.'

There was a pause as the engine in her heart stalled mid-flight.

Faith was fundamentally honest to the core, even when overwhelmed by love. She regularly told Rory how talented he was because it was true, but she knew his limitations.

'You mustn't do it!' she blurted.

'What?' he scoffed incredulously.

'The horse is too difficult.'

There was a disbelieving pause. She could hear him breathing. She wanted to feel those warm breaths against her her skin so badly.

'This is my dream, Faith,' he said eventually, his voice so low she could barely hear it over the noise of the Dutch boys watching television. 'This is the thing I have dreamed of doing all my life, and I can do it this week.'

'Please don't.' She was frightened for him, all the hairs on her body suddenly needle sharp, her every instinct bent against this, just knowing he would get hurt.

'Nell wants me to do it. It's her horse now. She is the reason I have this chance and I have to ride for her.'

The needles of fear all stabbed into Faith's skin simultaneously. 'Forget Nell! She *isn't* the reason Dillon has done all this for you—'

'Says who?'

'I know!'

He was starting to get annoyed too: 'You bloody don't, Faith. With respect, you're a good kid, but—'

'I am not a kid! I'm eighteen. I've left home, I can vote. I drive and drink – just not all at the same time, unlike you. I can marry, hold a shotgun licence and have cosmetic surgery!' There, she'd said it. The blood pumping through her head almost deafened her, so it took her a few moments to realise that he was chuckling.

'Just not all at the same time,' he said, his anger quite forgotten.

'Oh Faith, you always cheer me up. Now I'm going straight to bed, I promise.'

'No!' she bleated, desperate for reassurance.

'I'm getting up before dawn to drive to Berkshire and prove to Hugo that I won't let him down. And I won't let you down either. But you can't talk me out of this. I've dreamed of doing this for far too long.'

Faith's burning heart was exploding. You have The Fox, she wanted to scream. You have Rio. Be patient. Just wait. They'll take you there.

'Come and support me next weekend,' he said suddenly.

'I can't.'

'Surely you can get time off?'

'I've got a medical appointment.'

'Cancel it.'

'I can't, it's . . . really important.'

'God, are you ill?' He sounded alarmed.

'No – it's just that . . .' Her racing mind flicked through a hundred excuses before honesty and terror got the better of her, 'because I'm having a boob job!'

His gales of laughter made her hold the phone away from her head, panic rising. She thrust it under her duvet and counted to ten. When she finally pressed the battered little Samsung to her ear again the other end was silent and she thought he must have hung up, but then she heard him breathing.

'Faith, are you there?' he asked, clearly not for the first time.

'I'm here.'

'Tell me this is a joke?'

'It's no joke.'

There was a sharp intake of breath. 'Don't do it.'

'What?'

'It's dangerous.'

'No it's not.'

'You mustn't do it to yourself.'

'Why not? Men like boobs. You like boobs. I have no boobs.'

'You don't need them, Faith.' He sounded suddenly very sober. She hadn't heard this serious tone of voice since Whitey's accident.

There was a pause, and Faith longed to ask him to explain whether he meant that she had no need of boobs because he thought

202

she was perfect already or – as she suspected – because she was a lost cause, but every time she tried to say it a big fat frog in her throat jumped on her vocal cords.

'You don't *need* to ride at Burghley,' she said eventually, trying to make him understand, 'but the chance of a lifetime is there, like you say, and you're taking it.'

'That's not the same thing!'

'It so is. And it's far more dangerous than a boob job if you ride that horse.'

'Okay,' Rory conceded. 'You promise me you won't go under the knife, and I won't declare at Burghley.'

That big frog in her throat was wrapped up in her heartstrings like a kitten in knitting now, pummelling furiously.

But Faith had heard his hollow promises before. 'Promise me on what honour? Twitch's life?'

'Don't be stupid.' There was telltale clinking in the background as he filled his glass. 'This'll cheer you up . . .' He started speaking again, and it was a while before she realised he was talking about something else entirely. '. . . Sylva Frost came for a lesson today and brought an entire documentary team with her. Can you believe it? Man, she's an act.'

The frog finally jumped from Faith's throat as jealousy took over. 'What does she look like in the flesh?'

'Incredibly pretty and positively stacked.' In his hurried attempt to cheer her up, he didn't think through what he was saying. 'Magpie found it a bit unbalancing with all that bouncing around above her, but she'll learn to live with the suffering.'

Faith had heard enough.

'Put the drink down and step away from the glass, Rory,' she told him wearily, hanging up.

The following day Rory rode better than he'd ever ridden in his life. In the cool early morning, a low sun striping the Haydown stable arena through the poplars, he had the big, unpredictable bay horse dancing like Nureyev.

'Sweet Jesus! Was he up all night with Anke Brakespear?' Hugo laughed as he watched him. 'Talk about riding your Heart out.'

Beside him, Tash felt that giddy anticipation again. 'He could do it, couldn't he?'

Hugo nodded. 'I take it back. They'll go round that Burghley turf like they own it.'

So they were both astounded when Rory rode up to them a moment later and announced: 'The horse is great but you're right, Hugo. We should save him for Pau. I'll call Nell.'

Hugo and Tash turned to look at each other. They were flabbergasted.

Nell's reaction came as an even bigger shock to Rory. 'Good! Dillon's stuck up a mountain so Burghley's off anyway. I'm going to bring the horse over here to my brother's yard. Piers can take him hunting for a season, back him off with some big Lodes Valley hedges. He sounds far too full of himself.'

'You can't!' Rory yelped in horror.

'He's my horse.'

'What about Pau?'

'Dillon will be in Japan by then, after that it's Australia and South Africa.'

'But *you* can come and watch us,' Rory pleaded, longing for support from one of his oldest friends.

'Forget it. I'm going to bring the horse back here. If I can't have Dillon near by I'll bloody well have his Heart.' She rang off furiously.

Rory glanced across at the Beauchamps' inquiring faces and flashed a nervous smile. He'd just lost one of the most exciting rides he'd ever had. He hoped to God it was worth it.

Walking behind the strawberry-pink coach house for some privacy, he crouched down to text Faith, his heart strangely swollen. He had to think so long and hard about what he was going to say that he could see Tash peeking around the wall to check he was okay. In the end, he carefully tapped out: *Keeping my end of the bargain. Will you promise to keep yours?*

The reply came back as swiftly as a knee in the groin. *It's my life, loser.*

He reread it in disbelief, biting his lower lip so hard that he drew blood.

When his phone then rang he pressed 'answer', not pausing to check caller ID, convinced it was Faith calling to make up for the text mistake.

'Darlink, can you fit me in next weekend?' purred a seductive Slovak voice.

Rory tilted his head up to watch a pair of buzzards circling against the darkening sky. Every cloud had a Sylva lining, he guessed ruefully. 'As of today, I'm totally available . . .'

Faith rushed out of the tack-room loo and checked her phone, which she'd left beside the bridle she was cleaning. 'That's funny, I thought I heard a text come through.'

'Must have been mistaken.' Carly had just had time to delete the message log on her friend's phone memory after replying to Rory. As far as she was concerned, the moment Faith got some decent tits and a pretty nose she wouldn't need Rory any more. She'd turned up at Kurt's yard today specifically to have a pre-op pep talk and keep Faith focused on Double-D Day, which she sensed was in danger of being eclipsed by homesickness and missing Rory.

As inspiration, she'd bought Faith a copy of the most recent unauthorised Sylva Frost biography, *No Sylva Spoons*, but Faith showed no inclination to read it, so Carly was recounting the life story of one of her all-time heroines like a Jackanory narrator.

'It says here that Sylva Frost has had no less than twenty cosmetic procedures.'

'Maybe I'll phone Rory in a minute.' Faith went to hang up the bridle.

'D'you know, Sylva was a huge pop star in the Baltic – bigger than Kylie is over here?' Carly told her, silently elbowing Faith's Samsung into the tack-cleaning bucket while her friend's back was turned. 'Before that, she was shortlisted for the Olympic modern pentathlon squad.'

'So she's quite a good rider then?' Faith showed a spark of jealous interest, which Carly pounced on.

'At nineteen she threw in all that fame to get on a bucket flight to Stansted with her mother, and then queue for eight hours to audition for *Star Factor*,' she sighed in awe. 'Being secretly shacked up with one of the judges by the time she reached the final ten was inspired. I still rate her cover version of "Like a Virgin" as better than the original. And she only ever took her top off *after* she was famous here, not before. That's seriously cool.'

Still replaying what Rory had said the night before, Faith wasn't listening. What if Mr Ali Khan made a mistake and her new boobs started to leak or, worse still, they set as hard as hooves?

'She's such a role model,' Carly enthused. 'She went from nothing to marrying Strawberry.'

'Who?' Faith lent half an ear at the silly name.

'Strawberry – duh! Faith you are *so* out of the loop. He's just the Premier League's top Slovak striker, Alojz Strieborny, six foot three of muscle and tufty blond hair signed to Chelsea for record-breaking transfer fees. Our girl bagged him after they met in a Chinawhite VIP room and their wedding was in *Cheers!* over four weeks – I bought them all. It was held at this fabulous spa hotel. She was lowered to the aisle on a gold trapeze entwined with roses, wearing a dress embroidered with over three hundred thousand baby blue Swarovski crystals. They hired in white tigers in cages and fire-eaters.'

'Traditional, then.'

Carly ignored her. 'Then he broke his leg in a foul and lost his place on the bench and she started doing glamour modelling to keep the Chelsea roof garden over their heads, but she had to stop to have their baby boy. *Then* it turned out Strawberry had blown all his millions on fast cars and call girls, and she stuck by him through the bad press while their baby was being born and everything. Six weeks after the birth she was already out at work again, doing a semi-nude photospread in a ladmag.'

'What an achievement.' Faith was searching around for her phone. 'Strawberry must have been proud.'

'No. Get this. When Sylva started earning back their lost fortune by posing for the ladmags and *Playboy* looking a million dollars (with the fake tits that *he* had bought her as a wedding present) our sweet Strawberry announces that the marriage is over in a *Mirror* exclusive.'

'The celebrity equivalent to Relate these days.' Faith rooted through her coat pockets.

Carly sighed, thinking of Grant's betrayal. 'He was such a hypocrite, saying that he was a good Slovak boy who couldn't bear to be married to a woman who showed her body to any man on the street, and that he was divorcing her to be with his childhood girlfriend from Bratislava. Then he demanded the DNA test for their son, claiming Sylva had slept around throughout the marriage.'

'Not quite a fairytale ending, then.' Faith started searching the surfaces.

'But it's a plot twist to the fairytale, get it? That's why every little girl wants to be her. She has already been a sporting superstar, a famous singer, a *Star Factor* finalist, a WAG and a model, right? After that, she became an entrepreneur who would make Deborah Meaden look like an underachiever, with her own lingerie and homeware range, ghosted children's books and bonkbusters, and two autobiographies by the age of twenty-five – at one point she had a third of the *Sunday Times* bestseller lists sewn up – plus a perfume and a swimwear range. You name it, she does it. The woman can merchandise.' Carly held up the biography open at the photo section, where there was a publicity shot of Sylva sitting on a pile of her own books as high as a juggernaut.

This, at least, paused Faith's search for her phone as she looked grudgingly impressed. 'She must work bloody hard.' Then her eye caught the facing page and she yelped with alarm. 'What's Rory doing in there?'

'That's not Rory!' Carly snorted with laughter. 'That's the actor Jonte Frost. Sylva married him two years ago.' She held up a photograph of the couple looking very chic and retro on the steps of Chelsea Registry Office.

'He looks like Rory.'

'No he doesn't,' Carly said huffily. 'Jonte used to be the face of Burberry. Anyway, they divorced when he shagged a co-star on location while Sylva was pregnant. He's notoriously shabby. You can tell, really, can't you?' She studied the photo. 'It's in the face. That type of man. They have that untrustworthy look about them.'

Faith gave up looking for her phone for a moment to snatch up the book and take a closer look. 'I think he's quite dishy.'

'*Definitely* a boob man.' Carly played it to her advantage. 'They call him "Plus Two" in Hollywood.'

'Why?' Faith looked up blankly. 'Does he shoot?'

'Like, *duh*.' Carly pulled a face at her friend's ignorance. 'Over there, Plus Two is a man who'll only invite a date to be his 'plus one' at a party if she's got two big assets.'

'Is a double date a Plus Four, then?'

With Faith's trusty little Samsung drying out on her gayfather's Aga, she and Carly set out for London on Saturday morning, telling everyone they were spending the day shopping. Walking into Mr Ali Khan's consulting room with her boob scrapbook tucked under her arm, Faith focused hard on the thought of metamorphosing from tomboy to glamour girl like Sandra Bullock in *Miss Congeniality*.

She turned to the esteemed surgeon. 'Is it true you did Sylva Frost's breasts? One set, at least?'

'I am not at liberty to say.' He looked away, admiring the fingers that had created such masterpieces.

Her 'procedures' were booked for ten days' time, immediately after having her pearly white veneers fitted in a nearby dental clinic, but Faith kept quiet about those because Carly was worried that Mr Ali Khan would object to her having so much work in one day. 'They're just ultra-cautious about anaesthetic and stuff. You'll be fine.'

'He says I shouldn't muck or ride out for a week after the op,' Faith said worriedly as they drove back.

'I'll help you out. All we have to figure out is how to get you away for forty-eight hours without Kurt and Graeme smelling a rat.'

As Double-D Day approached, Faith became more and more uneasy. Having missed the live television coverage, she leapt on *Horse & Hound* when it arrived in the Thursday post and read the Burghley report, scouring it a dozen times before she was finally convinced that she wasn't mistaken. Rory had not been there.

Her phone had finally dried out enough to work again, but its screen was irreparably water damaged, too white to read or write texts.

She called him with shaking hands.

After what felt like for ever, a voice answered.

'Yes?' A female purr, distinctly foreign.

'Is Rory there?'

'He is in the shower. You want to leave a message, darlink?'

'Tell him Faith says it's all going tits up,' she said in a strangled voice, hanging up.

Chapter 18

'Who was that calling?' Rory walked into the bedroom of his cottage, towelling his wet hair as he sat down on the edge of the bed.

A moment later he was beyond caring as Sylva lifted her shapely leg, swung it across the firm, muscular expanse in front of her and mounted his half-mast cock with a delighted squeal. It expanded eagerly into her.

'Wow! Oh wowowowowowowowow!' Rory gasped, rendered inarticulate by the frankly amazing things she could do with her vaginal muscles. He hadn't been sure he could go again so soon, but she was always guaranteed an encore, it seemed.

He'd had a great many lovers for such a relatively young stud, yet none had been as skilful as Sylva Frost and her pornographic proficiency. He was frankly very intimidated – rather like riding Heart in front of the Beauchamps – but while it felt this good he was more than grateful for the distraction.

That afternoon Upper Springlode was swathed in a grumpy grey mist that wiped out the stunning view and permeated everything with its vile, clammy wetness. It was far too cold and damp to ride, so Rory and Sylva had discovered a very fun alternative.

Rory didn't care that he was just a passing fancy to her: he was wholly content to be her temporary plaything. He was grateful that that she was bored and lonely in her Cotswold weekend house, that it was damp and old-fashioned and that nobody in the area apart from a few village hoodies, a bunch of paparazzi and Rory seemed remotely interested in her.

The locals were being killingly snobbish about the new celebrity arrival, clearly thinking that Sylva's WAG-turned-glamour model status was outclassed by Kates Winslet and Moss, Raffertys junior and senior, Liz Hurley and even the Llewelyn-Bowens. Her recent move to the Cotswolds might have been splashed all over the red-tops and women's weeklies all month but, as she lamented to Rory whenever he coached her on horseback, filmed by her television crew and snapped by the paps throughout the session, none of her new neighbours read that sort of publication or watched her hit show on the Celebrity Channel. Most of them didn't even have a satellite dish because it contravened their Grade II listings. Sylva was definitely not feeling at home in the area and, as always when she was low, she sought male attention. Rory was more than gratified to be her warm welcome and country pursuit on a cold, damp autumn afternoon.

He needed cheering up after forfeiting Burghley and losing Heart as a result. Nell had sent a transporter to collect Cœur d'Or while the Beauchamps were away in Lincolnshire. Hugo was livid, and blamed Rory for handling her badly.

Now Rory was desperate to post a good result on one of Dillon's horses to prove his worth. He was pinning his hopes on the final three day event on the UK calendar, the three-star trials at Blenheim, immediately after which he would relocate to Berkshire. But Humpty was still not quite one hundred per cent, and his preparation was being plagued with setbacks, not least the appalling weather. He was struggling more than ever to get all the work done around the yard. His casual helpers were no match for Faith's efficiency and inexhaustible energy, and he was now spending stupid amounts of time on the phone going through checklists with Jules, Dillon's caretaker-manager who seemed to know alarmingly little about running a yard. She was taking over at the beginning of next week – another interruption to his Blenheim schedule.

His sex life was also getting in the way of competition preparations, but he didn't resent that.

'WOWOWOWOwowowoWOW – oh – WOW – WOW – *WOW*!'

He came with a delicious explosion that firecrackered his body with shuddering aftershocks. Then he slumped back into the pillows, face high with colour, grinning up at Sylva. 'You are ama*zing*!'

She had hardly broken a sweat, her cascade of hair perfectly in place, make-up immaculate, her pink frilly bra still holding her magnificent breasts against her deliciously curvy body.

Rory marvelled at her sexy, sanguine serenity. It was the same when she rode, never seeming to exert herself, yet showing true ability. At first he'd started her off on Magpie, the resident safe hairy cob, but was now happy to let her ride anything on his yard day or night, most especially himself. She was as consummate in the saddle as she was in bed.

Dismounting neatly, she half-passed to the dressing table to reach in her Kelly bag and extract a tissue. Three previous lovemaking sessions with Rory had taught her to bring her own supply – he couldn't be relied upon to have anything absorbent in the house. Toilet paper and kitchen roll were rarities, along with fluffy towels, fresh food, soap and bath plugs. But what he lacked in home comforts, he more than made up for in sex appeal, enthusiasm and charm.

'God, your arse is peachy.' Rory, lolling half off the bed and watching her upside down with his hair on end, let out a wolf whistle.

She wiggled it for him as she piaffed into her pink g-string.

In fact, her arse was veering dangerously towards what the magazines in which she featured on a weekly basis liked to dub 'Sylva's Beefy Backside', 'Sylva's Cellulite Horror' and 'Sylva Weight Gain Shock!'

They had already salaciously reported her flit from the Chilterns to the Cotswolds: 'Heart-broken Sylva Hides Away to dry her Tears after Hollywood Lover Outed!'

Last week the media had also duly taken her bait when she'd appeared at a celebrity film premiere wearing a too-tight Hervé Léger rainbow dress. She now featured on the front cover of almost every showbiz publication. Teeth freshly bleached, forehead botoxed, hair extensions reweaved and body clay wrapped to taut splendour, she looked good and had the bills to show for it, but she also looked every inch of her size-ten dress label. Printing the most unflattering pictures of the occasion that they could buy, the weekly rags were unable to resist speculating the cause of Sylva's 'rocketing weight gain', her 'secret junk food binges', her endless 'misery eating' and her 'piled-on pounds'. With the help of those ubiquitous 'insider sources', they blamed everything from the end of her relationship with the Brit actor to her children having health scares, and all of them claimed to have the 'exclusive' answer, but none of them knew the real truth – she had gained weight to get column inches.

It had been a great week. She was IFOP, IFOJ and very, very far IFOKK. The paparazzi were in her pocket. She had them on side again. She had two photoshoots – one with and one without the kids – scheduled for the following week to disprove the depression claims and show how fabulous her life was. She had initially intended these to take place at her new retreat, Le Petit Château in Upper Springlode, but she couldn't face the idea now that she knew the place better and so had instead hastily rearranged one to a swanky country-park hotel, and before that a high-profile family outing to Blenheim Horse Trials, where she intended to publicly establish her connection with the sport Dillon patronised, and privately to support Rory. He was the one upbeat thing about this place, but he was leaving.

She hated her Cotswolds retreat. On paper, Le Petit Château had seemed the ideal base, an eccentric folly of a house perfect for a princess, with its French-inspired turrets and towers hidden in a wonderful walled garden on the outskirts of the pretty little village. But in reality it wasn't much of a fairytale. What had looked like the mellow gold of locally quarried stone on the glossy brochure photographs was in fact Bradstone and on close inspection almost as ugly as the Duckworths' Coronation Street cladding. The house was not the historic mini castle she and Mama had imagined: it was more of a theatre set, an eighties fabrication designed with no eye for practicality or light. Inside, it was a rabbit warren of small, dark rooms that smelled of mildew. The big open fireplaces were fake, the mullions were fake and the beams were fake. It had originally been custom-built for eccentric seventies glam-rock star Barry Bullion, who was now a tax exile living with a posse of alarmingly young housemaids on an island off the coast of Sumatra. It was only after she'd moved in that Sylva discovered Barry's reputation was as tarnished as his fake gold taps. Rumour had it that the now-empty, ivy-clad pool house had once housed orgies of rent boys and cocaine-snorting schoolgirls, and that the house was said to be haunted by Barry's depressive stalker Queenie, a transsexual who'd hung herself from the fake Japanese pergola shortly after he emigrated.

Brought up on the twofold superstitions of high-grade Slovak folklore and devout religion, Sylva took the restless souls of the undead very seriously indeed.

She refused to stay in the house alone for more than a few minutes at the time, grateful that she had, as usual, travelled with as many members of her entourage as custom-made baby blue Louis Vuitton suitcases. Along with two PAs, her cook and her stylist, she had brought three burly Slovakian cousins with her from Buckinghamshire to clear up the place and redecorate, leaving Mama, the boys and the army of nannies at home in Amersham until the Château was more family friendly.

Her first fortnight in Upper Springlode had brought her no closer to Dillon Rafferty, apart from by her proximity to his home. He was overseas and Sylva had been trapped in her house with just his farm shop, their snooty neighbours, a few rides around his neighbourhood and his playboy eventing protégé to distract her. She felt she would have more chance of bumping into him if she had spent the fortnight hanging around the VIP lounge at Heathrow.

This Cotswold recce had been designed by Mama to be a path-building exercise profiled by her TV crew, with Sylva seen to be chatting up the locals, hacking prettily around the leafy lanes, buying organic veggies and designer cheese from Dillon's farm shop, maintaining a high media profile as the Lodes Valley's loveliest new resident and generally establishing herself as the perfect future wife for the heartthrob rock star turned farmer. Instead, she had got wet, scared and saddle sore, and had largely been overlooked. Rory's obvious desire and admiration was in refreshing contrast to local snobbery.

'You'll have to come and see me in Berkshire,' he said now, head still upside down as he watched her dress, sleepy pewter eyes crinkling appreciatively.

She flashed a non-committal smile, knowing that dabbling with Rory at all was very risky indeed – Mama would have a fit if she knew that her girl was bedding Dillon's sporting interest. But Sylva had always enjoyed dangerous sports. She felt confident that Rory was far too focused on his competitive career to get clingy or committed. Nor would he be indiscreet, too wary of the nature of her fame to want that sort of press attention; it would blow his concentration and his competition prospects. Sylva trusted him. He was a lovely, flirty plaything overflowing with energy that was perfectly suited to converting into sexual endeavour. Sylva's mindset had been much the same when she had been travelling through Europe to compete as a part of the Slovakian modern pentathlon youth squad. Her sexual awakening had come with fellow team members, most of them strappingly good-looking army boys who fell in love with her and fought each other over her. The black eyes and broken noses on the medal podium had been the cause of great speculation when Sylva was among Slovakia's elite junior pentathletes. Like Rory, she'd known no shame or restraint, but she had also been far too selfish and focused upon her sport for real relationships, making her short, passing affairs very discreet. Her taste for sportsmen dated back to those days, although experience had since taught her they made better bedmates than soulmates. As was the case with Rory.

He was a pleasant pick-me-up and very good for the ego while she was carrying so much surplus weight, but her main target was Dillon and she knew that she could not let Mama down by getting distracted. It was good that Rory was moving away from the village. Sylva had to concentrate on the Cheese-maker, as she now thought of her future husband, both musically and as a farmer. Having had a brief pop career herself, Sylva was more of a Madonna fan and found all that guitar-heavy sentiment a bit embarrassing. But Dillon's edible as opposed to audible cheese was certainly delicious and one of the reasons for her continued mysterious weight gain.

Inadvertently forewarned by Rory, Sylva was on full alert for Dillon's only trip home during her stay in the area. He had flown in with daughters Pom and Berry and brought them straight to the farm for a long weekend, disappearing behind the high gates and not coming out.

Sylva spent a frustrating, rain-lashed afternoon on one of Rory's horses trying to get close enough to West Oddford Farm to encounter the family, but the boundaries were impenetrable. Her rather vague, fanciful plan to fall (very carefully) off her horse and land prettily at his feet in Restoration heroine fashion was thwarted.

Instead, she decided to ride back to the stables via Fox Oddfield Abbey, knowing that there was a big bridle path there known locally as God's Corridor, which ran almost past the front door of Pete Rafferty's new stately playpen. She figured that rather than have an entirely wasted morning, she might as well check out the in-laws. Sylva had always thought Mask's former frontman wildly sexy, having grown up with all the band's albums that could be bought on the black market reverently stacked beside the hi-fi in her parents' apartment and a poster of that iconic Warhol image of Pete's wild-haired, laser-eyed face pinned to their kitchen wall.

But her horse had barely trotted twenty yards beneath the dripping branches of the oak trees along the unmarked byway when a flat-capped man in a pick-up brimming with barking dogs, gun racks and halogen lights roared up behind her and ordered her away.

'This is surely a public right of way?' She laid on the Slovak glamourpuss charm but he was impervious, his cap pulled so low over his wide-jawed face that he was unable to see above her booted ankle.

'S'not a bridlepath no more, misses, so youz best go back the way you come.'

Sylva tilted her head winningly. 'And you are?'

'Castigates, they call me. New boss don't want trespassers.' He jerked a big thumb in the direction of the Abbey.

'Is your boss Pete Rafferty?'

'None your business, missus, with respect.'

Apologising politely, Sylva trotted away to drop the horse back at Overlodes and consulted a map in Rory's cottage while her clothes dried over the Rayburn and Rory set about warming her up.

Soon she was lying back across the map with her legs around Rory's waist, but she already had no doubt that she'd taken the correct path marked with the green dashes. Father and son both liked their privacy, it seemed. She would struggle to get anywhere near their inner circle without a personal introduction. Rory might be far from ideal on that front but, being a great gossip, he was at least a superb fount of information and had already told her that the only time Dillon Rafferty was guaranteed to be at home these days was when his two pony-mad little girls visited from the States. Her own sons were frustratingly too young to befriend them, but she was certain there was a way in.

By the time she was dressed again, Sylva had figured out exactly what the password to his inner circle might be, and who might say it best.

Zuzi.

As she walked back from Rory's yard across the little village green known to all as the Prattle, she pulled her mobile from her pocket and called her older sister in Slovakia, her mother tongue sounding curiously out of place in this mist-laced corner of a quintessentially English parish. 'It is time you joined us here, Hana.'

'I cannot leave my family!' Hana's soft voice was strangled with fear as the day she had long dreaded suddenly arrived without warning.

'*We* are your family. Mama is here, and all your cousins,' Sylva insisted. 'I want you here with us. And Zuzi.'

'But . . . but . . .'

'She must come to this country. Think of her education and her future. You cannot deny her any longer. My PA will book a flight for you both. She will email you details.'

'What about Pavol?' Hana asked about her husband in a tiny voice.

'He will stay behind. He has a job.'

'I have a job, Sylva. I am a classroom assistant. I have never left my husband's side in ten years.' She was barely able to whisper for the encroaching tears. 'Zuzi will be heartbroken to leave her friends, her school, her home.'

'She has a new home now.'

The sobs had reached her sister's voice. 'The press will find out, Sylva. The secret will get out. It will ruin your career.'

Sylva stared at a fat Mallard duck waddling towards the pond pursued by several ducklings. 'Perhaps it is time for that too, Hana. Our sad little story would not affect my career now, I think. They may even see this as a happy ending. You will come and then I will decide whether we tell the truth at last.'

There was a small gasp of horror, but Hana knew better than to protest further. Sylva financially supported everything that she and her husband held dear – their home, their holidays, their car and their only, beloved daughter.

After ringing off Sylva watched the ducklings swimming behind their mother, stripes rippling from their tiny slipstreams.

Her groin still hummed from its joyful union with Rory's eager thrusts, fluttering twitches of pleasure lingering inside her like those ripples upon the water's surface. She patted her rounded belly, which was spilling very slightly over her skinny jeans. It was time for self-denial again – sexual and nutritional. She must forfeit occasional sex for regular exercise with her personal trainer, fasting and dieting back down to her usual size. As she walked the last few hundred yards to her horrible faux château, she wondered whether it was finally time for a tummy tuck. Three pregnancies would eventually take their toll, even if one did a hundred abdominal crunches a day, as she did. She wasn't eager to revisit the surgeon's knife again – the last time she'd flown to LA for a few discreet adjustments, she'd had a reaction to the anaesthetic from which it had taken her weeks to fully recover. But plastic surgery was a necessary evil these days, she reminded herself. No pain no gain, as they said in this country. Like childbirth.

'Two pregnancies,' she reminded herself as she reached into her pocket and pressed the remote control for her electric gates.

Chapter 19

Lying awake the night before her marathon dentistry-then-surgery makeover, Faith rehearsed a call to Mr Ali Khan, explaining that she couldn't possibly go through with it.

But the following morning, as she looked at her boyish chest in the mottled mirror of the mobile home's badly lit bathroom, she was less certain. If she had breasts like Sylva Frost a whole new world would open up to her, along with Rory's fickle heart.

Carly's escape plan worked perfectly. Kurt and Graeme were away competing in Germany. At her friend's insistence, Faith texted them to say that she had been kicked in the face by one of the young stallions and was going to have to get her nose re-set and her teeth fixed, but that they mustn't worry because Carly's family would look after her. As her father was a dentist, the gayfathers assumed she was in safe hands. They had no idea that Carly's parents were in fact away in Spain. Now Faith could legitimately disappear for forty-eight hours.

Carly bustled her and her pre-packed hospital bag into the pink Mini Cooper and accelerated along the half mile of tree-lined drive like a getaway driver, long before the other seven staff members at Piaffe Court could notice a thing.

In less than an hour the girls were walking into the Harley Street dental clinic that was the first port of call in turning Faith into the woman of Rory's dreams.

'Can I get you anything?' Carly asked caringly just before Faith temporarily lost the power of speech in order to gain the power of a whiter than white smile.

'A new phone.' Faith thrust her purse at her.

By teatime, now in Mr Ali Khan's care a few hundred yards along the same illustrious street, dopy from a pre-med and her mouth still floppy from her veneer fitting, Faith was waiting in her private room. Carly had gone to have her hair extensions reglued, leaving her friend with a fluffy pink good-luck teddy bear and strict instructions not to play with her new mobile phone.

Faith pulled it from its box and groaned. It was baby pink. Groggily she slotted in her old sim card and switched it on in case there were any messages, but its sleek face reported nothing apart from a low battery.

Unable to stop herself, she texted Rory, whom she knew would be arriving in Blenheim that day. *Good Luck.*

It took all her will power not to add a line of *x*s. The pre-med was making her feel horribly maudlin. Tears filled her eyes and her vision was so blurry that she struggled to read the reply. The nurses had appeared to wheel her through to the operating theatre now.

'You'll have to leave that here, love,' said one, trying to take the new phone away from her.

'No!' She snatched it back and blinked several times at the screen in front of her.

Miss you.

Suddenly overwhelmed with certainty and relief, she grabbed the nurse's arm urgently. 'Tell Mr Ali Khan I've changed my mind. I don't want boobs like Sylva Frost after all. I want boobs like my mother. And a nose like my mother.'

The nurse looked agitated, knowing that perfectionist Farouk, now scrubbed and waiting, would go mad at any last-minute change. 'What are those breasts like?'

'Beautiful,' Faith struggled upright. 'I want to look just like my mother. She's beautiful.'

'Do you have a photograph, perhaps?'

Faith scrabbled woozily for her bag and brought out her little leather-bound wallet of snapshots, opening it up to reveal a photo-graph of a young Anke with her Olympic gold. She held it out triumphantly.

'Dear child' – the nurse's eyebrows shot up – 'this woman looks just like you.'

Chapter 20

Beccy had slept in the strangest of places all over the world with some unusual bedfellows, from cosying up with Mongolian hosts in yurts in the hinterlands to keeping close quarters with twelve Vietnamese siblings in boat houses in floating villages, from head-to-toeing with tropical insect life in hammocks in the rain-forest to watching nocturnal rats investigate shanty shacks in city slums. But sharing the sleeping quarters of a horsebox with Rory Midwinter in a bitterly cold corner of a windswept field in Oxfordshire looked set to be a night she would never forget.

Her first impression of Rory was of a pro skier's physique, a big, mellow smile and gorgeous sleepy eyes, and the prospect of work-ing with him at Haydown was initially a very uplifting one. All too briefly. Then Twitch the terrier attacked Karma the Labradoodle puppy and everything changed.

Rory was unrepentant and even had the nerve to laugh when poor, terrified Karma, trying to escape, became stuck fast behind the chemical loo in the horsebox shower room, her fluffy coat attaching her to the Velcro towel holder. He was, Beccy decided, arrogant and selfish, and took nothing seriously. He was supercilious, spoiled and very rude. He called Karma a 'shagpile on legs' a 'posh mongrel' and a 'twit'. Beccy was so hurt that, to her shame, she burst into noisy tears, which at least silenced an astonished Rory.

Later, when he had found the manners to apologise, and tried to make amends by asking her about herself, he fell asleep while she was talking.

Beccy now thought that he was, quite simply, vile.

She knew it was unsportsmanlike, but she hoped he fell off. His lovely young coloured horse, Humpty, who had settled in his tem-porary stabling with much less fuss than his master, was far too good for him, as was his famous owner, along with his host and coach, Hugo.

She had also taken against Rory because he was unapologetically hijacking Hugo's bunk in the horsebox. For a brief and very excit-ing moment before that, it had looked as though just Beccy and her brother-in-law were going to share the state-of-the-art Oakley with its slide-out pod that projected from the side of the lorry at the press of a button to double the luxury accommodation, wood panelling, power shower and flat-screen television. But then Rory had driven up beside them in his ancient, leaking bus of a horsebox belching diesel fumes and Hugo had insisted his new protégé stay in the Oakley while he headed off to the Woodstock bed and breakfast to brave the family room with Tash and the kids, hoping for at least a few hours' sleep before each day of the competition. Jenny was sleeping in a nearby horsebox with her German-rider fiancé Dolf. That left Rory and Beccy sharing the state-of-the-art penthouse on wheels.

After fiddling with everything from the DVD player to the microwave – and breaking them, Beccy was certain – Rory wandered off with Twitch at his heels for the riders' briefing and a first cross-country course walk, leaving her to wrestle with all his badly packed trunks of horse paraphernalia. To her horror, Hugo had told her that she was going to groom for Rory while Jenny did everything for him, assisted by Tash.

'But Tash has two babies to look after!' she had pleaded.

'She has her au pairs, plus Sophia is around to help. Tash's focus will be entirely on me.'

Beccy wished *her* focus could be entirely on Hugo, as it longed to be, but she was stuck with the ever-yawning, big-headed Rory.

And her focus was about to shift dramatically to the North Island half way across the globe, from which she received her first text in almost a week.

Horses and Lem on way to airport. Going to sort things out and follow on. L

Beccy let out a whimper of fear. She hadn't heard from him since the night he had phoned to talk about his father and she'd told him not to come.

She quickly checked through her saved messages and found the one sent three weeks earlier, listing his arrival dates and details. Reading it again she groaned and sat down heavily on a tack trunk.

She'd somehow thought that if she ignored the situation it would go away, but instead it was about to blow up in her face.

Her hands shook as she tried to fashion a reply that would put him off, but she knew it was far too late for that. In the end all she could think of was: *Our conversations never took place. Hugo must never know. If you say anything I will deny it.*

He replied in an instant, even though it was the early hours in New Zealand: *Don't be frightened, Tash, I know you are unhappy. Want to change that.*

She tried to picture him sitting surrounded by the detritus of packing. She somehow imagined a little weatherboarded farmhouse in the middle of wooded, windswept hills. His horses had been loaded up in the middle of the night and taken away for their long journey across the world, leaving him all alone, packing up his few possessions and saying farewell to his family and friends, to his long-suffering mother and freeloading father.

Beccy already had a clear picture of him in her mind, a vignette of the sexy Devil on Horseback from the wrong side of the tracks, the loner, the self-starter who had succeeded against all the odds in his professional and sporting careers – driven, ruthless, touched with genius. It was a very sexy daydream. But now she had been caught napping and the daydream looked set to become a living nightmare, she was terrified.

She was about to switch off her phone when another message came through.

I won't give you away. I promise. Saved you once before, remember? Can do it again. Counting the days. L

Beccy held down the power button to make it all go away. If he worked out exactly whose life he had saved, she really was in deep trouble.

Not long after unpacking her case at the Woodstock bed and break-fast and noticing that, while she had brought endless changes of clothes, comforters, nappies and even DVDs for the children, she had failed to pack so much as a change of knickers for herself, Tash concluded that she probably wasn't quite ready for such a marathon undertaking as supporting Hugo at a three day event with the children in tow.

Worse still, she had left her purse on the kitchen table at Haydown and only had Hugo's spare cash to keep her going. Forty pounds and a lot of loose change that he had been only too grateful to relinquish didn't get you far in the Blenheim food stands when catering for the faddy tastes of two mute Czechs and a toddler, let alone fund a capsule wardrobe suitable for a supportive eventing wife and groom.

She would have asked Veruschka if she could borrow some clothes were it not for the fact that the twenty-something from Bohemia only seemed to possess size eight lemon yellow tracksuits and bootlace-strap vests with *Hot Lips* spelled out on the front in pink sequins. Vasilly, at six feet tall with a Budvar beer belly and shoulders like a shot-putter, was more Tash's size, but lived in very tight stonewashed jeans and a donkey jacket the likes of which hadn't been seen in the UK since *Boys from the Blackstuff* was on television.

The Jelineks were clearly finding it hard to settle in at Haydown. Homesick, insular and disapproving, they combined extreme politeness with a deep suspicion of all they found. While they worked like Trojans, their very fixed ideas and the language barrier meant that they rarely did what she asked of them. Veruschka was singularly determined to disinfect everything in the house using the strongest chemicals at her disposal, regardless of whether she was wiping down a highchair or an oil painting of one of Hugo's ancestors; Vasilly seemed set on an equally ambitious mission to run the petrol strimmer over every inch of Haydown's many hundreds of acres, strapping himself into his goggles and ear-protectors at dawn and marching off like a man possessed. Hugo thought they were hopeless and called them the 'Blank Czechs', but Tash appreciated their efforts and obvious love of children, and was trying her best to include them in every aspect of family life. Away from home, however, it was a much greater strain to look out for them, or 'keep them in Czech' as Hugo put it. They clearly had no idea what to make of a large scale horse trials in operation, and Blenheim Palace itself left them open-mouthed.

'Queen liff here!' Veruschka told Cora excitedly when they first set eyes on Blenheim Palace, and no amount of painstaking explanations from Tash would convince the au pair that the historic home of the Spencer-Churchill family was not Buckingham Palace.

Having arrived at the Oxfordshire venue on a September morning as cold as any January night, Tash had since endured a non-stop pandemonium of crying children and lost Czechs. Now Hugo insisted that she walk the course with him, promising to take it slowly to allow for her gradual return to fitness. With a double buggy and a brace of confused Eastern Europeans in tow, photographing everything with their mobile phones to text back to their relatives, Tash hardly helped Hugo's concentration and her own was far too shot to think straight.

'I'd aim to go the direct route on both horses here,' she told him at a particularly technical-looking run of three huge logs shaped like the Greek letter Xi.

'Are you sure?' Hugo blew a plume of condensed air through his teeth as he closed one eye and cocked his head at the double bounce. 'That's a big ask for Vix.'

A full sister to The Fox, Vixen was as beautiful as she was changeable; spooky, weather-dependent, capricious and flighty, she nevertheless had speed and heart on her side and was quite brilliant on her day, but she could need nursing round on a bad day and her cross-country routes always needed meticulous planning. As her biggest test to date, the Blenheim course had to be carefully masterminded.

'The alternative route is ridiculously long.'

'I guess you're right.' He gave it another sceptical look, but Tash was already kicking off the brake of the empty baby buggy and chasing after Veruschka, who had just gathered a mewling Amery in her arms and was jogging towards the next fence with him pressed to her sequinned chest while, alongside her, Vasilly bounced a rather alarmed and unstable Cora on his shoulders. They saw course walking as accelerated sight-seeing and were keen to press on, whereas Hugo needed time at each fence to look at the options, plan sightlines and talk tactics.

Hugo caught them all up at a big new drop fence with a second, skinny element almost immediately upon landing.

'Need to put the brakes on here.' He studied it thoughtfully, knowing that his second ride – Sophia and Ben's half-share horse Sir Galahad, an ex point-to-pointer with a fearsome hold – would be a nightmare to slow down enough to take the fence safely, particularly if he had taken the direct route at the Xi.

'Good point,' Tash agreed breathlessly, applying the buggy brake while she harnessed the reclaimed Amery back into the safety of his padded seat, ignoring Veruschka's protestations that 'he cold'. With a fluffy buggy sleeve and two blankets, she thought he was far more snug and secure in her personal care.

'We hungry.' Vasilly appeared at her side to hand over Cora.

Tash offered him a tenner, imagining they could navigate their way to a food outlet.

He looked as though he was going to cry.

'Okay – I'll get you food.' Smiling reassuringly despite her reluctance to leave Hugo's side, Tash resigned herself to queuing for the food before Vasilly's sugar low made him even more of a burden.

'Can you get some more cash out for me later?' she asked Hugo as she prepared to desert him just half way around the course.

'I *said* I would,' he hissed, dumping all the dog leads on her so that she was forced to take charge of the Bitches of Eastwick and the Rat Pack as well as the buggy, suddenly finding herself feeling like a arctic sled driver pulled in all directions by a team of mismatched huskies – particularly given the chillingly cold look Hugo cast her over his shoulder as they went their separate ways.

She hastily bought fish and chips for her au pairs and then breast-fed Amery in the back of the car while Cora wolfed down a packet of crisps and sang the first line of 'Baa Baa Black Sheep' repeatedly until Tash could hear nothing else in her head for the rest of the day.

That night was even worse.

Amery, just six weeks old and feeding every three hours, already had lungs like a town crier and could wake the dead at three in the morning, let alone light-sleeping Hugo and daughter. With one muttering cursed oaths and the other chirping 'Daddy!' and 'Baby' while she struggled to stand up in her Grobag in the travel cot, they kept Tash awake between feeds, guiltily wondering why she had agreed to come. Lying awake late at night like this was when her mind played tricks, obsessing about the flowers Hugo bought that weren't for her, and the texts he received from the mysterious V, whom she was no closer to identifying. Yet, as she well knew, the dead of night during a three day event wasn't the moment to tackle such things. She was here to support her husband and rediscover the golden era of the Beauchampions.

At four in the morning, Hugo – also wide awake and re-walking the course in his mind for the fifth time – muttered, 'Sod this. Let's have sex.'

They had only made love once since Amery's birth and, to Tash's shame, she'd lost enthusiasm half way through. The mind had been willing – Hugo always got her heart and groin revving excitedly, and after a glass of wine and a very passionate kiss on the sofa she'd been practically dragging his clothes off – but the body hadn't been quite ready. She'd soon become acutely aware of her wobbly stomach, new stretch marks and big, ugly pants and nursing bra. Hugo, as enthusiastic and bold as always, had taken a while to register her change of heart, by which time she had unequivocally wanted it all to stop, stupid hormonal tears bubbling up as quickly as her libido died down.

And again, her instant response was one of electric excitement and anticipation. Amazingly, the children had both gone to sleep in the past ten minutes and the room was a dark, exciting cloak of sexual energy. Hugo's warm, hard body pressed to hers, his breath on her neck, hard-on rising into the hollow of her back, a warm, steel-hard thigh sliding between her legs.

As he reached around beneath her arm to caress the swell of her breast, she gasped with apprehension and freefall lust. She didn't want the spell to break, that mounting desire to fail her, her body to recoil, the children to wake and distract her from lover to mother.

Spooned tight against her, he slid every long, luscious inch of hard cock into her with slow, patient self-control, letting her eager body suck him up further and higher.

Leisurely, rhythmically, he claimed her back until her heart was roaring and racing, pulse drumming, her body as desired and desirable as it had ever been, filling up with the first effervescent bubbles and pops of an orgasm.

'Baa Baa Black Sheep . . .'

Cora was awake.

The bubbles instantly went flat and the dark cloak lifted.

'Mummy – baa baa – baby!' The little girl trilled.

On clue, with barely a snuffle of warning, Amery started to bawl at top capacity.

'Fucking great!' Hugo muttered under his breath as he withdrew and lay back against the pillow with a frustrated groan.

Tash, suddenly feeling very wobbly in every sense of the word, pulled on her baggy sleepwear and crawled out of bed to settle them.

As soon as she left the bed, her warm patch was occupied by Beetroot, who crawled up from the foot of the duvet on her belly to adoringly kiss and lick Hugo's arm and ear.

'Thanks for the offer, Beet' – he tucked her under his arm and scratched her proffered chest – 'but I'd rather your mistress was doing that.'

His eyes gleamed in the dark as he looked over Beetroot's head to where Tash was breastfeeding Amery on the little armchair between the travel cots, while quietly singing Cora to sleep.

'I've got more chance of winning on Sunday than rogering the missus this week,' he sighed.

Beetroot wagged her thin tail sympathetically and licked his chin.

★

In the horsebox park on the Blenheim estate, another dog was determined to lick his bedfellows. Eager to make amends with Karma, Twitch the terrier would not settle with Rory on the bunk above the Luton cab. Instead, he had scrabbled up on to the foot of Beccy's bed and was trying to penetrate the sleeping bag in which Karma and her mistress were companionably snuggled.

Amazingly, Karma snored and grunted contentedly, fast asleep.

Unable to sleep at all, Beccy listened irritably to the snuffling and whining as Twitch scrabbled and nibbled at the zip near her ankle. There was a distinctly damp sensation penetrating the layers of duck down.

Across the darkened living quarters, Rory let out a yawn. 'Beccy,' he called in a soft but arrogant drawl. 'Can you roll over? You're snoring again.'

'It's not me!' she hissed back indignantly. 'It's the dog.'

'Okay, whatever. Roll the dog over.'

'Which one?' she muttered, aiming a sly kick at Twitch through the sleeping bag, but he gripped on to her bunk with his claws, still whining in what he clearly thought to be an endearing fashion, and Rory fell silent, trying again to sleep.

Beccy gazed moon-eyed into the darkness and weighed up the relative merits of Hugo and Lough Strachan. On paper it was a closely fought thing, with Lough coming out fractionally ahead because he wasn't married, wasn't a father and had sexy tattoos. But in her sleepless heart there was no contest. Hugo won every time. She sighed dreamily and thought about his face, imagined it hovering above her, tilting to kiss her mouth, muttering 'I love you Beccy, I love you with all my heart.'

'What?'

She blinked in alarm at Rory's voice breaking into her fantasy. Had she said something out loud?

'Nothing!' she whispered, heart hammering.

'I thought you said something?'

'No. Just having a dream.'

'Okay. Well please dream more quietly.'

After another ten minutes, during which Beccy tried very hard not to breathe too loudly, not to think about Hugo and not to listen to Twitch whinging and scrabbling at her feet, she suddenly became aware of a strange lapping sensation around her toes. Twitch had broken through the toughened two-way anti-arctic zip and was doing a little soft-soaping en route to his Labradoodle target.

Beccy started to giggle, the combination of tickly tongue and sleepless silliness heightening her muffled hysteria.

Twitch slurped all the more eagerly, knowing that he'd finally broken down the defences and was making headway in his charm offensive.

'Oooh!' Beccy let out a little squeal and pulled her foot away as a sharp tooth caught her toenail.

'Oh, for God's sake!' Rory muttered. 'If it's not enough that you snore, whine and scratch at your bed like the first Mrs Rochester, the horny groaning thing is just too much.'

'What?' Beccy gulped, suddenly horrified that he might think his dog was pleasuring her.

But the truth of the situation was almost as bad.

Rory thought that she was masturbating.

'Look, I'm a pretty impenetrable sleeper as a rule,' he grumbled now, 'but tomorrow's a big day and I haven't had a drink tonight, so the hangover I arrived with earlier is turning into bloody delirium tremens up here. I have to sleep this mother off to get through that dressage test, so I'd really appreciate it if you drop the volume on any gusset typing going on down there. I'm all for that usually, too – especially if I can watch – but frankly tonight's killing me. Pax?'

Beccy was too frozen with mortification – not to mention white-hot anger – to reply.

She booted Twitch off the bed, feeling slightly guilty because it wasn't really his fault and she was projecting her anger on a small, irritatingly persistent dog when it was his master she wanted to kick squarely in the balls.

Closing her eyes tightly and burying her face in her pillow, Beccy found that she could no longer fantasise about Hugo's rearing manhood thrusting towards her and was instead visualising the toe of her foot thrusting towards Rory's precious man-package. It was a surprisingly satisfying way to pass the sleepless minutes and before she knew it she was dropping into dreamland and Rory's package took on a life of its own, swept along by her subconscious into the most extraordinary shapes.

Chapter 21

The first day of dressage at Blenheim was marked by high winds and uninterrupted autumnal sunshine. It was far colder than usual for this time of year, and the northerly gusts stripped golden leaves from trees and paper wrappers from bins like metallic particles in a giant glitter lamp, but it made for beautiful scenes in the ancient park as the lake rippled like a giant silvery salmon skin, the blue skies flattered the magnificent palace and horses with the wind up their tails performed airs above the ground.

Hugo's first ride was no exception. The young Vixen, one of Snob's progeny, had none of her siblings' sense and practically turned herself inside out with fear as the dressage arena flower arrangements flew past at ear level. As all dressage tests are marked the same regardless of the weather, Hugo received a cricket score of penalties and was well down the field.

Rory, graced with an after-lunch slot during which the wind dropped and the sun strengthened, benefiting from the judges' post-prandial generosity and emboldened by the arrival of Sylva Frost to cheer him on, rode the test of his life on Humpty, whose back end was as bright white as his front was glossy black, making him look as though he'd galloped into an ink pot.

Left holding his warm-up bandages and his mobile phone as Rory danced around the arena like a gay hussar, Beccy tried to be critical but she knew he was riding magnificently and the horse was responding with something truly magical. He looked like a Red Indian on a celebrated warhorse, and the audience – a smattering of dressage devotees and chilly shoppers taking a break from the retail village to eat their burgers in the stands – lit up.

Rory's phone was also lighting up in Beccy's grip as text message after text message poured in from the same source. Faith.

Never one to respect privacy, Beccy read them all with a raised eyebrow and little interest as a procession of *How's it going? How RU? Tell me how UR getting on?* messages floated past.

Eventually, tempted by her mischief gremlins, she sent a reply. *Been arrested for public sodomy in palace grounds.*

When Rory seemed genuinely surprised and rather overwhelmed to find himself briefly topping the leaderboard, Beccy felt a needle of guilt at her behaviour, but then he ruined it by swaggering off with a glamorous posse to have champagne in the members' tent without so much as a thank-you, let alone a personal introduction, leaving her to do all the work to prepare Humpty and his kit for the gruelling day to come.

The arrival of Sylva Frost, her family and supporters, her documentary crew and a *Cheers!* photoshoot team effectively took over the members' tent and soon threatened to hijack the entire event but nobody complained – at least not openly – because the press coverage was so immediate and so phenomenal. It was predicted that cross-country day attendance could increase by as much as ten per cent if she stayed around. On a cold weather year when the event clashed with a rugby international, this was invaluable exposure.

Sylva was feeling rather bad-tempered. First, because she had not eaten anything but cabbage soup in three days; secondly, because Dillon was not there; mostly because Mama *was* there, along with the children.

'You must be seen with them,' Mama had hissed as they rushed between chauffeur-driven cars and private marquees, her golden-bullet hairdo safely pegged down by a Chanel scarf.

'They cramp my style,' Sylva hissed back, weighed down by eighteen-month-old Hain rather than the usual designer handbag.

She knew her mother was right, but she still resented being manipulated and wanted to be child-free to get to know Rory's event team, particularly his handsome coach, Hugo Beauchamp.

As it turned out, she hardly exchanged two words with Hugo, who eschewed the champagne tents in favour of the stable lines, from which Sylva's entourage was banned.

Rory, however, was a welcome distraction. Sylva was only too happy to flirt in return, despite Mama's disapproval and the fish eyes of so many cameras trained on her. She felt rebellious and light-headed from lack of food and so, accepting an impromptu invitation to the formal reception in the magnificent Orangery that evening, she arrived in a moss green velvet tube dress and six inch heels that showed off her temporary curves. Unhampered by children, she flirted outrageously with Rory all evening.

Riding high on his dressage score and his new-found celebrity as Hugo's protégé, Rory was on fire. His ego was well flocked enough to believe that Sylva's solitary reason for attending the trials was to see him, and the thought fuelled his drive to win. Amazingly, he stayed sober a third night running, although he had no such abstinence in other departments.

Erection pressing urgently into her side, he steered Sylva into a dark corner of the neglected coat check, both hopelessly excited by the risk of public exposure.

'Where are you staying tonight?' he breathed into her ear between kisses.

'A hotel near Oxford.'

'Is your driver waiting outside?'

'Yes, but we cannot go there – my children are there. We must go to your horsebox.' The novelty of it excited her enormously.

'Beccy is there.'

'Who?' Her eyes flashed with gratifying jealousy.

'Hugo's groom.'

'Make her wait outside.' She unzipped his fly and reached inside.

Rory groaned as all the blood from his body seemed to rush towards her touch.

'I can't do that.'

'Then maybe she would like to join in?'

He groaned even louder, attracting the attention of a passing waitress. She'd teased him before that she liked threesomes, but he had no great desire to share Sylva with strange Beccy and her self-pleasuring, dog-hugging weirdness.

'Definitely not your type,' he laughed.

'Then, my darlink,' she giggled, hand closing firmly around his balls, 'we will do it right here.'

Sidling behind a clothes rail and pulling a brace of long coats across to cloak them like curtains, the couple hastily and breathlessly united, rattling Barbours, Puffas and finest worsted tweed on their hangers.

Just as they were thrusting and gasping towards an exquisite photo-finish, the coat hangers were swept aside and a very dog-eared Haggart shooting coat pulled from a hanger.

'Don't mind me!' laughed a bright voice. 'Oh, hi Rory. I haven't seen you since you were in the Pony Club. You *are* doing well. Super dressage. Give my regards to your mother.'

'Who was that?' Sylva squeaked, terrified that it was someone who would expose her to the press and thus scupper her plans to bag Dillon Rafferty.

'Don't worry. It was just Penny Moncrieff. She won't have a clue who you are.'

'Thanks.' Sylva wasn't sure whether to be relieved or mortified, but she was certainly put off her stroke sufficiently to lose interest in Rory and their mutual pleasure amid the country clothing.

Returning to the horsebox in a foul temper, Rory found Beccy watching a DVD of last year's Blenheim, snuggling up to Karma and loyally sewing the seams of Hugo's best cross-country breeches.

'Who rained on your parade?' she asked.

Rory was too glum to answer. Gathering Twitch to his chest, he clambered up into his bunk and pulled the covers over his head.

Tactfully switching off the DVD, Beccy picked up her phone and took Karma outside for a final run, daring herself to check if there were any messages.

She switched the phone on and jumped sky high when it beeped an alert, but it was just listing missed calls. One, predictably, was from her mother. Two were from Lough. She checked the log details, calculating that he had called in the early hours of the morning New Zealand time, which was odd because she knew his flight times and he should have been airborne.

She leaned back against the horsebox, tilting her head up to look at the stars and shivering as the cold wind bit at her skin. She could hear chattering and laughter in the lorries around her that glowed like a miniature city set up in a windblown Oxfordshire field. She suddenly felt horribly excluded from it all, a stranger forced to watch life from the outside, much as she had felt all her life.

Save me again, she texted Lough.

When Beccy's phone finally beeped with a reply, Rory woke up and started grumbling at her to switch the bloody thing off. *I'm the one who needs saving now.*

Feeling very cold and very panicky, Beccy switched her phone to silent mode. An hour later another message came. *I've screwed up. Totally screwed up.*

Chapter 22

Blenheim was lashed by rain and high winds on the second day of competition. As a result, the dressage suffered from low spectator numbers and high penalties. Last in the arena, Hugo's horse Sir Galahad was just as unforgiving as his previous ride and failed to reward Hugo's loyal, sodden followers with anything spectacular as he squelched around the rectangle like a reluctant teenager dragging his feet through Peter Jones for a school uniform fitting. When a burger container flew between his front legs as he cantered up the centre line, Sir Galahad swerved, bucked and then planted himself on the spot. Hugo's score was even worse than on Vixen the day before and left him too far out of contention for any honours unless he could pull off a cross-country miracle, by riding clear inside the time while everyone else took the scenic route.

The last thing he wanted to face as he emerged from the riders' tent with his dismal test sheet was a barrage of photographers and a film crew, but such was his fate when Sylva Frost shimmied up to him, trout pout curling into a devilish smile that rained scented air-kisses around him.

'Uuugo,' she laid on the Bond Girl accent, employed as always when faced with an attractive but disinterested man. 'You have been avoiding me! I think you don't vant to sell me a horse.'

With a baby blue cowboy hat crammed on her platinum extensions, and wearing a matching baby blue Puffa, fake tan darker than a teak woodstain, and brown leather jeans so tight and shiny that her slender legs disappearing into Ugg boots resembled sapling trunks planted in terracotta pots, she cut a ludicrous figure amid the mud, rain and wind-whipped canvas. Hugo had neither the time nor the inclination to get involved, particularly with a man waving a vast, insect-like camera at him from one shoulder like a grumpy extra from a *Star Wars* battle scene.

Hugo couldn't take Sylva seriously and was certain that any non-sense she was spouting about buying an event horse was purely for publicity, but he was far too well brought up – not to mention aware of recent blights to his public image – to be rude to her face, particularly in front of her camera crews.

'Indeed, nothing would give me greater pleasure. Why not walk with me, and we'll talk . . .' He strode ahead and she was forced into hot pursuit, shapely Rear of the Year captured from every angle as it raced after him.

Hugo wanted to have a quick word with Ben and Sophia, who had brought family and friends to come along to support their horse, believing Sir Galahad was really in with a chance. He felt it only right that he commiserate and give a thorough explanation before he got wrapped up with other commitments, but the Merediths were nowhere to be seen and Tash had his phone.

He'd reluctantly agreed to make an appearance and a short speech at a drinks reception being hosted by his sponsors, followed by a rather tedious photocall at Mogo's trade stand. His natural instinct was to find Tash and walk the cross-country course with her once more, putting his lousy dressage behind him, but with any renewal of the sponsorship deal so precariously poised he knew that he had to keep the clothing label sweet, particularly as Rory was proving a rather wayward member of the Mogo team. He was the first person Hugo spotted in their sponsor's hospitality tent, flirting with the managing director's wife. He could see Tash making a valiant attempt to distract the attention of the managing directors away from the overexcited Rory, but with both children and the Czechs in tow, she wasn't doing the Beauchampions any favours. Sensing an uphill struggle ahead, Hugo braced himself.

What he hadn't anticipated was his sponsors' delight when Sylva Frost arrived after him; it was rather like Camilla arriving as guest of honour at a charity fundraiser, only to be followed in by The Queen.

Immediately swamped by Mogo VIPS and unable to get close to Tash, who not only had his heart in his pocket, but also his lifeline in the form of his mobile phone, Hugo was forced to introduce Sylva to the throng. He did this with a polite, stiff-jawed respect, but it was obvious that he didn't want to be associated with her. A few, especially the snobbish older eventing fraternity, concurred with a cold handshake, but when the flavour of the month arrives to sweeten a rather embittered little mix, it's a mouth-watering moment guaranteed to get tongues wagging.

Across the tent Tash tried, and failed, to stop jealousy slice through her when she saw who was prowling around her husband as excitedly as a kitten rubbing its whiskers on catmint. Sylva was so sylph-like and petite that you could fit the whole of her into one leg of Tash's jeans.

Hearing Hugo's phone beep in her pocket, she resisted the urge to dive behind a lifesize cutout of her husband receiving his Olympic team gold and check if the text was from V. Hugo's new handset was far too tricky to navigate quickly, besides which she had promised herself that she wouldn't dwell on the V texts or Waitrose flowers, which were undoubtedly perfectly innocent. This week was all about offering unconditional family support and she was determined to tame her suspicion radar.

Beside Tash, and oblivious to the small media storm at the entrance, Vasilly and Veruschka were devoting all their attentions to the children and the buffet respectively. Both had quickly tired of the delights of three day eventing. Veruschka complained that their bed was too soft, the breakfast in the B and B was too greasy, and that the weather was too cold. Vasilly, a more laid-back character from what Tash could surmise, was apparently suffering from chronic fatigue brought about by lack of nutrition. He seemed to be busy remedying that right now as he laid into the buffet common to all these events: vast silver foil trays crammed with sandwich triangles, still sweaty and flat from too-tight cling-film and canapés that looked suspiciously like something a Nolan sister and Christopher Biggins would advertise in *Coronation Street* ad breaks.

'He will be ill, I tell him,' Veruschka said to Tash with a jerk of her head towards her boyfriend. As she did so she laid Amery out on a stretch of white tablecloth, changing bag at the ready. 'He ees greedy peeg.'

'What are you doing?' Tash asked in alarm as she suddenly realised that her au pair was stripping her baby in full view of her sponsors' most valued clients, family and friends.

'He haff dirty nappy.'

'Not here, Veruschka!' Tash hissed.

'I weel not change baby in plastic lavatory box!'

'Of course not. We can go back to the horsebox.'

'He is miles away.'

'Then I'm sure the waiters can find us somewhere more discreet behind—'

Too late. Amery was naked from the waist down and a nappy

containing something resembling piccalilli was thrust at Tash while Veruschka delved in the bag for wipes and Sudocrem.

She found herself holding the laden nappy out in front of her as Vasilly turned to her, big cheeks bulging and half a dozen chicken skewers between his fingers like unlit sparklers.

'Ees good!' he spluttered approvingly.

For one ludicrous moment Tash thought that he was going to dunk a skewer in the offending nappy, but he simply beamed at her.

Cora let out an approving shriek from knee height as she wobbled around pulling at the tablecloths and peering beneath the trestles.

Hugo finally closed in on her, the baby-blue Barbie at his side. 'Tash! At last. You haven't met Sylva yet, have you?' He immediately peeled off towards the buffet, having not eaten all day.

'No – we missed each other yesterday – hello there!' Tash held the nappy behind her back and looked down at the cowboy hat, beneath which she could see only a glossy pout. For a brief moment jealousy and low self esteem curdled in her belly, then Sylva disarmed her with a single blow.

'These are your children? They are so beautiful!'

Sinking down on to her haunches she cooed at Cora, who was now playing peekaboo amid the overhanging tablecloths. Instantly identifying an audience, the little girl twirled, giggled and ducked behind the white damask, only to bob her head up a moment later with shrieks of delight. Sylva giggled along with equal enchantment. Even Amery, now with a fresh nappy and buttoned back into his pramsuit, was lifted upright in time to see the magical blue figure with the big white smile straighten up, home in on him and kiss his nose. He gurgled in appreciation.

Tash's heart was won.

Not so Veruschka, who snatched the baby to her chest and glared at Sylva over his downy head.

Meanwhile, still in possession of a full nappy and an uncertain smile, Tash was making introductions.

'This is Veruschka and this is Vasilly.' She managed to attract the attention of the big Czech who was now guzzling his way through a tray of stuffed cherry tomatoes. Noticing Sylva for the first time, his eyes bulged and he started to choke.

'You come from the same country, of course!' Tash fumbled on like a demented hostess, realising that her social skills were as out of practice as her supportive-wife ones.

'You are from Slovakia?' Sylva asked in English, rather pointedly, her native accent nowhere to be heard – she had a disconcerting ability to drop it at a moment's notice.

'*»eški*,' Vasilly muttered, spitting tomato juice on to the brim of her cowboy hat.

'Neighbours, then?' Tash corrected her gaffe.

Saying nothing, Veruschka made a strange hissing noise that was part tut and part snarl, and turned away to gather the children and spirit them away for a walk.

When Sylva called something out in Czech – or Slovakian, for all Tash knew – there was a distinct waving of a finger over one yellow shoulder.

'I'm so sorry,' Tash bleated, then squeaked in pain as Vasilly blundered after his girlfriend, canapés flying, big feet crashing down on Tash's as he passed by at speed. 'They're terribly nice, but they've only just arrived in this country and some things don't translate, I think.'

'It's okay. I'm used to it.' Sylva shrugged with surprisingly sanguine air. 'In the Czech Republic, they think they're better than us poor Slovakian neighbours.' Then she nudged Tash with her elbow which, given their height difference, meant jabbing her in the hip. 'Your husband does not fuck that nanny, I take it?'

Tash stood, momentarily open-mouthed, before gratefully spotting her sister approaching.

Dressed in an immaculately tailored long tweed coat with a nipped-in waist and a kick skirt, Sophia looked absolutely the part of the wealthy owner, from her fur collar to buttoned cuffs, and from the neat ponytail in her blue-black hair down to her brown leather Le Chameau boots.

The same could not be said for Tash. Mascara smudged and hair on end, her Mogo team coat covered in horse slobber and baby sick, she made an uncharacteristically loving lunge towards her sister. At the same moment, Hugo's phone rang in her pocket – a newly assigned ringtone that she didn't recognise. For a moment it sounded as though there was an angry troll in her jeans.

Thus Tash and Sophia embraced with a lot of strange grunts and roars emanating from below.

'It's a haka,' Sophia told her as Tash groped for the rubber-cased phone that Hugo had acquired because it was waterproof and rugged.

'A what?' She stared at the phone, which was still grunting.

'Maori chant. I recognise it from All Blacks matches. Ben watches enough bloody rugby for me to be able to recite it like the Lord's Prayer.'

Finally Tash worked out how to answer the call, turning away to try to hear better and gesturing for her sister to introduce herself to Sylva.

Feeling magnanimous, Sophia stepped towards Sylva Frost with a smile.

'We've met.' She shook the little Slovak's manicured hand while examining her cosmetic work in close detail. It was flawless. 'Polo, I think.'

Sophia was in her element at Blenheim, although not particularly horsy herself. Having only ever been a hobby rider, and rather nervous, she'd gratefully hung up her boots after marriage, but she was now serving a long internship as a Pony-Club mum, and loved the country houses and tweed of the eventing scene. Having a sister and brother-in-law ranked so highly in the sport lent one a certain gravitas, along with owning a half share in a horse like Sir Galahad. He'd somewhat underperformed today, but any disappointment Sophia felt was counterbalanced by the fact that Miranda Rock had just greeted her like an old chum and asked her when they were going to host a horse trials at Holdham, making her truly feel one of the clique.

But Sylva, who already thought uppity Sophia Meredith far less likeable than her sister, undermined that sense of well-being in an instant. 'Forgive me, I meet so many people . . . your name is?'

Sophia looked hugely put out. 'Actually, I'm Lady Malvern.'

'How lovely – like Lady Gaga,' Sylva teased, knowing perfectly well who she was.

Stranded together, the two women – former models, mothers and expert self-publicists, but almost a generation apart – looked around desperately for a distraction.

It came in the form of Mike Seith, the Mogo managing director, banging on a glass at the PA mic in the corner and introducing Hugo to his eager guests: '. . . our Hu-gold medallist, our Beau-champion, our Mogo team captain who represents what this brand stands for – tough, resilient, outstanding performance, top of the ranks, an out-and-out winner and, of course, incredibly good looking. Please welcome Hugo Beauchamp!'

Hugo sent a titter of laughter through the tent by politely requesting that his wife get off the phone. Then he ran a hand through his thick tortoiseshell hair and stepped forward to charm the room.

'Good afternoon. Those of you who saw my dressage test earlier might not agree with Mike's wonderful appraisal, but in my defence I have to say that if the rules allowed the horse and I to compete in Mogo waterproof wear we'd be home and dry. Very dry.'

Primed to respond to any Mogo name checks, his captive audience laughed obediently.

But Hugo wasn't at his best. Usually a natural, witty public speaker and excellent raconteur, he was suffering from lack of sleep and from the blow to his ego after two appalling dressage tests on horses that were expected to do much better.

His competition strings were suddenly looking frayed. He'd sold two four star horses and retired another one in the past month, actions for which he took full responsibility but that were starting to seem foolish if these lower-ranking horses didn't progress. Based on today's performance, he could be left with just one four-star horse next year. And his sponsors were already in possession of itchy feet.

He knew that delivering a lacklustre speech was hardly going to win Mogo approval, but as soon as it started to go wrong he found that he couldn't do anything to rescue the situation.

He hadn't really thought through what he was going to say and now, instead of finding that the adrenalin rush from that lack of preparation gave him great off-the-cuff one liners as it had in the past, he just felt distracted and ill at ease. He was aware that, across the room, Rory – who'd posted a far better test than his trainer – was not listening to a word he was saying, instead flirting loudly with Sylva and Sophia Meredith. Most distracting of all, Tash was holding his mobile phone as though it was an unexploded bomb and making discreet hand signals.

Then, just as he was finally starting to win over his audience with an anecdote about losing his way in a foreign championships and finding himself tangled up with a bunch of carriage drivers, he heard a strange barracking from the floor, accompanied by what sounded like a slow hand clap:

'*Ho ri ti! Ha ho ripe! Ka mau! Hi!*'

Directly in front of him, Tash let out a squeak of recognition and looked at the phone in her hand.

Don't answer it, Hugo thought desperately, somehow still talking into the mic.

But Tash had the phone to her ear and was making her way towards the exit.

Hugo's knuckles whitened and he glowered at the audience, muttering, 'It was all a bit of a fuck-up, basically.'

There were a few titters. Mike Seith covered his eyes. Rory let out a seal-bark of laughter.

Mood blackened beyond repair, Hugo carried on, praising the Mogo product range by half-hearted rote and making it abundantly clear that he would rather be standing anywhere else than right there. The applause when he finished was more from relief than praise. He couldn't wait to get out on to the course with his wife and dogs.

But, to add to his ire, Tash had other plans.

'I think Lough Strachan's arrived at Haydown!' she announced breathlessly the moment he left the Mogo tent, handing his mobile phone back.

Hugo wanted to hurl the thing into the nearest puddle.

'I must get back to Maccombe!' she panted, all too eager to escape.

'Absolutely not!' he insisted. 'Send someone else.'

'There is no one else.'

'Jenny can go. Or Beccy – send Beccy back.'

'It hardly looks good sending poor Beccy. It has to be one of us.'

'Well, for God's sake take someone with you,' he said, making it sound like they'd had a break-in rather than an unexpected arrival.

'I'm taking the Czechs and the children of course,' she pointed out, before adding guiltily: 'It'll be much easier for you to concentrate without us getting under your feet.'

'You'd better buzz off home then. And I'd prefer it if you don't answer my calls in future. Let it go to voicemail. Better still, turn the bloody thing off when I'm speaking in public.' He stomped off to gather his dogs from the lorry park without so much as a farewell.

Tash almost ran after him to try to pacify him, and to offer to walk the course with him before she left, but she held herself in check, unwilling to put herself up against his bad mood. Hugo was only being vile because he was so tense, this week's task playing on his nerves far more than usual. The Olympic gold medallist was expected to shine but his horses were uptight and underpowered, his sponsors increasingly unimpressed and his wife wholly distracted. It didn't make his behaviour any less immature, but Tash understood it. She'd suffered from competition nerves far more than her husband and at times had battled to stay positive. Over the years, Hugo had played a large part in controlling her tension until it had almost totally disappeared at the peak of her success, but now that he needed her to return the favour she was helpless.

He needed the old, practical Tash by his side, upbeat and focused, who could read a course and solve potential problems with a keen eye and instinct; she understood the way he rode better than anyone, along with each individual horse's way of going, meaning that her help was invaluable. But that Tash wasn't here this week and she knew it. This Tash was a distracted, over-emotional mother whose first instinct upon seeing the track she'd completed many times in the past in its differing incarnations was to wonder why on earth anyone would want to undertake such a dangerous endeavour. All the fences looked monstrous to her and she was genuinely scared for Hugo.

Coming to Blenheim to support him had been a big mistake, she reflected, especially bringing the children plus the Czechs and their Eurovision Song Contest wardrobe. Any excuse to relieve Hugo of it all seemed heaven-sent. She hoped he could focus on the competition without all her distractions that got on his nerves and disturbed his preparation. She would make it up to him when he returned to Haydown, she promised herself, already craving home and routine and domesticity, even if there was a strange New Zealander there.

'Mr Beauchamp, he stay here to ride horses in Queen's garden?' Veruschka asked as they left the park, craning over her shoulder for the last glimpses of Blenheim Palace through the rear windscreen.

'Yes, he's staying a few more days.' Tash glanced towards the lorry park, where she could just make out the green and gold livery of the Beauchampions lorry. 'We're all rooting for him.'

But the thin wedge that had edged between them during the summer splintered wider as she drove away far too enthusiastically, firing up the heated seats, an Eurythmics CD on the stereo and the sat nav pointed at home.

Singing along to 'Sisters Are Doin' It For Themselves' and telling herself that she was doing the right thing, Tash tried not to feel too grateful for her liberation. Away from the lorry park gossip it was much easier to put jealous thoughts from her mind, to stop dwelling on their deferred sex life and Hugo's active text life, and to enjoy being the great woman behind the great man.

'Sisters are doin' it for themselves!' she repeated, only hoping that Beccy would cope without her.

Unaccustomed to being so far down the leader board on the eve of cross-country day, Hugo was sorely tempted to drive home to handle Lough Strachan's arrival himself, certain that the man had timed it deliberately to coincide with Blenheim. But it wasn't in his nature to wimp out and so he girded his loins and resolved to salvage some dignity with good, fast clear rounds the following day. Dusk falling, he walked the course as he intended to ride it – quickly, efficiently and with no distractions. He refused to think about Lough Strachan and the secrets they shared; he couldn't afford to. When he got back to the start–finish area he set out once again and walked the course afresh, head bowed against the driving rain. It was now dark, but he trudged on, his exhausted, sodden dogs trailing behind him. In his pocket his phone rang continually – different ringtones to identify the callers – Tash from Haydown, Rory's mobile, Jenny, Ben. He ignored them all.

Yet, knowing a little camaraderie would help on such a day, he decided to sleep on the spare bunk in the horsebox that night. The room in the bed and breakfast, with its empty cots and the scent of Tash still lingering, depressed him too much to stay there. But when he arrived at the lorry park with his bags and the Rat Pack at his heels he found Beccy, Karma and Twitch waiting outside on the step to the groom's compartment, teeth chattering as they leant together for warmth.

'I wouldn't go in just yet,' she warned.

But Hugo, black-tempered and yawning widely, swept past the gathering on the steps like Ranulph Fiennes yomping through a cluster of mountain goats in the foothills.

Shortly afterwards there was a brief girly shriek, an outraged bellow and then – rather surprisingly – uproarious laughter all round.

Beccy took her phone out of her pocket and checked it. She'd heard nothing from Lough for twenty-four hours now. She felt increasingly sick.

As the gales of laughter continued inside the horsebox Beccy wearily clambered up the steps and opened the door. They were all gathered around the table drinking cheap rosé.

'There you are!' Rory greeted her like an old mate despite having unceremoniously booted her out earlier on. 'Join us! Bring Cooler!'

'Karma.' She perched awkwardly in a free spot, wishing it were closer to Hugo who was behind the table with his back to the window, customary fag dangling between his lips.

'Tash has gone home.'

'Oh yes?' She tried not to betray how much the news made her heart lift.

'It seems Lough Strachan's arrived to join our happy Haydown team.'

'He's in England?' Her heart was jet-propelled into her throat.

'So it appears.' Hugo's blue eyes were glacial as they narrowed and focused on the wine bottle. He topped up his glass and then poured one for Beccy. 'Here, you look like you need one of these as much as I do. Is grooming for Rory that awful, you poor darling?'

Beccy's face flushed deep red. Suddenly the freefall panic of thinking that Tash was with Lough Strachan right now paled to nothing as she took the glass from Hugo and looked him in the eye. He still had her heart so totally kidnapped she couldn't care less if Lough had Tash tied up in the Haydown cellars demanding to know why she had led him on.

It was one of the most exciting evenings of Beccy's life, watching Hugo get drunk and rant a lot, particularly when Rory walked Sylva back to her waiting car. Her ten minutes alone with Hugo was thrilling, not least because among his ramblings he dropped a gem of an indiscretion.

'Lough Strachan's a total shit!' Hugo announced in one of his more lucid moments. 'If he touches a hair on Tash's head I'll kill him.'

'Why would he want to touch Tash?' Beccy asked with more feeling than she intended.

'Because I lost her in a bet,' he mumbled, burying his face in his hands.

She wasn't sure that she heard this right, but it made no difference because a far more immediate, more spine-tingling moment came when he slumped across the table and, reaching out, gripped her hand in his.

Like a reflex, she pulled his fingers to her lips and kissed them. They tasted of cigarettes and horse.

Hugo lifted his face from the table and stared at her in surprise.

Which was when Rory walked back into the horsebox, kicking mud from his boots. 'How about that then? A pre-match shag from Sylva. Result!'

The fact that both Beccy and Hugo jumped sky-high bypassed Rory entirely.

'What a woman!' he announced theatrically as he sagged down on the seating. 'I'm going to win this for her.'

'You have about as much chance of that as young Beccy here has of winning Miss Singapore.' Hugo snapped, the drink making him cruel.

'Want to bet?' Rory scoffed.

But to his surprise, Hugo almost bit his head off. 'Yes I fucking well bet! And this is one wager I know I won't lose!'

Mortified, Beccy mumbled something about giving Karma a run and bolted outside. It was still raining. The going would be awful tomorrow, she realised.

Her phone was beeping again. Nervously she fished it out and felt cold shame drench her as she read Lough's name. He and Tash must have rumbled her.

She read the message with wide-eyed surprise, wondering whether this was some sort of joke: *Lost my Dad. Losing my liberty. Never had you to lose – my greatest regret. Will not come to England. As the song says, there's nothing you can save that can't be saved. I apologise for everything. L*

Chapter 23

When Tash watched Rory lift the Blenheim trophy live on television she had a Kiwi at her side, but it wasn't Lough Strachan. It was his head groom, a small ball of high-camp energy called Lemon, who reminded her rather quaintly of Mickey Rooney in *National Velvet*, although with far more piercings and a rather alarming bleached yellow Mohican sprouting from his otherwise conventional mousey short back and sides.

'Is that why you're called Lemon?' She pointed to the hairy yellow shark's fin.

'No, my real name's Lemmy. My parents are big Motörhead fans, yeah? Not great when you're the Abba-loving only son of a sheep shearer growing up in the middle of nowhere, yeah?'

Tash nodded sympathetically and they both lapsed into silence as they watched Julia Ditton interviewing Rory, who replied 'Bloody brilliant!' to every question.

'When I was fifteen, I ran away from home to work for a racing yard near Matamata,' Lemon went on. 'They called me Lemon there because I'm small, round and have an acid tongue, yeah? You can call me Lem if you like. Lough does. He was one of the veterinary team who used to come to the yard. That's how we met.'

Watching the hands slapping Rory on the back on screen, and realising Hugo wasn't among them, Tash wasn't really listening properly.

'Lough?' she asked eventually, wondering if she should try to call Hugo again. He obviously hadn't stayed on to support Rory. He'd be on his way home, having show-jumped before lunch.

'Scottish mother,' Lemon told her. 'His father wanted to call him Roto, which is Maori for lake, but Ma Strachan insisted on Lough.'

'But she used the Irish spelling.'

'What?'

'The Irish spell it with a "gh".' She stood up to leave. 'The Scottish with a "ch".'

'Lough's mum left Glasgow when she was three, so I guess she never knew that. She's not the brightest spark.' He looked at her with surprising directness. 'Why're you so interested in Lough's name?'

'I'm a pedant. I like clarification.'

'That's what Lough's mother's called.'

'Sorry?' Tash turned back in the doorway.

'Clara Fecashean,' Lemon hammed a bad Scottish accent.

'Really? Isn't that an Irish name?'

'Duh! Like, joke!' He was laughing so much he almost toppled his chair over, pointing at her in glee. 'Clarification. I can't believe you fell for that. You are so gullible.'

Tash flashed a weak smile and went out to phone Hugo, but his mobile was going straight to voicemail. She left another message saying that there was still no word from Lough Strachan, let alone any sign of him arriving in the UK.

Lemon seemed remarkably unfazed by this turn of events and was more than happy to make himself at home and enjoy the hospitality on offer. He grabbed the remote and switched to an old episode of *Baywatch* on satellite, making himself at home amid the squashy cushions on the quadruple sofa, ogling both The Hoff and Pamela Anderson.

Lough's non-appearance on the flight from Auckland was a mystery his head groom didn't seem able to solve. Lemon had travelled with the four horses on a specialist air-freight flight while Lough stayed behind a further night, aiming to catch a passenger flight that would get him into Heathrow to coincide with his precious cargo being passed fit, rested and ready to travel on to Berkshire via horse transporter. Lem and the horses had arrived on schedule; Lough had not. He wasn't answering his phone and had left no message.

'Any news?' she asked eagerly as he received a text on his bright yellow mobile.

'He handed the keys over to his landlord and set out for the airport.' He pocketed the phone again. 'After that, nothing. He didn't check in.'

Tash was perplexed. 'We weren't expecting you to arrive this weekend.'

'Lough's pretty oddball, but he defo sent details – I was there,' Lemon assured her. 'And he's spoken to you, yeah.'

'Not to me.'

Lem's eyebrows shot up towards his Mohawk. 'He'll be here,' he promised easily. 'He had some family stuff to sort out. He must have missed his flight and be in such a fuck-off bad mood he doesn't want to call until he's sorted it.' He settled back to watch *Baywatch*.

At a loss, Tash located Veruschka in the kitchen entertaining Cora with the peg bag while she hung the washing on the ancient pine airer that could be winched up to the ceiling. Tash was embarrassed to spot her biggest, tattiest post-Caesarean pants swinging among Hugo's far nattier black boxer shorts.

'Those can go in the tumble drier,' she snapped more crabbily than she intended.

'Huh? Is not okay?'

'Oh, don't worry about it,' she replied, settling the mewling Amery on a bouncy chair where he began chirping and admiring his own hands.

She picked up the phone and checked the dial tone. It purred reassuringly, and she dialled Hugo's mobile. Straight to voicemail again.

It was no wonder he and Lough got on so well. They were both lousy at answering their phones or explaining their whereabouts.

Not that she was entirely convinced that Lough and Hugo *did* get on that well. From what Lemon had said earlier, she was amazed that they had come at all.

'You'd have thought they were sworn enemies after the Games. But then he went to see his mum in Auckland for a few days and when he came back he said we were coming here.'

Lemon was fabulously indiscreet. He had already passed on some salacious gossip about several notable Kiwi event riders, had confirmed or refuted well-worn rumours that Tash had never quite believed, and was equally eager to know all about the Haydown set-up.

'Rory Midwinter's a bit of a dish, isn't he? Is he gay?'

From what Tash had seen of Rory so far, she very much doubted it.

Reassured that the children were okay, and aware that Veruschka – who hated being watched while she worked – was giving her the evil eye over Hugo's socks, she grabbed a coat and headed outside to check on Vasilly, who was clearing out the old lodge house for Rory. Previously rented as a weekend cottage by a pair of London solicitors who had tightened their belts as a result of the credit crunch and relinquished the tenancy, the little brick and flint cottage by the Haydown entrance gates had been unoccupied for almost three years. Tash had harboured vague plans of a holiday let, but hadn't found time to do anything about it through her two pregnancies, and now it was dusty and neglected, smelled of damp and mice, and was filled with oddments of furniture. Worse still, the ivy almost covered the windows in places and the garden was waist high with couch grass and nettles, the path tangled with ground elder like a cargo net on an army assault course.

Rory – who had been moving across in a very chaotic, one-horse-at-a-time fashion – had been staying in the house whenever he was at Haydown. But the return from Blenheim would mark his relocation proper, and Tash wanted to make his new home more welcoming.

When she had left Vasilly in the lodge that morning he'd been wearing goggles and waving his beloved strimmer around in the garden, looking as though he knew what he was doing. Tash had pointed out the ivy that needed cutting back, and some broken furniture to mend.

Walking around the crumbling wall that separated the main garden from the little lodge one Tash smelled the familiar tang of bonfire smoke. Then she got a faceful of thick, acrid fumes and stopped in her tracks.

The garden was stripped bare. Everything had gone – the ancient rhododendrons, the herbaceous borders that teemed with lupins, delphiniums and foxgloves in summer, the hollyhocks and rose bushes, the hebes and the fruit bushes were all gone. As was the ivy – every last leaf of it hacked from the walls that had worn their green foliage like an old lady hanging onto her fox fur for over a century. Now, pale, bony and pockmarked, veined with old ivy trails and riddled with strange stains, the cottage looked like it had been the centre of a gun battle.

Vasilly, who was busily feeding the entire contents of the garden through the mulcher, looked very pleased with himself.

In the centre of what had once been a pretty, if overgrown, lawn a pyre raged. Poking from it like dismembered limbs, Tash recognised various items of familiar furniture.

One glance inside the house confirmed her fears. Vasilly had taken all the contents and set light to them.

'I do good?' Vasilly asked when she came out, not noticing that she was white with shock. His big, red face was wreathed with proud smiles. He was sweating heavily from the effort of such hard work.

★

247

'It's all my fault, not his,' Tash hurriedly explained when Hugo finally returned to see his pretty lodge descaled and gutted. 'Please don't tell him off. He tried really hard.'

'He's devalued the place by about ten grand in a day!'

Rory, meanwhile, found the whole thing hilarious. He thought his new quarters 'quite charming – and very Zen'.

Red-faced, Tash explained that he would have to share it with Lough when he finally arrived: 'I thought he and Lem were a couple,' she whispered indiscreetly, 'but it seems not. Lem insists he won't live with him, and says he prefers the company of women so I've put him in the stables flat with Beccy.'

Rory preferred the company of women too, but after Blenheim he was happy to forfeit the company of Beccy, with her strange moods, undisciplined dog and awful hippy hair.

Tash prepared a special welcoming and celebratory meal for their new rider – and for Lemon – but Hugo blighted it by remaining silent and sour-faced throughout, and complaining that the fish smelled off. Rory was equally lacking in appetite. Having remained sober for almost a week to keep sharp-eyed and focused on the competition, he was intent on making up for it as quickly as possible.

Only Lemon appreciated the effort:

'Lemon sole. That's so cute. Shame I'm a vegan.'

'Oh no, really?' Tash was mortified.

'Nah. Only kidding. You're so gullible! I love it, yeah.'

'He's odious,' Hugo muttered when he and Tash were alone in the boot room, as he returned from yet another trip to the cellar to slake Rory's bottomless thirst and she fetched the lemon cheesecake she'd left setting in the old meat safe. She was rather embarrassed that she'd hit upon the food theme, and Hugo clearly loathed the new arrival.

'You knew what he was like when you invited Lough over.'

'More's the pity.' A muscle was slamming in his cheek. 'I never spoke to Lemon.'

'I'm sure he gets easier to be around when he relaxes. We're all a bit tense. Can't you make more of an effort?'

But Hugo's exasperation seemed unshakeable. He wasn't usually a bad loser, but both his horses had put in silly run-outs across country that he knew were his fault. To Tash's frustration he seemed to blame her for his poor scores, insinuating that if she had not fled back to Haydown on the slightest excuse he might have put in better cross-country performances and pulled up through the ranks. Unwilling to enter a full-blown row in front of the Haydown's new team members, Tash let it go.

His other dining companions were already winding him up enough as it was.

'Always a tough call when the apprentice has more magic than the sorcerer,' Lemon joked, earning the dirtiest of looks from Hugo and an ill-timed 'hear hear!' from Rory.

Nobody there could deny the skill of Rory's performance, least of all Rory.

Having struggled for so long with little support, he didn't really know how to take success. He was accustomed to living alone and talking to his terrier, or relying upon the adoration of his many female fans and clients like Faith. What's more, he was positively reeling from the on-off attentions of Sylva Frost at Blenheim (culminating in a definite 'on' with another knee-trembler in the back of the horsebox after he loaded the victorious Humpty for the journey to Berkshire). His urge to brag won him no favours with the Beauchamps at a very tense supper table.

'Julia Ditton called me the next Fox-Pitt, did you hear? And Brian Sedgewick was all over me after the prizegiving, so it can't be long before I get called up for my team uniform fitting.'

'You can borrow Hugo's,' Lemon joked. 'He won't be needing it for a bit!'

Lemon flirted shamelessly and pandered to that ravenous new-found ego for all it was worth. Mohawk bobbing, he asked endless questions about Rory, his horses and his life, subjects on which Rory was all too happy to dwell with barely a passing reference to Hugo, or indeed the elusive Dillon Rafferty and his millions.

'It's been tough. I've nearly given up so many times – when I smashed my leg, when the money's run out, when Whitey almost died. This is a reward for all the hard times.'

'Yes, congratulations.' Tash smiled at him warmly. 'We're all really proud of you.' She tried not to notice that Hugo was paying far more attention to reading the messages on his indestructable mobile than listening to the new arrival.

Lemon raised his glass, but there was a menacing glint in his pale-lashed eyes. 'So many in this sport are rich buggers with no idea how easy they've got it. Just look at this place. No disrespect, Hugo, but if you knew the shit Lough has been through to stay in the sport you'd thank your lucky stars to have been born into this.'

Casting his phone aside, Hugo gave Lemon a look that clearly said he'd be seeing stars if he carried on this line of conversation. Eventually he could take it no more and stomped off to do night-check.

Tash was dying to casually tidy up Hugo's mobile and nip into the boot room to frisk it for messages from V, but Lemon thwarted her plans by picking it up to admire it. 'These are great bits of kit.' He proceeded to take endless photographs of the kitchen, the dogs and Rory with it, while Tash hovered in frustration, finally giving up and making coffee.

When Hugo reappeared he found Tash loading the dishwasher while Rory and Lemon flirted over brandies at the kitchen table. On the baby monitor little snuffles and grumbles indicated that Amery was starting to dream about his next feed.

'Beccy's in floods of tears out there, threatening to leave,' he told Tash in an undertone, leaning down beside her to slot glasses into the upper rack.

Tash looked across at him in alarm. 'Why?'

'Search me.' Hugo straightened up and went to fetch himself a nightcap, bypassing the brandy and reached a bottle of malt from the dresser. 'I didn't ask.'

'I told you we should have asked her to join us tonight.'

'You know I can't stand that pouting expression of hers, and the way she just *stares*. Anyway, you said you didn't have enough fish.'

'Oh hell,' Tash groaned as Amery started to mewl loudly. 'Go back out and find out what's the matter while I feed him, will you? I'll be down as soon as I can.'

Hugo rolled his eyes at the prospect, but nobly reached for his yard keys. However, as soon as Tash was gone he was distracted by Lemon and Rory.

'Lough reckons she's the best woman rider in the world,' Lemon was saying.

'Who?' Hugo snapped, draining his scotch on the way to the door.

'Someone like Marie-Clair Tucson is much more stylish,' Rory countered.

'Lough's shagged her,' Lemon sniggered.

'Who are we talking about?' Hugo repeated witheringly.

'Tash.'

'Lough's shagged Tash?' Rory hooted, deliberately misinterpreting.

Lemon joined in, almost weeping with laughter. They shared an appallingly silly sense of humour.

A scotch glass was slammed down on the scrubbed pine between them with such force that it cracked clean in two, leaving behind a dent like a horseshoe.

Outside, Beccy stood shivering beneath the clock-tower arch, which afforded her a clear view through the kitchen windows of the main house, where she could see Hugo, Rory and the little New Zealander having an animated conversation. She knew that Lough had not arrived as expected, but she was still fuming with indignation that she hadn't been included in that night's meal – even as a gesture of thanks for her contribution to Rory's success at the competition. All Tash had said was that she must be wiped out after all her hard work, so was bound to want an early night. She didn't want an early night. She wanted to be a part of the action. She felt as alien as the Czechs, currently moving about above her head in the little clock-tower apartment and, from the sound of things, having a heated argument while listening to strange, yodelling folk music.

But Beccy envied them their togetherness. At least they had each other in the overpoweringly selfish world of the Beauchamps. Beccy only had Karma, and the disloyal minx had now formed an unshakeable attachment to Beetroot, following her around adoringly.

'Well, I'm not following bloody Tash around,' Beccy fumed.

She took out her mobile phone and scrolled through the half-dozen messages she'd received from New Zealand in recent days. Jealousy bubbling in her hot blood and tears drying on her face, she re-read them all, pretending that Lough knew that he was really sending them to her and not Tash.

One sentence from that final, heart-wrenching message ran past her eyes again and again imprinting itself there: *Never had you to lose – my greatest regret.*

Feeling strangely calm and composed, Beccy pressed Reply.

You haven't lost me, Lough . . . you just haven't found me yet. I am here. It's easy, as the song says.

Despite sleeping just a few metres apart in the stables flat, their bedrooms to either side of the little galley kitchen, Lemon and Beccy didn't speak properly until the following morning, packing down the muck-heap into stepped layers. It wasn't the most glamorous spot to bond, but Beccy later reflected that it was rather apt given Lemon's love of what he openly called 'shit-stirring'.

'You know, I reckon Hugo's happy that Lough's lost in transit. You'd think he was the Home Guard about to get a German prisoner of war. Christ, he's a bad-tempered bastard.' He threw up straw, compact little biceps bulging in his tight sweatshirt. He might have a face like a cherub, but he had arms like a boxer. 'Lough's gone AWOL before: he once went walkabout for a month after a horse of his got killed at Puhinui trials. He gets like that sometimes. I reckon he'll turn up soon enough.'

'It's a bit weird, though, isn't it?' Beccy was thinking anxiously about all the frantic texts she had ignored. 'Could something have happened to him?'

'Nah. He was sorting out some shit to do with his dad, but that's nothing to do with it, I reckon.'

'What shit?'

'Not this shit, that's for sure!' He flicked a forkful of droppings at her.

Shrieking, Beccy flicked some back and soon they were having an all-out dung fight. Afterwards, breathless with giggles, they looked like swamp monsters and smelled so noxious they had to shower before breakfast.

Lemon was childish, crude and cocky, but Beccy thought he was the most entertaining thing to happen at Haydown since Dillon Rafferty landed on Flat Pad in a helicopter.

Over coffee in the flat, while he gelled his Mohawk back into place and she dried her dreadlocks with a towel, he eyed her with interest. 'Aren't you a bit old to be a working pupil?'

'I travelled a lot.'

'Ever come to New Zealand?'

'No,' she muttered. Then, eager to change the subject, 'I like your hair.'

'Lough says I look like a Yellow Crown Amazon – that's a bird we have in New Zealand, yeah? He knows all that sort of shit.'

'Is he a twitcher then?'

'A what?' he laughed.

'A bird fancier.' She blushed, remembering Lough's birds-of-a-feather text after her quacking gaffe.

'Nah,' Lemon was predictably coarse. 'Only birds he fancies have tits and arse.'

'So he's a ladies' man?'

'A *ladies' man*!' he cackled, mocking her voice. 'Nah, he's too obsessed with horses and winning. He once told me he lost his heart years ago, but I reckon it grew back while he wasn't looking.'

Beccy hoped so. She really hoped so. However fraught with danger and deceit, her texts with Lough felt incredibly special and, even though she knew it was only ever really a fantasy, she treasured the early ones.

And now her heart was glowing like a freshly stoked fire from having Lemon around. It was a long time since she'd had a friend.

He soon called her Limey and flirted relentlessly. 'You're really beautiful, you know that?'; 'Christ, you have a hot body, Limey'; 'Fancy a quick roll in the hay, yeah?'

On the surface she took it all with a pinch of salt – the limey compliment to his tequila-slammer humour and down-in-one flattery – but deep down it opened the flues of her heart and kept the fire burning there. It was nothing to the all-consuming flames of her love for Hugo and the burning shame of her strange, *Cyrano de Bergerac* relationship with the missing Lough, but it made her fingers and toes tingle as she embraced the working day with enthusiasm at long last.

Chapter 24

'Voila!' the *Cheers!* photographer's assistant finally made the reflective umbrella stay put beside a large marble urn in the Garden Suite at Eastlode Park.

Lounging on the vast four-poster bed – carved from a six-hundred-year-old oak for a mistress of Charles II, it was said – Sylva regarded the two different teams shooting her with impassive calm, despite being dressed in no more than a loose-stayed corset, silk cami-knickers and silky striped over-the-knee 'sockings', a new hosiery trend that was proving a triumph of branding over practicality.

'I can see some nipple on the right!' the *Cheers!* photographer called out, causing a stylist to leap into frame and start adjusting.

'I can move my own breast,' Sylva muttered as tit tape and curses landed upon her massive mammary.

'Yes, but I'm paid to do it,' the stylist snapped. 'You're paid to lie back and take it. I'm sure you've done that plenty of times before.'

There was a time when Sylva would have had the girl fired for less than that, but she was mellower these days – and she had her documentary team's cameras trained on her.

Today Rodney was in his element, enjoying a terrific, unexpected angle to this particular episode of Sylva's reality show that came from the fact that Eastlode Park – normally a bastion of discreet efficiency – had double-booked. For while Sylva Frost, the nation's favourite single-mum superstar was being captured by *Cheers!* curled up with a down-filled bolster in one wing of the Palladian mansion, supermodel-turned-child-adopting-global-campaigner Indigo Rafferty was in the opposite wing, holding up a glass of vintage Dom Perignon and steaming in the spa with a tame photo crew from *Hello!*

Fed up with her husband's failure to officially move into his new Oddlode pile, Indigo had decided to take matters into her own hands and announce their arrival at the Abbey with a glossy photo spread featuring all eight of her adopted children. Naturally reluctant to reveal her newly redecorated inner sanctum to the masses, she had elected to host her Cotswolds photoshoot at the nearest five-star spa, where oiled water now slid from her dusky skin in the fabulous evening sunlight that streamed in through the pool wall of Italian glass.

Pete was, predictably, nowhere to be seen.

'Probably busy searching for the third Mrs Rafferty,' muttered Sylva at the opposite end of the hotel when news of the Rockfather's absence reached her.

A clash was inevitable. Throughout the day the women, aware of one another's presence, edged closer like prize fighters unable to resist a pre-bout showdown.

Indigo's crew set up in the vast marble-clad reception hall where she dangled from the *bianco carrara* pillars in designer cocktail dresses like a pole dancer warming up. In the neighbouring ball room, Sylva's two crews caught every aspect of her posing in diaphanous silk against a backdrop of sun-drenched parkland caught through floor-to-ceiling Georgian windows so that every curve of her glorious body was cast in silhouette. The two photo shoots finally met on the battlefield of the long gallery as Sylva's team set up one end with a suit of armour, a bell-sleeved Guinevere outfit and an orb, while Indigo's posse noisily arrived at the other complete with fake-fur rugs, primitive musical instruments and small, beautiful children.

'It's like *The King and I* meets *The Jungle Book* over there.' The photographer's assistant whistled from the medieval end just as Indigo swept in on her endless glossy legs, wearing a leopard-print body stocking and what appeared to be a headdress of antlers. 'Wow!'

'Is it panto season already?' Rodney scoffed, eager to get a furious-looking Sylva on side.

Indigo was an intimidating and breathtakingly beautiful figure. A hybrid of a gerenuk and Medusa, she had golden bronze skin, fierce ebony eyes and unsmiling lips so rosebud plump her mouth was a perfect circle. Her trade mark snaked, braided hair was just visible beneath the antlers.

Several nannies and assistants were attempting to attract the interest of the children, who were gazing rapturously around the room at the portraits, coats of armour and tapestries. Seemingly in charge of this mêlée came a diminutive Chinese man in an expensive suit and sunglasses, who removed the 'Do Not Sit' sign from a George III Chippendale armchair and settled delicately upon it before clapping his small hands together and ordering 'Music!' like an oriental emperor holding court. With a lot of huffing and puffing, the childminders brought the instruments to life. The children took no notice.

The little group at Sylva's end ducked for cover.

Pauline, the older and tougher of Sylva's two PAs, a bull mastiff of a woman who had been known to headbutt more invasive members of the paparazzi, set out to silence the din but Sylva called her back.

'It's time I introduced myself.'

Watched by her ranks of supporters, Guinevere swept majestically along the gallery.

She reached the leopard-stag and stood at its hip, a mere five foot five Lilliputian to the seven feet six of former supermodel plus horns.

'We haven't been introduced.' Sylva extended a hand, bell sleeve dangling.

Indigo's blue-black eyes bored into hers.

For a moment the urge to say 'I am your future daughter-in-law' almost overwhelmed Sylva, but she managed to control herself and summon a gracious smile.

'I'm Sylva. I know you are Indigo. Two colours that compliment one another absurdly, as I hope we shall. Your children are beautiful; I wish mine were here to meet them. Now that we are neighbours, I trust we can be friends.'

Caught off guard, Indigo's eyes flashed. She didn't have many friends. Pete disliked her having girlfriends in the same way he disapproved of her wearing jeans and trainers or plain white underwear. He thought them dull.

'I hope so,' she purred, reaching out to snatch the proffered hand in a brief salutation, more like a high five than a handshake, that left both their palms buzzing.

Sylva lingered briefly, vaguely hoping for an invitation to coffee at the Rock Palace, but the horned one was sharpening her talons on a faux tiger-skin throw now, so she decided to float away and leave their brief encounter as a marker card. She'd made the first move. That was what counted. The Rafferty poker circle was within her grasp.

And her trump was still up her bell sleeve.

Zuzi. Children were power in the Rafferty clan.

On the short drive back to the château in her chauffeur-driven car, Sylva called her sons at home in Buckinghamshire, cutting the call short while her heart was singing from hearing their voices, just catching herself before she choked up for the want of seeing them again.

Then she texted her sister in Slovakia, saying how much she was looking forward to welcoming her and Zuzi to England. Hana was putting up a lot of resistance and refused to take her daughter out of school before the end of term, but Sylva had no doubt she would get her way, even if it meant that she had to travel to her motherland to collect them. Finally, she called Tash Beauchamp.

'It was so lovely to meet you last weekend, darlink. We must have lunch soon. I want to pick your brains about buying a horse.'

Lunch was obviously an alien concept to Tash as she sounded gratifyingly excited: 'I normally just have a Cup-a-Soup when I come in to give Amery his feed.'

'You must bring your children,' Sylva insisted. 'My nannies will look after them while we gossip.'

'And your documentary team, will they be there?' Tash asked worriedly.

'No, no. Just a quiet girls' lunch.'

A quiet lunch involving a convoy of cars, nannies, bodyguards and PAs with the paparazzi camped outside, Sylva predicted. Tash would probably be overawed. Indigo Rafferty would have no problems handling it, but Sylva had decided against inviting her too, knowing that it would make her look overeager. She needed to play a long game with Indigo.

They agreed a date the following week. 'Hugo and Rory will be in France then,' Tash chattered breathlessly, 'but I'm sure I can play hooky for an hour or two. God, I must phone Rory to remind him to pick up his passport while he's at Overlodes this week.'

'He's in the Cotswolds?'

'His new yard manager isn't coping too well, I gather. He's had to go back for a couple of days to sort her out, which is no bad thing because he came here with ten kit boxes full of equipment for his horses, and just an overnight bag for himself. He's so sweet.'

As soon as she finished the call Sylva rang Rory's mobile.

'I can't see you,' he pleaded half-heartedly. 'I head back to Berkshire first thing tomorrow. Dillon's friend is here so I have to behave. I'm even *sober*, can you believe?'

'I'll take care of that.' Sylva told her driver to stop off at Oddbins in Market Addington.

When Rory saw her, a bottle of cask-strength twenty-year-old Ardbeg and a certificate eighteen smile, all bursting from the back of a dark Mercedes like air confined in a bubble too long, his self-control vanished.

She had unzipped his flies before they were even through the door.

257

'Steady on!' he laughed, tripping over his bags of winter clothes that were lined up, waiting to be taken to Haydown the following day. 'We have company. She's only just gone upstairs for a bath.'

But, pinning him against the wall and dropping to her knees, Sylva wasn't listening. Accustomed to the total privacy of his cottage, her lips already on the tip of his delicious dick, ready to lure it into life.

'The water's cold,' came a laconic voice from the top of the stairs.

Hard-on wavering between four and two o'clock, Rory was in no mood for social mores: 'Jules, stay there – the immersion switch is in the airing cupboard next to you.'

But Sylva had already stopped lapping his foreskin like a kitten at a milk-bottle top and looked up sharply. She knew that voice.

To Rory's disappointment, she sprang upright. 'Verne!'

Feet pounded down the stairs and Jules, a square-set girl with attractive short blonde curls and a freckled nose like a naughty schoolboy, regarded Sylva in amazement.

'Plath!' She let out a strangled sob of a laugh.

'You know one another?' Rory asked, big hand wilting to six o'clock as he hurriedly zipped up his fly.

Dillon's record-industry friend was fresh from rehab, in need of a new direction, and clearly desperate to make her stay at Overlodes a success even though she had no apparent qualifications to run a yard apart from an ancient British Horse Society assistant instructor's certificate dating back to her teens, a horse of her own and a lot of recently purchased books about stable management. Her lack of experience alarmed Rory. Her association with Sylva astonished him.

'You could say so.' Jules was now doing a laughing-crying thing that further surprised Rory, to whom she had only spoken in a sardonic monotone since her arrival. 'We met on the pentathlon circuit as teenagers. I called her Sylvia, which drove her mad, but used to get her all the latest CDs from the UK for her Discman so she decided to forgive me.'

'Then Jules became a record promoter,' Sylva laughed as the two women fell into a hug that, to Rory's slightly paranoid and for once sober mind, was distinctly Sapphic.

'And Sylva became a pop star.'

'That nobody west of Vienna had ever heard of,' she giggled, pronouncing it 'vest of Wienna'.

'And *I* suggested you came here seeking fame and fortune,' Jules boasted, like a schoolteacher reminding a former pupil turned megastar that their history classes had once been their reason for living.

'You always told me to come here,' Sylva purred into her shoulder. 'Always making this little Slovak travel far from home. My Jules Verne.'

'And you are *still* attracted to utterly unfaithful, untrustworthy and beautiful men, I see, Plath.'

'I am very trustworthy, I'll have you know!' Rory said indignantly, although he was secretly rather chuffed by the summary.

'We're not,' Sylva giggled again, nudging Jules who snorted with laughter, both transported back to teenage friendship.

He watched as they tilted their heads back and stared at one another's faces with tearful affection in what he decided was a very tATu fashion – he could almost see the chain link fencing and the school uniforms.

'In that case, early start tomorrow and all that. I might just go to bed and crash out,' he announced grumpily, adding half-hopeful, half-joking: 'Unless you two care to join me?'

Still giggling, Sylva and Jules glanced at one another. 'Okay.'

Even as he opened his mouth, Rory knew that it would be incredibly uncool to cry 'Hallelujah', so he managed to limit it to 'Ha!', which was all the cue the girls needed to take his hands in theirs and drag him towards the cottage's little staircase door.

They bounded upstairs, clothes flying. As they hit the bed, the long-case clock in the room beneath them was ringing out midnight and Rory's cock was proudly confirming the time, ready for action.

'Ding dong,' Jules leapt aboard first, which was no bad thing because Rory couldn't last long for darling, sexy Sylva. For Jules, he could hold hard and enjoy the show. She was, in fact, rather spectacular in a cobby sort of way, and reminded him rather excitingly of Clare Balding. She effortlessly rolled him over and bounced on top of him like a wrestler.

Rory wrestled back some sexual authority by pressing his elbows into the pillows to either side of her and showing off his power drill.

Gratifyingly, Jules eyes widened and she let out an amazed wail, arms flailing around, gasping breathlessly, reaching out for her beloved Plath.

Twelve o'clock was threatening to ring out again when Sylva slithered aboard, her full lips on Rorys left earlobe and her thighs resting against Jules' wide freckled cheeks. It would all have got far too deliciously confusing if it weren't too wonderful to bother to decipher.

Rory had the night of his life, watched disapprovingly from the threadbare wingchair in the corner of the room by Twitch.

Having moved back downstairs to catch up while Rory slept, Jules and Sylva were still curled up spine to spine together on the dog-eared sofa at three in the morning, both dressed in Rory's freshly laundered hunting shirts, pulled from the rack above the Rayburn.

'I can't believe you're here,' Sylva purred, blowing the steam off a camomile tea. 'In this little backwater, in this little village.'

'The Cotswolds are the new Kensington and Chelsea,' Jules reminded her as she sucked the froth from an instant cappucino. 'I have plans for this place – The Stable Diet and Detox. I'm going to get urban fitness fanatics to come here to tone up and chill in all this fresh country air – mucking out is a great work out, after all, and Londoners love all this rural simplicity stuff. I've already got bookings through to Christmas. One record label is sending their entire sales team.'

Sylva was impressed. 'You always could make a silk purse out of a cow's ear as you say in England.'

'Sow's ear. But I'm making a pig's ear of it right now,' Jules groaned. 'I'd forgotten how much hard work horses are. I only agreed to do it as a favour to a good friend.'

'Dillon Rafferty?' Sylva made the connection smoothly.

'You know him?'

'Not yet, but we are close neighbours and have a lot in common so I am sure we will meet soon. Through our children, maybe, or our interest in horses.'

'If you're angling for an invitation, forget it,' Jules picked imaginary specks off her white shirt. 'You'll annihilate him. He's as soft as those cheeses he makes.'

'I'm merely interested in getting to know the locals. I think Dillon will be a close friend.'

Jules studied her face sceptically, knowing the old Sylva too well to believe she'd changed in recent years, 'Is Mama behind this?'

Sylva turned away irritably, realising they'd been rumbled.

Jules sighed. 'I've known Dillon a great many years and, believe me, he is not your type. If you want to get to know your neighbours, target the Abbey. Pete's old school: you'll fancy him much more.'

'I know his wife,' Sylva said pompously, based on their one encounter. 'I would never do that to Indigo and her babies.'

'And Nell Cottrell?'

'Oh, I have no respect for her, she broke darlink Rory's heart once.' Sylva stood up and stretched luxuriously before heading upstairs to fetch her clothes.

When she reappeared, Jules watched her dress, marvelling at her beauty. She was a breed apart and always had been, even as a teenager on the pentathlon circuit, where her self-possession and ambition had been legend. Then, as now, she had treated sex as sport.

Jules recalled reading that the poet John Betjeman, as an old man, had been asked whether he had any regrets and replied, 'Yes – not enough sex.' Sylva had more than enough sex; it was regrets she had always lacked.

'Don't screw with Dillon, Plath,' she now warned in a low voice. 'He's far too straight for you, and he's still hung up on his ex-wife. His daughters mean everything to him.'

'As do my boys to me.' Sylva zipped up her baby blue leather jacket as far as her lacy cleavage.

Having seen Sylva's sons plastered on the cover of the weekly gossip magazines since birth, Jules could guess just how much they meant to her. 'If you need publicity, pick on an easier target, one that's in the UK more than a few days at a time for a start. Use me if you like. I have nobody to hurt and it'd be great publicity for this place.'

'You're not famous,' Sylva muttered.

'At least give it a try,' Jules urged. 'I'll give the redtops a story that makes you look quite adorable and will, of course, be set so far in our distant past that nobody will blame you for having a little dalliance during your teenage sexual awakening.'

'Not *so* distant past,' Sylva laughed, starting to warm to the idea. 'Mama will hate it.'

'Not if you're on all the front pages looking gorgeous.'

'Okay, we'll do it,' Sylva shrugged, walking across the room to an old desk beneath the casement window where she rooted through the drawers and drew out Rory's passport. Then she dropped it into one of his bags.

'He needs someone to look after him,' she told a surprised Jules. 'Not you, though?'

Sylva shook her head with a ravishing smile. 'I need a grown up, darlink. A real man. I'll be here at seven-thirty tomorrow, yes?'

'What?' Jules yawned, looking at her watch and balking.

'The Stable Diet and Detox,' she headed for the door. 'I need to lose a great deal of weight. Your system will be perfect.'

'But Plath, you're not remotely—'

The door slammed.

'—overweight.'

Chapter 25

When Kurt Willis attended his regular dental check in Chelmsford's most exclusive practice, he naturally took the opportunity to thank his dentist for all his help after Faith's accident.

'We were so grateful Carly was there and enlisted your help. Faith's teeth look amazing. In fact, I was wondering if we couldn't spruce up my veneers to look like that? That new smile quite transforms her face.'

By the time Kurt's teeth had been probed, scraped and polished, the girls' web of lies had been exposed and Faith was about to have the smile wiped off her face. Not that she had smiled much in the recent weeks of driving rain and twelve-hour days, but she'd ridden some amazing horses, worked hard and gained invaluable coaching. Assiduous, talented and gutsy, Faith had all the makings of a top rider, but now Kurt's trust in his stepdaughter and working pupil was quite shattered.

He and Graeme called her into their massive open-plan bungalow for an inquisition, taking up position on opposite sides of the forty-foot room on suede Eames sofas that matched their colouring, blond for Kurt, dark brown for Graeme. Faith was forced to perch on an orange Flocks pouf in the middle of the room while they rounded on her.

They were *seriously* mad.

'You told us a stallion kicked you.'

'I know.'

'It didn't, did it?'

'No.'

'We labelled that horse a danger! All so you could indulge your vanity.'

Faith shrank back, knowing it was the truth. However much she'd tried to play it down, to get on with her job and put that weekend behind her, the guilt she felt wouldn't go away. A good horse had been sent back to its breeder in Germany as a result of her lies.

'Why did you say it?' Kurt demanded.

'It wasn't my idea!' she bleated, starting to explain about Double-D day and Carly's elaborate plan to enable the makeover.

But before she'd got beyond describing the dash for the gate in the Mini, Kurt covered his eyes in horror. 'You went for a *boob* job?'

'Yes, no, that is—'

'I'd ask for your money back,' Graeme sniped. Admittedly, Faith wore a lot of baggy layers to ride, but he coached enough artificially enhanced Essex housewives to know that her physique was still more Vincent Price than Katie Price.

'How can you *hope* to be a professional rider with *tits*?' Kurt howled.

'But I didn't—'

'You've let me down,' he stormed, standing up and stalking across a vast expanse of cowhide rug to the ten-foot-wide pebble fire, where he paced beneath a life-size portrait of himself and Graeme riding a pas de deux and flicked his highlights about for effect. 'You've let down your darling mother. You've let your*self* down.'

Kurt loved a big scene, imagining himself Scarlett O'Hara in *Gone with the Wind*. It was months since he'd had the opportunity to flounce quite so theatrically. In secret, he was grateful for an excuse to lay in to Faith at last. He might claim to want a protégée, but this one was sullen and ungrateful, despite having the makings of a superstar rider. Her talent was all the more frightening because she seemed to care so little about it. Nobody on his yard was more dedicated or put in longer hours, yet he sensed Faith's heart and ambition lay elsewhere, and that she was merely treading water with him. He wanted some of that fire he knew she possessed, but here in Essex, she was all cool water, a trait that had sometimes handicapped her ice-queen mother.

'Do you want to be as good as Anke was, Faith? Better, even?' he asked now, striding from his fireplace to his Rennie Mackintosh desk, which he leant against with dandyish aplomb. 'Do you *really* want success?' He lifted his chin, fully expecting her to take the baton as they reached a breakthrough. 'Because if you do, you're going to have to fight for it, honeybunch.'

Faith looked him square in the eye, saying nothing but thinking back to the past few weeks of simply throwing herself into the work to make up for all those unanswered texts and late and lonely nights sitting in the caravan, or occasional dreadful evenings out on the town with Carly trying to be something she wasn't. She thought about Sylva Frost and her high-maintenance glamour, seducing her dreams away. She thought about her beloved Rio relocating to the Beauchamps' fantastic Berkshire yard along with half a dozen other Overlodes competition horses. She felt increasingly like poor White Lies who had been left behind, overlooked because he was no longer considered useful.

Faith still remembered the first time Rory had let her ride Whitey in open country, and the sheer speed with which he'd powered over hedges and ditches. 'We would have won the Foxhunter Chase if we'd stayed in racing,' Rory had laughed afterwards. But when Faith had asked why he hadn't done just that he'd looked at her askance. 'Just because you *can* win something doesn't make it the natural choice. Where's the challenge in that? It's what you *want* to win that counts.' It was one of the wisest things she could remember him saying, and the reason she'd decided Rio should swap from dressage to eventing.

Faith had been bred to be a dressage rider. It was in her genes, just as being flat-chested, ginger-haired and long-legged were part of her make-up. She'd come away to reinvent herself, but instead of becoming more feminine and beguiling she'd found her body toughening to muscle with all the hard work, her resolve hardening and her skin thickening as she reverted to type. Yet her heart was utterly unchangeable; it wanted to break out of the arena and gallop across country.

Kurt strode back to the fireplace, where he stood facing her, hands on hips, issuing the challenge again. 'So what's it going to be, Faith? Are you going to fight?'

She had a sudden ludicrous image of them grappling one another down on to the designer hearthrug to battle it out like Grecian wrestlers while Graeme watched on, a poodle to each side of him. It reminded her of the film *Women in Love*. She wasn't sure if she had grown from girl to woman while she had been away, but she knew she was in love.

'I want to have a go at eventing,' she said in a small voice.

Kurt's handsome, tanned face lengthened with disappointment and he looked away.

On the sofa, Graeme snorted with laughter. 'Oh God, it's worse than we thought. Not only has she been under the knife in the name of love, now she wants to pop logs with hunting toffs and farmers from the colonies.'

'It's the best test of horse and rider!' Faith flared. 'Four-star eventers have more courage and skill than anyone.'

'You won't get anywhere with that attitude, smiler,' Graeme snarled back, though he was quietly thrilled by this turn of events, having already lined up a lovely young Swedish rider as Faith's replacement.

Faith rounded on him. 'I *like* my attitude!' She cocked her chin, displaying some of that fire at long last. '*And* I like my teeth. In fact, I wish I'd had more work done!'

'Why not?' sneered Graeme. 'You'll have plenty of time now you're out of a job.'

Faith's mouth hung open, showing off her very white teeth as she registered what was happening.

Confirming her fears, Graeme looked victoriously at Kurt. 'In the words of Alan Sugar . . .'

With a shrug of regret, Kurt nodded. Graeme had been impossibly jealous since Faith's arrival, having never really dealt with Kurt's previous marriage or his stepchildren. He was all for an easy life. There was no point having a protégée if she wasn't ready to be tamed, and he really preferred riding the horses himself. But he would miss Faith's pure, raw ability.

She hung her head. 'I really am sorry about the stallion. I hated lying.'

To her surprise, Kurt waltzed forward and took her face between his hands. 'My darling child, you have a *lot* to learn. But your attitude – and your teeth – are quite dazzling. What better for the girl who always bites off more than she can chew?'

Later that same drizzling grey October morning, Faith made the long, traffic-choked drive from Essex to the Cotswolds. She had never been so mortified. Before today, she hadn't been given so much as a detention or an official reprimand of any kind. Now her gayfathers had just fired her.

Her eyes barely focusing on the road beyond the sweeping windscreen wipers, Faith deeply regretted her shabby behaviour towards Kurt and Graeme. They had been good to her. They were family, and she'd abused their trust. Her mother would be livid.

Yet a part of her couldn't help feeling liberated. She longed to see Rory and was desperate to get back to the way things had been before. She would never let him down, or desert him, again.

Turning on the radio, she found Samuel Barber's *Adagio for Strings* playing on Classic FM, so absurdly romantic and yet saddening that rare tears almost blinded her progress along the M40, her battered heart at bursting point.

The truth hit her with every passing slip road. She wasn't going home to Rory. He had gone to Berkshire without looking back. He had taken her horse. He had sent just a one-line text to let her know. Worse than all of that, he had played with the ultimate Slovakian sex kitten. Rory, her beloved, her only Rory, was increasingly a stranger.

She took a deep breath, blinking to see, wishing that she had asked Mr Ali Khan for massive Sylva Frost boobs after all, as well as a tiny button nose and buttock implants. Carly had been right all along, she needed some mileage. She had an awful lot to learn about men and sex. An eighteen-year-old virgin had no hope of bagging a seasoned playboy.

Faith drove the last few miles home to Wyck Farm on autopilot, running straight past her waiting mother and shutting herself in her bedroom.

There, back in her familiar surroundings, looked down upon by walls decked with posters of dressage and horses, pictures of Rory, rosettes and one solitary Brad Pitt photo ripped from one of her parents' Sunday supplements, she felt hollow with inexperience and ignorance.

Now she was determined to wise up, to be as cool as Sylva Frost. Even if she could never hope to be that beautiful, she could try to be that assured, to acquire a little of that attitude and sexual poise.

'I love him, I love him, I love him.' She exhaled, her breath a dragon puff of hot, scorching truth.

Anke was not at all pleased to have Faith home in such disgrace. She'd been appalled to learn from Kurt and Graeme that her lovely, athletic, handsome daughter had sneaked off for cosmetic surgery to alter the way she looked for ever.

When she hadn't emerged from her room for almost an hour Anke took up a cup of tea and knocked on the door before going in to perch on the edge of the bed. Faith was texting Carly to let her know the latest.

'How could you do it to yourself, *kaereste*?' she asked, trying not to stare at the vast, gravity-defying hemispheres jutting through Faith's polo shirt.

With a sigh, Faith cast her phone to one side and started to pull up the shirt.

'No – please don't!' Anke looked away, unable to bear seeing that body she had created from her own now so mutilated.

Something warm and rubbery landed in the palm of her hand.

Anke looked at it in wonder. 'What is this?'

'My fake tits. I put them in today because I thought I might see Rory. Even though he told me not to have the operation, he is such a boob man that I have to try something. Then I remembered he's not here any more.' Her face pinched with disappointment, she looked away.

'Rory talked you out of surgery?' Anke gasped in disbelief, tears springing to her eyes as she realised her beautiful daughter wasn't really altered at all, apart from very white teeth and a very black mood.

'Men are such hypocrites!' Faith fumed. 'He said "don't do it to yourself, Faith", but his latest lover is so plastic she'd melt if she sat too close to a radiator.'

Anke stroked her back. 'Men can be like that, *kaereste*. What they want with their hearts and want with their eyes doesn't always match up.'

'Do you think Rory might want me with his heart then?'

'Maybe one day.' Anke stretched forwards to give her daughter a rare hug, immensely grateful that there was nothing fake to get between them. 'But you must give him time to find that out for himself.'

When Anke went back downstairs to tell Graham the good news that his stepdaughter was not quite as distorted as they first thought, he was surprisingly disappointed.

'You've got to admit it would have been an improvement,' he said.

'There's nothing wrong with the way she looks.'

'I'm not saying that. I'm just saying cosmetic surgeons are God's way of touching up His handiwork. What girl wants a flat chest and big nose?'

'She inherited those features from me, Graham.'

'Nonsense,' he blustered. 'They came from her father's side, I reckon, along with that wilful streak of hers. She's put you through all this worry over nothing, and now she's lost her job in the best dressage centre in the country. She'll have to make up for it.'

Anke found his comments very hurtful, but she did back up his determination to keep Faith on a short leash for the time being.

'You'll have to get another job, of course,' Graham told Faith when she emerged from her bedroom to check her email account on his computer. 'You can't mope around here for months on end until you go to university. We had enough of that with your brother.'

'I'm already looking for work. I've posted an ad on yardand-groom already. That's why I'm checking email.'

Graham was pleasantly surprised, although he needed more control. 'You will work with your mother at the bookshop.'

'I don't *think* so.' Faith was already online and accessing Hotmail. 'We agreed I could work with horses this year.'

'That's before you let us down so much.' Anke was peering over her daughter's shoulder, surreptitiously trying to read her messages. 'I can't trust you on your own again.'

'It was my money to spend as I like.'

'Not during work hours, it wasn't. D'you know how many young riders would sell their souls to train with Kurt and Graeme?'

Faith had stopped listening as she scrolled through her mail. She'd had quite a few responses to her ad, although none of them were in the discipline she had hoped.

'Racing!' Anke managed to read one. 'You cannot go and work in racing!'

Faith had to admit her size was against her – she weighed more than most racing staff – but she was a good rider and a hard worker, plus the National Hunt yards that were dotted all around the downs close to the Beauchamps' base were not as weight-obsessed as the flat yards.

'You cannot work in racing!' Anke said again.

Faith knew that the hours were awful and the pay was worse, but the geography was perfect and from what she'd heard a busy National Hunt yard full of red-blooded lads living in close proximity would be the perfect start for her sexual learning curve and development of Sylva Frost attitude.

'I would rather be based in an eventing yard, but there's nothing on offer now it's the end of the season,' she pointed out as she started typing enthusiastic replies to the enquiries, suggesting she could start as soon as they confirmed the job and accommodation.

'Eventing?' Anke sounded even more appalled.

'Yes, I've gone off dressage,' Faith said coolly, practising her attitude. It sounded good.

Anke bit her lip. She knew full well that this was about Rory, and she could tell that fighting it was hopeless. Graham was right: Faith had a wilful streak that had no link to her mother's fair-minded Danish blood. At least if the family supported this change of discipline Faith was unlikely to revisit notions of going under the knife. Big breasts might be a disadvantage in dressage, but they were a positive danger in eventing.

'Wait there! I'll make a couple of calls,' Anke insisted, rushing into the kitchen for her old Filofax that contained numbers dating back to her professional career when she had been dressage coach to most of the top event riders in the South of England.

Chapter 26

Every year for almost a decade Tash and Hugo had taken a family holiday in France after Pau three day event, letting the grooms take the horses home in the lorry while they headed to Alexandra and Pascal's manoir in the Loire Valley. There they would rest and eat and drink and talk themselves hoarse before heading home. It was a hugely relaxing break, and Tash always looked forward to it immensely, never more so than this year with a new baby to show off to her ever more remote mother.

But then, just days before Hugo and Rory set off for the Pyrenees, a postcard arrived from Tibet, featuring a large yak lying down, wearing a brightly coloured blanket. *Taking a year out with P & P, so you will miss your R & R, darling ones. But I will have such tales to tell my wonderful grandchildren when I come home! xxx*

'She's *where*?' Hugo laughed when she showed the card to him.

'She and Pascal must have gone travelling with Polly and her friends,' Tash gasped, hardly able to take it in. 'I know she was incredibly worried about letting her go backpacking, after what happened to Beccy.'

'Isn't this a bit extreme?' He studied the card. 'Surely a good global roaming mobile and Hotmail account would cover it?'

'She's always loved travelling. Pascal retired this year so they have the time now.'

'Knowing your mother, they're doing it in style, with hot and cold running Sherpas and a fully loaded portmanteau.' Hugo seemed impressed, having always admired Alexandra's spontaneity and sense of adventure.

'She could have told us what she was planning.' Tash felt terribly hurt. 'They've been gone weeks.'

'We had the Olympics and then the new baby all over us – they probably didn't want to stress you out even more.'

Nevertheless, Tash was shocked. She and Alexandra hadn't spoken in weeks, but she'd been pinning her hopes on the holiday, knowing that her capricious mother could be hard to contact but that she wouldn't dream of missing the opportunity to meet her grandson at last.

She hurriedly phone Sophia to see what her sister knew about it all.

'It comes as no surprise, frankly. You know what she's like,' Sophia assured her airily.

'She hasn't even *seen* Amery yet.'

'Linus was practically out of nappies by the time he met his grandmother, remember?'

'That's because Mummy fell out with his father. We haven't fallen out.'

'And she's always been *very* protective of Polly,' Sophia gave a jealous sniff, having long struggled with the youth, beauty and monopoly of their halfsister. She then changed direction sharply, on to the subject of Hugo's surprise fortieth birthday party. 'You still haven't given me a *clue* about numbers and budget, Tash. I simply can't organise it *all* myself!'

Tash pretended the baby was crying and rang off. She couldn't think about that right now, particularly with Hugo standing close by, barking into his mobile.

She suddenly felt tearful. Her mother was rather wayward and fickle, avoided confrontation and could be very impulsive, but she was never usually this neglectful.

It was a few moments before she realised that Hugo was speaking in French. For a brief and thrilling moment she thought that he had somehow managed to summon Pascal to the phone in the Himalayas and was giving him a piece of his mind about this 'year out'. But then she picked up enough to realise that he was trying to rescue their holiday plans. Her heart sank as she guessed exactly which hostess he would call for a last-minute invitation.

'That's settled!' he announced triumphantly as he rang off. 'MC would love to have us to stay after Pau.' His old eventing friend Marie-Clair Tucson owned a stud farm near Angers. 'We'll meet up there after the trials.'

Tash secretly dreaded spending any time with MC, who had once been a lover of Hugo's, swam naked, smoked cigars and regarded small children as vermin. Thinking that he was missing the point, and feeling even more tearful, she suggested they stay in a family-friendly gîte instead.

'Don't be silly, Tash. MC is a fabulous cook, and we can look at some of her young horses while we're there.'

'But this holiday is always totally *away* from horses,' she reminded him, voice strangled with emotion. 'We agreed we need one week a year without a horse in sight.'

'That's hardly going to happen on a stud farm, is it?'

'Which is why I don't want to go.'

'It's agreed now.'

'Well dis-agree.'

He gave her a withering look. 'I know you're upset about your mother swanning off like this, but—'

'You have no idea how I feel!' she wailed, tears finally spouting.

271

'I don't want to go to France at all if Mummy's not there. I want to stay here.' Nowadays, her default position when upset was to cling to home and the familiar.

But Hugo, who had spent the autumn dashing to competitions all over Europe and Ireland, couldn't understand Tash's thinking at all. He knew that living out of a lorry was tough with such a young family, but surely all the luxuries of MC's fabulous farm would appeal to her?

He tried hard to make conciliatory noises. 'It's been a tough season and God knows we all need a break. I can see how tense you've been since Blenheim.'

'*I've* been?' she laughed incredulously. Hugo was the one who had been impossibly short-tempered, snapping at Rory, berating Beccy and, most of all, ragging poor little Lemon, who seemed as stumped as the rest of them as to where Lough Strachan could be.

'Let's get to France and let our hair down, huh?' He put his arm around her. 'It'll be like old times.'

For a moment, Tash longed for it to be true. But she already knew the reality. With no au pairs or grandmother to help with childcare she would be constantly guarding a small baby and rampaging toddler while Hugo demanded equal attention and stimulation. Yet the thought of being all together was a rare opportunity.

'It'll be hard work with the children,' she started to weaken.

'We can leave them here with the Czechs.'

Tash couldn't believe her ears. 'What?'

'Just for a few days. My mother will oversee them.'

'Amery is still breastfeeding!'

'Can't you express?'

Tash was too staggered to speak. Her jaw was still swinging when the phone rang.

'I've solved your staffing shortage,' Penny's cheerful voice greeted her as soon as she picked up. 'You can borrow our new working pupil, Anke Brakespear's daughter. Howzat?'

Tash managed a grateful sob.

'You okay?'

'Having a domestic.'

'Righti-ho. Hang on in there, and if he claims you're driving him away hand him the car keys and tell him to do it himself. Always brings Gus to heel.' She rang off, leaving Tash glaring at Hugo.

'I am not going to France without the children.'

'Fine,' he shrugged, as though they were just talking about packing extra socks. 'Bring them along.' He picked up his phone and read a text that has just come in.

'Only if we stay in a gîte.' Tash craned her neck to see if the message was from V, but he'd pocketed the phone before she could read a word.

Suspicions flaring, Tash took an even more stubborn stance. They were still arguing when Beccy appeared, pink-faced, at the door to say that they were both needed on the yard because one of the part-timers hadn't turned up, the muck heap was full, they needed haylage bales moved and the tractor wouldn't start.

'We're hopelessly behind,' she apologised breathlessly. 'Nothing's been groomed yet.'

'It's okay, we'll finally have some more hands on the yard next week,' Tash promised.

'What?' Hugo looked at her crossly.

'Lough Strachan?' Beccy asked, turning pinker.

'No, someone from Lime Tree Farm,' she pulled on her coat. 'And me.'

'You'll be in France.'

'No, I won't.'

As Hugo opened his mouth to protest, his phone beeped with yet another text. Stalling by the door, Tash bristled while he read it, longing to grab the indestructible device and try out its manufacturer's guarantee.

'I shan't tell MC you're a "*non*" yet,' he said as he read it. 'After all, I'm sure someone else will take your place if I RSVP a royal *oui* now.'

'Who?' She felt faint, the V in RSVP raging in her head.

'Rory,' he suggested lightly, typing a response to the text as they headed outside. It was obvious he didn't believe that she would stay behind, but Tash's obstinate streak was firmly in play.

The following day, when she still refused to change her mind, Hugo appeared with a vast bunch of roses, star-gazer lilies and asters held out like a shield in front of him as he pleaded with her to reconsider. But her reaction alarmed him all the more as, spotting the label, her eyes narrowed. 'They're from Waitrose.'

'So?'

Looking highly disapproving, Tash took them without another word. Later that day they appeared, neatly arranged in two pewter vases, on Snob and Bodybuilder's graves in Flat Pad, and Hugo realised he had done nothing to further his cause, although he had no idea why.

'Are Waitrose flowers politically incorrect?' he asked Beccy, baffled.

'They do it for me.' She sighed, giving him a bashful sideways look that was wasted on Hugo as he stalked off, muttering about living orchids.

By the end of the week, Haydown was bursting with blooms, but Tash was no more willing to go to France. 'Someone has to stay behind and water all these plants,' she pointed out mulishly.

Chapter 27

When Faith arrived at Lime Tree Farm in Fosbourne Ducis, her chicken fillets and attitude were firmly in place. She immediately kicked up a dust cloud of controversy as an ageing and unfit grey Thoroughbred gelding that she had apparently kidnapped from Rory's Cotswolds yard was dropped off by a passing local trainer on his way back from Cheltenham.

'How did she get Charlie to agree to do that?' Gus was staggered and secretly quite impressed that one of the meanest Lambourn stalwarts had taken a twenty-mile detour for an unprepossessing kid like Faith.

'Flashed her fake tits at him probably,' Penny muttered.

'Has she got falsies?' Fascinated, Gus couldn't wait to take another look. He'd never seen fake breasts close up before and, being a leg man, would need them pointed out rather like Prince Philip touring a factory and told that he was looking at a bottling machine.

'I definitely heard that Kurt fired her because she took time off to have a boob job,' Penny nodded, having been to her dressage trainer for a lesson just that week and got all the gossip. 'I hope Anke's right that she's a bloody hard worker and knows her stuff. When I told her she can't have her own horse here d'you know what she said?'

'He's not my horse, I've just stolen him,' Gus laughed, having overheard. He liked Faith's style. Opinionated, domineering, defensive and obstreperous in equal measure, she was a tough cookie even in the notoriously hardened world of event riding.

'She's just like her bloody father.' Penny was not looking forward to life as unwitting guardian to the irascible new cuckoo chick. 'Thank God she's going to start off at Haydown,' she sighed with relief. 'She can take that pensionable horse with her for a start. Tash has a knack with these stroppy girls, and Lord knows she needs the help with Hugo away so much. There's no way she can cope alone, whatever he thinks.'

'What about Lough Strachan?' Gus asked. 'Won't he be there?'

'Not arrived yet.'

'*Still?* Jesus. Has he been abducted by aliens?'

'Don't joke.' Penny dropped her voice, having enjoyed a long gossip about it with Jenny when out cubbing that week. 'That little punk groom of his is behaving as though this is all perfectly normal, but of course nothing is being paid for. Hugo's threatening to sell one of Lough's horses.'

'Shouldn't they at least check he's still alive?'

'Lemon seems to have heard from him, but he's a shifty little character. I wouldn't trust him.'

'You don't trust anyone,' Gus said with feeling.

'Hardly surprising, being married to you,' she muttered, stalking off to check Faith hadn't taken delivery of any more stolen horses.

Walking away after a barbed comment was becoming Penny's stock in trade. It was as far as she ever pushed the panic button on their marriage, fearing that if she pressed any harder it would trigger the eject seat and she'd find herself bereft, with no Gus and no Lime Tree Farm. Their marriage had been heading towards a tailspin after Burghley, but was spluttering along just above the tree line now that the UK horse trials season was almost over and Gus had fewer opportunities for stolen moments in moonlit lorry parks. Penny was certain that whoever it was he was having an affair with either rode, groomed or owned an event horse. While the woman's exact identity remained a mystery, she was convinced it was an open secret on the circuit.

Worse than the disloyalty and betrayal, she found, was the humiliation: the thought that people in the sport knew, that riders and organisers she had competed alongside for so many years were laughing at her.

Yet she had spoken to almost nobody about her fears, not even her sister Zoe or Tash. The only person that she had breathed a word to, *in vino* and in a stupidly overwrought state, was the handsome young man she had met at Haydown after the tipsy wedding-anniversary lunch. He turned out to be just about the most famous pop star in England, which was typical of her luck.

Perched on the top of the hay bales stacked in the Dutch barn, which seemed to be the only place with any decent reception on her mobile network, Faith sent out a blanket text to let her friends know about her new job. Then she began composing a separate message to Rory, agonising over how to phrase it and explain to him about bringing Whitey with her. But she had to abandon it when Penny started shouting for her. Phone already beeping with replies, she clambered down to be told that she would be working most days at Haydown.

'I've just spoken with Tash and your horse can be stabled up there in the short term, but you'll live here at Lime Tree Farm. We've promised your mother we'll keep an eye on you.'

Faith wanted to hug her. It was better than she could have dreamed: she would be working right alongside Rory again. With Penny still banging on about the arrangements, she surreptitiously checked the texts that had come through. Amazingly, Dillon Rafferty was one of the first to reply and wish her luck. She'd only ever added his number to wind up Carly when they'd been playing with the settings of her new phone.

Realising that Penny had fallen silent, she looked up to find her glowering. 'You're going to have to sharpen up your ideas, Faith. If Hugo catches you texting during work hours he'll send you straight back here. And if *I* catch you texting in work hours, I'll send you straight back home.'

'Yeah, sure.' Faith's new attitude was holding out despite the knots of fear and homesickness in her belly. As always when she was nervous, she was overly assertive. 'It's just Dillon Rafferty wishing me luck. He came to my eighteenth. We're mates. I was the one who told him to buy The Fox.'

Penny looked shocked. 'You know him?'

'We're like this.' Faith pinched her thumb and forefinger together.

'I've told Tash you'll go straight up to Haydown to introduce yourself. Why not stay all day?' Penny turned and stalked away.

Faith's heart sank. She was dying to impress Penny Moncrieff, who was a doyenne of the sport. Instead, she'd just made herself look like a name-dropping idiot.

When Faith first set eyes on Haydown's blushing brickwork, Flambards atmosphere, family heartbeat and quality horseflesh, she thought she was in heaven. But then she found that her *raison d'être* was missing.

'Rory left for Pau with Hugo yesterday,' Tash explained when showing her around. 'They'll be in France a couple of weeks – Hugo's arranged a stay with MC, that's Marie-Clair Tucson. They'll be back for the Express Eventing Challenge.'

'But that's not until the end of November!'

'I know.' Tash sighed, looking strained. 'Hugo's off to Adelaide straight after that, but Rory will stay here, and Lough Strachan should have finally arrived by then, so we'll have more help.'

Faith was too disappointed about Rory to be interested in Lough, who the Moncrieffs seemed to think had disappeared into the Bermuda Triangle.

Tash was introducing a pretty girl with dreadlocks. 'Beccy will show you the ropes. You must excuse me if I dash off,' she apologised, already backing away. 'The au pairs have discovered the steam cleaner and I'd have to get back in the house to stop them vaporising the dogs.'

'She's not on the yard much,' Beccy told Faith after she'd gone. 'Prefers having babies and painting pictures to horses these days.'

Faith was surprised. Tash was one of her all-time heroines – meeting her was a secret thrill – and she thought she was lovely. But sacrificing horses for domesticity was a crime in her eyes.

'She was supposed to be in France now too,' Beccy went on, grateful to have someone new to gossip to. 'But they changed their plans at the last minute – something to do with Tash's mother not being around. She's got a house there. There was a huge row and Hugo left in one hell of a bad mood. It's their anniversary next week.'

They were walking through the yards now, and Faith's eyes were on stalks. Haydown was her Mecca and it didn't disappoint. The horse facilities were out of this world.

'It's a bit quiet here today,' Beccy pointed out the obvious as they toured empty yards. 'Everything's turned out apart from the injured ones. When Jenny comes back with the Pau horses next week there'll be more going on.'

She turned and blushed as Lemon hacked into the yard, parakeet Mohawk squashed beneath a racing helmet with a yellow bobble-top silk. Having trained as a jockey, he still rode with his stirrups very short.

'Got lost again!' he lamented as he jumped off. 'Fucking downs – why are they called that when there are so many hills? And they all look the same!'

'It's 'cos they get you down when you're lost.' Faith stepped forward to hold the horse while he unsaddled.

'And you are?' he demanded camply.

'Faith.'

'I'm Lemon. Great tits.'

Faith bristled. She was now more sensitive than ever about her bust, which was, today as every day since arriving in West Berkshire, crammed with her biggest chicken fillets. It was her new body armour, along with her attitude. 'Are you always this rude?'

He winked at Beccy who was giggling nearby, clearly thinking him hilarious. 'No, you misunderstand me. I'm a twitcher. Saw some great tits when I was out riding just now.'

'Is that a fact?' Faith snarled, hackles rising further.

'Getting colder, isn't it? Might see blue tits later.' He dumped his saddle on a stable door, ready to take his horse from her to lead him to the wash box. 'We twitchers love all tits.'

Beccy was still sniggering.

Faith held on firmly to the rein he was trying to take from her.

'One more tit comment around me and you won't be twitching any more, buster. You won't even have a pulse.' Her voice was pure ice.

Lemon blinked, taking a proper look at her for the first time. Then he smiled widely, realising he'd met his match.

'Frightfully pleased to meet you. Faith,' – he held out his hand, aggrandising his Kiwi accent to finest old-colonial Queenstown – 'you have my word that I will not mention those indigenous British birds in your presence again.'

'Thank you,' she shook his hand, dropping the snarl to smile back. As he walked away, leading the horse, she added: 'Great arse.'

Beccy adored Faith and her attitude. Working on the yard became even more fun with her sparking off Lemon. Having become the straight man to the little Kiwi's pushy humour, she delighted in witnessing him take massive doses of his own medicine. Despite being ten years their junior and always working at twice the rate, Faith still managed to stick up for Beccy at all times and backchat faster than a cobra strike when Lem was being domineering. Within a week she had him in check and he became increasingly Lemon cordial.

Beccy felt no immediate threat to her position as Lemon's number one Limey because he still flirted with her all the time, play-fighting and telling her how sexy and beautiful she was. Faith refused to join in that game.

'I don't know how you put up with it,' she grumbled one day after a particularly full-on flirtation session involving a pitchfork and the hosepipe. 'It's so fake when gay men flirt with women like that.' Her blunt self-assurance made Beccy feel stupid at times.

'He told Jenny he was bisexual, apparently.'

'Oh c'mon, I've been involved with dressage too long to fall for that one,' Faith sneered. 'Gay men always say that to make girls fancy them. It's good for their egos. Kurt did it for years. Still does.'

The following day, as the girls took a tea break after mucking out and sat on a log to watch Tash loose schooling one of the home-bred youngsters for the first time in the round pen, Faith sprang a surprise question on Beccy. 'So, do you fancy Lemon, then?'

Beccy was about to laugh, but something stopped her and she watched the straw dust dancing in the light from an early ray of sun that was radiating from beneath the stable yard's arched entrance. Autumn was still putting on a magnificent show, the copper leaves sweeping down and littering the grass around them, like God's pencil shavings as he frantically sharpened between sketching in the grey lines of winter.

'No! Well, hmm. A bit, maybe,' she found herself saying, and it came as a shock even to herself. She guessed she must be such a desperate old virgin that she fancied anything with a pulse these days. She wasn't about to admit to her feelings for Hugo or her secret text life with Lough. Lem called her 'sexpot' and told her she had the most beautiful eyes. It made her feel good.

'Crikey. You and I will be great mates.' Faith turned to her, grinning stupidly.

'Yes?' Beccy was thrilled.

'I thought you'd be after Rory.'

'God no.' Beccy was about to announce that she found Rory vile, then realised that was perhaps not wise. She knew she wasn't always good at reading people, but she had enough sense to realise that Faith was very touchy on the subject of Rory.

'You want to have a drink in the Olive Branch tonight?' Faith suggested. 'We'll ask Lemon.'

'Oh. Okay.' She felt suddenly plagued by ridiculous butterflies.

In the round pen Tash called the young horse back to her, rubbing him between his eyes and scratching his neck once she'd caught him.

'Has she said anything about how it's going in Pau?' Faith asked casually.

'No idea. I sense she and Hugo aren't talking much,' Beccy told her with satisfaction.

'Is it that bad?' Faith was shocked. The Beauchampions were her idols.

'Things have been very shaky since Blenheim,' Beccy confided in an undertone, then shut up as Tash led the youngster passed them and paused to point out in her gentle but nonetheless certain way that they should both be working.

Beccy glared at her stepsister's retreating back, hoping that things were set to get even worse in her marriage. It gave her hope.

Any feelings she had for Lemon were mere surface scratches compared to the mortal wounds of loving Hugo.

That evening in Fosbourne Ducis, the Olive Branch's landlord couple, Italian chef Angelo and his English wife Denise, observed the raucous new trinity of Haydown and Lime Tree yard staff with suspicion.

Faith and Lem were getting louder by the minute. As designated driver, Beccy was sober and deflated. Her mobile phone had packed up after too many rain-sodden days stored in her pocket while working on the yard; she had fallen off that morning, her bank balance was zero while her credit-card bills topped almost four figures, and she felt her new-found crush fading fast as Lemon and Faith bonded more and more.

Faith was lovely when sober – tough, acerbic, straight-talking and funny. But she had no head for drink whatsoever and became a monster after one vodka and coke. And Lem had immediately spotted an opening to take advantage.

He encouraged her to join him in his favourite pastime of slagging off Hugo. 'He's such a reactionary'. . . 'Tash is a saint to put up with that shit' . . . 'Beccy says the marriage is on the rocks.'

'I said no such thing!' Beccy squeaked at Faith, appalled that her indiscretion was now being broadcast within earshot of locals who knew the couple well. 'He's just been away a lot. After the Olympics he was in Ireland, then France for Fontainebleau and Le Lion d'Angers, plus Holland for Boekelo, now back in France again.'

'Avoiding being at home,' Lem said knowingly. 'Classic sign of a shaky marriage.'

'Classic sign of being an event rider,' Faith shot back.

'My dad used to disappear for weeks on end before he and my mum divorced,' he told them. 'He was a shearer and used the excuse that he was away working, but they couldn't stand each other. Mum didn't realise he'd left her until she found out he'd been living with the woman across the road for three months.' He and Faith seemed to find this screamingly funny, whereas it made Beccy want to cry.

'You think Hugo shags around?' Lem pondered.

'Undoubtedly,' Faith asserted, 'they all do on the eventing circuit. Mum used to coach Hugo years ago, before he married, and says he was notorious. He was known as Clear Round because every woman in eventing wanted to jump him. He once even shagged Julia Ditton in the commentary box while she was live on air, but nobody ever guessed. Every time a horse jumped a fence she let out a shriek of delight.'

They both fell about.

Beccy felt like a small child trapped with her two ASBO parents.

When not slagging off Hugo and counting down his marriage, Faith and Lemon were having conversations that not only verged on the obscene, but left Beccy feeling sexually ignorant and prudish: 'You ever got your period while riding out?' . . . 'Never. Have you ever come?' . . . 'Come first, come second, come third, me. You?' . . .

'I always come first' . . . 'I'd like to see that someday' . . . 'You'd have to work on it' . . . 'You should see me in action. These fingers are pussy poetry. All that mane plaiting' . . . 'And your tongue runs away with you, too' . . . 'I give good head' . . . 'Head or tails?' . . . 'Depends who's asking . . .'

'Beccy says you're bisexual,' Faith told Lemon with a hiccup.

Beccy felt her face flame.

But he wasn't at all fazed. 'Yeah – lucky me. If I reach down the front of someone's pants I'm always satisfied with what I find.'

'Well that's good news, huh, Beccy?' Faith gave her a thumbs-up. She flashed a very weak smile.

'Afraid *I'm* off limits,' Faith told Lem.

'Why's that?'

'Never wear pants.'

Beccy felt totally out of her comfort zone, longing to be back at Haydown with Tash, a huge meal, her copy of *Cheers!* and an old eventing DVD playing on the kitchen telly.

At that moment, landlady Denise bore down on them to collect empties and pointedly wipe the table, as though trying to clear away the loud, indecorous chat from her well-mannered country pub. 'Can I get you folks anything to eat?'

'Just another round, gorgeous.' Lemon hammed up his New Zealand accent, gazing up at her through his pale lashes and bright yellow fringe.

Denise shuddered and gave Beccy a sympathetic look.

'I'm going outside for a smoke.' Lemon lurched off.

Faith grinned at his retreating back then turned to Beccy. 'You're right. I think he is bi.'

Beccy raised an eyebrow, deciding the new friendship was off. 'Thanks for playing cupid. I really appreciate it.'

The sarcasm wasn't lost on Faith, who blinked a few times to get her head together. When she spoke again, her voice was slurred, but she knew exactly what she was saying.

'Okay, here's the deal.' She glanced towards the door to check that Lem was still outside smoking. 'I have to be honest, Beccy. You're way too cool for him – look at you. Gorgeous. Sussed. Older woman. Travelled the world, seen all sorts of things, slept with maharajas and Masai warriors for all I know. You even smuggled drugs, for chrissake. Oh, sorry, you probably don't like being reminded of that. Anyway, Lemon's not for you. He's funny, but he's not even in your league.'

Beccy gaped at her.

Eventually, Faith waved a hand in front of her companion's face: 'Hello? Are you there?'

'You think I'm a cool older woman?'

'You are! You are way cool. I'm such a geek. This is all an act, but you're the real thing.'

It should be easy to take a compliment, but Beccy had never taken the easy route. It was why she had travelled for so long on such a solitary path. 'Faith, I'm not cool. I'm a twenty-seven-year-old virgin with no career path and a chip on her shoulder.'

To her surprise, Faith raised her glass in a salute. 'Beccy, you and I have *so* much in common.'

Beccy's mouth was still formed in a little surprised 'o' when Lemon rejoined them, reeking of fags, knocking back his tequila and eyeing them both mischievously.

'I did a naughty thing just now when I was having my smoke.'

'Oh yes?' Faith was only half interested in his practical jokes.

'I texted Lough that Tash and Hugo have split up.'

She snorted in surprise. 'You what?'

His porcine eyes glittered. 'I reckon I've had it the wrong way round, you see, – telling Lough what he doesn't want to hear: "You're in deep shit. Hugo's spitting blood." Maybe this'll work. Carrot and stick. Tell him something he *wants* to hear.'

'Why would he want to hear that Tash and Hugo have split up?' asked Faith. 'Have I missed something?'

Beccy felt her face flame.

Lem looked at her thoughtfully before turning to Faith. '*Ka mate kāinga tahi, ka ora kāinga rua*, as the boss says.'

'Meaning?'

'When one house dies, another lives.' He raised his glass. 'Lough comes from a broken home, yeah. He likes to take on damaged horses to try to rebuild them, same goes for people. He doesn't really care for something unless it's broken.'

On cue, 'All You Need is Love' started playing over the pub's sound system.

As Faith and Lemon crooned along, Beccy had to sit on her hands to stop them shaking.

Chapter 28

In the Pyrenees, Hugo threw his phone on to the table of the little hotel bar and reached for his wine glass. He'd tried to call Tash while he took a cigarette break outside, but the reception was lousy and it had started to rain. Now he raised his glass at Marie-Clair, grateful for her company.

She raised hers in return. He knew that look in her eye of old. Lusty, excited, red-blooded and fantastically unfettered by any morals. Her rich American husband was in another time zone, and as far as she was concerned that placed her beyond reproach. She wanted to be extremely naughty tonight.

She'd looked exactly the same throughout the two decades they'd been friends, with her sunshine complexion and knowing eyes, her body still as fit and lean from riding horses and lovers daily. MC had always possessed an unashamed appetite for sex, food and wine, and as well as friendship she and Hugo had shared a bed several times, but that had been before his marriage.

Tash was in his blood, his head and his heart, but he had never felt as distanced from her as he did now. He ran a dry tongue along his teeth and tasted his mounting unease.

Beside him, Rory looked as though he could only taste success, washed down with his fourth glass of Buzet. Hugo envied the young man his carefree attitude. His dressage that day had been a disaster, yet he remained enviably upbeat. Another time, Hugo might have laid into him about slipping off the wagon but he knew he was hardly leading by example as he leaned across the table to refill their glasses.

In fact, Rory was far from happy, but the wine was acting as an anaesthetic, and he had been brought up not to sulk, however bleak his heart. Sylva had dumped him by text that morning. Theirs had never been anything more than a playful fling, but because Rory played with all his heart he felt bruised by the brush-off, and insulted that she felt it necessary to dismiss him like a superfluous employee. The press had found out about Jules, she said, and it was all about to blow. She wanted his name kept out of it and insisted it was best to cease all contact.

Cease all contact. It made him feel like a stalker under threat of a court order. When he'd replied that there were no hard feelings his text had come back as undeliverable. She had blocked his number.

His mind had been in the wrong place all day and his dressage on Rio had been a shambles. He knew that he'd let Hugo down. He was feeling so low that he'd wanted to crawl to bed early that night, but Hugo insisted that he come along to supper with Marie-Clair Tucson. His bleak mood made him uncharacteristically tongue-tied, even more so because he was dining with one of his teenage pin-ups, a woman so intimidatingly carnal that every man in the restaurant seemed to loosen his collar upon looking at her.

He'd long admired MC, and had coveted the chance to get closer to her for years. Once the undisputed glamourpuss of the sport she was still a formidably sexy figure – part Sophia Loren, part Jacqueline Bisset and wholly built for sin. She must be over fifty now, but she had amazing glossy olive skin, and rumpled bed-head hair the colour of Nutella that snaked down towards a cleavage as welcoming as two profiteroles. He was immensely excited at the thought of ten days in her company at her family's Loire retreat, which purportedly had an indoor pool, Jacuzzi, hot tub and sauna as well as four-poster beds as big as snooker tables.

No longer competing at four-star level, she remained one of the most respected and influential female riders of her generation, not least because her marriage to an extremely wealthy, horse-loving American businessman, himself a long-term sponsor of the United States Eventing Association, had enabled her to become a great patron and benefactor of the sport. The couple had homes in Florida and Montana, as well as MC's magnificent stud near Angers.

A holiday in France was just the time out Rory needed, and would suit Sylva, who clearly wanted him as far away as possible. It also delayed his return to Haydown. He knew Faith was going to be there: she'd texted him earlier that day to break the news and demand to know why he hadn't told her Rio was competing at Pau. The truth was, Rory had no desire to encounter the all new, grown-up, altered Faith with her plastic additions and her Essex attitude. He preferred the kid he remembered. He had a feeling the all-new Faith could be almost as scary as MC, who had the same ballsy, outspoken grit and free spirit. But MC had grown from child to woman many years ago and Rory had no problem seeing her curves, carnality and corruption as assets. He fancied her a lot, despite the fear factor.

He was happy to sit back and watch as she and Hugo spent the evening chatting alternately in French and English, gossiping, joking and spatting – not always in an entirely friendly way – and lifting Rory's spirits. He loved the way she reached out to touch whoever she spoke to, as automatically as someone stroking an attractive dog lying at their feet. When she touched Hugo he had a habit of batting her away without realising it, as though her hand was a fly that kept landing on him. Rory suspected his irritation came more from the fact that she accused him of losing his competitive edge since having children.

'Thees boy, he ride with more balls than you now, huh?' She reached out and stroked Rory's hair, making the balls in question tighten deliciously.

'That's your opinion,' Hugo snapped. 'But we all know you ride with the biggest balls of all, MC. I'm amazed you can stay in the saddle.'

'I am ze belle of ze big balls, no?' She laughed, winking at Rory.

'Alarm belle maybe,' Hugo muttered dismissively, but there was affection in his voice.

'*Ta belle époque est terminé, chéri.*'

'*C'est la pitié qui se moque de la charité.*'

'Eh?' Rory was lost.

MC turned to him again, this time touching his cheek. 'I tell him he is past his prime, and he tell me zat I ze pot calling kettle black, *oui*?'

'Nonsense! You're perfect. Beautiful.' He admired her gloriously high cheekbones.

'You are sweet boy.' She smiled, revealing fabulously white teeth with a seductive gap between the front two. 'When we were lovers, I taught Hugo many French sayings which now come back to – how you say – haunt me?'

'You two are a great double act,' Rory said. 'Why d'you never marry?'

'I asked her once,' Hugo told him truthfully. 'She said I'd be too unfaithful.'

Rory laughed uproariously at this. She was *just* like Faith.

'Maybe that trait is not so bad for me now.' Marie-Clair's sexy chocolate eyes gleamed with mirth. 'And I am ze one asking all ze questions tonight, huh Hugo?'

He shifted uncomfortably.

'And do you have an answer for me?' She licked her lips, plump and moist and temptingly carnal. 'Shall we do it again for old times' sake, or must I wait for your wife to give you your balls back?'

Hugo said nothing.

'Have I missed something?' Rory was baffled.

But neither of his companions answered as they carried on regarding one another with a mixture of long-standing respect, lust and confrontation. Rory sensed a subtext.

'Is this the point at which I should make my excuses and leave?' he joked.

'Stay, *chéri*.' MC reached out and stroked Rory's leg with strong, warm fingers that edged excitingly close to his crotch.

Rory stayed.

Hugo tapped his phone against the table, glaring at its darkened screen, a muscle fluttering in his cheek.

'Okay.' He looked up, suddenly smiling in that way that transformed his masked face and made all the waiting staff fall over one another to get to the table first. 'We'll do it again.' He called for more wine.

MC let out an ecstatic purr. 'Is that a promise?'

'You have my word.'

'And your wife? Will she want to join in this time?'

Convinced he was listening in on a sexual assignation, Rory's eyes bulged at the thought of a threesome with MC and Tash. Now that would be heaven. It even outranked his romp with Sylva and Jules.

'I need to work on Tash. For now it's just you and me – and perhaps Rory can join us.'

'Ah, yes. Hmm. Perhaps not.' Rory started to panic. Wrong sort of threesome. He'd never had Hugo down as a daisy-chain man, but in this sport it never did to assume. Rory fancied MC, but he genuinely liked Tash and, while not averse to a little off-limits carousing, this was too far out of line. Realising this was all getting too hot – and adulterous and kinky – for him to handle, he made to stand up and announce he was off to bed, but MC's hand kept him clamped down by the groin.

287

'We are having another drink, *chéri*,' she insisted throatily. 'Then I need you to come and help me open the bathroom window in my room. I like to have extremely steamy baths, and ze catch mechanism is very, very stiff.' The hand stroked higher and Rory felt his own mechanism stiffen in sympathy.

'Is Hugo checking the catch too?' he asked in a small, anxious voice.

'Why should he? *Ou es-tu homo?*' She sighed disappointedly.

'No! I thought you and he just agreed . . .'

'Hugo will 'ave to wait his turn, *non?*' She was practically sitting in his lap now, which Rory found impossibly thrilling. MC was the most predatorily sexual woman he'd ever encountered, and far more his type than coquettish, manipulative Sylva hiding behind texts, high walls and her entourage.

'Besides, Hugo, 'e is an old man now – he needs to preserve his energy for ze cross country tomorrow, *non?* I sink you need a work-out instead.'

Rory's face suddenly lit up with understanding. 'Oh, right – one at a time. Great! Me first then.' He couldn't think of a lovelier way to get over being dumped.

'*Non, chéri.*' She laughed throatily. 'Where are your good manners you English are so famous for? *I* always come first.'

At Haydown, Tash was grateful to have an evening of solitude, without the customary obligation to provide a meal for Beccy and Lemon, or her mother-in-law who had a house guest that weekend.

Aching from a day lunging and long-reining young horses, she settled by the easel in the study to finish a painting of a brace of red setters, listening out for the phone. She'd already tried to call Hugo, but his mobile was going to voicemail. She knew they both longed to make peace, but it was proving hard, and she was still livid that he'd suggested holidaying without the children.

Equally, he'd been so furious when she refused to join him in France that he'd left without even saying goodbye. They'd spoken daily since then, but these had been curt, mandatory updates with no affection. The last she'd heard, he and Rory had got into trouble for riding two borrowed mopeds around the Pau horsebox park at three in the morning on the first dressage day. As it was their home-bred hopeful Cub's first four-star CCI and Rory's first real test on

The Fox, she was not best pleased, but she knew that Hugo's default setting was juvenile hell-raiser when the marriage hit a sticky patch. It somewhat reassured her that, if he was drunkenly pratting about in the early hours, at least he wasn't having illicit liaisons with the mysterious V.

Ever-mindful of the V texts, Tash was desperate to put the row behind them. All evening she conducted imaginary conversations with him, alternating between indignation and affection. She knew he was struggling to understand the way that she was right now, her clawing fear of getting back in the saddle and her desire to stay at home, which was at such odds with the Tash he knew so well, who'd shared his competitive and physical passion for so many years. Her fitness and confidence had recovered so quickly after Cora was born that she'd taken it for granted that the same would happen a second time. Instead, she was ever more introspective and deeply selfconscious, and couldn't hope to explain to Hugo how much her saggy, untoned body appalled her, certain that by doing so she would just bring it into sharper relief. They'd only made love a handful of times since Amery was born, and she'd been far too busy trying to hold in her stomach to really enjoy it. As her mother-in-law kept telling her, 'Yummy mummies are all very well, but if they can't close the nursery door at night baddy daddies start to look elsewhere.'

Another hour crawled by with no call. His mobile was still unobtainable.

In Tash's overactive imagination, Hugo was no longer repeating the moped escapades of the previous night, and was instead sitting astride quite another racy plaything. Now entertaining paranoid visions of Hugo pleasuring a mistress in Pau, she painted faster and faster to blot out the products of her mind's eye. Soon, the two red setters on the canvas in front of her began to take on the facial expressions of a married couple, one as bashful as the other was sexy and roguish.

She was so carried away that she might have added a Cavalier King Charles rampantly in heat and wriggling on her back between them had the phone not rung.

Picking it up to hear a really crackly line from a mobile, she almost sobbed with relief.

'I'm so glad you called! I've been thinking about you all day. I so wish I was sharing your bed tonight.'

'Tash, are you okay there?' It wasn't Hugo's voice; this was a deep, unfamiliar drawl yet with an accent recognisable to all three day event riders: a New Zealander. 'Your mobile number's been dead all night.'

She coughed nervously. 'Actually, I don't have a mobile right now. Is this—'

'I've just got Lem's message. I can't speak long. I'm still in some deep shit here.'

'Are you okay?' The conversation was surreal.

'I'm not allowed to leave the country yet. Where's Hugo gone?'

'France.'

'Has he taken the horses?'

'Yes. Of course.'

'Shit. And the kids?'

'They're with me. Can I just check, is this—'

'I haven't forgotten a word you said,' he interrupted urgently. 'I'll be with you by Christmas, that's a promise.' There was a beat's pause then, his voice dropping, 'I wish you were sharing my bed tonight too. I've got to go.' He hung up.

Tash scratched her head and tried Hugo's mobile number again. This time he picked up the call, predictably bad-tempered.

'Hang on . . . go outside . . . no blood . . . reception . . .'

'I think I've just heard from Lough. It sounds like he's in hospital or something.'

'Hope . . . broken his neck. Save . . . from wringing it. All okay there?' The bad line made him sound even more distant than ever.

'Yes. You?'

'So so. Rory ballsed up his dressage this afternoon. Rio freaked out at the stadium, and by the time he settled him Rory was so wired he forgot his test.'

'At least he posted top-ten with Fox yesterday,' she placated, 'and you've got Cub in contention.'

'Think I should go for it tomorrow?'

They'd already agreed tactics for the young horse, but she could tell Hugo was dying to be competitive.

'Take it steady and give him confidence,' she urged. 'He's still green.'

'Hmmph. Need to get . . . owners . . . next season . . . decent four-star horse . . .' He disappeared into crackling interference again.

'There's plenty of time,' she reminded him.

But the line was breaking up badly now and he was talking across her:

'. . . been thinking . . . drive the kids and . . . in the Loire . . . next Monday . . . bring Verruca, yes?'

'Don't call her that,' she said automatically. 'And I can't come. I've got an important lunch next week.' It was the perfect opportunity to remind him that she was meeting Sylva Frost and to sound him out about which horse they should try to sell her. She could be just the new owner he needed.

He'd moved to get better reception again, his voice suddenly a crystal-clear bark. 'Cancel it. You're coming to France. MC's dying to see you.'

Tash knew Marie-Clair of old, and doubted she'd notice if Tash was in the room doing a tap dance on the table.

'So you're definitely planning to stay on there?' she asked in a small voice, realising he was truly taking a stand.

'She's invited Rory too.'

'Oh yes?' Hardly a reliable chaperone, she felt. The three would be drunkenly debauched from day one.

'Come and join us, Tash.'

She wanted to say 'we need you here' but her throat was too choked to speak the words. It was all she could manage to croak 'No.'

He hung up without a goodbye.

Tash clambered wearily into her boots and pulled on a coat to do night-check with the baby monitor in her pocket, walking outside just in time to see Beccy's sporty little car driving far too fast into the first courtyard and parking at an angle in front of the door to the stables flat. Then she practically carried Lemon from the passenger seat and through the door.

The lights were glowing above the archway and the sound of the television indicated that the Czechs were still up, wrapped up in one another and their cloak of shared language.

Tash went around each stable, making sure that the automatic drinkers were working, that hay racks were topped up and rugs correct.

Afterwards she stood for a long time staring up at the dark sky, wishing that she was going to France. She missed Hugo so much it hurt. They were both so stupidly stubborn at times. But if she thought about Marie-Clair's lifestyle and her forceful sexuality and ribald humour, the late night meals, early hours drinking sessions, wild pranks and desire to spend all day in the saddle she knew that there would be no place for her and the children there. She was appalled that Hugo couldn't see it too.

The following morning, somewhat jaded from a long night with the extremely demanding MC, Rory thought any chances of victory were blown when The Fox overreached badly just three fences into the cross-country and pulled up lame, forcing them to retire. As usual he couldn't get hold of his owner to report the bad news, Dillon currently being somewhere in Japan with his mobile switched off.

Yet that afternoon he climbed no less than twenty-three places on the leader board after a blistering ride across country in appalling weather on the brave but inexperienced Rio.

By equal contrast, this horse's owner sent a text almost before Rory had dismounted. *Saw it all online. Bloody amazing. Love my horse! Big it up for the boys. UCnDoMgc. F x*

Rory felt uneasy under such Big Brother scrutiny. And since when had Faith started saying 'Big it up' or whatever gobbledegook UCnDoMgc meant? It must be one of her Essex affectations, along with silicone and stilettos. Nevertheless, he saved the message to his phone memory, alongside the *Bonne chance* MC had sent him just before he set out. Then, stifling a yawn, he handed Rio to Jenny and went to study the scoreboard.

Earlier in the day, Hugo had posted a safe and solid round on the equally inexperienced The Cub, racking up some time penalties but still securing the top slot. But now Rory had bolted home so fast he'd climbed two points above his trainer the night before show-jumping. On another occasion Hugo would have been praised for his caution, for putting the horse first and thinking more long-term for once. But such was the cruelty of contrast that critics immediately chorused that he had lost his edge and that younger men like Rory were riding more boldly and bravely in the traditional spirit of the sport. In the post-competition interviews one journalist accused him of selling out and losing his nerve. It seemed he couldn't win their approval either way.

Chapter 29

Hugo: 'I CAN'T WIN!' shouted the *Horse & Hound* report on Pau CCI★★★★, which featured a thumbnail of him looking very grumpy as he and Cub sailed over the Fontaine Jump. The large photograph of Rory clearing the last show-jump on the flashy stallion Rio was much more flattering, and was captioned *'Pau . . . sers!'* The commentary pointed out that the Midwinter string looked likely to take all next year, and would bring the recently failing fortunes of the Beauchamps' yard a much-needed boost, particularly as Lough Strachan had apparently changed his mind about coming to the UK.

Tash scanned the rest of the report as she waited for Sylva, who insisted on collecting her and the kids for their lunch date, but was now over an hour late. It didn't make great reading. Hugo came across as a terrible loser, with his quote taken quite out of context. She only hoped that she could cheer him up by bagging Sylva as a new owner by the time he returned from France.

'Rory did good, yeah.'

Tash jumped, realising that Lem had wandered into the house and was standing right behind her, reading over her shoulder. She wished he would knock first. It never bothered her when Beccy or Jenny came in unannounced, but something about Lem made her edgy, especially with Hugo and Rory away. He was become increasingly proprietorial.

'My girls want to know what to ride after lunch,' he said now.

'It's written on the office board,' Tash told him, disliking the way he used 'my girls' for Beccy and Faith. The three had formed a little clique that she privately thought brought out the worst in them all, particularly Beccy, who was ever more distant.

'Do you know anything about this?' Tash pointed to the reference to Lough in the report. 'I had a very strange call from him the other night, but he definitely said he was still coming.'

'He's had a spot of bother with his passport,' Lemon said airily, before changing the subject. 'You look great, Mrs B. Going somewhere nice?'

'Lunch with a prospective owner.'

Stressed out from a morning spent battling the yard's broken-down tractor, and then embarking on a rescue mission to collect the

Czech au pairs who had got stranded in Marlbury's multi-story with the Beauchamps' decrepit Volvo that they used as a runaround ('a total death trap' to quote the AA man), she wasn't feeling as serene and ladies-who-lunch-tastic as she might have hoped. She couldn't get the black crescents of oil and grease from beneath her stubby nails despite minutes of scrubbing with a nailbrush – but at least they matched the dark crescents beneath her eyes.

'La-di-da. I'd better get back below stairs, m'lady.' Lemon doffed an imaginary cap and headed towards the back lobby, poking his tongue out at Cora as he passed to make her laugh, but the little girl burst into tears instead.

'So Lough definitely is coming?' Tash checked as she gathered Cora into a hug.

'Yeah, yeah.' He stalled at the door. 'Don't panic. He's half Maori, remember. They see time differently.'

'Well perhaps the non-Maori half could get his arse in gear,' Tash snapped, realising too late that she sounded just like Hugo.

Lem stopped and looked back at her over his shoulder.

No longer crying, Cora was ramming her Elmer Elephant down her mother's top and giggling furiously as she pointed out 'Mummy's boobies!'

'Lough's risking everything to come here.' Lem's voice had lost all its jokey edge. 'You'd do well to remember that as you sit here in your big house with your rich husband, playing happy families.'

'Hang on a—'

'Lough and Hugo have a deal. I know you upper class Brits think life's all one big game, but Lough plays hardball, yeah?' It sounded like a threat.

Clutching Cora tighter, Tash glanced nervously out of the window and was relieved to spot a vast four-by-four with blacked-out windows rolling up outside followed by a huge, shiny Hummer.

'Well if he doesn't get here soon any deal is off,' she told Lem curtly, gathering her children and ushering him out of the house.

'He can't leave New Zealand yet.' Lem stood in the doorway.

'And I can't leave this house until you step aside.'

He turned away angrily, hissing to himself. 'From what I hear, Lough's the least of your worries.'

Tash wanted to run after him demanding an explanation. But she had a child under each arm, and cars waiting.

Sylva, who was on the phone, blew kisses and smiled.

Immediately separated from her children who were whisked into the back of the Hummer along with their car seats and encased behind its blackened glass with a small army of Eastern European nannies, Tash found herself sliding about on a vast expanse of leather beside Sylva in the back of the four-by-four. She was still giving whoever was on the end of the line a very hard time. 'I will fire you if this happens again, you understand? This is not the sort of publicity I need right now. You should have handled it completely differently. You are an idiot, and you're on borrowed time . . .'

Still trying to calm down from her conversation with Lem, Tash gazed straight ahead at the back of their driver's head. He had no perceivable neck, and his arm muscles were as big as pit-bull torsos, she noticed. The radio was blaring Dillon Rafferty's new single.

Sylva came off the phone at last and barked something in Slovakian at Pit-Bull Arms, who turned off the radio and switched on the sat nav.

'The driver is my cousin Olaf,' she explained to Tash. 'He has no sense of direction, which is why we are late. I won't introduce you because he speaks no English and he is nasty.'

Tash caught two eyes studying her in the rear view mirror and smiled awkwardly before turning to Sylva. 'Are you okay? That sounded a tricky call.'

'It's all good. No publicity is bad publicity, after all – but they didn't have to know that.' She flashed her gorgeous smile. 'I have been looking forward to today so much. This has been a horrible week. You must cheer me up with talk of horses, Tash.'

Then before Tash could get a word in Sylva started listing her grievances. As the sat nav guided them with soothing Slovakian tones through West Berkshire and over the border to the Oxfordshire Chilterns, she complained non-stop about her disloyal friends who all talked to the press, her cold-blooded documentary team, her lazy agents (she had several), a swimwear launch she'd just starred in, her useless PAs, her horrible Cotswold weekend retreat, the illustrator for her latest children's book and – most of all – her mother, who had wanted to come along that day.

'I say no. Mama, I am allowed to haff friends of my own. I tell her you would not like her, Tash, because you are posh and she is trash.'

Tash found her alarmingly outspoken. She craned around to

check that the Hummer carrying the children was still behind them and realised in a panic that it had gone.

'It's okay.' Sylva rested a warm hand on her arm. 'My nannies are taking them to a lovely play area while we have lunch. They will look after them.'

'Are they all family too?'

'Yes. We are a close family. My sister Hana is bringing my niece Zuzi to live with us too. She will be my Cotswolds housekeeper.'

'Your niece?'

'No, she is just a child. Pretty child. Very like her mother.'

'She and Hana must be stunning if they're anything like you.'

'Hana is very plain,' she said confusingly, then made Tash jump by reaching up to pull out the clip that she had crammed into her wild hair to keep it off her face. 'But you are very beautiful, I think. There! Much better.'

Tash's hair spilled over her eyes and she blew an embarrassed raspberry to stop it tickling her nose. 'Well at least it hides my face, I guess.'

With a few quick flicks, Sylva's expert fingers styled the wayward bed-head to one side so that it just fell over one eye, then she leaned back to admire her handiwork. 'It's a very sexy face. I like sexy friends.'

Tash pondered this for a moment while Sylva whipped out a compact and checked her immaculate make-up. Feeling she should keep her end up, Tash fished around in her bag but found that all she had were a couple of old hairbands, a cherry lipsalve and a broken comb with what appeared to be a boiled sweet impaled on its teeth. She settled for applying some lipsalve and admiring Sylva's brightly knitted mohair peplum jacket over a black and white striped catsuit and red boots with heels as long and narrow as Visconti fountain pens.

Amazingly, she realised, she was on trend today. Her own outfit of bright, clashing jewel colours and monochrome, inspired by the fashion pages of the *Sunday Telegraph* supplements that her mother-in-law stockpiled in her loo, had looked rather cutting-edge and cheering in the dusky mirror in her room, although when she'd later reassessed it in the less flattering mirror in the brightly lit downstairs loo it looked like she'd been styled by a colour-blind parrot fetishist with jumble-sale rejects.

Sylva's outfit worked much better, not least because she had no baby sick on her shoulders or tractor oil on her cuffs.

Yet Sylva, who handed out compliments in almost every sentence, made her feel surprisingly good about herself. She said she envied Tash's clear skin, her fabulous bone structure and – when they tumbled out on to a tarmac turning arc in front of a very exclusive Thames-side restaurant near Henley – her height.

'My goodness, I forgot you are so tall – your legs finish where my arms begin, and I'm wearing my highest Jimmy Choos!' She gaped up at her lunch companion in awe.

Lunching with Sylva was not a low-key event. Everybody in the restaurant turned and stared as she walked past, despite its exclusive reputation. She was just too famous – and too gaudy – to ignore. And she was demanding, insisting that their table be changed twice, that the flower arrangement was removed 'because I cannot see my beautiful friend through all that foliage', that she ate food 'off menu' and drank cocktails made to her own recipe.

At least all the attention-seeking and posturing took Tash's mind off the whereabouts of her children.

And Sylva's cocktails – apparently a mixture of vodka, coffee liqueur and coke – were strangely delicious. They drank two before lunch, followed by a bottle of vintage Cristal.

The champagne acted like a truth drug on Tash, who never normally drank during the day unless Hugo won a four-star, and who had barely touched any alcohol since Amery's birth. Allowing herself this rare treat, she got tight incredibly quickly. Any attempt to sell Sylva the idea of owning an event horse rapidly lost focus, although Sylva remained gratifyingly interested in everything she said. Tash was surprised by how clever she was, and how knowledgeable.

'Rory got me riding again, and I like your sport,' she explained. 'He has a very good owner, of course. Dillon Rafferty is a big fan of eventing, yes?'

'God no – Rory never hears from him,' Tash admitted. 'But that's how most event riders like it, as long as the bills get paid. The less interference the better. Although we treat all our owners really well at Haydown,' she added quickly, reaching for her drink.

'Maybe Dillon will visit his horses this winter, now that they are with you there?'

'Maybe.' Tash nodded, taking a swig of champagne. 'He's a lovely man. So unaffected, and he's such a champion of the countryside. Perhaps I should invite him to our shoot? We usually ask a couple of owners.'

'Oh, I love shooting!'

'You could come too,' Tash suggested eagerly, taking another gulp of champagne, which went up her nose. 'It's a Christmas thing, so you'll probably be away—'

But Sylva already had her phone out to put it in her diary as waiters bore down on their table with oversized white tableware.

Afterwards, Tash couldn't remember exactly what she ate, if indeed she had eaten anything (although the tomato soup stains all over her lap and breadcrumbs in her bra indicated that she had at the very least handled her food thoroughly).

By the time their plates were removed and a fresh bottle of Cristal placed in the cooler beside them Tash was rambling freestyle about eventing and event riders, joking about their reputation for infidelity.

'Sounds like showbusiness.' Sylva nodded at the waiter to refill Tash's champagne glass, while she helped herself to more water. 'And is the reputation justified?'

'Oh yes. Some riders are beyond redemption.'

'What about Hugo?' She was typically direct.

Startled, Tash looked at her over her glass, her mind full of sudden, horrible visions of Hugo seducing his way around the lorry parks.

'I don't know,' she admitted in a frightened voice. 'I thought I could trust him with my life, but lately he's been behaving so strangely. I think he might be . . .' She couldn't say it out loud.

Those big blue eyes radiated sympathy across the table. 'Darlink, you are talking to a world expert on unfaithful husbands. Now tell Sylva everything.'

'I really don't want to bore you.'

Nonetheless, cocktails and champagne surging through her veins, Tash found herself telling her dining partner about her concerns over her marriage.

'He's become so distant, and he always has so many women running after him. We used to live in each other's pockets but now we're apart so much it's like we're in different orbits. It's been worse since Amery was born. He wants things to go back to the way they were, but we've changed. I've changed.'

Sylva's advice on matters of the heart was predictably uncompromising.

'You are a beautiful girl, but you do not make the most of yourself. Man likes to fight for his meat like a bear, you understand?'

'Are you suggesting I disguise myself as a salmon and leap out of rivers at him?'

She laughed. 'You are funny. Men desire us before they marry us like a member of an audience watches an act – we showgirls come out and flaunt a bit of arse, strike a pose, flirt over the footlights. But after we marry he only wants the private performance, yes?'

'I guess.' Tash didn't think she'd ever posed over the footlights, but she let that pass.

'Seduction is a gladiatorial sport played out in a huge arena. Marriage is a duel in a private room.'

'We're event riders. We do it in the open.'

'You make jokes to hide your true feelings.' Sylva sighed. 'It is so British. Both my marriages ended when the showgirl became a married mother. Strawberry was paranoid that I was having an affair. He thought our child wasn't his, but still wanted sex three days after he was born. When I refused he said I was a bad wife. Then I found out he had another woman all along. And of course the world knows that Jonte was being unfaithful before our baby's umbilical stump fell off.'

Tash thought it terribly sad that a woman who was still so young had been through such a bad time. 'You must hate men.'

She shook her head. 'I love men. I love women. It's what we do to each other I hate. When we were very poor in Bratislava my mother kept a little money aside in a secret place, but my father always found it and drank it, you know? He said it was his right. One time, we were so broke that she sold her hair, her beautiful long blonde hair – just for food for her family. My father was so angry he beat her black and blue, then he took the money and bought a whore for the night. He boasted about it to her afterwards, saying that she was too ugly to love any more without her hair.'

Tash was too appalled to speak.

Sylva held up her hands apologetically. 'He was not always such a bad man, my father. He became bitter that my mother always loved her children more than him. So many men are like that.'

'And you still want to find the right man to love?'

'Oh yes!' Her pretty face lit up at the thought. 'I have promised myself that, and my children. But the next man, he will already be a father, you know? They understand the way things work, that children change things. It's funny: I liked Jonte's father; and we almost became lovers. He loved me very much. He asked me to run away with him but I am not unfaithful, *ever*, in my married life.'

Tash's jaw dropped. 'Your father-in-law asked you to run away with him? Jonte Frost's father!'

'Keep your voice down.'

'Sorry.' She glanced around at their fellow diners as she reached for her glass and took a bolstering swig.

'When Jonte got wind of what was going on it was the only moment he really wanted me back, when he clocked that his own father might steal the jewel from under him. D'you see what I'm saying?'

'Not really. Hugo's father died ages ago, and anyway he was a horrible old goat.'

'We have saying in Slovakia, "*Nič nepovažuj za svoje, čo môžeš ztratí*". It means, don't take for granted anything you may lose.' She fixed her with a determined look. 'Make your husband see what he's got and what he stands to lose if you're neglected. You must take pride in yourself – wear sexy lingerie, pamper your body, dress better and value yourself. Make *him* value you. Make him jealous!'

Sylva reached across the table and took Tash's hands. 'Another saying from my country is: "*čo máme, o to nedbáme a za iným sa zháňame.*" We disregard what we've got, always chasing what we've not.'

'You think Hugo is chasing something else?'

'No, darling Tash.' Sylva rubbed her thumbs on Tash's wrists, at the acupressure point known as the Very Great Abyss, a focus for loss, longing and regrets. 'You are the one who is chasing something else.'

Tash smiled at her squiffily, not really understanding. 'So if I get better undies and spend a few more minutes each day in front of the mirror things will get better?'

'You need an admirer, Tash.'

Tash shook her head violently. 'I couldn't have an affair!'

'We're not talking infidelity here, darlink. Just flirtation. The two are very different things.'

'I really don't *do* flirting.'

'You will flirt with me,' Sylva ordered.

Tash snorted with laughter.

'For practice,' she insisted smoothly.

Tash hiccupped. 'If it means you'll buy an event horse then I'll flirt my socks off.'

'That's the spirit, darlink!' Sylva laughed, signalling for the bill.

Once they were back in the car, being smoothly chauffeured by Olaf, Sylva gave Tash a crash course in flirtation.

'If you talk to a man like this,' she told Tash, sitting respectably beside her on the hand-stitched leather upholstery of the back seat, 'then he thinks nothing of it, but if you talk to him like this,' – she slid closer so that her slender body connected alongside Tash, warm and soft – 'he takes notice; and if you talk to him like *this*,' – she turned her head so that their faces were inches apart, lips and eyes on a level, her breath warm against Tash's skin – 'then he gets the message.' Her voice had dropped to a husky purr. 'And if you talk to him like this,' – she suddenly slipped a long, slim thigh over Tash's knees and swivelled up so that she was astride her lap, facing her, their lips just a millimetre apart – 'he knows you mean business.' She cocked her head and smiled cheerfully. 'You see?'

Tash had her arms up as though being held at gunpoint by the double barrels of Sylva's vast cleavage, her torso pressed back against the seat. 'Yes, but you're Sylva Frost,' she pointed out nervously. 'No man would complain about you doing that to them. Most men I know would have me sectioned.'

'You are very beautiful, Tash,' Sylva purred, her big blue eyes so close to Tash's that she could have counted those perfect, individually applied false eyelashes.

Just as she was starting to look around for a panic button, Olaf suddenly pulled into the staff car park of a big Georgian boutique hotel. They parked in the delivery bay by the kitchens.

'The kids are all here,' Sylva said briskly, climbing off Tash and pulling out her trusty compact to check her make-up, tease out her mane and reapply her glossy lipstick. 'The press are all out front. They think we haff been here all along. Your babies will be okay with flash cameras, yes?' Not waiting for an answer, she hopped out of the open door being held by her gum-chewing cousin, who spat on the tarmac beneath after she'd shot past.

Forgoing her own cherry lipsalve this time, Tash clambered out less elegantly but no less speedily as she realised that she was going to see her children.

The nannies, toddlers and Amery were in an amazing soft room filled with luxurious padded climbing frames and ball pits, shelves piled high with books and toys for the offspring of wealthy guests who wanted them entertained out of sight for long hours. Cora hurled herself at Tash like a small missile; Amery was asleep.

'I use this place a lot,' Sylva told Tash as she gathered her two adoring boys to her chest. 'We will go out by the main entrance. The cars will be waiting for us, but I warn you it will be a stampede. My driver will take you and your babies home – I have a photoshoot this afternoon with my beefy boys here.' She nuzzled Kol and Hain, who both had her blue eyes and amazing cheekbones and giggled deliciously. 'We are going to prove that Mummy is a responsible parent, aren't we guys?'

'Have you done something particularly newsworthy, then?' Tash asked.

'This is why I love you.' Sylva laughed. 'You really have no idea, do you?'

Tash shook her head.

Sylva let out a big sigh, eyebrows raised somewhere between self-mocking and martyred resignation. 'An ex lover has done a kiss and tell about our relationship.'

'How awful.'

'She is an old friend. We'll work through it.'

'She . . .?' Again, Tash's face coloured as she thought of her recent flirtation tutorial.

At that moment the doors to the hotel opened and the cameras started flashing frenziedly, catching her looking as though she was having a menopausal flush.

Tash would never forget the bustle, the shouting, the endless click-click-clicking of digital cameras. She had never encountered anything like it, even when her relationship with Niall had been under massive media scrutiny. Her children, thank goodness, seemed oblivious. Amery was still asleep and Cora was much more interested in the alpacas that the hotel had in a small paddock beside the drive than the pack of yelling minotaurs with the vast telephoto lenses grouped in front of her.

'I will text you!' Sylva promised Tash as they posed briefly for the clamouring masses.

'I don't have a mobile phone,' she apologised.

'Email me then.'

'I don't really do email either.'

'Twitter? Banter? Facebook?'

'What?'

'I'll call you!' Sylva promised, with lots of blown kisses.

By the time Tash got home, there was already a message on the phone from Sylva – bored to shreds in make-up – telling her that she must get herself better connected and networked, 'then we can stay in touch all the time, darlink!'

Which was in direct contrast to Hugo who, no doubt languishing by the super-heated indoor pool in MC's Loire retreat, had not deigned to call all day.

Still decidedly tight, Tash automatically picked up the handset to ring him and stopped herself, instead taking her time feeding and bathing the children before pouring herself a vast glass of wine and looking through her wardrobe for inspiration. She strutted in front of the flattering bedroom mirror in her few favourite dresses, striking model poses and hearing Sylva's fabulously Bond-girl voice saying, 'You are beautiful woman.'

Still wearing a much-loved pale green Ghost dress bought for her by her sister that dated back to her honeymoon and was fabulously forgiving, she floated downstairs, poured herself another glass of wine and fired up Hugo's computer.

Twitter took just a few moments to join; its irreverent little-sister site Banter was even easier. Both offered to find her 'followers' by checking her email address book. These were almost all Hugo's contacts, but Tash just pressed 'yes to all' and went to do night-check.

After lurching around, cannoning off walls and falling over buckets, she sought sanctuary at the stable door of Dove, her favourite broodmare, who was expecting the last of Snob's foals the following spring – an embryo transfer from her top mare, Deep River, that meant there would be a half-sibling to Fox, Vixen and Cub.

The lunch with Sylva had cheered Tash up enormously, but also made her feel more unsettled than ever. She couldn't shake the image of Sylva's father rejecting her mother when she sold her hair for food, or of Sylva, so desired by every man in the country yet spurned by two unfaithful husbands. Where did that leave her?

Backing unsteadily away from the stable door she glanced up at the stable flat, its windows glowing.

She was tempted to march up there and demand to know what Lemon had been talking about that morning, but she was too tired and drunk, and too much of a coward. She found him rather frightening, although she knew that was silly. He probably felt far more vulnerable than she did, trapped here in England with his boss thousands of miles away and totally reliant upon the Beauchamps for income and security. He was bound to lash out.

There was an odd smell in the air. She wrinkled her nose and sniffed to try to identify it. Then she looked down at her hands and realised that she had picked up an air freshener instead of the baby monitor. She rushed inside, where all was uncannily quiet, including the house phone. She glanced at it resentfully. I will not phone Hugo. I will not phone Hugo, she told herself, determined to do as Sylva prescribed.

En route for bed, still in her dress, she realised she hadn't switched off the computer. Twitter was still active, and there were tweets left, right and centre, with more followers than a religion. Banter had an equal number of rants.

Tash suddenly realised why. It was the Sylva effect.

Now that Britain's most-Googled celebrity single mother had left a row of kisses on her previously blank Facebook wall, no less than two hundred people had requested to be her friend.

Tash didn't care what anyone else thought. Sylva was going to be good for business.

Chapter 30

'Bloody hell look at this!' On the flight back from France, Rory stopped leafing through a copy of *Cheers!* he'd found abandoned on his seat and thrust it at Hugo.

In it, just before the six-page spread of Sylva posing with her boys and opining about her teenage bisexual 'experimentation' was a big photograph of Tash, dressed like a bizarre parrot with orange stains on her crotch and loo roll trailing from her heel, towering over Sylva Frost and a gaggle of excited-looking children as they left a chavvy boutique hotel. *Single mum Sylva supports new best friend Tash* ran the caption, and beneath it was a short piece insinuating that 'openly bisexual' Sylva had been comforting Tash through marriage difficulties.

'Who the fuck is saying we're having marriage difficulties?' Hugo waved the magazine around furiously at Tash as soon as he got home.

'They make these things up,' she bleated. 'We were having lunch to talk about her buying an event horse.'

He looked at her as though she'd just driven a muck spreader through the kitchen. 'That ghastly woman will give eventing a bad name. We have to think about the good of the sport. For God's sake put her off.'

He was on a quick turnaround. In two days he was heading to Cardiff with Sir Galahad for the Express Eventing Cup, an indoor competition that was to three day eventing what Twenty20 cricket was to test series, and which carried a huge cash pot that he was determined would swell the Haydown coffers. Then, as a part of the Olympic gold-medal squad (and soon-to-be-disbanded Team Mogo), Hugo had taken up an invitation from Equestrian Australia to ride at Adelaide three day event before taking part in a two-week lecture-demonstration tour across the country. He would then fly to New Zealand for Puhinui Three Day Event before returning home just before Christmas.

'You can fly Lough Strachan back here,' Tash told him, but that just put him in a blacker mood.

'Man's an unreliable shit. He can stay in Auckland as far as I'm concerned. Ten to one he'll be competing at Puhinui on some new wonder neddy trying to make me look like a berk. I think he just sent his parakeet groom here as a joke at our expense.'

Faith had been up since dawn in her little Lime Tree Farm attic room, readying herself to see Rory again. She was wearing her new shell jacket for his return, its zip lowered despite the November chill to just the right height to show off her chicken-fillet-enhanced cleavage. She'd matched her tightest metallic pink breeches with long leather boots that showed off her great legs and had teased out her now shoulder-length hair in a sexy cloud. Then, as a finishing touch, she'd put on a slick of lip gloss to draw attention to the straight white smile and detract from the nose, which was still undeniably bulbous despite hours of careful shading as Carly had taught her.

When she drove into the Haydown courtyard to start work he was already there, standing by Whitey's stable. Her heart roared and she threw herself out of the car and ran up to him as eagerly as his terrier Twitch.

To her dismay, he was uncharacteristically angry and wouldn't even look her in the eye.

'Who gave you permission to bring my horse here?'

Faith reached instantly for her attitude as protection.

'You brought *my* horse here without permission,' she pointed out hotly.

'That's different. I compete Rio for you; we have an arrangement.'

'Actually, I think you'll find that I agreed to leave him at Overlodes, then went back to find you'd both gone!'

'So you thought you'd "borrow" my old horse, is that it?'

That was it in a nutshell, but Faith wasn't about to admit it. 'That Jules woman is useless. The other horses are tough enough to cope, but Whitey needs specialist care to stay in work.'

'He's retired.'

'You said last summer that he still has a three day event in him.'

'That was just idle talk. He's too old and knackered, and he's had too much time off through injury. You should have left him be to enjoy his old age in peace.'

You just don't want him – or me – here cramping your style, Faith thought furiously, pulling up her zip because her heart was beating so hard her chicken fillets were slipping.

Rory still wouldn't look at her.

Across the courtyard, Beccy and Lemon were observing the reunion with interest.

'So *he's* the reason she's here.' Lemon sighed, noticing the way Faith's whole body cleaved towards Rory when they were talking, even when she was yelling at him.

'I think it was just coincidence that the Moncrieffs asked her to help out here,' Beccy pointed out.

'In the magical universe there are no coincidences and no accidents,' he said flatly. 'Nothing happens unless someone wills it to happen.'

'William S. Burroughs!' She recognised the quote in delight. His writing had kept her sane when travelling. Lemon was a kindred spirit.

'Who?' Lemon was still watching Faith, adding distractedly. 'It was written on a postcard in Lough's place in New Zealand. He kept it propped up on the mantel.'

He sauntered across to get a closer look, noticing Rory had picked up on Hugo's mannerisms while they'd been away together: the way he ran his hand through his hair, the arrogance of his tone and the legs astride, hands on hips army captain stance were all pure Hugo. It made him less likeable.

'Good to have you back, yeah, mate.' Lemon slapped him on the back so hard that Rory nearly fell over. 'Don't put our girl here off her work – we're short-staffed enough as it is. If you guys want a long catch up, we'll all meet up in the pub tonight.'

'Who does he think he is?' Rory asked in surprise as Lemon swaggered away.

'So are you coming?' Faith demanded aggressively.

'What?'

'To the pub.'

'I guess so.'

'Fine.'

'Fine.' They turned and walked in opposite directions, both deeply disappointed by the reunion.

On that first day home, Hugo rode the young Haydown horses back to back, from dawn until late evening in the floodlights to get a feel for their training levels and what to prescribe for them next season. Soon they would all get a winter holiday, and Hugo always liked to stop on a good note so they came back fresh and enthusiastic in the New Year.

'You should be doing this,' he told Tash as she watched from the rails in the driving rain, hood plastered to her head and eyelids windscreen-wiping her contact lenses.

'I haven't got my nerve back yet,' she admitted.

'Well, get it back. It's like sex. The more you do it, the better you get.' It was a very barbed comment.

Acutely aware that they weren't making love much at all – and with Sylva's words still ringing in her head – Tash donned the Ghost dress and a sassy attitude that night for seafood linguine and too much Brown Brothers Riesling, attempting to be flirtatious and yet enigmatic.

Perplexed by all the eyelash-batting and hair-twizzling, and the fact that she kept talking to him with her face millimetres from his, Hugo asked if she had forgotten to put in her contact lenses, or was feeling overtired.

Within minutes of joining Faith and her new friends at the Olive Branch that evening, Rory regretted coming out. He'd quite liked camp little Lemon when he'd first arrived at Haydown, but he'd become cockier and cruder, bedding in like a virulent weed while Rory was away in France.

'These are my hos,' he bragged as he settled between the girls and put his arms around them in a show of ownership. 'Limey's my older woman, and Eff's my tom-boy friend.'

Faith's appearance was far from tomboyish, in a clingy top from which her unfeasible cleavage jutted accusingly, with the tightest of skinny jeans, ultra high heels and too much make-up. Rory couldn't bring himself to look at her for long or scrutinise the changes close up. The thought of her cosmetic surgery shocked him. This all-new Faith was like a stranger, more assertive and bolshy than ever. When he asked her what had gone wrong in Essex she just snarled, 'I got fired.'

'Can't be a top dressage rider with massive bazookas,' cackled Lem, who had no idea they were detachable.

Under a similar delusion Rory cleared his throat and stared at his glass.

'Big boobs get you noticed,' Faith retorted, determined to wear her chicken fillets for life if she had to.

'Shame Kurt Willis is more of a bicep man,' Lem cackled, turning to Rory. 'So tell us about *la belle France*,' he goaded, enjoying the atmosphere. 'Is Marie-Clair Tucson as big a bitch as they all say she is?'

Having slipped from the wagon in France, Rory raced through his drinks, hamming up his tall tales of his time in France because he was ill at ease.

'MC is seriously cool,' he enthused. 'She has to be the sexiest woman in eventing.'

'Oh come on!' Faith was combative as ever. 'Lucy Field is the pin-up now – or Zara. MC is ancient.'

'She does it for me.' He didn't look at her.

'Hugo was in a foul mood in France,' he went on, addressing Beccy now. 'Barely said a word the whole time we were staying with MC – just buggered off running for hours on end. Thank God for MC. She cheered me up enormously. Sensational woman. Looks like Lollobrigida and rides like Lester Piggot. Just my type.'

'So you said,' Beccy reminded him, glancing worriedly at Faith.

'She has some amazing contacts in the States,' he went on. 'Hugo's taking me out there after Christmas to train with Janet Madsen. We're going to be based at MC's Florida barn for a few weeks before flying to Virginia to stay with the Johanssens.'

'Oh, Virginia's beautiful,' Beccy said. 'I always wanted to go ranching there.'

'Didn't you fit that into your eight-year world tour?' Faith asked bitchily, jealous that she was hogging Rory. She couldn't bear the idea of him going away again so soon. 'I'm sure you'll love playing the cowboy, Rory. You can re-enact that scene with the man galloping down the cliff in that film you love. What's it called? *Ride on Snowy Mountain?*'

'*The Man from Snowy River,*' he said hollowly, mortified by her scathing.

'That pile of Aussie shit!' Lemon shrieked with horror. 'Give me *Brokeback Mountain* any time.'

'Oh shut up!' Rory snapped.

Lemon gasped. 'Homophobia alert! Homophobia alert!'

'If you'd just make up your mind on that front, I'd have more respect for you.' Rory stood up, raised a hand and walked out, leaving Faith's heart blazing in his wake.

'Tosser,' Lem sniped at his retreating back. 'He's trying to be all macho like Hugo.'

'Maybe that's a good thing,' Beccy said placatingly, thinking Rory had been rather better company than usual that night, especially as he'd singled her out for attention. 'He obviously respects Hugo, and he can learn a lot from him.'

'Yeah, like how to be an even bigger tosser!' Lem sneered.

'C'mon, Hugo's the best rider in the world.'

'He fucking isn't!' Lem's anger flared so brightly, she cowered back. 'He's a typical stuck-up dickhead who's bought his way into the sport. So is Rory. Lough has ten times their talent and is no piker. He's tough. He'll squash Hugo when he gets here. Just you wait.'

Swallowing uncomfortably, Beccy was happy to wait indefinitely.

Tash's romantic dinner derailed when she found out that Hugo was taking lascivious livery Venetia Gundry to lunch the following day. Jealousy stubbed its toes on each one of her ribs as they ate, before running up and down them and giving her a stitch. Even the fact that Hugo's jolly and bibulous trainer chum Kelvin would be at the lunch failed to comfort her as she imagined him getting too drunk to notice Hugo and Venetia playing footsy beneath a table in the Olive Branch.

'I could come too.'

'It's the Czechs' day off. You have no childcare.'

'The children can come too.'

'That would be completely unprofessional. Venetia is one of our best clients and Kelvin's a part of the support team we rely on. They don't want you breastfeeding between courses.'

Tash regarded him levelly. 'Is that how you see me? As a milk cow?'

'Of course not. It's only when you're with the children.'

'We have children together, Hugo.'

'Yes, darling, and we run a business together too. I have to keep going out trophy-hunting to make ends meet. Perhaps we should each concentrate on our areas of expertise, huh?'

'I'm bringing in new owners,' Tash pointed out.

'Yes. You're new "bisexual" best friend,' he said caustically.

So that was it, Tash registered with surprise. He felt threatened. Sylva had fulfilled her prescription in the most unexpected way, making him jealous already.

To Hugo's surprise she suddenly smiled wantonly across the table. 'Let's go to bed. I have something to show you.'

Hugo might not approve of his wife's new friendship, but he certainly approved of the Per Una underwear purchased at the same time as their M&S meal. What was underneath those frilly layers, however, came as a shock.

'What *is* that?' he gaped at his wife's pubic hair, reduced from its normal lush, neat triangle to a racing stripe.

'I went for a bikini wax and they got a bit carried away.'

'It looks like you've had a hunter clip.'

'It's a Brazilian, apparently. Don't you like it?'

'It's certainly different, but I'd rather you stuck to a full English in future.'

Her face flamed, but then Hugo kissed each one of her polished new angles with interest and she lay back delightedly. A moment later, however, he had turned his head away and was rubbing his lips with the back of his hand. 'What have you put on here?'

'Just perfumed body lotion.' It was from Sylva's signature range. 'Don't you like it?'

'I prefer your natural smell. It's like going down on a jar of pear drops.'

It was last orders at the Olive Branch and Faith was horribly downcast as she revealed to her friends the true scale of her feelings for Rory, mascara slipping and lip gloss chewed away: 'I just get so mad that he doesn't fancy me, I can't help myself. I want to punish him. I am *so* crap with men.'

'Me too,' agreed Beccy sympathetically, patting her arm.

'Me three,' Lemon put his arms around them both, 'and I *am* one.'

'Only a token one,' Faith muttered.

'Less of that!' he growled, forgiving her cattiness because she had shoulders like an oarsman that felt good to hang on to.

They huddled together for a moment, staring at their glasses, sharing one silent thought.

'A pact.' Lem squeezed the shoulders to either side of him. 'We will all get laid before the New Year.'

He received a muted response. Faith stared at the floor. Beccy stared at the ceiling.

'C'mon, what's so bad about having a shag? It'll cheer us all up.'

Faith, bravest and most honest, laid her cards on the table first. 'Thing is, Lem, I've never had – that is, I'm not very experienced. Fuck it, I'm a virgin. There. I said it.'

'Cool,' Lemon kissed her on the top of her head.

'Me too,' Beccy mumbled, knowing Faith was already in on the secret.

311

'You?' Lemon's eyes were like saucers. 'But you're really *old*.'

'Thanks for that. The opportunity just never arose.'

'Ker-ist.' He turned from one woman to the other. 'We really need to do something about this situation, yeah. You see,' – he screwed up his peculiar, munchkin face in a grimace with the effort of ditching the wisecracking act and admitting his own home truth – 'my opportunity has arisen many, *many* times but there have never been any takers.'

'Are you saying you're a virgin too?' Beccy gulped, amazed.

'Keep your voice down,' he hushed, looking around. 'I am just very choosy.'

'You're bisexual,' Faith pointed out. 'What's choosy about that?'

Lem shot her a sideways look. 'I still say we make a pact.' He cleared his throat. 'Let's lose our cherries. How about it, girls?'

Faith and Beccy looked at one another uncertainly.

'Well, I wasn't planning to throw mine away just like that,' Faith muttered.

'And I've hung on to mine long enough to want something a bit special,' said Beccy.

'I'm not suggesting we cruise down to the docks and pick up low-life.'

'Only docks round here grow in hedgerows,' joked Faith

'Exactly. This is the Royal County of Berkshire, the heart of the jolly old home counties.' Lemon camped up his bad British accent. 'The talent round here is fabulous! Jockeys, artists, writers, models, actors, City boys . . . all bursting with sexual energy.'

'Put like that, it does sound rather tempting.' Beccy flushed delightedly.

'Maybe we should do this,' Faith agreed, certain that Rory would fancy her if she was sexually experienced like Sylva. 'It could liberate us.'

'Liberation,' Beccy echoed, having long suspected that losing her virginity would be to cast the albatross from her neck.

'Libido liberation!' Lemon raised his glass hopefully.

The girls joined in the toast with gusto.

'Libido-ration!'

Late that night, Hugo's eyelids were pinned back despite the exhaustion clawing at his bones. Tash had been behaving very oddly all evening, and now lovemaking had yet again been interrupted by Amery bawling for a night feed.

He felt a stranger in his own home. His children barely recognised him; his wife was wary and hostile and his yard staff were near-strangers. He wished to God he wasn't going away again so soon. Coming home suddenly felt more akin to staying in a Travelodge with a bunch of unknown commuters.

Tash had taken Amery down to feed him in the kitchen by the Aga because the house was so cold and Hugo disapproved of the baby coming into bed with them. She flipped open the laptop and looked at Twitter and Banter, her new addictions. Sylva had left her several private tweets reminding her to make Hugo jealous.

He is already, she tweeted back, excited by progress. *But resisting.*

He's such a dinosaur! Sylva tweeted immediately from her jewelled Nokia.

Says bikini wax is 'suburban'.

A cave man! Me hunter, you gatherer. Make him sweat more! Cau xx

On Banter, there was lots if eventing gossip among the rants, but one post made her feel freezing cold again despite Amery's warm skin against her chest and the nearby Aga.

You Beauchampions are so up yourselves. Pride comes before a fall.

Tash hastily flipped the lid down on the computer.

Risking Hugo's wrath, she carried Amery upstairs and into their bed, where she cuddled him tightly.

His back turned to her, Hugo didn't stir.

Chapter 31

Hugo missed out on a win in Cardiff by just a fraction of a penalty, but at least he regained some much-needed pride and garnered good press.

Upon his return, Tash laid on a belated anniversary supper of their favourite Thai treats – deep-fried breaded oysters zinging with lime, lemongrass chicken sweetened with coconut and pandan leaves, and slivers of rare beef in her own home-made red curry – all washed down with lots of vintage cava.

Hugo did sweat, as Sylva had prescribed. In fact, he sweated rather a lot, both from Tash's rather over-enthusiastic use of red-eye chillies in her curry sauce and the rather thrilling lovemaking across the kitchen table and then, after a break to settle Amery, in the bath, and later in bed.

'I can't believe you're going away again,' she said soulfully as she pressed her cheek to his hot chest, feeling its rise and fall. He barely puffed after riding a horse at full pelt across country, but riding his wife lately had been such a rarity, his adrenalin peaked sooner and he worked up a muck sweat.

'I'll be back for Christmas,' he promised.

Tash found herself thinking of Lough Strachan saying almost the same words.

'I might be riding by then.'

'You must,' he said. 'Our business will suffer if you leave it any longer.' It was the first time he'd admitted it openly, and they both knew he was right.

While she'd been pregnant with Amery they had sat down with a year planner and committed to all the lucrative foreign trips for Hugo in the belief that Tash would soon be back in the saddle. Instead, she had been hijacked by nerves. The thought of getting on a horse made her feed giddy with fear.

She counted to ten, letting the panic that was buzzing in her ears gradually fade away. 'I *will* be riding by Christmas,' she promised.

He shifted across the bed to kiss her hard on the mouth, fingers running through her hair to the hollow behind her ear, where his thumb rested idly on her jumping pulse. Then he kissed on so tenderly she felt lightheaded. When they finally broke apart his cool blue eyes were gleaming with happiness. 'God I've missed you!'

She felt tears of relief pricking. 'I miss you so much when you're away, too.'

'That's not what I'm talking about.'

Tash settled her cheek back in its nook and stared at his chest, eyeing the little hairs scattered there, the familiar moles, the areolae and nipples and the jut of his collarbone.

'I haven't *been* anywhere,' she reminded him.

But he was already asleep, dreaming no doubt of those distant horizons he had to cross in pursuit of glory while she was still struggling to gather her thoughts and cross the divide that kept opening up between them.

A week later, left alone at Haydown again, Tash cheered herself up by indulging in a shopping spree. Spending several late nights on the laptop monitoring Hugo's progress in the Southern Hemisphere's only four-star three day event, she honed her online retail skills buying uplift and control undies from online stores in between checking the Adelaide scoreboard. How anybody could spend so much on kinky, corrective and seductive underwear in one week appalled her afterwards, but Tash was soon all too familiar with the hazards of the click-and-buy culture. By the time she knew the final score in Oz, she had plundered La Senza, Agent Provocateur and Victoria's Secret.

But her late-night vigils weren't in vain. Hugo rewarded her nocturnal support with his best four-star result of the year, winning the Adelaide trials on Oil Tanker, a wiry little young thoroughbred borrowed from Australian rider Sandy Hunter.

In another time zone, Hugo was also discovering the delight of impulse purchases. He liked the little bay horse he had ridden to victory so much that he'd struck a deal with Sandy then and there, certain he could secure an owner back in the UK.

Tash phoned him on his mobile shortly after the awards ceremony.

'You stayed up!' he laughed.

'I have a great surprise for you when you get home,' she promised him after demanding a blow-by-blow account of the competition, fighting not to let her yawns be heard.

'I'm bringing a surprise back with me too.'

'I just want *you* back.'

'When you ride, think of me,' he spoke into the phone in a hair-tingling whisper.

While Hugo was away, Tash tried and failed to summon the nerve to get on a horse again, using the excuse that most of the horses were having their annual holiday and she still had commissions to finish – besides which, Rory was more than capable of taking up the slack now so many horses were turned away on their winter breaks. Back on the wagon and getting early nights, he was riding the newly backed babies brilliantly.

When she was working on the yard, Tash was too preoccupied by her own worries to pick up much on the atmosphere there, not noticing the unholy trinity of Beccy, Lemon and Faith sniping in one corner while Rory and Jenny were trying to ignore them in another. As Rory's dislike of Lemon intensified, so the little Kiwi increasingly froze him out and sought to get Faith on side with nights out at the Olive Branch or the Marlbury metroplex.

Still struggling daily with the tractor, Tash found herself relying on Rory.

He drove the ancient, cantankerous Massey Ferguson with indecent speed and unfair skill, whipping huge haylage bales, straw bales and pallets of feed in and out of the courtyards with balletic grace. Tash and Vasilly couldn't even get it started.

'Tractors, horses, women – I ride them all brilliantly,' Rory boasted.

Tash appreciated his company in the evenings, which stemmed her loneliness and somewhat limited her increasing addiction to Banter and internet shopping. Rory was great company and, underneath the bravura, far less big-headed than at first impression.

'Hugo says that if I don't stay sober he won't take me to the States in the New Year.'

'The States?'

'For winter training with MC and the Swede . . . Jensen Stefansen?'

'Stefan Johanssen. He's won Kentucky three times. Married to Kirsty.'

'Yeah. Them. They're coached by Janet Madsen. She's a legend – you know how hard it is to get a session with her?'

'I've trained with her out there.'

'Of course. But Hugo says you won't be going this year, so I get to play in MC's barn instead.'

'Good for you.' Tash nodded encouragingly, although her heart was hollow at the thought of Hugo being away for most of January and all of February. 'I have the kids to think about, and this end to run.'

'Exactly.' Rory hugged her gratefully. 'You have no idea how much this means to me. I just pray that I don't goof up.'

'Why should you? You ride brilliantly.'

'Got to prove myself.'

'I think Hugo realises how good you are.'

'Not just Hugo, everyone. My family, the selectors, Dillon, Faith.'

'Faith?'

Rory's cheeks striped red and he changed the subject, asking how Hugo was getting on in Australia.

'Good. He's off to New Zealand tomorrow.'

'Bet you wish you were competing out there, too.'

She shrugged.

'We talked a lot about you in France. MC reckons you'll never come back to competitive riding. Says you're not at all like those steel-thighed old four-star mothers that take two nags round Badminton three months after dropping a sprog. You're more of an earth mother, a home-maker. I see you baking Victoria sponges and leading toddlers around Haydown on Shetlands. You're so solid, Tash. You're great.'

Staying up late to track Hugo's progress at Puhinui, Tash threw herself into her painting, and occasionally sought solace on the internet as she waited for the online scoreboards to update. Her 'click to buy' shopping habit was getting out of hand.

Addiction planted, she decided to find out whether it was possible to buy a tractor online. It was. So she did.

Fascinated, she looked for a replacement car for the au pairs. One was secured and paid for via secure server in less than half an hour.

'Jesus! Thank God you can't buy horses this way,' she gasped, terrified and exhilarated by what she had just done.

Then . . .

She had to force herself to take a break before she added two Shetlands for the children, plus a safe cob for herself, to her virtual shopping basket.

'Please don't tell me you've bought this one as well?' she asked Hugo when he woke her with a call at six the following morning to announce that he'd come second in Puhinui. There was talking and laughter in the background; he was obviously celebrating with connections.

Yet his response was muted. 'I've just found out why Lough hasn't come to England.'

'Is he there, then?'

'Of course not. Nobody's seen him for weeks, although I gather he was in custody for quite a while.'

'Custody?' Tash sat bolt upright. 'Are you saying he's been arrested? What for?'

'Nobody seems to know, but it's not exactly news to anybody over here. He's so far on the wrong side of the tracks he has his own branch line.'

In her room overlooking the courtyard, Beccy was awake in the early hours, as she often was these days, panicking about everything and anything, though she knew that these worries would disappear with daylight and common sense. Padding around restlessly, she went to make herself a cup of tea and was surprised to find that the kettle had only just boiled. She cocked her head to listen for sounds of life from Lemon's room, but all was silent until the water began to bubble. She took her tea and a big bowl of cereal back to her room and picked up her mobile phone to look at her old texts from Lough. They no longer gave her joy, instead curdling the panic in her belly. She'd been such a childish, hot-headed idiot creating her own fantasy world, unable to conceive that it would threaten to impact so horrendously on real life. But that was how she'd always approached life, and was probably why she was where she was now, rattling towards thirty with nothing to show for it except a pact that she'd finally start copulating.

Faith and Lemon seemed so much more self-assured than Beccy felt, for all her world travels. They also made her feel left out, their upfront attitudes and angry energy such a direct match, whereas she was secretive and vacillating, taking refuge in her daydreams. Every time she thought about the Libido-ration pact, she was riven with shame and fear. That wasn't in her romantic game-plan. But then, she reminded herself, just look where her romantic game-plan had got her.

She composed another text to Lough: *Please send Lemon and the horses back to New Zealand. Do not come here. You are not welcome any more.*

But she couldn't send it, frightened of what it might kick off. She preferred to bury her head in the sand, or beneath her pillow, if only she could sleep.

Yet, quite incapable of leaving the itch alone now that she'd let it twitch against her nerve endings, she sent a different message that simply read *How are you? Where are you?* She wanted to know how much imminent danger she was in.

Beccy paced around her little room some more, chewing her nails until, unable to bear being alone with her thoughts a moment longer, she got dressed and went outside.

When Lemon appeared on the yard at six-thirty to start putting out morning feeds, he realised that the lights were on in the indoor school.

Beccy was riding one of the youngsters, both so absorbed in their work that they didn't see him come in. The horse was going well – really well. Last time Lemon had seen him, he'd been tripping around with his nose in the air like a real baby; now he was carrying himself properly, his body a curved bow of growing strength. Beccy had a real talent with the novices, showing a quiet courage and steely determination at odds with her usual vague manner.

But the illusion was shattered when Tash burst in to the school, still in her pyjamas, a groggy child in each arm.

'Lem! There you are!'

At that moment Beccy's horse shied and stormed up to the far end of the arena, fly-bucking with alarm and despatching its rider into the sand.

By the time Beccy had caught the horse and led him back to the mounting block, Tash had dashed out again.

'What was that all about?'

'I just had to convince her it's all cool with Lough, yeah.'

'Why? What's going on?' Beccy panicked that it had something to do with her text.

'He's been in serious trouble. He was detained trying to fly out of Auckland and his passport taken away. But he can leave the country now.'

'Detained for what?' Beccy demanded, her skin icy.

'I don't know.' He looked shifty.

'He hasn't done anything seriously wrong?'

'I guess not.' Lemon shrugged. 'After all, they can't find a body.'

'A *body*?'

Chapter 32

'I am *not* spending Christmas with your ex-wife!' Nell screamed at Dillon. 'Not, not, not, NOT!'

'I think that's clear.'

'Just what does the bitch think we have going on here? A fucking kibbutz?'

'It's the first time I'll have my daughters in the UK over Christmas. Fawn has come a long way.'

'Well she can fuck a long way off if she thinks she'll be getting a turkey leg and a chipolata off my family.'

'We're not spending Christmas day with your family.'

'Says who?'

'Me.'

'But everyone will be there!'

'Everyone? Joseph, Mary and Barack Obama? Angelina Jolie and Oprah? Madonna and her orphans?'

'Trudy will be there.' She sounded pleading. 'You love Trudy.'

'And I have children with Fawn,' he pacified. 'I owe it to her – and them – to break bread at Christmas. We'll all be here at West Oddford. I want you to be a part of that, Nell.'

With that the last word on the matter, he wandered off to have a meeting with his farm manager.

But Nell couldn't let it rest. She secretly hated Fawn. In truth, she even struggled with Pom and Blueberry, who were sweet little minimes of Fawn, with their mother's East Coast accent and prim smartness.

She hadn't seen Dillon for almost a week while he was yet again spending time with his children and taking advantage of the Johnston's Malibu guest lodge, and now she faced the prospect of Christmas with his family *including* the ex in-laws.

Taking Giselle for a play-date with young Garfield Belling, Nell had a heart-to-heart with her friend Ellen in her cosy Oddlode cottage, which smelled of the pine, holly and ivy that decorated its heavy beams. Carols were playing on the radio and there were freshly baked mince pies cooling on a rack in the kitchen.

'He's so bloody pig-headed.' Nell stomped through to the sitting room to claim the best sofa before raking scatter cushions on to her lap to hug for comfort.

Ellen, heavily pregnant, waddled after her bearing mugs of tea, with Postman Pat puzzles and Thomas the Tank Engine books clutched beneath her arms for distraction purposes. 'He's a rock star that wants to be a farmer.' She handed the books and puzzles down to toddlers Garfield and Gigi.

'So?'

'I married an ex fraudster playboy who always wanted to be a cartoonist.' She sank gratefully into a chair. 'And I get the speech bubbles, not the crime thrillers.'

'Spurs is divine.'

'We're a boring married couple these days. You have to decide if you want to be a farmer's wife.'

'I want to be Dillon Rafferty's wife.'

'You think he's going to propose?'

'I think he was close to it in South Africa: really gentle and sweet, wanting to be alone together. But the PR team there were amazing and there were *so* many parties it just didn't happen for us.'

Ellen gathered Gigi into a giggling hug of butterfly kisses and raspberries. 'You have to ask yourself whether it's Dillon you really want?' She knew Nell well and loved her dearly, and wasn't alone among those many friends worrying that this relationship was very damaging for her.

'Of course I want him!'

'And what about Milo?'

'He's married.' Nell glared at the Christmas lights shaped like little angels that were draped from the big stone mantel.

'Doesn't mean that you have to be married to compete.'

'Yes I do. He always has the upper hand.'

'The upper hand in marriage,' Ellen sighed. 'Do you love Dillon more than Milo?'

'Differently.'

Ellen rested Gigi on her lap and pressed her chin to the little girl's head, staring fixedly at her friend. 'I want you to think very, very hard about this, Nell.'

Nell thought very hard for a nanosecond.

'If it weren't for the cheese, he'd be so totally, totally perfect,' she sighed.

'A farmer's wife must like his cheese.'

Nell let out a sceptical snort. 'He makes one called "I love Ewe" that's shaped like a heart. It's flavoured with cranberries. Horribly tart.'

'And what about Dillon's heart?'

'Oh I have that already,' she giggled. 'I just haven't figured out what to do with it yet.'

'Don't abuse it, Nell,' Ellen warned, her voice unusually stern. 'If he'd rather be Old MacDonald than Ol' Blue Eyes, you mustn't punish him for that.'

Dillon loved the Dorset Horns: they bred year round, meaning they were reliable milkers. His new miniature cheeses wrapped in local wild garlic leaves, branded I Owe Ewe Lodes, were flying off the farm shop's shelves this Christmas. It was a far more exciting prospect for him than his Christmas single, a reworking of the old David Essex classic 'A Winter's Tale' that was being downloaded by his target female audience faster than if it was a George Clooney striptease on YouTube. Dillon hated his over-produced, rocky version with a vengeance, but he cynically agreed with his record company that it would be a smash hit, and perfectly timed to cash in on his high-stakes success.

He was exhausted from ever-shifting time zones. He seemed to have been on the publicity circuit in perpetuity. So many names to remember, so many anecdotes to tell and re-tell, so few hours in which to sleep, so little time to share with those he loved. These days he found he had more peace and time to think in the Johnston's Malibu guest lodge than he did at home in the Lodes Valley. It was starting to become his refuge from Nell.

He had barely noticed her driving away earlier, although now he realised she was gone he registered a sense of relief familiar with her absense these days.

Dillon had allowed idle thoughts to drift in the direction of splitting up with Nell for a long time. But he'd never been good at ending relationships; like removing splinters, he preferred other people to do it for him. Instead, he retreated behind his BlackBerry and work schedule as often as possible. The relationship that had been so good on paper no longer stood up in an increasingly paper-free world. Nell crowded him in cyberspace when he was away, continually texting, emailing, PMing and video-calling. If she could have projected a three-dimensional image of herself into his hotel suite he suspected she would. When she travelled with him she ransacked his headspace like an over-zealous customs official going through a suspicious suitcase. Yet her body thrilled him. Sex was never better with Nell than in hotels. She got off on hotels.

She fitted into the landscape in the Cotswolds like one of his gorgeous rare livestock, an old breed with class and sense and local knowledge. But the Lodes Valley bored her. She loved travelling the world and living out of suitcases, networking and partying and hanging out in VIP rooms.

In South Africa he'd almost plucked up the courage to end their relationship. It was going nowhere and, while the sexual kick still stirred him from his apathy occasionally, it hadn't blossomed into the supportive family unit he'd hoped for. Nell's jealousy was starting to impact upon his relationship with his daughters and ex-wife.

Lately she'd started accusing him of being boring and parochial, and he guessed she was right. He was happiest here in the Cotswold drizzle, up to his gumboot-tops in sheep droppings, talking lambs, milk yields and field rotation with his stockman.

Tomorrow he was flying to Abu Dhabi to sing at a wedding for so many million dollars he couldn't have refused, but his body ached to stay put in his beloved farm and sort out his personal life.

He took a photograph of a winter lamb springing past and mindlessly texted it to Faith, who he knew missed the Lodes Valley desperately.

Ever-reliable, she replied within thirty seconds.

Where the hell have you been? Rory obnoxiously big-headed. Been out hunting today. When are you coming here to see your horses?

He texted back *Boxing Day*, although wasn't at all sure if he'd be there. His PA had accepted the invitation to the Beauchamps' shoot on his behalf while negotiations with Fawn had still been ongoing. Now that he definitely had his children, ex-wife and current girlfriend to juggle, he doubted he'd get them all to Haydown alive if Fawn and Nell had to share a car, and he was certain that guns were a very, very bad idea indeed.

His phone was beeping. Faith again, this time with a blurred, lopsided photo of something that looked like a Christmas turkey, plucked and trussed a week early.

? Dillon replied.

My arse says you'll never come here.

He grinned and saved the picture to his gallery, getting into the Christmas spirit at last.

Dillon made the mistake of laughing when Nell found the trussed-turkey photo on his phone.

'How dare you keep another woman's bottom on your mobile!' she screeched.

'It's obviously not a real arse,' he pacified, fighting amusement.

'You saved it!'

'Because it made me laugh – it's an armpit or knees or something.'

'So you've studied it quite closely then?'

'No.'

'There! I've deleted it.'

'Oi, that's my phone!' He made to grab it, but she threw it over her shoulder.

They were in his bedroom at West Oddlode Farm. Gigi was back with Granny Dibs and Nell had just changed into a very tight electric blue sweater dress and black patent high-heeled boots. She looked fantastic.

'I'm taking you out to dinner,' she now insisted. 'I can't let you go to Dubai on a row.'

'Abu Dhabi,' Dillon yawned. Frankly, he wanted to be alone. Nell's idea of taking him out to dinner was inevitably a very overpriced Michelin-starred country house hotel where he would be recognised and pointed out before having to pick up the bill for a lot of food and champagne she'd rejected. Then she'd announce that she had booked a room and he would follow her meekly, knowing that the sex would be phenomenal in their temporary quarters, as Nell insisted on trying out the bed, the bath, the dressing room and, quite possibly, hanging from the beams. He only wished she was as inventive at home, but his beloved house and fantastic, huge bedroom no longer seemed to inspire her. He was half tempted to put a minibar in one corner and lay out a tray of miniature toiletries in the en suite to see if it would spice things up.

It had always been his Achilles heel; he couldn't end relationships calmly and sensibly. It was the big joke – the rock star incapable of breaking hearts. Infidelity was his only Get Out of Jail Free card, and right now he had no takers and no inclination to take. His failure to get it right with Nell just saddened him, and he longed to be alone.

But he forced himself out tonight, determined to show some guts at last and tell her that it was time to call it a day. Lately even Fawn had been advising him what to say to end the relationship, convinced that Nell was making him depressed.

To his surprise, Nell took him to the New Inn in Upper Springlode, where they sat in one of the discreet oak panelled booths eating Gloucester Old Spot bangers and mash followed by a massive board of local cheeses, including several from the West Oddlode range.

'I love you,' she told him simply.

He gazed at her beautiful, fine-boned face. Those sea green eyes invited him to dive straight in with a siren's call.

'I'm sorry I've been such a bitch lately,' she went on. 'I think it's time I started looking after your heart more carefully.'

The end notes to their relationship died on his tongue after that.

That night, he lay back on his own bed in his beloved farm and studied the exquisite cello curve of her back as she straddled him, his endpin sliding out of sight, the rise and fall of her buttocks accelerating, her ankles forcing his legs further apart so that she could drive him deeper, her head tipping back on her long neck. Her hair, still wet from a hot shower, was so short that he could study the delicate nape, the clasp of her necklace resting at the top of her spine and several little moles clustered beneath it. He reached up and touched them.

'You're so beautiful,' he breathed, and to his shame found tears in his eyes.

He was only grateful she was facing away from him. By the time she lifted off and repositioned herself facing him, he was back in control, knowing the show must go on.

That she could look him so directly in the eyes while the dark blush spread up through her chest and throat, her fingers between her legs, lips parting, inhibitions utterly abandoned always thrilled him. She so wilfully grabbed her pleasure and rode it hard home. It still blew his mind – and his wad – even if his heart was starting to lock itself away.

★

While Dillon was playing wedding singer in Abu Dhabi, Nell headed to her brother's yard to see Cœur d'Or for the first time in weeks.

Piers Cottrell had grown surprisingly fond of the horse with the wild eyes and the heart-shaped star, despite the fact that his early shots at riding him had left him on the deck. He was quite the best-looking animal on the yard, and after a few fierce arguments this Vale of the Wolds stalwart had put the strongest bit in his possession in the French horse's mouth and risked a morning's hunting to see what he would make of it. The horse – and Piers – had loved every minute. Now they were a regular partnership in the field and Heart was shaping up to be a true master's horse.

Piers was therefore supremely reluctant to let his sister ride the animal. 'Just a quiet hack,' she pleaded. 'He's my horse.'

Nell had always been able to bend her older brother to her will.

'I'll come with you,' he eventually relented. 'There's a shoot going on today; I don't want you riding through it. Give me half an hour.'

But Nell wanted to be alone with Dillon's Heart and so, while her brother was distracted on the phone, she quickly tacked up, hopped into the saddle and slipped away.

There were many who'd accused Nell of riding too recklessly over the years. She had always loved speed, often at the expense of safety. However, since taking a crashing fall out team-chasing while pregnant with Giselle, she'd calmed down greatly. She did exactly as she had told Piers, hacking along God's Corridor past the Abbey, marvelling at the horse's long, easy stride.

She stared up at the big house as they passed, wondering if Dillon's father would ever move in or was just intent on owning it to wind up his son, as Dillon maintained. She was far too distracted staring at all the changes the Rockfather had wrought to remember Piers's warning about the shoot.

A hundred yards away, a single gunshot cracked through the woods.

When Cœur d'Or took fright Nell wasn't fazed, and she was quietly determined to stop him without heroism or hysterics.

The horse bolted the full length of the woodland bridleway, over a five-bar gate and out into open country. There, in a huge set-aside field punctuated by just one lone oak and a startled pair of fallow deer, they hurtled around in wide circles. Nell knew the horse would eventually run out of puff, but he was hunting fit and so there was an awful lot of puff to get through. Round and round the perimeter of the field they sped until she was close to exhaustion. He was one indefatigable horse, but she was determined to hang on.

By the time Heart finally slowed down enough for Nell to take control, both were close to collapse. Nell rode away from the sound of the guns and found a gate at the far end of the field. It was padlocked. For a moment she thought about jumping it, but the horse was on his last legs. Instead she found a gap in the hedgerow a few yards away and urged him through it, not seeing the gaping ditch hidden beneath a tangle of dead bracken and brambles. But Heart saw it and put in an enormous leap from a near standstill, clearing it easily. Caught unawares, her legs and arms still like jelly from her recent exertions, Nell pitched forwards. As the horse landed his neck came flying upwards and smacked her firmly on the nose. She heard it crack, a strange sound that seemed to come from inside her head like a thought bubble popping.

They hacked back to the yard with the horse almost on his knees, his ears flopping sideways with utter fatigue.

'What have you *done*?' Piers was appalled when he saw the state of them both, dried blood congealing across his sister's chin and chest, while Heart shambled through the gate so stiffly Giselle could have walked faster.

He put an urgent call through to their brother Flipper, an equine vet, before taking Nell to hospital to have her nose reset. To her credit, she didn't complain once about the pain, but Piers was nonetheless livid. 'You bloody little fool!'

However much she protested that the horse had just taken off, he didn't believe her. Nor did the rest of her family, especially Flipper.

'He's tied up behind and blown both his front suspensory ligaments by the look of things,' Flipper reported when they got back. 'He won't be hunting again this season, let alone eventing. The tendon injures will take months to heal.'

'How many months?' Nell asked her brother anxiously.

'Hard to tell. At least six, probably the best part of a year, possibly never.'

'My poor, dear Heart.' Nell cupped the horse's muzzle in her hands, feeding him mints and kissing his star. Rare tears of remorse dropped on to her chest. She seldom wept over anybody, but horses were another matter.

'Chances are, he'll be fine.' Flipper patted her back. 'Many even get back to top-level one day. We'll get him back to Haydown – Hugo has the facilities for laser- and hydrotherapy to help him.'

She turned tearfully to her brother. 'Dillon will think it's my fault. You *all* think it's my fault. But he just kept going with me, Flips! He wouldn't give up.'

Flipper knew his twin sister better than anyone. He placed a firm hand on both her shoulders. 'And did you try to stop him?'

She looked at him sharply, opening her mouth in protest. Then she closed it again as she realised what he was saying. Very slowly, she shook her head. 'I never try to stop them. I just wait until they get too tired to carry on. It's what I always do.' They both knew she wasn't just talking about the horse now.

Chapter 33

Sylva Frost was unwittingly walking in the direction of the Fox Oddfield shoot. The black-skied December drizzle depressed her utterly. In Slovakia, her home village would be covered in thick snow, its preparations for Christmas magical and steeped in history. In Upper Springlode the duck pond had overflowed to turn the little village green into a mud bath, the fairy lights outside the New Inn had fused and the windswept Christmas tree had blown over. She thought longingly of her fifteen-foot fibre-optic designer tree in the vaulted hallway of the Buckinghamshire mansion, stretching up towards the chandelier and decked with a thousand pounds' worth of brand-new Swarovski-encrusted decorations.

Coming to the Cotswolds had been a waste of time. She wished she had never agreed to host an intimate Christmas here. Despite the fact that her mother and the boys arrived tomorrow, and Hana and Zuzi were on their way, Sylva was tearful and dispirited. Even the sight of her fourteen-page Christmas *Cheers!* shoot, published that day, hadn't cheered her up because she was convinced her Botox was wearing off and, with her pet beauty technician in the

Bahamas until New Year, it was too late to get a top up for the festive parties ahead.

She wearily retied her designer scarf around her neck, climbed a stile to her right and changed direction, cutting across a field once used for strip farming that rippled up and down like a fluffy green slide.

She couldn't even go and see Jules to offload because the paps were all over the village and they were playing down their friendship since the exposé. Mama had been incandescent with rage about that particular story, even though it was such fantastic publicity – Sylva had been IFOJ for weeks now. The paparazzi had certainly got a lensful earlier, when Sylva set out on a stroll in the sodden countryside looking lonely and sad. The public would love it: their very own Dorothy, blown out of Kansas, lost and lonely and looking for her yellow brick road, perfectly timed for the customary Christmas screening of *The Wizard of Oz*. She *was* lonely; now even the paps had retreated back to their cars, their trainers heavy with water and mud, eager to email the first shots to their agencies for the scoop, and then to follow her by car or motorbike. This far off-road, however, she was totally alone.

The official path hooked to the right, running around the edge of a big private wood belonging to the old Fox Oddfield Abbey estate before climbing back up towards the Springlodes. But Sylva stealthily clambered over a gate marked 'Private – Keep Out' and dived into the gloom.

It was sheltered and peaceful in among the trees. The wood was a commercial plantation of Scotch firs looming up as regularly as girders in a warehouse, the tracks between rows as wide and straight as American intersections. After ten minutes of trudging, she found herself passing between big game enclosures with high, chain-link fences like prison exercise yards. She could hear guns in the distance, at least half a mile away, going off with the regularity – and the accompanying whistles – that indicated a well-organised driven shoot, no doubt suits from London.

Cynical locals believed that the Abbey estate was running as a money-making theme park for City boys to play at being country squires. They said that Pete Rafferty had no intention of ever setting foot there, which disappointed Sylva.

She moved past the game pens to a section of old, broad-leafed wood where the ground rose steeply up in front of her like a huge leaf-scaled tidal wave. She turned to walk alongside it, reluctant to climb and now quite eager to find a spot to take a pee.

On the edge of the woods she crouched down behind a holly bush, keeping a safe distance from its prickles, and dropped her trousers.

A loud whistle shrilled immediately behind her. Moments later male voices rose up in catcalls and gruff whoops, sticks crashed against tree trunks and through bracken.

The beaters were making their way along the ridge above her head, sending up pheasants to the guns in the field just beyond the sparse hedgerow in front of her. She was slap, bang between guns and game.

The first shot rang out, so close by that she was momentarily deafened.

With a shriek, barely pulling her trousers beyond her knees, she dived under the holly bush and not a moment too soon. As guns exploded all around her, she was showered with shot and feathers. A twitching, blasted bird landed with a thump by her face, hot and bloodied, another ricocheted off her foot.

An eager black Labrador was the first to unearth her, with a cold wet nose on her shot-pecked, part-exposed buttock. Then a picker-up with a rasping Cockney accent shouted: 'Dead woman, dead woman, dead woman – murdered, raped, dead!' before running away.

Hastily trying to extract herself from the holly bush, Sylva found that her scarf had got caught up in its prickly leaves, tying her there. The more she fought to unknot it, the closer she came to asphyxiation.

'Here.' A leathery hand reached down towards her and Sylva let out a shriek as she saw the glint of a fierce-looking hunter's knife.

The man calmly sliced through the silk scarf and freed her so that she could scrabble to her feet and pull up her trousers.

With a bleat, Sylva found herself looking into the ferocious, untamed eyes of Castigates the gamekeeper.

'You okay, missus?'

'Fine.'

'Something happened to you?' He looked her up and down, taking in the dishevelled appearance.

She hastily did up her belt, shaking her head. 'Just . . . got a bit lost.'

Castigates narrowed his eyes. He never forgot a face. 'I've told you off for trespassing before.'

'Sorry. I will go.' She turned to run.

'Stay there!' he ordered, turning back to his beaters and pickers-up, who were hanging around longing to see more of the pert tanned buttocks in a purple g-string that had been glimpsed through the foliage. 'I'll drive you back to a public path once these men have got back in the trailers. The guns are breaking for lunch now, so at least you haven't interrupted sport.'

There followed a lot of shouting and ordering about, which Sylva watched with mounting delight. Close up, Castigates was an impressive stamp of a man. Wide-shouldered, bullish and taciturn, he reminded her of the Slovak pentathletes from her younger days. He was younger than she'd first thought, perhaps in his late thirties, with a fantastically chiselled jaw, straight dark brows and classic Grecian nose. Most excitingly, as he lifted off his flat cap to readjust it he revealed a mane of dark curls. He looked just like the bronze copy of the Apollo Belvedere that had pride of place in her Amersham hallway.

So when he finally led her to his pick-up truck, she laid on the charm, thickening her accent.

'Vy do they call you Castigates?'

'None of your business, missus.'

'C'mon, it's not your real name.'

He had climbed in, started the engine and began to drive before he answered. 'That's Mr Gates.'

The big pick-up bounced along the wet, rutted tracks.

She studied his wonderful profile again. He was really very rugged and manly. She adored old-fashioned machismo.

'You can get out here,' he ordered, pulling up at a road gate. 'If you walk left along the lane you'll get to the Oddlode to Springlode road.'

Sylva stayed put.

'Is the Rockfather here for Christmas?' she asked casually. He pulled his cap lower over his eyes and lit a small cigar.

'That's his lot shooting today.'

'Pete Rafferty is among the guns?'

'He was the one what found you, missus.'

'Oh,' she felt a deliciously shameful body blush course through her.

'He doesn't shoot no more. Says his hands shake too much after all the boozing years. Likes to pick up.'

'Women mostly, I hear,' she said lightly. His marriage to Indigo was again rumoured to be on the rocks after he'd been photographed leaving a Dublin nightclub with a Russian call-girl.

Castigates picked a strand of tobacco from his teeth with amazingly strong, calloused fingers. 'A lot of pretty girls here this weekend, right enough, and a lot of men old enough to know better.' His loyalty was clearly being stretched.

'Anyone I know?'

He reeled off a list of half the members of the Rock and Roll Hall of Fame, many of whom Sylva had assumed died from overdoses years ago.

'Wow. That must be amazing.'

'Not when you see them shooting. Pete's got the hands of a surgeon compared to half of that bunch of old rockers with delirium tremens. You're lucky you're alive, missus.'

'My name's Sylva.' She thrust out her hand.

'I know who you are.' He didn't shake it, instead leaning across her to open the passenger door.

Close to, he smelt of cigar smoke, peat, wet tweed and gunpowder, a combination that spirited her back to childhood so unexpectedly and violently she felt faint with longing.

'So the Rafferty family are all here for Christmas?'

'If you don't mind, I need to get on.' He nodded towards the door.

She grabbed his arm. 'I must thank you for saving me, at least. Are you free for a drink later?'

He regarded her from beneath his cap. Make-up free, platinum extensions hidden beneath a khaki boonie hat, now minus her garish scarf and camouflaged by her waxed cotton and moleskin layers, Sylva looked fresh-faced, earthy and incredibly pretty.

'I usually taker the beaters for a pint.'

She rested a hand on his tweed thigh and encountered very exciting muscles.

'Tell them something's come up.' She slid the hand higher, feeling

332

that drumroll of anticipation start to thrum between her legs. 'And I can feel it coming up as we speak.'

Once she had hopped over the gate to the lane Sylva called her driver, forgetting that he was half way to Stansted airport to collect her older sister and niece.

'Okay, carry on – but take them to Buckinghamshire,' she instructed Olaf in Slovakian. 'Tell Mama there's been a change of plan. Christmas is delayed.'

'Delayed?' He was shocked.

'That's right. They must all stay away until *Štědrý večer*. They can come here for the *velija*.'

'That is Christmas Eve,' he protested.

'Yes. I must have time to . . . change my menus.' Sylva felt marvellous. Uncovering a wild game dish was far more exciting than waiting for cheese to ripen.

At Stansted, Hana embraced her cousin Olaf.

She had spent a tiring journey with Zuzi. Their entire baggage allowance was taken up with Christmas presents for all the family, most important of which was the one for her sister. She had thought long and hard about what to get Sylva that would be significant, that would help convey the many emotions she had exploding within her in recent weeks. Convinced that Sylva wanted her quite simply to hand over her daughter, she knew that she had to remain strong and resolute, and keep control.

Earlier that week, she and Zuzi had travelled into Bratislava to sit for a photographer in a studio near the castle. After striking poses that had made them giggle as they rolled around the floor, played piggy-back and touched noses, they had come away with a folder full of images of mother and daughter, the invincible double act. Zuzi then chose an arty frame in a quirky gift shop in the Old Town before they stopped for lunch in a café where Hana started to quietly explain the truth about the little girl's heritage. Afterwards, they had walked along the banks of the Danube and talked more.

Zuzi was amazingly calm, Hana thought proudly, so wise and stoic. Just like her aunt.

'You will always be my *bábätko*,' she told her.

Her daughter held on to her hand and nodded. 'You will always be *mamička*.'

They agreed that nothing would change – unless for the better.

'Two mothers are better than one,' Hana promised her.

'I think I only want one mother,' Zuzi had replied.

Now, as they were told that Sylva was 'too busy in the Cotswolds' to see them, and were conveyed to the main house in Amersham, Hana felt strangely elated. There had been no tearful reunion at the arrivals gate, no photocall. Perhaps Zuzi would be allowed to have one mother after all. She hugged her to her side and listened to the Christmas songs playing on the radio; both pointed in amazement at houses lit up with fairy lights like fairground rides as they passed them.

While shots of her looking sad and alone before Christmas were being syndicated, Sylva felt like the fairy on the top of a very big spruce as she anticipated climbing aboard Castigates' huge, smooth trunk. That evening she flirted outrageously over mulled wine in a dim corner of the New Inn, her Bond-girl accent at full strength: 'You are *very* strong. Like athlete. So many muscles.'

'Gateses are known for their build round here,' he told her, coughing uncomfortably.

'I haff always loved swinging on gates – the bigger the better.' She laughed delightedly.

'I'd better not introduce you to my cousin Amos, then,' he muttered, glancing at his watch.

To Sylva's fury he only stayed for one drink before thanking her and saying that he must hurry home because he was expecting his wife back from a trip to Lapland with her sister and three nieces. And so, instead of coupling like two rapacious animals in front of the spluttering wood-burning stove of his little estate cottage as she had planned, Sylva was alone in bed by ten o'clock.

She squirmed with frustration, knowing that she would meet Dillon Rafferty in just a few days' time, taking aim at the hand-reared game instead of playing with the keeper. As soon as Mama arrived she would take over the action plan and make sure Sylva behaved. She was relieved that she'd put her mother off, along with Hana and Zuzi, who reminded her all too vividly of her past. She needed a few more days of freedom.

Sylva lay in the semi-darkness, fingers illuminated by her telephone screen, telling all her Twitter followers and Facebook friends that she needed a man, and smiling as a wave of offers came back, including a host of teenage fans offering their fathers. Feeling cheered, she made a quick call. 'Darlink, I know we're not officially speaking, but unofficially, I'm *sooo* bored and lonely.'

The reply was laced with laughter just as warming as a log fire. 'Come over and help me choose what to pack for Malta. You always had much better taste than me.'

Chapter 34

When Nell collected Dillon from his Abu Dhabi flight wearing a strange white beak made from surgical tape and gauze, he assumed she'd had a nose job. So did the gathered paparazzi, who captured it from every angle. Therefore her attempts to garner sympathy backfired and she was set on a serious damage limitation exercise.

The less she said about the circumstances of her accident the better, so she told Dillon that she couldn't remember much about it.

'Were you knocked out?'

'Probably.'

He was contrite, blaming himself for buying the horse in the first place – 'I'll make it up to you, darling Nell' – but he had that weary look in his eye that she knew spelled trouble.

'Mummy's got Gigi for the night,' she told him as they pulled into the West Oddford Farm drive. 'I've cooked pheasant stew.' Actually her mother had cooked it, but Nell needed all the points on offer.

'I'm not hungry.' Dillon yawned, still stuffed with wedding banquet and airplane snacks. 'I just want a bath.'

'Then I'll run it for you and rub your back.' She rushed upstairs, pulling out all the stops to make up for skating around the truth and over ever-thinning ice. She lit candles and added half a bottle of Penhaligon's Blenheim Bouquet scented oil.

Soon Dillon was slipping around in the big claw-foot bath like the last sardine in the can.

Perching on the side she rubbed his back and shoulders, sliding her strong fingers around the knotted muscles.

He sighed, closing his eyes and knowing that he had to have some guts. 'Nell, we need to talk.'

It was the ultimate cliché. Her fingers were carefully removed.

'I don't like talking.'

'We have no choice.'

'Sure, but I need you to soap me first. It's your turn.'

He opened his eyes to find that she had stripped to her stockings and was bending over beside the bath, face carefully averted to hide the comedy nose. She had such a perfect heart-shaped backside and there, in that magical hollow, the exotic fruit was bursting to be touched and tasted.

His fingers, inches away, lifted without thinking, scented water dripping as he traced the skin towards that delicious opening. She perched obligingly on the lip of the bath and stood on tiptoe.

Slipping around precariously, Dillon managed to position himself for entry, but just as he plunged in, knowing that he couldn't keep a grip on either the sides of his bath or his sexual appetite, the door shot open.

'Dillon, my son!'

Framed within the doorway was the legendary figure of the Rockfather, clad in skinny jeans, cowboy boots and a granddad shirt, his dyed-black hair on end above his wide-eyed, oh-so-famous face.

'Here you are! Your PA told me to come on up.' He marched in, waving in two shadowy figures behind him. 'I brought your uncles Lenny and Dave to see you. Get the bimbo to sling her hook for a few hours, huh? We've got catching up to do.'

'Dad! Fuck offffeeeiighhhoohhhhh . . .!' Dillon slipped back in the bath with a great whoosh, banging his chin hard on the enamel edge.

With a laconic chuckle and a swagger of his narrow hips, the Rockfather admired Nell, who had grabbed a towel and was gaping at him over one shoulder as she wrapped herself up in it.

Then Pete peered down over the rim of the bath.

'Merry Christmas to you, too. Son – Dillon – *son*? Fuck!' he turned back to Nell in a panic as he reached into the water to haul out the incredibly slippery Dillon. 'Get some clothes on, girl, and call an ambulance! He's knocked himself out!'

'Man, it's like Brian Jones!' croaked Dave in a rasping voice.

'More like Jim Morrison,' droned Lenny in a nasal whine.

Sending both of them flying in her wake, Nell dived for the phone. Behind her, Pete slithered about on a wide slick of Penhaligon-scented water and fell into the bath with his son.

Dillon had swallowed a great deal of Blenheim Bouquet but was otherwise unharmed. The paramedics were sent away with a hefty donation to the air ambulance fund and an apologetic explanation that, after so many years on drugs, Pete Rafferty was prone to seeing things.

'As soon as I get here, people start trying to die on me. Just my luck!' Now wrapped in a dressing gown while his clothes dried on the Aga, Pete told Dillon the much embellished story of the dead girl under the holly bush at his weekend shoot.

Their rapprochement might have got off to a sticky – slippery – start, but the two men were making an effort, and Pete was clearly genuine in his desire to build bridges.

Nell was less impressed. Coming from a world where women were as disposable as razors, Pete treated her like a fluffer available to all that night. The other men had similar attitudes.

'You done topless modelling?' asked the weasily one with the whining voice.

'No.'

'You should – great kahunas. Small but sweet. Shame to waste them. You need to lose the beak, though.'

She felt as though she might as well still be naked. They just looked straight through her and talked over her.

She clutched Milo to her chest and went to the kitchen to fetch a drink. Amazingly, all the men were knocking back orange juice and she needed something stronger.

Typically Dillon had almost no alcohol in the house. She unearthed a small bottle of cooking brandy at the back of the larder and helped herself to a slug.

He appeared in the kitchen, hair dried flat from so much bath oil, a big bruise forming on his chin. It made him look strangely young and vulnerable.

'Sorry about Dad. I need to deal with this, y'know. I have to give him a chance. He bought a bloody stately home up the road just so he could stage this number. The least I can do is play along.'

'Sure.' She fetched her coat.

'I'll make up for it.'

She nodded, not looking at him.

He patted her shoulder in a curiously detached gesture, then tickled Milo's ears with far more affection. It didn't go unnoticed.

But when she popped her head around the door to the big, comfortable sitting room to wish Pete and his friends farewell, the old rocker threw her a lifeline.

'What are you lovers doing for Christmas?'

'We're staying here,' Dillon said firmly, not looking at Nell. 'Fawn's bringing the girls to stay.'

'That stuck-up cow.' Pete winked at Nell.

Dillon smarted, the reunion already under threat. 'It means a lot to the girls to have their parents together over Christmas.'

'Come and see my new gaff,' Pete offered, studying Nell's body again.

'Your new gaff's my old gaff,' she told him winningly.

'Eh?' He looked blank.

'You bought the Abbey from Nell's family, Dad,' Dillon explained. 'She's Nell Cottrell.'

'You're from that bunch of criminals?' he cackled. 'Great! Invite them too. Boxing Day.'

Dillon shook his head. 'We can't. We've been invited shooting with friends.'

Nell elbowed him hard but he ignored her. She couldn't believe he would stay loyal to an invitation from people he hardly knew, when this was the dream opportunity to combine both their families in the perfect setting.

'At least think about it.' Pete shot Nell's body a hot look, which meant that she would soon be thinking about nothing else.

Dillon towed her away to the front door. 'Please don't rise to it. Dad does this to all my girlfriends. It's his thing. He wants you to fancy him.'

'Of course I'm not interested in him,' she lied.

Dillon looked sceptical. 'Fawn would never look twice at him. It's why he hates her.'

Nell flared at the bait. 'He is *so* not my type.'

He looked incredibly tired again.

'So we're still shooting on Boxing Day?' she checked.

His blue eyes met with hers, so honest and full of regret, and suddenly she knew he was about to say something that she didn't want to hear. Kissing his kiss-off away, she jumped in her car and drove away before he could do it.

Dillon trailed back into the house.

Pete and his friends had turned on the television and were watching a repeat of *The Old Grey Whistle Test* on an obscure satellite arts channel, marvelling at long-lost friends.

'Good to see you again, son,' Pete rasped, patting the sofa beside him. 'Nice little crib you've got here. Not sure about the bird with the beak, but you always had shit taste in skirt.'

'Touch her and you're dead,' he warned, knowing his father's penchant for stealing his girlfriends only too well. He needed to do something about Nell, but not like this.

Pete raised a hand in respect, then let out a distracted wail of protest as Lenny surfed the channels, settling on an Edith Wharton adaptation that featured one of Fawn's Oscar-nominated performances.

Dillon's face froze as he watched his ex-wife on screen in a corseted dress, parasol aloft, flirting demurely with Daniel Day Lewis.

His father grabbed the remote and flicked on to live racing from the States. 'Take it from one who knows,' he sighed. 'If marriage is a triumph of imagination over intelligence, *second* marriage is a triumph of hope over experience. Don't hurry into it.' He studied the horses being posted into the stalls. 'Now *these* nags, I like.'

'I've got a few in training now,' Dillon couldn't help boasting. 'Event horses.'

'That's my boy!' Pete patted him on the back. 'Chip off the old block.'

Beside them, Lenny was tilting his head back in a reverie. 'I found my *third* marriage the best one,' he remembered fondly.

'That so?' Pete flashed a pirate smile. 'Maybe I'll take your advice, Len, and give that a go.'

Chapter 35

'Welcome home!' Tash burst through the Heathrow crowds in arrivals and dashed towards Hugo, gearing up for her running jump. This was going to be her moment, her Meg Ryan leap from *Top Gun*, the ultimate demonstration of how pleased she was to see him. She eyed up her landing spot and took off beautifully. It was only during the split-second she was in the air that she realised he was carrying a large parcel under one arm. As she landed on target, embracing him lovingly, she crushed the parcel flat with an ominous breaking sound. Her ultra-supportive elastic bodyshaper chose the same moment to roll up from her thighs to her armpits, leaving her with a large Lycra sausage encircling her chest like an over-tight rubber swimming ring, and she hastily slithered back on to her own two feet again.

Hugo took it all in good spirits, grateful that he'd stayed upright, although the Lalique horse he'd bought her for Christmas had been smashed into a hundred pieces. 'I knew I should have sent it back with Oil Tanker, with travel boots and its own in-flight groom.'

'Was it terribly expensive?' she asked worriedly as he binned the parcel on the way to the car park.

'I'll buy you something else.' He eyed the strange bulge that was making her walk with her arms held away from her sides like an ape. 'Is that strapping around your chest? Did you fall off?'

'No, just a new bra.' She didn't have the nerve to tell him that she hadn't got back *on* a horse to fall off it yet. 'Rather uncomfortable, actually.'

'Let's buy you some new underwear for Christmas then,' he offered as she pointed the key fob at the Shogun to unlock it.

Flashing him a worried smile, she was equally reluctant to admit that she'd already spent a small fortune on smalls. 'I'd rather have a new watch.'

'Don't tell me you've mislaid another one?'

'You know me.' She scuttled around to the far side of the car to try to discreetly roll down her body-sock while he heaved his case in the boot. 'Always making up for lost time.'

Tash was not good at Christmas shopping. Traditionally, she would visit Alexandra in Paris for a few days in late December and, with her shopaholic mother's help and guidance, buy everything that the family needed for the festive season in one Galeries Lafayette hit. But Alexandra was still away globetrotting and her daughter, reluctant to admit how disoriented and stressed this made her, was showing distinct signs of dysfunctional behaviour.

This year she'd decided to buy all her Christmas presents on eBay. Tash thought the auction site a marvellous invention, although thus far only a pair of earrings for Beccy and a golfing book for her father had arrived in the post. The gadgets she had bought for Hugo from Hong Kong and all the pretty Tang horses from China that had seemed such good value had yet to materialise, which was a bit worrying just two days from Christmas, but she was sure they'd make it.

Having gone unchecked while Hugo was away, Tash's internet shopping habit was by now thoroughly out of control. Hugo was staggered to return home from the Antipodes to find a new tractor, along with a second-hand Mini for the Vs. It was one of the many things they were soon arguing about on a daily basis, along with her ongoing failure to start riding again and the fact she had let Rory take over so much of the running of yard, the au pairs take over the house and her family monopolise Christmas. She had invited them all this year, trying to make up for the gap her absent mother would leave at the table.

They also argued about Lough. That morning, Hugo had told Lemon that he and the horses must leave; Tash had told him to stay.

'We can't throw him out just before Christmas!'

'He lied to us!' Hugo raged.

'I genuinely don't think he knew much more than we did.'

'Well Lough certainly lied.'

'He didn't lie; he just didn't say anything at all. They've let him go without charge, so let's all start with a clean sheet when he gets here.'

'There are no clean sheets around Lough for long, trust me,' Hugo had hissed, stomping off to take out his pent-up aggression on the new tractor, which was so much more powerful than the old one that he unintentionally knocked over the wall of the muck heap by reversing too fast, which hardly improved his temper.

Tonight, Tash wanted to put all the arguments behind them. She was determined to be positive and get in the Christmas spirit.

Hugo would soon be back from driving around the estate farms and cottages delivering the usual bottles of scotch, hampers of food and Christmas boxes. It was a tradition, dating back long before Hugo's father's stewardship, that all estate tenants and workers received a personal visit.

The Czechs had disappeared to a long church service, Jenny had flown off that afternoon to visit Dolf and his family in Germany, Rory was having supper with a cousin in Wantage, and Beccy and Lemon were out clubbing. The children were asleep and even the dogs, stupefied by stealing all Tash's cooling, pastry-heavy mince pies from the kitchen table, were unusually subdued. Hugo and Tash had all of Haydown to themselves for once, and he was the only Christmas present Tash wanted to unwrap early.

'We can run around naked all over the garden,' she told him as soon as he got back.

'Not in this weather, we can't.' He peeled off a sodden waxed jacket. 'The Ding Dongs and the Singalongs send their love.'

'I hope they didn't mind that there were no mince pies this year,' Tash fretted as he squelched to the Aga to warm up.

He shook his head so that water drops scattered everywhere. Then, looking up at her through wet eyelashes, he caught sight of her properly for the first time since he'd come in and whistled.

Tash's internet shopping sprees had provided some rich spoils. The magic control underwear indeed cast a spell that had enchanted her. These figure tightening creations might be torture to pull on, but the effect was mesmerising, both for her confidence and Hugo's appreciation. While the elastic bodyshaper was a non-starter, Gok Wan's Basque in Glory combined with Trinny and Susannah's Magic Knickers were miracle-workers. Most of her pre-pregnancy clothes fitted again.

Tonight, she had tracked down an incredibly figure-hugging, wasp-waisted little black dress that her mother had bought at ludicrous expense from a Paris catwalk collection over a decade earlier to mark her engagement to Hugo. It had seemed rather too old for her at the time, but now it looked sensational – Isabella Rossellini meets Juliette Binoche.

'Wow.' Hugo reached out and pulled her towards him. 'You're quite breathtaking.'

She smiled, her belly flipping and skipping beneath its hefty support. She was finding it hard to take deep breaths, but it was worth it.

They stumbled along the back corridor towards the stairs, kissing all the way.

While Hugo loved all this new dressing up his wife was doing, he was less enamoured of the effort it took to undress her. The last time she had worn this dress – many, many years ago – he had simply had to reach beneath it to encounter the delicious sensation of stocking top, soft thigh and lace. Now he found industrial packaging. Hauling her out took both of them many minutes, but at least it was worth it.

They hadn't made love this frenziedly since Amery was conceived. It was heaven, climaxing loudly and lovingly in short succession on the unmade mattress in a distant, barely used room, far enough away from the children not to be heard.

Yet, less than twenty minutes later, they were back in the kitchen and arguing once more because Sylva Frost had just tweeted Tash to say that she wanted to buy Oil Tanker, the Australian horse Hugo was importing. He had other ideas.

'I've already sold two third-shares.'

'Who to?'

'Ben and Sophia, and a . . . secret investor.' He pulled an apologetic face.

'Why "secret"?' Tash's suspicion radar was instantly on full alert.

'She doesn't want her identity revealed,' he shrugged.

'Not even to me?' So it was a 'she', she realised, feeling increasingly paranoid that it was the mysterious V.

He held up his palms. 'What can I say? She insists that's how it is.'

'Well, I think that's ridiculous.' Tash had taken a microwave meal out of the fridge and was angrily stabbing its cellophane cover with a carving knife. 'And why didn't you tell me you've already syndicated the horse?'

'I'm telling you now.'

Leaving the microwave heavy breathing as it heated luxury paella, she headed into the study and sent Sylva a private message. *Horse part sold. One third left.*

Tash called up the happy face of eBay to cheer herself up. She'd won several bundles of winter clothes along with a Sheridan bridge table for Alicia.

'What are you doing?' Hugo appeared suddenly over her shoulder as she was checking her purchases, several of which were for him. She hit the minimise button in a hurry.

'Buying the Vs' Christmas presents. They still have no decent winter clothes, and how those trainers stay so white is beyond me.'

'Verruca bleaches everything,' Hugo said in a bored voice.

'Don't call her that.'

Just then, Sylva tweeted: *I want a whole horse. Find me a pretty one. A palomino! See you on Boxing Day. Cau. X*'. She was declared offline a moment later.

'Well that's a relief.' Hugo read the message over her shoulder. 'I don't want her involved with Oil Tanker.'

'She's not going to *ride* him, Hugo.'

'That's what Dillon said about Heart and look what happened to him.'

Tash said nothing. She blamed herself for the fact Heart had just arrived back with them so lame in front that he was barely able to walk. Rocco Naylor was threatening to sue Hugo or Nell or both if the horse wasn't one hundred per cent sound by the end of the lease.

'You're not going to ride Oil Tanker either,' Hugo said idly as he carried on reading her Twitter page.

'Why not?' Tash thought he looked a straightforward horse.

'Because you don't ride.' His tone was light but unmistakeably sarcastic.

'I need more time.'

'For Christ's sake, it's been four months since the boy was born.'

'He has a name. Amery. Our son. I know you hardly see him, but that's no excuse for not using his name.'

Hugo had stopped listening. He was reading Sylva's message again. 'What does she mean, "see you on Boxing Day"?'

'We've invited her to the shoot,' she reminded him.

'That's a family thing.'

'Yes, and she's bringing her family. So is Dillon Rafferty.'

'Christ, why don't you put a poster up welcoming all and be done with it?'

'Don't be like that, Hugo. They're worth a lot of money to the sport.'

'Well, I hope you all have a jolly day out. I'm going hunting.'

'You can't!'

'I always go to the meet,' he said witheringly, heading back to the kitchen where the microwave had pinged so long ago, the supper was entombed coldly in its plastic casket awaiting the afterlife.

'So meet me half way.' She followed him.

'I never do anything by halves.'

'Except half-passes.'

'At least I'm still riding them.'

They shared the meal in silent discord, both desperate to make up but unwilling to budge off their high horses. Tash wasn't even sure whether she was qualified to occupy a high horse any more. She knew Hugo's antagonism came from a genuine worry that she wasn't yet back in the saddle, and he was right to be concerned. She longed to talk to him about her paralysing nerves but she just didn't know where to start. Instead, she waited for him to go outside to do night-check, then headed upstairs to change into her pyjamas for Amery's late feed.

Hugo found her curled up in bed with their baby son, wearing just her pyjama bottoms. She looked beautiful in sleep.

He had been going to ask her advice about one of the pregnant mares that was causing him concern, but he couldn't bear to wake her.

Instead, he went downstairs to call the vet, getting through to the after-hours service and then heading into the study to check his mail, virtual and snail, while he waited for the duty vet to ring him back. It had been a long time since he'd caught up. His laptop was covered with paint, he noticed, as he logged into the email account.

Tash may have come on in leaps and bounds on the internet but she still ignored email and so Hugo was greeted with a plethora of unread messages congratulating him for his eBay purchases. Sandwiched between these and the usual fan mail and marketing offers were an alarming number of poison pen letters.

You Beauchampions are so spoiled, Hugo read a line from one. Another threatened: *Prepare to suffer.*

None were very original, but the sheer quantity rattled Hugo. *Watch your backs,* they taunted. *You are riding for a fall . . . I am watching you . . . Keep your doors locked at night. I'm right outside . . . I know your secrets.* All came from the same Gmail account that belonged to someone called Shadowfax. And the most recent was unpleasantly close to the bone: *Your marriage is over.* Thinking back to the summer and the Olympics, Hugo felt a claw rip at his temples.

Deleting the lot, for once grateful that Tash was no IT girl, he determinedly dismissed the messages as junk and turned his attention to the vast pile of bills surrounding the laptop. They were all final demands. While he'd been away, the office had descended into chaos, part crèche, part artist's studio with piles and piles of unopened post. Tash seemed to live in here, yet do nothing but dream and play. He lifted the dust sheet on the easel and found a portrait of a family there – a happy, laughing bunch he didn't recognise. A commission, no doubt. He was pleased that she was at least painting again. She seemed to do precious little else while he was away teaching and competing non-stop.

Then he spotted a neat pile of canvases stacked against the wall and stooped to investigate.

There were over a dozen portraits. Horses, dogs, children, families, houses – they were all there, painted in Tash's characteristic style, so vibrant and lifelike, so utterly truthful. They were stunning. She must have been working every hour she could to get so much done. All her commissions were completed, ready to be sent off as soon as she convinced herself that they were good enough. Tash always took for ever to decide her work was worthy, often hiding it somewhere obscure only to unearth it many weeks later and decide that it really was pretty good, much to her own and the client's surprise and delight when it arrived at long last.

Drawn by a half-remembered likeness, Hugo lifted the sheet on the easel again.

It was *them.* It was himself and Tash and the children and all the dogs, looking happy and relaxed and content as they lounged beneath the cedar at the top of the old parkland pasture now known as Thirty Acres. The likenesses were uncannily, brilliantly there: the way his blue eyes seared into nowhere as they restlessly longed for distraction, the way she ducked her head but looked up with such honesty and intensity, Cora's cock-headed humour, especially little Amery's delicious gummy smile. Even the bloody dogs were spot on.

His eyes filled with tears. 'Bloody fool.'

He needed a cigarette.

Gratefully remembering that the mare needed checking and the vet was coming, he went in search of his yard boots, coat and fag packet.

Outside, there was a frantic kicking coming from the rear yard. One of Lough's horses had cast itself, trapped in a corner of its box after rolling and unable to free its legs to get up. Hugo hurried inside, dodging flying hooves as he shouldered its flanks and heaved to free it. At last the horse stood up, shaking, eyeing him warily from beneath a thick dusting of shavings. When Hugo stepped forward it almost mowed him down in fright, dancing this way and that against the rear wall and kicking out.

'That's fine, don't thank me,' he muttered, heading towards the door. He marched off to check the mare, wishing that he had sent Lemon and the horses back to New Zealand that day. The thought of Lough finally arriving made him very jumpy indeed.

Chapter 36

In Rumorz nightclub in Marlbury, Libido-ration was not happening for Faith. The cube-like building had once been a gym, adapted into a club when it went bankrupt with a tiny dancefloor crisscrossed with coloured lights. The music was anonymous techno anthems, interspersed with two lurching ballads an hour to get the clients necking. Just to keep them on their toes, a DJ also occasionally broke through the rhythmic beat to shriek something along the lines of 'Party on, Marlbury girls and boys!' which was singularly inappropriate given that there were only eight people in there for most of the night, three of which were the gang from Maccombe.

Burping at regular intervals from so much Diet Coke and fizzy water because she was driving, Faith was dying of boredom. The clientele – two lads from a National Hunt yard on the downs, two IT boffins from a company called Wigitex in the thriving Marlbury silicon valley and a man called Gutter who winked a lot and said he was a council operative – had all tried and failed to chat her up. She was medusa to all who approached.

For all Lemon's lecturing, she wanted Rory to be the one who claimed her cherry in the pact. Anything else seemed like cheating, and strangers were too stomach-turning to contemplate. She just didn't want to know them.

Lemon, however, was determined to have fun. He'd bought an ecstasy tab from one of the bouncers, which he shared with Beccy. Faith refused to touch any of it. Her Brain Candy night had put her off drugs entirely.

Lemon washed his fragment back with Mexican beer.

Beccy slugged hers with a WKD.

Faith texted Rory. *Wish You Were Here.*

He didn't reply.

Leaving Lemon and Beccy eagerly awaiting their high, Faith went and danced alone in a dark corner. When Gutter started rubbing up against her she decided to go and sit in the car with the doors locked and Radio Three for company, reaching on to the back seat for an old sweatshirt and bodywarmer because it was freezing cold. She extracted her chicken fillets and threw them on the passenger seat before locating a packet of tissues in the glove compartment to wipe off her make-up. Then, with Handel's *Messiah* for company, she played loves me loves me not with passing car headlights on the nearby flyover.

The half-hourly ballad struck up just as Beccy and Lemon were reaching the perfect pitch, and Dillon Rafferty's version of 'A Winter's Tale' raunched its way through the cube.

The floor was theirs.

The club had finally started to fill up, but nobody was occupying the small laminated square as they wrapped their arms around one another and camped it up.

Beccy could feel the blood in her veins, the love in her heart and the beat through her feet.

When Lemon's lips connected with hers it seemed beautiful and right. When his tongue circled hers, so muscular and wholehearted, she joined in with abandon.

Their bodies ground together. Somewhere, in that hollow cube, libido-ration was unleashed in Beccy.

Her breasts tingled, nipples so electric that she was certain a blue arc could be seen crackling between them; her groin throbbed with the beat as though she had her own personal drummer in her g-string. She felt wholly, all-consumingly sexy.

When cheesy but sexy Rafferty was replaced with Massive Attack and far more dangerous 'Inertia Creeps', Beccy kissed for all she was worth. Lemon responded with alacrity. It was heaven.

She closed her eyes and imagined it was Hugo's lips on hers, his body moving with hers, sinew and muscle and hot skin, the promise of pleasures untold and passion unlocked.

They broke off for a moment to breath, sharing sweet gulps of the same air.

Hugo was still in front of Beccy, her mind's eye projecting him there.

'D'you fancy me more than Tash?' she breathed, hardly aware she was saying it.

'I don't fancy Tash,' he nibbled her ears. 'Too bloody tall to do this to for a start.'

She giggled, 'And married, of course.'

'Yeah, to a total shit.' He pressed his lips to her neck.

'Oh, don't stop,' she sighed.

'He doesn't care about anyone but himself.' The bitterness that cut through his voice was pure venom. 'He doesn't deserve any of it – his wealth, his beautiful wife, or his victories. He was just born lucky. Lough should have won gold.' He stepped back, eyes semi-focused.

'I meant don't stop kissing me,' Beccy craned forward to be embraced again, giddy with lust.

This time his mouth was hard against hers, biting at her lips, tongue lashing angrily past her teeth. Beccy found it dizzyingly exciting, passion sparking as her Hugo fantasies ignited further and her head spun.

Then, suddenly Lemon pulled away. 'Fuck, I'm going to be sick. Sorry Becs.' He lurched off towards the loos.

She didn't see him again. Libido-ration stalled.

Cast adrift, she saw shapes and sounds drift past. Strangely her sense of happiness and wellbeing didn't immediately desert her, but she missed having Lemon at her side, that stout little bamboo cane that had held up her flowering blossom head tonight. She was out of control and top-heavy.

Suddenly she wanted to go home. She looked around for Faith, but she – and Lemon – were missing. They must be together, she realised with a heart-stab of jealousy.

'Are you all right?' One of the little racing lads who had been chatting up Faith earlier was looking at her worriedly.

'Have you got a car?'

In Wantage, Spurs Belling was having supper with his cousin, an event usually guaranteed to be a raucous catch up, but Rory was noticeably lacking his usual happy-go-lucky outlook.

'Now Hugo's back throwing his weight around I feel like a bloody yard hand,' he complained. 'I've been running that place with Tash while he's away, not that I get any thanks from him or the others. Tash is sweet about it, but she's always so busy. Lemon is pure poison and Beccy's frankly weird.'

He snatched up his phone as it rang out with a message alert. As he read it, Spurs noticed the colour in his cousin's cheeks.

'Secret lover?'

Rory shook his head, 'I wish. My love life's dead in the water. It's just Faith with one of her weird texts. Drives me mad: she ignores me all day, then sends these strange messages that make no sense. I think she's on drugs. It's such a waste.'

'I thought she worshipped the ground you canter on?'

He looked up in surprise. 'In between being incredibly sarcastic, maybe. It's got worse since hanging out with her new cronies. They're all out 'clubbing' tonight. They invited me, but I'd rather assault my eardrums in private, where I don't have to pay a fiver for a bottle of water. Man, I wish I were back in my own yard. I'm not good working with other people.'

'You worked with Faith at Overlodes.'

'She was different then.'

His cousin looked at him levelly. 'Do I detect a growth spurt?'

'She's certainly "blossomed".'

'I was talking about you.' Spurs raised his black brows above his distinctive silver bullet eyes. Having grown up cheek by jowl, he and Rory were almost as close as brothers and he sensed a sea change. Going to Haydown had been good for Rory, he realised. He was taking control at last. As a teenager, Rory had been forced to grow up very fast, very young, whereas it was Spurs who'd gone off the rails. Obliged to work hard and live independently Rory had never rebelled, but he had a fatalistic outlook that had been allowed to run riot. In a way it was why he was so brilliant at what he did – he was a fearless rider with no dependants, whose passion for horses had always eclipsed personal relationships – but it also meant that he didn't look after himself, was easily seduced and rarely valued what he had.

In many ways Rory was very like his father, who Spurs remembered idolising for his dashing charm and wild riding, and the succession of beautiful women he had dated. James Midwinter's great mistake had been to marry capricious Truffle, who already had one failed marriage, to a polo player, behind her and a reputation for taking flight at the slightest sign of trouble or ennui. James worshipped her, but married life was never easy for this free-spirited, boozy, philandering charmer and Truffle left him many times during their time together. For seven years James always managed to forgive and talk his wife back to the decrepit farmhouse he'd inherited high on the Foxrush ridge. Eventually, however, Truffle ran away for good, to live with a point-to-point trainer near Great Tew, keeping Rory with her until he could be sent off to boarding school like his sister Diana. A succession of marriages and love affairs followed, with Rory largely overlooked by his reluctant stepfathers and discouraged from spending the school holidays at home.

Occasionally he stayed at his father's farm, which grew damper and more dilapidated in tandem with his father's descent into drinking and gambling. More often, Rory was despatched to stay with friends or other members of the family, such as Aunt Isabel 'Hell's Bells' Belling and her son Jasper.

Spurs remembered Rory as a tough, awkward little boy who wet the bed, broke toys and struggled academically, yet who lit up with such talent when he rode that he found salvation in the saddle, becoming a Pony Club favourite, adored by mothers and daughters alike. In horses, he seemed to find the love he so craved at home. Rory barely appeared on Truffle's radar unless her ex-husband's school-fees cheque bounced again; Diana ran away from home when he was just eight; and James Midwinter loved scotch more than his son. But horses never let him down.

Not long after Rory's tenth birthday his father drowned in the bath after a protracted drinking session. He was forty-one. It was a dishonourable departure for a man who had once been so fêted. Rory, white-faced and silent, had not cried at the funeral. Afterwards his aunts patted him on the back and said, 'Well done, jolly brave', as though he'd just successfully completed his Pony Club B Test.

The majority of the Midwinter farm was sold to pay off debts, except Horseshoe Farm Cottage and its stables, where Rory's Great Uncle Gerald, known to all as Captain Midwinter, had taught small children to ride for as long as anyone could remember, with military ferocity, a long leather-clad cane clamped under his arm at all times and a voice incongrously like Noël Coward addressing a dim-witted chorus line. The captain was a stickler for manners and went to bed at eight o'clock each evening, but had a good heart beneath the bluster and nurtured his nephew's riding talent. He had once famously ridden around Badminton on three horses in the same day, a feat Rory dreamed of matching. Horseshoe Cottage became Rory's spiritual home in his later teens, and his uncle was the force behind him joining a point-to-point yard as a sixteen-year-old apprentice instead of struggling on at school as his mother wanted.

When the Captain suffered a fatal stroke at home in bed after a long day's hunting, Rory had inherited the run-down riding school. Still in his early twenties and forging a good career as an amateur jockey, he'd returned to the Lodes Valley to rechristen the yard Overlodes Equestrian Centre and take up event riding, which had always been his greatest ambition. Since then, he'd slipped into a lot of bad habits, many of which were inherited.

Spurs had watched with concern as his cousin grew more lackadaisical, and increasingly like his father whose life had been such a tragic waste. Tonight, he was showing a little more Midwinter fighting spirit at last, and Spurs was delighted.

'You are wising up, Rory,' he told him.

'Meanwhile everyone around me is dumbing down.'

'You sound like the Captain.'

'Do I?' He laughed. 'Christ, I'm turning into a grumpy old bachelor. Uncle Gerald was probably a closet gay, I think. I remember all the Pony Club mums hanging round him eagerly, batting their eyelashes. Why do women do that with camp men? Is it the unattainable thing?'

Spurs shrugged. 'A bit of femininity makes them feel safe, I guess.'

'Faith's like that with Lemon – and you should see him. He looks like an Oompa-Loompa, but the girls are all over him. No matter how well I ride, how hard I work, Faith is more impressed by his bad jokes than anything I can do. I might as well not be there.'

'Maybe she's trying to make you notice her?'

'Say again? By ignoring me?'

'It's what you do with horses, don't you? "Join-Up". You chase the buggers around hassling them until they're fed up and exhausted, then you ignore them and they come and stand by you and follow you anywhere.'

Rory laughed, 'So you think Faith's trying Join-Up with me?'

'You're pretty tough to break in,' Spurs pointed out. 'All those bad habits from years of having it all your own way.'

Rory's phone beeped again. This time the colour drained rapidly away. 'Fuck. Faith's lost Beccy and Lemon's passed out cold. She needs help.'

He leaped up, throwing a wad of cash on the table.

Spurs leaned back and smiled up at him, hands aloft. 'I rest my case.'

Rory was too flustered to listen. 'Great to see you. Love to Ellen. See you in the New Year.'

'Aren't you home for Christmas?'

'To drink dry Martinis at teatime and share my mother's spare bedroom with that china doll that looks like Myra Hindley? Not if I can help it.'

Waving him off, Spurs hardly blamed his cousin for wanting to stay away from his immediate family. Widowed twice and divorced twice, Truffle now lived alone in her chocolate-box Georgian townhouse and was never short of dinner dates, most recently enjoying a very flirtatious liaison with retired Danish bookseller Ingmar Olensen. At one point it was rumoured within the family that the pair had secretly married, but Truffle wasn't letting on and Ingmar had already forgotten. She remained a contrary character and spared her son little affection. Both Truffle and Diana had let Rory down badly over the years, breaking promises, abandoning him, pursuing their own goals at the expense of his, yet he never seemed to blame them, he simply retreated into his own world, trusting horses more than people.

It often worried Spurs that Rory was sitting on such a well of unspoken anger. He feared that he would self-destruct like his father unless he dealt with it soon.

The two boys Beccy had picked up in Rumorz were kind souls really, barely out of their teens and good Catholic lads fresh from

Ireland offering a pretty girl a lift home. Still high on her e, Beccy was giving out strong come-hither signals. Lady Gaga on the car stereo made her squirm and giggle. She was a wreck, but she was blonde and buxom with a twinkle in her eye – and she had her own little flat above a stable yard in one of the classiest villages on the downs, compared to the lads' static caravan. They thought Christmas had come early when she asked them in for a drink.

'You sure?' asked the younger lad as they climbed out of the car, music still blaring from the stereo. Two huge dogs were bearing down on them.

Beccy giggled, whistling the dogs away and then wrapping her arms around him. 'Sure I'm sure.' She kissed him, her nerve endings still tingling, grateful to be home and feeling fabulously serene once more.

'Hey, don't leave me out of this,' heckled the other one.

Beccy found herself in a jockey sandwich beside the car, dancing to the music. One of them was sucking and licking her neck while the other fumbled in her bra – or was that the same one? A hand was between her legs. They both smelled of perspiration and cheap aftershave. She started to feel slightly less serene.

'Um . . . actually . . . I think I might just . . .' She struggled to break free and found that one boob was bobbing about outside her plunge-neck top.

Suddenly the yard floodlights came on, illuminating the three-some like escaping prisoners making a dash across the exercise yard.

'What in *hell* do you think you're playing at?' a voice boomed from the shadows beneath the arch.

The lads were back in their car and driving away in less than a minute. Beccy quailed as Hugo strode across the yard towards her, but he marched straight past to close the gates and watch the tail lights retreat along the driveway.

Realising her tit was still hanging out, she hastily tucked it back in and shivered.

The rain had lifted at last and left a skin-biting freshness just off a frost and a lowering mist that floated down around them like gossamer.

Hugo turned back to her, rubbing his hair wearily. 'Look, I have no problem with you bringing boyfriends back here,' he said, sounding almost apologetic. 'But I would request that you take them one at a time, otherwise it frightens the horses.'

'I *am* twenty-seven!' she blustered, feeling the last of her ecstasy high and the Libido-ration opportunity abandon her. She was massively relieved that the lads had gone, but she wasn't about to let Hugo know that.

'With respect, Beccy,' Hugo's voice was cool and dispassionate, 'you have purple dreadlocks and believe in reincarnation. Your taste in men is up for debate.'

'Don't you like my dreadlocks?'

'I dread Loughs,' he said idly.

'Eh?' She was still quite stoned.

'Nothing.' He shook his head, starting to walk away. 'Frankly, I don't like them, no, but my opinion hardly counts.'

'It's my life!' she shouted after him, absurdly hurt.

He held up his hands. 'Your life.' He marched back under the archway to the second stable yard, killing the lights as he passed. 'Go to bed. I just thank God I have at least a decade before I go through this with Cora.'

Beccy breathed in and out three, four times, realising that, suddenly, her opportunity was so golden again it was radiating light above her head a thousand million watts brighter than the yard light.

'What if you're dead by the time Cora grows up?' she screamed after him. 'My father was!'

He stopped in his tracks. She knew that he didn't want to hear this, but now that he had he was honour-bound to react.

He was beside a stable that had its internal light on, glowing in true nativity fashion, golden beams catching the natural blond streaks in his hair and the plumes of condensing breath coming from his mouth. For the first time, it occurred to Beccy to wonder why he was out here on his own so late, but she was on too much of a mission to ask.

Making her way beneath the arch, she shuffled alongside him and looked over the stable door, almost blinded by the sense of him against her side, the warmth of his body and his smell. He was everything she had dreamed about for years, and he was here.

He reached up and turned off the light, heightening her sense of nearness even further.

'Why d'you think I ran away and kept on running?' she asked him in a breathless whisper, desperate to keep him there.

'You don't have to say any more.' He put a warm, strong hand on her back and Beccy felt as though she was sprouting angel wings.

'I want to say more! I want you to understand!'

He rubbed her shoulders distractedly, much as he would comfort one of the dogs, but a divine warmth unfolded those angel wings. 'You must talk to Tash about this, Beccy. She's better than me on this sort of stuff.'

Beccy's eyes narrowed. 'I don't think so.'

'She's there for you.'

Beccy said nothing, staring into the gloomy stable ahead of them and realising for the first time that there was a horse in there, lying quietly in one corner. It looked dead.

'Almost lost her foal,' he whispered. 'The vet had just left when you got back.'

It took her a while to register that the horse was the broodmare Dove.

'What—'

'Placentitis. I spotted her running milk at night-check. She's full of anti-inflammatories and antibiotics now, but it will be touch and go.'

'She might *die*?' Beccy wailed, but Hugo covered her mouth quickly with his hand as the horses around them kicked and snorted, coming to their doors to see what the noise was about. His fingers smelled of hay, of horse, of cigarettes and of cologne.

Beccy held his hand tight to her mouth and kissed it with all her love.

'Stop that.' Hugo's fingers slid away.

She looked at the mare through her tears.

'Don't tell Tash about this just yet.'

For a ludicrous, heart-leaping moment, Beccy thought he meant about her kissing his hand, but then sense prevailed.

'This will be Snob's last foal, yes?'

'If it survives.' He nodded, unlit cigarette dangling between his lips.

She felt tears flooding her eyes, scoured with her own self-pity as she tried and failed to blink them away. 'I was in prison when he died, you know.'

'Bad luck.'

Beccy felt a rip of anger in her chest. Hugo could be so damnably upper class.

He regarded her for a moment, the pathetic figure hunched over the stable door in her party clothes, big blue eyes glistening with tears.

'Time to go to bed.' He plucked the unlit cigarette out of his mouth and stepped forward to peck her on the cheek.

Beccy had had few moments of perfect timing in her life, but this was one rare opening. She turned her head at exactly the right moment, her lips parted and she felt Hugo's brusque, muscular kiss land on her tender, open mouth like a bee diving into nectar.

Before he could register what was happening, Hugo felt the most delightful of touches on his lips, a soft, sweet draw that took him wholly by surprise.

'Happy Christmas!' Beccy pulled away and skipped off to her quarters.

Chapter 37

By the time Rory arrived in Marlbury, feeling like a superhero to the rescue, his heroism was no longer fully required. Beccy had texted Faith announcing that she was safe and at home, and Lemon had been discovered in the loos at Rumourz. A bouncer had extracted him from his foetal position on the floor of a cubicle and carried him outside.

Rory spotted them shivering on the steps of a nearby warehouse. Lemon had his head between his knees. Beside him, all Rory could make out of Faith was those endless legs clad in disturbingly tight leather jeans with killer heels. He suddenly felt unaccountable nervous. Then she stood up and he realised that she looked quite normal from the waist up, swathed in tatty layers, her hair pulled back from her scrubbed face. There was something different about her shape, too. Rory thought he hadn't seen her look this pretty for weeks. But, as usual, she was first on the attack.

'You took your time. He won't stand up and I can't get him to the car park,' she announced through chattering teeth. Then she hastily zipped up her bodywarmer and crossed her arms in front of her chest, hurriedly turning away from him.

'Here – you're cold.' He uncurled his scarf and wrapped it round her neck, breathing deeply. She smelled glorious, a heady combination of horses and expensive scent. 'I like your perfume.'

Not looking at him, Faith ducked away and nodded at Lemon. 'Let's get him back.'

Hauling the drunken and stoned little Kiwi over his shoulder in a fireman's lift, Rory carried him to the car park, ignoring the groaning protests that he wanted to be left to die with his Faith intact. Whether he meant his religion or his friend was uncertain.

Soon Faith was joining in the protest.

'Not my car!' She barred the passenger's door of her little yellow VW, arms still crossed in front of her and her eyes darting from Rory to the seat inside.

'Why not?'

'You're going straight back to Haydown, so you can take him. Besides, my interior's just been valeted. Yours is a tip.'

'So you're saying it doesn't matter if Lemon throws up all over my car?'

'Basically.'

Rory looked at her over Lem's thigh, trying not to notice the long curves of her body silhouetted by the tungsten light behind her. 'I cut short a dinner date to rescue you.'

The whites of Faith's eyes flashed in the dark. 'I'd do the same for you. That's what mates are for.'

Rory was at a disadvantage. He had a small, moaning man thrown over one shoulder and a heart burning like a furnace. 'I'll hold you to that some time.'

'You do.' She nodded and dived into her car, so anxious to take something from the passenger seat and thrust it into the glove compartment that she ripped her waistcoat. Rory watched her anxiously, hoping it wasn't drugs. All he could glimpse were two shiny bags the same size and colour as the ones in the cop shows containing large quantities of heroin or some such narcotic.

Just as she was about to slam the driver's door he called 'Hang on!'

In the dark, her eyes glittered.

'Have you ever done "Join-Up"?'

Medieval Christmas vespers were booming from her car stereo and she leaned forwards to lower the volume. 'Depends if you're talking handwriting, thinking or training.'

He stared at her in confusion, shrugging Lemon higher up his shoulder as he started to slip. 'Horses.'

'Mum always uses Join-Up – she went to California and trained with Monty Roberts long before it was fashionable,' she told him, glancing at him and then quickly away again. 'You look like a cowboy standing there, a bounty hunter with Lem your fugitive.'

'Call me Butch Cassidy,' he swaggered.

'He was one of the outlaws,' she smiled, reaching for the door handle. 'Text me when Lem's tucked up safely in bed.' The door slammed.

On Rory's shoulder, Lemon lifted his head groggily and muttered into his ear, 'Face it mate, she's way too clever for you.'

The little car engine sparked and Rory stepped back, waving Faith off like a stiff-spined army officer, before manhandling Lemon into his own car and driving him back to Haydown.

Increasingly lucid now, but still intoxicated, Lemon rambled about Faith on the journey home. 'She'd never be happy with a stupid man. She's such a smart cookie.'

'She was dumb enough to go under the knife to get laid,' Rory muttered.

'So she can fake big tits, but you'll never fake any brains, yeah? She has twice your fucking heart. She's a good kid. You need to leave her alone.'

'*Me* leave her alone?' Rory was tempted to stop at a lay-by and push Lemon out. 'I *do* leave her alone. I've never tried it on with Faith. Why are you telling me all this?'

'Because, dickhead, she thinks you're where it's at, yeah. But you're not. You don't understand her at all.'

'And you do?'

'Yes, posh boy, I do.'

Rory gritted his teeth, but his heart was soaring, the words 'she thinks you're where it's at' going around and around in his head. She might have a very odd way of showing it, but being where it's at for Faith was exactly where Rory wanted to be.

Beside him, Lemon was on a rant. 'You're all the same, you British toffs. You think you're better than us. You think you still rule the world. Hugo's the fucking worst, but he knows fuck-all about women, and neither do you. Faith will never fall for all that. She's way too cool.'

As soon as Lemon was safely in the stables flat, Rory texted Faith: *Bitter Lemon is home.* As usual, a reply came flying back in less than a minute. *My hero. Thank you. Owe you a Christmas drink. Need a lift back to Oddlode this week?*

Suddenly, staying on at Haydown to help out the Beauchamps over Christmas held little appeal. It was a long time since he'd seen his mother; he owed it to her to make an effort. She'd mellowed these days, after all.

He texted Faith straight back. *Let's join up.*

Truffle was less than gracious about her son's change of heart when Rory called her the next morning: 'I've made plans now. You can't stay beyond Christmas Day – Diana will have to have you after that. I'm visiting friends. Don't you race on Boxing Day anyway?'

'I'm an event rider not a jockey, Mother. You came to Scotland to watch me in the summer, remember?'

'Rather boring, I thought. Til says there's no future in it. You should have gone into the army. Are you bringing anyone with you?'

'Just Twitch.'

'He'll have to sleep in the car. The Pekes can't tolerate other dogs in the house. Thought you might bring a gal. Time you settled down, or you'll drink yourself to death like your father.'

Rory could tell he was in for a tough season of goodwill. 'I'm off the booze now, Mummy.'

'You are *not*,' she ordered. 'What's the point of having you here if we can't share cocktail hour?'

Hugo's reaction to his rider's change of plans was even more caustic, even though Rory laid it on thick that his mother was very lonely.

'Why not take all your horses with you to keep her company over Christmas? That'll save me, Tash and Beccy having half a dozen more to muck out.'

'Lemon can do mine,' Rory told him, figuring the little Kiwi owed him a big favour right now.

'He won't be here. He's spending Christmas with Faith's family,' Hugo pointed out sourly.

When Faith arrived at Haydown later that day, tarted up to the nines and her chicken fillets out of the glove box and back in her

Wonderbra, the car sprayed liberally with perfume and a range of specially selected Rory-friendly driving music ready loaded in her iPod, she was dismayed to find him throwing his overnight bag on to the back seat of his old banger.

'You're getting a lift with me.'

'Sorry, I'll need my car with me.' He glanced up as Lemon minced out of the stables flat and laid claim to the passenger seat of Faith's Volkswagen, complaining loudly about his hangover.

Faith's face fell. 'What about that drink I owe you?'

'I'll call,' Rory promised, walking with her to her car. 'I'm not sure what my plans are after Christmas lunch. My mother's got friends to see. I'll call,' he repeated vaguely, holding open her door.

'Here, you might as well have this now.' She reached into the car for a little gift bag, which she thrust at him embarrassedly. 'Merry Christmas.'

'Christ. Thanks, Faith. I wasn't expecting—'

'Don't mention it. It's only little.' She turned to get into the car.

'Wait a minute.' He caught her arm and turned her back to kiss her cheek, 'Merry Christmas.'

She was wearing so much perfume his eyes smarted. Yet when his lips touched her warm skin they wanted to rest there, breathing in her positive energy.

Just then, Bach's *Christmas Oratorio* started blasting out as Lem fiddled with the iPod dock.

'I love this!' Rory stepped back in surprise, almost changing his mind about going with them, but Lemon cut the music as abruptly as it started. 'Christ, Faith! Is it all this shit?'

Just for a moment her eye caught his and Rory thought he saw his old friend there, but then she turned to Lemon and laughed. 'Yeah – it's all heavy crap on the 'Pod. Let's listen to Kerrang!'

As her little Volkswagen joined the A34, Faith's cheek was still buzzing as though she'd left her electric toothbrush stuck in there.

Lemon had finally stopped complaining about the content of her iPod and was staring at her grumpily. 'Rory's a lost cause, yeah? He's like Lough: the sport will always come first. Give up on him, mate.'

It wasn't the message of Christmas cheer Faith wanted to hear.

'I *am* over him,' she said hotly. 'We're just mates now.'

'Good. You've got Lemon Aid here. And I'm so looking forward to meeting the in-laws.'

Faith chewed her lip awkwardly. 'Before we arrive, Mum's asked me to explain to you that my little brother Chad has a new girlfriend at school, who's called Pansy.'

'So?'

'He's so in love, he's taken to writing her name all over his arms with felt-tip pens like a tattoo. Quite sweet really, but Mum doesn't want you to get the wrong idea.'

'Why? What have you told her about me?' Lemon looked shocked.

'Just that you're my mate.'

'Like Rory's your mate, yeah?'

'Sort of.'

When Rory unwrapped the tissue paper around Faith's present, he found a tiny antique bronze of a Jack Russell terrier, barely bigger than his thumb but cast in exquisite detail. It looked just like Twitch. He adored it.

He knew he must give Faith something in return, and he'd already decided exactly what it should be. The porcelain horse he'd picked up in a Cotswolds antique shop years ago that reminded him of Whitey, which he'd gone ahead and bought even though he'd misread the ticket and found it was ten times as much as he first thought. It was one of his very few material possessions that he hadn't been given or inherited. It was still at his cottage with Jules, but he could go up to Overlodes and fetch it while he was staying with his mother. It would also give him a chance to check how his yard was doing.

When he called her mobile, however, Jules was in Malta, and happily reported that she was holidaying with friends for the whole festive season.

'I've left the yard with two of my regular guests,' she told him.

'Guests?'

'The Stable Yard Ashram – it's really taken off. We're turning over a mint as Londoners will pay a fortune to come and muck out horses for a week. Gary and Phil booked Christmas weeks ago so they can detox before their New Year in the Maldives.' When she told him how much the couple were paying, he wanted to weep.

'Do you let them stay in my house?'

'No, that's the best bit: guests stay in the old static caravan. It's all part of the rustic, farm-worker atmosphere they're buying into.'

Rory couldn't wait to find Hugo and tell him the bizarre success story, but he wasn't remotely impressed with it as a solution to Haydown staff shortages. 'I already have one flaky hippy here and she's next to useless. I don't want any more.'

Wheeling a barrow out of a stable behind him as he said this, Beccy hid her flaming face behind her dreadlocks and rushed to the muck heap. Abandoning the barrow there, she fled to her room. Lemon had deserted her; Hugo despised her. Their kiss had clearly meant nothing. She was dreading Christmas.

Where are you? she texted Lough tearfully. *I need you here. I need you so badly.*

The reply came within the hour. *This time nothing will stop me.*

Chapter 38

By late afternoon on Christmas Eve, Tash had a ten-kilogram monster goose lying, fat and naked, in the meat safe, along with sausages, forcemeat stuffing and mountains of earthy vegetables. There was an un-iced cake in the larder, an eighteen-foot Norwegian Spruce lying on its side in the hall, the study was full of presents from eBay waiting to be wrapped, none of the spare beds had been made up and piles of unwashed laundry waited in skips by the machine.

Listening to the Festival of Nine Lessons and Carols on the radio, and singing along to 'Hark the Herald Angels Sing' as she frantically crammed wet sheets into the tumble dryer, she was overwhelmed by the enormity of the task ahead.

It was her first full Christmas as host to so many of the family, previous years being traditionally alternated between Sophia and Henrietta – her father, sister, brother, stepsisters and their families were all staying at Haydown, with Alicia and the Czechs joining them for lunch to round up the numbers to an even twenty, plus assorted children. She hadn't for a moment anticipated how much work was involved, especially with almost all of the yard staff away.

Hugo was flat out looking after the horses, with only Beccy to help him, while the Czechs had two days off.

She had no choice but to rope in her family and house guests to help, and so as soon as the various factions arrived, anticipating mulled wine and carols, they were allotted tasks.

The sight of her sister-in-law Sally cheered Tash enormously. Ever-smiling and easy-going, Sally was the best foil for the more prickly elements of Tash's family, and her eighteen years as wife and production assistant to uptight documentary producer Matty had lent her tremendous resilience, along with a warm common sense born of bringing up their three children. Pink-cheeked and upbeat, she immediately helped dish out orders and Bucks Fizz, deflecting protests all round.

Sophia was furious to find herself, her daughter Lotty and step-mother Henrietta making up beds, while James was equally perturbed that his welcome scotch was forfeited in favour of deco-rating the tree with Em and his youngest grandchildren.

'At least you were deemed too senior to help out on the yard,' Sally pointed out brightly as she whisked past with a pile of freshly tumbled sheets. 'Matty, Tom and the other chaps are all mucking out. Oh, they got that tree up. I wouldn't hang anything to the left, though, it looks jolly lopsided.'

Sally loved huge family occasions like this, all the more so for Tash's lack of organisation. Christmas with Sophia at Holdham Hall was always so well organised and staunchly patrician that it felt like being on the upper decks of the *Queen Mary*; Henrietta's Christmases at Benedict House were similarly regimented. Sally loathed hosting, and was happy to use the modest size of her house and lack of parking as an excuse to avoid it.

Aside from spending Christmas with Alexandra and Pascal in France – a treat that hadn't happened for many years now – Christmas with Tash was shaping up to be quite the closest and best substitute. Like her mother, Tash was scatty, muddled, a great cook and warmly welcoming. It also helped that she was married to Hugo, a man who poured massive drinks at fabulously regular intervals, just as Pascal did.

Henrietta and Lotty were industriously making up the bunk beds in the old nursery for all the boys. Sally tracked Sophia down to a twin room along the corridor, where Lotty and her cousin Tor would sleep; she was perching on a window seat and studying Sylva Frost's huge Christmas photoshoot in *Cheers!*

'There you are!'

'Shhh – shut the door. Listen to this: "Sylva is a keen horse-woman and has recently developed an interest in three day eventing thanks to her close friend Natasha Beauchamp, wife of gold medal-list and horsy pin-up, Hugo. 'I am buying a horse this year to compete,' says Sylva, who once represented Slovakia in the sport of modern pentathlon. 'If I can, I would like to compete at the next Olympics.' Sylva, who is a devoted mum to Koloman and Hain, says that she is not worried by the dangers involved in this high-risk sport that has claimed several lives in recent years, pointing out that the Beauchamps are the best in the world and will look after her."'

'So she's Tash's new best friend?'

'She's coming to the Boxing Day shoot, apparently.'

'Typical! We have to be at my parents' house by mid-morning. I always miss out on all the fun.'

Sophia was flipping back through the glossy photographs of Sylva and her children dressed as pantomime characters and posing in a fairytale Scottish castle. 'She's had *so* much surgery already and she's not even thirty.'

'Looks good, though. I like the platinum blonde.' Sally perched beside her and automatically reached for her mousey blonde hair, which was now liberally scattered with grey.

'Very unforgiving for older skin. And you need a strong com-plexion. Look at the colour of her fake tan; she's like a satsuma.'

'Very festive. You remember when we were little and got satsumas in the feet of our Christmas stockings? So old-fashioned and quaint.'

'I still do that.' Sophia looked affronted.

'Yours still have stockings?'

'Of course. And Ben. Don't yours?'

'Tom has a cheque, Tor wanted a donation to Greenpeace and Linus has asked for a horribly violent DS game, but don't tell his father, who thinks he's getting Advanced Brain Training.'

'Tash will be pleased. That means you'll have lots of free time to help her wrap. Beccy promised to do it, but she's skedaddled as usual.'

'Beccy?' Sally suddenly registered the absence with a flash of guilt. 'I haven't even seen her yet.'

'Hardly surprising,' Sophia whispered, eyeing the door, aware that Henrietta was just along the landing.

'Meaning?' Sally was agog.

'*Very* unstable still,' Sophia said in a breathy undertone. 'Strictly *entre nous*, Hugo told Ben she brought two men back with her the other night.'

'Well, that's just greedy.'

The last cut before Christmas to be performed by Traycee at Marlbury's ultra-trendy Bed Hedz salon looked set to take her all afternoon, and the stylist wanted to close up for the festive break. But her client was very exacting in her requirement.

'Are you sure about this?' Traycee asked her again. 'It's a very unforgiving cut.'

'It's what I want.'

'Well I suppose anything's better than what you came in with,' Traycee commented bitchily, painting bleach on to short layers before folding them into foil. 'Asked for anything nice from Santa this year?'

'My brother-in-law.'

'That's nice.' Traycee glanced up at the clock and slapped colour on bigger sections of hair to hurry things along.

In the Haydown study, Tash pulled out several tubes of garish metallic lime green paper scattered with glittery holly sprigs and white snow that were already covering everything in a sparkling dandruff. 'Fifty pence a roll on eBay. Amazing value.'

'One man's rubbish . . .' Sally muttered as curious objects started appearing at an alarming rate from jiffy bags to be encased in the shedding glitter wrap.

Soon the room was swirling with a sparkling mist and Tash and Sally had so much glitter in their hair, on their skin and on their clothes that they looked like they were about to take part in a *Dancing on Ice* Christmas special.

Sophia popped her head around the door. 'Hugo's taken all the chaps to the village pub and I can't find what's intended for supper. Why are you all glittery?'

'We've been glitter-eBayed.' Sally stood up. 'I'll mix more drinks.'

Tash rolled out another length of paper. 'There's salmon and olive pie in two enormous baking dishes in the gun room because there was no room in the fridges or meat safe. The key's on the ring hanging by the kitchen phone. Just bung them in the Aga for forty mins.'

Sally was back a minute later. 'Would that be the gun room with the door wide open and three fat Labradors looking rather pleased with themselves?'

'Oh hell, not again! I locked the door!'

But when Tash investigated she was more alarmed by the fact that a gun was missing than the theft of the salmon pies. 'It's the Webley, not one of the expensive ones – the twelve gauge Hugo uses for rough shooting.'

'Maybe he's taken it?'

'To the pub? Hardly! Oh God, he'll go mad.'

'There'll be a perfectly simple explanation,' Sophia assured her.

'Probably hunting some supper for us seeing as the Bitches of Eastwick have polished ours off,' Sally giggled.

It was too late to dash to the supermarket, so Tash called Angelo in the Olive Branch kitchen and threw herself on his mercy.

Thus Hugo and the men arrived home half an hour later with a boot full of the finest frozen lobster tails and wild Alaskan salmon from the pub's catering stores. Tash didn't dare think about the cost.

'Just like being with Alexandra and Pascal.' Sally sighed delight-edly as they all joined together in creating a feast in the huge kitchen, drinking their way through so much wine that by the time they sat down around the enormous table they were all in roaring spirits.

'To Tash and Hugo, and this wonderful time together!' Sally raised her glass enthusiastically.

As soon as Tash picked up her fork Amery let out a furious wail through the baby monitor and she rushed upstairs. He took an age to settle, not helped by Em's two older children thundering around the landings as they dashed from window to window to look out for Santa Claus. When she finally got Amery off to sleep there was a wail from Cora's room as the little girl woke from a bad dream and found her cuddly Elmer missing. A long hunt ensued and he was finally tracked down in the bathroom, tucked behind somebody's toiletry bag.

By the time Tash got back downstairs the table had been cleared and everybody was putting on coats and scarves to walk to midnight mass in the ancient Maccombe church.

'We'll babysit,' Sally offered, taking the monitor from her. 'You go with Hugo and the others. Matty is allergic to organised religion, as you know.'

'Has anyone seen Beccy yet?' Tash asked as she went in search of a coat.

'Been and gone faster than Santa on his rounds,' Sophia said, handing her a scarf. 'She was wearing a very strange hat throughout supper.'

'A hat?' Tash was surprised.

'A rainbow-coloured witchy thing.' Her sister said, then dropped her voice. 'Is she all right? She looked very spaced out. Nobody knew what to say to her.'

'I'll go and see her. Ask her along to midnight mass.'

But Sophia shook her head, buttoning up Tash's coat for her. 'She was adamant she didn't want anything to do with it. Isn't she some sort of Buddhist?'

Stomach rumbling, Tash followed the others into a cold, dense mist, groping into the darkness for Hugo's gloved hand, which felt big and safe and firm. It wasn't until they all stumbled past the lodge cottage and set off the motion-detector floodlight that she realised she was holding her father's leather-gloved hand. To her surprise, he looked terribly pleased.

'Merry Christmas, Tash. Thank you for taking us all on.'

'It's a real pleasure.' Tash reached up to kiss his stubbly jowls and, for the first time that day, she really meant it.

Standing side by side in the Beauchamp family pew she and James belted out the carols and got terrible giggles when one of the old vergers, reading haltingly from Luke, quoted the Angel Gabriel as telling the shepherds that they would find an 'infant sapped in waddling clothes'. On her other side, swigging discreetly from his hipflask, Hugo sang along flatly, yawning widely in between having a tight-lipped argument with his mother, who reeked of gin, was smoking a sly Rothmans and kept asking loudly whether the female vicar was 'that old queer, Reverend Coles, in drag'.

That night Tash stayed up until past three wrapping gifts. It was only as she climbed, exhausted, to bed at last that she remembered the missing gun. Hugo was too sound asleep to disturb, so she made a note to ask him about it first thing in the morning.

Then she remembered Beccy.

In the stables flat Beccy stared at her reflection, contemplating her new look.

The dreadlocks had gone. In their place was a highlighted crop.

Left longer on front, urchin short behind, streaked at the crown with silver blondes that almost made her look grey and near-black at the nape of her neck, Beccy knew it looked awful, but it was what she had asked for. It had looked sensational in the photograph that she'd ripped out of *Vogue*. She'd refused to listen to Traycee's advice, determined to transform from hippy to vamp for Hugo. But it was still her round, babyish face staring out at her, now crowned with this monstrous creation that was part Phillip Schofield, part roadkill badger.

She hated it. Hated it, hated it, hated it. She wanted to die.

She fought back the tears again, knowing that she couldn't concentrate if they took hold.

In front of her was the gun. So dark and sleek and deadly.

She picked it up, slid her hands along the cool metal barrel, around the trigger mechanism and stock. It was beautiful.

Her romantic notion, spun at her lowest ebb, had been to go in to the woods with it. Blowing her brains out had never been on the agenda, but blasting a few trees would feel good. For that, however, she would need shotgun cartridges, and in her haste to grab the gun undetected she'd forgotten those. She'd tried to steal some during supper but there were too many people and she hadn't wanted to hang around in case anyone spotted the disaster zone lurking beneath her hat. So now she was a useless waste of space with an unloaded gun and a hideous haircut.

At that moment, she heard light footsteps on the stairs up from the yard and gripped the gun tighter.

Karma let out a disloyal, welcoming bark from the end of her bed. Something landed with a thud just outside her door. Then a voice whispered, 'Beccy, are you awake in there?'

Thrusting the gun under the duvet, Beccy stole to the door.

'What do you want?'

'Are you okay?'

She opened the door a fraction. There was a stocking outside –

or, more accurately, a lumpy pair of old tights filled with wrapped presents shedding glitter everywhere. Above it Tash's mismatched eyes, pinched with tiredness and hidden behind her out-of-hours specs, regarded her anxiously. 'I saw your light on. Ohmygod! You cut off your dreadlocks. Wow. That's so lovely.'

Beccy stared at the stocking again, tears gripping her. She hadn't had a Christmas stocking in over a decade. She hadn't had a proper Christmas in over a decade. She didn't really know what to do about it or with it. She felt out of control.

'I haven't bought any presents,' she blurted.

'This is a beautiful present to all of us.' Tash reached up to touch her short hair.

Beccy jerked her head away sharply. 'It's vile.'

Now that she could study it more closely, Tash clearly couldn't disagree. 'It's very trendy,' she said diplomatically.

'It's vile.'

'And the colour's a striking mix.'

'It's vile.'

'Would you like me to have a go at calming it down for you?'

'You'll only make it look worse.'

'I promise I won't. I've cut hair for lots of riders on the circuit who never get time to go to a salon. I can even do colour if you want to have another go at dyeing it.'

Beccy thought about the gun in her bed and suddenly felt very silly and very tearful again. 'Would you mind?'

It was the early hours of Christmas morning. Tash had a limited number of products at her disposal but a willing heart. 'Of course not. Put the kettle on and I'll be back in five minutes.'

Using the yard's best plaiting scissors and a colourant advertised by a Desperate Housewife that she'd bought at the supermarket to give her own hair some winter lustre and had never got around to trying, Tash trimmed the David Beckham nineties curtain fringe to a tufty Agyness Deyn/Erin O'Connor crop and toned down the unforgiving white blondes to flattering biscuit shades.

'I wish I could cut hair,' Beccy sighed as her stepsister worked, thinking it unfair that Tash could paint, cook and even dress hair well, whereas she had no great talent.

'I'll teach you,' Tash promised. 'It's as easy as clipping a horse or pulling a mane once you know how.'

Having blow-dried her handiwork until they were both pink in the face, she wrapped her arms around Beccy's shoulders and smiled at their reflection.

Beccy let out a little gasp of delight. Her eyes shone out beneath the flattering urchin cut so that they now seemed huge, lending her face a Manga quality. She looked prettier than she had in years.

'Happy Christmas.' Tash kissed her on the top of her head.

Cautiously, Beccy covered Tash's hands with her own. 'Happy Christmas.'

A text message came through on her phone, making them both jump.

'Must be one of your travelling friends from Australia or New Zealand,' Tash yawned, gathering up her scissors and the little plastic bottles, gloves and pots. 'They're already washing up after Christmas lunch there.'

Beccy nodded, almost strangled with nerves.

'I must go.' Tash hurried for the door. 'If he wakes up, Hugo will think I'm kissing Santa Claus under the mistletoe, and I'm in his bad books enough as it is.'

Beccy brightened, guessing there was tension between the Beauchampions.

Once Tash had gone, she leaped on the phone and read the message. *Merry Christmas from Hong Kong.*

What was he doing in Hong Kong? she wondered as she wearily crawled beneath her covers and then screamed in shock at finding herself sharing her bed with a shotgun.

Chapter 39

The Beauchamps enjoyed a joyful Christmas Day despite the stress drone humming in the background. The family rallied together, cooking and laughing, helping out on the yard, walking through the park, drinking copiously and sharing gifts. The goose was cooked to perfection, the pudding set alight and sung around, the crackers pulled and the jokes read aloud.

And the most dazzling sugar plum fairy was definitely Beccy, told so many times that she looked better without her dreadlocks that she was left in no doubt it had been the right move to have them cut off, even if she had needed a little help to perfect the look – not that she or Tash admitted that to anybody else, although they exchanged smiles that meant as much as the many gifts exchanged that day. Beccy felt strangely naked without her dreads, but she was starting to appreciate the light-headedness and freedom. And she must look good because James used the digital camera he had been given as a Christmas present to take shots of Henrietta and her daughters for the first time in years, and Beccy posed beside her mother and Em positively beaming. Only Sophia, tipsy on champagne, managed the odd bitchy backhander, comparing her stepsister to Kelly Osbourne 'in her *Dancing with the Stars* stage', and then later saying she looked like Aled Jones 'now, of course, not when he was a choirboy'.

Beccy, who had always hated Sophia, wanted to push over the huge lopsided tree on top of her, but settled instead for tuning her out and concentrating on Hugo, who provided by far her most thrilling moment of the day and best Christmas present ever when he bestowed a festive kiss on her lips and told her she looked 'quite ravishing'. She played with the words all day, repeating them whenever she was alone, in her flat, on the yard or even in the loo. 'Quite ravishing, Quite, quite ravishing. Ravishing. Ravish, ravish, ravish.'

She hadn't needed a gun to kill Beccy the ashram hippy, just scissors. Long live the new Beccy.

Now, as yet another blanket of cold mist swooped down to tuck the evening in, and Tash was again trying to get through to her mother on the telephone to wish her, Pascal and Polly a Happy Christmas, Beccy slipped outside and danced toward the yards, still whispering 'ravishing' to herself.

At the kitchen table, Sally and Sophia were sharing the last of a bottle of Cointreau and agreeing that Alexandra had never been a great one for Christmas.

'She and Pascal are bound to be in Mauritius or Dominica or somewhere.'

'Always forgets to send cards.'

'Much better at birthdays.'

'Just not Jesus'!'

They both fell about.

Fed up with their unhelpful background talk, Tash stalked

through to the dining room, where the table was still littered with the meal's fall-out and Henrietta, sitting at the top end of the long stretch of antique linen tablecloth, had nodded off with her cheek pressed to the pile of napkins she had been gathering.

Quietly backing out of the room and making a mental note to wake her in half an hour, Tash checked on the rest of her house guests. Aside from the babies and toddlers, Matty had been the only adult sensible enough to go to bed for forty winks after the marathon meal. James and Ben were snoring loudly on adjacent sofas in the drawing room and the older kids were sleepily watching *Madagascar 3* in the snug along with Em and her husband Tim, who were already writing thank-you cards on behalf of their children. Alicia was stretched out on the Chesterfield in the old snooker room beneath the portrait of her late husband, Beefeater the pug tucked under one arm and a bottle of his namesake under the other.

Ignoring the heaps of washing up as she headed back through the kitchen, Tash went outside to help Hugo bed down the last few horses for the night. He had already been out there for over an hour.

It was like walking through dry ice, the mist was so thick. She could barely find her way to the arch, but she could tell from the blackened windows overhead that the Czechs were also sleeping off the excesses of their first British Christmas lunch, which they had eaten with the suspicion of food testers at the court of a particularly unpopular king, just as they had opened their glittery packages of winter clothes and hats with polite smiles that barely concealed the fact they would much rather stick to pastel jogging suits and marbled denim.

Hugo was in with Dove, who was expecting Snob's last foal.

'Is she okay?' Tash checked, still unaware that the mare had been ill.

'Fine – all quiet.' He came out and closed the bolts, looking strangely shifty.

There was a step beside her and Tash realised that Beccy was there, her unfamiliar hair gleaming gold in the overhead work lights.

Just for a moment, caught unguarded, she gave Tash a look that made her step back in alarm. It was poisonous. But then she smiled her sweet, child-like smile and Tash guessed she must have imagined it. It had been a long day for all of them.

'Thanks for lending a hand Beccy – we really appreciate it.' She reached out to squeeze her stepsister's arm.

'Pleasure.' Beccy shrugged, looking uncomfortable. 'I'll leave you two to it now.' She practically ran to the stables flat.

'Was it something I said?' Tash laughed, turning to Hugo.

'She probably knows what I'm about to do.' His eyes glinted in the dark.

'And that is?'

Lifting his hand to cup the back of her head, his mouth met hers in the longest and deepest kiss they'd shared in months, tongues delving, lips tasting, his body hard against hers. It was a very sexy kiss; Tash would have happily dragged him into a stable had there been one free.

'Talk about having it away in a manger,' she gasped as she came up for air.

Together they walked around the rest of the stables in the main yard, checking everything was settled and the horses warm, with forage and water for the night.

'Are you really going hunting tomorrow?' she asked, trying not to sound too hurt.

'Yes, but I'll only stay for the meet. I'll be back before lunch. I might even bag some birds.'

Tash curled an arm around his waist and stretched up to kiss him on the neck, breathing in his familiar, but still intoxicating, smell.

But, just as he joined in the kiss and it began to hot up again, she remembered the missing gun.

Hugo was furious, all the more so because she had left it so late to tell him.

'You should have called the police!' he raged, storming back to the house.

'It was Christmas Eve.'

'So? If there's not a simple explanation to this I'm going to call them now and it's Christmas fucking Day.'

Tash had a sudden vision of Hugo gathering all their house guests in the drawing room like a butch Miss Marple until the culprit was exposed.

But when they got to the gun room the Webley was back in its place, locked in the stand, as though it had always been there.

'It was definitely gone . . .' Tash was baffled.

But it was obvious from Hugo's withering expression that he didn't believe the gun had ever been missing.

Chapter 40

On Boxing Day morning, yawning widely and still wearing her pyjamas, Tash finished plaiting horses while Hugo pulled down the ramp of the horsebox, dressed in his scarlet Berks and Hants jacket.

'You're a life-saver,' he said as he leant over the stable door. He'd never been able to plait quickly, and he was running late as it was. Both his horse, Duck Soup, and old Mickey on whom he had been planning to mount his niece Lotty were off lame, and so he'd been forced to find alternatives.

Tash wasn't sure it was wise to take out two of Lough's boggle-eyed New Zealand thoroughbreds without permission, but Hugo argued that they were fit and clipped and needed the exercise, to which she could only agree. It was also so lovely to have him in a genuinely good mood that she was loath to break it by arguing.

'You've done the most amazing job this week,' he told her now, admiring her bottom as she stretched up to plait Rangitoto's fore-lock to his bridle. 'I'm really proud of you.'

Tash felt her face flush happily. 'I hope the shoot goes okay.' She had a nasty feeling that, having bitten off more than she could chew over Christmas, today had another mammoth portion of chaos lying in wait.

'I'll get back as soon as I can,' he reassured her as she carried her plaiting stool out of the stable.

'Promise?' She glanced up quickly, about to turn back to fetch the horse. But something about the sight of him in hunting gear made her pause, loving the old fashioned Christmas card quality, the whiteness of his breeches against the red wool, the shininess of the mahogany-topped boots.

He caught hold of her sleeve and pulled her up against him. 'I promise.'

Wheeling her way beneath the stable yard arch with a barrow

loaded with two bales of shavings, Beccy was just in time to witness a very steamy clinch. Hugo, looking so cruelly handsome in all his regalia, was kissing Tash very thoroughly, his hand inside her thick fleece top and his white thigh creeping between her legs as he pinned her against the wall.

A jealous stitch winding her, Beccy quietly set down the barrow and turned away, deciding to abandon mucking out and claim one of the cooked breakfasts her mother was dishing out from the Haydown Aga.

She met Lotty coming the other way, prim and proper in black hunting coat and white silk stock, her dark hair confined in a net.

'I'd hang back a while,' Beccy told her crossly. 'Hugo's squiring the wife.'

Agog, Lotty rushed on in the hope of seeing rakish Uncle Hugo doing something terribly depraved, but when she rounded the corner Tash was leading Toto out to be loaded beside his stable-mate in the yard's tatty old hunting box, a far cry from the state-of-the-art luxury coach they used for competitions.

'We'll come straight back after the first draw.' Hugo kissed her before clambering in beside his excited niece and driving away, leaving Tash to hurry back to the house to get dressed, checking en route that her game pies were still safely locked in the boot of the Shogun, where she was sure the dogs couldn't possibly get to them.

The Czechs, thank goodness, were back at work again that morning, loyally wearing the stiff new moleskin trousers that Tash had bought them for Christmas. As soon as breakfast was cleared away Veruschka took charge of the children. Not trusting Vasilly to handle shotguns, Tash told him to look after the dogs and commandeered Beccy to help her bag cartridges.

Still sulking from witnessing such a hot kiss between the Beauchamps earlier, Beccy distractedly muddled up different gauges.

'Won't Lough be angry that Hugo's taken two of his horses hunting?' she asked.

Tash rolled her eyes. 'He's hardly here to ask, is he?'

'You've heard nothing from him then?'

'Not even a Christmas card.'

'How rude,' Beccy muttered into a big box of cartridges, turning pink.

When Sylva arrived, using Haydown's front carriage sweep for dramatic effect, Tash joined the rest of her family gaping from the drawing room windows and let out a yelp of horror as Sylva's huge entourage emerged from the three cars. 'Do you think they'll all want lunch?'

But nobody was listening, as they watched Sylva Frost stepping from the back of her Porsche Cayenne in all her glory.

Dressed in Ralph Lauren plus-twos and knee-high Stella McCartney boots, with a low cut, wasp-waisted tweed jacket from which a lot of lacy bra was frothing, and a leather shooting waistcoat that was more rough trade than rough shoot, she looked as though she was about to pose for a *Playboy* spread, draped over a shooting-brake bonnet undoing a button at a time.

Tash was too relieved by the sight of all the super-efficient Slovakian nannies to care that the rest of her family were gaping at Sylva in horror, or that Rodney and his crew were pulling a camera and sound equipment from the boot of a Freelander.

'Daarlink!' Sylva enveloped Tash in a reassuringly tight hug of silicone and bone. 'I have been so looking forward to this! Is everybody here? Am I terribly late?'

'Dillon's lot aren't here yet,' she reassured her as they walked to the house.

'How rude,' Sylva huffed, her much-planned entrance wasted.

A little girl raced between them as they reached the steps up to Haydown's rather pretentious portico (a legacy dating back to Hugo's great-grandfather who fantasised himself Andrea Palladio), bounding up to them to pirouette beneath the grand entrance and chattering away in Slovakian.

'My . . . niece, Zuzi,' Sylva laughed, calling out to the girl in Slovak.

'She's beautiful!' Tash exclaimed as Zuzi spun to a halt in third ballet position and held out her hand to shake her hostess's.

'*Dobrýden!*' she chirruped, tilting her head. With her huge eyes, rosebud lips, heart-shaped face and thick blonde curls she was a miniature of her aunt.

'She refuses to speak English,' Sylva complained as Tash crouched down to talk to her, but before she could address her the girl was whipped away by a dark haired woman muttering oaths.

'Hana, my half sister,' Sylva explained almost apologetically as the woman carried the little girl away, casting Tash a furious look over her shoulder. 'She doesn't speak English either. I send her for lessons, but she says it is a horrible language. Sophia, my *darlink*!' She spotted Tash's sister just inside the house and rushed forwards to greet her like an old friend. Sophia, who had been bitching throughout Christmas that Tash was selling out, looked mortified as Sylva air-kissed her extravagantly. 'So lovely to see you again. And this gorgeous man must be a new husband?'

'This is Daddy,' Sophia quacked.

James looked thrilled.

Within twenty minutes, Sylva had them all charmed, demonstrating that the unique appeal which kept her at the top of the tabloid popularity stakes despite her gaudiness was her ability to disarm and appeal to all sexes and ages. When she pulled out the big guns and put on the Sylva show, she was irresistible.

The shotguns, meanwhile, lay idle on the rack in the back of Alf Vanner's pick-up as they waited for Dillon Rafferty.

Tash started to fret that her shooting lunch, already scheduled for three o'clock, wouldn't happen until nightfall. The Bitches of Eastwick, having seen the guns come out, had for once snapped out of their usual stupor and were going beserk with excitement, barking loudly and wagging tails so vigorously that decorations were volleying from the tree with pings and smashes.

She dashed upstairs to check on Amery, who was having his mid-morning nap.

'Vasilly's put the dogs in the back of the car to keep them quiet,' Ben told her when she came back down.

Tash froze. 'Which car?'

'The big red bugger, I think.'

'My game pies!' she wailed, sprinting outside.

Dillon was running over an hour late. The argument with Nell that had started on the phone first thing that morning was still blazing as they belted off the A34 and on through the downs lanes to Maccombe.

Furious that she had been excluded from the family Christmas at West Oddfield with his children, Fawn and her family, Nell had decided that Dillon should devote his Boxing Day exclusively to her. She loathed shooting, big lunches and boorish horsy families like the Beauchamps. She wanted rock 'n' roll and wild adventure.

But Dillon was adamant that they would go, making her feel as though she came a paltry second to his social calendar. He'd urged her to bring Giselle – 'There'll be lots of toddlers and children there' – but she'd arranged for her mother to look after her, thinking that at least they could stop off somewhere romantic on the way home for supper and sex, little realising that, when he collected her that morning, the back seat would be occupied by Pom and Berry, looking as blank-faced and beautiful as their mother. Wrapped up in their dual-screen DVD player, they had headphones clamped over their little ears, which at least enabled her to give Dillon a piece of her mind without fear of being overheard.

Her only consolation was that he hadn't brought along his ex-wife and in-laws, who were by now on their way to visit relatives in Scotland.

Even turning into the Beauchamps' driveway between two spectacular brick and flint gateposts with lions rampant, her jaw kept moving as she complained that he might as well hire a girlfriend by the hour for all that he made her feel special. But Dillon had long since tuned out.

He was surprised by how much he was looking forward to seeing the Beauchamps again and being enveloped in their enviably hearty, straightforward life. He only hoped that Nell would appreciate it too.

What he saw as they finally drove into Maccombe didn't disappoint. The weather was perfect – a misty frost burning off to reveal blue sky with just a few dark clouds over the downs on the horizon hinting at the snow to come later. A scene reminiscent of a Merchant Ivory production greeted their arrival, with tweedy types and Labradors striding around various off-roaders and trailers in front of that exquisite strawberry pink house that lifted his spirits as surely as the sight of a beautiful woman. He was looking forward to the day ahead.

Tash rushed forwards to greet him, looking far slimmer than he remembered her, and those odd eyes sparkling warmly.

'What beautiful children! Hello!' She kissed them all. 'We have smalls inside, and games galore. And you must be Nell.' Tash gathered her arm beneath Nell's to lead them inside. 'I'm afraid I didn't manage to find out whether you shoot or not. Do you want a gun today?'

'Only if Dillon behaves really badly,' she replied glumly.

As Dillon took his little blonde girls to meet the host of other children that seemed to be milling about like something out of *The Sound of Music*, Nell grumpily fingered the hard little heart at her throat and wondered whether she should have brought Gigi after all, but decided it would have just stressed her out. Even though she knew that things were bad with Dillon, when he had produced a little Tiffany box she had somehow still hoped that it might be a ring. Instead it was a gold heart pendant; very pretty but quite probably chosen by his PA. She couldn't hide her disappointment.

She supposed she should be grateful that he hadn't given her another horse. It made her edgy to know that beautiful and mad Cœur d'Or was here at Haydown, recovering from his injuries and facing an uncertain future.

She was even more disconsolate about the day ahead when she realised that neither darling Rory nor sexy Hugo were in evidence. If it hadn't been for the off-putting presence of Pom and Berry she would have insisted on joining the children in the house with an army of jolly nannies who were setting up quaintly old-fashioned activities like apple-bobbing, musical bumps and mask-making. Finding herself standing beside a dark-haired woman in a velvet jogging suit that was so unfashionable it had to be catwalk cutting-edge, and taking her to be another of Tash's high-calibre sisters, she pulled a sympathetic face. 'Not coming out with us?'

The woman said nothing, glowering at the floor.

Realising now that she must be one of the help, Nell reached in her bag and pulled out a couple of twenties. 'Make sure the little blonde girls are exhausted,' she said, pushing the notes into the woman's hands.

They were pushed right back. 'Get lost,' she whispered, her accent so thick that it was a while after she'd turned and walked away that Nell realised what she'd said.

At *last*, Sylva had her moment. She had waited months for this and had rehearsed it many times over Christmas, drilled by Mama to get it absolutely right first time.

When Tash made the introduction to Dillon Rafferty – discreetly filmed by Sylva's documentary team, who were lurking behind the Christmas tree – Sylva had Zuzi at her side and Hain under one arm. She smiled at him with such lovely, natural, engaging warmth (practised endlessly in front of the mirror at home) that the air around her practically glowed and it wouldn't have surprised anyone if small animated birds hadn't twittered down from above to form a sweetly singing halo about her head.

Dillon had a daughter to either side, both of whom were eyeing Zuzi hopefully.

Close up, he was less charismatic than Sylva had hoped, and far shorter. Despite the trademark stubble and piercings, he had a baby face and shy expression. Newly accustomed to Castigates's exciting height, breadth and ruggedness, Sylva found Dillon disappointingly diminutive. The smile when it returned fire, however, was quite devastating.

'I gather we are almost neighbours these days,' he said.

'Yes, I have a house in the Lodes – a place to escape with my family.' She introduced Zuzi who, already briefed by her aunt, obediently led Dillon's daughters away to play.

Dillon was pulling faces at Hain, who gave him the benefit of his giggly laugh, laying a pink cheek on his mother's magnificent chest and looking up at the stranger through the longest, lushest lashes available to any toddler – creating an effect far better than Sylva could have hoped to achieve herself. Mama had insisted Kor be kept away because, just as his little brother had inherited his actor father's flirtatious charm, Sylva's older son had his footballer father's belligerent tendency to kick strangers.

The plan worked like a dream: Dillon was at their mercy. By the time one of Sylva's nannies appeared at her side to unobtrusively whisk Hain away, his eyes were quite lost in her face.

'Let's shoot,' he said in a sexy undertone.

For a moment, as their blue gazes played together, Sylva thought her tactics had been so successful that he was suggesting they both leave inconspicuously by a back door, but then Dillon turned to follow their hostess who was trying politely but firmly to herd them all to the shooting brake, much as she encouraged young horses up a horsebox ramp.

Gathering her shooting party together, Tash hoped that Hugo would get back soon. He'd promised to come and find them after he returned from the meet. It was just a walk-up family shoot, a traditional part of any Beauchamp Christmas, and so there were no beaters or organised drives – more of a big ramble with guns, but with only Alf and Vasilly around to help and so many guests she knew she'd still struggle to control it. At least only experienced shots got to carry guns. She had an unpleasant feeling of trepidation, as though something truly calamitous was about to happen.

She cast a worried look across to the horizon now, knowing the snow wasn't far away. The Cotswolds had already been dusted with it when they had left, according to Dillon.

'Oh, I love snow,' Sylva said excitedly as she clambered into the brake, making sure Dillon got the full benefit of her perfectly shaped rear in the skin-tight plus twos. 'It reminds me of my home. So romantic.'

'Ah yes, the reindeer and sleigh-bells of old Amersham,' Nell muttered, hopping in behind and making sure she was wedged between the little Slovak and Dillon. Just like Tash, she had a very nasty premonition that something bad was about to happen, and she was going to do her damndest to stop it.

Chapter 41

The Haydown family shoot was surprisingly fruitful. They bagged Mallards and snipe by the huge trout ponds; gundogs sent up pheasant and partridge from the copses; and Ben even claimed a brace of woodcock.

The impromptu arrival of Hugo's mother with a houseguest almost caused carnage when Alicia took a few random pot-shots at a telegraph pole and brought down her own phone lines, but as her houseguest pointed out, 'you never answer the damned thing anyway'.

His aim improving all the time, Dillon was having a superb afternoon and felt more relaxed than he had in weeks, despite Nell sulking and Sylva Frost's rather overpowering presence with her camera crew's lens constantly trained on him. When he politely requested that they stop, they reluctantly acquiesced and Sylva was profoundly apologetic: 'I forget they are there these days, but of course your private time is very precious.' To her credit she was a crack shot – far better than any of the other women there – and single-handedly accounted for five brace of pheasant and a couple of crows.

Increasingly petulant at the sight of her lover lapping up the attentions of an orange-tanned bimbo, Nell set about flirting to make him jealous, but mistakenly chose Tash's affable but dim brother-in-law Ben Meredith, who had absolutely no idea what was going on and, assuming that she really *did* want his advice on how to handle that 'terribly big gun', started to bore her rigid on good shooting practice.

By the time Hugo joined them, still in his breeches and stock, but now teamed with Dubarry boots and a big tweed shooting jacket thrown over his shoulders, the party was marching out of Pinnock's Copse. He made a beeline for Tash.

'Who let Mother join in?' he asked in horror as he spotted Alicia waving a gun around, Beefy panting eagerly in her poacher's pocket while the Bitches of Eastwick cowered behind her.

'I can hardly have her removed,' Tash pointed out.

'When's Rory getting back?' he asked in an undertone as they moved on towards the edge of the old forestry that usually provided great cover and rich pickings for the fattest, laziest pheasants. 'I could use his help on the yard. Beccy's on her own.'

'No idea – sorry.' Tash had more pressing concerns as she handed him her gun. 'You take over: I've got to take a car back to the house to rescue lunch. The dogs ate two of the game pies, so I need to raid the freezers and improvise like mad.' She kissed him on the lips to stop his bark of protest.

Moments later, Hugo had spotted a late pheasant lifting from the safety of the copse, and claimed it before any of the others could even lift their guns.

It started to snow properly as Tash drove back across the estate, big flakes whooshing towards her windscreen.

Back at the house, the children were having a riotous time dashing in and out of the tall glazed doors to catch the snowflakes, impatient for enough snow to fall so they could make a snowman.

Tash kicked off her boots at the back door and headed straight across the rear lobby to the old pantry that housed the two big chest freezers, pulling a big bag of local sausages from one, followed by two huge plastic pots of the chicken soup that Henrietta always brought with her when she visited, and which Tash and Hugo always forgot to eat.

Holding them in place with her chin, she teetered precariously into the kitchen and then stopped in the doorway.

A man was standing with his back to her, thick black hair full of snow. His shoulders were as wide as rower's, his hips as narrow as a jockey's. Just above his collar, on the back of his tanned neck, she could see the black edge of a tattoo. She knew instantly who it was.

'Ohmygod, Lough Strachan! You're here!'

As he turned to face her, his black eyes smouldering like coal, a slow smile widened across his face, a smile so exultant it seemed to heat the room.

His voice seemed as deep as a blue whale's call as he dipped his head apologetically. 'Sorry it took me so long.'

Tash found her smile matching his, genuinely delighted to find him so warm. The Devil on Horseback had ridden in at last, but with sunshine rather than hellfire.

'Welcome.' She hastily dropped her frozen spoils on the kitchen table and went to shake his hand. Hers were icy from clutching sausages straight from the freezer, his as warm as toast. As he pulled her towards him to land a kiss on her cheek, Tash was caught by surprise and tilted her face the wrong way, so he ended up practically sucking her nose. He smelled deliciously of aftershave and mints. Turning pink, Tash backed away, her nose damp and her face glowing.

'You've caught us on the hop – there's a shoot here, and it was the big meet this morning, so we're all over the place – oh!' She suddenly remembered that Lough's horses had gone in place of Haydown ones. 'Actually, I should mention something straight away . . .'

As she tried to explain the last-minute switch she got the impression that he wasn't listening. His eyes were focused on her face, but they had a faraway look. She guessed he must be feeling quite jetlagged. 'Boxing Day meets are really just a procession,' she told him, 'so the horses did no more than stand about, trot out of Marlbury and have a quick canter across a couple of fields.'

Lough's dark gaze was fixed on hers.

'You're even more beautiful than I remember,' he said suddenly.

Tash gaped at him, wondering if he'd been drinking a lot during the flight, but guessing he was just a typical eventing roué. He was certainly nothing like she'd expected, having heard he was rather moody and tongue-tied.

'Beccy will be washing off your horses now. You'll want to see them, I'm sure. Or would you rather have a cup of tea or coffee first? Something to eat?'

He said nothing, staring at her for what seemed like forever.

Tash was secretly dying to get her sausages in the oven and start defrosting the soup, but it seemed rude to whisk about like Delia Smith when he had just arrived and was being so nice to her. She edged towards a cupboard to fetch out a roasting tray.

'You must feel terribly out of sorts getting here after so long in . . . er . . . transit,' she fudged, turning away, knowing she needed Hugo alongside to tackle the topic of his arrest. 'But it's just lovely to have you here now.'

He watched her long neck bending as she stooped down to reach to the back of the cupboard. 'Nowhere you can be that isn't where you're meant to be,' he said softly.

'Sorry?' Tash was clattering through the baking trays.

'"All You Need is Love", remember?'

'Oh, right. Super.' She looked up at him over her shoulder and smiled awkwardly, finding him incredibly nice but rather odd. 'I'll just get this food on then I'll take you out to see your horses. I'm sure Hugo gave them a fun morning out.'

The mention of Hugo's name seemed to snap him out of his reverie. 'Out where?'

'At the Boxing Day meet, like I told you. He took my niece, Lotty. She's on the Pony Club dressage squad, so is a super jockey.'

Lough's eyes narrowed. 'They took *my* horses?'

His deep voice was a rumble of thunder now, the coal eyes burning like furnaces.

She nodded nervously.

'Where the fuck is Lemon?' he raged, turning to storm back outside.

Abandoning her frozen sausages, Tash dashed after him.

Beccy was in a stable applying leg wraps to Lough's rangy bay mare Tinks when she heard raised voices approaching outside.

Every nerve ending on her body tightened as she took in the New

385

Zealand accent, the growling bass notes and the obvious anger. 'I get here after all these months of shit to find my head lad is missing and your fucking husband has taken my top two horses out for a day's sport!'

Tash sounded out of breath, her voice further away. 'Oh Christ, I know it seems unforgiveable, but—'

'Too right it's unforgiveable. I'll bloody kill him.'

'We had no idea you were coming!'

'Don't fucking lie, Tash.'

Beccy crept to the back of the stable as the voices grew closer.

'We've been expecting you for weeks, of course,' Tash was saying, 'but we had just that one call and suddenly it's Christmas. Lemon said nothing. I didn't know you could fly here from New Zealand on a bank holiday.'

'The plane was scheduled to land on Christmas Eve, but it developed a fault and we got grounded. I spent Christmas Day in Hong Kong.'

'How awful for you.'

They had reached the block where his horses were stabled. Beccy could hear him walk into the stable beside hers, greeting the grey Rangitoto who was now hosed off and wrapped in warm rugs, pulling on a haynet and apparently very happy after his short morning's entertainment.

'Hey boy, how's my superstar?' His voice was soft now, and she stifled a sob of fear and excitement as she remembered it speaking to her late at night, talking to her from thousands of miles away. Now it was so close, her ears filled with the sound of her own rushing blood.

She shrank back further into the shadows as Lough loomed over the door, a silhouette of such broad-shouldered, wild-haired heroism that she thought her heart would stop beating. When Tinks let out a whicker of recognition right beside her she almost fainted with fright.

With a click of the bolt he stepped inside and approached the horse, running a hand along her neck and pulling affectionately at her ears as he cast an eye over her. Her mane was still curled from its plaits and her coat damp from being washed down, but she looked a picture of good health, eyes bright and contented, body gleaming and fit.

Lough made clicking noises under his breath as he fished in his pockets for mints, clearly incredibly moved to see her again.

His sheer physical presence was incredibly intimidating, although he wasn't that big; maybe an inch or two shorter than Hugo, and smaller-framed despite the amazing shoulders, yet it was as though a tornado had blown into the yard, sending up the snow and melting a path in its wake.

Then he suddenly spotted Beccy cowering behind the mare.

'Thanks for looking after her for me.'

Nodding mutely, she felt as though her heart had stopped beating.

'This is my stepsister, Beccy.'

'Hi.' He smiled tiredly and reached up to brush the snow from his pelt of black hair, his anger finally evaporating. He suddenly looked absolutely shattered, the dissipating adrenalin taking his last reserves of energy with it.

Tash was eager to make amends. 'We're about to have a big lunch – some friends and family are here shooting, but they'll be back soon because of the weather. Please join us.'

He shook his head. 'Is there somewhere I can just crash out for a couple of hours? The flight's beaten me. I haven't slept since Auckland.'

'Sure – Beccy, could you show Lough the lodge cottage? You know where the keys are, so give him that set. You'll be sharing with our work rider Rory,' she said, turning to Lough, 'but it's a big cottage – plenty of space.'

'Haven't had a lot of that lately.' He looked more exhausted than ever, but his deep voice lost none of its power as he fixed Tash with a long look. 'Forgive me. I can't think straight right now.'

'Take as long as you need.'

His eyes flashed, searching her face again for more than just the kind smile there. 'Tell your husband I'll speak with him as soon as I'm rested.' Then he turned to Beccy. 'Lead on . . . sorry, I missed your name.'

'Beccy,' she gulped, not looking at him.

'Beccy,' he repeated, and suddenly she felt she had the most beautiful name in the world.

She kept her head down and her hat pulled low over her face as she hastily led Lough to the cottage, terrified of being alone with him for long in case he recognised her under closer scrutiny. She hadn't prepared herself for meeting him in person and while it was over-whelmingly exciting, it was also terrifying.

When he had stepped into the stable earlier, full of heat and fury like an erupting volcano, she'd thought she'd forgotten how to breathe. Her head was still spinning, but self-preservation had kicked in. *Act normal*, her instincts told her. *You look nothing like you did in Melbourne. He won't recognise you. And he thinks that Tash is the one he's exchanged messages with. You're just a groom.*

He had to quicken his step to keep up. 'Hang on, my hire car's back there.'

'Fetch it later,' she insisted as she swung through the iron gate and crunched up the front path, leaving a trail of footprints in the virginal snow.

'Very chocolate-box.' Lough was gazing up at the little brick and flint cottage with its shingle roof, far removed from the tin-topped cabin he had rented on twenty acres of prime New Zealand horse country, or more recently his temporary accommodation in a suc-cession of cells, interview rooms, cheap hotels and his mother's Auckland apartment.

'Yes, it's quite pretty,' Beccy spouted, trying so hard to sound dif-ferent from her Tash phone voice that she was now squeaking like Tweetie Pie. 'You'll have to remember to keep the Rayburn and the sitting-room fire lit because it gets seriously cold and the night stor-age heaters are hopeless. Rory's room is upstairs on the— Well, it's obvious. You get the other big room. There's bedding and towels in the cupboard in the bathroom.'

Not looking at him, she stepped back on the doorstep and thrust the keys in his direction.

As his hand covered hers to take them they both jumped at the static shock that stung at their palms. The keys dropped to the ground. Stooping to retrieve them at the same time, they banged foreheads. Then, to her embarrassment, Beccy's felt her feet slip in the snow and she tipped forwards, head-butting him again before reaching out to save herself and finding her splayed hand landing firmly in his crotch. His eyes watered with pain.

'Sorry!' She scrabbled back, slipped again and landed on her bottom.

Lough held out a hand to help her up. For a moment, as he looked directly in the face of this shy, red-cheeked creature who'd just accidentally battered his tired body, he started with surprise. 'Have we met before?'

Shaking her head furiously, she ducked her face away and went into reverse. 'Never. I'll leave you to look around. Shout if there's anything you need.'

Grateful that she obviously wasn't going to come in and start fussing around, Lough nodded a polite dismissal. The girl scuttled away down the path behind him as he kicked snow from his boots and stepped inside. His new housemate thankfully seemed to be out, so he closed the door on his worries and made his way upstairs, not caring about the cold. One room was clearly occupied, so he made his way across the landing to an empty room with duck egg blue walls, containing just a brass bed, a chest of drawers and a small bedside table. There was a charming oil painting of a horse above the bed – incredibly delicate and accurate. It was a few moments before he realised that it was one of his horses.

He walked to the window, which looked out across the white winter gardens to the main house, only the topmost windows of which were visible over a high wall.

It was all so alien to him, this English country life with its grand houses and long family pedigrees. He knew that was the mainstay of eventing in the UK, but it still came as a shock to him how formal it all was. Tash had behaved like a total stranger, so British and polite. It had really thrown him.

He closed his eyes and groaned. Why had he been so angry? He shouldn't have taken it out on her, but he just couldn't stop himself. It was just so strange, seeing her at last. Their secret exchanges felt like a dream, these past few weeks so horrific and surreal.

In a sudden moment of sleepy penitence he pulled his phone from his pocket and texted her.

So muddled up and fucked up being here. Seems unreal. Glad I am here, though.

She texted straight back. *Me too. xxx*

'Me too,' he breathed, looking up at the little picture of the horse. 'Me too.' And he was asleep.

Driving back to Berkshire in the billowing snow with her car boot half open and Lemon fretting on the passenger seat was not Faith's idea of fun.

'Lough is going to murder me!' he said for the tenth time.

Faith ignored him.

Behind her, the rear seats were folded down and a large wheel-barrow and shovel bounced around beneath their bungee straps. Because they were too big to fit in with the boot closed, Graham had tied the boot ajar and cold air was blasting in.

Faith understood that she had only got a token Christmas present this year because her birthday car had been so generous, but had they needed to get something quite so embarrassing? The Haydown mob would laugh themselves hoarse over it; Lemon had certainly had tears in his eyes when she'd pulled off the acres of wrapping to reveal the barrow, which her stepfather had sprayed bright turquoise to match her cross country colours, then customised with Danish, British and Irish flags and slogans like 'Bottoms up', 'Kick on' and 'Leap of Faith'. The shovel was similarly adorned. A great deal of care and love had gone into it, but she couldn't help wishing that they had just given her the new breeches and waterproof over-trousers she had asked for instead. At least it would give Rory a laugh; he hadn't been in very good spirits lately.

She concentrated on the twilit road ahead, its sludgy grey tracks disappearing away through the snow and white flakes spinning brightly in the headlights, trying not to worry about Rory travelling back in his old banger. It wasn't so long ago that he'd got his licence back after a ban, and he was an appalling driver.

'He'll murder me!' Lemon covered his eyes and groaned yet again.

'Oh, c'mon,' she snapped. 'It's not your fault Hugo took his horses out.'

'Yes it is. They're my responsibility.'

But, in the end, Lough was still sleeping off his flight in the lodge cottage when they arrived, his hire car parked on the yard where he'd left it, and thickly coated with snow.

A late lunch was still in progress in the house. Lemon and Faith peered through the glowing windows and observed at least twenty at the kitchen table, with various free-range children and dogs milling around.

'That's Dillon Rafferty.' She pointed out a dark-haired figure leaning away from the attentions of a platinum blonde. 'I might have guessed Sylva Frost would be all over him.'

'She's *hot*.'

At this, Faith let out a low snarl. Rory wasn't among the late lunchers and his car wasn't back, so she wearily set about skipping out his horses so that she could return to Lime Tree Farm before the weather closed in totally – not that she would mind being snowbound in Maccombe for a few days; it felt more like home than Lime Tree Farm, although that was set to change from New Year. Once the horses were in full work again the Moncrieffs would need Faith in the team and she'd move White Lies to their Fosbourne Ducis yard too. She was dreading the change and the separation from Rory.

Still gibbering with fear, and casting anxious looks in the direction of the lodge, Lemon started on Lough's horses.

The Haydown shooting lunch proved riotous fun, despite the strange selection of food on offer. Acting as cook and waitress, acutely aware of her sweaty face and uncombed hair, Tash tried not to feel offended that nobody lifted a finger to help her, nor mind that Sylva alternated between flirting with Dillon Rafferty and turning her laser-beam attentions on Hugo. He seemed mercifully oblivious, far too preoccupied with fuming about Lough Strachan's arrival. Tash was playing down how angry the Kiwi had been about Hugo hunting his horses, but there was no doubt that fireworks were in store.

'He can't just turn up without a bye your leave,' he muttered now as she leaned past him to offer round the last few home-made chocolate brownies with hot fudge sauce.

'I think he's terribly dashing,' Sophia admitted from across the table. 'We saw him at the Olympics and he's the most breathtaking rider.'

'Jolly talented horseman for a foreigner,' Alicia agreed loudly, the contents of her hipflask having long since rendered her politically incorrect. 'Gather he's a bit of a firebrand, but the best often are.'

'Is Lough the one you said should have won?' James asked Henrietta.

'Hugo won the gold,' Tash reminded them awkwardly, feeling Hugo bristle beside her.

'This cake stuff is splendid, Tash,' congratulated Ben, helping himself to a fourth brownie as he tried valiantly to deflect any tension.

'Jolly good spread you've laid on, especially those tasty little game goujons with the spicy sauce. You must give the recipe to Sophs.'

'They were Captain Birdseye's chicken dippers, Ben,' Sophia informed him in an ungracious undertone.

'Terrific.' He looked blank. 'Better ask him for the recipe then. Any relation to Clarissa Byrd-Sligh?'

Sylva giggled, trying to catch Hugo's eye again, but he was gazing fixedly at the darkening dusk beyond the window so she settled for smiling at Dillon, who flashed a nervous smile before returning his attention to his plate of cheeses and biscuits. He was sweet, but Sylva found Hugo far more macho and exciting. No wonder Tash fretted about keeping him; he was even sexier than she remembered him at Blenheim. The day had got far more thrilling once he joined the shooting party, and the late lunch was great entertainment as the Beauchamps and their guests chatted and laughed and barracked and gossiped. Nobody wanted to leave, but it was finally forced to break up when Olaf came into the kitchen for the third time, covered in melting snow, to say that he had yet again cleared the front drive with the help of Vasilly and two shovels, but that it would be impossible a fourth time if the snow continued at this rate.

'Oh, darlink people I must leave you!' Sylva stood up, blowing kisses.

To Tash and Henrietta's embarrassment James blew loud kisses back and raised his glass. He was having quite the jolliest Christmas in years.

'You must come again!' Alicia warbled from the head of the table, having automatically resumed proprietorial rights as she always did when eating at Haydown. 'You remind me so delightfully of those gorgeous European girls one knew from noble families that had to flee communism after the war. Lovely gels. So pretty and gay. Always made dreadful marriages.'

'Touché.' Sylva beamed at her, having bonded with Hugo's mother during the shoot. She had a wicked sense of humour, along with the sort of class and connections that money could never buy.

Equally, Alicia thought that the little Slovakian was a complete poppet and planned to cultivate her as a plaything to entertain her friends. 'Come for New Year. We always have a frightfully jolly party, don't we Hugo?'

'Not here,' Hugo pointed out.

'Of course not.' Alicia was sparking up a Rothmans despite horrified looks all around her. 'It's a local landowner's jolly.'

'Bollocks it is!' he laughed. 'It's the Moncrieffs bash,' he told Sylva. 'Very local.'

'Terribly jet-set,' Alicia countered winningly, having taken to Sylva big time, especially the strong scent of new money that emanated from her. 'That lovely Irish actor, Neal O'Thing is always there.'

'Niall O'Shaughnessy,' Tash corrected, earning a dark look from Hugo.

'Do come.' Alicia batted her eyes at Sylva through the smoke-screen. 'You will be my personal guest.'

'I'll check my diary,' she promised, gathering her shooting waist-coat from the back of her chair and winking at Dillon.

Pretending not to notice, Dillon glanced across at Nell, relieved that the party was breaking up, however much he had enjoyed the day. The greatest surprise had been Sylva Frost. From what little he'd read, he had always assumed she'd be a hideous, fake creation, but at close quarters she was a lot more down to earth yet, para-doxically, a lot more complicated. He liked her directness and obvious intelligence. She was sensual and intriguingly wise.

'You will call me,' she insisted now, pressing a card into his palm. 'We should be allies.'

He nodded, hastily pocketing the card while Nell was looking away before politely standing to take part in the procession of kisses that accompanied Sylva's departure. Moving in beside him, Nell calmly reached into his pocket, took out the card and flicked it behind her into the open fire. 'We should have spent the day with your father.' Her eyes narrowed as she watched Sylva Frost politely kissing her hosts at the door. Another card was pressed into Hugo's palm as she did so.

Dillon saw it too and smiled to himself before turning to kiss Nell firmly on the mouth. 'Thank you for putting up with today,' he breathed into her ear, 'I know it wasn't your thing.'

She touched the Tiffany heart at her throat and felt somewhat cheered. At least his children had stayed well out of the way, and she hadn't had to see any of his horses, especially the one she'd injured.

'Is Rory not here?' Dillon double-checked as they prepared to leave, making Nell hold her breath.

Tash shook her head apologetically. 'You'll probably pass him on the way home.'

Beccy tracked down Lemon and Faith to the stables, where they were skipping out the furthest row of boxes. Flushed pink from kitchen heat and whisky macs, delighted to be a part of the inner circle as opposed to the stable hands, she couldn't wait to impart all her news.

'Lough is *so scary!*' she gasped, making Lemon turn even paler. 'You should have heard him shouting at Tash. I'm sure he made her cry. Hugo's spitting tacks about it all in there and is dying to take him on, so there'll be fireworks soon!'

'Can't wait,' Lemon said faintly, guessing that he would personally be tacked to the Catherine wheel.

'You never said how goddamned *sexy* he is!' Beccy was too tight to censor herself much. 'He's so hot the water troughs bubble like Rotorua when he walks past. Even the horses were batting their eyelashes at him.' She was still thrilled he hadn't recognised her, imagining their slate wiped clean and ready to be written upon again.

'Oh, he's sexy all right.' Lemon sighed sadly. 'But too hot to handle, trust me.'

Beccy felt the familiar mix of fear, shame and excitement curdle in her belly and knew that she was willing to give it a try. If any man could exorcise her crush on Hugo, then surely Lough was the one. She couldn't wait to see them square up to each other.

'Has Rory called at all?' Faith was asking.

'Oh, put him back in your doll's house, Faith!' Lem suddenly snapped.

'What?'

'You're so pathetic, chasing after him all the time, worrying about him. You're like a fucking stalker. No wonder the poor guy wants some distance.'

'How dare you!'

But all the pent-up anxiety, fear and frustration that Lemon had been suppressing about Lough's return was bursting out and needed a target.

'You need to grow up, girl,' he snarled at Faith, marching out of the stable. 'Get real and see that Rory does not and will never fancy you. You're. Just. Not. His. Type. He told me so himself, that night he brought me home from the club.'

Faith was a fighter and, attacked on any other topic, would have held her ground, but this had always been a subject she was too sensitive to take. Throwing down her shavings fork and turning on her heel she sprinted through the snow, sending up great puffs of flakes in her wake as she headed for her car, already an indistinguishable mound of white. Scraping the windscreen with her sleeve, she jumped in and started the engine before reversing with an even bigger puff of snow and slithering from the yard, headlights swivelling.

'Shouldn't you have tried to stop her?' Beccy asked impassively.

'Shouldn't *you*?' he snapped back.

'Not my fight. I hope she doesn't get stuck.'

'She's only going as far as Lime Tree Farm,' Lemon muttered. 'Anyway, she's still got her Christmas present in the back – she's safe with that.'

'Don't tell me, she got a toboggan?'

'Close.' Lemon stared past Faith's black tyre tracks to the darkened Lodge Cottage. 'Was he really mad when he arrived?'

'Spitting.' Beccy shivered with an almost sexual tingle at the memory.

'Christ.'

In the back of her chauffeur-driven Cayenne, which cut an easy swathe through the snow, Sylva curled up deliciously against the heated leather upholstery and rang Mama.

'Did it work, *mačička*?' her mother demanded breathlessly as soon as she picked up.

'Yes, Mama.'

'When are you meeting again?'

'It will take a little more time for that, I think.'

'You did something wrong then!'

'No . . . no, but it's complicated.'

Mama wouldn't listen, launching into a tirade of Slovakian as she always did when she was upset, insisting that Sylva should have tried harder.

Holding the phone away from her ear, Sylva decided that now was not the time to mention that she didn't really fancy Dillon very much. Mama would insist that was totally irrelevant. This was business, after all.

Sylva was far more attracted to men like Hugo, who had so much energy and willpower, and who was so overwhelmingly male. Metrosexual family guys really didn't do it for her. She'd rather have a woman.

Mama had fallen silent at last. With a few soothing words and a promise that she would try harder next time, Sylva rang off and texted Castigates to suggest a snowy meeting the following day, but the reply that came back was wholly dissatisfying: *For pity's sake, leave me alone at Christmas.*

Irritated, Sylva deleted the message. She had nobody to play with. Perhaps coming back to Haydown on New Years' Eve was not such a bad idea after all.

Not a single strand of Lough's intricate body art was visible as he knocked at the back door of Haydown later that evening. Dressed in a thick black Merino sweater, suede Puffa, cream jeans and brown boots, he was a picture of country respectability. When Sophia answered, she positively shivered with delight.

'You must be Lough. Come in out of the cold. Did you have a good sleep?' Today was turning out to be such fun – first dishy Dillon, who was gloriously rock and roll meets Roquefort and organic bread roll, and now luscious Lough, who was a heavenly mix of Kiwi and Byron.

'Tash and Daddy are propped up together in the snug, snoring away like troopers,' she announced as she showed him in, 'but Hugo's around somewhere. Drink?'

Having followed her through the warren of old domestic rooms to that big kitchen again – bigger than the courtyard of his old stable block at home – Lough found a glass of white wine being pressed in his hand.

'Cloudy Bay – thought you'd appreciate it.' Sophia eyed him excitedly. She was exquisitely beautiful, with Tash's bone structure and colouring in a finer, more symmetrical package.

'Thanks.' He forced a smile, although he was more of a beer man.

'Tash tells us you were terribly delayed?'

To Sophia's mounting excitement, Lough's deep, deep voice was hypnotic and too bad-boy for words. 'There was a bit of a mix-up and I found myself behind bars for a while.'

'In a Hong Kong hotel, yes, so Tash said – thank goodness for those bars, eh? They serve some terribly good cocktails out there. Must make spending Christmas in transit a little less wretched.'

He regarded her for a moment, eyebrows aloft, then those big black thunder eyes softened to teak brown.

'Didn't it just?' He raised his glass and smiled at her, revealing a gold crown just behind one canine tooth.

Sophia tingled and belted off in search of Hugo, grateful that Ben had fallen asleep in front of *Lawrence of Arabia*.

Lough looked around the kitchen, at the many framed photographs and portraits – horses, family, friends, mostly in that familiar style he recognised from the painting in his room. It astonished him that a room so big could be so filled with life, with a family's identity and style stamped everywhere – and it smelled just delicious. The rest of the house, so huge and so historic, intrigued him now, and he could only guess at its matching warmth and flair. He'd imagined that Haydown would be a cavernous mausoleum housing the empty heartache of a failed marriage, but if first impressions were anything to go on it was overwhelmingly welcoming. A part of him wanted to run away, but his *taniwha* heart kept him standing still, waiting, knowing that the wave would come to sweep fate his way.

He stepped closer to a photograph of Tash and Hugo on their wedding day, hung at an angle above a long bookcase crammed with cook books. Tash looked smoky-eyed, tousle-haired, excited and beautiful – like a top-class mare who had run wild all her life only to find herself corralled, broken in, mounted and ridden away just in time for the annual fiesta parade.

'Seven years ago,' a voice drawled behind him, 'and no itch yet apart from the willingness to scratch each other's backs. Lough.' Hugo held out his hand and shook Lough's firmly, his own grip an equal match to the Strachan crunch. He'd just fired his first warning shot. 'Welcome to Berkshire. And Merry Christmas. Your horses had a great pipe-opener this morning.'

'You could have asked.' Lough kept his tone light, but both men's grips tightened. 'I always ask permission before I take things that don't belong to me.'

Hugo's blue eyes frosted and for a moment he looked as though he was going to hit him, but he had better manners than to flatten a guest the moment he walked through his door, however unwelcome they might be. 'You could have rung ahead to let us know you were arriving two months late.'

'I've been delayed,' Lough apologised far from humbly.

'Understatement.' Hugo turned away to fetch the wine bottle from the fridge. 'In fact, better never than late.'

Lough didn't hear, and Tash suddenly appeared in the room.

Having just awoken at Sophia's prodding insistence with such a cramp in her foot that her limping entrance was reminiscent of Sarah Bernhardt late for her cue, Tash was groggy, sticky-eyed and bad tempered.

'Do you want something to eat?' she asked rather brusquely, blinking madly because a contact lens appeared to be dangling from her eyelashes and she could only see half the kitchen in focus – the half in which Hugo was scowling and stalking around as opposed to the half containing the brooding Lough Strachan. But she didn't have to see him to know that he was truly the most devastating package; Sophia was behind her, panting like an eager Labrador.

'*Do* stay,' she echoed Tash more winningly. 'There's Tash's famous blue cheese and walnut risotto, lashings of rare beef fillet and winter salad, and honey-glazed figs for pud.'

Tash glanced over her shoulder at her sister in alarm, wondering where she'd whipped that fantasy from (although it had admittedly been on her original written list for the day, still pinned to the fridge door). There was shooting lunch leftovers.

But Lough was already shaking his head, staring at Tash with those molten dark-chocolate eyes. 'I just came to the house to apologise for my behaviour earlier. I was sore-headed and I was mean to you. I'm sorry.'

'Forgiven.' Tash smiled kindly, closing one eye and trying to focus on him without looking too much like a winky perv. No wonder Sophia was like a cat with its tail up, and still ogling his dangle-from-me shoulders and his wrap-your-thighs-around-me hips from over her shoulder. He was ravishing. She could feel her sister's hot breath on the back of her neck.

'So what, exactly, kept you?' Hugo enunciated carefully.

'I was arrested boarding the plane in September,' he spoke matter-of-factly. 'And I've been in and out of custody for almost two months. They finally let me go last month, but I had no home and no passport and they wouldn't let me leave New Zealand until this week.'

There was a shocked silence.

Sophia, ever the social butterfly, attempted to find a positive angle first: 'Gosh, how dreadful. I remember when my darling interior designer was caught in a similar pickle coming back from St Petersburg with a few knick-knacks that turned out to be priceless icons. He was detained for yonks – missed the Caledonian Ball and two weddings. What on earth did they try to pin on you?'

'Murder.' He drained his glass. 'Now, if you don't mind, I must go and talk to Lem.'

As he walked out, leaving Sophia open-mouthed with shock, the phone rang out. Tash answered it. A moment later, she was sobbing the happiest of tears.

'*Mummy*! Happy Christmas. Oh, it's so good to hear your voice. Where *are* you?' Suddenly she started to laugh. 'New Zealand! Now there's a coincidence . . .'

Chapter 42

Faith didn't drive to Lime Tree Farm. Instead, blind with tears and anger, she drove almost a third of the way back to the Cotswolds without thinking. It wasn't until she was crawling along the A34 in nose-to-tail traffic, accidents in front and behind, severe weather warnings on the radio, that she wondered what in hell she was doing.

She couldn't pull up or turn around – there was nowhere to go – but the longer she inched forwards at a snails' pace, the sillier she felt for running home to Mummy and the angrier she felt with Lemon.

Yet she knew he was right. Dillon had said as much six months ago, at her birthday party, and how much had she learned since then?

Faith closed her eyes and groaned as she realised that she had missed seeing Dillon at Haydown – one of those rare moments when their paths crossed and she could remind herself she had friends with influence, and ones that she really liked. She had thought that

Lemon was her friend, had started to think of him as her very best friend, but now all that had been shattered.

Her mobile phone rang deep in her Puffa jacket. No doubt it would be Lemon with an apology. She scrabbled for the hands-free earpiece.

'Faith?' The voice was very muffled, the signal appalling.

Faith was edging towards the exit for West Ilsley, where she knew that she could cross back over the flyover and start the arduous task of crawling back to Maccombe.

''s me,' the voice croaked. 'Promised I'd call.'

'Rory?'

'Yup.'

'Where are you?'

'Not sure. Snowed onmycar.' He sounded very drunk.

'You're not with your sister?'

'Godno. SheshwithAmosshorrible family. Ishaw Aunt Bell and SpursandEllen andwhatever their babieshcalled butithinkthey want-edmetogo, so I drove here to pick up your present, but Jules wassnthere and then I drove into a tree.'

'You did what?'

'Droveintoatree.'

'Where are you?'

'Dunno.'

'Stay right there,' she ordered, cancelling her indicators in a cacophony of car horns as she swung back out from the slip road. 'I'm coming to get you.'

When Faith got to the outskirts of Upper Springlode she tried Rory's number again, but it was going straight to voicemail.

She pulled up in a gateway opposite the Prattle, away from the drifts, wondering what to do. It was pitch dark and, although it had stopped snowing, the wind was whipping the fallen snow around and the landscape was uniform white with just a few brave tyre tracks crimping the thick covering on the lanes. No snowploughs or gritters would pass through a backwater like Upper Springlode for hours, if at all. She had no idea where Rory was.

She had almost come off the road several times, and was tired and over-emotional. She thought about calling her mother to beg for help. Graham would launch a search party, and Magnus and Dilly were still around, both of whom had an army of local friends to call upon.

Then she remembered Jules at the stables, and she set the car in first gear to make her way to Rory's yard by the white lanes.

The driveway up to the yard was so deep in drift that she was forced to leave her car behind and wade through by torchlight, the snow biting far above her wellington boots as she stepped into it, her jeans soon soaked. Again she cursed her mother for not giving her the waterproof trousers she'd wanted for Christmas.

At last she reached the cottage, stooping beneath the fruit tree branches that were usually high overhead and now, weighed down with snow, created an alien landscape of white arms stretching out to bar her way.

The cottage was locked up and in darkness.

Fighting her way back through the garden, her legs now sodden, chilled and numb, she made it into the American barn where the warm air was infused with familiar scents that soothed Faith – hay, straw, shavings and warm horse.

There was no sign of human life.

Outside again, she suddenly noticed that the static caravan, unoccupied for several years, was glowing away cheerfully beyond the high stack of glossy black haylage bales.

Crunching forwards through another drift, she got within a few feet before stopping in her tracks and backing away. Two figures inside were doing nefarious things up against a mock-teak cabinet. Neither was Rory.

She stepped back further and jumped as an indignant yelp rang out.

Spinning around, Faith saw a small, dark shape in the snow by her feet.

'Twitch!'

Rory's nervy little Jack Russell terrier writhed with joy, wagging his stumpy tail so vigorously that his whole body waved from side to side in the deep snow and created a small clearing.

Faith stooped to pick him up. He was freezing cold, like a little hairy block of ice. She unzipped her coat and tucked him inside to warm him up.

'Where's your master?'

He inserted a very cold, wet nose beneath her jumper neck.

She checked underfoot with her torch beam.

Apart from her own footprints, the only obvious tracks in the drifting snow were those of Twitch.

She started to retrace them.

They ran almost parallel to hers, leading her back along the drive and straight past her car.

He must have trotted along just minutes after she had parked, bound on an arrow-like path back to the home he had known best. Wherever he had come from, Rory, she was certain, was waiting.

Knowing that she was far safer staying with her car, she got in and followed the pawprints along the lane with her headlights, Twitch sitting importantly beside her on the passenger seat. No other cars, humans or animals were out in this godforsaken weather. She had the village to herself, the place that had once been her second home now rendered her silent, empty kingdom.

When the tracks disappeared a part of the way along the snow-covered lane that ran alongside Broken Back Woods, she parked and climbed out, eyes immediately watering in the bitter wind. There were no signs of a car passing here apart from her own – the drifting snow had long since covered any tracks.

She called out, the words snatched back into her mouth. Great wads of snow landed on her head as they were dragged by the wind from the tree branches overhead; elsewhere snow dusted down like icing sugar. She shouted and hollered. Nothing.

Then she reached for her phone and called his number.

Somewhere, just audible above the howling wind and creaking, freezing snow, she heard 'Ride of the Valkyries' ring out to answer her.

Faith fought tears of relief. He hadn't changed his ringtone in two years – not since she had shown him how to download tones, using Wagner as an example, a lesson he had immediately forgotten. He hated that ringtone, but it was now his life-saving siren. As she neared her target, she used her mobile phone to call Rory's again and again so that she could close in on the muffled melody coming from one of the piles of snow ahead of her.

At last she found his car, a fattened cartoon shape, totally covered in white and wedged into a tree. Beneath its thick snowy jacket it was twisted and bent, the damage revealed as she brushed its white-iced perfection away.

And there was Rory. He was unconscious.

The driver's door was jammed closed by the snow and stoved in by the impact. On the opposite side, the passenger's window was partly wound down and Twitch had obviously burrowed out from it, but Faith couldn't hope to get close to it through the undergrowth and snow.

Pulling her frozen hand into her sleeve, she hurled her elbow at the window in front of her and yelped as pain razed through her, but at least it cracked and she could smash out the glass, trying not to let too much shower over Rory inside. He stayed totally still and corpse-like.

Heart hammering like a machine gun, Faith felt for a pulse and listened for breath.

Both were strong and even.

The smell of whisky was overpowering. There was a litre bottle of expensive-looking malt on the passenger seat, which was almost empty. Beside it lay the little bronze dog she had given him, and a broken porcelain horse.

For all her love, she spared him little sympathy now, so angry and terrified that she might not have ever found him and that he might have died there. She trudged back to her car and grabbed her Christmas shovel to begin to dig him out, hurling great showers of white over her shoulder until she could wrench the door open at last.

Then she fetched the shiny barrow and hauled Rory into it to push him back to her car.

Only then did he briefly regain consciousness. 'Where am I? Haydown?'

'Yes, Rory,' she replied through gritted teeth. 'I'm shovelling shit as usual.'

He started to sing: *'In the bleak midwinter, frosty wind made moan . . .'*

He lapsed back into unconsciousness for the journey to Berkshire and Faith debated taking him to A & E, but she was terrified that he had done something illegal, and she knew his drinking habits well enough to gauge this stupor as one he could sleep off, albeit with pretty major tremors. If Hugo found out – as he inevitably would, should Rory get arrested – then Rory would probably be out on his ear. Better to risk it, she decided, stopping off at an all-night garage to stock up on dextrose tablets, bottled water and caffeine drinks.

'Bad night to be travelling,' the cashier sympathised.

'They say travelling hopefully is sometimes better than arriving,' Faith replied bleakly, carrying her goodies back to her unconscious passenger, who had Twitch under one arm and the broken horse figurine under the other.

By the time they arrived at Haydown Rory was starting to come to, with nauseous, delirious confusion. It was not a good moment to meet his new housemate. But Lough was just emerging from the steamy bathroom, a towel wrapped around his waist and a toothbrush poking from his mouth, when Faith hauled Rory upstairs.

'What the fuck is going on?' he bellowed.

For a moment Faith was dumbstruck. She was staring at his tattoos – although that was far too prosaic a word for the amazing body art that adorned at least half of his muscular biceps and torso from the collarbones down, intricate Maori patterns and symbols, arm bands and moko designs, almost all on just one side of his body. It was breathtaking.

But just at that moment Rory opened an eye, groaned and threw up on his feet, which wasn't the greatest first impression.

'Food poisoning!' Faith apologised, dragging Rory into his room while Lough retreated back to the bathroom.

He could tell – and smell – that it wasn't food poisoning. He hadn't heard a lot about Rory Midwinter: in fact his very presence at Haydown had not even been brokered when Lough and Hugo first agreed any tenancy deal, but that was a long time ago now, of course. Lem was clearly not a fan, and during his brief catch up with his boss earlier had already let slip that Rory was on his last chance and had to stay on the wagon to remain at Haydown. From what Lough had just seen, Rory Midwinter was about to go as cold turkey as the Christmas leftovers in the Beauchamps' fridge or he'd be out on his ear.

When Lough re-emerged from the bathroom, the girl was scrubbing the sick from the landing carpet.

'I'm Faith.' She pulled off a yellow rubber glove and held out her hand.

'Lough.' He took it in a vice-like grip that made her wince before stepping past her with a swish of towel and a waft of hot, showered male skin that even Faith noticed was scented with such uncompromising testosterone that he would make the *Top Gear* team look like the cast of *Priscilla, Queen of the Desert*.

She checked on Rory, washed his face and lips as best she could, lined up his dextrose tablets and water, and kissed him on the freshly wiped cheek before backing quietly to the door. He still had the broken china horse under one arm, she noticed, hoping that he wouldn't cut himself.

Just as she turned to reach for the door handle he called out her name.

'Yes?' She looked over her shoulder, but his eyes were still closed and seemed to be asleep. She turned wearily away again.

'Thank you. I love you.'

Faith froze, knowing that drunks said that to everybody. Yet her heart sucked it in, pounding it joyfully through her ears.

'I love you too. Now sober up and see if you remember that.'

Trailed by a hopeful, tuck-tummied Twitch, she slipped out and fed him a packet of stewing lamb from the fridge (no doubt put there by Tash who was under the illusion that Rory could cook like Jamie Oliver) and then headed outside, determinedly not screaming when she got tangled up with two feathery, freshly shot pheasant hanging from the porch – also, no doubt, a gift from Tash.

After checking on Whitey and the rest of Rory's horses, she mixed their morning feeds and then drove back to Fosbourne Ducis through the drifts, hardly noticing as her car jack-knifed this way and that on the now icy roads.

She had never been more grateful to see Lime Tree Farm glowing a welcome, the Moncrieffs and their houseguests all curled up on threadbare sofas and sag-bags amid the piles of old horse magazines and schedules in the farm's sitting room, warming their toes by the huge open log fire, swigging mulled wine and taking it in turns to have baths when the immersion had heated enough water. All had been hunting earlier in the day, forced to return when the weather changed. They were very pink-cheeked and jolly.

'Get what you wanted for Christmas?' Penny stretched out an arm in welcome, her bright berry eyes mischievous.

Faith paused in the doorway as she passed, suddenly finding a tired smile on her face. 'I got something I've been dreaming of for years.'

'Good for you.' Penny waved her away cheerfully, already reaching for the phone to call Anke and report that her daughter was back safe.

In her chilly little attic room Faith changed out of her still-damp clothes into two pairs of pyjamas, two sweaters, several pairs of socks and a woolly hat before crawling into bed, her teeth chattering and her body starting to shake uncontrollably. Guessing Rory was shaking too, she sent him a message to remind him to drink water, before conking out to have a disturbing dream that Lemon was holding Rory down in a tattoo parlour, insisting that he have 'I Love Sylva Frost' inked across his forehead. The tattoo artist was Lough Strachan.

Rory took almost two days to recover enough to venture out of the lodge cottage. Faith appeared sporadically to check in on him, bringing fresh supplies of fruit, biscuits and bottled water. He told her he had flu. She seemed to believe him, and told him his horses would be fine in her care until he recovered. He could remember almost nothing of Boxing Day. He had no idea whatsoever how he'd got back to Haydown.

But when he finally emerged, feeling very weak and shaky, Faith wasn't there. She was working at Lime Tree Farm all day, Beccy told him when he headed on to the yard.

'I've had flu,' he explained. 'My new housemate probably brought something bubonic over from the colonies.'

Beccy flashed a wary smile, very jumpy on the subject of Lough.

'I like the hair. Suits you.'

'Thanks.' Beccy blushed, deciding he was getting nicer these days. She felt rather sorry for him, being ill. He looked truly terrible. 'Hugo and Lough are riding in the indoor school if you want to see them.'

'Thanks, but I'll pass.' He'd gone very grey and had to lean against a wall for support.

Lemon led out a horse behind him, tacked up ready for Lough to swap rides.

'You're still alive then.' He looked disappointed. 'Food poisoning, wasn't it?'

'Flu,' Rory corrected, deciding he really needed to go back to bed.

'No wonder you got a chill, driving into a snow drift like that.' Lemon eyed him resentfully.

Rory had no idea what he was talking about, but that might start to explain the voicemail message he'd received from his brother-in-law Amos, asking if he wanted his car removed from Broken Back Woods before the police impounded it.

'Mate,' said Lemon as he stepped closer, voice dropping to an accusing hiss. 'Faith could have died saving you back there. I think you deserved to freeze, frankly.'

Before Rory could ask him what he was talking about, there was a clatter of hooves as he led the horse away.

'Take no notice of him.' Beccy reappeared from a stable with a barrow. 'He's in a foul mood because the big bad boss has finally arrived to make him the whipping boy again. He shouts at Lem all the time. He must be tricky to live with.'

'What?' Rory was finding fragments of Boxing Day floating through his conscience at last.

'Lough?'

'I've barely spoken to him. Been too ill.'

Beccy wheeled away, relieved.

Over the coming days Rory's mind gradually started filling in the blanks. Oblivious to the cross currents swirling around the yard like the hay strands blowing in the ever-changing wind, he spent an uncharacteristic amount of time on his own, riding Rio who couldn't enjoy a long holiday in the fields like the others because his stallion's wanderlust meant he would only tolerate being turned out for a few hours at a time.

He barely noticed Hugo legging a very reluctant Tash up onto her old grey, Mickey Rourke, and making her ride in the school, her face so frozen with fear and her body so stiff that she looked like a mannequin taped to the saddle. Nor did he spot Lough watching them in his silent, black-eyed way. He avoided Lemon, who was spoiling for a fight, and Beccy did her disappearing act most days. But he made time for Faith, the flu lie sitting awkwardly between them.

He didn't know what to say to her or how to thank her. His humiliation was total; he'd completely self-pitying and out of control and now he was so deeply ashamed he longed to wake up again and find it was all a dream. But he didn't.

He rode over to Fosbourne Ducis on New Year's Eve, a bright, blue-skied afternoon, the snow now pushed back to the verges in grubby piles like royal icing peeled back from its marzipan and fruit mix, but it was still uniform Christmas-cake white across the fields. Lime Tree Farm was in disarray as the Moncrieffs prepared for their annual party.

'Bloody Faith's sloped off to Marlbury without saying when she'll be back!' Penny told Rory as she rushed past with a case of wine. 'Put that horse in a stable and help me out while you wait for her.'

Rory did as he was told, not thinking to ask why Penny knew that he had come to see Faith in particular.

'Here – take this.' She thrust a box at him when he reappeared. 'You're coming tonight, aren't you?'

Rory found himself swaying under the weight of six bottles of cheap scotch, his personal poison.

'I can't make it,' he apologised, carrying the case into the house like a ticking bomb. 'Something's come up.' Just the clank of the bottles made him break out in a cold sweat.

He was forced to head back to Haydown when the light started fading.

'I'll tell Faith she missed you.' Penny waved him away distractedly. 'Happy New Year. Got any resolutions?'

'Sobriety,' he said with feeling.

When Faith got back to Lime Tree Farm to find that Rory had been there looking for her, she called him straight away.

'You saved my life,' he answered without preamble.

Faith listened to him breathing as he walked. She guessed he was still with his horses on the yard.

'Hey, it was nothing,' she said eventually.

'It was everything to me. I wanted to thank you in person. You're amazing. Amazing.'

Her chest tightened with fear and pleasure. 'No worries.'

She could hear him clanking through a door. Terrified that he was going to ring off at any moment, she blurted: 'Why were you at Broken Back Woods in the first place?'

He coughed and clattered about some more. It was clear he didn't want to talk about it, or didn't remember enough to be able to. Faith could hear him scooping out feeds in the background, the rattle of pasture mix falling into buckets.

'I'm sorry for what I did. I'm sorry I put you through that. I'm sorry. I owe you big time. Anything. Name it.'

Oh, the temptation. Faith ran through her options, all the time knowing there was only one. Immediacy. 'Come to the party tonight.'

For Rory, it was the one chamber with the bullet in it. 'I can't.'
'Why not?'

He said nothing for a long time, and Faith tortured herself with all manner of hot encounters he might have lined up.

'Hugo's just told me he wants Lough to go to the States instead of me.'

Faith caught her lip beneath her teeth. She knew it was a devastating blow to him. But to her it was salvation. If he didn't go to America with Hugo she'd have him close by. She couldn't keep the elation from her voice. 'Let's just all celebrate New Year first.'

'I'm not quite ready to party again yet,' he apologised.

Chapter 43

Tash prized Gok, Trinny and Susannah over her festive curves before reaching for the red suede dress that Sophia had given her for Christmas, assuring her it was by a designer who was 'brilliant at hiding post-natal bumps'. But not crotches, it seemed. She tugged the very short skirt down towards her knees and studied her reflection in the long mirror. It was years since she'd worn something this revealing. Yet her sister had been quite right about the figure-hugging creation. A leggy, wasp-waisted vamp stared back. She pouted and threw a model pose, then squeaked in delight. This would surely cheer up Hugo.

In the adjacent bathroom, he was out of the shower and complaining loudly about Lough as he towelled his hair dry.

'He's so bloody-minded. He won't last five minutes in the States if he behaves like this.'

In the past week Lough had spent his days avoiding his hosts, ignoring the yard rules and working horses at the opposite end of the indoor arena to everyone else like a rival warming up for a jump-off, all of which drove Hugo mad. They'd barely exchanged a word for days, so the prospect of taking the New Zealander out to a New Year's Eve party needled at Hugo's usual generosity. He'd already torn a strip off Tash for offering Lough and the rest of the Haydown contingent a lift to the Moncrieff's farm.

'I think he's terribly shy,' she told him now, striking a few more poses as she added distractedly, 'please try to be nice to him tonight. It could be just the ice-breaker you two need.'

'Plenty of ice around here, so every chance of a serious breakage.' Hugo appeared at the door, the towel falling from his head as he took in her scarlet harlot dress.

'What d'you think?' Tash asked, eager for approval.

There was a telling pause before he answered in a terse voice. 'Very smart. Where's the skirt to go with it?'

'It's a dress.' Tash wilted, Gok's sterling support digging into her deflated ribs. She really must be mutton dressed as lamb, she realised. In her fantasises Hugo had scooped her up and thrown her on the bed, saying the party could wait. In reality, he just turned back to the bathroom to clean his teeth.

She painted her lips red with shaking hands then she looked at her reflection again, tugging down the hem. She could hear a text message coming through on Hugo's phone, which was lying on the chair in the bathroom. A moment later the door was pushed closed.

Tash tried and failed to persuade herself it was perfectly innocent and had nothing to do with V.

To take her mind off it, she added another layer of kohl around her eyes, masking her fear a little more.

In the bathroom, Hugo angrily replied to MC's text, telling her that Lough *was* better suited to the American lecture–demo circuit than Rory, and if she didn't like it she could fuck off.

Then he cleaned his teeth so angrily that he loosened a front crown dating back to the day he'd knocked a tooth out falling off Snob at their first World Championships.

He spat out toothpaste and glared up at his reflection, knowing that he should tell Tash how beautiful she looked tonight. She took his breath away. Yet jealousy had punched the words from his mouth. He could hardly bear to look at her, certain that every day which passed was counting down their marriage. He wished she was wearing a baggy sweater and leggings as usual, or had lost a front tooth too.

Unable to resist, he reached up and tested the loose tooth, and to his horror it fell out into the basin beneath with a clatter, leaving his gap-toothed reflection glaring back at him like a medieval village idiot.

Hastily retrieving it before it disappeared down the plughole, Hugo wedged the crown back as best he could, grateful he'd soon be in the States where he could get it fixed by the best in the business. It was one reason for still going, at least.

When he came out of the bathroom Tash looked even more beddable, hair teased out, red lips moist with anticipation, positively quivering as she weaved up to him to kiss him.

Afraid that his tooth would fall out again, Hugo kept his lips tight shut.

Abashed, she quickly turned away and picked up her handbag from the bed.

The New Year's Eve party was well underway at Lime Tree Farm by the time the Maccombe contingent arrived, reversing along the village lane to find a space on the thawing verge because the farm's driveways and arrivals yard had long since filled up with cars.

In the back of the Beauchamps' four-by-four, Beccy fought carsickness and nerves, aware of every millimetre of her body that was brushing against Lough's as she sat crammed between him and Lemon. She was equally aware of the back of Hugo's neck ahead of her, the neatly trimmed hair at its nape, the crisp cotton collar of his shirt and the familiar scent of lime-sharp aftershave rising from it.

Increasingly on edge, Hugo insisted that his Christmas gift from Ben be played on the car stereo at full blast for the short drive, Mask's *Best Ever Best of The Best* CD, thus they arrived to Pete Rafferty's legendary gravelly voice rasping the track 'Infidelity'. The famous anthem, which claimed that all lovers would cheat if they could, was cut off in its prime as Tash turned off the engine. The song still ringing in all their ears, they spilled from the car and picked their way around the potholes and remaining snowy islands.

Feeling wretched, Beccy trailed along in the rear with a subdued Lemon, her heart thump-thump-thumping at such closeness to Lough. She was accustomed to it with Hugo, but she was still adjusting to it with Lough. All week, her blood pressure had been leaping and dropping crazily in his presence, with the usual Hugo-triggered hyperventilation to boot. Her body couldn't take much more.

Dressed in an early sales bargain that she had thought wildly sexy until she'd seen Tash looking like something out of a fashion spread, she was suddenly aware of her big, raw shoulders that would be exposed by the strapless bodice of her dress as soon as she took off her long coat, and her chilblains grating and boiling beneath the Spanx pants that she'd prized on to neaten her butt. Worst of all, her newly short hair that Tash had re-dyed at Christmas now appeared to have turned a strange shade of khaki; every time she washed it, it looked more green. She wanted to go home.

'Tonight's the night,' Lemon suddenly reminded her.

'For what?'

'Bye bye cherries, *chérie*.' He looked up at her, pale eyes suddenly luminous in the security lights. 'We get laid.'

Faith hung back when the Haydown mob walked in, her eyes scanning the group for Rory. He wasn't there and her heart ripped wider. Hugo and Tash, looking amazing, were predictably hailed from all sides, along with Lough, who knew many guests from international championships and was also pulled straight into the mêlée.

Faith had barely spoken to Lemon since their Boxing Day argument. But he was refreshingly upfront, marching straight up to her with Beccy in his wake, Mohawk at its sharpest and tight leather trousers making him mince whether he wanted to or not.

'You look fantastic, Eff. Great dress. Sexy.' He kissed her on both cheeks, smelling deliciously of Hugo Boss aftershave and strawberry–lime gum.

Faith smiled abstractedly. She'd been a bit uncertain about the strapless dress she'd picked up hurriedly in a Marlbury chain store sale that morning – it was a clingy, garish mix of black, white, green and orange, but it had been less than twenty pounds, fitted and suited her figure absurdly well. Without Rory there, it hardly seemed to matter.

Loitering behind Lemon, her face as red as her hair was green and her expression oddly crestfallen, Beccy eyed the dress in horror.

'Hi Beccy.' Faith gave her friend a kiss on a cheek that was blushing hotter than ever. 'Let me take your coat.'

'No! I'll wear it, thanks.'

'But it's boiling in here.'

'I'm fine,' Beccy insisted, clutching her manky waxed jacket closer around her. 'Where can we get a drink?'

'Here, I'll show you.'

Beneath the coat, Beccy was wearing the same dress as Faith, two sizes bigger and far less suited to her figure. She wished that they had compared notes beforehand, but they didn't have that sort of girly friendship and, even assuming they had, it probably wouldn't have made any difference. Worse still, when Beccy had asked what Tash was wearing she had interpreted 'a dress Sophia gave me which is a bit out of my comfort zone' as meaning Tash would look hideous, whereas she looked as beautiful as Beccy could ever remember her. Jealousy bubbled inside her. She missed her dreadlocks. She wanted to get very drunk.

At the opposite end of the farmhouse, Hugo was set on an equally lethal course of self-destruction, especially when the first person to loom out of the crowd in the sitting room, sexy smile playing on his famous lips and dark eyes sparkling, was Niall O'Shaughnessy, Tash's charmingly rakish ex lover.

'Hugo, my old friend!' He gave him a double hand-shake before turning to Tash. 'Angel! You look incredibly beautiful. It's just grand to see you both in such good health, so it is.' His kisses lingered indulgently on Tash's cheeks, making Hugo want to swat him away from his wife like a bee. 'Zoe will be thrilled to see you – she's in here somewhere.' He scanned the crowded room and then gave up, turning to admire her once again. 'My goodness, but you're breathtaking. You get more gorgeous every year.'

Aware that Niall was paying his wife the compliments he should be bestowing himself if he weren't feeling so stupidly uptight at seeing her vamping it up, Hugo stalked off in search of champagne, hoping to return with a magnum and side-swipe Niall with it.

But before he could get across the room he was commandeered by his mother, who had brought a surprise guest.

It took Hugo a few moments to recognise Sylva without her documentary team, Slovakian contingent and – most noticeably – her waist-length blonde hair.

She had gone brunette. It suited her fantastically. She looked like Penelope Cruz.

Sylva planted a lingering kiss on his cheek which was so plump and perfect that it left a flawless cherry-pink lip stamp that could have been painted by a pop artist.

Hugo drew his mother aside, knowing her habits of old. 'Mother, please don't tell me you've adopted a new pet?'

Alicia, who was looking extraordinary in a Dior dress from her deb days and a peacock feather fascinator perching jauntily in her peppery Carmen waves, gave a discreet shake of her head. 'She's wildlife, I assure you. Like feeding a badger or a fox. Not pet material.'

In tears of happiness, Zoe was hugging Tash as tightly as she did her daughter India when she'd flown home from her first backpacking trip.

'You look sensational!' Her short blonde bob swung as she tilted her head to admire her friend. 'Two children in as many years and – wow! It took me at least a year to lose the baby weight last time, but just look at you . . .'

'It's got a built-in corset,' Tash admitted without guile. 'And anyway, you had twins. Takes twice as long.'

Zoe kissed her again. 'God, I miss you. Where's Hugo? I've told Niall that he *must* buy a horse for you two to compete so we have an excuse to see you more.'

'I'm not competing.' Tash turned away, looking for Hugo and spotting him with Sylva Frost.

'You and Hugo not competing?' Zoe laughed. 'How do you keep love alive? I thought that's what sparked you.' Her gaze followed Tash's. 'My goodness, that looks like Sylva Frost—'

'It is,' Tash said artificially brightly, surprised by the new dark hair and understated yet beautifully tailored wool trouser suit in deepest plum. 'She's a . . . family friend.' Realising she was being watched, Sylva glanced across and gave a regal wave before turning back to Hugo. She was standing very close to him, Tash noticed. The diminutive Slovak was practically inside his jacket.

'Gosh.' Zoe had noticed it too, but then her eyes drifted through the room, taking in all the unfamiliar faces. 'You are moving in different circles these days. All these strangers. But your new work rider is a dish, isn't he? *So* sexy. Where did you find him?'

Tash guessed she wasn't talking about Rory, for all his insouciant blond charm. Sure enough, Zoe was admiring Lough perched on the arm of a sofa, chatting quietly to his hostess, who was hugging a scatter cushion and looking positively skittish under his intense gaze. He was certainly one if the most charismatic forces in the room, a tamed jaguar in jet-black jeans and long-sleeved T-shirt that revealed the muscular contours of his torso. Several female guests were practically climbing on to the sofa as they angled for invitations, all of whom Penny was gamely ignoring.

'New Zealand.'

'How heavenly,' Zoe sighed. 'When Niall was filming the Ptolemy Finch movies we pretty much lived there for eighteen months, as you know. Such a beautiful country. Very good-looking men.' She winked. 'Maybe Penny can give Gus a taste of his own medicine, d'you think?'

'Sorry?' Tash said vaguely as Lough looked up and caught her gawping at him. There was no regal wave this time. His eyes scorched paths across the room. He really was incredibly intense, she thought as she raised her glass clumsily and turned back to Zoe's earnest face.

'You eventers are worse than movie stars for flirting on set,' she was saying, clearly fishing for something, 'or perhaps you'd say "on course"?'

'How d'you mean?' Tash gulped, casting Hugo another anxious look and gratefully noticing that he and Sylva had parted company.

But Zoe wasn't talking about Hugo. She checked Niall was still busy talking to old village friends before dropping her voice to a whisper, 'What's Gus playing at, Tash?'

Tash had heard enough rumours by now to guess it was more than idle talk, but she still looked deliberately blank, desperately hoping it wasn't true.

'Penny says there's nothing to worry about,' Zoe whispered. 'But I'm her sister and I know her too damn well. You're friends with both of them. Is Gus really serious about this other woman, do you think? Penny says temptation is a part of the sport, especially with such a high ratio of young, sexy women to men who should know better. It's like actors, and Niall is appallingly hard to control, of course. Is Hugo the same?' Do you have to say "down, boy" when the girls crowd around him?'

'I don't think – that is I'm not . . .' Tash tried to stop her lip wobbling as she stared at her glass. 'We don't really talk about all that. It's been a bit tricky lately.'

Zoe's big eyes widened like warm spa pools eager to soothe away

Tash's stresses, and she hooked her arm around that sexily corseted waist to lead her somewhere quiet. There were famously no quiet spots at a Lime Tree Farm New Year's party – even the horses had to cope with the annual shock of sharing their stables with necking couples and their fields with cavorting revellers – but experience born from many years living and partying there had taught both Zoe and Tash precisely where to go.

They were shut safely in the larder within minutes, Tash breaking into a comforting packet of ginger nuts while Zoe started to ask probing questions.

Left unmarked, Niall was an open target for Sylva. Having peeled away from Hugo and Alicia, she locked on target and laid on the charm with its slickest lubricant – a bottle of champagne, two flutes and her cutest smile – as she shot like an arrow to his side to introduce herself.

'I'm Sylva.'

'Plain old Irish bog peat, me,' he laughed.

'Is Niall just a stage name then?' Sylva was confused by the joke, but she didn't let it deflect her. 'I think you can tell a lot from a name. Pete is a sexy name. I have a silver tongue and a silver lining and here I am talking to a star of the silver screen. It's fate.'

'Is that a fact?' Niall regarded her impassively.

He politely deflected her, totally unaffected by her charms. It was the first genuine brush-off she'd had in many years and it jolted her. The most famous of flirts would not play her game.

Compared to A-lister Niall, Jonte had been distinctly end-of-alphabet. He had needed Sylva as much as she needed him, their careers and profiles guaranteed to rise to new orbits together; Niall was so established that he only needed friends who genuinely entertained him and had nothing to gain from him. Sylva's ambition was like neon above her head, and he just wanted to get on and talk to his friends, some of whom he so rarely saw, including local actor Godfrey Pelham, who bore down on him now: 'Dear boy – what *have* you been doing lately?' 'Biblical epic with Scorsese. You?' 'Village panto. Mother Goose. Went down a storm. Shame you missed it.'

Sylva drifted off through the party, hoping that coming here had not been a mistake. Accustomed to being the centre of attention, she was thrown by her sudden anonymity in such alien surroundings. They were really *very* horsy here. The Moncrieffs' farm was such an unlikely gathering to find the nation's favourite single mum on New Year's Eve that she'd even managed to give the paparazzi the slip, although she had no doubt that at least one unscrupulous guest would soon spread the word that Sylva Frost was here at a green-wellies backwater to party with James Blunt playing in the background and weak punch on tap.

She pursed her recently saline-plumped lips at the notion of the press getting hold of the story, but then reassured herself that Niall O'Shaughnessy was here too and the media would naturally link their names together, like prom king and queen, because they were the only celebrities: of course they *had* to be there for each other. Being linked to Niall would do her image no harm, even if, in reality, the man wouldn't even talk to her.

Sylva's mood was rapidly blackening. She had only agreed to come here to avoid the annual exodus to Slovakia for New Year. Mama had chartered a private plane to take her grandsons, plus Hana and Zuzi and the rest of the mob, to Bratislava for two nights, booking all four of the exclusive Tulip House Hotel's pent-house suites, plus five further suites. It would be noisy and chaotic affair, with relatives visiting non-stop, a constant babble of Slovak, laughter and tears, gifts and – in Mama's case – lots of showing off.

So Sylva had hyped up this party as an excuse to stay behind and had dug in her heels, persuading Mama that it was an essential part of her Dillon plan and hinting that he might even be there, but of course he wasn't. There were just hundreds of haw-haw event riders and locals, and a disproportionate number of adolescent boys following her around and taking photographs with their mobile phones. A few were even brave enough to ask if they could pose with her while they handed their camera phones to guffawing friends.

'My nephew invited rather a lot of his school chums,' Gus, her likeable host, apologised, helping himself to a top-up from her champagne bottle. 'Great boys, but it's a terrible age. Tell me if they're bothering you and I'll get Hugo to rein them back.'

'Hugo?' Sylva giggled at the idea of one so arrogant being put in charge of teenage discipline.

'Also my nephew's name – Hugo or Huey,' Gus explained. 'Parents beware: not a name to bestow lightly. Would you like Hugo Junior and his pack to back off?'

'No, it's fine,' Sylva assured him, thinking how nice he was, like a big, shaggy blond bear that had lost most of its stuffing. From what she could tell, these event riders were all sexy rogues.

She needed attention like oxygen, but teenage boys were very thin air, and she liked her testosterone as chilled and vintage as her champagne.

As Dillon wasn't here and she had got the brush off from Niall O'Shaughnessy, Sylva was determined have some fun this evening. She drained the last of the champagne and went to fetch another bottle, eyes scouring the faces around her. She was going to flirt with the most handsome man in the room.

The males of the English country set were not, on the whole, the most stylish figures, particularly given their propensity to dress in ludicrously bright trousers and waistcoats.

Which led her to a dilemma. By far the most tempting and sexually attractive man in the room was the prototype for all dashing, daredevil and very English horsemen, Hugo.

Only for the briefest moment did her friendship with Tash hold her in check. Friends were transient; sex was a life force. She quickly appropriated her second bottle of champagne and repositioned her biggest smile before setting her missiles on full lock.

Hugo was having a stiff-jawed argument with a dark-haired man as Sylva approached, both far too intent to pay more than cursory attention as she played waitress with her champagne bottle.

'. . . Florida next week,' Hugo was saying firmly as he held out his glass for a refill, then noticed who she was. 'Lough Strachan, Sylva Frost.' He introduced her as little more than a punctuation mark in his argument. 'You're coming to the States, Lough.'

'First I've heard of it,' Lough said dryly, not even looking at Sylva.

'If you'd got here sooner we might have been able to talk it through,' Hugo snapped.

But Lough shook his head. 'I only just got here, mate, I'm not budging. I've hardly sat on my horses yet.'

'You can bring two horses. It's all arranged. We're teaching clinics with MC and Stefan Johanssen through January and February, and training while we're there. It's seriously good money and unbeatable prep work.'

'Sounds great!' Sylva interjected, starting to get irritated that she was being ignored.

But Lough blanked her, suddenly realising what Hugo was trying to do. 'This is Rory's gig we're talking about, isn't it?'

Hugo returned his accusing stare levelly, not denying it. 'He was the sub. Now you've finally joined the Haydown team he stays on the bench.'

'Rory must go to America.'

'Yes, Rory will love America.' Sylva dived in again. 'I am—'

But Hugo talked right across her. 'Nobody's heard of Rory over there. You're Olympic silver medallist and World Champion, Lough. I'm gold medallist. That's a dream ticket. We could double the profit.'

'I'm staying here.'

Hugo held Lough's glare until Sylva thought she might have to erect a screen between them to stop them fighting like two stallions.

'What amazing sportsmen!' She was determined to wrest attention this time. 'As I am Sylva, that makes two silvers and a gold. So much precious metal. I smell money, don't you?'

The stallions snorted, stamped their hooves and repositioned to sniff the new mare.

Sylva had found the stand-off thrillingly sexy. Her whitest smile seemed to grow even whiter as her eyes widened. 'Hugo, can I take you aside for a moment to talk about buying a horse?'

Hugo was still looking like a thundercloud, especially when Lough muttered something about spotting an old New Zealand teammate and shot off.

Glaring at his retreating back for a moment, Hugo then turned to Sylva with a mannerly apology, but his eyes took a telltale second too long to focus, revealing that he really was quite drunk.

'You want to buy a horse?' he said carefully.

Sylva manoeuvred him to the farm's back door amid a sea of boots and coats, one of the quietest spots in the house while all the guests were still safely contained inside and only the smokers were braving the elements, clustered in the front porch at the opposite end.

'I want to buy a three day eventer,' she insisted, standing much closer to him than necessary so that she had to tilt her head right back to see him – always very flattering to the facial bone structure.

'So Tash tells me.' He had a fantastically devilish smile, she realised as he looked down at her.

'Money is no object.' Sylva flashed her eyes and moved forwards, positioning herself directly beneath Hugo's chin.

'I can find you a horse to own if you're really serious.' He stepped back so that he was almost enveloped in the coats hanging from the rail behinds his head.

'Oh, I'm serious.' She let her very pink tongue stroke her upper lip for just a second, her eyes not leaving his. 'Tell me, do you ride women as well as you ride horses?'

He suddenly barked with laughter, catching her by surprise. 'Are you trying to seduce me, Mrs Frost?'

Sylva stalled for effect, adoring his straightforwardness. She knew that he had never liked her very much, but that was part of the challenge.

'Yes, I am,' she admitted. 'But I want to buy a horse more.'

Drunk, bad-tempered, aroused and in no mood for mind games, Hugo wondered where Tash had disappeared to. Lough and Niall were both on the prowl, and now he had Sylva Frost to deflect. He couldn't help finding her enticing, and he knew that he could sell her a horse at a massively over-inflated price if she were seduced a little, but he wasn't in the mood right now.

'I'm going outside for a cigarette,' he excused himself with an apologetic shrug, knowing it was the best means of escape from situations like these.

But he hadn't accounted for the fact that Sylva was accustomed to her Slovak cousins on fifty Mayfair a day. 'I will come with you. I need the fresh air. You can show me around the stables here.'

In the larder, the conversation was coming to a close and Tash had found a convenient pile of paper napkins to use to blow her nose and mop up the mascara from her cheeks.

'You really think I should tell Hugo how insecure I'm feeling?'

Zoe nodded. 'Silence just breeds misunderstanding. Don't wage war with a great lecture or pity-me monologue, but simply say that you know things aren't great and it's time to do something about it –

oh, here . . . shh.' She handed her another napkin as Tash started to cry again. 'Admitting it is half the solution.'

'D-do you think he could be having an affair?'

'I don't know him well enough,' Zoe hedged. 'But talking will help you find out. Look out for lines like 'You're too good for me' and 'I don't deserve you' – classic giveaways that he's got a guilty conscience. Equally, he could get hyper-critical about everything you say and do, trying to find excuses for his behaviour.' She was a world expert, for all she loved her own philanderer.

Tash nodded. 'He's been so cold and angry. It was pretty bad over Christmas with my family staying: he seemed to resent them all, except perhaps Ben. But he's been *much* worse since Lough arrived.'

'Your sexy New Zealander,' Zoe smiled knowingly. 'Now there's a surprise. Is it true he was arrested on suspicion of murder?' She had heard enticing smatterings of gossip.

'Well, he didn't actually reveal a lot about it. He's not a great talker and, as I say, Hugo's been so horribly offhand with everyone since he arrived that we've hardly seen anything of Lough.'

Zoe shook her head with a rueful smile. 'And you wonder why your marriage is suffering? You might be harbouring a murderer in exile right now, and you're "too busy to talk about it" and besides, the suspect "isn't a great talker"! Somebody has to start talking, Tash. It might as well be you.'

'You think I should speak to Lough about his arrest?'

'No! I mean, yes, maybe, but talk to Hugo first. Please talk to Hugo first. The sooner you put it out there, the sooner you sort it.'

Beccy was still wearing her coat, which was starting to smell pretty dubious. Sweating heavily and feeling increasingly sick after drinking a lot of punch, she was desperate to go outside and cool off, but the others refused to join her.

'It's freezing out there,' Faith pointed out, and Lemon agreed, putting an arm around her bare shoulders.

'Well I'm going,' Beccy huffed, hoping that they would follow her if she fled looking upset.

They didn't follow. They'd been doing their 'exclusive' thing all night: Lemon flirting with Faith and her goading him in return, doubly so because she was in a bad mood that Rory wasn't there. Beccy felt excluded and very hurt.

Outside, she lurched around in the slush for a bit, cannoning into cars, before her head cleared and her body cooled sufficiently for her to focus a little better.

Then she realised that she wasn't alone in the darkness.

Beccy stopped to listen. A couple laughing as they moved closer sent her scuttling behind a car.

'Told you there wasn't much to see,' drawled an all-too-familiar male voice.

'It is interesting,' purred a Bond Girl voice. 'So different from your beautiful stables.'

'This is still a top set-up. The Moncrieffs know their stuff and you could do a lot worse than finding a horse through them. I can have a word if you like.'

'I want to find a horse through *you*, Hugo.' Her voice dripped with entendre. 'A pretty one.'

Beccy felt a jealous squeeze in her chest as she peered out through the darkness, but there was absolutely no moon tonight and they were too far from the house lights, so all she could see was a brief spark, flame and red glow as Hugo lit a cigarette.

'I'll find you a horse if you really want one, but they're not like shoes, you know. You can't throw them to the back of the wardrobe and forget about them.'

'I never throw my shoes to the back of my closet – I have an auto-mated carousel that carries one hundred pairs.'

'I bet you do. So it's just skeletons in the closet, then.'

'Care to come and look?'

'Tempting, but no thank you. My wife might be more interested in seeing your closet and shoe carousel in action.'

'Her feet are much bigger than mine.'

'So don't try to fill *her* shoes.'

She let out a hot gurgle of laughter. 'I'm not trying. I always walk tall and fuck barefoot.'

He laughed too. 'Spoken like a true peasant.'

Sylva's voice was pure honey now. 'If you're so well-heeled, Prince Charming, why not take the weight off your feet and drive it deep into me?'

Beccy gasped. She'd never heard anything like it, a come-on as audacious and ballsy as it was vulgar and – she had to admit – sexy.

There was a long pause and she strained to hear sucky kissy

sounds, but there was nothing. She saw the cigarette end glow again. Then a door opened and closed, briefly beaming light across the farm yard. Hugo was now standing alone, smoking his cigarette in solitude.

Beccy longed to casually wander out from behind her shielding car and accidentally bump into him, to have him confess his utter desolation – unhappily married, no longer in love with Tash, propositioned by Sylva Frost but impotent to her lust because he had secretly always loved her, Beccy.

But she stayed glued to the spot, crouching low to the ground, discreetly sniffing her coat and realising that it still had an odour that was more mackerel than MAC fragrance. She hated waxed cotton.

Jerking her head away from the pong, punch still swilling through her system, she lost her balance and lurched back against another parked car, sending its alarm suddenly blaring, its lights flashing.

'Who's there?' Hugo demanded, flicking away his fag and stepping forwards.

Beccy backed into rapid retreat, shuffling through several more cars until she was up against the exterior wall of the main stable yard. There was more light here and she could see Hugo's shadow moving towards her through the cars. Within seconds he would find her and realise that she had been eavesdropping on him and Sylva, a secret party to their high-grade flirtation.

There was a small door directly beside her. She tried the handle and it opened, letting her dart inside. She was immediately faced with a steep, narrow staircase in the pitch darkness. She scrambled up it, working by feel, until she reached a wooden boarded upper level that appeared to have rugs and old haynets piled everywhere. Stumbling blindly across the floor, Beccy slumped on to a quilted stable rug and listened to her heart crashing wildly in her ears.

Gradually, the adrenalin began to wear off and, away from the cold fresh air, the punch kicked in again, clawing at her head and making her feel groggy and sick. She could hear a horse moving around beneath her, another kicking its door just feet away: she was in a room above the stables, safe and alone. She sagged back against the rugs and opened her coat to cool off, head tipped back and nostrils flared as they sought more air.

'You okay?'

She ducked her face away as it was struck by the white, focused glare of a little halogen torch. 'Please turn that off!'

The beam was cut.

Once extinguished, she was in absolute darkness again, uncertain if she was imagining things or if it really was . . .

'Hugo?'

'Yes,' he sounded surprised to be identified.

She hadn't heard him come up, but the blood was still rushing so loudly through her ears that she wouldn't have heard a SWAT team crashing in.

'Want a drink?' A champagne bottle was thrust at her through the gloom. He sounded different, the drawl a little lighter and croakier.

'Sure.' She took it despite her heaving stomach, anxious not to break the magic of the moment.

There was a long silence.

She swigged more champagne, guessing he must know that she had overheard and want to ensure her silence.

'I won't say anything, I promise,' she said carefully.

The champagne was making speech tricky again. She took deep breaths to stop the room spinning.

'You're hot,' he said, crouching down beside her.

'I am a bit sweaty,' she agreed, although it came out rather slurred, and could have equally been 'slutty' or 'sweety'.

'Really hot.' He sat down next to her in the pitch darkness, the smell of his aftershave easily drowning out the coat's fishy smell. She couldn't remember Hugo smelling so strongly of Ralph Lauren Safari before, but she knew it was one of the bottles that was lined up in his dressing room because she had seen it there, along with the gold cufflinks, ivory-backed hairbrushes and several watches that she sometimes tried on when she sneaked in to snoop around.

She took another swig from the bottle and fought over-excited nausea as she registered the heat of his body next to hers. Her Hugo. Here with her. A dream come true.

'Mind if I sit down?' he joked, already leaning warmly against her.

'Be my guest.' She handed back the bottle and giggled: 'Why don't you take the weight off your feet and thrust it straight into me, big boy?' she quoted, badly.

The kiss that landed on her lips was harder than the bottle neck which had just left them, his grip on her shoulders urgent, as was the way he wrestled with the hem of her coat hoiking it and her dress up to reveal her rib-to-knee control pants.

Breathing hard now, he tried to prise them back like a particularly tough avocado peel to reveal the ripe flesh of the fruit beneath.

It wasn't quite the seduction Beccy had anticipated, but she was really feeling too gratified to care. Hugo was on top of her, his weight pressing down on her, ready to take her cherry, kept perfectly ripe just for him to pick. Her years in exile had been rewarded.

At last the Spanx were lowered in his honour.

'Do you have a condom?' she asked as he pulled her knees apart.

His breath was coming out in excited little bursts but he managed to pull his wits together with great effort.

'Don't go away.' He straightened up and fumbled behind him for the pockets of the trousers that were around his ankles.

There was no real light in the store room, but now that her eyes had become accustomed to the dark Beccy could just about make out an outline and was surprised how much smaller than expected Hugo looked. She had very little experience of a semi-naked man at such close quarters, but she had somehow imagined him to be more imposing and – manly. But when she tried to focus through the dark, her head began spinning again and she felt sick.

He was fiddling about for ages, cursing and muttering angrily to himself now.

Beccy started to feel paranoid. Perhaps he had lost his erection? He didn't fancy her that much – she was a poor substitute for Sylva after all – and, when it came to the crunch, he couldn't carry through.

'What's wrong . . .?' she asked shakily.

'Nothing,' he cleared his throat.

'Come here,' she purred, but the anxiety in her voice made her sound like a member of the Monty Python team pretending to be a woman.

After what seemed like an agonising pause, he moved forwards and Beccy found her face level with his crotch, the very dimly lit configuration in front of her definitely closer to the small, limp man-hoods depicted in her biology textbooks as a teenager than the huge, rocket-like ones she'd espied on the internet. Oh God, he *had* lost his erection.

She determinedly didn't panic or cry, thinking instead of those internet images she had seen and what the women had been doing in some of them. He was saying something now, but her heart was hammering too hard to take it in as she sat up taller, licked her lips, and reached out for that unfamiliar bundle. She located the warm, creased little dough finger tucked in its sticky, scratchy basket of soft rolls and guided it towards her mouth to help it rise again.

He gasped in joy, his voice sounding even more unfamiliar as it thickened with lust. 'Yeah, baby. Here he comes again.'

Beccy's mouth was suddenly filling up with firm, sinewy muscle that tasted of salt and – unpleasantly – stale underpants. She'd thought Hugo would be delicious. And the commentary was deeply off-putting, too. She tried to blot it out.

'That's it, baby. Wow! Keep sucking the meat. Swallow me.' He sounded as though he had been looking at the same website as she had.

Beccy was alarmed to find his hand on the back of her head now, forcing it forwards, making her gag. The salty flavour was getting stronger, his balls scratching her chin, her nose bent sideways with pubes up her nostrils. She pulled away, gagging, and he pushed her back against the pile of rugs, his calves forcing her legs apart once more, a hand reaching down to start kneading and fingering her crotch, trying no doubt to fire up her clitoris but in fact just making her sore. She wanted to pull away, to make him to stop.

At that moment, voices cut in directly below them:

'This is the grey I was telling you about, Hils – a real find. Only cost a couple of grand from the bloodstock sales and went Intermediate in his first year. Gus wants to flog him to Hugo for one of his rich clients, but he'd probably kill them. Nightmare to ride. Here – let me turn on a light.'

Rolling away from Beccy like an SAS commando, Hugo had his trousers up and was taking the stairs two at a time by the time the lights came on, shooting panes of light up through the floorboards in the loft space above the stable.

Sitting in this weird laser-land Beccy was left reeling, knickerless, with her legs wide apart and a bad taste in her mouth, wondering what had hit her.

At ground level Penny Moncrieff continued showing her sister-in-law, Hils, around the horses, grateful for some fresh air in the last half hour before the midnight countdown. 'This mare is a sweety – came from Val Lancaster's yard.'

'Val Mackesy as was, of course!' said another voice, even more cut-glass than Penny's. 'I remember her from Pony Club! Hugo's at school with her son, Alec.'

'Alec's not one of the mob here tonight, though?'

'God no – he's two year's above Huey, so a different species. I am sorry he's invited so many ghastly, spotty friends by the way. We said no more than two.'

Penny laughed and their footsteps started to move further away. 'I'm only sorry we don't have any spotty girls to offer them as entertainment.'

'Ah but you have Sylva Frost. The boys are delirious with happiness – even *I've* heard of her and I'm just a mink and manure housewife from the Cape peninsula.'

'*I* didn't invite her.' Penny sounded arch.

'Who did?'

'Hugo Beauchamp's mother, I think.'

'Gosh.'

Their voices had started to drift out of earshot. Beccy could hear 'horse' and 'affair' and 'publicity' before the rushing blood in her head drowned everything else again.

Chapter 44

Rory walked around the Haydown yard with Twitch at his heels, listening to the rhythmic crunch of his horses eating their hay, the snorts and tail-swishes, the occasional bang of a hoof striking timber. He stroked Whitey's long, pale face hanging over his half door to greet him, his ghost horse brought back from the brink of death and now teaching Faith valuable lessons. He moved to Fox, his back turned away as usual, content to keep his own counsel. He let sentimental Humpty rest his chin on his head, then yard comic Sid lip at his cuffs in search of treats, pulling silly faces. One by one Rory moved along the stables, checking them all and drawing comfort. Cœur d'Or's heart-shaped star bobbed in the half light behind the grille of his corner stable as he pulled angry faces, furious at his prolonged box rest, and pathetically grateful to see Rory and get some attention at last. He reminded Rory curiously of Faith, always so pleased to see him yet always so cross with him.

Rory let himself into the box and checked the horse's stable bandages and rugs. Once someone got close up to Heart he inevitably stopped playing up and pretending to be menacing, and became very soppy indeed.

Rory pressed his forehead against the horse's warm shoulder and breathed in his power. Heart hadn't been clipped because he wasn't in work, so his coat was as fluffy and soft as a teddy bear. Horses had always been Rory's comforter, since infancy when his father had bought him his first Shetland, strapped him into a basket seat and taken him out hunting. He had never been attached to toys – they always got lost or broken – but he had treated his ponies like best friends, little gods that gave him speed and flight and power, that made a wimpy little boy with a bad home life into a superhero, attracting girls and plaudits, adult respect and, ultimately, glory. He knew the power of the horse. He understood horses far better than he understood humans.

He closed Heart's door and walked beneath the arch to the yard that housed the stallions in their own covered barn, which was partitioned into big, walled stalls with ornate rails and finials dating back to Haydown's heyday of carriage horses, hacks and hunters kept ready for action by a small army of grooms, nagsmen and ostlers.

Rio was waiting for him, coat as black as the night sky, his clever head slightly cocked as he watched Rory scuff his way along the aisle. He was by far the brightest horse that Rory rode, with such a sharp sensitivity about him that he could be almost impossibly volatile on a bad day, but was equally the best of the lot on others, so attuned that his ability to read Rory's mind and body seemed far faster than Rory's ability to think and act for himself. He blew Rory away, and he was almost frightened by how good he was. He secretly thought he was better than million-pound Fox any day. He was in a class of his own.

He pulled off his glove to feed him a mint and felt the horse's breath warm his hand.

'Your mistress needs us to show her how good we are,' he told him. If Hugo took Lough to America instead of Rory he might as well pack off back to Overlodes and drive in to a few more trees.

He closed his eyes. He didn't want to think about that. A week later and his body was still suffering. Boxing Day had marked an all-time low, a great wave of anger breaking inside him, crashing down memories of his father's pathetic death, of his mother's endless search for security through rich men, and his older sister who, over two decades earlier, had run away from home on Boxing Day, leaving a distraught eight-year-old brother secretly blaming himself for some childish prank that he was certain had made her leave. Christmas often had a negative effect on Rory. It had few good memories. His great uncle who, despite his austerity, had been Rory's greatest ally had died three days after Christmas.

His family was now barely tied together by more than a scrap of brown paper and a few loose strings compared to the Brakespears and Beauchamps, who were all wrapped up in ribbons and garlands.

But falling off the wagon on Boxing Day and letting the runaway coach and horses drive in to a tree was unforgivable, and he knew it. His sister Diana had wanted to celebrate her birthday with just Amos, and Rory had felt like that eight-year-old again, rejected and at fault. Diana was still like a stranger sometimes, consumed by her amazing love affair, possessing the same curious detached manner as their mother.

For the first time in his life Rory wondered if he had the same trait. Perhaps it ran in the family, but unlike his mother and sister, who preferred to devote themselves entirely to their men, Rory devoted himself to his horses and his sport.

One of the horses called out from another yard and Rio raised his head to return the whinny, raising his upper lip to show his front teeth as he tasted the air inches from Rory's face.

'I'm looking a gift horse in the mouth,' he said out loud, realising it properly for the first time. Faith had given him her horse to ride. He had never realised the scale of the gesture until now. Last week she'd saved his life.

The least he could do was be there tonight to thank her in person. She'd asked him to be at the party for New Year, and he was just moping.

He looked at his watch. If he hurried he could make it to Lime Tree Farm not long after midnight. He had no car, but he knew the combination to the machinery shed padlock, and the quad bike was in there.

He raced out to the yard and then, remembering that he had a present he wanted to give her, ran to his cottage to fetch it, Twitch yapping excitedly behind him.

'Ten minutes to go!' a voice shouted above the din downstairs as Faith queued for the loo. She had been waiting so long that Lemon came in search of her, bringing brimming glasses of punch.

'Perhaps someone's passed out in there?' he suggested.

'You don't suppose it's Beccy?' Faith replied in an anxious whisper. They hadn't seen her in a long time.

'Nah, she went outside.'

Increasingly desperate for a pee, Faith banged impatiently on the door. They were in the little attic corridor next to her bedroom at the very top of Lime Tree Farm. She had no idea who was hogging her bathroom, but she wasn't impressed.

At last, the occupant came out. It was Gus's teenage nephew, Huey. To Faith's surprise he took one look at her and gulped, 'Look, I'm really sorry about what just happened – about – everything. It was all my fault. I blew my load too quick, then my mother appeared on the scene and . . . Let's just forget it, okay?' And he bolted downstairs.

'What "just" happened? What load?' Lemon demanded jealously.

'No idea,' Faith's bladder was too full to care. She handed her drink back to him.

Lemon was lying on the little single bed in her room when she reappeared, leafing through the Pippa Funnell biography that made up her bedside reading. He'd found the Melody Gardot tracks on the MP3 player that her brother had given her for Christmas and her sultry, sexy voice filled the little room.

He looked up at her over the book as she sat down heavily on the bed. 'Looks like we'll never make it.' He rested his feet on her lap and sighed deeply.

'Speak for yourself,' she countered. 'I plan to be just as successful as Pippa.'

'I was talking about the pact.' He lifted his watch to show her the dial. 'We've got less than ten minutes to lose our virginities.'

'Oh, that.' She slumped down, staring up at the ceiling, his feet still on her lap. 'I think I'll save myself for Rory after all.'

'Like he's saving himself for you?'

Faith said nothing.

She had been certain he'd turn up, but it was now almost midnight. He clearly wasn't coming.

'He'll be with someone right now, I reckon,' Lemon predicted.

'He said he was staying in.'

'Yeah! Like when have you ever known Rory "stay in"?'

Faith felt her heart deflate.

'It'll be some tasty married bit. You know Rory. Venetia Gundry, maybe? She's not here tonight, is she?'

'Lem, can we not have this conversation?' Faith snapped, feeling sick suddenly. She knew she had no hope of competing on a sexual scale with Venetia, who had two marriages and a host of event riders under her belt.

He shrugged, looking peeved.

'The pact was a dumb idea anyway. We'd never have done it.'

'We still could.'

'In five minutes?' She checked her bedside clock.

'If we trust each other on this one.'

'How d'you mean?' She turned her head to look at him.

His round, jokey face was bright red. 'Lose it together?'

'Yeah!' She laughed dismissively.

'I can't be sure, but I think it's a safe bet that I'll come in at under two minutes first time around.'

Faith propped her chin on her elbow and stared more intently at him. 'You're not serious?'

'I fancy you, Faith.'

Faith looked at him, uncertain what to say. She had never felt attracted to Lem physically, but she suddenly wanted to have sex very badly indeed, like wanting to jump six feet and not caring which horse she rode to clear it. This was a goal within her grasp. The thought made her feel fantastically empowered.

'I guess it's worth a try.' She suddenly felt a pulse of energy thrum its way from her heart to her groin.

'Do we kiss first, or undress?'

'Both, I think.'

By the time the countdown had started far below them, Faith and Lem were naked on her little bed and enjoying a thorough, unexpected and truly enlightening exploration of one another's erogenous zones, tickly bits and never-been-touched-by-another's-hand intimacies.

'Crikey, it's all a bit undignified, isn't it?'

'Feels good though, yeah?'

Lemon had underestimated himself. He lasted considerably longer than two minutes, and Faith appreciated every second of extra time. This all took quite a bit of getting used to, she decided, as Lemon's rising trot increased rapidly. It wasn't perhaps quite the thrill of jumping a six-foot gate that she'd hoped for, but it was good to get it over with, and she was grateful that it was with a mate. At least they could laugh when his thrusts became so wild he kept slipping out, or when Faith discovered that the strange slopping noise accompanying them was because she was lying on her hot water bottle, still in the bed from the night before. In fact, losing one's virginity was so fantastically absurd and preoccupying that they totally missed midnight.

'. . . Three, two, one, Happy New Year!'

Cheers, party poppers, whoops and 'Auld Lang Syne' replaced Big Ben's bells as the Lime Tree merrymakers saw in another year.

Lough Strachan, more sober than most, received lot of kisses, more than he could remember in thirty-two successive New Years. He didn't particularly like kissing, but he was careful not to kick up a fuss.

His eyes sought out Tash as they had all evening, feeling safe in her proximity and also fiercely protective. He was appalled at how negligent Hugo was towards his wife. When not flirting with Sylva Frost he was carousing with his dreadful, loud friends or knocking back glass after glass like a drunk at a public bar. Enmity soured in Lough's veins.

'Happy New Year – I hope you have a good time in England. A successful year.' At last the only kiss he wanted arrived on his cheek, so tantalisingly close to his lips that he could almost taste it.

'Happy New Year, Tash.' He flashed his rare smile, but only for a moment.

A voice cut through the din around them like an army officer in a parade ring.

'I believe it's customary for a man to kiss his wife at times like this!'

Lough couldn't watch as Hugo, hair dishevelled and eyes unfocused but still ludicrously handsome, grabbed Tash like a mannequin and threw her back into the crook of his arm to kiss her, almost pitching her straight on to the floor.

Lough felt punched in the throat. He left the room without a backward glance as the revellers clapped and cheered in delight at the sight of Hugo giving Tash such a thorough kissing that when she finally emerged, pink-cheeked, minus her lipstick, flustered and yet beaming deliriously at such a demonstration of propriety, she didn't even notice that her incredibly tight, short dress had risen to reveal very jaunty red lace control knickers.

'Be hanging from their bedpost later,' Gus said in amusement to Penny. 'Any chance of your sensible waisties making a rare appearance on ours?'

'Oh bugger off and phone your mistress to wish her a Happy New Year,' Penny snapped as Niall loomed up broadside to kiss her.

'Happy New Year, angel. Any resolutions?'

'To give up hope,' she muttered, casting Gus a weary look and turning heel to look after their guests.

Lemon managed a second performance a few minutes into New Year, at the climax of which he howled like a coyote.

Faith opened her eyes, all attempts to visualise Rory scuppered. With her own pleasure points still largely unexplored territory, she was secretly rather relieved the encore was coming to an end. Lem was never going to light her touch paper. But she had been enlightened, and for that she was grateful. He was also unwittingly funny, with his running commentary and his animal soundtrack, making the whole experience somehow sillier and less sordid than it could have seemed. She only wished he was Rory.

'Yow, yow, yeeeeow!!!!' he hollered.

'Shhh!' She giggled beneath him as the bouncing mattress jiggled her around. 'That's seriously off-putting – ah!' He'd suddenly pulled up her knees so she shot further up the bed.

'Good, huh? Yeaaaaawwww!' Lemon plunged on.

'Stop! Shh!' She held up her hand urgently and covered his mouth, tilting her head towards the door. 'Did you hear someone knock just now?'

Lemon shook his red face beneath her hand.

'It could be Beccy,' Faith whispered. 'We abandoned her.'

'She'll be fine.'

They both looked at the door. The shadow of two feet moved away.

'Whoever it was has gone,' Lemon said obviously, starting to plunge and howl again.

Beneath him, Faith fretted that Beccy must have heard what was going on – it was hard not to with Lemon making such a din – and was bound to feel hurt and isolated.

She looked up at that round, red face and felt suddenly guilty. She had jumped the six-foot gate at last but it now felt like she'd got the stride wrong. Lem was fun and eager, and it had been incredibly educational – she'd had no idea how manic men got at climax, for a start – but the whole process made her feel strangely detached, like it was a simulation on a computer game. It didn't feel real. When Rory had kissed her on the cheek before Christmas she'd thought her body would melt right into the ground. Lemon was still grinding around inside her and yet she felt almost nothing.

'Cherry picked.' She kissed his nose and almost lifted him off her, her arms so strong from hauling shavings bales that Lemon's solid little body was easy to manoeuvre to one side, where she rubbed his cheek affectionately, much as she would a horse, then patted his arm and closed her eyes again, immediately thinking of Rory and how much closer she must be to his world now that she had cast off her virginity and joined the team of players.

Letting Faith doze, Lemon got up, feeling unbelievably good about himself as he swaggered to the little attic bathroom to take a pee wearing Faith's dressing gown, which was rather practical and fluffy – he'd have preferred red satin – but was still rather excitingly feminine against his naked skin. He admired his reflection in the bathroom cabinet, deciding he looked part Leonardo DiCaprio, part Pink. The party was still raging on downstairs, with a drunken ensemble giving a rendition of 'Bohemian Rhapsody'.

It was only when Lemon wandered back along the corridor that he spotted the glittery little gift bag hanging on the doorknob of Faith's bedroom. Quietly lifting it by its handles, anxious not to alert her, he took it back to the bathroom to examine.

Inside, wrapped in tissue paper, was a white porcelain horse, its rider glued on rather wonkily after what looked like a crashing fall. The note was scribbled in almost indecipherably bad handwriting. *To my beloved St Bernard. I haven't forgotten what we said. Always. Rxxx.*

Lemon scrunched up the note and flushed it down the loo before hiding the china horse in among the clutter of dusty tankards, bottles, tarnished old trophies and assorted bric-a-brac the Moncrieffs kept crammed around the beams and sills in the bathroom. Thank heavens they were such messy buggers; Faith would never see it there.

He went back to the bedroom, hoping she would be up for a third bite at the cherry. He was certainly game.

A quad bike overtook Lough on the lane back through the downs to Maccombe as the New Zealander trudged along the frost-dusted verge with his hands deep in his pockets, his hair, coat and jeans as black as his mood.

The red brake lights lit up and the bike waited, engine ticking, a terrier barking in the crook of the driver's arm.

As Lough drew level he realised Rory was aboard.

'Hop on – you can have a lift,' he called out.

'I'd rather walk, thanks. Need to clear my head.'

'Get on,' Rory insisted. 'The others will be coming back soon. Tash might be sober, but she doesn't have the best eyesight in the world and you're bloody difficult to spot.'

Lough clambered on, deciding he'd rather be home and warm, not that the lodge cottage was ever really warm. But surprisingly the solid-fuel Rayburn was still lit and a fire glowed in the grate.

'I was here until half an hour ago,' Rory explained, crouching down and raking through the ashes to encourage the fire to burn down. 'Not really in a party mood.'

'Me neither,' Lough said, heading for the stairs. 'Thanks for the lift.'

Rory looked over his shoulder. 'Tell me, is Hugo taking you to the States? Nobody will give me a straight answer.'

Lough shook his head. 'I won't go. It's your gig. I told him tonight.'

'Good.' Rory turned back to stab angrily at the embers, making them spark. 'Suits me. I can't wait to get out of here.' Then, as Lough moved away again, he added suddenly, 'Is Lemon trustworthy?'

Lough ran his tongue along his teeth doubtfully. 'Depends what you entrust him with.'

'Faith.'

'Ah.' Lough nodded, pausing to think. Lemon was as crooked as dog's hind leg, yet fiercely loyal to those he cared for, most of them equine rather than human. He had few lasting relationships, but that's why he and Lough had always worked so well together. 'She's one of his mates,' he told Rory now, 'and he looks after his mates. They have fun together. I reckon you can trust him to take care of her.'

Rory blinked and nodded, briefly still staring at the fire, his shoulders hunched miserably.

Three steps up the stairs, Lough paused again. 'I'll keep an eye on her if you like.'

'Thanks. Happy New Year.'

'You too, mate. Hope you get what you want.'

Rory looked at the last glowing specks of red, matching the burning in his heart. He'd figured out what he wanted, but as usual he was too late. He'd missed the stroke of midnight and Cinderella had run off with one of the footmen before he got there.

From now on he was going to stick to what he knew best: his horses, his sport and the occasional passing Fairy Godmother.

'Beccy was very weird on the way home, don't you think?' Tash said as she and Hugo undressed in the early hours, yawns ripping at her jaw.

She had hoped that he might undress her but his black mood and drunkenness was clearly not going to cooperate.

He grunted, hopping around as he pulled off a sock.

'I hope she's all right. She seemed terribly out of sorts.'

He said nothing.

'Hugo?' She turned to check he was okay.

He was lying on the bed, squinting at her because he was having trouble focusing – but what he could see he obviously liked. His erection was on full alert.

'You. Are. Beautiful,' he breathed.

'Thank you. So are you.'

'Then why don't you take the weight off your feet and lower it on to this?' He indicated his magnificent flagpole.

Tash bit her lip, a giggle escaping out of one side of her mouth like a burp. She pressed her lips together to hide it, but it snorted out of her nose. Unable to stop herself, she bent double with laughter.

'What?' he wailed indignantly, flagpole lowering rapidly.

'That is just such . . . a . . . *bad* . . . line.' She was getting a stitch from laughing.

Hugo sulkily turned off the light.

Groping her way into bed, Tash located his mouth to bestow a pacifying kiss. It deepened deliciously. Then suddenly she felt something hard land on her tongue.

'Oh Christ!' she yelped, sitting up and spitting the little bullet into her palm. 'It's a tooth!' Her panic-stricken tongue immediately probed her mouth for a gap.

'Mine.' Hugo retrieved it. 'The king has lost his crown. Easy enough to fix. For now I'll put it under the pillow and wait for the tooth fairy to grant my wish.'

Tash stared into the darkness, remembering how heroic he had looked after he lost the tooth falling from Snob, his beauty all the more obvious because of that gaping flaw in his once perfect smile. She'd fancied him almost more than ever then.

'Come to America with me,' he spoke into the darkness. 'I can't leave you on your own here.'

'I won't be on my own. There's a team here now. I'll be safely under Lough and Lemon,' she joked, kissing him again.

Hugo's lips yielded for a moment, revealing that delicious flaw, a temporary reminder of how dangerous his day job was, of how brave he was and vulnerable they all were. Tash found it a thrillingly sexy kiss. But the flagpole resolutely refused to raise its colours again.

'Too many New Year toasts,' Hugo muttered, falling almost immediately into a drunken sleep.

Trying hard not to feel rejected, Tash lay awake, thinking back to her conversation with Zoe and worrying that by avoiding walking on the cracks in her marriage she was going to fall flat on her face. She soon worked herself up into a panic, convinced that he was put off by her mumsiness, that he no longer saw her as sexually desirable and so he was playing away with increasing regularity.

'Hugo,' she prodded him urgently at three in the morning. 'We need to talk.'

It took several more prods to get any response.

At last he groaned in his sleep, apparently mid-dream: 'Your bloody deadlock.'

437

Tash's hyped up mind immediately made word associations: deadlock . . . wedlock . . . stalemate . . . he must think they were in a terrible rut. 'What deadlock, Hugo?'

'Your bloody deadlock,' he repeated, 'if you lay a finger on her . . .' His voice trailed away into muttered nonsense.

'It's not a deadlock if we talk about it,' Tash bleated, suddenly even more insecure. Was he warning her off handbagging V while he was away in the States?

She prodded and shook him for a response, but he was too deeply asleep to rouse.

Also lying awake, just a few hundred yards away in the lodge cottage, Lough abandoned counting sheep – New Zealanders could always count more than anybody – and instead calculated the hours until his housemate and landlord crossed the Atlantic and left him alone at Haydown with Tash. Less than a hundred.

He could start the countdown, knowing he must watch and think.

Chapter 45

Not long before the first daylight of the New Year, Lemon and Faith arrived for work at Haydown in her little Volkswagen, having slithered up the hill from Fosbourne Ducis on black ice and frozen snow, both feeling deliciously deflowered but determinedly not in love.

'This won't change anything, right?' Faith checked, automatically looking up at Rory's window as they passed to see if the curtains were still closed. They were.

'Nothing at all, yeah,' he agreed, hoping that they could do it again very soon.

They were surprised to find no sign of Beccy, who always woke unnaturally early and would usually have started putting out feeds by the time Lemon got going or Faith drove in. But today the yard was deserted and the horses were banging on their doors. Jenny was still away in Germany with her fiancé's family; Rory, Lough and Hugo weren't yet in evidence.

Lemon and Faith cranked up the yard radio and set to work, a bounce in their step, sharing knowing smiles as they passed.

But by the time they had fed, watered and hayed the horses and were gathering barrows to muck out the smiles were faltering.

'We have to check on Beccy.'

When they went up to the stables flat she was in her little bed-sitting room, under her duvet, clutching Karma and shaking uncontrollably.

'Are you ill?' Faith reached for her forehead in concern.

'Alcohol poisoning? Bad food?' Lemon guessed.

But Beccy shook her head wildly, imploring them to leave her alone.

'What is it, Beccy?' Faith pleaded, kneeling down beside the bed. 'You must tell us.'

For a moment a blade of panic lanced her chest as she wondered whether Beccy had been the one outside her room last night, had heard her and Lemon and was reacting like this because she was jealous.

But then she whispered 'Hugo' and started crying.

'What about Hugo?' Perching on the opposite side of the bed, Lemon stroked Beccy's shoulder the same way as he did when handling one of the more nervous horses: not his usual brash, tactless self at all.

'It was all my fault,' she sobbed. 'He kissed me, but then it all went wrong.'

Lemon's gaze met Faith's across the bed, his pale-lashed grey eyes bulging in alarm.

'What went wrong?' Faith asked carefully.

But Beccy was muttering and sobbing nonsensically now '. . . in the stable yard . . . all those filthy rugs . . . so ashamed . . .'

'Did Hugo attack you, Beccy?'

'No! It was a bit rough, maybe, but he was frightened of getting caught. I feel so terrible. It was all my fault.' The sobs stopped her being able to say any more.

Lemon opened his mouth but Faith hushed him with her hand. 'She's had enough right now – we'll talk more later. Make her a cup of tea, Lem. She can stay here. We'll keep checking on her, and as far as the others are concerned, she's ill today.'

There were no bank holidays for horses. From first light, Lough and then Hugo appeared looking somewhat the worse for wear and began working in the indoor school. When he finally appeared on the yard Rory looked terrible, making Faith think that Lemon was right; he must have spent the night womanising. But he was the only one of the three men to notice that Beccy was missing.

'Beccy overdo it last night?' he asked.

'Something like that,' Lem replied.

'Bloody lightweight,' Rory grumbled, tacking up Rio to follow the others into the indoor school, which was the only safe surface until the frost thawed.

Lemon and Faith went into a huddle once he was out of earshot. 'Hugo doesn't look remotely shifty or worried.'

'Why should he?' Faith sighed. 'He doesn't think he did anything wrong.'

'He tried to *rape* her!'

'Keep your voice down,' she hissed. 'We don't know that for certain.'

'As good as! You heard what she said. She should report it.'

'What, her word against his? A highly strung ex drug trafficker with a proven history of dishonesty and unpredictable behaviour up against the nation's favourite gold-medal-winning, happily married toff? I think not.'

Lem reluctantly conceded the point. 'I won't let this drop. Hugo's a heartless shit.'

Faith lowered her voice to a breath: 'We're going to have to take care of her, Lem – prop her up. And that means she mustn't know about what happened between *us* last night.'

'Good though, wasn't it?' Lem growled, eager for a repeat performance at their earliest convenience.

'It was great,' Faith said quickly, 'but we mustn't tell her, and we *mustn't* do it again.'

'Why ever not?'

'She's sensitive. She needs to feel included right now. If we're to stand a chance of finding out what really happened to her last night we have to support her totally. Totally.' With that, Faith headed off to groom Humpty for Rory's second ride.

Watching her retreating back, Lemon groaned, hoping that they uncovered the full story as quickly as possible so that he and Faith could resume their sexual co-education.

He took his frustrations out on the sack of rock salt by the horse-walker, hacking at it manically with a shovel to split the plastic before digging it in and throwing showers of it down on the rubber track so that they could get some horses moving safely in the mechanical exerciser to make up for the frozen fields.

Unlike the dissolving salt, Lem's hatred and resentment towards Hugo had crystallised still further. It had been building up slowly over weeks, but what had happened to Beccy, combined with Hugo's murderous mood since Lough's arrival, had accelerated the chemical reaction.

'Fucking Hugo.' He dug his shovel blade deeper and deeper into the split belly of the salt sack. 'Stuck-up bastard. He deserves a fucking big fall.'

But it was Rory who took a fall that morning when bringing Rio back to the yard. The horse caught a vein of untreated ice under one shoe, his leg slipping right underneath him so that Rory was forced to kick out the stirrups and bail out, landing on his feet before his own heels encountered the ice and upended him on to his bottom.

'Emergency dismount!' Rory joked when Faith raced over in alarm to check he was all right. It was an embarrassing fall, but both horse and rider were fine. 'Guess I need some of that superglue I used to mend the china horse.'

Faith looked at him blankly, wondering what he was talking about. She led Rio away to his stable, leaving Rory kicking the edge of the ice, lifting it with his toe into little sharp shards.

When Hugo cornered him later that morning to confirm that he was the one going to the States, he felt only relief.

'MC is very much looking forward to seeing you again.' Hugo gave him a wise look.

Rory sighed, realising that as one door closed, another *porte* had opened in the storm.

The following week, five of Haydown's top horses, including Rio and The Fox, flew out to Florida accompanied by Jenny. Hugo and Rory were to follow two days later.

Hugo had been making this annual excursion for many years with Tash, traditionally leaving his staff to get the top competition horses fit at home. The decision to take the best of the four-star horses to the States with him this time was a new tactic that he was using as a part of their fitness campaign, taking advantage of the warmer climate and the early competitions to start tuning them up himself.

Determined to break the deadlock Hugo had drunkenly alluded to, Tash planned to use her wifely wiles to give him a send-off that would linger in his mind. She knew they needed to talk more, but didn't want a last-minute showdown, and she was secretly terrified of hearing something she couldn't handle. Instead, she felt actions should speak louder than words.

But her attempts at romance were blighted from the start. Her first proper period since Amery was born arrived that week, coinciding with a streaming cold that she must have caught from a New Year's guest. Soon her temperature was leaping well over a hundred and she was wiped out with fatigue. With spare tissues, cold capsules and panty-pads lined up in the bathroom, she donned her best new La Perla combination for a final seduction, but was a vision of snotty-nosed, red-eyed, sneezing ill health. Hugo charitably declined to take advantage, so she gratefully knocked back more paracetamol and slumped into a deep, feverish sleep while he headed downstairs to gather more riding gear to pack.

When he finally rejoined her in the bedroom, clanking about so noisily she woke up, it was the early hours, but she was feeling far too ill to worry what he'd been up to, or that he had to set off for the airport at dawn. Her throat full of razorblades, she got up to refill her water glass and take painkillers for her stomach cramps. The reading light was on and Hugo was sitting up in bed when she returned, making notes on a printed list.

'I'm leaving written instructions.' He looked up as she staggered around the bed. 'I don't trust Lough to do anything I say.'

'I'll make sure he does,' she croaked, sagging back against the pillows, sweaty and shivery from her excursion.

'No. Leave him alone, Tash. He can figure it out, and Lemon's been here long enough to know the score. I want you to keep away from them both, understood?' The harshness in his tone surprised Tash, but she was too weak to argue. She just longed to sleep again.

But for once Hugo had chosen this moment to open up. Casting the list aside, he wrapped an arm around her and pressed a kiss to her clammy temple.

'You mustn't trust Lough,' he said softly. 'He's a loner. He hates people, especially women.'

Grateful for the warmth of his arm as her body fought to regulate its temperature, Tash nodded vaguely, lead weights of tiredness on her brow and eyes.

'He has his own agenda.' Hugo's voice was so quiet it acted as a lullaby. 'He understands horses a lot better than he understands humans. He uses people, and I don't want him to use you to get at me.'

Drifting off to sleep, Tash's cold-filled brain took a while to register what he was saying. Now, her itchy eyes reopened. She was suddenly feeling very hot.

'Why would he want to get at you?'

There was a long pause. She swallowed flaming ashes, her face burning, sinuses screaming with the effort of staying awake.

'That's not important.' Hugo stroked her sweaty hair. 'It's what he might do that matters.'

Pushing away his arm, which was making her overheat like mad, Tash struggled to sit up, head spinning. 'You don't think he's going to hurt us, surely?'

'No, of course not,' he said quickly. 'I'd just rather you kept your distance.'

She sagged back against the pillows. 'What is it between you two?'

A muscle was slamming in Hugo's cheek, although his voice stayed calm. 'He has a lot of secrets, none of them very nice.'

They could hear snuffling on the baby monitor, indicating that Amery, who also had the cold, would start bawling at any second, but as Tash peeled back the covers ready to go and comfort him, Hugo reached across and tucked her back in. 'You need to rest. I'll go.'

Soon she could hear him on the monitor, whispering to his son as he settled him back to sleep. She closed her eyes in relief, not sure if they were streaming so much because of the head cold or the panic tears that were starting to mount. Within minutes her nose was an unstoppable tap as she used tissue after tissue, trumpeting and snorting like a drowning elephant. Hearing Hugo's soothing noises on the monitor made it all the worse as she thought about their young family, her little fortress of love that was under threat from Lough.

Nobody could deny the enmity between the two men. Tash had put it down to Lough's appalling travel delays and the controversy surrounding them, but now she started to suspect there was more to it.

When Hugo returned the bed was piled high with tissues and Tash was hiccupping madly, her throat so sore she couldn't speak. She looked at him blearily, taking in the beauty of his cool blue eyes and those long, strong limbs that wrapped themselves around her now, so secure and reassuring, the ultimate safety net.

'What secrets does Lough hold against you?' she finally managed to whisper.

'Let's not talk about it any more.' His voice was low and hoarse as his kissed her wet cheek. He reached away to switch off the light.

Tash wanted to wail 'I have to know!' but her head felt as though it was being boiled in hot wax, so all she could manage was a groaning sob. Then, to her shame, her eyes and nose started to spout again.

Hugo was forced to turn the light back on before they both drowned. He reached for fresh tissues and handed them to her, his face drawn and tired. There was a long pause, during which Tash blew her nose a lot and Hugo ran his hands through his hair, unspeakably tense.

At last, she cleared the torrent. 'Is it V?'

There. She had said it.

But Tash's cold had done her enunciation no favours, and thinking that she was blaming herself, Hugo immediately launched into a rebuttal: 'No, it's not you. Darling Tash, you are perfection, although you are too bloody self-deprecating by half. It could never be you. I don't deserve you.'

Remembering Zoe's recent words of warning, Tash let out a horrified croak. 'I don't deserve you' was a giveaway of infidelity.

There was an agonising pause, during which Beetroot unsympathetically re-nested at the end of the bed, turning around and around, nosing the covers this way and that and then plumping down and commencing a noisy clean-up of her paws.

Tash's throat was as dry as her nose and face were wet.

'I know you buy flowers in Waitrose!' she suddenly blurted.

He looked at her, rubbing his head in confusion. 'Is that against the law?'

She turned away, too strangled by tears to speak.

'I don't know what you have against them, Tash, but if it helps I promise to use the florist in Marlbury High Street from now on.'

Tash was appalled by this apparently open admission of regular flower purchases. Her eyes itched and stung so much they were practically fused shut, and her nose was poring forth non-stop. When she tried to ask him again about the secret he shared with Lough and whether it was that he had a mistress, she had a coughing fit that gripped her for almost a minute. Hugo waited it out.

'You're ill and we're tired,' he said eventually in a low voice, leaning across to kiss her sweaty forehead. 'Let's leave it for now. We all have nights we regret.' He reached out to turn off the light again.

Tash knew he wasn't talking about tonight, but however many times the voice in her head screamed for more information, her pounding heart denied it. She could only take the truth in tiny doses, like Lemsip and throat sweets.

Pulling the covers up to her chin she turned to face him in the darkness. His lips were the best analgesic she had taken all night.

Even though the kiss was marred by the fact that Tash was so snotty that she had to breathe through her mouth in rapid gulps, it was the most intimate they had shared in many weeks, a deep draw of love that transcended colds, cramps, his loose crowns and Beetroot loudly moving on from cleaning her paws to hoovering her rear end. Tash only wished she felt sexier, but although Hugo's flagpole raised hopefully against her side she had to hold up the last white handkerchief and surrender to sleep. As they dozed through the brief hours until dawn wrapped in one another's arms, she found her head full of disturbing, muddled dreams in which her husband had a harem of women to equal his string of horses, and Lough Strachan was trying to steal them all like a rustler in a bad Western.

Almost as soon as Hugo set out to the airport, the cold lifted and Tash stopped bleeding, making her sure that fate had conspired to leave him with an off-puttingly sickly parting memory. She was now doubly determined to make him proud of her while he was away, and then welcome him home with the grandest of seductions.

Chapter 46

The January weather was as changeable as a chameleon running across a chequered floor. Frequent snow showers gave twenty-four hours of picture postcard white before melting away in one sunny day. The ridge above Oddlode resembled a Swiss mountain-top one moment and a Toblerone bar the next.

Determined to cash in on her Boxing Day encounter with Dillon Rafferty, and egged on by Mama, who had returned from Slovakia hellbent on a spring wedding, Sylva stayed put in the loathsome fake château in Upper Springlode with her children and the inner circle of family helpers, and started riding again. Every day she poured herself into ultra-tight baby blue breeches and took out two of Jules's horses: Gaga, a sturdy go-anywhere cob with hooves like snowshoes, and an amazing little Icelandic pony called Björk for Zuzi, the thought of which terrified Hana who was convinced that the girl might get hurt.

With an eager Zuzi on the leading rein, Sylva explored the bridlepaths around Dillon's farm. They were mostly very dull and muddy. By the second week Zuzi was bored stiff and no longer wanted to go on their chilly rides. Sylva explained to her that they were on a secret mission.

Zuzi brightened at this, seeing a point behind all the interminable plodding. 'What do I do?'

'If anybody tells us that we are trespassing – remember that English word, it is important – *trespassing*, then you must fall off your pony and pretend to faint.'

'I might get hurt.'

'You'll be fine. Watch, I'll show you how.' She subtly slipped her feet out of her stirrups, pressed her hand to her forehead, let out a few fake groans and slid elegantly to the ground, making sure that her arms were around Gaga's neck all the time, to allow her to swoon safely.

For the first time since she had arrived back in England from her New Year holiday, Zuzi giggled.

Sylva opened one eye and stared up at her, holding out her arms. 'Now your turn.'

A couple of dog walkers in Broken Back Woods reported to their families afterwards that they had encountered the strangest woman and child there, repeatedly sliding off their horses and dissolving into fits of giggles before remounting and starting all over again.

But, despite their many rehearsals, Sylva and Zuzi failed to make a positive sighting of Dillon in coming days, let alone stage their performance. It was like hunting the elusive Scottish wildcat. Yet Mama insisted they keep trying, unaware that he and Nell had secretly jetted off to the Caribbean straight after Christmas to try to melt the cold war between them.

Mama's plans were often doomed to failure. Even Sylva's documentary team had stopped bothering to turn up if they knew that she was going riding.

Sylva saw an advantage in this. She'd also tired of the Dillon plan, but knew there were other places in the area to explore on horseback, some thrillingly forbidden. She missed the excitement of dangerous liaisons. Since her brush-off from Hugo Beauchamp on New Year's Eve she'd hungered for the ruggedness of a tough, no-nonsense man. She also craved publicity, her lifeblood, which badly needed replenishing. Sylva suspected that both were very close at hand if she just reset her compass twenty degrees.

She took Zuzi to the Fox Oddfield Abbey estate one spectacular sunny afternoon, carefully selecting one of the public bridlepaths that ran close to the house. The low gold sun sliced in through the young fir trees, striping the horses so that they resembled zebras, treating their riders to a strobe show as they cantered along the wide, springy avenues, hooves hollow on the pine-needle carpet beneath them.

As predicted, Castigates soon roared up in his mud-splattered pick-up, waving his twelve bore around and trying to sling the two riders off the estate. Having been warned off Sylva by his wife – several times, and without the safety trigger engaged – he wanted her gone as swiftly as possible.

'You're trespassing!' he roared.

Sylva winked at Zuzi.

On cue, the little girl slid to the ground and crumpled in a heap.

But, before Castigates could react, a figure burst out of the undergrowth behind them, startling the horses as she ran forwards, wailing, to gather the little girl in her arms.

It was Hana. Unable to bear waiting at home each day while

Sylva stole Zuzi away from her, she had followed them through the woods on her mountain bike and now witnessed them being held at gunpoint.

'My darling, my darling!' she sobbed in Slovak, clutching the little girl to her chest.

'I am fine, Mama,' Zuzi whispered back through tight lips, her eyes still closed. 'It is a mission. Our lives depend on it. You must go away.'

Hana had seen enough and, snatching up Björk's reins, lifted her daughter back into the saddle before mounting behind her to ride away, hissing to Sylva over her shoulder that she would never allow her to use her little girl this way again, and that they would both be on the first plane back to Bratislava if she tried.

Sylva turned furiously to Castigates. 'Now look what you've done!'

'Me?'

'This is a public right of way and you frightened the poor girl so much she fainted. You can't go pointing a loaded shotgun at a six-year-old. I'll have to report this. I insist that I speak with your boss.' She licked her lips.

Castigates uncocked his gun and tucked it under his arm, eyes shadowed by his flat cap. 'He's not here.'

'Then I shall get his attention another way. He will hear about this.' She turned to catch Gaga.

'As you wish.' He collected the abandoned bicycle and handed it out to her.

'I can hardly carry it on horseback,' she laughed, reaching for her stirrup. Then, unable to resist, she turned to purr over one shoulder: 'I'll come back for it later.'

'You stay away, missus.' Castigates finally lifted his chin high enough to watch her with his untamed dark eyes. He remained far too strait-laced to play games.

Sylva regarded the wide-shouldered gamekeeper with regret. He was so magnificent physically that she would relish the conquest, but that wasn't entirely why she had come here today. She had another use lined up for him, knowing that it was time for radical action in order to make Mama's plan work.

'You know I have every right to ride this path whenever I like.' Sylva eyed him closely.

The flat cap lowered again, his expression unreadable. 'I'm just following orders, missus.'

She had a suspicion that Castigates disapproved of his boss's predilection for obstructing public access to the Abbey's land. He clearly loved his job, but he was a reluctant henchman.

'I need your help,' she told him, stepping closer. 'I'm going to make Pete Rafferty put a stop to all this trespassing nonsense.'

'He'll fire me.'

'It's okay,' Sylva assured him. 'Your name can stay out of it, and I guarantee you'll make enough of a nest egg to forget I ever goosed you. All I need is a little information . . .'

Later that evening, Sylva settled down at her computer with her mobile phone cocked to her ear, her Twitter and Facebook pages minimised while on screen she composed a mass email to her huge address book of media contacts.

Upstairs, Hana was reading Zuzi a bedtime story, having been persuaded by Mama (using every means at her disposal bar torture) that they both must stay in England for now. And now Mama was hovering behind her favourite daughter, waiting for a break in the non-stop telephoning to demand an explanation for the day's events. She listened in with a pale face as Sylva spoke, her accent barely discernible as she became Britain's favourite hardworking mum talking up a media storm.

'Yeah, that's right. Illegally closed. The gamekeeper can't be blamed – he'll be sacked if he doesn't carry out orders. He's a working man, like I'm a hardworking mum. It's Pete Rafferty who thinks he is above the law . . .'

At last, Mama pounced on her between calls. 'Just what do you think you are doing, *mačička*?'

'Taking on Dillon's father.'

Mama's hands flew up to her shaking head with a groan of despair, but Sylva reached up to reassure her.

'This is the only way, Mama. I am doing something that he wishes he could do himself. He *will* notice me, I promise.' And so will Pete, she added silently to herself.

'But will he love you?'

'Not yet.' Sylva squeezed her mother's arm with its loose, creasy skin over sinews of steel. 'But he will. Now be quiet, I'm phoning Rebekah.'

Within forty-eight hours, Sylva was once again IFOP, her public popularity souring as the nation's favourite single mum took on its mad, bad old Rockfather amid a huge press campaign (and lots of photo opportunities for herself and her children in green wellies).

Returning home from the Caribbean in early February, Dillon was amazed to find that Sylva Frost had mounted a public challenge to reopen all the illegally closed Fox Oddfield Abbey footpaths. Ramblers, riders and locals suddenly adored her.

Dillon called her to add his support, although he drew the line at making this public: 'Dad couldn't handle that: a beautiful woman taking him on is one thing, his own son quite another. I hope you understand.'

Sylva said that she did, although she privately thought it was a bit wet. But she was nonetheless quick to issue an invitation to Dillon and 'all the family' to lunch, 'and of course your lovely Nell, who knows all the paths so well – I must pick her pretty head about them'.

Nell, who did indeed know the footpaths and bridleways like old friends, was grudgingly impressed by what Sylva had done. Still glowing from a month of exclusive attention in Dillon's gated villa with its own private bay, soaking in the St Croix sun and sea while he wrote new material and the hired nanny tended Giselle, she was feeling so conciliatory that she was, for now, happy to play the perfect country girlfriend, cheese-lover and stepmother.

She even acquiesced to Sylva's play-date lunch invitation to Le Petit Château during Pom and Berry's next stay. The girls could play with Zuzi, and Giselle with the boys. It suited Nell to have Dillon's girls farmed out; she found their presence at West Oddford Farm oppressive, and the *Cheers!* reader in her was dying to have a private view of Sylva's weekend retreat, which she was convinced would be so bad taste that she would dine out on it for weeks.

But as soon as they arrived it was clear that Sylva had engineered it so that Nell was immediately encircled by her Slovakian posse and press-ganged into childcare while she annexed Dillon, steering him straight to the turret office from which she was co-ordinating her Fox Oddfield Abbey for All, or FOAFA, campaign.

'Come and see all my hard work in action!' she purred at him while Nell, a toddler on each hip, had a Peppa Pig mask plonked on her head.

'So much for picking my brain,' she fumed as her boyfriend was taken hostage.

Over an hour later, briefly granted freedom to enjoy a traditional Slovakian lunch of peppery goulash soup followed by sausages and potato salad, and then fantastically sweet fried jam dumplings, all of which Sylva claimed to have made herself, Nell didn't like the glint in Dillon's eye. She knew full well that the route to his heart via his stomach was a fast-track that they had never shared because she saw food purely as an enemy to beauty. When Sylva then produced a huge wooden board laden with oozing, stinking, award-winning cheeses from Dillon's own organic shop she knew for certain that she had walked into a trap. It had strong echoes of her own bangers and mash reconciliation before Christmas, but with a far more personal touch.

'We must go,' she told him, clutching her temples. 'I have a migraine.'

Sylva was more than a match for gameplay like that: 'You must lie down first,' she insisted, calling to one of the family army and issuing instructions in Slovakian. Moments later, Nell found herself frogmarched into a darkened room by a very beefy Slovak woman, who pressed a pill into her hand and poured her a glass of water. Crumpling under pressure – she would have made a hopeless prisoner of war, besides which she *did* have a headache – Nell swallowed it and sat down on an antique day bed, relieved at least that she didn't have to go back to play with the under-tens. Left alone, she could regroup and plan her defence strategy. But whatever was in the pill was potent stuff and within five minutes she was fast asleep.

Left unmarked downstairs, Dillon started to weaken under the all-out Sylva charm offensive. He knew precisely what she was up to and he wasn't going to let it happen, but that was no reason not to briefly enjoy it. His daughters were having a fantastic afternoon, and Nell was getting a much-needed reality check. In his most duplicitous secret heart, he was also starting to wonder if he had found his Get Out of Jail Free card at last.

In St Croix, despite wild sex and stunning sunsets, he had suddenly begun to see the startling similarities between Nell and his monstrous stepmother Indigo, who saw being the wife of a celebrity as a profession in itself, and who was as high-maintenance as the houses she constantly redecorated, the body she constantly rejuvenated and the adopted children she constantly restocked. Nell still showed no enthusiasm for helping him with the farm, or his great passion for the best organic food. The local landowner's daughter was not an earth mother, after all, but a luxury-loving rare breed with no meat on her and no sustainable by-products apart from her beauty and sexual appetite. She was a wannabe rock chick surrounded by free-range, corn-fed chickens.

It had brought him up short to see Sylva in action. Ambitious Sylva never let up, both supporting and supported by her huge family. She was a workaholic who juggled her busy career with her loving private life. She was refreshingly upfront. And she enjoyed her food. He couldn't help but be impressed.

'They drugged me!' Nell complained groggily on the way back to West Oddford.

'You're overreacting.' Dillon had become immune to her tantrums.

'Fuck you.'

'Shh!' He indicated the girls behind them.

On the back seat, Pom and Berry were hyper with excitement. 'Can Zuzi come to a sleepover next time we're here? Can she? Can she?'

'God preserve me,' said Nell. 'I'm going to Amsterdam to see Milo next time you're here.'

'Why would your *dog* be in Amsterdam?' piped Pom.

'Not *that* Milo.'

Dillon was temporarily spared his peacemaker role as his hands-free rang. It was his father calling from Ireland.

'Who is this Sylva Frost bitch, eh? Should I be worried?'

'On the evidence I've seen, Dad, you should be very worried.' Dillon hung up, deciding that for now he would store his Get Out of Jail Free card under the game board. Having Nell in play might mean three hotels in Mayfair and landing in Bond Street more often than he'd choose, but Sylva had a Community Chest and Fleet Street in her pocket, and that was infinitely more dangerous.

Chapter 47

Left in charge of thirty horses, Tash knew she had no choice but to start riding again, as well as mucking in and mucking out, clipping and grooming and sorting paperwork. Still gripped by fear, she put it off as long as she could, even though Hugo inevitably asked after the horses' progress every time he called from America.

'They're all going great,' she'd say vaguely.

'And Lough?'

'Hardly see him,' she could report more truthfully, knowing that if Hugo thought about it he'd realise that if she were riding, she'd inevitably cross paths more with Lough who was on a horse most of day, but it was easy to avoid him on two feet.

The New Zealander certainly showed no signs of wanting to engage in conversation, and worked incredibly long hours. Tash often saw the lights of the indoor school still glowing late into the evening. She gave him a wide berth, both because Hugo's warning had made her fear him and his secrets, but also because she was too embarrassed to let anybody see her on a horse, least of all the current eventing world champion.

The first time she got back in the saddle she chose Mickey Rourke, the steadiest ride on the yard, and waited until everybody was out of the way to tack him up and lead him to the mounting block, where she stood beside seventeen hands of dappled grey stupidity, palms sweating. She felt so sick and anxious that she nearly flunked it, but Beetroot – ecstatic to see her mistress getting in the plate again – had already walked purposefully to the main gates where she was waiting, milky eyes blinking and tail wagging in anticipation of a long run across the downs. Tash didn't have the heart to let her old dog down, although all her nerves could take was a short loop around the village, which suited Beetroot, who was starting to suffer from arthritis as well as poor sight. Afterwards, the dog gratefully flopped down on a discarded stable rug and gazed up as Tash dismounted, her legs like jelly and her ankles aching, feeling as though she had just ridden around Badminton, not Maccombe. She was absolutely victorious, but also dismayed to realise just how unfit and unnatural she now was.

Over the coming fortnight, she steeled herself to hack out alone on the safest horses, deliberately timing her exit so that the yard staff would be busy and she could avoid company.

Yet she soon found she had a regular outrider because Lough had a disturbing habit of appearing from nowhere, hijacking her solitary excursions like a ghostly highwayman. Despite Tash's best efforts to ride alone without the scrutiny of any critical eyes, he'd suddenly trot up alongside her out hacking or reappear from his lunch break after just ten minutes, riding into the indoor school when she'd been certain she'd have an hour to herself. He never said anything beyond a grunt of a hello to accompany the nod of his head. He existed so deeply within himself he hardly seemed to even notice her. Yet Tash, who was used to co-riding with Hugo, swapping observations and tips, found this silent presence threatening.

'Isn't it funny we keep choosing the same route?' she said to him when he'd ridden up beside her for the third day in a row, even through she'd deliberately chosen a bridleway nobody used much because of its fiddly gates.

'Not particularly,' he shrugged, looking across at her with those amazing dark eyes, always so watchful and guarded. She had a feeling that he was waiting for her to say something else, but she was too nervous to risk it, continuing the ride in all too awkward silence, trying to pretend he wasn't there.

Afterwards, she couldn't help worrying that by being so unfriendly she would in fact exacerbate any tension between him and Hugo. The Beauchamps had hardly been welcoming hosts, and Lough had clearly been through a nightmare before arriving. His stern aloofness was understandable, particularly if she was fuelling the fire by coming across as cold and snooty. It might all be so easily overcome with a few kindly gestures.

Although Hugo had her warned against being over-friendly, she saw no harm in making a peace offering, and so crammed a basket with jams and biscuits from the farm shop, along with a slightly burned home-made sponge cake, which she left outside the lodge cottage door.

There was no word of thanks. When he appeared in the indoor school the next day, she asked him if he'd received them and he looked at her curiously: 'I gave them to Lem. I hate jam. You know that.'

Trying not to feel offended, Tash probed the staff as casually as possible.

'Is he very shy?' she asked Lemon, but he laughed at this so much he couldn't speak. Then she asked Beccy if she found Lough stand-offish, and her stepsister blew a sarcastic raspberry, saying, 'And some!'

'And some is as handsome does,' Tash muttered, none the wiser and feeling increasingly uneasy.

She redoubled her efforts to stay out of sight when she was in the saddle. Her cowardice appalled her, and didn't melt away as she had hoped after a few more hours on horseback. If anything, she felt even more frozen, stiff and incapable. Her fear and lack of fitness made her increasingly withdrawn and uncommunicative with every-one on the yard, not wanting to undermine morale by showing that one half of the Beauchampions had totally lost her nerve and her knack.

Beccy was sensitive enough to see what was going on, but she said nothing, even when Lemon began to grumble that Tash was too grand for them. Since the fated party he had become her closest ally. They were both feeling the effects of Faith deserting the Haydown yard to work more hours with the Moncrieffs. On a practical level, those days that she didn't drive up the hill the yard looked scruffy and slipshod, and everybody was left chasing their own tails. On an emotional level, the bond between Beccy and Lemon became increasingly close as Faith's sensible judgement was not there to call upon and Lemon had to deal with Beccy's mounting insecurity and neediness on a day-to-day basis, most especially her guilt, which he felt was completely misplaced.

'I can't even look Tash in the face,' she lamented tearfully one evening as they shared cheesy microwaved baked potatoes in their flat.

'Hardly surprising, the way she's riding,' he sneered. 'She is *so* bad. I can't believe she was on the British team once. She makes Hugo look good.'

'I can't bear it that he's gone,' Beccy then sobbed.

Lemon waited patiently for the tears to abate, polishing off her potato while she snivelled her way back to sensibility. He missed Faith's company more than he cared to admit. Beccy was okay com-pany on her less flaky days, and he felt very protective around her, but Faith was his sparring partner. She defused his tetchiness.

Having Lough in England and being accountable to him again

made the little Kiwi very tetchy indeed, because he could clearly see what nobody else had even noticed: Lough was infatuated with Tash.

'How are the horses going?'

'Great – River's flatwork really moved up a notch today,' Tash exaggerated.

'What botch?'

'Notch!'

'What?'

'Up a notch!'

Tash missed Hugo's company so acutely that she day-dreamed conversations while she worked, and at night dreamed of erotic reunions in all sorts of bizarre settings, from her late grandmother's apartment in Paris's seventh arrondissement to a horsebox parked on the hard shoulder of the M4. In contrast, their real-life phone conversations were frustratingly prosaic, not helped by Hugo's tendency to call her from horseback, meaning she had to shout to be heard.

'I knew you'd fall straight back in to it as soon as you started again,' he said now, having at least stopped trotting so they could speak normally.

'It's falling straight back off I'm worried about,' Tash replied, knowing she was still far from back to her old self, but Hugo was already chattering about life at the Johanssens' winter training barn. The lecture–demos were a sell-out, he reported; the horses were doing great; Rory was trying his heart out and impressing everyone with his dedication, especially MC and Kirsty. 'Women love that boy. Can't think why – he's totally cocksure and thoughtless, but has so much charm and talent they fight each other to flirt with him.'

'Sounds like you before marriage changed you,' Tash reminded him, but it came out sounding wrong, as though getting married had somehow gelded him. She was uncomfortably aware that he was currently based with not one but two ex lovers, having dated Kirsty not long before they got together, when Tash was still with Niall.

She'd briefly played with the idea of taking the children to Florida and turning up out of the blue, even for just a week. Their marriage needed a big gesture to get it back on track, but it was impossible to leave the house and yard. Her big gesture right now was the silent, all-consuming one that took place behind the scenes as she worked twelve-hour days on the yard and in the office.

'The children send their love,' she told him now. 'Well, a "gaa" from Amery and a "wery beeeg keeess" from Cora, who's developing a Czech accent,' she giggled.

Hugo was less amused. 'Better knock that on the head,' he told her before he rang off, leaving Tash feeling irritated that juggling yard, office and home now also involved toddler elocution lessons.

No longer fazed by the eccentricities of England and the Beauchamps, Veruschka had taken increasing charge of domestic life at Haydown. The little Czech micromanaged the children and the running of house with supreme efficiency, and had made it her mission to take control of the Haydown mess through the winter months, using Vasilly as her strongman. Spending ever longer hours in the saddle, Tash's grip over her home life slipped further and further from her fingers. She felt like a stranger in her own home and kept falling over furniture that had been moved while she was out.

Tash complained about it to Sophia when she called one evening to discuss party-planning.

'You have to exert your authority,' Sophia insisted. 'I briefed all my nannies regularly.' Absurdly, this made Tash think of supplying her au pair with a weekly quota of knickers. But her sister's focus remained on Hugo's fortieth birthday. 'I knew there was no point waiting for you to come up with a guest list, so I photocopied your address book when we were staying with you at Christmas, and also sent myself Hugo's email contacts. I've whittled it down to about two hundred.'

'Isn't that rather a lot for a surprise party?' Tash gulped, trying not to think of the cost.

'Not a problem if one plans it right by staggering the list – closest friends and family spring the big reveal, then the remainder of the guests arrive afterwards. I've already sent the invitations to be printed, and I've contacted Marysia, who does all my outside catering, and she's come up with a price for her lovely banqueting buffet that is jolly competitive. Ben's wine merchant chum Dicky Chester-Lewis can let us have all his bin-end cases practically at trade, which is such a saving because I know you're trying to keep costs low. With a few waiting staff hired in from Marlbury, portaloos, insurance etcetera, we're looking at no more than twelve or thirteen thousand.'

Tash closed her eyes, wishing that she had the guts to shout 'No!

Stop this now! I just wanted twenty close friends, love and laughter, shepherd's pie and good Rioja and Hugo to feel relaxed and happy for once, not all this!'

But in the same way that she couldn't stand up to Veruschka about the domestic blitzkrieg, she certainly couldn't stand up to her sister.

Instead, she tried to convince herself that a surprise party for Hugo would show him how much she cared. It was her big gesture.

But as more days passed, their transatlantic phone calls remained horribly stilted and full of practical detail, from her blow-by-blow accounts of dealing with emptying the muck heap and poulticing a hoof abscess, to his long-winded and enthusiastic descriptions of training sessions with Janet Madsen that she wished she could be a part of. But they wanted to keep hearing one another's voices, even if they weren't really coming up with what needed to be said. When they did, it inevitably led to conflict:

'How are the horses?'

'Great. We hacked up to Jester's Copse today. The blackthorn blossom's out already.' She'd been joined yet again by Lough, who predictably blanked her chatter about the good sloe gin to come. Now she simply had to talk to Hugo about her worries: 'I think Lough's very lonely.'

'So? He's a loner. Leave him be.'

'I think I should socialise him.'

'He's not a hound puppy.' Hugo sounded annoyed.

'He needs to meet other people involved in the sport here.'

'He'll meet plenty once the season starts.'

'We have to keep our profile up too, Hugo. We need to make the owners feel loved. You've been away so much since last autumn that some of them will be wondering what we look like. At least let me invite them to visit, and introduce them to Lough.'

'And let him steal them off us?'

'Why should he want to do that? We're all on the same team now.'

'He has no scruples. Look at his reputation. He sailed very close to the wind in New Zealand, believe me. He's untrustworthy.'

After they rang off, Tash found the house especially lonely, the children asleep and the paperwork beckoning. The evenings seemed interminable.

She'd stopped thinking of the computer as a fun distraction. Its screen lay as dark as the television in the snug most nights; she preferred real company. But Beccy had become more withdrawn recently, acidic little Lemon unsettled her and Lough was even more intimidating. The big, regular suppers for family, friends and staff were becoming a distant memory.

Despite Hugo's disapproval, her social conscience hung heavy. Lough was forking out good money to be based at Haydown and had diligently paid off all his back rent upon arrival, so she felt she owed him more of a return. She could be introducing him to useful contacts during this traditional quiet time in the eventing calendar, when riders partied, hunted, hitched, hatched and holidayed. Networking Lough was a task that would improve her current social life, too; she and Hugo had piles of invitations propped up on the mantelpiece in the hall, but Tash was reluctant to go to anything alone. It seemed ridiculous to ignore the company on her doorstep.

Defying Hugo's advice, she decided to offer Lough another peace offering, a savoury olive branch this time, its fruits pressed to oil and used to create something more appetising that Lemon and Beccy could enjoy too.

When he next hijacked her on one of her solo hacks she turned to him with a determined smile. 'I'm going to cook all of us supper. Just because Hugo and Rory are away, it doesn't mean Haydown has no team spirit. It's much more fun to share food with other people, and I don't feel I know you at all yet.'

But Lough's reaction was even more frosty than usual.

'You know me,' he muttered into his collar, which was turned up against the chill. Then he kicked his horse into a smart trot and Tash found her youngster cantering and crabbing excitedly alongside, any further conversation rendered impossible as her nerves gripped at her chest and her hands closed in to tight, defensive fists on the reins, making the horse fight for his head. It took all her concentration to remember to breathe and hang on tight until they got back to the yard, where Lough immediately handed his reins to Lemon, who was waiting with his next horse ready, before riding off to the furthest sand school.

Left with a sweating horse and a hammering heart, Tash cursed him under her breath and decided Hugo was right; it wasn't worth the effort.

★

But, to her surprise, Lough was sitting on the dog-eared sofa in the kitchen when she came down from putting Cora to bed that evening, leafing through the latest issue of *Eventing* magazine. His hair was still wet from a shower and he'd dressed in smart brown jeans and a cashmere sweater.

Still in her filthy breeches, knee-high spotty socks and one of Hugo's ancient sweaters, Tash hastily poured two massive gin and tonics and apologised for being so disorganised. She was far too polite to point out that her supper invitation had been a general plan, not specifically for that evening, and besides that his reaction had made her think he preferred eating alone. Now he'd caught her wholly unprepared.

She fought an urge to rush out to the stables flat and beg Beccy and Lemon to join them and liven up the atmosphere a little; she could see Faith's little yellow car parked alongside Beccy's and knew it had the makings of a fun night, but Beccy wasn't answering her mobile, and abandoning Lough to go and recruit more guests looked terribly rude. But Lough in isolation was very hard going.

It was soon patently obvious that he didn't do small talk off a horse any more than he did mounted as Tash chattered nervously about the season ahead, about Hugo's news from America and about horses that she was working. He responded in monosyllables, if at all, watching her from beneath those dark brows as she chopped onions and fried them off, tripping over the dogs.

'It's only chops, I'm afraid.' She scraped the onions to one side and dropped in two chunky cuts of Berkshire pork from the farmers' market. 'If I'd known you were definitely coming I'd have defrosted something better.'

'You invited me to supper.'

'Yes, of course.' She felt silly, and also ridiculously nervous, as though she'd willingly invited a predatory animal into her house.

'About time, too.' He looked up at her, his big dark eyes impossible to read.

'Sorry – yes, very rude to be so antisocial, but with Hugo in the States . . .' Red-faced, she fetched potatoes from the larder and began peeling them over the sink. 'It's such bad timing that he and Rory went away so soon after you got here, just as you're settling in. But of course we had no idea when – if – you'd get here in the end.'

'You know why I couldn't come.'

Tash turned, peeler aloft, head to one side. She had never fully got to grips with the details of Lough's arrest and detention. 'I'm not sure I *do*, to be honest.'

'I'll tell you some time.' He stared at his fingers, which were badly chapped from long hours outside and the nails bitten right down.

Tash nervously opened a bottle of Marlborough red, her own fingers clumsy on the foil. She should have listened to Hugo. The man was a bad-tempered misanthrope. She should never have invited him in.

The wine seemed to loosen his tongue a little, however, and he outlined his plans to enter a few modest one-day trials to settle his horses as well as competing at the bigger pre-Badminton three-star CCIs. 'I'm going to lease a box so I can get about independently.'

'You're part of the team here. You can travel to competitions with us.'

'I prefer my own company.'

'We all muck in together,' she said carefully, 'there's no room for modesty or ego.'

'Are you competing this season?' He looked across at her.

'I've got no choice.'

His dark eyes were on her face, not quite catching her eye but focusing on the seed pearl stud in her left earlobe.

'Then you need help.'

'I beg your pardon?'

His flat, laconic voice had a strange thread of emotion woven through it when he spoke, addressing his own hands with passion: 'You're in trouble, Tash. You have a lot of talent and that doesn't go away, but when your nerve goes it's dangerous in our sport. You look a mess out there. Believe me, I've been there big time.'

'Really?' She was fighting to keep the sarcasm from her voice, deeply hurt despite the fact she knew he was speaking the truth.

'Yeah, I'll tell you about it some time.'

That was obviously his line to avoid any lengthy inquisitions.

'I'll get you through it,' he offered.

'That's really kind, but—'

'It's not a suggestion.' He refilled their glasses. 'It's a guarantee.'

'Thanks.' She smiled nervously, certain Hugo would disapprove. But in truth she badly needed help. 'I sometimes feel I've forgotten how to ride these days.'

The voice was gruff and flat, rendering the quotation unrecognisable: 'Nothing you can do but you can learn how to be you.'

'I'm sorry?'

He looked at his hands. 'It's easy.'

'I do hope so.' She stood up hurriedly, realising she'd forgotten to put any vegetables on to boil.

Lough watched her crossing the room. 'Tash, why are you doing this to me?'

'Doing what?'

'I know you said you'd deny everything, but we're alone now. Hugo's thousands of miles away. We don't have to pretend any more.'

She was too busy digging around in the fridge for supplies to concentrate. 'I'm not pretending anything.'

'C'mon. You opened your heart.' His deep voice held sharp flints of irritation as well as the heat of affection. 'We're birds of a feather. What's changed? Help me out here: I've been drowning since I arrived.'

For a moment Tash wondered if this was some elaborate wind-up, and that Lough shared Lemon's bizarre sense of humour after all. But one glance over her shoulder told her that this was no joke as his big, dark eyes burned holes into her face.

Carrots and broccoli hugged tightly to her chest, she dashed to the sink, her mind racing as she tried to figure out why exactly he thought they were birds of a feather. She suddenly felt very vulnerable, alone with him in her big, silent house, the children sleeping upstairs. She could see the lights on over the courtyard – the Czechs and Beccy and her gang, all just out of earshot if she screamed.

She shuffled along the kitchen surface with her colander of rinsed veg and selected the biggest chopping knife to slice them down to size.

'Honestly, I don't know what you're talking about,' she said carefully.

'The phone calls. The texts.' Anger was rippling through his soft words now, building pressure. 'I risked my liberty to keep in contact with you. I thought you felt the same in your prison, too.'

Tash stopped chopping. 'I can't send a text, Lough – not without referring to the manual. Ask anybody.'

'Bullshit!' He exploded, standing up.

'It's true,' she bleated, keeping a firm hold of the knife handle.

He marched straight past her and started pacing up and down in front of the window, a caged panther pressed up against its bars. 'You said you needed rescuing. You said you were unhappy. You begged my help.'

'I did no such thing!'

He pulled a mobile phone from his back pocket and started punching its buttons. '*You keep me sane; I wait up all night to hear from you; You have the key to me.*'

'What's the caller's number?' Tash demanded.

'Yours. The one you gave me.'

'When?'

'The first time I phoned to say I was coming. You'd just had your baby and said you were bored and all alone.'

'I definitely didn't take that call.'

'Well who did?' He sounded disbelieving.

She thought back, raking her memory. It was the day that Dillon Rafferty had dropped in by helicopter and life at Haydown changed completely; the day they learned Lough was coming. 'Beccy spoke to you,' she remembered.

'*Beccy?*'

'What's the number?'

But he pocketed his phone again. 'Forget it.'

'I'll talk to her about it tomorrow,' Tash promised. 'I'm sure there's a perfectly simple explanation.'

'No,' Lough insisted. 'You stay out if it. This is between me and her. I'll sort it.' He stood up. 'Thanks for the wine. I've lost my appetite.'

Left alone, Tash fed the burned chops to the slavering Bitches of Eastwick before locking all the doors and retreating upstairs for a bath, terrified that she'd just lifted the lid on Pandora's Box. She wanted to somehow warn Beccy, but she didn't want to embarrass her, especially when she had her friends with her.

An hour later, in another shouted conversation from a sand school in Florida, Hugo had a badly timed change of heart: 'You're right about Lough. We need to get him a social life. Get some locals over, and owners. Introduce him to Lucy and Venetia, the Stanton girls and all the hunting lot . . .' He started outlining plans that could keep Tash busy every night for weeks, entertaining most of their contacts, and especially any ravishing single women they knew. She supposed it would at least enable her to spread the word about the surprise party for Hugo's birthday.

'I've already asked the Moncrieffs to help you out,' he told her. 'Gus can take my place, and Penny will chaperone Lough so that you can concentrate on hosting. She'll make sure he meets the right people.'

Tash knew she was being stage-managed, but the thought of having a social life again delighted her.

In the stables flat, Faith stifled yawns as her two companions fell about with unbridled laughter. That evening, Beccy had persuaded Lemon to dress up in drag to see if he'd have more chance of attracting a man if he dressed as a woman. The verdict was a resounding no. He looked like Donatella Versace. But the little Kiwi groom clearly loved the fake lashes and bling, singing along to Lady Gaga with a hairbrush as a microphone and Beccy providing backing vocals.

'I wanna take a ride on your disco stick . . .' he howled as he minced past, stooping to shimmy in front of Faith. 'C'mon, join in, Eff!'

Faith might be almost a decade younger than her friends, but she found them incredibly juvenile at times. They were bunny-hopping side by side now the song came to a close, hands on crotches, re-enacting the video. These days, with Rory in America and the Moncrieffs utilising her more at Lime Tree Farm, time spent at Haydown thrilled her less, and Lemon and Limey were becoming increasingly bitter and twisted. The two had grown very close since New Year, she noticed, with Beccy acting as the ever-more straight man to Lemon's camp vitriol. That struck Faith as unhealthy, but she was very sensitive to how much Beccy had regained confidence since the Moncrieffs' party and didn't want to undermine that. Faith had expected Beccy to be withdrawn for weeks, yet she seemed to have blossomed, which was in reverse proportion to her own flagging energy as she found her party cherry-popper with Lemon increasingly regrettable.

Her heart gave a timely lurch as Beccy's iPhone burst into life beside her with strains of 'Two Souls'; it was the ringtone she had designated to Rory on her old Samsung. Picking up the phone to pass to her friend, Faith was surprised to see a photograph of Lough lighting up the screen.

'Aren't you going to answer that, Becs?' Lemon struck a pose and flicked his wig.

Beccy had turned pale. 'No. It's nobody I want to speak to.' 'Two Souls' abruptly stopped.

They all jumped as somebody banged loudly on the bedroom door.

'Come in!' Lemon giggled nervously.

Lough walked in, his face as stormy as a thundercloud over Mount Cook.

'Oh, shit. I can explain . . .' Donatella went into sharp reverse, but there was nowhere to hide.

Barely affording his cross-dressing groom a second glance, Lough held up a hand to silence him, his phone still gripped in it. 'What you do in your spare time's your concern, Lemon – just don't let the horses see you like that. Beccy, we need to talk.'

She was cowering in a corner, wearing a feather boa and a sulky expression.

'What about?'

'I'd rather this was in private.'

'Well I'd rather not,' she answered, her voice brittle.

'Then we can talk in front of your friends if you'd prefer.'

'No!' she wailed, and to his alarm burst into tears.

Glaring accusingly at Lough, Faith jumped up and put her arms around Beccy. 'Now isn't the time for this, whatever it's about.'

'Tell him to leave me alone!' Beccy pleaded, burying her face in Faith's side.

Lough hesitated, clearly thrown by the girls' reaction. Even the daft-looking curly-haired dog was barking at him now.

'You've upset Karma!' Beccy sobbed.

When he didn't immediately leave, Faith passed the shaking, sobbing Beccy into the arms of Lemon and marched up to Lough, backing him out of the room and into the dark corridor.

'This way,' she hissed, jerking her head for him to follow her into the kitchen where the debris of an Indian takeaway littered every surface.

'I need to speak with her,' Lough demanded quietly.

'She's in a bad way,' Faith whispered, her eyes narrowing. 'Whatever this is about can wait.'

'Says who?'

Faith cursed under her breath, fixing him with a determined stare that could twist lesser men's scrotums. She pushed the kitchen door to behind her.

'It's taken us weeks to get her to start to open up again,' she whispered, running a hand through her frizzy hair so that it stood up on end. 'Tonight has been a breakthrough. Don't fuck that up by laying into her about turning one of your horses out in the wrong rug or some other shit. She's on a hair trigger.'

'So, funnily enough, am I,' he fumed. 'Now tell her to dry her eyes and come in here, and we can sort this out quietly and calmly.'

Faith wasn't about to be intimidated. 'Sort what out?'

He hissed through his teeth. 'Let's start with deliberate deceit, misrepresentation, impersonating someone el—'

'Fine!' she cut in angrily. 'Not as serious as murder, then?'

Lough's expression darkened.

'Or sexual assault?' a voice spoke from the door, making them both jump. Lemon had quickly changed back into jeans and washed away Donatella, although he still had mascara stains under his eyes.

Faith shot him a warning look, but he ignored her.

Lough's dark eyes were wide with shock. 'Sexual assault?'

Lem nodded. 'Beccy was assaulted at New Year.'

'She doesn't want anyone to know,' Faith reminded him in a whisper. 'Where is she?'

'In the bathroom.'

She pushed past him to check, pausing to whisper in his ear. 'Don't say another word until I get back.'

As soon as she was out of the room Lemon closed the door and leant against it, his panda eyes regarding Lough intently. 'You'll have to excuse Faith. She gets pretty defensive around her friends, yeah, especially when they've been through a hard time.'

'Christ!' Lough felt a blast of concern and anger run through him. 'Was Beccy hurt?'

'Only up there.' Lemon tapped his head. 'But Beccy's pretty sensitive up there.'

'So I'm finding out.' He blew out through his lips, trying not to think about those amazing, electric texts. 'Do you know who assaulted her?'

Lemon's eyes hardened. 'Hugo,' he breathed. 'It was Hugo.'

Lough started in surprise. He saw the man as an incorrigible player, but assault wasn't his style. 'Are you sure?'

His little groom looked belligerent. 'Beccy might think it was all star-crossed stuff, but that's bullshit. Yeah, and maybe she led him on, but he took advantage of her.'

Lough imagined the enticement from Beccy, and the thought saddened him. He wondered if she sent Hugo texts too. She was clearly out of control, but that was no excuse for what Hugo had done, both to her and to his family. 'Poor bloody Tash,' he breathed.

'Poor Beccy,' Lemon countered in an angry hiss. 'Hugo thinks he can pick up anything he likes and drop it again, not caring whose lives he destroys in the process. Somebody needs to teach him a lesson.'

'Not me.' Lough shook his head.

'Why not? I thought that's why you came here.'

Lough was still shaking his head. 'I've destroyed enough lives myself,' he said with feeling. 'I came here to save one. I thought I was invited. Turns out I was wrong.'

'So are we going home?' Lemon asked hopefully.

Lough gazed out of the little kitchen window, across the cobbled yards, frosted white and lamp-lit by the moon, and ran his eyes along the darkened upper windows of Haydown, wondering if one was shielding Tash from the cold.

He contemplated going back to New Zealand, even if that meant facing the demons he'd left behind. It was the obvious solution. Nothing was as it seemed here; he felt as though he had walked into a hall of mirrors. But when he had left Auckland, he'd barely been able to face his own reflection. At least here the demons had new faces, and he was too close to something he had wanted for so long to turn around and leave it behind.

He had to protect her from Hugo. The man was a monster. He had to protect them all.

'We're staying.'

They could hear Faith banging on the bathroom door, insisting that Beccy had been in there long enough and demanding she come out.

'I'd better check they're okay.' Lemon turned away.

As soon as he'd left the room Lough reached for his phone and sent her a text, knowing for the first time that it wasn't her at all.

Beccy, let's forget this ever happened. I don't know why you did it, but I'm glad you did. It saw me through. It brought me here. It brought me salvation. Now you and I must forget and keep confidence. L

Just two letters came back from the depths of the bathroom. *OK*.

As he walked back to the lodge cottage, Lough edited the number in his phone from 'Tash' to 'Beccy'. Then, one by one, deleted the stored texts.

His mind kept returning to that night with Hugo, before he'd been misled into thinking Tash was the one replying to his messages.

'She's all yours,' Hugo had told him.

She had been his guiding light in recent weeks, that drunken bet taking on life-changing proportions. Since arriving in the UK Lough had seen the way Tash struggled on a daily basis to hold her family together, to temper Hugo's waywardness and to overcome her nerves, yet her fortitude and kindness never faltered. She remained the only truly innocent one among them all. To Lough, she seemed to grow more beautiful with each day that passed.

He wanted to win the bet more than ever.

Much later, Beccy lay in her bed clutching Karma, debating whether or not to run away. She could be packed and gone by morning. Nobody would miss her. She had screwed it up with Hugo and now she'd screwed it up with Lough.

That he was willing to forgive and forget brought no real relief to the scalding shame and loss she felt. She'd been so childish to mislead him, and yet she'd sensed a real bond. Now that had been completely destroyed, she was lonelier than ever.

She got up and paced her room, uncertain what to do. She could hear Lemon's music two rooms away. He must still be awake.

Padding through the flat, she knocked on his door.

When he opened it, looking comfortingly cuddly in purple pyjamas, his eyelashes still smoky with mascara, she stifled a sob. 'Can I please have a hug?'

Lemon didn't really do hugs, but he made an exception; it would be easier to handle than yet more tears. Having been in touch with his feminine side tonight, he was feeling conciliatory. He even dropped a comforting kiss into her hair.

Safe in his arms, Beccy decided to stay.

Chapter 48

When Tash rode into the indoor school at lunchtime the following day, Lough was already in there on his big ugly bay mare, Tinks. He barely nodded hello, warming up alongside her as though they were both going to work around one another in silence as usual. Then he came up and started to ride with her.

'Breathe in with the stride beat, out with the beat, feel your pelvis lowering. That's it. Track left.'

'Lough, about Beccy—'

'It's sorted.'

'But I—'

'Forget about it. I have sorted it. Now use the leg yield to open your hips more. Follow me across the arena. Great.'

Together their horses' hooves created parallel geometric patterns in the silica sand as they rode circles and diagonals.

'Relax your knees and try to connect more from your seat-bones to the front of your pelvis – that's fantastic.'

Within half an hour, Tash and River were beginning to rediscover the connection that had taken them around the biggest four-star tracks. The mare's ears flopped obediently in front of Tash as she relaxed and listened, and the smile on her rider's face widened with delight.

'You're a great teacher.' She looked across at Lough. 'I can line up lots more clients for you.' It would be a lucrative source of extra income.

'I don't want any more clients,' he told her tersely. 'I hate teaching.'

'What's this then?'

'Essential maintenance.' He gave a ghost of a smile. It was the closest he had come to a joke.

Back on the yard, she leaned over his stable door. 'I'm going to be inviting some eventing mates to supper over the next couple of weeks to meet you.'

'I'm not much good in company.' He didn't look up from removing Tinks's boots.

'They're all good fun, I promise. It's the least I can do after you've helped me.'

'You wait. I've hardly started.'

He was waiting for her in the school at exactly the same time the next day. And the next. His poker-faced cool was a far cry from the chatty, gossipy coaches she usually favoured, but the effect he had on her riding was undeniable. By day four, she found herself watching the clock all morning to make sure she was there on time.

He worked his horses hard and he expected her to keep up, but his calm encouragement stopped her busy head panicking and started to produce results as Tash and her horses relaxed. Small talk wasn't allowed, nor jokey self-deprecation – Tash's standard defence mechanisms. With her entire focus on her horse, she started to ride out of her skin.

All the time, Beetroot sat loyally on the sidelines, fading old eyes seeing what her mistress couldn't. This man meant business. In his quiet way, he was taking over the yard.

Tash did notice a change in Beccy, however. She was getting up as early as possible to do yard work, wearing her hoodie up and her iPod earphones in at all times, head down and eyes averted. She had also started going walkabout again, leaving Lemon and the part-timers to cover her absences.

'Please tell me what's been going on between you and Lough,' said Tash when she managed to corner her one afternoon. 'I want to help.'

'It's nothing. We're cool.' Beccy was giving nothing away, apart from a blush that told Tash there was more to it than anyone was letting on.

'That's a relief.' She eyed her stepsister disbelievingly, knowing from experience that it would be nigh on impossible to get past her defence shield. But she had another tactic. 'In that case, I've got a few drinks and suppers lined up to introduce Lough to the locals and I wondered if you could lend a hand?'

Beccy's blush deepened. 'I'm doing stuff with Lem. Sorry.'

'What, every evening?'

'Pretty much.'

'You two are very close these days.' Tash wondered if that had something to do with the disagreement with Lough, but at least any misunderstanding now seemed forgiven.

Beccy shifted awkwardly, now crimson in the face. 'He's fun.'

Tash had never quite caught onto Lemon's brand of humour, but she was genuinely pleased that Beccy had a close friend and an active social life; she was looking forward to reactivating her own.

'How are the horses?' Lots of background noise. Hugo was on the Interstate, travelling to a show venue to present a demonstration.

'Great. Took six to Kelvin's gallops today and they all felt the benefit.' No need to tell him she'd chickened out of riding, leaving that to Lough and Lemon.

'Started jumping yet?'

'Just out hacking. Logs and things.'

'Got to move things up a gear – season's not far off. I hear you've got Mary and Charles for supper tomorrow.' He had clearly been speaking to Gus. 'Give them my love.'

'And the children?'

'What?'

'Do they get your love, too?'

'Goes without saying.'

'No it doesn't,' Tash complained, but he had already hung up.

Thrilled to have a social life again, Tash brought in the local set to introduce to Lough – the Moncrieffs, the Stantons, the hunting set like the Cubitts and Oare-Austens, farming families Bell and Carroll, local trainer Kelvin Meech, beloved clients past and present such as the Seatons, Elf Reddihough, Lord and Lady Buckland and even the dreaded Venetia, who turned up in tight leather jeans and a see-through top, much to Lord Buckland's delight.

Lough was a reticent but polite guest and remained understated throughout. He arrived on time, left early and spoke little. That didn't stop Tash's guests all being quite bewitched by this taciturn talent from the other side of the world, a reclusive world champion who had won Olympic silver. They found him wildly sexy and issued invitations to parties, hunt balls and charity fund-raisers, all of which he declined. Tash found him very difficult to mix, like absinthe.

'I can't figure him out at all,' Tash confided in Penny after a rather sticky evening when Lough had blanked a very influential horse-trials organiser.

'He just doesn't suffer fools,' Penny defended Lough, who she'd come to admire over several evenings co-hosting suppers with Tash. 'I think that's admirable. The man has more talent than any of us mere mortals. He doesn't need to kow-tow to anyone.'

'I don't know why I'm bothering trying to give him a social life then,' Tash replied grumpily as she contemplated another mountain of clearing up.

'It's obvious why. If one has a tiger captive, one can't resist showing it off,' Penny winked. 'Besides, Hugo was most insistent we all entertain the masses until he gets home.'

'He was?' Tash looked up as Gus came back in from waving away the departing guests.

'Safety in numbers,' he laughed, helping himself to the last of the open wine.

Tash felt far from reassured, particularly now she was investing so much trust in this anti-social interloper. Working in the school was one thing, but out with him in open country she felt more vulnerable, equally frightened of the horsepower beneath her as the manpower beside her. Lough had at least stopped unexpectedly appearing on her hacks, and they now rode out together each day. As she started working the horses harder and faster to get them fit, she needed company, however intimidating. And Lough seemed to have a sixth sense for when she was losing control or her adrenalin was peaking, setting a pace that never overwhelmed her yet pushing her a little more each day.

Haydown had a full cross-country course at its disposal, built up over many years with a plethora of obstacles of differing heights and combinations to tackle, from skinnies to arrowheads, corners, big galloping flyers and turn upon turn upon turn, yet Lough rode on past them each day as though they weren't there, only to catch Tash unawares out on the downs with a suggestion of popping a stone wall for fun.

It was a clever tactic that worked. Had it been Hugo, Tash knew that they would have worked their way around the cross country course a jump at a time, tens of dogs (and possibly Alicia with a picnic) in attendance, with much briefing, tactical talk and encouragement, and then great pressure each time she approached a fence. This way, there was no weight of expectation, just a great gush of self-confidence and an energising sense of achievement. She wanted the feeling to last for ever.

Entertaining night after night was giving her less of a buzz, however, as the novelty quickly wore off and fatigue set in. Within a fortnight she had cooked her way through most of the contents of the freezer. She loved seeing old mates, but she seemed to spend her life swapping between riding gloves, oven gloves and washing-up gloves. She wasn't getting enough sleep.

It was the morning after a particularly raucous kitchen supper that she fell off for the first time. It was nothing dramatic: Vixen – who was notoriously spooky – suddenly twisted sharply away from a hedge when she spotted a sheep peering through it at her. Normally Tash would have sat the leap, but she was half asleep and had been distractedly wondering whether to invite some of the British-based New Zealanders over to supper the following week. The next thing she knew, she was sitting in a very wet, very muddy tractor rut.

Lough spun back, his horse half-rearing in surprise. 'Are you okay, Tash?'

She found herself laughing with relief. 'Absolutely! Thank God for that. I needed to fall off.'

Less than impressed, Lough caught the loose mare and brought her back.

'You weren't concentrating. Next time, you might not be so lucky,' he told her as she remounted and they moved off again.

'I'll be fine. I'm through the worst case scenario now: I've fallen off.'

'You reckon?' Lough's eyes glittered.

In an instant he urged Toto from a steady walk to flat-out gallop, mud splattering on to Tash and Vixen as horse and rider streaked away. Before Tash could take in what was happening, the little chestnut mare threw herself into hot pursuit, ears flat back, instinct telling her that this was a flight for life. Tash had no control whatsoever.

'Stop, Lough. Stop!' she screamed, but her words were whipped straight back from her mouth. The sheer speed at which they were travelling almost winded her.

Over the ridge of the downs they raced and on to the old public gallops, faster and faster, clods of turf flying in their wake. Tash had been bolted with before, but this was different; this time the horse had a target to follow. She tried everything to check the mare, but she wanted to follow her stablemate at all costs.

Then, just as suddenly as he'd set off, Lough pulled up to a steady canter, gradually easing Toto down.

Tash had less smooth control. Plunging around like a lunatic beside him, she only just held on as Vixen fly-bucked and threw her head.

'What the hell did you do that for?' she demanded.

'Just interval training.' He turned to her, dark eyes dangerous. He'd made his point.

They hacked home into a dropping sun, Tash's heart taking minutes to stop lurching in panic. 'Don't ever do that again without warning me,' she muttered.

He said nothing, but as they rode back into the yard, metal shoes ringing on the cobbles, he said in an undertone, 'You need to concentrate more on your riding and less on your dinner parties.'

Tash bristled. 'Last night's meal was in your honour! It was for you.'

'No – tonight's for me.' He rode away before she could ask him what he meant.

That evening, he was waiting in the kitchen again when she came down from putting the children to bed. This time he was standing at the Aga, stirring the contents of a casserole. Whatever was in it smelled delicious.

'My turn to feed you,' he told her, not looking up.

Tash yawned, too polite to mention that she'd scoffed all of Cora's rejected fishfingers and half a packet of biscuits earlier, and had been really looking forward to vegging out in front of *Sylva's Shadow* on television this evening.

Instead, she settled at the table and watched him warily. She was quite accustomed to people taking over in her kitchen – Veruschka did it daily – so it felt quite normal to see a relative stranger waving her peppermill around. Realising that he was probably doing this as a peace offering to apologise for their terror ride earlier, she tried to be friendly.

'I didn't know you cooked.'

'My mum taught me. It relaxes me.'

'Glad something does.' She rubbed her brow tiredly.

The big, dark-chocolate eyes glanced across at her.

Feeling ungrateful, she propped her chin up on her palm. 'Tell me about your mum.'

'What do you want to know?' He was typically unforthcoming.

'Everything.' She stretched the fingers of her free hand across the table, studying her battered wedding ring. 'From start to finish. What makes Lough Strachan tick.'

He took a long time to respond, setting the lid back on the cooking pot, resting the spoon in the drip catcher and turning to lean against the Aga rail to look at her, his gaze guarded. 'What's the point in you knowing that?'

'It would help me understand you better.'

His eyebrows shot up, but he made no further objection. Instead, for the first time since he'd arrived in England, he started talking in more than just single sentences. Over quite the most sensational lamb stew Tash had ever tasted, he told his story with minimal emotion or self pity.

'Mum's family was from Scotland originally, but I never knew them. They cut all contact when she moved in with my dad.'

'He's Maori, yes?'

'Yeah – his family reckons they're noble stock, but he's a waste of space, always drinking and womanising. He used his fists on Mum and us kids.'

'He beat you?'

He nodded, not looking at her. 'Mum got it much worse, usually trying to defend us. I remember the day he almost blinded her in one eye just because she'd spent their last twenty dollars on new shoes for my sister. I came home from school and there was blood everywhere. She tried to pretend it was an accident, but I knew. I told her I'd kill him if he ever touched her again.'

'How old were you?'

He shrugged. 'Ten, maybe. But I meant every word. I started bunking off school to keep an eye on the house, so I could be there to defend her if he rolled in drunk at lunchtime. He picked on me more then and I wore my bruises like badges of honour. Pretty soon, the authorities started asking questions. It was around that time Mum threw him out for good.'

'You were very brave.' Tash stared at him, unable to imagine a life where Amery was forced to defend her against violence. 'Your mother has an amazing son.'

But he shook his head. 'I went off the rails for a long time – some might say I never got back on.' He looked up with a rueful smile. 'I wasn't home much as a teenager.'

Lough had spent his teens in South Auckland dreaming of being a jockey, he explained, pursuing his single-minded ambition through long, lonely bus journeys out of town that had cost him as much as his meagre riding wage. But he was thrown off too many yards for aggressive behaviour, and then grew too tall and heavy, his only compensation being that his brain grew just as big and bold as his body. After years of bad behaviour and truancy he buckled down and went back to school where, against all odds, he won a scholarship that enabled him to train as a vet.

'I was base metal, but a bloody amazing alchemist of a teacher called Simpson fought my corner, and more often fought me, to get me there,' he told her, without sentiment. 'I was a fish out of water at Massey University. I was chippy and destructive and introvert and money was always way too tight for comfort – Mum took on extra jobs and I did night shifts in a convenience store – but I worked like stink on the academic stuff, and I had to; it didn't come easy. I won't pretend I was a great vet after I graduated, but once I started working with horses again it started to make sense.'

His competitive riding dreams had been reignited through a trainee job at a practice in Wairarapa, working in the exclusive North Island eventing circles, which had quickly provided him with his first real opportunities to ride again. Thus the Devil on Horseback was born, a young local vet with no fear and an innate, almost supernatural ability to get a horse to fly across country.

Competing with ferocious success on chance rides, he rapidly earned himself a reputation as a king-maker of difficult horses. He'd taken work wherever the rides were, but almost dropped off the edge of the sport many times through injury and lack of funds. Despite his ambition, his bloody-mindedness won him few allies and he seldom hung on to sponsors and patrons for long. His talent kept rides coming, but he had endured bitter disappointments.

'When I was twenty-four I spent every cent I had flying a horse across to compete at Melbourne,' he told her carefully.

'I rode there a couple of times. What year?'

'You were there.'

'Did we meet?'

'My horse went lame in transit.' He got up to help them both to seconds.

'Bad luck.'

'It was a bad year for me,' he said quietly, ladling out stew.

A favourite horse had been sold from under him in the same season that he lost two to injury, one to poisoning and a lover to a rival. His was stony broke, homeless and jobless.

'That's when I lost my nerve. I was starting from scratch again. I began doubting myself and my riding suffered. I thought about quitting.' His big, dark eyes regarded her with empathy. 'It took a long time to beat, but I got over it. It does get better.'

'I hope so.' She looked down at her plate, not wanting to dwell on her own failings. 'You must have had good owners to see you through.'

'I had no owners. I still don't.'

'But how could you afford to keep going?' She looked up.

His dark eyes didn't leave her face. 'By bending the rules.'

'You cheated?' She was appalled. 'How?'

'I knew I couldn't stay in the sport without regular money coming in – and a vet's salary was never going to cover my costs, especially with all the time off I needed. I'm a clever bugger, but I'm still a little cross-breed from the ghetto. My career meant nothing next to competing. Then I met Lem and realised the only way of staying in the sport was by offering a unique service.'

'What service?'

'I'll tell you about it some time.' He stood up and cleared away their empty plates, leaving her hanging.

There was a single coloured show jump set up in the arena when Tash rode in the following afternoon, mounted on her goofiest youngster, a coloured mare called Lauren Bacall – or Lor – who was as beautiful as she was neurotic and stubborn.

'I'm not going near that,' she told Lough when he rode in after her on his little intermediate horse, Hex.

'Sure.' He started trotting round, warming up and ignoring her.

Tash wobbled about, getting increasingly tense and disagreeable with Lor, who set her neck left and crabbed furiously, almost falling over every time she caught sight of her reflection in the mirrors at the end of the school.

By now, Lough was sailing over the jump, which was set up at a good four feet, a ground pole placed well back from the approach which he was using to alter his stride pattern in – sometimes four, sometimes three, sometimes five strides from its stripy boundary.

Quite suddenly, Lor decided that she wanted to get out of the arena – if necessary backwards, on two legs.

Tash clung on, trying not to draw attention to herself.

'I think we should swap.' Lough suddenly appeared beside her. 'You take this boy over that a couple more times and I'll see if I can sort her out.' He hopped off.

She was so grateful to get help with Lor that she didn't really question what she was taking on. Which was why, two minutes later, she sailed over a jump that was way beyond her comfort zone and barely registered what she was doing apart from feeling a lovely rush. She was too busy looking over her shoulder to watch Lor trotting obediently down the long side like a dressage schoolmaster.

'Whatever you're on, I want some,' she laughed.

'I'll cook you that tonight,' he promised.

The food – and the life story – kept coming. Over successive nights of spicy seared salmon and meltingly tender beef fillet, Tash guzzled his food and listened as he carried on the story.

Dragging himself up to four-star competitive glory again had meant bending the rules more than just a little. He'd sold his soul, or at least his professional ethics.

'My nickname, the Devil on Horseback, I figure I earned it twice over. I met Lem, and he opened a lot of doors – back doors – into the racing industry.'

His constant, crippling lack of funds had been solved by a reluctant but inexorable passage into corruption as an equine vet: 'Dodgy blood tests, illegal beta blockers and anti-inflammatories, faked post-mortems, I did it all.' He made enough money to rent his own yard and secure fast-track access back into the sport he loved. Tipped to be the next Mark Todd because of his natural ability, he soon became an unwitting New Zealand celebrity, a pioneer in breaking stigmas against the Maori, against mixed-raced riders and elitism in sport. All the time his corruption and duplicity had threatened his sanity.

'The one thing I never, ever did was drug my own horses,' he insisted. 'They were fit, sound and healthy and winning everything I entered. I got to the Olympics, for Christ's sake. We got tested. Toto was clean. But by then it was obvious I was under closer watch than most, if you get my drift.'

Tash steepled her fingers over her nose, not knowing how to take it all in. Hugo would go spare. But then Lough said something that made her blood run cold.

'Your husband knows all this.'

'Hugo knows?' She stared at him, bewildered.

He nodded, face hardening. 'He made it quite clear that it would be in my best interest to come to the UK. He'd heard talk that I was under suspicion in New Zealand, that the authorities would soon be after me but it was being kept hushed until after the Games. A lot of rivals in the sport had information that could damage me. Hugo had access to all that information too.'

She was finding it hard to believe her ears. 'Are you saying Hugo blackmailed you?'

'Let's say he gave me a very good reason for coming. I told him I'd think about it. We struck a deal.' He looked up at her, watching her face closely as he often did these days, no longer too shy to look her in the eye. He had a way of running his gaze from hers to her mouth and up to meet her eyes again that was wholly disconcerting.

Tash licked her lips nervously. 'But then you went back to New Zealand anyway?'

'And got arrested,' he nodded. 'I thought it was the horse-doping. When they said suspicion of murder I laughed at them.'

'What happened?'

'I'll tell you some time.' Again she was left frustrated.

As soon as he'd gone, Tash phoned Hugo, staring at the clock and calculating Florida time as it rang through.

'Is this urgent?' he answered irritably.

'What are you doing at six in the evening that's more important than me?' She tried to sound light-hearted, but the anxiety in her voice made her squeak like a mouse.

'Addressing the USEA central committee on rider safety in

four-star international horse trials; I'm about three-quarters of the way through the Q and A, if you'd like to add anything.'

'No – you carry on!' She rang off, mortified.

Later that night, he called back in high spirits. 'How are the horses?'

'Drug free, I hope.'

But when she tackled him about what he knew about Lough's rule-breaking, Hugo's reaction threw her: 'Don't believe a word he says. That's not why he came over to England. Do *not* trust him, Tash. He's got his own agenda. I don't want you spending time alone with him, is that understood?'

'Understood,' she whispered, suddenly feeling very vulnerable.

But it was like leaving a book with the last chapter unread. She had to know.

The following day, Lough said nothing about cooking her supper. They worked around one another in near silence, riding out together, schooling side by side, utterly focused on their horses. Yet she knew that he needed to tell the rest of the story as much as she needed to hear it.

He was sitting at the kitchen table when she came downstairs from bathing the children, opening a bottle of wine. There were already two big bowls of Thai soup laid out. She fetched two wine glasses and sat opposite him, trying not to show how frightened she now felt at being alone with him.

But Lough picked up on it as swiftly as fear in one of his horses. 'You've shown me such kindness, Tash.' He looked across at her, eyes filled with concern. 'Talking to you is helping me get a lot of things straight in my head. I probably come across as an ambitious, heartless shit to you.'

She shook her head. 'Olympic medals and ruthlessness go hand in hand.'

'Your husband won the gold,' he reminded her.

Tash looked at him sharply, finding her apprehension eclipsed by curiosity. 'You don't like him very much, do you?'

Lough shrugged. 'I don't trust him.'

'Funnily enough, he feels the same way about you.' Tash laughed, relaxing a little as she perceived male egos at play. 'Yet you accepted his offer to come here.'

Lough picked up his spoon and looked at it. 'When I flew back to New Zealand with silver I was welcomed as a hero, but I knew it was a mistake to stay.'

'Because you were about to be busted?' She lapped up her soup, eyes watering because it was wildly spicy. It was one of the most delicious things she'd ever tasted.

It was his turn to laugh, that deep, rich sound which was as relaxing as it was rare. 'Because life there has lost meaning. I'd done what I set out to do: I became world champion and an Olympian without forsaking those shores. But sometimes what you really want is across the sea and you have to travel to get it.'

'So you *do* really want to work with Hugo?' Her nose was starting to itch from the soup's chilli punch.

He looked into her face thoughtfully, gaze travelling slowly from green iris to amber iris to pink nose to stinging, wet lips and back to her mismatching eyes. 'He and I will always compete. We want the same things. This time, I want to play by the rules.' His voice was so low Tash had to lean forwards to hear.

Realising her tongue was poking out of her mouth, she tucked it back in and nodded. 'Lots of rules in British Eventing, but all good. It's a much safer sport these days.'

'I don't feel safe with safe. Maybe I get that from my father.'

'He's the one you . . .' She stopped herself, realising that adding 'were accused of murdering' would be beyond tactless.

He was still tracking her face, eyes to nose to mouth, an eternal triangle that kept that dark gaze occupied for what seemed for ever as she ate greedily, amazed by the flavours, equally fascinated by the story.

Now those black eyes alighted on hers and stayed put. 'You're so beautiful.'

Tash spluttered soup everywhere, making him duck.

'Sorry!' she coughed, eyes streaming. 'I must have misheard you.'

'You're hearing's fine.'

Nerves on full alert again, she carefully laid her spoon aside.

But before she could speak, Lough started talking again: 'A couple of days before I was going to fly here, my dad got in contact out of the blue, wanting to meet me. I knew it was a trick, but I hadn't seen him in almost twenty years and I figured it was my last chance to face those demons, so I went along with it.' He refilled his glass, hand shaking.

'We met at some slum bar he hangs out in near the harbour the night before I was due to leave. He's a waste of space, my dad – typical Otara lowlife. Claims he's never used his fists on Mum, but I saw the bruises, know how scared she still is of him. Most of his memory is pretty much white noise apart from anything involving dollar signs. He'd read about my success in the papers and wanted a slice of it. He threatened to make Mum's life a misery after I'd gone if I didn't pay him off. I gave him three grand in cash and told him to leave her alone, but he said it would cost me a lot more than that. It made me so mad, so demented, that he'd left my mother for dead all those times, I lost it big time . . .'

Tash caught her breath, staring across the table at him. 'What did you do to him?'

He rubbed his brows with shaking fingers. 'I spiked his drink.'

'What with?'

'Ketamine.'

'Ketamine?' Tash recognised the drug from working with horses, and she'd seen enough newspaper articles to know that the animal anaesthetic had a recreational following for its addictive – and illegal – opiate effects.

'Yeah, I sent Papa through the K-hole.' He let out a hollow laugh. 'I wanted to fuck with his head as much as he's fucked with mine. And I just wanted the truth.' He looked up at her, making her heart rake through molten ashes of compassion for him.

'And did you get it?'

He shook his head. 'Just a load of shit about *his* father and how shit his life had been and how he could have had what I had if he'd only had the breaks. He was pretty out of it, talking in *te reo* – in the Maori language. Then he started throwing his fists about and hallucinating so I beat it, figuring he'd come out of it again soon enough, sleep it all off.'

'But he didn't?'

Lough shrugged. 'He disappeared that night. Next thing I know, his freaky girlfriend was telling the police I killed him.'

'And he's still missing?'

'As far as I know.'

'Where do you think he is?'

'Floating around Manukau Harbour, maybe, feeding the fish?'

She stared at him in bewilderment. It was hard to take in, all these secrets and lies. He was taking a huge risk by telling her, and it was a responsibility she found hard to bear. He was one of the most talented, instinctive riders in the sport, but what he had done would be career-ending if word ever got out.

He let out another hollow laugh now, as sad as a fox bark. 'When the police picked me up at Auckland International twenty-four hours later, I thought someone had shopped me for doping horses. They'd already been to my place and found a load of illegal drugs in the incinerator. Then they started bandying the word "murder" around and I freaked out. A lot of people had seen me and Dad drinking together the previous night, they'd seen me hand money over and us arguing. His girlfriend swore blind he must be dead, spouting a lot of shit about me coming after him for having a bust-up with Mum. It was enough evidence for the police to detain me and then stop me leaving the country. Of course they couldn't hope to make any sort of murder charge stick, but they still wanted to get me for the drugs and malpractice. I was held in custody for as long as they could get away with. Finally, they decided against bringing any charges. Turns out nobody would turn evidence against me after all, not even my greatest rivals. I guess winning the country a medal has its good points.' He smiled ruefully. 'Finally I got my passport back and flew here. Lemon covered for me.'

'He knew all along?'

'Only about the racing industry stuff. He's been involved in that side a long time, and he got me into it in the first place. When I quit vet work to turn professional I tried to clean up my act – both our acts – but it never make any difference to Lem. He was still dealing drugs and doping right up until we left Auckland.'

'And you brought him *here*? We trust him with all our horses!'

'He wouldn't do anything to harm them.' He shook his head. 'Lem's not the problem. It's his boss who might be a murderer.'

'Don't say that.'

'Why not? It could be true, couldn't it? They haven't found a body and until my dad turns up, I might have bloody killed him for all I know.' He buried his face in his hands.

'But he was alive when you left.'

'I drugged the man to oblivion and then abandoned him.'

Tash reached across the table and took his hands. They were

shaking so hard that she had to grip them tightly, feeling their size and weight, twice that of hers, the nails bitten down to nothing.

'Christ, Tash,' – his dark eyes lifted to look at her – 'do you think I killed him?'

'No!' Scraping her chair back, Tash rushed around the table to wrap her arms around those wide, shaking shoulders. 'Of course you didn't.' The truth was, she didn't know.

Yet she cradled relief to her chest as she hugged him, certain that Lough's confession must be one of the 'nights we regret' Hugo had alluded to before he left for the States. That was the secret the two men shared, so dark and threatening that Hugo had tried to protect her from it, wanting her kept apart from the New Zealander at all costs while he was away and fearing for her safety until he could assess the situation. But Lough had a fierce heart and great honour, and she didn't doubt his integrity. Hugo's fears were groundless, as he would soon find out. She was incredibly proud that he'd stuck his neck out to take a risk for this talented rider. It was typical of his generosity and guts. She couldn't wait for Hugo to get home and see that Lough was such a safe and trusted part of Haydown life.

Chapter 49

Sheltering from the rain beneath the courtyard arch, Beccy stared across at the glowing Haydown kitchen window and shivered, her teeth chattering and her head pounding. She could clearly see Tash with her arms around Lough, framed perfectly by Queen Anne sash-work. It was like watching a scene from a sugary feel-good movie, but this particular tableau didn't make Beccy feel at all good. She felt like Cyrano watching Roxane and Christian getting together. She wanted another genre, crime, war or even sci fi; a space ship swooping down to gobble Tash up and spirit her off to Mars would be ideal.

Beccy pulled her dressing gown tighter and wished she'd put on more than just a fluffy bathrobe and Ugg boots. She felt as though she'd been dropped in a tank of ice cubes. The rain was turning to hail to match her mood.

Watching the embrace made her jealous heart split – one half for Hugo, one half for Lough. How *dare* Tash get them both?

She wanted to run in and scream at them, but of course she had too many shameful secrets of her own to risk exposure.

She tied her dressing-gown cord tighter and went back up to the flat to knock on Lemon's door before walking straight in, desperate for distraction.

Lem quickly shut his laptop, looking shifty. 'Jeez, you made me jump, yeah?'

Beccy's lip wobbled.

'You want a hug, I suppose?' He sounded snappy and defensive, as though she'd just barged in to borrow a fiver.

She shrugged, not caring what website he'd been looking at. She was sure it could contain nothing worse than what she'd just witnessed. Her lips were wobbling out of control now.

With a sigh Lemon padded across the room, arms outstretched. She sank gratefully into them, feeling his hard little wrestler's body against hers, a rock in her stormy sea.

'Whassamatter?' He rubbed her back.

Falteringly, she told him what she had just seen. 'Hugo should know what Tash and Lough are up to behind his back,' she finished tearfully.

'Leave Lough out of this.'

'What do you owe him?' she sobbed. 'He's horrible to you most days. You could get a better job grooming for someone else over here. We both could.' She loved the idea of running away with Lemon, who had been so kind recently, who sometimes even seemed to be able to see right into her muddled mind.

'We'd never get a flat as good as this one,' he deflected.

She put on her best suburban-housewife voice: 'We've got the place just how we want it.'

'We're like an old married couple.' He tried a voice to match. 'I love tinkering with my mains pipe, and you like to dust your knick-knacks with the curtains drawn.'

'Nobody else around to dust them,' she giggled.

'Shame the marriage was never consummated.' He let out a theatrical sigh then pressed his lips to Beccy's head, breathing in its shampoo scent. She used Johnson's baby shampoo – he had seen the bottle in the bathroom and always found it fitting because her attitude was so childlike. He thought wistfully of Faith and her boyish body, now so cruelly denied to him.

Beccy's surprisingly womanly body was getting decidedly hot and bothered against his. 'You really think it's a shame?'

'Nobody dusting my beautiful Limey's knick-knacks?' Lem exclaimed, still camping it up. 'A crying shame: you were built for luxury. You need a woman who does.'

'I need a man who does more than my husband,' she corrected, wriggling out of the hug and blushing furiously.

Lemon kept hold of her arms. 'Your husband would do anything for you, you know that.'

They exchanged a lingering smile, Beccy bashful and cautious, Lemon suddenly cocksure, his excitement mounting as he looked at his sidekick from an entirely new perspective. He'd been barking up the wrong tree all year, he realised, trying to climb the prickly acacia rather than the weeping willow. Lemon was no druid, but Beccy was no flower fairy, as he'd learned in recent weeks. All that flakiness hid a stubborn will. She still refused to accept that Hugo had taken advantage of her at the Moncrieff's party, although it was obvious she was deeply damaged by it. Lemon was starting to tire of the constant comfort she craved. Tonight, however, he saw the perfect antidote to her neediness and his own ongoing sex drought. He was now feeling so cocksure that his pyjama bottoms had developed a front canopy.

'Do you love me?' Beccy asked suddenly, putting him off his stroke.

'Yeah,' he said vaguely.

Beccy's heart, so bruised from seeing Tash cradling Lough in her arms while her beloved Hugo was away, beat hard and fast against her ribs. Lemon was safe and familiar; he surely deserved access to that secret part of herself she'd never quite let loose. It was kicking so hard against the stable door now, she had to free it. Libido-ration beckoned.

Two dressing gowns were dropped in record time.

Beccy found him surprisingly confident and adroit. She had spent a decade trying to find herself, but within minutes Lem was finding parts she never even knew existed.

'I've only had a couple of lessons, but I had a very exacting tutor,' he panted.

'I thought you were a virgin too?'

'We're neither of us virgins now,' he said a moment later as he thrust eagerly inside her.

Soon Beccy didn't care whose cherry had been picked first, if it felt this thrilling. When she caught sight of their reflections sliding together in the wardrobe mirror, illuminated by just the dim bedside light, she let out a gasp of pleasure.

Lemon joined in, howling like a coyote.

As her body went from unexplored territory to conquered empire, Beccy could almost feel her mood shift from black clouds to blue sky. She was making love. She loved Lemon.

Five minutes later, he was ready to go again. Unlike Faith, Beccy's enjoyment increased with each encore.

What Lemon lacked in stature, he more than made up with in eagerness and ability to go again and again. Beccy simply couldn't get enough of his stubby, wide and very active spring-loaded cock.

They were still making love at dawn, the horses kicking hungrily for breakfast outside.

'If Faith's your tom-boyfriend, what am I?' Beccy asked leadingly.

'You're my best-girlfriend.' Lemon, pumping away happily, kissed her nose.

Beccy felt marvellous. She had a boyfriend. It didn't quite soothe away the panic she had felt at seeing Lough and Tash embrace, but it made life a whole lot rosier.

When he issued his last coyote wail of the night, rolled off her and sagged back against his pillows, sated and jubilant, she covered his sweaty face with kisses. 'I'll go and put out morning feeds,' she offered, 'then I'll come back and cook you breakfast before we muck out.' She went out, humming 'Two Souls'.

Waiting in bed, Lem reflected that, for a gay man, he was getting an awful lot of girl action – certainly more than his straight boss. If Lough wanted to get hooked on a married women, that was his loss. Goey virgins were where it was at.

Thinking about Lough and his fixation on Tash, Lemon's eyes narrowed, but he no longer felt so threatened by the situation. Wrapped in a post-coital glow, he felt invincible. Hugo had stolen a gold medal from under Lough's nose. He'd taken advantage of Beccy who was so vulnerable. That he deserved to have his charmed life wrecked had never been in doubt, so Lemon could hardly complain if Hugo's wife now performed that duty with her characteristic lack of guile, cuckolding the arrogant Brit by mounting the most talented rider in the world. Any romance between Lough and Mrs Beauchamp would never last, after all. They were both far too easily led. Lemon had more chance of living happily ever after with Beccy.

The thought made him chuckle as he settled back beneath the bedcovers and looked forward to his cooked breakfast.

Outside, still humming 'Two Souls', Beccy wafted around on a cloud.

Staying up all night and falling in love might have improved her mood immeasurably, but it had done nothing for her concentration. She gave horses the wrong feeds, reeling around happily, still smelling Lemon's body on hers. Dancing into Heart's stable, she plonked his feed bucket at his stamping feet. A moment later his hooves were lifting off the ground.

Beccy screamed as the horse, scenting escape, made a lunge towards the open door. Instinct told her to stand up, but suddenly his chest was right in her face.

She stood, frozen in horror. Before she could move a pair of arms closed around her and rugby-tackled her to the ground, pinning her there as the horse jumped clean overhead and clattered away across the yard, whinnying delightedly.

The arms let go and Beccy looked up at Lough's furious face. For a moment, the déjà vu was so intense it almost blinded her.

'You okay?' came a bullet-shot enquiry.

'Yes,' she spluttered.

He was gone in an instant, grabbing a headcollar and crossing the yard to catch Heart and lead him back. He looked furious. 'You should never leave his door open. You know that.'

She nodded, moving to one side of the stable as he led in the overexcited horse, and feeling very silly. Her face flamed so much she was surprised the shavings bed didn't combust around her.

Lough waited for her to go out before following her and bolting the door. 'You sure you're okay?' His eyes studied her red face. 'You look a bit spaced out.'

She nodded again, feeling incredibly awkward. It was the first time she'd been alone with him at close range since he discovered she was behind the texts and phone calls. She stared at her shoes.

'I'm really okay,' she gabbled, her mouth starting to bolt faster than Heart from the door. 'Really, really okay. Fabulous, in fact. Never better. Thank you for asking. Appreciate it. And thanks for rescuing me back there. Super job. You're so amazing with horses.' She peered up at him, hoping she'd said enough to convince him.

Lough's rare, guarded smile touched his eyes and mouth. 'It's easy.' He gave her a mock salute and walked away.

Beccy caught her breath. 'It's easy,' she repeated. Suddenly 'Two Souls' had been replaced in her head by 'All you Need is Love'. Over and over again that four letter word repeated tunefully within her. She reeled back against the clambering roses, knowing that she really was very much in love. It was knowing who, exactly, she was in love with that troubled her.

Chapter 50

Sylva admired her latest *Cheers!* photo-spread. This week's issue was emblazoned with the lines 'Skinny Sylva Denies Anorexia Jibes – "I am just a healthy, campaigning and hard-working mum in search of true love" she tells *Cheers!* exclusively from her lovely Cotswolds retreat.' On the front cover was a heavily airbrushed photo of a coppery, fake-tanned Sylva beneath a fluffy baby blue Cossack hat, her arms around two small, fluffy-hatted boys and in front of her, for the first time, an exquisitely pretty girl in a pink Cossack hat on which Sylva was resting her chin. Inside were pages of her fake château shot from lots of flattering angles in the snow with Sylva and her kids tobogganing, playing snowballs and looking like a re-enactment of an Abba video.

Her cabbage water, green tea and vitamin tablet diet had gone rather too well and now she was in danger of emaciation. Barely even a size four, and now weighing just under seven stone, she knew she had to start eating soon. Her periods had long since stopped, her face was getting hairy and her breath was starting to smell of acetone. Any more punishment and her very expensive veneers would begin to fall out. Her sex drive had vanished, but that was no bad thing as her ambition to bed a pop star had also diminished. In fact, she hadn't eaten a full meal since Dillon had come to lunch all those weeks ago.

The *Cheers!* team had done a good job, however. She certainly looked incredibly slim, but despite the hollow cheeks, lollipop head and unnaturally tiny frame, a combination of clever styling and winter layers made her look more captivating than ever. The newly dark hair worked fantastically against winter whites and her trademark baby blue. Sylva was pleased with the results. Mama, however, was not.

'Dillon Rafferty should be in these pictures by now!' She threw the magazine back at Sylva when shown it.

Sylva sucked her teeth. 'I think he is not the right husband for me, Mama.' She'd found their play-date lunch wholly tedious. 'My campaign is a big success. The Rockfather has agreed to open all his paths and donated woodland to the local people. He has been so very generous.' She dared herself to say it. 'I think maybe we have chosen the wrong Rafferty?'

'Nonsense!' Mama was incensed, astounded that her daughter would dare question her judgement. 'The plan is perfect as it is. Saddle the horses, *mačička*. You will ride to the farm now. The villagers in Oddlode post office say Dillon's at home this weekend.'

'The horses have already gone out,' Sylva sighed, having long since handed over the reins of now pony-mad Zuzi's daily hack to a deputy.

Dillon had done nothing but drive his new scramble bike around his farmland for days on end.

He sped out of the orchard in a flurry of mud and zipped along the headland of the biggest pasture field towards the woods at the far edge of his boundary, where a gate accessed a neighbouring farm's overgrown water meadows. Taking the gravel track alongside the low-lying marshy wasteland, he headed up towards the public byway that led to the ridge.

Riding the bike made him feel better about the Nell situation, but it didn't make it go away. He was reliably informed through his loyal PA mafia that his publicity team was now gearing up to take control of their biggest artiste's love life. If Dillon slipped any further into an antisocial depression because his current relationship was well past being on the rocks and was now washed up, bloated and decomposing on the foreshore, they would step in like eco-warriors to replace it with a sunset scene. It was like being a panda in a zoo. If he dumped her, he knew he'd be prey to every publicity-hungry PR team with a matching mate. At least having Nell around gave him protection from that, even if he could hardly bear to be in the same room as her. This week, she'd taken herself off to Amsterdam to visit her ex, Milo. It was obvious she was trying to make Dillon jealous. He only wished he cared more.

He was sweating heavily under his leathers, which felt constricting and uncomfortable. Braking briefly, he unzipped the top half and pulled it down, the rugby shirt beneath clinging wetly to his arms and chest. He'd put on weight lately, a sure sign that he was unhappy. His record label was on his case to shift it, and shave off his winter beard, blaming his slipshod image for slipping sales. To show willing, Dillon had installed a range of state-of-the-art gym equipment in the newly converted milking parlours. Yet he hadn't even taken the plastic wrapping off the treadmill, bench press and weights, unlike the scramble bike that he put to work as soon as it came out of the delivery truck. Its angry engine was the perfect accompaniment to his thudding head as he sped around his farm and beyond, high above the valley. It was the closest thing to riding a horse that he had found, and he loved it.

He pushed the throttle as far as it would go, skidding and skittering over potholes and through puddles and he climbed the track, shooting around a dog-leg and then, far too late, seeing a woman and a child riding towards him.

The back wheel slid away and, despite the breakneck speed, in that strange, suspended snatch of time just before impact Dillon had time to spot his landing on stony ground, to curse the fact that he wasn't wearing a helmet and that his leathers were dangling around his waist, and to register that he definitely knew the woman and her child. Then he hit the ground at such speed that he started sliding, rolling and turning over like a rag doll toward a blur of horse legs.

The air was knocked from his already stinging body with an almighty punch as something landed on him. He heard hooves pounding away. The weight was still pressing down on him. His bike engine was ticking over nearby, its sedate 250cc putter strangely incongruous after such high drama.

Groggy but conscious, with a mouthful of mud and blood, he took a while to realise that the woman who had been riding had landed on top of him. She was now calling out at the girl in a foreign language, seemingly telling her to stay calm, that she was okay, that she would help her down. But she was tangled up in Dillon's loose leathers, one slim ankle having slipped into the armoured sleeve and jammed so that when she went to stand up, she collapsed back down on him.

'Ow!' he wailed. That hurt more than falling off the bike.

A little voice called out: '*No, mama. Je mu! Je to šlovek. Sylva je princ! On je princ!*'

Hooves were suddenly banging about close to Dillon's head again.

'No, Zuzi, no!' the woman cried.

He peered up in time to see a set of mud-splattered pony legs nearby and then, to his surprise, a little girl fell very gracefully from the saddle and landed in a heap alongside them, her pretty eyes fluttering shut with what he could almost have sworn was a giggle.

'Zuzi! Zuzi!' The woman was shrieking and crying out in panic, starting to flail about and inadvertently kicking Dillon in the kidneys and ribs.

'Woah, woah – steady on!' He quickly unzipped the waist of his leathers so that the jacket came free and she could scramble away to pull out her leg. Then, in a blur of flying dark hair and red Puffa jacket, she rushed to the girl, who opened her eyes and smiled. Gathering her into her arms, the woman burst into tears.

'Hana?' Dillon struggled upright, recognising Sylva's sister at last. She started spitting something incomprehensible at him in Slovak.

She had a nasty gash on her forehead and lip, he noticed, but landing on him seemed to have cushioned her from serious injury. Little Zuzi, meanwhile, was sitting up happily and watching her mother shout at Dillon with interest. She looked terribly pleased with herself for some reason.

Despite her recent protestations, Mama was secretly starting to harbour doubts about her marriage plans for Sylva. For all his soft cheese, Dillon Rafferty was a hard target. She had even begun to leaf through her Husbands file for alternative ideas.

But then, like a miracle, he appeared through her daughter's electric gates in a huge Land Rover with Hana and Zuzi bouncing around beside him as the car sped over the cattlegrid to park directly in front of Le Petit Château.

Mama hastily dragged Sylva away from executing fifty ab flexes with her personal trainer just as Hana marched in, covered in cuts and bruises, and brushed past them without a word, carrying Zuzi in her arms. The little girl, who was smiling widely, gave her aunt a big thumbs-up.

Mama thrust Sylva outside to corral Dillon.

'You must come in,' she offered half-heartedly, aware that she was covered in sweat, had no make-up on and was wearing an unflattering Lycra workout suit.

'I can't.' He backed off nervously. 'I'm due to pick up my daughters at Birmingham airport in an hour.'

'Even better!' Sylva responded to Mama's sharp prod from behind. 'Why not bring them here to play with Zuzi and the boys this week?'

'They all got on *so* well last time,' Mama droned behind her like an eager bumble bee.

'Sure, the girls would love to see Zuzi. But you must come to West Oddfield this time.' Dillon headed towards his car. 'They can all splash in the indoor pool. Bring the family – Hana, too. Just no cameras, okay?'

'Sure. Great!' Sylva waved him away casually.

Behind her, Mama waited until his car was out of sight before letting out an excited shriek and punching the air. 'Go upstairs and get out all your bikinis,' she ordered Sylva. 'We will choose something together.'

Sylva trailed upstairs, leaving Mama looking up to the sky and thanking the saints.

'You have done a very good thing,' she told Hana when she went back into the house. 'He will be your brother-in-law soon.'

Hana gaped at her. 'No! He is not at all right for *mačička*.'

'He *is*, and your opinion is not wanted on the subject. Now shoo.'

Hana shook her sore head as Mama bustled her away. Dillon was a very good man, but not the one to make their pretty kitten happy. She could hear the *boom-boom* of music upstairs in Sylva's dressing room, and then raised voices as mother and daughter argued about what she was going to wear to ensnare Dillon Rafferty. Hana was suddenly reminded of their family apartment in Bratislava; Mama and Sylva had been like this then, so close yet forever scrapping. And even the music had been the same – the band that her step-father had loved, with its sexy, grinding rock anthems and bad-boy reputation. Mask, she remembered. The band had been called Mask.

Nell retied the scarf around Giselle's neck and kissed her daughter on the nose, pointing out a windmill as their boat chugged from Volendam to Marken, an antiquated Dutch fishing village where, Milo promised, some of the inhabitants still wore traditional costume.

'We can even visit one of the few remaining cheese farms,' Milo told her.

'Oh please let's not,' she shuddered. 'No cheese.'

Milo laughed, putting his arm around her. But then, as Giselle ducked down to play with the little Dutch dolls that he had given her that morning, he lowered his voice and turned to Nell. 'You must end this silly affair.'

She took his gloved hand and felt to the hard band around his third finger through the leather. 'And if I do, will you leave your wife?'

'You know that won't happen.'

She stared murderously out at the grey sea. No matter how many times she had asked him that question over the years, he gave her the same answer.

'I will never stop loving you,' he offered truthfully.

'Love has no security.' She turned to look at Giselle, so full of sweetness, not twisted and spoiled by disappointment like her mother.

'Leave him,' Milo urged. 'He's made you so unhappy, my darling. He'll be losing the most beautiful girl in the world, but that's just his hard cheese.'

She nodded and let a small, sweet smile drift on to her lips. 'He'll be very cheesed off.'

'You'll have to go Caerphilly.'

She nodded. 'He probably Camembert it.'

They stole a long, giggling kiss while Giselle played at their feet.

Sylva knew that her chosen bikini was a sure-fire winner – baby blue and sheer with a halter neck that emphasised her magnificent chest and shapely shoulders, and tie-sided micro shorts that skimmed her buttocks at just the right height to tantalise with two peachy curves. The tiny triangle tops and Brazilian-cut tanga bottoms all stayed firmly in her drawer, vetoed as too unflattering while she was so thin, although she did lend some to Hana who didn't have a swim-suit. Hana stayed submerged to her chin at all times, mortified.

But nothing could look as silly as Mama's outsize bathing dress and bright pink flower-petal hat.

Sylva, who had allowed herself to start eating again and whose body was consequently zinging with energy, was still so svelte that she made everyone else look like goliaths, even the children with their puppy fat and round, happy faces.

Dillon, in baggy knee-length surf trunks and a fortnight's beard was far from the lean, buff, gym-fit star that had recorded the sexy 'Two Souls' video a year earlier, and today he had made no effort whatsoever, compared to the hours of work that had gone into getting Sylva ready for this casual family play-date. She'd waxed and bleached and epilated, she'd exfoliated and moisturised and fake-baked, she'd manicured and pedicured, wrapped and face-masked.

Sylva and Mama had planned the day like a military operation, well aware that this was their best and possibly only chance of a romantic coup. With Nell away visiting a friend, they had an open target.

Pom, Berry and Zuzi were having a ball, overseen by Hana, while two of the nanny army looked after the boys and Mama prepared to launch her floating offensive like huge pink war ship, cutting off Dillon and Sylva from vital supplies.

'Let's have a game of water polo!' Mama clapped her hands above her head, bingo wings flapping. 'The little ones, Bozka and Dalena will join me as one team, and Hana and the girls are the other team. Sylva and Dillon can find prizes for the winners and runners-up, and Bohemian champagne for us all.'

Nobody ever questioned Mama, such was her self-assured tyranny, and so a somewhat puzzled Dillon led Sylva along the glass-roofed corridor that ran through one side of the smallest kitchen garden and linked the pool complex to the main house.

'What plants are these?' She pointed to fruit trees trained to neatly espalier their budding branches along the old south-facing wall beside them.

'Apricots.'

'They must produce amazing fruits under glass like this.'

'Not bad, but you should see the old Victorian hothouses. They're something else. Cost a fortune to renovate, but it's like a tropical climate. We already have grapes ripening in there.'

Hearing Mama's imaginary cry of 'go' in her ears, Sylva knew that she had her cue.

'Show me!' she urged.

'We'd have to go outside.' He looked down at his wet trunks, paired with just the open shirt and Crocs he'd thrown on to walk to the house. She was still in only her bikini and white flip-flops. It was barely above freezing beyond the glass.

'Oh, let's go!' Sylva purred, her nipples already standing to attention at the thought of the cold air. 'That can be the water-polo prize – home-grown bunches of grapes. How perfect is that?'

She had him exactly where she and Mama wanted him: at home, relaxed and unaware that he was walking straight into a trap.

Unable to resist showing off his beloved hothouses, Dillon led her to an arched door in the old wall, slid the bolts and latch and warned 'Brace yourself!'

Whooping, they crossed the larger of the two walled gardens, racing along the pebbled tracks that divided raised beds, dug-over for winter and insulated under piles of rotting manure. Lashed by icy rain, they jumped down terraced steps two at a time, dived between scratchy, topiary box obelisks and finally made it to the door to the first of the two interconnecting hothouses occupying the garden's south wall.

Inside it was indeed sub-tropical, the thermometer on the wall reading over seventy. It was hotter than the pool complex.

Shelves groaned under the weight of orchids and other wintering exotics. Nectarines and lemons were starting to form absurdly early on branches against the walls beside them; above their heads, vines hung with fat grapes, already turning the deepest of reds. Sylva reached up, but was a good foot too short.

'Here – let me.' Without thinking, he put his hands around her and lifted her up like a ballet principal. She was as light as a feather. His fingers almost met around her tiny waist. But before he could settle her back down again, two slender legs slipped around his hips and gripped tightly as she plucked a grape and held it to his mouth.

Laughing, embarrassed, he ate it, expecting a sour burst of sharp acid in his mouth, but it was as sweet as Muscat and honey. She fed him another and he stepped backwards, off-balance until his shoulders found support against a peach tree trunk.

'You know I have a girlfriend.' He gave her a mock-critical look.

'And we both know that's as good as over.' She popped a grape in between her straight white teeth and fed it to him.

Up until that moment Dillon still would have struggled to say whether he fancied Sylva Frost or not. So much about her was anathema to him: her fakeness, her brassiness and vulgarity. But the moment those plump, glossy lips touched his, the sexual kick that rocketed through him at a voltage he hardly knew existed told him there was no going back.

She was breathtakingly adept. Like a very carnal monkey, she took hold of a peach tree branch, braced her feet against the wall and, a weightless shaft of golden muscle and glossy skin, reached down to loosen his trunks.

Afterwards, Dillon wished that the shame of knowing his staff were so close by, along with her family and any number of people that could have stumbled upon them had not heightened the excitement, but that would have been lying. The thrill of being at home, surrounded by all that was familiar yet having this new, exquisite woman lowering her beautiful body against his and slotting his cock into the sweetest, wettest, most skilful pink booty it had ever plundered was almost overwhelming. He felt like Adam being seduced by Eve. It seemed utterly right, and the liberation it granted coursed through him as he climaxed.

Sylva couldn't keep the smile off her face when she and Dillon finally made it back to the pool laden with grapes and bottles of the sweet Bohemian champagne her mother loved so much that she'd brought her own case along today.

Mama was still bobbing about in the pool, which surprised her. And surely there hadn't been that many children before? Not of all those different colours; it was like a Benetton advert. Some of them were frighteningly familiar, along with the oriental man in the handmade suit perching on a sunlounger, manicured fingertips steepled against his nose as he scrutinised Sylva. And Mama, purple in the face, was giving out distress signals. It seemed they had unexpected company:

Beside her, Dillon let out a groan. 'Oh shit – it's Dad.'

Sylva's heart revved.

'There you bloody are, you little rascal!' hailed a gravelly voice of such achingly familiar depth and timbre that it could have been whooping over the sound system at the start of a live concert recording.

Cigar poking from his mouth, face wizened as a date but still sexy as a demi-god, with the towering blank-faced Indigo beside him, the Rockfather had come to visit his son for only the second time since his relocation. 'Dillon, my boy!' He swaggered forward to give his heir apparent a double handshake and look approvingly at Sylva in her bikini. 'How come every time I call by, you're squiring a piece of top skirt, huh?'

'Dad, the kids!' Dillon hissed, but his father waved away the warning and held out his hand to Sylva. 'No need to introduce yourself, Trouble. I should be calling my lawyers, by rights, but you are far too gorgeous. Wow.' As a mark of his respect he lowered his dark glasses for only the second time in almost a decade to look at a woman more closely, the last time having been Indigo on their wedding day. 'You. Are. Choice. The pictures don't do you justice.'

Sylva smirked and offered him a grape, surprised to find that, even compared to the ecstatic shiver that had coursed through her when finally claiming Dillon, the charge that was shooting lightning bolts to her nerve endings now was immeasurable. The Rockfather was just *so* sexy. She cast a guilty look towards her children and then Indigo, but that smooth bronze face was giving nothing away.

Mama, meanwhile, was as wrinkled as the Rockfather from spending so much time in the geyser-hot swimming pool. A lifelong Mask and Pete Rafferty fan, she was quite gunned down by humiliation to find that the amazing opportunity to meet her hero was presented to her when she was wearing a pink bathing dress that revealed her sagging, blotchy body in all its decrepitude.

Hana, in her Brazilian bikini, was by the far pool ladder, loyally holding out the largest towel that she could find, her mother's vast satin kimono over one shoulder in readiness, but Mama was too embarrassed to admit that she couldn't actually climb the ladder and would need to wade out up the tiled steps at the shallow end.

Sylva took in the situation in an instant. As quick as a lifeguard spotting a drowning child, she appropriated the towel and robe and guided her mother from the depths with minimal cellulite, saggy bum and bingo wing flashing.

'I got him, Mama,' she whispered as she wrapped her up.

Mama's chlorine-reddened eyes sparkled beneath her dahlia in bloom swim cap. 'We must secure an invitation to the Abbey straight away,' she hissed. 'That way, he will see you as family.'

Sylva was thrilled at the challenge. It was her easiest yet. She and Pete had a lot in common, after all, and she knew the way to his door only too well. The Rockfather, meanwhile, wanted Sylva in his lair as fast as he could get her there.

'You beat a public path to my door!' he rasped huskily, 'and now my private quarters are all yours.' Then, aware that his wife was shooting him daggers, he raised his voice: 'Bring the kiddies up to play with . . . ours.' He always struggled with the notion he had paternity over the many children Indigo had acquired while he'd been away touring, much as she went out shopping for handbags and shoes. 'I should get to know my granddaughters better, hey girls?' he called to Pom and Zuzi, who burst out giggling while Berry scowled behind a sunlounger. 'I love kiddies.'

For a moment, the whites of Indigo's eyes flashed luminous with distrust, but then she reset the mask.

She stepped close beside Sylva who was pouring frothy wine into champagne flutes. 'You want father or son?' she whispered.

Sylva looked up sharply. 'Is holy ghost not an option?'

Indigo's mouth pouted into an oval.

Sylva looked at Mama, so puffed up with pride. 'I want the son, of course,' she lied. 'But how?'

'Watch me.' Indigo melted away.

Two days later, with Mama dressed in bright orange Anna Sholtz crepe, a mohair wrap, patent boots and trilby, a get-up that she fantasised would make the Rockfather throw his skinny young model wife into the nearest skip and claim her as his own, the Szubiaks and Raffertys joined forces beneath the portico of Fox Oddfield Abbey, where two grand, zig-zagging stone staircases met in front of its imposing black gloss and glass Regency double doors. The eighteenth-century Rock Palace, freshly sand-blasted and re-pointed, looked as though it had only been built a week ago.

Dillon and Sylva had only spoken once since their hothouse play-date, and that was for the steamiest, dirtiest phone sex he could ever remember. But after he had hung up he'd thought guiltily of Nell, still in Amsterdam and blissfully unaware of events in Oddlode.

To Sylva it had been an unsatisfactory call, even though she'd made it in the first place. Mama had been breathing down her neck throughout, eager to find out whether he had ditched Nell, and Sylva had rung off none the wiser.

But today, as soon as they saw Pete swagger towards them waving a chastising finger, they were left in no doubt where the relationship was going.

'You two lovebirds didn't tell the father of the groom the good news!' he tutted, kissing them both, his lips lingering on Sylva's ear and cheek long enough to breathe, 'Not too late to change your mind, Trouble.'

'What are you talking about, Dad?' Dillon demanded, but Pete ignored him, playing mine host with theatrical aplomb.

'The difficulty with having famous kids,' he told Mama now as he steered her into his house with the cigar that was wedged between his fingertips smouldering at her shoulder, quietly burning holes in her mohair wrap, 'is that the only way you find out what they're up to is by reading it in the papers.' He had champagne already poured into flutes on a long, polished oak side table in the Abbey's marble-flagged entrance hall. He handed a glass to a positively skittish Mama, and reached for one brimming with orange juice to raise himself. 'Congratulations, you two. My PR rang just now to tell me the *Star* has already been in touch saying you're going to do it here, which is news to me, but you'd be most welcome for a modest, ahem, fee.'

Dillon looked at him questioningly. On cue his mobile rang. They could all hear Nell squawking in the background. 'Bullshit, we are!' he finally got a word in. 'No, that's tosh! I haven't called because you're in Amsterdam with Milo. Yes, I know he's a friend, and Sylva's a mate of mine. You know our kids all get on. Who called you? *They said what?*' He strode away from earshot, his voice start-ing to hiss urgently.

'What is this all about?' Sylva asked Pete as the children were all ushered upstairs by the nanny army.

'My son's posh totty's just heard you two are getting married,' he said cheerfully.

'We're *what*?'

The faded blue eyes held hers for a lengthy pause. 'It's all over the internet, according to my PR, and it'll be in all the papers tomorrow, darling. You and Dillon getting hitched.' He gave her body a lingering look. 'And I, for one, can't wait to kiss the bride.'

Now it was Sylva's phone's turn to ring, shortly followed by Mama's, Pete's, Indigo's and even two of the nannies'.

Only Hana, at the top of the stairs, had no phone call, allowing her to hastily shush Pom, Berry and Zuzi away from the shouting match that was suddenly firing up below.

For a moment Dillon glanced up at her, his blue eyes in turmoil. Hana managed a brief, reassuring smile and placed her hands on his daughters' blonde heads, nodding at him to let him know they were in her care. He nodded back, then turned to the babbling, blustering family.

Before he could open his mouth his phone rang out again. 'Tania – thank God! Why didn't we know about this earlier?'

On the opposite side of the vast entrance hall Sylva finished her call and turned to Mama. 'The paparazzi have been all over the Amersham house since dawn. Now they've just turned up at Le Petit Château, so Pauline says not to go back there until she's sent more cars here as decoys.'

'Where did they get this crazy story from?' Mama was delighted.

Beside them Pete cackled, making Mama jump and Sylva quiver.

'No smoke without fire,' he said hoarsely, proving his point by puffing on his cigar and winking at Sylva like Lucifer in a plume of sulphur.

Helping himself to more orange juice, he wandered out on to his grand front steps to breathe in an exquisite frosty morning and admire the Ferraris in his drive, so shiny and red against the snowdrops and frost.

'The press linked me with Madonna once,' he told Mama, who had followed him out like an eager pitbull. 'One rag even said we was getting married, although she's just a mate of my daughter, Kat, who designs shoes for her tours. We're way too old for each other, of course – her toy boys' and my ex-wives' combined ages wouldn't add up to one of our birthdays – but the publicity was a boost.'

Inside the house, Dillon was finding the situation far less amusing as he cut his call. 'The papers are determined to run with this, whatever we say. Apparently the source of the story came from within the family – so close that they say it's beyond refute – but of course nobody's naming names.' He glared through the doors to Mama, who was now puffing girlishly on Pete's cigar.

Sylva meanwhile looked sharply across at Indigo. She gave a ghost of a wink in return.

'We have to issue an immediate statement making it clear that this is a total fabrication,' Dillon was saying in urgent tones.

'Stay calm,' Sylva soothed.

'We have our children to protect here, our families and loved ones.'

His phone rang again. This time it was Fawn, considerably cooler than Nell had been, but nonetheless furious to have been awoken at dawn on set in Quebec with news that her ex-husband's engagement had been announced while their children were staying with him.

'Why wasn't I told?' she asked now. 'We need to break these things to them gently, not spring it. They're just little kids and they still dream that Mom and Dad are gonna get back together. This could seriously damage them. I mean, do they even *know* her?'

'No,' he admitted hoarsely, 'and neither do I.' He promised to sort it out, but had no idea how.

Sylva called legendary PR guru Clive Maxwell, who she only hired in for big gigs, like her break-ups with Strawberry and Jonte, her rumoured affair with a married racing driver and Jules's recent lesbian kiss and tell.

'It's all cool,' she told Dillon after she had spoken with Clive at length. 'He says let the papers have their fun, keep a very dignified distance with no interviews or photo calls, issue a simple statement that there's no truth to the current marriage rumours and leave it at that.'

'That's all?'

She nodded. 'He also wanted to know whether there *is* a relationship here.'

He flashed a big white smile, but nervously, like a weapon. 'And is there?'

'I reckon so.' Checking nobody could see, she reached between his legs and cupped his groin, her thumb stroking his cock through his jeans, feeling his balls tighten above her fingers.

Both their assets were rising, she realised happily. The publicity was going to be superb. She was IFOP for the foreseeable future.

'What did Nell say?' she asked.

'That I can go hang. It's over.'

Sylva had the tact to look contrite as Dillon headed upstairs to see his girls, knowing that he had just swapped a relationship that looked so good on paper for one that looked good *in* the papers, but both of which weren't worth the paper they were written on.

Later, Sylva abandoned Mama to a guided tour of the renovations from Indigo and joined Pete on the front steps, where he seemed to be taking up permanent residence.

'Like my pretty cars?'

She did. Ferraris had always turned her on.

'I'd offer to take you for a spin, but your fiancé might get jealous – knows his old Dad's a terrible roué.' Pete tilted his head and contemplated the giant cedar just beyond his cars, as big as a cooling tower, which he was pondering turning into a totem pole with the faces of Mask's late, great band members carved into it.

Sylva watched him, loving the vigour in his battered face. 'You like it standing out here, admiring your parkland?'

'Prefer Wandsworth Common.' He sighed, turning his back to lean against the palisade wall and look up at his house's façade. 'Pretty gaff, this, I'll grant you, but I only bought it to be closer to the lad. I prefer Ireland. That's my spiritual home. Dillon's mum did it up lovely there. I won't let Ind touch it with her animal prints and raffia crap.' He jerked his head towards the Abbey's doors. 'Have you seen it in there? It's like a scene from *Zulu*.'

Sylva suddenly understood why he preferred standing outside, and why he so rarely stayed here. The Abbey was Indigo's pet project. It was her fantasy and his nightmare.

'Tell you the truth,' – he drained his glass – 'I only asked you up here today to try to get in your pants, but I reckon you and Dillon are more serious than I realised so I'll lay off. I always used to nick his girlfriends when he was a kid and it drove him mad. They were underage then, of course, not all grown up and gorgeous like you, Trouble.'

'Don't call me that.' She looked up through her eyelashes at him, deciding that she would very much like him to try to get in her pants. If only she had known that all those weeks of campaigning against his bullying landowner tactics could have been resolved so pleasurably and quickly with one face to face meeting.

'I was never much cop at school,' he admitted as they looked up at his beautiful house, 'but I do know when something spells trouble.'

Following his gaze, Sylva saw that there was an inscription carved into the stonework above the door. It appeared to be in Latin.

'And what does that spell?'

'Some crap Indigo thought up,' he shrugged, and then chuckled. 'Probably "divorce me and I'll keep your balls as earrings".'

Things were definitely on the rocks in the Rafferty marriage, Sylva deduced excitedly.

She looked across at him and, to her fear and surprise, felt her stomach drop and flutter, her heart swell in her chest and her clitoris thrum. She couldn't remember desiring anybody this much in years, this gloriously preserved rock fossil who had survived against the odds both professionally and medically, who was famously impulsive, forgetful and womanising. She fancied him rotten.

Looking back at her levelly, his wise, craggy face so famous yet exclusively his, the eyes incredibly similar to Dillon's but more hooded and bloodshot and carnal; the testosterone-loaded smile not nearly so white and straight but ten times more gut-kicking, he ran a surprisingly pink, healthy-looking tongue along those famous teeth.

'Good job you're not still blonde,' he said, rasping voice seeming to stroke all her nerve endings.

'Why's that?'

'Never could resist a blonde.' He flashed his ladykiller smile again. 'But I've had to give them up now, like the booze. The wife doesn't trust me around either.'

Looking into his eyes, Sylva found herself wishing with all her heart that she was still blonde.

He returned her gaze and let out a long, regretful sigh. 'Fuck.'

The electric charge between them could have powered every light in the house.

'Fuck,' she agreed, walking away before she did something she might regret, her heels echoing through the hallways as she fled in search of Mama and rescue.

★

Indigo pounced on Sylva from behind a life-size carving of a water buffalo on the landing. It took Sylva all her powers not to scream.

'What have you done with Mama?' she asked nervously.

'She's trying out Pete's massage chair.' Indigo slid her arm through Sylva's. 'I have someone very special for you to meet.'

The expensively suited oriental man that Sylva had previously seen with Indigo was sitting at one end of the huge nursery, occupying a vast throne that appeared to be made out of animal bones. At the opposite end of the room the children were playing with Hana and the nanny army.

'Dong is my resident child psychologist,' Indigo told Sylva, introducing her to the diminutive Chinese-American.

Not taking his eyes from the children, Dong held up a hand to Sylva with almost papal grace and for a moment she wondered whether she was supposed to kiss it.

'A child psychologist?' She shook the limp hand suspiciously. She had a great many nannies and assistants, a personal stylist, trainer and driver, but this was a new one on her.

'Dong is responsible for the mental nutrition of all my children,' Indigo said coolly.

Sylva looked from Dong to the children. Indigo's huge brood were shrieking with delight along with Pom, Berry and her own kids as they splatted organically sourced food dye paint hand-prints on a huge canvas laid out across the floor. 'I take it you don't like getting your hands dirty?'

'My role is to observe, not interact,' he told her in a measured Californian drawl.

'And what do you observe right now?' Sylva asked as Kor and Hain spotted their mother and charged up to her and wrapped their arms around her legs.

Dong looked up, hooded eyes taking a long time to profile her face and body.

'That you are perfect.' He turned to Indigo and they exchanged warm smiles. 'Quite, quite perfect.'

The Rockfather was having quite a sociable time on his front steps. No sooner had Sylva departed than his son joined him, limping backwards and forwards as he smoked a rare cigarette.

505

'What do I do, Dad? Nell's in bits. I like Sylva, but this is way too fast-track.'

'Chill out, kid. She's a great-looking bird. Your kids get on. So what's the problem? Go with the flow. The story will blow over.'

Dillon flicked away the barely puffed Marlboro that he'd bummed off one of Sylva's bodyguards. 'I have a bad feeling about this.'

'So do I, but it's probably just the gout.' Pete sighed, kicking out his stiff leg to get the bloodflow going again and then patting his son on the back. 'If you really want her off your hands, there could be a vacancy coming up here quite soon.'

'Don't even *go* there.' Dillon looked murderous.

'Joke,' Pete laughed, holding up his hands. Having tested the water and found it boiling he was happy to let it cool a bit. He put his arm around his boy, admiring his Ferrari again for comfort. 'Now tell me what you've heard from Kat lately. You know she just texts me once a month, saying *"still alive"*. I thought she was refer-ring to herself until she started adding a question mark. Bloody cheek!'

In a hotel suite in Amsterdam, Nell blew her nose, composed her-self and phoned Milo at his office. 'It's over with Dillon.'

His monotone response was as businesslike as ever. 'Good. I'll buy you and Gigi lunch at Envy.'

'I'd rather you bought me a flat in London,' she said petulantly.

'You need to learn to stand on your feet, my darling girl.'

Nell was livid. 'That's not what you said when my legs were around your neck.'

Not long ago, when she found out that she was pregnant with Giselle and seriously contemplating marrying Magnus, the father, Milo had offered her a serviced apartment opposite Green Park. But the recession had hit since then, and he played his assets more cau-tiously these days.

'Meet me half way.'

'I will. You just watch me: I can go Dutch!' She hung up and immediately set about finding the number of a good publicity agent. She knew that Sylva used Clive Maxwell, so she chose his arch rival Piers Fox. A vague friend of the family – he'd even asked her on a date years ago – he was more than delighted to receive her call.

'Of course I can help,' he assured her in his cougar-smooth growl. 'Let's meet for a quiet dinner to talk about it.'

'I'm in Amsterdam.'

'I'll phone my pilot. I can be at your hotel by eight.'

'I have my little girl with me.'

'Book a listening service.'

Nell was impressed, and remembered that Piers had an incredibly attractive aura, even if he was six inches shorter than her and extremely ginger. It was, at least, an encouraging start. She had no intention of standing on her own two feet when lying back and letting a man take the strain on his elbows was so much easier.

On cue, Milo texted her. *When I said meet me half way, I meant an apartment in Paris.*

Nell smiled and looked at Giselle napping on her hotel bed, a tiny perfect doll on a huge raft of white linen. She had both their futures to think about. Milo would never leave his wife. Piers Fox, as far as she was aware, was between marriages.

I'll think about it. Je t'aime, she texted back, settling back beside her daughter on the bed. Even though Giselle was sleeping, she decided to tell her a story.

'Once upon a time there was a fox and a crow,' Nell whispered. 'The crow found a fantastically tasty piece of cheese and flew into a tree to keep it safe from the greedy fox. But that fox was very cunning . . .'

Chapter 51

March's blustery weather brought out flocks of cumulus that raced across the sky so that the bright sunlight was switched on and off in perpetual camera flashes, lighting up the Berkshire Downs, urging the sleeping landscape to pose and preen after its long winter hibernation, and to bring its jewellery out to adorn throats and wrists. The snowdrops and crocuses that lined the village rides were soon joined by daffodils and tulips; wild primroses clumped in the wilder verges at the base of the downs; the woods burst with rising sap and waking wildlife bent on flirtation.

All the Haydown team were working flat out as the eventing season kicked off. Tash and Lough had started taking horses out two or three times a week to dressage and show-jumping competitions along with the early trials. They also loaded the lorry at least once a week to head for the all-weather gallops for really fast work and more concentrated interval training for the more advanced horses. Lovebirds Lemon and Beccy stayed behind and worked with the horses at home, supervised by the ever-trusty Jenny, who had returned from the States a week ahead of the others to help where she was most needed.

'I'll miss her,' Tash confessed to Lough as they set out for a competition in Hampshire. 'She's getting married in June. I should start advertising her position soon, but Hugo's old head groom Franny emailed this week saying she wants to come back. I need to talk to him about it when he gets home.'

Lough wasn't listening. He was watching the way her mouth moved. It was just beautiful, those small teeth and the exquisite curve of her upper lip with its distinctive bow and sharp incline to her nose.

She crashed through the gears trying to find second as they slowed for the Fosbourne Ducis turn. 'Hugo hates me doing that. He won't let me drive the HGV unless it's an emergency. I've got my operator's licence, but I'm frankly crap.'

She was so excited about Hugo's imminent return that she unwittingly mentioned him in every other sentence. Lough felt every reference like a knife in his chest.

Sitting between them, Beetroot gave Lough a long-suffering look. Not long afterwards, she and Lough fell off the seat when Tash swung the lorry too sharply into the competition venue's gateway. In the back, there was a lurching and stamping of hooves and a few furious whinnies.

Tash's appalling nerves were holding her completely to ransom now that she was out competing again. By the time she had parked up, been to the secretary's box and walked the course, she was too frozen with fear to think straight.

'Just imagine you're at home, doing it for fun – no pressure,' Lough calmed her. 'Don't get distracted.'

Tash tried to draw on her reserves and focus on his voice as she did at Haydown, but there were too many familiar faces wanting to catch up with her, questions about how Hugo was faring in the States, people crowding around angling for an introduction to Lough.

The Moncrieffs were out in force, fielding a horsebox full of contenders including Faith on Rory's old elite horse, White Lies. Unlike Tash, she was so focused on the task ahead that she was ignoring everybody around her, determined to post a good score by Rory's return. The only time she became distracted, for just a moment, was when she overheard Penny asking Tash when Hugo and Rory were flying home.

'Two days,' she spouted happily. 'I've spent the last week eating nothing but cabbage soup – Sylva Frost always swears by it.' Since Tash had started riding so many horses each day, the baby weight was dropping off and she couldn't wait for Hugo to see the changes.

'Ah, young love.' Penny sighed. 'If Gus goes overseas I change the locks and get out the Ben & Jerrys.'

Lough rode up hurriedly, having just come out of the dressage arena. 'Tash! They're calling your number. You have two minutes or you'll be disqualified.'

'Oh God.' The nerves seized her, along with blind panic because she must have misread the start times and the horse wasn't worked in properly.

She rode so defensively that both her horses failed to get close to the placings, although she was just grateful that she hadn't fallen off.

'You'll do better next time,' Lough told her as she drove them home. He was in a black mood despite winning prize money on his rides.

'I'm sorry I let you down.' She chewed her lip guiltily, knowing that he'd sacrificed a great deal of time to work with her and her horses in recent weeks, and so far all her competition results had been dismal. Hugo was bound to be disappointed.

When they returned to Haydown at dusk with aching muscles, Beccy and Lemon helped them unload in a high state of animation.

'Nell Cottrell's done a kiss and tell on Dillon Rafferty in the papers!' Beccy waved the *Mail on Sunday* in front of Tash as she was unloading batty Lauren Bacall, making the horse pull back and almost wrench her arm from its socket. 'She says that Sylva Frost will basically shag anything that moves, including . . . wait for it . . . Rory! His photo's in here. *And* you and Hugo get a mention.'

'Oh Christ, he'll go mad.' Tash took the paper, but their names were merely listed as part of the eventing elite with whom Dillon and Sylva now socialised, and had contributed to their love affair.

She tried to visualise this inner circle, but if she and Sylva were to be depicted in a Venn diagram these days, they'd occupy two separate circles. Sylva had quite lost interest in her since New Year, despite a few tentative phone messages from Tash, including a request for her cabbage soup recipe. She felt quite hurt, but consoled herself with the notion that Sylva was the sort of friend who called ten times a day when she was bored and never at all if she was busy, as she clearly was now.

Once the horses were settled, Beccy and Lemon mucked out the lorry while she and Lough cleaned their competition bridles in the huge tack room, the wood-burner glowing away in the corner.

'Lem and Beccy make an odd couple don't you think?' she asked idly.

'Not for me to say.'

'But they're lovers now, don't you think?'

'No fucking idea,' he said brusquely, uncomfortable with the topic.

'I always assumed he was gay.'

She looked at him questioningly, but Lough didn't reply, making Tash jumpy given all the bad things she already knew about Lemon. If Lough wouldn't be drawn on the subject, it didn't bode well. She was worried about Beccy.

'Surely you two talk sometimes?'

'Only about the horses. Don't you talk to your sister?'

'Not a lot,' she admitted. 'She's a complicated character.' She dropped her voice in case Beccy came in and realised she was being talked about. 'She's had a tough time in the past few years.'

Lough watched Tash clean a saddle, turning it this way and that to cover each curving surface with a damp, soapy cloth.

'Beccy's grown a lot calmer since she's been here,' Tash went on. 'I think this place is good for her.'

Lough said nothing, watching silently as Tash gripped the saddle between her thighs like a cello and rubbed saddle soap into the panels, long neck bent as her head lowered in concentration, hair falling into her eyes. It was so unintentionally erotic, he was spell-bound.

'Lem had better look after her,' she said, looking up.

'It's her life,' he muttered.

'Hugo will disapprove.'

He looked away.

'He hates relationships on the yard. He says they get in the way of horsemanship.'

'You two should divorce then.'

'Not *us*.' She dropped her sponge back in the soap tub and glanced at her watch. 'I must take over the children's bath time.' She stood up to leave. 'Do you want supper later?'

Lough looked up in surprise. 'Cabbage soup?'

It was over a week since they'd eaten together because Tash had been on her crash diet. She looked sensational, her cheekbones heightened in her face, her waist more defined in that long, languid body, but Lough preferred sharing her table to admiring her from a distance any day. His spirits lifted like hot ash at the thought of one last meal together.

But then she ruined it. 'I'm trying out a sea bass recipe I want to cook for Hugo the night he gets home. I thought I'd invite Beccy and Lemon too. We can see if I'm right about them.'

'I said I'd meet Faith for a drink at the Olive Branch.'

Tash nodded, surprised to find herself feeling jealous. She'd wanted to make amends for letting him down today, and for being such lousy company recently. She had used the excuse of her cabbage soup diet to keep him away all week, but she knew a lot of it was fear. Lough's intensity frightened her, along with the life he had left behind in New Zealand. She badly wanted to talk to Hugo about it. Now that he was almost home, she felt more confident that Lough would fit in and prosper at Haydown, and she told herself that she mustn't resent him having his own social life.

'Faith is lovely,' she said encouragingly, heading for the door. 'Enjoy your date.'

He said nothing.

That evening, blown out not only by Lough, but also by Beccy and Lemon who had gone to the Basingford multiplex together, Tash put the sea bass in the freezer and decided to give the diet another day. Feeling virtuously slim, she tried on clothes to select something to welcome Hugo home in, starting with the most important layer.

But all the sexily supportive, figure enhancing underwear that she had bought before Christmas no longer fitted, her figure so altered by increased fitness and decreased comfort eating that she looked silly in the vast lacy pants and bras that bagged around her now-modest boobs like tropical butterfly nets capturing two humble cabbage whites. No longer breastfeeding, her belly almost completely flat and her buttock cheeks as hard as bowling balls from so many hours in the saddle, she had no need of control lingerie. Yet her laundry-faded pre-pregnancy Sloggi knickers and sports bras were far less appealing.

She stood naked in front of the mirror, trying to remember what she had done with the basque and suspender set that she'd worn beneath her wedding dress. Hugo had loved it, but she hadn't worn it since.

'Seven years,' she said out loud, brought up short by the realisation that so much time had passed.

The months and years had seemed to accelerate once the children had arrived, propelling her through life almost too fast to keep count. Amery was six months old now, yet it seemed a moment ago that she was carrying the floppy, toasty little newborn around on her collarbone like a fat little brooch.

She stared at her naked reflection, amazed her body had recovered from so much trauma, although she had her scar and a few tell-tale stretch marks just above her hips, already fading from red to silver.

She still recalled pointing out her mother's stretch marks for the first time, on holiday at the age of about ten and asking her what they were, to which Alexandra had barely lifted her head from her sunlounger to say: 'They're baby brushstrokes, painted there to remind me how lucky I am to have my three beautiful children.'

Suddenly Tash hit upon an idea. She could add to the baby brushstrokes. Hugo would love it, and it was far more personal than badly fitting underwear or elaborate sea bass. She could practise tonight.

Lough only stayed for one drink in the Olive Branch, though Faith was at least a brooding, malcontent ally.

He felt bad that he'd done so little to follow up his promise to Rory to look out for her, although he always got the impression that she was the ultimate self-preservationist.

She was muttering furiously about Nell Cottrell's *Mail* exposé: 'Rory and Sylva were hardly secret lovers; Sylva used him for sex. He gets that a lot: women exploit him'. She also grumbled about Lemon and Beccy: 'They're so horribly loved up, have you noticed? He calls her Limey. "Lemon and Limey", I ask you! Ugh!'

So Tash had been right. He hadn't even noticed. He wished that he was eating with her now in the vast, messy Haydown kitchen. But he knew he had to immunise himself against Hugo returning to take over, a plague that would sweep through the yard and take control, wiping him out if he wasn't prepared.

Faith was talking about her plans for the season. The Moncrieffs obviously worked her far harder than she had at Haydown, but gave her more direction and guidance to compensate, with daily lessons, lots of outings and a competition plan for White Lies.

'He's a bit of a crock and he's been off the circuit for a few years, but he was four-star in his heyday so Gus thinks he'll enjoy it. Whitey's nothing to Rio's raw talent, of course, but he's safe and steady.'

'Tell me, why d'you let Rory ride that stallion of yours while you struggle with his cast-offs?' Lough asked.

She looked at him levelly. 'Unrequited love. Go figure. It's the pits.'

He watched her closely, but she then reached out and dug him jovially in the ribs.

'I do it because Rory rides better than me,' she laughed. 'And he's got Hugo's Mogo sponsorship deal covering him, which picks up the biggest tabs.'

Lough thought Rory was unbelievably spoiled, his silver spoon still poking out of his mouth. If he was dreading Hugo coming back, the added weight of Rory reappearing – and sharing his little safe house once more – demoralised him utterly.

But Faith was clearly as excited as Tash about the Haydown duo's imminent return, still chattering about Rory's talent as she stomped outside with him to say goodbye, pulling a woolly hat over her head and pausing to admire the old Yamaha Bandit he'd picked up cheap at auction.

'Gus has just bought himself a motorbike too,' she told him. 'Bright green thing. He says it's his mid-life crisis, but Penny says he had one of those years ago and she calls the bike AWH. Gus thought that was really cool until she explained it stood for Accident Waiting to Happen. They are funny. Thanks for the drink.' She clambered on to her modest bicycle and pedalled back to Lime Tree Farm.

Lough sliced through the lanes, wishing he had some of Faith Brakespear's self belief.

When Lough came in through Haydown's electric gates, the Roadies snarled and snapped at his tyres as usual, thinking he was planning to make off with all the tack and red diesel.

All the downstairs lights in the main house glowed welcomingly, and his stomach let out a longing rumble.

It wasn't yet nine. He could just put his head round the door and pass on the Lemon and Limey comment, which wasn't his style at all, but was the only reason he could come up with for seeing Tash.

The kitchen was deserted, the Bitches of Eastwick crowded on the sofa as usual, the Rat Pack clawing and grinning at his legs.

Lough wandered along the back lobby, stooping to stroke Beetroot who walked into him lovingly from the direction of the study, where Tash camped out at all times when she was in the house and the children were asleep, painting and doing paperwork, checking online scoreboards if Hugo was competing abroad.

He pushed the door.

She was totally naked, her back to him, focused upon her reflection in an old gilt-framed mirror propped up on a chair. She was painting with such absorption that she didn't realise he was there. It was the most amazing canvas he'd ever seen.

Her torso was covered with intricate swirls, flowers, horses and wildlife, painted with incredible lightness and delicacy. They reminded him of the most beautiful Maori tā moko work.

For a long time he risked detection, unable to drag his guilty eyes away, so torn apart by love and longing that his heart felt ready to rip itself out of his chest.

The radio was on – a digital channel playing some sort of back-to-back bluesy folk. He recognised the song but not the artist. 'Fields of Gold'. The voice was smoky and rich, laced with life and love and regret.

Lough backed reluctantly away, stealing through the house and out into the night where yet another spring frost lit by a full moon was turning the gardens, parkland and home paddocks into fields of silver.

Chapter 52

While Jenny was dispatched in the horsebox to Heathrow Animal Centre to collect the horses that had just flown back from the States, Beccy was allotted the task of meeting the passenger flight later that evening.

'You'd think Tash would go herself,' she grumbled to Faith, who had hacked up from Lime Tree Farm to see if they were back yet, only to find Beccy bad-temperedly clearing out the tiny boot of her car. 'I'd be desperate to see Hugo after all those weeks apart.' She hid her blushes in frantic tidying.

Faith was light-headed with anticipation, knowing that however much she kept reminding herself she must play it cool and not crowd Rory, fate had intervened. She couldn't let Beccy be sent as a taxi service to Hugo after the New Year's Eve encounter. It would be cruel.

'I'll meet the flight if you like,' she offered as casually as she could.

'Would you?' Beccy looked relieved. 'Lem and I want to see the new Percy Jackson film tonight.' Then she cast a look at her watch. 'You'll have to get a move on, though. The flight lands at five.'

Faith cantered all the way back along the cross-country route to Lime Tree Farm to fetch her own car, jumping hedges and ditches, grateful that Whitey was so trustworthy and easy to handle, unlike his master.

She wished she could tart herself up, but by the time she had washed off Whitey, skipped out her charges, made up haynets and feeds, and persuaded Gus to let her finish an hour early, she could do no more than clean her teeth and cram in her chicken fillets.

As it was, she was almost an hour late, and Hugo and Rory were waiting in the arrivals hall, as fantastically lean and bronze as two adventurers after a far-flung expedition. Both were surprised to find

Faith welcoming them home in muddy breeches, hay poking from her frizzy hair and a strong horse pong drawing sideways glances from the private-hire drivers around her, some of whom discreetly lifted their name boards over their noses.

'Where's Tash?' asked Hugo, striding forwards first.

'Waiting at home,' Faith told him. 'She said something about the children being in bed? I volunteered.' She was trying not to stare too conspicuously at Rory.

He'd arrived back in the UK like an avenging angel to unrequited love, far more intimidating that she had anticipated. He seemed suddenly very grown up, and for the first time she felt the ten-year age gap between them. He seemed gratifyingly pleased to see her and kissed her sweetly on the cheek, making it sting with longing. Then he thrust a bag of Duty Free scent at her, which was generous, but made her feel like he was making some sort of point about her lack of femininity.

Hugo was certainly not pleased by Tash's non-appearance, and his black mood worsened when he found himself crammed in the back of a bright yellow Volkswagen that reeked of perfume, and sharing the seat with a dementedly excited Jack Russell.

'You brought Twitch!' Rory was close to tears, which would have pleased Faith had it not been for the fact he'd greeted her with such comparative cool. She realised sadly that he meant she rated lower than the dog.

As they drove through the Heathrow underpass towards the M4, Hugo closed his eyes on the back seat and feigned sleep. He felt profoundly hurt that Tash hadn't come to collect him. What's more, Rory was suddenly behaving very oddly indeed.

Faith had imagined this drive home all afternoon, rehearsing all the things she would tell Rory about life at Lime Tree Farm, Whitey, the start to the season – and planning all the questions she would ask him about Florida, the lecture tour, the competition and training.

Instead her tongue was tightly knotted and there was an awkward silence as she digested the fact that there was something totally different about Rory. It wasn't just the tan, the sun-bleached hair or the fabulous waft of spicy aftershave. Nor was it the great clothes – the suede jeans matched with a cowboy boots, the faded denim shirt and scuffed leather jacket that made him look like he'd just walked off the set of one of Dillon's pop videos. The most noticeable thing about him was the silence. He had yet to say a word.

It took him until they were past Reading Services to speak.

'Your horse is well.'

'So's yours,' she managed to splutter, abandoning plans to give him a fence by fence description of their cross-country round at Tweseldown.

'Stefan and Kirsty promise to take good care of him.'

It took her a moment to register what he was saying. Then her tongue gratefully unravelled itself from its knot faster than a cobra lunging.

'You *left* Rio in America?' she cried with a familiar burst of anger.

Tash let the brush stroke her skin with quivers of anticipation as she imagined Hugo's eyes on her new, taut canvas. She added a curl to her thigh and a butterfly to her navel. Looking at her reflection in the mirror, she marvelled at the artistry.

She reached for her wine glass and realised it was empty. When she reached to top it up, she found the bottle was empty too. But instead of feeling pleasantly tipsy she felt dizzy and sick with nerves. She'd been painting for a long time and had a crick in her neck from craning round to add flowers and horses on her buttocks. When she'd had to go to the loo earlier, several roses had transformed into something that looked like nappy rash. She had carefully wiped them clean and repainted them, and now she was standing naked with her legs splayed and arms out, praying that no yard crisis brought Jenny or Lemon to the door before Hugo got home.

She was grateful the children had gone to sleep so easily that night. Amery's pink cheeks forewarned teething or a cold, but the monitor remained silent and she'd had plenty of time to perfect her creation.

But now she looked at her reflection one final time and panicked.

Imagining Hugo's eyes on her again, she suddenly doubted what she'd done. She looked like one of those freakish women at tattoo conventions, inked from collar to ankle. She wasn't sure it was Hugo's thing at all, returning after more than a month away to find his wife shuffling towards him plastered with paint. She should have stuck to a sea-bass supper.

She contemplated rushing upstairs for a bath but, looking in the mirror, she wavered. Her handiwork was too beautiful to waste. She'd painted with such love and attention; it had taken her so long.

She decided to open another bottle of wine.

But just as she was taking wide-legged steps out of the study, she heard the buzzer go in the kitchen to indicate that the main electric gates were opening. He was home.

Waiting for the Haydown gates to swing apart, Faith willed them to slow down so that she had more time to climb off her metaphorical high horse and tell Rory that he was forgiven for leaving her real horse in the States, but her heart was still crashing so violently in her chest she couldn't speak.

She'd overreacted to the news, as she so often did, the adrenalin-pumped excitement at seeing him again combusting alongside her anger that he'd so obviously changed and was even further beyond her reach. She wanted the old Rory back, dishevelled and chaotic, not this cool, calm demi-god posing as a young Robert Redford who'd proudly announced that they'd left Rio behind because Hugo wanted the duo to compete at Kentucky next month. Even though that was a dream come true for both her horse and her greatest love, Faith felt left out and furious that the decision had been made without her. She understood they'd left the stallion with the Johanssens, along with Hugo's Kentucky hope Oil Tanker, in the belief that it would be better to have them fine-tuned by Stefan than fly them back and forth across the Atlantic. That all made sense. But Rory suddenly sounding horribly mature and sensible, like her mother, *didn't* make sense. She'd ended up reacting much as she did during any confrontation with her mother, shouting so much that Rory had shut up, and they'd spent the past half-hour in stony silence. Now, as the Haydown gates opened, with the Roadies barking at her headlights like Cerberus, she knew she had to make concessions.

'Why didn't you tell me earlier?' she asked in an undertone, punching the VW into gear and kangaroo-hopping through the gates.

'I wanted it to be a surprise.' His voice was flat with disappointment, having clearly believed the news would wow any owner. 'I thought you'd be pleased. Rio's enjoying five-star care and even has a webcam in his stable so you can keep an eye on him. I know how you fret.'

Which made Faith feel like a maiden aunt stressing over her cats. As she pulled up behind the main house Rory fished out a postcard from his pocket and thrust it at her. 'Here – I wrote down the URL for you.'

Faith briefly studied the single line of indecipherable scrawl before flipping it over. The card featured a photograph of a cowboy with a saddle slung over one shoulder.

'I was going to write something personal and post this to you,' he explained sheepishly, 'but you never read my cards, so I figured it was best to say it.'

Before Faith could ask him what he was talking about he turned around to wake Hugo, whose feigned sleep had rapidly dropped through the trapdoor to real, deep slumber, with Twitch curled in his lap. 'We're home on the range.' Rory shook his shoulder.

Hugo straightened up, taking in his familiar surroundings. 'At last.'

Inside the house, Tash waddled hastily back to the study to repair any of the damage and check her reflection from all angles. Now she heard doors bang and voices call.

She crept to the central passageway in the house, shaking like a leaf.

She could hear Hugo's voice. He was clearly trying to persuade Rory to come inside.

She froze.

His voice grew closer and there were footsteps through the kitchen. 'Come and say hi to Tash. Where is she? I thought she'd at least be outside. Tash? *Tash?* Look in the study, will you, Rory, and I'll check upstairs.'

With a yelp Tash dived back into the study and dragged on her dressing gown just in time as Rory wandered in, looking amazingly blond and tanned.

'Oh, there you are, luvvie,' he yawned, walking up to give her a kiss on the cheek and then a friendly, tight hug that made her want to cry as the towelling robe rubbed against the artwork beneath; he gave her shoulders an extra squeeze and arms an affectionate pat for good measure. 'You been having a nap?'

'Sort of.' She trailed behind him out into the main hallway. 'Good flight?'

'Bloody awful. Hugo! Found her!'

He bounded down the stairs two at a time, which matched Tash's missed heartbeats as she looked up to see those long legs for the first time in ten weeks, followed by that long body and beautiful face with its laser-sharp gaze burning with love and indignation.

Without thinking, Tash engaged Meg Ryan's *Top Gun* run. Like a reflex, it was always her first reaction after separation. She burst forward, arms flung as wide as her smile, but then she suddenly remembered her beautiful body paint, all ready to be admired. Forced to re-think at the last minute, she slid to a halt directly in front of him and, momentum still propelling her onward, performing a high kick to either side of him.

Hugo was visibly shaken. 'Don't tell me Lough's been teaching you the haka while I've been away?'

Not waiting for an answer, he gathered her into a kiss that she was certain would melt the floor beneath her feet and cause the ceiling above her head to fall down. Her body sizzled like a hot plate, the paintwork sliding fast. When he pulled back to look at her he suddenly noticed the dressing gown. 'What are you wearing that for? Are you ill?'

Despite being exhausted and feeling the first temple-biting symptoms of jet lag, Hugo and Rory were in that state of travelling camaraderie that doesn't want the adventure to end, so they dragged out the last hours of their expedition over vast mugs of longed-for PG Tips, telling Tash all about Stefan and Kirsty and MC and Janet Madsen, about the adventures and the training sessions, about the competitions and the seminars, until she was the one fighting sleep. Then, suddenly, they both seemed to empty out. Rory yawned so widely his eyes almost rolled back into his head. It was all he could manage to kiss Tash on the cheek and stagger out towards his cottage.

Hugo was practically on his knees going upstairs.

He crashed, fully dressed, into bed with a rapturous Beetroot on his chest, both looking blearily across the room at her.

Tash dared unknot her belt and let her dressing gown drop.

'Bloody hell.' He blinked a couple of times to make sure he was seeing straight. 'You're filthy. Better have a bath. How d'you end up in that sta—' and he was asleep.

Tash went into the bathroom and looked at her body under the harsh, critical light of the neon strip above the mirror.

She had painted it so carefully – the horses leaping across her breasts and belly, the lush meadow grass on her hips, the flowers and butterflies and blue sky and soft clouds adorning her shoulders. All were now smudged and rubbed beyond recognition. Hugo was right; she just looked like she'd been rolling around in the mud. Wearily, she ran herself a hot bath, grateful at least that it might soak away the aches that were corkscrewing through her shoulders and lower back from twisting around in front of a mirror to paint daisies and buttercups on her bottom.

Chapter 53

From the moment he arrived home, Hugo had a mountain of commitments both on the yard and the estate. For all Tash's determination to get married life back on track with a big bang, he seemed equally eager to simply slot her in for a quick service.

On his second evening home, when she popped into the bedroom to fetch another layer, he emerged from the shower fully cocked, talking on his mobile in the seemingly never-ending succession of calls that had started the moment he landed.

'Yes, darling – he's fit and raring to go, I can assure you. Quite understood. Uh ha . . .'

He held up his hand to make Tash wait, blowing her a kiss which made it clear what was on his mind. As she loitered, she grew uncomfortably aware that he was talking to Venetia Gundry which, given his impressive hard-on, served only to arouse her suspicions rather than her libido.

'Yes, Ven . . . totally . . . okay . . .'

Hand and erection still aloft, he indicated with his eyes for her to get on the bed.

'What?' she mouthed. She hadn't started cooking supper. Cora was still awake in her cot with her beaker of milk.

'That's right, Ven. Burnham Market, then Badminton.' He covered the mouthpiece and said, 'Take off your clothes.'

Tash gaped at him. Along the landing Amery, who was cutting a tooth, had started to cry. She went out to settle him.

Having finished his call with Venetia, Hugo wrapped a towel

around his hips and followed her, shouldering the door, a silhouette against the light of the landing as Tash straightened up from dabbing Anbesol on their son's red little gums.

'I've invited Rory to supper,' Hugo told her.

'I see.' She tried not to feel cheated out of the romantic dinner she'd planned. 'And Lough?'

'What about him?'

'You can hardly invite Rory and not Lough,' she said quietly, eager not to disturb Amery, who was dropping off again.

'Of course I can.' His face was still in shadow, but his tone was unconcerned.

Tash could imagine how aggravated Lough would be by the snub.

'They're both our work riders,' she protested in a whisper, coming out and pulling the door ajar behind her. 'They're living in the same cottage.'

'Lough probably already has plans.' He turned away, sauntering back into their bedroom. 'Surely he's out cavorting with half the Young Riders' team every night after all your social introductions?'

Tash followed him. 'I can at least call him and ask.'

'Don't bother.' The towel dropped again. 'Let's screw instead.'

Tash did an about turn as Amery started to bawl at full pitch once more, secretly grateful that she had just avoided the moment. She felt they both deserved a more seductive build-up than that.

But Hugo's nose was clearly out of joint, and it was a tricky supper, despite the presence of Rory, as upbeat and oblivious to cross-currents as ever. Tash tried to divide two sea bass between three as inconspicuously as possible, still worrying that Lough would feel offended because he hadn't been invited too. Not that he would appreciate the conversation if he had been there.

'Lough's so bloody uncommunicative,' Rory complained. 'It's like sharing a cottage with a Trappist monk.'

'He'd better have been behaving like one,' Hugo muttered, looking at Tash.

'He's been very well behaved,' she said carefully, longing to talk to him about Lough's confessions, but it was impossible with Hugo in such an edgy mood and Rory there.

'I can't believe Lem and Beccy are an item!' Rory gossiped. The news seemed to have made his day. 'What *do* they see in him?'

'They?' Tash looked at him curiously.

'Women.' His cheeks coloured.

'Don't they have some sort of threesome going on with the lanky girl who works for the Moncrieffs?' Hugo drawled.

Tash noticed Rory's tightly masked face. 'Of course not. They're just friends. They share a lot of secrets.'

Hugo's fingers were drumming on the table. 'Three may keep a secret if two of them are dead.'

She looked at him sharply. 'What makes you say that?'

'Nanny used to say it.' He reached forwards to answer his ever-ringing mobile.

Tash swallowed anxiously, wondering how many secrets Hugo had that she didn't know about. While he was away in America she'd imagined her husband's pre-departure talk of regrets and lies was all about Lough and his troubled past in New Zealand, secrets she now shared, but suddenly she wasn't so sure. The safe haven Hugo had offered Lough still harboured half-truths and stormy seas.

Hugo's mood was strange and edgy that evening in the few moments he was off the phone. Tash found herself drinking too much wine.

By the time a sober Rory thanked her for supper and took his leave to return to 'the monastery' as he called the lodge, Tash was decidedly drunk.

'He obviously loved America.' She began squiffily loading the dishwasher with a clanking disregard for the Beauchamp family Spode.

'He worked incredibly hard and rode brilliantly, but he's been a bloody pain,' Hugo replied. 'Always sloping off to meet MC in motels or moping about miserably when her husband was around.'

'MC and Rory?'

He nodded, laughing. 'You'd think she'd eat him alive, but she's terribly fond of him. And Rory knows he's on to a good thing, squiring the first lady of eventing. He's learned a lot in and out of bed, I'll bet. She's incorrigible, and as gorgeous as ever.'

Tash crashed the pudding bowls together. 'And what does MC's husband think of all this?'

'From what I've seen he's just as bad. I suppose infidelity cancels itself out if you're both doing it, like being a drunk. Frightfully bad form if you're the only one at it in a marriage.'

It was a typically flippant Hugo comment, but nonetheless Tash worried that he was suggesting they both become alcoholic adulterers. She finished loading the dishwasher, vowing not to plunder the wine so much in future. The easy understanding between them had become even more dislocated while he was away; it desperately needed coupling again. She knew she must rekindle that lost romance.

When they finally went to bed Tash rushed into the bathroom to soften and scent herself, anticipating a wild night of passion, but Hugo was already asleep by the time she came out, still jet-lagged and now doubly exhausted from hitting the ground running. His phone was still clutched in his hand, mid-text.

She prised it out and checked that he hadn't been messaging V. The recipient box was still blank and he had only got as far as writing *If I hear that you've touched* before stopping.

Tash placed the phone on the bedside table and climbed into bed beside him, curling her body alongside his warmth and lying awake plotting her seduction strategy. Just as she was falling asleep, she felt him turn around and slide a hand between her thighs. For a moment a hot spark ignited her senses but then, just as suddenly, it fizzled and died as she felt overwhelmed by tiredness. To her shame, she kept her eyes tight shut and pretended to be asleep, even throwing in a couple of snores when his fingers started tracing her nipples. He soon gave up and fell asleep again, arms growing heavy on her skin.

She needed a big scene to kick-start her libido. She wanted to feel desired, worshipped, wanton and rampant, not just readily available.

The following evening, Tash revisited the idea of sexy underwear. She had just that week discovered the lingerie section of Asda, to which she had swapped her allegiance because Waitrose made her think of Hugo's secret flower purchases. George was her new fashion guru. Despite the early morning frosts that glazed the fields outside, the rails of the Basingford superstore were already full of pretty summer dresses and strappy shoes, and the undies were to die for. Frothy little combinations in jewel-bright colours, costing less than a free-range chicken, had found their way to her bedroom which, thanks to Veruschka's continued military sweep of the house, was looking fresh and seductive with its polished floors and antique furniture shining like burnished metal, fresh daffodils creaking open in an old Delft jug on the dressing table, the old bedspread replaced with a fabulous claret fake-fur throw that had been a wedding present from an owner.

That afternoon, Hugo and Rory had taken two horses for a pipe-opener at Kelvin's all-weather gallops, staying on to have a drink and catch up afterwards. Lascivious livery Venetia had insisted on going too. Meanwhile, Tash was eager to pull out all the stops and she planned to drape herself on the fake fur throw for Hugo's return, clashing joyfully in a bright yellow basque and cami-knickers trimmed with orange ribbon. As soon as the children were in bed she bathed and oiled herself in readiness and donned her outfit.

When the horsebox failed to reappear by seven o'clock she started to worry. She was cold and hungry; Amery, still cutting his tooth, had taken ages to settle. She couldn't shake the image of Hugo and Venetia entwined together, ecstatic to be reunited after his trip.

Wrapping herself in the wispy chiffon robe that had come as a part of the set, she headed downstairs to snaffle some crisps and open a bottle of wine, deciding to drape herself in front of the fire in the snug instead, although it stubbornly kept going out.

By eight o'clock she was really starting to fret. Hugo's mobile went straight to voicemail and there had been no calls to the house. She'd now had time to work out a complete adulterous scenario for him: the Moët would be flowing at Kelvin's house, and he and Rory would be drunk (Rory was no doubt still easier to push off the wagon than a baddie in a spaghetti western). Able to sneak away undetected, Hugo and Venetia were canoodling ecstatically in Kelvin's state-of-the-art hot tub and sucking champagne off one another's slithery bodies.

Her cheap underwear itched uncomfortably at the thought.

She pulled on a long coat and her boots, hung the baby monitor around her neck and stomped outside. The yard was in darkness, the old work lorry still missing. Lights glowed from the stables flat and the archway apartment, and she could hear the Czechs' television as usual.

'Everything okay?' asked a voice in the gloom, making her jump.

Lough walked out from an unlit stable a few feet away.

'Hugo's not back. He and Rory left hours ago. Have they called the yard at all?'

'Not while I've been out here.'

She hurried into the office to check the machine. There were plenty of new messages, but none from Hugo.

Lough had followed her in and was looking in the veterinary cupboard. Tash tried not to eyeball him too obviously to see if he was pocketing restricted substances. Her suspicious mind was in overdrive tonight. But he pulled out the bottle of brandy stored there for human emergencies and went in search of two mugs.

'I don't want any thanks.' She shook her head, knowing that she'd already had too much wine.

Lough poured himself three fingers and knocked back most of it in one go, wincing as it burned his throat.

Tash watched him guardedly. 'I've hardly seen you this week.'

'Figured I should keep my distance. Don't want Hugo thinking I'm monopolising his wife.'

'Very noble of you,' she replied, thinking anxiously about her adultery scenario and helping herself to some brandy after all. 'I wish Venetia was so well mannered. I think she's finally cracked and tied him to the haynet rings in the back of the box to ravish him.'

He raised an enquiring eyebrow. 'Does she have a history of that sort of behaviour?'

'She certainly has a reputation for shagging other women's husbands, which is ironic for a divorce lawyer. They call her Marriage Misguidance on the hunting field.' The brandy was going straight to her head. 'Last year she bought a horse for Hugo to compete and named it Brief Encounter, which says a lot, don't you think?'

He looked at her with those ferociously honest eyes, as direct and brutal as Hugo could be flippant and oblique. 'Are you saying they're having an affair?'

'I bloody hope not.' To her horror, tears caught in her throat. 'But he's keeping something from me, that's for certain.'

The baby monitor suddenly crackled into life with a single plaintive wail that made Tash's heart squeeze tight. She clutched it to her chest, already hurrying for the door, but something pulled her back. For a crazy moment she thought it was Lough grabbing her coat and swung around to tell him to let go. Then she saw him still standing at the opposite end of the office, and realised that her hem had caught on the edge of a filing cabinet and tugged her to a halt, popping off the button. Much worse, it was now gaping open to reveal a full frontal of George at Asda's finest. Feeling her face flame, she whipped it closed again and gulped that she had to check on Amery before dashing back to the safety of the house.

Finally, at half-past nine, Tash heard an unfamiliar engine turning into the yard and hurried back outside, Beetroot at her heels. A small horsebox with 'Racehorses' emblazoned over its cab was discharging the two Haydown horses, with Rory supervising.

'Hugo's still with your lorry, waiting for the recovery truck,' he explained to Tash as she helped him settle two very startled horses. 'Brakes went on the way down Lamford Hill. We were bloody nearly all mincemeat – went over the ledge on the dogleg, ended up on our side in a field of sheep.' He looked shaken, and had cuts on his forehead and chin.

'Is Hugo injured?'

'Fine. Honestly, not a scratch.'

'And the horses are really okay?' She had checked them both over; they seemed amazingly unscathed.

'Pretty much in one piece, but it took over an hour to persuade them to get on this little wagon to come home, and who can blame them?'

Lough had appeared on the yard, his hair wet from the shower. 'What's happened?'

'Why did nobody call here?' Tash demanded.

'Hugo's mobile got hammered in the smash and mine has no charge,' Rory grimaced apologetically. 'But Venetia said she'd let you know what happened.'

'Well, she bloody didn't,' Tash snapped, anger and panic suddenly bubbling again. 'Is she still with Hugo?'

Rory shook his head. 'She went back to Kelvin's yard. I think they were both quite chuffed to have an excuse, frankly. They can't keep their hands off each other these days.'

'Kelvin?' Tash balked, finding it hard to imagine Venetia in a clinch with the much-married trainer who was about five foot three, had no teeth and looked like a warthog.

'Been going on for months.' Rory seemed surprised she didn't know. 'Since before we went to the States, but he's going through an expensive divorce and doesn't want to give the ex any more opportunity to make off with the chattels.'

It felt as though a pitchfork had been pulled from her side, but she didn't dare look at Lough. Instead she watched distractedly as Beetroot flirted with Twitch, still believing herself a hot act despite near blindness and advancing decrepitude.

'Darling, you look frozen through.' Rory noticed her teeth chattering. The long coat she'd chosen this time had a full complement of buttons, but was barely thicker than a shower curtain. 'Leave the yard to Lough and me. Hugo will be back soon, I promise.'

Back inside the house, Tash covered the kinky yellow undies with leggings and a sweater dress before preparing a vat of spaghetti bolognese, guessing Hugo would be ravenous when he finally got home. She turned off Radio Four, which was running a particularly depressing series about the disintegration of marriage in modern Britain, and selected a CD instead. Soon the mellow tones of Dillon Rafferty filled the room, telling her that he'd never loved anyone as much as he'd loved her, even though she could never be his.

Venetia was in love with Kelvin the trainer, she thought delightedly. Venetia, for all her transparent lust for Hugo over the years, was not 'V'.

Tash hugged herself with relief, wooden spoon still in hand and dripping sauce everywhere as she swayed in front of the Aga.

'You're in my soul, you're in my head, you're stitched through me like needle and thread . . .' Dillon sang, his fantastic, heartfelt voice making the lyrics so romantic and sexy, despite their ambiguity. 'You rip my heart with every smile, but I cannot leave while . . . I . . . am . . .'

'Addicted to you!' she sang along to the chorus with feeling, holding her spoon up like a lighter at a concert. 'I am a love junkie, addicted to—'

She stopped abruptly, spoon aloft, as it occurred to her that if Venetia wasn't 'V' then somebody else was. At the same moment as this unpleasant thought struck home, she realised she wasn't alone and swung around to find Lough standing at the kitchen table watching her.

'What is it?' she asked ungraciously, feeling foolish.

'I brought Beetroot back.' He nodded towards the dog, who was looking very pleased with herself. 'She followed us back to the cottage.'

Having gone over her bowl in forensic detail, Haydown's senior dog trotted across the flagstones to the dog sofa, ready to take on the Bitches of Eastwick.

'Thanks.' Tash bolted back to the Aga to stir her burning sauce. 'She has a crush on Twitch.'

'It's mutual.' Lough's voice was now so familiar, especially in this kitchen, yet since Hugo's return it felt like an alien invasion. Tash found herself letting loose a nervous laugh that sounded equally foreign, an escaped budgie shrieking in a quiet hedgerow as she sensed a sparrow hawk close by.

Scraping at the black crust on the base of the pan, she was aware of him coming closer. Typically, Dillon Rafferty chose this moment to stop singing about destructive love addiction and 'Two Souls' made its mesmerising way into the room.

'Are you okay?' Lough spoke quietly at her shoulder.

'Fine!' the budgie puffed up defensively. 'Sorry about earlier. Crazy of me to think Hugo's having an affair.'

'Why crazy?'

'You hear such rubbish.'

'Like what?'

'Oh, tittle-tattle . . .' she fudged, pulling the pan off the Aga and closing the lid. 'Anyway, he'll be back soon and we can have a laugh about it.'

'Of course.' He turned to leave. 'I'll see you both in the morning.'

Tash gripped the Aga rail, unable to stop her beak opening. 'Lough, is there something you know about Hugo that you haven't told me?'

He stalled. 'Ask me anything.'

Gripping the rail tighter, Tash was suddenly uncertain as to whether she wanted to know the truth.

After a long pause, Lough came to stand alongside her, his broad hands taking the warm steel rail so that they were like two teenagers riding a rollercoaster. His voice was deep and apologetic. 'You deserve better than this, Tash.' But whether he was talking about her marriage or himself was not clear.

Still she said nothing, acutely aware of his hand next to hers and the range heating her face and chest.

There was a step behind them.

'I see my childish superglue-on-the-Aga-rail prank has worked at long last,' said a dry voice.

They both turned to find Hugo behind them, a huge graze on his head and dew in his hair.

Tash was too relieved to have him home at last to check herself, surging forwards happily. 'Thank goodness you're safe.' She wrapped her arms around him. 'We didn't hear a car.'

'Evidently.' His sarcasm was lost on her. 'I walked back. That's why I'm so late – and ravenous. This smells delicious.' He breathed in the cooking smells, eyes drifting to the man still leaning against his Aga. 'Do I take it you're joining us, Lough? I'll lay the long-handled spoons.'

Saying nothing, Lough nodded farewell to Tash and headed for the rear lobby.

'Stay for a drink at least,' she found herself bleating, desperate to break the tension. But Lough was already through the back door.

'What did he want?' Hugo turned to her the moment he was gone, eyes like bullets.

Wearily, Tash told him about Beetroot while she put the pasta on. 'She's on heat.'

'Isn't she past all that?'

'The mind's still willing,' she yawned, suddenly feeling beaten up with tiredness.

Hugo gave her a rueful look and suddenly she laughed, putting her arms around him again as they shared a long, heart-lifting kiss that made both their minds very willing indeed. When they finally broke apart Tash ran her fingers through his hair. 'The accident sounds awful. I can't believe the brakes went like that. The box was only serviced last month.'

'Old lorries like that suffer if they're parked up all the time; they need taking out regularly.' Hugo wasn't really interested in post mortems, as his hands had slipped beneath the waistband of her leggings and discovered an enticing whisper of lace not quite covering her exfoliated, moisturised bottom. 'Like wives.' His hand ran up her spine to find the back of her lacy new bra.

Biting back the retort that being compared to an old lorry wasn't wildly flattering, Tash quivered with anticipation, feeling her supermarket undies heat up.

But by the time they had eaten supper and she was ready to show them off at last, Amery was in full cry again. It took her almost an hour to settle him this time and Hugo was long asleep.

*

The next day, Hugo bought a new mobile that the manufacturers boasted was even more indestructible than the last one, and completely waterproof. To prove his point, he took it with him as he schooled several horses around the Haydown cross-country course in the driving rain, and it even survived being trodden upon by Sir Galahad when it fell out of his pocket during a disagreement about a drop fence.

'Amazing bit of kit,' he enthused afterwards.

Finding it abandoned among his discarded clothes on the bathroom floor after his evening shower, Tash couldn't resist taking a detailed examination of the new device to make sure she knew how to check for V texts. She hastily locked the bathroom door and turned on the taps loudly to cover the sound of her beeping her way to his inbox.

To her mortification, she discovered that V had already been busy sending Hugo messages that day, asking after 'my hero' and saying that they had to keep 'our little secret'. Her eyes and chest burned as she read them.

'Is my phone in there?' he yelled through the door, making her jump so much that it shot out of her hands and cannoned into the bath oils lined up by the bath, which went flying like skittles.

'Why's it so slimy and wet?' he complained when she thrust it out at him.

'I was just checking if the manufacturer's boasts were true,' she said vaguely, examining his face around the door. Ask it, she told herself. Ask who V is. Ask him.

He wandered away, looking at the screen. 'Have you been fiddling with this?'

Her heart hammered. She felt guilty for spying, despite what she'd found. Tell him you saw, Tash. Ask for an explanation.

'Haven't touched it!' She bolted back into the bathroom, feeling like a naughty child who had fiddled and fiddled with a musical box to get at the mechanism and broken it, only to find it didn't play its sweet music any more. Now she wanted to slide it back on the shelf and pretend nothing had happened, waiting for the adults to come back in the room to mend it.

Chapter 54

Clusters of daisies now carpeted the Haydown lawns and hedgerows like harnessed clouds, along with little fire-lick flames of buttercups and dandelions, promising spring was ready to roll in with its lengthening days, bulbs, blossom and cheering optimism. Despite this, the accident with the horsebox spelled the beginning of a run of misfortune for the Beauchamps. Hugo's start to the competitive season, already delayed by his prolonged working trip to America, was blighted by bad luck: several horses came down with a mystery virus before the important trials at Aldon and had to be withdrawn; one of his terriers disappeared; the tyres of his newly fixed car were slashed when it was parked outside the Olive Branch. And his marriage wasn't in the greatest shape.

Tash already suspected a surprise party at the end of the month was the last thing Hugo would want for his fortieth birthday. He seemed to have returned from the States determined to exercise his authority, both on the yard and within his family. Having been given sole responsibility for running the yard in his absence, she found this unsettling. She longed for some romantic time out, but attempts were hamstrung as home life took a back seat to competitions.

Within a week of his return, Hugo and Tash were rarely at home together for longer than a few hours at a time as they travelled around the country competing two or three times a week. The Beauchamps had traditionally always travelled and competed together, but now they were seldom even at the same event, Tash running youngsters in a mixture of shows and one day events with Beccy acting as support and the children occasionally in tow, while Hugo, Rory and Lough took the top horses to the big trials backed up by Jenny and Lemon, often staying away for several nights.

Tash felt increasingly guilty that Cora and Amery saw so little of their parents, and Hugo clearly resented the fact that this guilt didn't seem to extend to him in the same way. Tash, however, was determined to hold out for a big set-piece seduction to show him once and for all that she was still all woman and all his. She'd planned it for too long to give up now, even if, on the few occasions they did have an evening together, there never seemed to be time to kick-start anything romantic. Either Amery was up all night teething, Hugo was stuck on the yard with a sick or lame horse, an owner popped in to catch up on the news from America or some other distraction cropped up. Their days started punishingly early and ended late. Her underwear went on and came off again faster than a stripper working back-to-back shifts, without Hugo getting to admire the show.

Out on the eventing circuit, the lorry-park gossips were relishing a winter of new material to chew over as term started in earnest again. Talk was all of those who had hatched, matched or dispatched divorce papers during the long break, along with inevitable rumours. Last season's quest to identify Lucy Field's married lover remained a favourite topic, along with great excitement that the Devil on Horseback was now in the UK and already kicking up dust at Haydown. Gus Moncrieff was already on the case with first-hand knowledge and eye-witness accounts, although his loyalty meant that he warned Hugo where talk was going early on.

'Lough up your daughter's, eh?' he joked as they stood in front of the CCTV in the riders' tent, watching the New Zealander scorch around the Bicton cross-country, a gaggle of admiring female riders and grooms gasping behind them. 'You must feel like King Arthur.'

'Meaning?'

Gus lit a cigarette, ignoring the complaints around him. 'The quiet ones are always the worst. He was a nightmare to get out of his shell while you and Percival were away warring. Talk about a square peg at the Round Table. Tash has the patience of a saint with him. And Penny adores him, of course, but she's always fancied herself as the Lady of the Lake.'

'What exactly are you saying?' Hugo asked coolly, his eyes not leaving the screen.

'Keep a close eye on Lancelot, Hugo.'

Hugo said nothing of this to Tash, but it hadn't escaped his attention that his wife had been behaving increasingly strangely, changing her clothes all the time, doing furtive things in the bathroom and endlessly checking his whereabouts as though she was afraid he would suddenly appear around a corner and catch her out. He didn't like it.

She was at least forced to overcome her Luddite urges and accept the BlackBerry that he bought her to enable them to stay in touch while on the road. Struggling to master it, she kept sending Hugo blank texts and emails which infuriated him because he was so quick-witted and natural with technology that he couldn't understand why she found it so hard. When not sending blank texts, she was having suspicious, whispered conversations on the thing that were cut short whenever Hugo came within earshot. With Gus's warning still ringing in his ears, he felt very jumpy indeed.

On the surface, Lough gave him no reason for suspicion. He kept his own counsel and seemed utterly focused on his horses. Apart from the evening Hugo had found him in his kitchen, he never ventured in the house and barely spoke on the yard, apart from monosyllables to Lemon about the horses' routines. He had his own transport and stayed away from socialising at competitions. He was, as everyone so often described him, a machine, and certainly gave no indication that he had any interest in Hugo's wife.

By contrast, Rory was always flirting playfully with Tash and any other female who crossed his path, partly because he was instinctively charming, and also because he was now embroiled with MC, who blew hot and cold faster than a faulty hairdryer and left most of her conquests in need of an ego boost. He snuggled towards Tash like a toddler in search of a comfort blanket, knowing she was soft and warm. But Hugo trusted Rory implicitly after their time away together, knowing he was a chip off the old mounting block of his legendary uncle, a war hero who had ridden round Badminton three times in one day. The chip on Lough's shoulder was four gigabytes of well-stored resentment, and Hugo watched him like a hawk.

But Lough didn't make a wrong move. It was Rory who inadvertently turned traitor.

'I've changed my mind about Lough,' he told Hugo as they loaded horses for a one day event near Salisbury. 'I like him a lot. He's a dark horse, but they say never judge a horse by its colour, don't they? And he's one hell of a gambler.'

Hugo looked at him in surprise. 'Don't tell me the Trappist monk's tipping winners?'

Rory shook his head, a big, easy smile breaking across his face. 'We were up until three this morning playing Bezique.'

'Cards?' Hugo was familiar with the game that his father-in-law considered as compulsory as sun-cream during holidays in the Loire.

'I was within one hand of winning the lot, and he turned it around and beat me. It's no wonder he's such a great competitor. The man has nerves of steel. He's a gambler that never gives in.' Rory started to haul up the lorry ramp. 'That's *seriously* cool.'

'That's dangerous,' Hugo snapped, feeling like he'd had another one of his loyal Rat Pack stolen.

Tash had noticed Lough's distance, but she was far too preoccupied to try to team build, especially when Hugo was so on edge.

With Sophia increasingly on her case, she couldn't stop the momentum of a party that looked set to rival one of Elton John's charity balls for glamour and expense, but she was desperate to be on a better footing with Hugo before they sprang the surprise of the year. As the big day fast approached her sister went into organisational overdrive, delighted that Hugo was away from home so much because she could party-plan at Haydown without fear of detection. It was a nightmare for Tash, however, because the eventing world was hopeless at keeping a secret. If one more person came up to her and asked, in front of Hugo, how it was going and whether he'd guessed anything about his surprise yet, she would scream. He had started to get quite suspicious, and the more he asked awkward questions or cornered her, the more defensive she became.

'Who was that?' he demanded when she yet again hung up on Sophia because he'd walked in, this time interrupting a spat about floristry.

'Voicemail,' she said vaguely.

'I heard something about roses?'

Tash, who had just been arguing vociferously that they did *not* need a thousand pounds' worth of flower arrangements, was forced to lie yet again. 'Just ordering flowers for Mother's Day.'

'To be delivered to China?' They'd recently had a postcard from Alexandra featuring the Great Wall.

'You'd be surprised what Waitrose can do these days,' she blustered.

He looked at her for a long time before turning to leave, muttering under his breath, 'You're lying.'

She could hardly deny it. It seemed they were both harbouring so many secrets in their marriage these days, the gangplank was fast becoming impossible to lower amid the jostle of burning boats.

The following Sunday, two dozen roses were delivered with the note, 'To the mother of all invention, from the bull in a china shop. You are perfect.' She wasn't sure whether to laugh or cry, but she knew she had to build bridges fast.

At Hyam Hall trials, the weekend before the party, they shared a rare night in the horsebox and Tash packed George's finest in anticipation. But that evening a stab of pain through her belly told her that the horny feeling which had been cooking away the previous night while Hugo was inconveniently addressing an after-dinner speech to a hunt supporter's club in Wiltshire was now at an end. True enough, when she checked in the loo, her period had come. Hugo never minded the occasional 'red shag', but Tash found it embarrassing, and certainly had no intention of enacting her grand seduction with a towel on the mattress and a tampon to hand.

He'd been back over two weeks and they had yet to make love.

Wearily, she called home to check how Alicia was coping with the children.

'I can't get that Kraut to leave the house,' she warbled, sounding three parts cut already.

'She's Czech.'

'Yes, keeps checking them, yes!' Alicia boomed, shouting as usual to compensate for her deafness. 'Says she will sleep here tonight. Won't take no for an answer. Is she staff? Do we pay her overtime?'

'No, no – it's fine. Let her stay.' At least Veruhska was conscientious. Tash couldn't help longing for her own mother. Alexandra had come to England regularly when Cora was a baby, looking after her when Tash started competing again.

'I miss her,' she told Hugo now.

'Are you saying my mother can't cope?' he demanded huffily.

'No, she's great! And she has the Czechs.'

'Quite the little domestic dream team. And let's not forget Lough manfully keeping the home fires stoked while I was in the States.'

'What?'

'I must thank him for keeping you company so often. I gather you two had lots of cosy suppers together.'

'Along with the Moncrieffs, the Stantons, the Bucklands—'

'But not every night.'

'Hugo, what are you suggesting?'

'You tell me.'

'What are you talking about? Absolutely nothing went on.'

He glared at her furiously. 'I just don't want to find you're keeping any secrets from me.'

Swallowing hard, Tash thought anxiously about the two hundred guests primed to arrive at Haydown the following weekend. She found she couldn't look him in the eye.

Tash battled hard with her competition nerves, eager to show Hugo how much she had bounced back into the saddle. It was the first time he'd seen her compete this season and she was in contention in both her sections after the dressage and show-jumping. But then across country she held too much back, riding over-cautiously on both horses and posting hopelessly slow times.

'Stop to chat to friends on the way round?' Hugo asked afterwards, which did nothing for her self esteem.

Lough was also competing at the trials, having travelled there in his leased Ketterer box and three of his four horses on board. When he caught up with Tash in the stable lines he gave her the sympathetic pat on the back she badly needed, and the understanding in his dark eyes was a huge boost.

'You did a good job out there. I was proud of you,' he told her. 'Better to be safe but slow when you're still building your nerve and stamina.'

She smiled at him gratefully. 'I'll be better after the party.'

'Party?' He looked blank.

She stared at him, hardly able to believe he could have been missed off the guest list. But she had left all that to Sophia.

'You must come . . .' She started to gabble about the surprise fortieth extravaganza, but after a while he held up his hand.

'I'll pass.'

'Please don't.' She reached out to grip his arm, steering the belligerent hand down. 'It would mean so much to me. I really want you and Hugo to get onto a better footing, and it's always lovely to have an excuse to dress up and celebrate.' She was certain a big party would cheer them all up, and help to break the ice between the two men.

He tilted his head to look at her fingers on his sleeve, her knuckles still dusted with scurf from being pressed nervously into her horse's mane over every cross-country jump.

'I'll think about it.'

'Thanks. Good luck for your round.' Tash squeezed his arm gratefully before dancing away, oblivious of the tens of eyes following her, hands raised to faces as the gossips started to speculate about just how close Hugo's wife had grown to his handsome Kiwi work rider during his prolonged absence.

Heading back to his horsebox to change, Lough found Lemon entertaining Beccy. Although they appeared to be doing no more than having a cup of tea, she still bolted as soon as she saw him, dashing past with her cheeks flaming.

'And g'day to you too,' he muttered, looking around for his cross-country kit.

'She's shy,' Lemon said breezily, standing up. 'She doesn't want to get drawn into the "love triangle".'

'The what?' Lough started zipping himself into his body protector while Lemon made his way through to the horse area of the box to fetch tack from the lockers.

'You're being talked about, didn't you know? It's all around the course. You and Mrs B are big news.'

Lough hurried after him. 'What the fuck have you been saying, Lem?'

'Nothing! Not me!' Lemon held up his hands, a bridle in each. 'But I can't stop other people talking. They've seen the *hot 'n' smokin'* way you look at her.' He hammed a Yankee accent. 'No smoke without fire, after all.'

'Only thing getting fired around here will be you if you talk like that again,' Lough snarled, grabbing a bridle and stalking out.

This put Lemon in such a sulk that he for once didn't wish his boss luck as he headed off across country, although Lough hardly looked as though he needed goodwill as he flew around the first half of the course. Heading to the finish to wait for them, Lemon found Beccy cooling off Hugo's horse after his round.

'How'd he get on?' He fell into step alongside her.

'Clear.'

'Bastard,' Lemon hissed, kicking at a divot. 'You should have left his girth slack.'

'I could never do that,' Beccy gasped.

'Of course not, Ms Goody Two Shoes,' Lemon sneered. 'Remind

me to buy you a new doormat for your birthday. The one on your face is looking worn out.' He peeled away to get ready for Lough's return.

Beccy battled tears, not realising that Tash was behind her and had heard this last comment.

'Let's take this chap back to his box.' Giving Beccy's back an encouraging pat, Tash steered her towards the stable lines, speaking in an undertone as they walked. 'Beccy, I don't want to interfere, but I'm really not happy hearing Lem talking to you like that.'

'Don't listen in then.'

'I'm sorry. I know you two are terribly close,' Tash went on carefully, 'but are you really sure he's boyfriend material? Wouldn't it be better to take it easy for a bit?'

'No it wouldn't!' Beccy flashed, making the horse start back. 'He *is* my boyfriend, so please keep your nose out of my business and leave us alone!' She led the horse away, leaving Tash standing in her wake feeling foolish for trying.

She was still holding the bucket of sponges, spares, wipes and sweat scraper. Suddenly it made a strange buzzing noise and started to vibrate, making her drop it in alarm, imagining a giant insect in there.

Hugo's phone fell out on the grass, a blue light flashing away on its rim to indicate new messages.

She hastily pocketed it and gathered the rest of the things back into the bucket before darting behind the portaloos to look at his inbox.

You are riding for a fall.

Tash took a couple of moments to take this in. Then she checked the sender, but it was from a caller listed as Shadowfax, with no contact details. Scrolling through his inbox, she found half a dozen similar messages such as: *Watch your back . . . Countdown to the final farewell* and – most worrying, and sent three days earlier – *Your wife is fucking the Kiwi.* For a mad moment, ludicrous images of herself with a green fruit sprang to mind.

It came as absolutely no consolation that there was nothing on Hugo's phone from V. That he'd never mentioned the messages appalled her.

Chapter 55

'How is it possible to send an anonymous text message?' Tash asked Beccy, her fount of all IT knowledge, the next day.

'Why d'you want to know?' Beccy looked wary, still mistrustful around Tash. 'Can you still not work your BlackBerry?'

'No – I just wondered.'

'It's easy. There are internet sites for it.'

'Why would anybody do that?'

'Because they *can*. It's great for chatting up people you fancy.'

'And threatening people.'

'I think they legislate pretty carefully against that.' Beccy eyed her suspiciously. 'I wouldn't go there, if I were you.'

Tash opened her mouth to protest her innocence, then closed it again, knowing that she had to keep quiet until she had done some detective work. 'You're right. I'll just send a strongly worded letter. Thanks Beccy.'

She checked the main Beauchamp Eventing email account that day. There was a host of malicious messages, just as there had been before Christmas, but these were even worse, threatening that horses would die, calamity strike and disaster crash down on them if Hugo didn't retire from the sport. She wondered what or who they could have upset so much, her blood running icy in her veins.

The worst email simply read: *Look after your family, Beauchamp. Those poor little bastards won't have a Daddy much longer.*

Hugo claimed the messages were nothing to worry about. 'We're in the public eye and the public get very misty-eyed about horses – somebody has probably seen YouTube footage of me giving a horse a clout and now wants to exact revenge in cyberspace.'

Tash found it impossible to believe this was a random cyber-crank. 'Somebody is seriously out to get us, Hugo. It's not just the messages. They slashed your tyres, they kidnapped one of the Rat Pack, they could have could have cut the horsebox brakes and poisoned the horses for all we know!' She was so terrified she clung to him like a child that night.

Hugo remained stoical. 'I'll guard you all like a lion. And whenever I'm away, I'll make sure Vasilly has a bloody big baseball bat near by at all times.'

After that, he made a concerted effort to delete all the malicious texts and emails that came through before Tash could see them, but his riding and competition commitments meant he wasn't always quick enough.

Privately, Hugo suspected Lough but couldn't prove it. They avoided one another completely on the yard and could still be in two different continents for all the contact they had. It was only at competitions that the gloves came off. At the three-star trials in Norfolk's Burnham Market, Lough triumphed over Hugo with a big win on his top horse, Rangitoto, and claimed another section on his second advanced horse, the little chocolate dun mare Pihanga.

A week later at the South of England trials, Hugo reversed the placings and forced Lough into second in three sections.

'It's not fair,' complained Lucy Field. 'They're not letting the rest of us have a look-in.'

'Stand well back,' Gus advised. 'With any luck they'll have killed each other by Badminton.'

The growing press speculation surrounding the professional rivalry between Hugo and his tenant rider soon had a nasty twist to it.

In the build-up to Kentucky, totally unfounded and very damaging rumours about Hugo suddenly started spreading through equestrian internet forums. Many said he was cruel to his horses; some that he was equally aggressive and violent to his wife. Within days, stories appeared in the sporting media, with claims of malpractice that even reached the nationals, who took delight in dredging up the photograph of Debbie Double-G, topless and tantalising, kissing Hugo at the Olympics.

All the allegations were immediately retracted once Hugo got his lawyers on the case, but the timing was awful and the mud had already stuck. Eventing was a very muddy sport, and when it dried on hard it could take a lifetime to wash off. A valuable new sponsorship deal with an accountancy firm fell through, and a lucrative television contract was cancelled.

As the date for the Haydown contingent's departure for Kentucky three day event approached, Hugo's status as British pin-up and ambassador for the sport looked ever more shaky.

'There's a very focused smear campaign being orchestrated against you.' Gus pointed out the obvious when he came up to

Haydown to use the cross-country course. 'You must know who's behind it.'

Hugo distractedly fed Gus's horse a mint from his pocket, watching with narrowed eyes as Lough rode out of the yard with Tash, Beccy and Lemon. Although Tash was hanging well back on the nutty Lor, and Lough was at the front of the line, there seemed to be an invisible thread between them. Hugo had noticed it before when they were riding together. They never spoke or even exchanged glances, but he was certain he wasn't mistaken. He was dreading the thought of leaving them at Haydown when he and Rory returned to the States, but he badly needed a good four-star result to salvage his reputation, and Sophia and Ben were flying out especially to support the horse they part owned. He had to trust Tash.

'Whoever it is can throw all they like at me,' he told Gus now, 'but if they touch my family I'll find them and shoot them.'

While Gus trotted eagerly back to Lime Tree Farm to pass on this latest news to his team, Hugo took a call from Mogo managing director Mike Seith that was guaranteed to intensify the enmity between himself and Lough yet further. The sponsors wanted a ride-off between the top Brit and his New Zealander team-mate. This was typical of the company, which often employed such tactics. Having at one time supported a team of six riders and started this year promising a Haydown exclusive, Mogo now planned to reduce to just one rider–ambassador – whoever ended up higher on the points board at the end of the season. Hugo was certain that Lough must have suggested the challenge. Having been away in the States at the start of the season, he was already lagging way behind.

That Rory wasn't even being considered in the Mogo sponsorship race didn't register with Hugo and Lough. They considered him well enough supported by Dillon Rafferty to survive. But to Rory, exclusion from the Mogo challenge spelled a very uncertain future and was a bitter blow to both his pride and pocket. Dillon hadn't paid a bill in a long while; the papers were full of pictures of him and Sylva Frost playing happy families. Rory left endless messages to no avail. Relying on individual patrons was notoriously risky, and Rory knew that he couldn't afford to keep paying his way at Haydown without more traditional corporate support.

Quietly getting on with his riding away from the Zeus and Poseidon rivalry, he'd scooped a decent cache of top-ten places in the spring events, but no plaudits so far this year. He wasn't sure how much longer he'd be able to keep going.

He badly needed a sounding board, and Faith was the first person to spring to mind, just as she'd been on his mind when he was on the other side of the Atlantic. But long gone were the days when she would send him twenty texts by lunchtime. He'd expected to hear from her as soon as she'd checked out the URL on the cowboy postcard, but she'd been ominously quiet of late. When asked, Beccy and Lemon said vaguely that she never got any time off, but Rory suspected she had a boyfriend, one of the Moncrieff's flash young blood City clients, or a National Hunt hell-raiser attracted to those terrifying fake boobs and her amazing vivacity. He hoped they didn't exploit her lion's heart.

Badly in need of advice, he turned instead to his latest fairy godmother. Marie-Clair had told him never to ring her at home even if he was dying, in case her husband answered. He left several urgent messages on her mobile, but she didn't return his calls.

He felt so down that he dared himself to text Faith after all, risking egg on his face. But gratifyingly she responded within twenty seconds of him suggesting they meet for a drink with *How soon?*

Yet even Faith had nothing great to offer in the way of wise counsel when they met in the Olive Branch for fizzy water, beer nuts and a game of skittles. 'You'll just have to win more, Rory. That's how it works.'

She'd become even more brusque lately, he noted. He blamed the influence of Penny Moncrieff, who was incredibly school-marmish and ragged Gus endlessly.

'I can barely afford the entry fees as it is,' he grumbled. 'I spent all my capital in America. Hugo's been paying for everything since then,' he revealed anxiously, firing off a skittles ball that missed its targets totally. 'If I don't have a win soon, he's bound to ditch me, especially now we know Mogo doesn't want me at the end of the season.'

'What about Dillon?' Faith was surprised.

Rory laughed bitterly, shaking his head. 'Now Nell's out of his life he's lost all interest in me. Owning horses was all about impressing her. And Sylva just pretended to be interested in eventing to get at Dillon.'

'That's not true.'

He lowered his head modestly. 'Thanks for imagining she saw more in me than a way to get at Dillon, but—'

'Oh, that bit's true.' Faith waved her hand at him impatiently. 'But Dillon certainly didn't back you because of Nell.'

'Whatever.' Rory was too dejected to care. 'He's not backing me right now, full stop.' He looked up at Faith again, drinking in the intensity of her gaze, the blue eyes sparkling to either side of her long noble nose like the beams of a lighthouse.

'Only one thing for it,' she told him dryly, selecting a skittles ball. 'You'll have to win the Grand Slam, starting with Kentucky.'

'No chance of that.'

'Why not?' She suddenly grew animated. 'You have a great horse waiting over there, you've been sober for weeks and you're running each morning – don't deny it because I've seen you. You've had the best coaching, support, ownership and expertise in the country at your disposal for months now. The least you can do is win the first leg.'

'Never been a leg man.'

Faith looked regretfully down at her endless slim legs and sighed, pressing her chicken fillets together instead as she bowled out her skittles with one toss. 'Just be grateful you're going to Kentucky.'

'You're invited too,' he pointed out, fingers strumming against his cheekbones as his tarnished-silver eyes stared at her indignantly.

She laughed. 'Don't talk crap. I have no money and no time off.'

'All paid for.'

'I have a full-time job.'

'Time off was arranged weeks ago.'

'Says who?'

Rory cocked his head, looking offended. 'Your horse, of course.'

'Eh?'

'Haven't you been keeping an eye on the webcam?'

'Since when did my horse have a webcam?'

'I *told* you about it as soon as we got back. It's on the postcard I gave you. I wrote the address down.'

Faith didn't have the heart to admit that she couldn't decipher his handwriting, even after many years of reading his feed charts at Overlodes. The postcard had been propped up on her bedside table since his return so that its picture was the first thing and the last thing she looked at each day, but the reverse was gobbledegook.

When Rory dropped her back at Lime Tree Farm he insisted on coming inside to assist in firing up Penny and Gus's ancient Mac. Showing unexpected reserves of patience throughout the technical glitches born of sluggish broadband and their combined ignorance of computers, Rory finally helped Faith locate the Johanssen's website with its live link to her stallion in his Virginia des res.

'This is their summer barn,' Rory explained, clicking the mouse for her. 'The horses all relocated there from MC's Florida place just before we flew home. There! Looks settled, doesn't he?' There was a surprisingly proud catch in his voice as he watched Faith's horse eat hay on screen. 'I asked Stefan to put him in this stall when I heard they had a camera in there.'

'Why?'

'Take a closer look.'

She squinted at the screen.

Pinned above Rio's hay manger, curling from the damp and dust, was a big sign that read: *Come and see me win in Kentucky, Mum. Your tickets are booked.*

Faith re-read it a dozen times before she started to take it seriously. 'You want me to go to America?'

'Blued my pocket money on a ticket, so I sure hope so,' he affected a Yankee accent.

She stared at him, realising what exactly he'd done for her. And what's more, he'd done it weeks ago, when he was still in America. She felt giddy.

'Why?'

'You're the owner.' He patted her on the shoulder with a respectful bow of his head, before looking up winningly through his lashes, a sheepish smile breaking on his face. 'And I need a groom.'

'You're not serious?'

He looked suddenly doubtful. 'Well, I could ask Stefan and Kirsty if they can spare somebody, I guess . . .'

'Like hell you will!' she whooped. 'I'm going to Kentucky!'

So delirious with excitement that she couldn't think straight, Faith kissed Rory a hundred times on his face, cheeks, lips, hands and even knees until he had to bat her away and tell her to go to bed.

'I hope your boyfriend won't mind you being away,' he said as he was leaving.

'What boyfriend?' She laughed. 'I have no time for stupid things like that.'

'Of course,' he agreed heartily, 'stupid of me to even think it.'

Faith was far too distracted to notice the relief in his face.

'I'm going to Kentucky!' she shrieked again, thundering up the stairs to her attic and inadvertently waking the entire house.

Riding home on Hugo's quad bike, which he'd taken to borrowing on a regular basis, Rory also felt pretty delirious.

Lough had to tell him off for singing 'Whip Crack Away!' at top volume in the lodge cottage bath. He bounded into bed that night feeling as though he'd just won the Mogo sponsorship deal, not been excluded from the race.

He was about to text Faith to remind her to pack her party dress when a text message came through from Dillon, making contact after many weeks of silence: *Hope all okay with horses. Sorry money late – girls in office snowed under. Cheque on way. Good luck in Kentucky. D.* He read it in amazement, marvelling at the serendipity.

The phone rang in his hands.

'*Chéri,* it is too bad you are so low.' MC's voice was a deep, sexual purr. 'I am going to cheer you up next week, *non?* I am on the ground jury at Kentucky so I will see you there. I am looking forward to it, *chéri.*'

Rory felt a quiver of anticipation course through him.

Chapter 56

'It's the big party at Haydown next week,' Sylva purred throatily at Dillon during one of their rare phone calls, which she was conducting via speakerphone in her powder blue kitchen while her documentary team filmed her. 'Just checking you'll be back?'

'I'll try,' he promised. 'Berry has chicken pox and her mother's away filming, so it depends how she recovers.'

He was predictably in the States, almost his second home, where he was staying with his ex in-laws in Malibu. Sylva didn't for a moment object to the amount of time he devoted to his daughters and to maintaining close links with their mother's family – she only wished her own children's fathers were as conscientious – but it played havoc with any attempt at a normal relationship. Not that anything about their relationship was remotely normal, from the imprudent announcement of their engagement to the ongoing civility between them, while all around the press slavered for scraps and their respective families went into overdrive.

Mama was still planning the wedding of the century, spending hours poring over brochures and dress designs, ordering his and hers Swarovski Grenade rings the size of gulls' eggs.

'But he hasn't really proposed,' Sylva pointed out after Rodney and his team had left.

Mama batted the objection away. 'It's publicity, *mačička*. We all know that. And you *will* marry him.'

Yet, up close and personal, Sylva wasn't so sure. She had loved Strawberry when they married. And Jonte had been exciting and a fantastic lover, if incapable of keeping his dick in his pants for more than a week on a film set. She'd cared deeply for both and borne them children. Dillon Rafferty, on the other hand, was boorish and twitchy in person, banging on about farming and food, uninterested in clubs, parties and the high life; he didn't even drink or take drugs. He was a very dull rock star, especially compared to his father. When Sylva had met Pete she'd known instantly that he had the power to snap her lingerie straps with one come-here click of his fingers.

As her darling Jules had foretold, Pete was the real deal, with his manic laugh and globe-trotting life. He was edgy rather than twitchy, a truly dangerous man rather than a bad boy, and head-spinningly untrustworthy. While Dillon's testosterone-packed smile was legend, his father didn't need to smile to ooze sex appeal.

But Pete was not the member of the Rafferty family driving the groom's side of the wedding train; that was his young wife Indigo, who played for the cameras quite brilliantly. She might guard the castle gates very closely when her husband was around, but he was most often in Ireland these days, and while he was away Indigo had made it her mission to cultivate her stepson's fantasy fiancée, for whom she had played matchmaker in the first place. She was a faultless stage manager, granting the tabloids limited but enticing telephoto opportunities, along with Sylva's film crew, who were gracefully but firmly manipulated along with their subject.

It had started with an open invitation for Sylva and her family to use the Abbey's new indoor pool and fitness rooms, and to ride the horses kept there. A series of shopping trips followed, along with pampering sessions at Eastlode Park, all accompanied by their many children, the nannies and the oleaginous child psychologist Dong. Most recently, Sylva had found herself joining Indigo on a succession of more intimate girls' lunches. Mama insisted Sylva go along, maintaining that the friendship could prove as beneficial to her as Posh's was to Mrs Cruise. The paparazzi certainly chased these photo opportunities eagerly, and Sylva was riding high IFOJ as a result of the alliance, but she was growing tired of the headlines that claimed she was best friends with her future mother-in-law when she barely knew her future husband.

Sylva found Dong's strange, watchful presence an impediment to the natural flow of conversation, and she thought he was a toadying sham, but Indigo trusted him implicitly. Just five feet to her six, they were an incongruous pair, but they seemed devoted to one another. Both apparently loved the sound of his quasi-Californian drawl.

'Dillon is your classic madonna–whore complex, just like his father,' he told them over lunch of clear soup and noodle toast at Eastlode Park. 'Distant mother, now deceased, making him put some women on a pedestal – the sort he perceives as a mother or a wife, almost desexualising them – while other women he sees as no more than depositories for his jizz.'

'And which category are you suggesting I fall into?' Sylva demanded.

'Hard to tell.' He eyed up her breasts. 'Superficially whore, because that is your public image, but you are also a mother, of course.'

'What exactly are your qualifications?' Sylva fumed, but Dong was impervious to any attack.

Her friendship with Indigo was as brittle as her love affair with Dillon, and both women were well aware that theirs was a careful game of chess being played out in front of the full media glare, with the kings held back for now. Sylva appreciated the challenge of taking on a grand master, at least. By contrast, what she had with Dillon felt like an online chess quickie in which both players had walked away from their keyboards. Their names remained up on screen, but they had no control over their pieces and no real care. Each just wanted to wait for the other to give up first and then log off.

For Mama's sake, Sylva tried very hard to stay in play for the Beauchamps' party. It was important that she and Dillon were seen out in public together soon. And she was surprised to find herself looking forward to seeing eventing's premier couple again; they provided the rare combination of a husband she found attractive and a wife she genuinely liked. That Sylva had once tried to poach one from the other didn't bother her now that she had Dillon caught in a snare. She could trust herself to behave impeccably. Surely taking him back to that beautiful house where they had first flirted over a champagne shooting lunch would give the lacklustre romance a little fizz at last?

She had her dark hair extensions re-applied, her natural blonde roots touched up to match and her lips plumped in anticipation, then enjoyed a lengthy Bond Street shopping trip with Indigo, who talked her into a very sexy Galliano smock matched with thigh-high suede boots instead of the more modest, retro Chloé cocktail dress she'd been favouring. 'Dillon will love this.'

'Are you sure?' Sylva turned round and the smock's diaphanous fabric swirled, revealing the first tawny curve of her Fake-Baked buttocks. 'They're quite a conservative crowd, darlink.'

'Dillon will *love* it, won't he Dong?' Indigo consulted her oracle, who was sitting in a plush velvet chair in the corner of the dressing room, sipping green tea.

He peered over his thick-rimmed spectacles. 'His father would love certainly it. Like son like father.' He thickened his Sino-American accent to make the Spoonerism sound like a Confucian proverb.

'There you go.' Indigo rested her case.

Sylva opened her mouth, about to protest that Dillon wasn't like Pete at all and hardly had the same taste, but then she looked at her reflection again and changed her mind. The dress did look sensational.

'It would work better with blonde hair.' Indigo was studying her critically.

Their eyes met in the mirror.

'I'll go blonde again for the wedding,' Sylva said evenly.

They shared half-smiles, barely perceptible amid the Botox-frozen perfection of their faces.

Watching them, Dong steepled his manicured hands to his nose and whispered, 'The dye is cast.'

Sylva wasn't sure what he meant, especially when, two days later, Dillon phoned to say that Berry was no better and Fawn's filming had been extended by a week so he couldn't get back in time for the party. Trying to sound serene, Sylva insisted that was fine and she would go alone – or, better still, take her new best friend Indigo with her.

'Good luck.' Dillon's laughter inflamed her bottled anger. 'My stepmother is allergic to horses.'

'But she has a dozen at the Abbey.'

'One in every colour, yes. She collects them, like children. She gets somebody else to handle them, just as she does the children.'

Indigo's reaction to Sylva's request that she be her plus-one bore this out. 'Who are these people?' she demanded as they bobbed in the Abbey pool, surrounded by nannies and children as usual.

'Lovely sporting heroes.'

'I am not interested in them,' Indigo coolly dismissed. 'And I am busy. Pete will be here next weekend.'

Sylva found herself perking up. Maybe she would give the party a miss too. She wanted to try a few more of the Abbey's horses for size for a start.

But Indigo was moving her chess pieces with consummate skill. 'You must go to America to see Dillon,' she insisted, swimming around Sylva like a crocodile. 'He needs to know you care. His father will approve.'

'Don't be silly, darlink.' Sylva made it to the steps and clambered out to consult her jewelled phone. 'I am working all this week and next promoting my new book. If I fly out on Friday night, I would only have time to meet him for a few hours before flying home.'

'So romantic.' Climbing out of the pool, Indigo wrapped herself in a fluffy robe and glanced at Dong, still in his suit on a sunlounger, smiling his enigmatic guru smile. 'Book a great restaurant. Wear your new dress. The press will go wild. Pete can read all about it in the Sunday papers here; he loves to catch up with his son that way.'

As soon as Sylva got back to Le Petit Château, Mama backed up Indigo's entreaty with the heavy artillery. 'I'll get Pauline to book your flights. You will take the pretty rings as a peace offering, *mačička*. This is a much better surprise for a man than a boring party.'

Sulkily, Sylva acquiesced.

Chapter 57

Five days before the best-planned party in eventing history, Sophia phoned Tash in an apoplectic fit. '*Why* have you cancelled the caterers?'

'I haven't,' she said in surprise.

'Marysia took the call over a fortnight ago, she tells me – *and* got confirmation from you in writing. Now they've got another booking. We'll never get another lot at this short notice, not for this number.'

'We can try,' Tash urged, wondering who on earth could have forged the letter, and why.

The next day, while Sophia was ringing desperately around her contacts to secure a new caterer, calls and messages started to come through on Tash's BlackBerry, commiserating for the family loss.

It didn't take a great deal of detective work to discover that almost half the guest list had been emailed from her phone to say that the party had been cancelled.

'I didn't send it!' Tash promised her sister, knowing that she left the thing all over the place at the yard and competitions, along with a piece of paper tucked into the case with the password and instructions because she kept forgetting how to work it. Anybody could have used it.

'Now we have no choice but to pull the plug,' Sophia told her in another phone call, which Tash had to take in the downstairs loo to avoid being overheard by an increasingly suspicious Hugo. 'It's in disarray and I will *not* have my reputation tarnished. I'll discreetly let all the guests know and ask them to all keep schtum so we can rearrange something for a later date. At least Hugo has no idea what's gone wrong. Just do something low-key instead.'

Working in the outside arena in brilliant spring sunshine later that afternoon, Tash spotted Lough riding across the road towards the downs track and decided to cool off River by joining him as far as the start of the first steep climb. This was one guest not on Sophia's list who Tash wanted to tell personally, although she had always suspected he wouldn't come.

Crows were rasping overhead, wood pigeons cooing and amorous hedge birds tweeting at one another closer by as River's mile-eating walk meant she quickly caught up with her stablemate, hooves quiet on the ridge of green that ran between the still-muddy wheel ruts. To either side of those, the first shoots of nettles and hogweed were starting to uncurl in the verges.

Lough didn't look round, but he knew she was there because he held up a hand to keep her from talking and then pointed across the pasture field to their left. There, a family of fallow deer were watching them, much closer than they would have ever dared stray had the riders been on foot. Tash could clearly see the pregnant bellies of the does, their limpid eyes watchful.

'Hugo's father kept a herd on the parkland – it was all the rage in his day,' she whispered once they had passed by. 'But lots escaped in the late seventies and now there are breeding herds all over the downs.'

'Good for them,' he murmured. 'Wild animals should run free, not be a rich man's pretty playthings.'

'The local poachers certainly like it,' she sighed, glancing over her shoulder. 'They eat a lot of prime venison round here. Lough, there's been a horrible mix-up.' She told him about the sabotaged party.

He gave no reaction to the news.

'It has to be deliberate, don't you think?' Tash asked.

'Why are you telling me about it?'

'I thought you might know something.'

At last he looked across at her and gave a surprised laugh. 'You mean, you think I might be behind it?'

'No!' she gulped. 'I just . . .' She looked away, embarrassed.

'I'm not your husband's greatest fan, but I wouldn't do something like that, Tash. What would be the point? I was going to come.'

'You were?'

'Sure.'

They'd pulled up by the downs gate. Ahead, the track sloped sharply upwards and the horses traditionally cantered or galloped it.

River was already jogging, despite the hour's work she'd already had. She was almost competition fit now and raring to go.

Reaching for the huntsman's latch and swinging the gate open for her, Lough made way for her to pass.

'I should go back,' she said, reluctantly looking at her watch.

'You won't get that horse fit enough for a four-star in the school,' he shrugged.

Knowing he was right, Tash guessed she could spare another half hour. Hugo was away coaching clients until four. Taking the challenge, she went through the gate and just about held on to River until Lough had shut it, then they were off, pounding along the parallel soft ruts up the steep flank of the downs, wind chilling their faces and ears, rhythmic hoof-falls, snorts and clanking bridlework creating a percussive beat. Tash felt no fear, just pure exhilaration. In a moment of showmanship she crouched higher over River's neck and pushed for a fast finish, the mare easily out-racing Lough's little horse.

When they pulled up at the top, Tash was speechless with delight.

A rare smile breaking across his face, Lough reached across and patted her on the back. They both remembered the day, not many weeks earlier, when he'd taken off ahead of her and she'd almost expired with fright as her horse bolted behind.

'I got it back!' she laughed.

'It never went. It was always in here.' He boffed her chest lightly with his knuckles. As he did so, his horse shifted sharply beneath him and he was unbalanced for a moment, forced to reach out to steady himself, and almost joining her in the saddle. Their bodies crashed clumsily together, his hand on her thigh and chin in her ear. Then he tipped back again, in balance once more, horse circling away beneath him.

Tash, who now found she could barely breathe, looked away to try to compose her face.

They both remained silent as they began to hack the short circuit home again, but when she finally glanced across at Lough, she knew he was just as tense as she was. This blood-rush was a lot more alarming than falling off.

Unlike his mute reaction, instinct made her start to chatter nervously. 'I'll think I'll host a big supper instead of a party. I'm going to invite the Moncrieffs and the Stantons, plus some other good chums and the team at home, of course. I hope you'll be able to come?' As soon as she said it she could have hit herself. It sounded appalling after the chemical reaction that had just occurred between them, like Sharon Stone taking a break from smouldering in *Basic Instinct* to suggest she and Michael Douglas have a cream tea.

He didn't dignify it with an answer.

'I have no idea what to give Hugo for his birthday,' she rattled on. 'I was really hoping the foal might be born by now, the one Dove's carrying – it's the last of Snob's line, and this one's embryo transfer.' She patted River's neck. 'That's really his present from me, but I'd better find something else too.'

Still saying nothing, Lough held open another gate. Their knees brushed as she passed through. It lit up her nerve endings and she half-expected her stirrups to send out sparks.

'I wish I could give Hugo some good luck,' she squeaked, her overheated brain determined to cool itself with a tide of words. 'He's had such a rotten month, what with the bad press, sick horses and some awful hate campaign going on. I'd love him to do well in Kentucky to give him a boost. My sister and Ben are flying out to support him . . .'

Lough had ridden closer so he could reach out to touch her arm. 'Tash, shut up.'

With another electric bolt passing through her, Tash did as she was told.

'I'm sure you'll give Hugo a great birthday,' he said quietly.

She nodded.

'And we're all looking forward to following his progress at Kentucky.'

'Yes.' She swallowed uncomfortably, not daring to look at him. The both knew that as soon as Hugo and Rory left for America they'd have Haydown to themselves once more.

This time, she was determined to give her husband a fantastic send-off. She only wished she could stow away with him.

If Hugo was somewhat disheartened by the hastily cobbled-together dinner party Tash organised to celebrate his two score years, his present from his wife was one he would never forget. She made him wait until after the last guest had departed before he could see it.

Utterly determined to get a four-star seduction on the scoreboard, Tash would let nothing stand in her way. Leaving the wash-ing-up piled in the sinks and the Bitches of Eastwick helping themselves to leftovers, she hoofed upstairs three at a time, telling Hugo to bring up a nightcap. In a spirit of wicked, one-night-only abandonment, she switched off the baby monitor and locked herself in the bathroom.

When she emerged, Hugo was lounging on the slipper chair in the corner of the bedroom, swirling cognac in a huge balloon glass and gazing into its contents. Looking up, a smile broke across his face like rays of sunshine through thunder clouds.

She had used the remaining tubes of ready-made coloured icing that Cora had squirted on her father's birthday cake earlier that day. It wasn't nearly as sophisticated a picture as the exquisite body-paint that she'd applied upon his return from the States, but given her artistic flair and her new-found, toned physique, it was more than enough for Hugo to feast his eyes.

Inscribed deliciously all over her body in bright icing were the let-ters and numbers that made up HAPPY 40TH HUGO and I LOVE YOU!

Self-conscious yet hopelessly excited, Tash hastily dimmed the bedroom light and edged towards him, hoping that he wouldn't notice her crab-like walk, necessary to try to preserve the H on the inside of one of her thighs. Behind her back was the unused tube of cherry-flavoured red that she planned to use to write MANY HAPPY RETURNS on his body.

'Take off your shirt,' she ordered.

But she was barely mid-way through writing the HAPPY when Hugo scooped her up and threw her onto the bed, his appetite for petites-fourplay ravenous.

He found the Ps and H's with greedy kisses, devoured the Os and Us and licked away each Y with two tantalising flicks of the tongue. By the time he reached the As, the G and the L, the icing was melt-ing in his mouth and on Tash's skin.

She had barely tasted a delectable sweet fix of M from the inside of his wrist before he discovered his 40th at the base of her spine.

'There's an exclamation mark somewhere,' Tash managed to gasp as he turned her over again and dived for the perfect V beneath her belly button.

He found the exclamation mark and more as his tongue traced

lower to taste the sweetest nectar, its icing swept away in a hot, slippery tide of excitement.

'You're something else,' he breathed into her ear when he resurfaced, looming over her, his face and body in shadow, such an eclipse of vigour and animal sex appeal that she felt willing to succumb to his every whim.

Hugo's every whim was thrillingly straightforward. Impatient and rapacious, they lifted hips and tilted pelvises to those familiar angles that slotted together so well, hot excited skin brushing faster and tighter, friction sparking, nerves jumping and trembling, their breath quickening as blood rushed south and oxygen whooshed after it. Hugo's eyes never left Tash's, her cries of delight as untamed as a wild bird lifting from cover, frightened and exhilarated by the sheer abandon of instinct taking over.

Afterwards, sticky with sweat and icing, curled in each other's arms, they said nothing. Tash could hear Hugo's heart in his chest, settling back into a steady rhythm after such a violent awakening that she was left in no doubt of his desire and love. At the far end of the bed, beyond a slumbering Beetroot, the Rat Pack minus one terrier was trying to scale the furry new counterpane without detection.

She smiled into Hugo's chest.

His voice lifted through his ribcage into her ear. 'What are you thinking?'

Tash held her breath in amazement. It was the first time in almost a decade together that he had asked that question. She remembered reading somewhere that real men never asked it unless they thought you were having an affair, or they feared that you had found out about the affair that *they* were having.

'I don't have time to think these days,' she evaded, 'just to love you.'

'Me too, but—' He laughed gruffly and closed his eyes, leaving Tash cemented to his side, getting cramp, until she realised that he was fast asleep.

'But?' She prodded him.

He was dead to the world.

Tash wearily unglued herself and went into the bathroom to sponge away the last exclamation marks. The dye from the blue icing had left a rather alarming stain across her throat, arms and belly, along with the purple on one cheek and her shoulder.

Making a mental note to exfoliate in the morning, Tash wrapped herself in Hugo's deep green dressing gown, switched on the baby monitor and carried it downstairs, trailed by Beetroot, to tackle the washing-up.

When Beetroot started running backwards and forwards from the Bitches' sofa to the terrier's floor-rug, she straightened up from loading the dishwasher and glanced over her shoulder in time to see her aged little dog performing strange hops and snarls as she danced out into the back lobby.

Following, Tash found that Beetroot was now standing at the boot room door, trying to inhale the air from under it and growling suspiciously.

Swathed in the gloom of the unlit back passage, she jumped as the yard security beam flashed on, its silver light-spill slicing in though the grubby windows and revealing a long shadow of a figure moving around.

Not thinking, Tash stepped into her boots and raced outside, Beetroot limping along in her wake.

The first thing that struck her was the cold, like an acid splash in the face, even though it was early April. There were even snowflakes in the air. She was still naked beneath Hugo's dressing gown and not really equipped to restrain armed robbers. But when she walked beneath the archway, she saw a light glowing from Dove's stable and gave a bleat of excitement.

Dove had given birth to a big, white-faced colt, still wet and crease-eared from the womb, his long legs trembling and limpid eyes blinking as he stumbled about in search of milk and succour.

'He's a beauty, isn't he?' A familiar, flat voice drawled across the yard as Lough appeared from the office, a can of antiseptic spray in one hand.

'Why didn't you fetch us?' she asked.

'You had guests. The old girl didn't want a load of spectators.'

She stepped aside as he pulled back the bolt and went in to sterilise the foal's umbilical stump. Watching the leggy newborn and proud, whickering Dove brought an unexpected catch to Tash's throat that made speech impossible. For a maddening moment she thought she was going to cry, but she stared determinedly up at the rafters and held hard to her emotions, knowing that maternal overload and birthday sentimentality were in danger of making a fool of her.

Lough came out through the door, his shadow falling across her.

'They haven't needed my help really. She's a great mum,' he murmured as Dove nudged the colt towards her milk.

Tash felt the tears brim again, a broody tidal wave that made no sense.

The baby monitor was still in the kitchen, she remembered, her own umbilical cord, not yet fully cut and cauterised. 'We should leave them to bond. It's late.'

'Sure. You must be frozen through.' Lough moved further out into the yard and stopped in his tracks as saw her in the light for the first time, cast in chiaroscuro but still visible enough to make him double-take.

'I *am* cold,' she laughed, pulling the dressing gown tighter and trying to stop her teeth chattering. 'I should get back.'

But as she turned away he caught her arm and held her under the glare of the security light.

'You're covered in bruises.' He reached up to take her chin in his fingers, tilting her face away from the shadows. 'Christ, you're black and blue.'

'Food dye,' she muttered embarrassedly.

Lough didn't seem to be listening as he examined the deep blue and purple stains on her cheek, throat and forehead. Then he touched her collarbone, still smudged with green where Hugo had recently licked an O from its curved ridge.

Still tingling with sexual after-burn, Tash was horrified to find her pulses leaping obediently, her cool, naked flesh drawing hot blood. As Lough drew back the collar of the robe to reveal more stains, ominously and deceitfully dark against her pale skin, her faithless heart hammered in her chest, ears and groin.

'What has he done to you?' he breathed, his eyes filled with pity as they examined the damning evidence.

'It's dye,' she repeated. His fingers were blisteringly hot against her skin, his kindness and care enveloping her. 'Here – taste.' Without stopping to think, she rubbed her forefinger against her neck, where there was still a smudge of icing, and touched it to his lips. The moment she did it, the moment his mouth was against her skin, she knew she'd crossed an invisible line. She snatched her hand away, but the boundary stayed crossed. In the dark side of her heart that told the bitter truth, she knew she'd been walking the line for weeks.

He was still pulling back her collar, but he was no longer looking for bruises. She could feel the cool air on the back of her neck and his warm hands on her shoulders.

Count to ten, she told herself firmly. On one, walk away. On two, run. By five, be back in the house with the door looked and in bed with Hugo by ten.

But even as she started counting, Lough had eased the robe over her shoulders, letting it drop to the ground. By two, Tash was naked, bar her boots.

Being a birthday cake for Hugo had made her fizz all over, forty little candles of hot lust licking at her skin.

Being naked in front of Lough, in the snow, made her feel as though her skin and heart were on fire.

His eyes, so huge and dark they were the blackest of wishing wells, didn't leave her face as he stepped towards her and gathered her gown again, wrapping it over her shoulders, his breath hot against her cheek. For a moment she felt his lips there. Her mouth craved contact with his so badly that she had to consciously hold her head as if in a neck brace to stop it tilting into his.

'I love you.'

He could have said it, or it could have been a trick of the wind, moaning softly through the archway.

'I know,' she breathed even more quietly, turning to flee.

Amery was bawling his heart out when she got back in the house, the monitor on the kitchen table lighting up like a mini disco. She ran guiltily up to him, gathering him in her arms to cuddle and love without question or restriction, her guilt-ridden heart hammering so badly that she felt as though it would burst.

Finally settling him, she went straight to bed. Too exhausted to care about the half-finished washing-up, she cleaned her teeth again and climbed into the heavenly cocoon.

Hugo woke groggily as her cold skin slid against his bed-hot warmth.

'Where've you been?'

'Dove had her foal.'

'Alive?'

'Of course. Why wouldn't he be?'

'Mmm, yes.' Hugo was already too distracted to pursue the topic, a rejuvenated hard-on pressing a demanding doorbell call, even though his conscious mind was still only just surfacing.

Tash found her own sexual energy defying tiredness as she arched her back, lifted a leg and drew him in with a pull of eager muscle that astonished her – as did the climax which came within seconds, rushing up inside her with such intensity it almost hurt.

When Hugo came, he collapsed back in bed and was asleep again almost immediately, leaving Tash with her eyes wide open, body pulsating and mind racing. It was Hugo in her body but Lough in her head, and she knew it. Lough had been in her head throughout. She hadn't felt sexual craving this intensely for years. Not since falling in love with Hugo.

Chapter 58

Faith was completely blown away by the sheer scale and intensity of America. She loved the country from the moment they pulled up at Stefan and Kirsty Johanssen's Virginia barn, nestling in a lush green valley at the base of Blue Ridge Mountain, with its white clapboard farmhouse and tree-shaded barn. She longed to run around their fields with her arms outstretched like Laura Ingalls Wilder. It was heaven. She wanted to live there.

They spent just one night with the Johanssens, which barely allowed them time to reacquaint themselves with their horses, pack up everything, share a gossipy meal and rest for a couple of hours before setting out in the early hours of Tuesday morning on the ten-hour drive east to Lexington. Their hosts led the way in a butch Freightliner truck, a big-nosed overgrown pick-up towing a gargantuan gooseneck trailer that was part horsebox, part caravan and part Greyhound bus, loaded up with four horses, three to compete and one that was transferring to a new owner. The Johanssen's called their rig Vegas because it was big, brash and American. It was their second home that transported them and their valuable horses all over the States, including on their bi-annual migration between Bluemont and Ocala, Florida, and they were rightly proud of it. Hunky working pupil Björn and their head girl Pia, both from Sweden, were travelling with them in the big crew-cab truck while Rory took the wheel of a borrowed Ford Ranger belonging to show-jumping neighbours of the Johanssens, along with their more modest trailer that housed just Rio and Oil Tanker, separated by a stall piled high with hay bales to stop the stallion picking on the Australian gelding. At the front of the trailer was just enough room to house Rory and Faith in excitingly close quarters; Hugo had, as usual, secured himself cushy accommodation in a hotel near to the Kentucky Horse Park. The Johanssens and their grooms had big enough sleeping quarters in Vegas to host the entire Swedish team and their families.

Driving in convoy along Interstate 81 as dawn broke, the journey reignited Faith's spirit of adventure, while the weariness that she had felt when putting her watch back five hours and keeping going with precious little sleep melted away. Cowboy hat tilted over her face, feet up on the dash, she felt her heart soar.

Having travelled out with Faith and Rory to Washington Dulles from Heathrow, Hugo had very little left to say to them and dozed through most of those early miles. Yet Rory and Faith had no trouble keeping up the flow of conversation as they cruised along, talking about tactics for Rio, what they needed to get out of the event, his long-term plans and all the training that Rory had put in earlier in the year in Florida.

They paused only to catch their breath as the sun finally spilled over the horizon, revealing the Appalachian Mountains in all their glory, as green as a pile of giant emeralds.

After breaking for a huge brunch that could have fed Faith for a month, Hugo took over the driving and his travelling companions carried on talking non-stop, while he gritted his teeth and tried to tune them out.

When they finally followed Vegas into the Kentucky Horse Park entrance, Faith gasped with delighted astonishment as she took in the magnitude of the place and the atmosphere. The venue was beyond her wildest imaginings, but then again everything about the States was beyond her imaginings. Even a day before the official start of the Rolex Kentucky Three Day Event, the atmosphere was absolutely buzzing.

As they drove through the park, skirting around a boggling number of arenas, sand tracks and tree-lined avenues and seemingly endless white-railed paddocks stretching away into the distance, she found herself gripping Rory's hand. To her surprise, he gripped tightly back. He had turned very pale and suddenly gone quiet as the scale of the task ahead of him started to sink in.

This was no muddy, friendly English event. This was all-American, super-efficient eventing on a mammoth scale at a tailor-made show site. The security alone seemed never-ending as they reached the stables office and went through the rigmarole of passport and preliminary veterinary checks, being issued with security wristbands and stable numbers while the grooms walked the horses in hand before finally locating their stalls, laying beds, brushing away the sweat and dust of the long haul, checking water and forage and unpacking trunks. All the time, familiar faces swooped in to say hello, to slap Stefan and Hugo on the back, kiss Kirsty and be introduced to Rory and then Faith. To her, the faces were the stuff of legend – international heroes, Olympic medallists, world champions and other eventing superstars who had been her pin-ups since early childhood along with dressage and showjumping heroes. She loved being called an owner, although her wristband meant she knew that it was her groom's hat she'd be sporting for the coming days as she supported Rory through the biggest challenge of his competitive life. Pia would double up her care for Kirsty's horse with looking after Oil Tanker, whose dressage time and cross-country slot were at opposite ends of the running order, with Björn looking after both of Stefan's rides.

Having had only a short time in Virginia to sit on their horses again, Rory and Hugo were keen to get straight on and stretch them through the park, leaving the others to set up a temporary home from home in the campsite at the far eastern reaches of the main boulevard that ran through the park, separating the southerly 'In field' from the northerly 'Out field', through which the majority of the four-mile cross country course ran.

There was so much to take in that Faith pressed her nose to the window like a child at a safari park as Björn drove the Ranger and trailer to the campsite for her, chatting easily in his strange, lilting voice about his ambitions to ride for Sweden one day.

'You want to ride for England, yes?' he asked her.

'Oh, not really – just well enough for the people I love to take notice.' She suddenly felt stupidly shy, and not just because strapping, blond Björn looked like a pin-up. Tiredness was stripping her of energy, and the ability to think straight.

The campsite was arranged in a figure-of-eight of neat, tree-lined lots, many already filled with high-tech horse trailers, others by RVs belonging to eager eventing fans. Björn reversed the trailer into the lot beside Vegas, which had already been uncoupled from its monster truck and was having its nose hydraulically lowered to create an amazing, private double bedroom for the husband and wife team.

Having thanked Björn, who then took one of the little mopeds that the Johanssens had transported in a locker on the cavernous Vegas and whizzed back to the stables, Faith took a better look at her sleeping quarters. Her legs now feeling like lead, she clambered inside the trailer and studied the very cosy mattressed sleeping area in the gooseneck nose, and the little sofa bench that converted to a miserly single bunk for her. It was hardly the stuff of romance, but to Faith it was the most heavenly opportunity she'd ever had, better than a weekend in a Ritz penthouse suite with anybody else. She and Rory were shacked up together in a small tin box. It was a dream come true.

She climbed up on to the sleeping platform to try it out just once before Rory claimed it, stretching out and imagining his body where hers was now, his steady, deep breathing, his wonderful smell and long, languid limbs.

Within seconds she was asleep.

Rory didn't notice her there in the shadows when he dashed in to change out of his breeches before going to meet MC, who had sent him several hot texts insisting that he must visit her hotel room before her husband flew in and before she had to be back on show wearing her official cap as a member of the ground jury.

Right now I am wearing nothing but my Dutch cap, her last message had read. Rory wasn't sure he found the image quite as erotic as she intended – it conjured pictures in his head of MC dressed in Amish costume.

Faith didn't wake up until after seven; it was dusk outside. She had a crick in her neck. The trailer smelled horribly of cigars and Bourbon, a legacy from the show-jumpers who owned it. Feeling nauseous, she groped her way into the little toilet cubicle, but she hadn't hooked up the electricity and water yet so the pump wouldn't work to wash her face, nor could she turn on any lights because the leisure battery was flat. Back in the living area, she fell over Rory's breeches, which he'd left where he'd stepped out of them. She hadn't even realised that he'd been back.

Björn and Pia were presiding over a barbecue that was smoking only marginally more than Stefan and Hugo, who were sitting in folding chairs in front of Vegas, which had sprouted awnings and pods galore and was lit up like its city namesake, even sporting fairy lights and rows of Swedish flags. Both men had bottles of beer.

'Don't tell the wife.' Stefan grinned, fag dangling from his thin, smiling lips as he reached behind him into a cool bag and held up a Bud for her. 'She made me give up smoking three years ago.'

'I insisted Tash give up' – Hugo took a long drag – 'but she didn't return the favour, alas.'

Faith politely shook her head to the proffered beer.

'Kirsty's in the shower.' Stefan nodded towards the trailer, slotting the fresh bottle in his jacket pocket. 'I turned the water pressure right down so I have longer to enjoy my sins, but she'll be out soon and we'll eat. We didn't want to wake you earlier, you poor lamb. You must be bushed and there's a lot of action ahead.'

'Where's Rory?' Faith asked awkwardly, the smell of cigarettes combined with charred raw meat making her want to retch. 'Has he gone to check on the horses?'

'Hardly,' Hugo drawled. 'He's still taking his French oral.'

'He's what?' she asked dubiously.

'Marie-Clair.' Stefan sighed nostalgically, having himself once engaged in an apprenticeship with eventing's premier lady rider in and out of the saddle.

Faith looked from him to Hugo for clarification, although a spasm of pain in her heart had already confirmed the worst.

Hugo raised his eyebrows at her, suggesting the subject was better closed, but she needed to lay it open.

'Are they lovers?'

He fixed her with his cynical blue gaze, but his eyes retained an edge of compassion. 'I'd hazard a guess that he's currently sitting through an optional talk on international codes of practice in eventing, poor lovesick bastard. Her husband's due to fly in by helicopter any minute to co-host the FEI delegates' dinner, so he might as well come back to eat.'

Rory didn't come back to eat, however, and as true darkness fell barbecues disbanded and all-important pre-competition sleep got underway. Faith's texts went unanswered. Hugo set off for his hotel in a golf buggy that one of his sponsors had procured for him for the event and which looked faintly ridiculous whirring away decked in their advertising banners, but certainly made the schlep from the campsite to the hotel a great deal speedier. Vegas glowed a little less brightly as the outside lights shut down, followed shortly afterwards by the little advent calendar windows one at a time.

Faith trailed to the stables to check on Rio. He was lying down on his plump bed, limpid eyes looking up at her curiously, as though wondering why she had bothered to pop by when he was obviously so content.

Back in her putrid-smelling caravan, too proud and humiliated to ask for help hooking it up to the water and electricity, Faith cleaned her teeth in the dark without rinsing and fought tears of indignation.

I'm his horse's owner, she thought furiously. Rio's the reason he's *here*.

It was almost midnight by the time Rory finally crept in, falling over his own tangled breeches which Faith hadn't moved.

She listened, every nerve alert as he fumbled about in the dark searching for his bag, clearly gave up and clambered up on to his bed.

Wide awake now, she couldn't bear to wait through the silence for his sleep-breathing to begin.

'Where have you been?'

'Is that you, Faith?'

'Of course it is. Who else d'you think's in here? Mary King?'

'I wasn't sure of the sleeping arrangements.'

'Where have you been?' she repeated.

'I tried to blag my way into some godawful dinner, but they were all ancient old eventing bores and they didn't want me there, so I walked the cross-country course instead.'

'In the dark?'

'Always find it the best way to memorise it. If you can find your way around in the dark, you have the edge.'

'Didn't anyone try to stop you?'

'Only the ditch monsters and the ground disappearing from under my feet. There are a lot of drops out there.'

'Are you drunk?'

'No. Nothing but Coca-Cola and sweet nothings have passed through these lips tonight. Can I go to sleep now?'

'One last thing . . .'

'Hmm . . .?' His voice was thick with slumber.

'Did you and MC have sex?' It sounded horribly clinical, but she could think of no other way of asking it.

'None . . .' he mumbled, making her heart leap hopefully, '. . . of your business.' And he was asleep.

Chapter 59

Tash put pressure on Beccy and Lem to eat supper with her each evening during the Kentucky run, determined to keep the laptop on the kitchen table throughout with links to updates of the scores, the Twitter feeds of sports journalists and riders, live video streaming and radio buffering, and even the gossipy forums. She insisted it was good for morale and team spirit, but in reality she didn't want to risk being alone with Lough. Later in the week they would be away competing together, but the cramped camaraderie of shared quarters in the lorry park held less danger for her than the intimacy of time spent in his company amid Haydown's many rooms and acres, especially after dark.

It was difficult enough riding in such close proximity by day. Whenever he and Toto fell into step alongside her and River in the arena, she suddenly found sitting trot impossible because the seat of the saddle seemed to have built up a static charge. She avoided hacking altogether, her head filled with far too many involuntary images of frolicking naked with Lough among the wild hyacinths in the beech wood. Instead, she threw herself into work and hosted big kitchen suppers.

She pulled out all the culinary stops with tastebud-soaking roasts and her range of killer puddings. Lemon readily accepted the invitation, dragging Beccy in his wake.

'We could see all this in the stables flat,' Beccy grumbled, not liking any control her stepsister exerted over her life – and Lemon's – these days. 'My laptop's higher spec than this.'

'Yeah, but your cooking's not a patch, and there's a dishwasher here,' Lemon pointed out as he tucked into a vast plate of mouth-watering food.

Beccy took consolation in the fact that Lemon liked winding Tash up so much, teasing her that Hugo and Rory must be up partying each night with all those slim-thighed all-American eventing girls. Tash pretended to make light of it, but Beccy could see it made her agitated, because she'd distractedly add grated cheese to the buttered carrots, or put out horseradish sauce with the puddings instead of cream. But despite the odd gaffe, the food was undeniably good.

On Wednesday both horses sailed through the initial vet check, and Tash's supper guests went online to look up photographs of Rory and later Hugo running alongside their horses in what the Americans called 'the jog' while she cooked and updated them with the latest news from Hugo.

'They schooled in the stadium this afternoon. You can get lost in there. It's bigger than a cricket field. Tanker was fine, but Rio was all over the place – they couldn't get him in. Hugo thinks Stefan's got the horse too pumped. They've galloped the legs off him now to try to settle him, but they only get that hour in the stadium to school and that's gone, so tomorrow is do or die.' She added vats of cream and butter to celeriac and sweet potato mash.

Watching her, Lough said nothing. Covertly observing him from the far end of the table, Beccy found her heart going out to him, understanding that as much as it hurt him to be there, he couldn't keep away. She felt much the same as she tried to blot out the noise of Lemon eating, making appreciative humming noises as he gobbled down the softest, sweetest roast pork. The way Lough's eyes almost devoured their hostess when she wasn't looking upset Beccy deeply. She knew nobody ever stared at her like that, not even Lemon. Increasingly, she found her own eyes drawn to the Devil on Horseback, so incongruous to her in a domestic setting. His hair had grown quite long now. He clearly hadn't had a cut since he'd arrived in the UK and it swept around his head in dramatic Beethoven fashion – not sleek and floppy like Hugo's, but a great sea crest of turbulent waves and tumbling black surf. It was far too untamed and disturbing.

'You need a haircut,' she told him.

He looked at her in surprise.

'I'd steer clear of Bed Hedz in Marlbury,' she recommended kindly.

'Thanks.'

'I'm pretty good at cutting hair, aren't I Lem?'

'So so.' Lemon spoke with his mouth full, already reloading his fork.

Beccy shot him a hurt look. 'I cut yours.'

'You run the clippers around my Mohawk, yeah.' He reached up to touch his yellow fin, winking at Tash. 'Great chow, Mrs B.'

Beccy flushed, her indignation rising. Lemon was deliberately winding her up. She might not have mastered cooking, but she liked to think her hairdressing skills at least were drawing level with those of her stepsister these days. 'I'll cut your hair,' she offered Lough now.

'If you like.' He looked uncomfortable.

'Tomorrow.'

'Sure.'

She looked at Lemon victoriously. He gave her a 'your funeral' look and turned to Tash again. 'So tell me, who's the hot redhead with Hugo in all the vet inspection photos?' He nodded to the laptop, open at the end of the table. The screensaver had kicked in and the Windows logo was floating around the screen. Lemon gave the mouse a nudge with his elbow and a photograph flashed up of Hugo and a pretty woman leaning their heads together as Rio trotted past.

'Oh, that's Stefan's wife Kirsty. She was a work rider at Lime Tree Farm years ago.' Tash carefully didn't add that she was also Hugo's girlfriend at the time. She eyed the photograph closely. They did look alarmingly intimate. She'd been too busy cooking to study it properly.

'Luscious-looking bird.' Lemon sighed, earning hurt looks from both Tash and Beccy. 'They're obviously *great* mates.'

'We're all close.' Tash cleared her throat and glanced at Lough, then looked hurriedly away. His eyes were so easy to fall into.

As soon as pudding spoons were settling back into bowls with hearty congratulations, and Beccy and Lemon made leaving noises, she announced loudly that she had to call Hugo to see how the course had walked and so they must all go, and could they do night-check for her?

Lough's eyes didn't meet hers as he thanked her for supper and wished her goodnight.

Hugo wasn't answering his phone so Tash went upstairs for a shower and an early night, forcing herself to read three more chapters of a very stolid racing biography before yawns finally raked her jaws and she fell asleep to dream that she was buried up to her neck in the sand arena with Dillon Rafferty's helicopter about to land on her head while Hugo and Kirsty ran naked around the Haydown cross-country course.

On the Thursday of Kentucky, Lough and Tash competed four horses at a small novice trials in Hampshire. With nobody on the ground to help them, it was a difficult juggle. Tash's heart-skipping jumpiness around Lough wasn't improved by having to change at high speed and in such close quarters between phases that she got regular eyefuls of his muscles and tattoos and he walked in twice to find her flashing her sports bra. Hopelessly distracted, Tash set off across country on one of Hugo's insane ex-racehorses with the wrong bit in his mouth and consequently had no brakes whatsoever. Perhaps inevitably, the increasing speed with which he was pelting into fences took its toll and they caught a leg at a big set of rails, propelling her out of the saddle and practically into the lap of the fence judge. Eliminated and muddied but otherwise unscathed, she took the horse back to the horsebox park, relieved at least that it was her last ride of the day.

Taking the wheel of the lorry because he said it was unsafe for her to drive after a fall, Lough insisted on navigating their way home, getting thoroughly lost somewhere the wrong side of Salisbury. The old hunting horsebox, patched up after its accident with new, improved brakes, didn't have such luxuries as sat nav, and Tash had left the printed directions somewhere at the event.

'I told you we should have brought my horsebox,' Lough griped.

'It costs twice as much in diesel,' Tash pointed out, misdirecting him into a business park.

They stopped in a layby on a busy bypass to consult the road atlas, but it was ten years old and appeared to pre-date the bypass itself. Traffic was building up around them as rush hour started.

'Oh crap and bugger!' Tash howled as she tried to make sense of the map, anxious to get back for the online Kentucky coverage.

Soon Rory would be embarking on the most demanding dressage test if his life, starting with the challenge of persuading Rio into the stadium in the first place.

'I'm fucking sorry, okay?' Lough snarled.

'It's not your fault we're lost,' she snapped back, although she knew it was.

He glared out of the windscreen and then slumped back in the driver's seat, the air and pent-up anger seeming to sigh right out of him.

'That's not why I'm sorry, Tash. You know why I'm sorry.'

She watched the traffic flying by and listened to the horses stamping in the back, only too aware that he wasn't referring to the fact that they were lost. But was he just referring to her apparent attempts to flash him every few days and the growing spark between them, or was he referring to something more sinister, involving threats and rumours?

'We have to talk,' he said eventually.

It was like Hugo in reverse, she realised with mounting panic. When she tackled Hugo, saying they needed to talk, he clammed up – now she felt exactly the same. She just wanted to get home.

'Sorry I've been a bit – weird,' she managed to mumble.

His eyes swivelled in her direction and the brows shot up.

'I get tense when Hugo's away competing,' she went on.

'Sure.'

'And I like lots of company.'

'So I gathered.'

There was an awkward pause.

'You trust Hugo when he's away?'

'Of course,' she said, untruthfully, now embarrassed that she'd confided her fears to him about Hugo playing away. She tried to make light of it. 'On eventing's moral scale, he's a saint.'

Lough's eyes scoured her face. 'I've not even got a ranking.'

'Well, your track record's not great,' she agreed.

'Yeah.' He gave a rueful smile. 'I know: horse-doping, money laundering, stealing other men's wives.'

His final words hung in the air.

'But all that's changed now?' she asked in a strangled voice.

He turned to look out of the driver's door at commuter traffic crawling past as rush hour intensified. 'My mother always wrote a

New Year's resolutions list then used it as a bookmark in the romantic novels she borrowed from the library each month. It was always the same, with Find a New Man at the top. Every year, my father would blast his way back through her life, wrecking her relationships, leaving her in a mess. None of her boyfriends was ever strong enough to stand up to him.'

'But you did.'

'I handled it all wrong.' He watched the high sides of a supermarket lorry slide past, its slogan boasting fresh value. 'Bullies like him just make me see red.'

In the back of the lorry, the horses were stamping impatiently.

Suddenly, a flash of anger sparked in Tash as she took offense at the insinuation that Hugo was a bully when she felt there were far worse culprits at Haydown. 'You should do something about Lemon, then.'

'What?'

'Don't tell me you haven't noticed how badly he treats Beccy?'

His fingers drummed on the steering wheel. 'Let's leave her out of this.'

'Out of what?'

'This.'

Tash could feel his eyes on her face again, but she didn't dare look at him. Another juggernaut drove past them, making the old box sway and groan like a boat in a storm. She suddenly wanted a lifejacket for protection, acutely aware of every movement of Lough's body beside hers in the cab. When he shifted forwards she was absolutely convinced that he was about to touch her.

But he just picked up the road map again to study it. 'Right, let's get going.'

Almost faint with relief, Tash realised their talk was at an end. Within seconds, her nervous reflex kicked in and she started to gabble: 'I'm sure Beccy will sort things out with Lem. She hates me interfering or worrying, and always insists she's tougher than she looks.'

Saying nothing, Lough found first gear and indicated to rejoin the bypass, sweeping aside a stormy black wave of hair to squint at a road sign ahead.

'She's right about your hair needing cutting.'

Without looking at her, he pulled back onto the dual carriageway. 'Tonight's the night, then.'

'I bet it'll feel great after waiting so long,' Tash said inanely, hoping Beccy was up to the job; she'd hardly done her own hair any favours before the dreadlocks came off.

His eyes didn't leave the road. 'It'll feel amazing. Trust me.'

It was several minutes before it occurred to Tash that they might not be talking about quite the same thing.

As soon as she came downstairs from showering and then kissing her sleeping children who had already been in bed when she got home, Tash opened a bottle of wine and set up the laptop to check the Kentucky action. Rory's test was still over an hour away.

There was no sign of the others yet, but she guessed Beccy was wielding her scissors on Lough in the stables flat, which at least gave her some time to relax. Lemon in particular made her feel horribly tense, and she didn't even want to think about Lough, although she hoped things might get easier now they'd cleared the air. She drank her first glass of wine rather too quickly and then poured herself another before getting out a big corn-fed chicken from the fridge, cramming it with garlic and onions, slapping it with butter, draping foil on top and slamming it in the Aga. She decided she'd cheat with the roast potatoes and use the frozen ones from the posh farm shop in West Fosbourne.

Washing her buttery hands then drying them on a tea towel, she picked up her BlackBerry and tried to fathom out how to send Rory a text to wish him good luck. Calling him this close to the test wouldn't be fair, but she wanted him to know that everybody at home was thinking about him. They'd become his unofficial family now. His own clan certainly didn't seem to be very supportive.

By the time she had typed out the message, she'd drunk the second glass of wine. She poured a third and realised that there was a new message in her inbox. It was from Beccy.

Going to Olive Branch for romantic meal. Tell Lough sorry about haircut. Please text Rory's dressage score. Bxx

She heard a step and looked up. Lough had come straight from the shower, hair still dripping water on to his shirt, making the cotton cling to his wide shoulders.

'Beccy can't come now.'

'I know.' He stooped to pat Beetroot, who had sidled up to lean

572

against his leg and squint up at him, tail whisking the flagstones. 'I told Lem to take her out.'

'Why?'

'You said he was mean to her, so he's treating her to a candlelit meal. I thought you'd be pleased.'

Tash gasped in horror. That's not what she'd meant at all.

'According to Lem, Beccy's just the apprentice. You're the real stylist, so you can cut my hair tonight.'

Tash wanted to tell him that she couldn't possibly do it, but it seemed an embarrassing overreaction, as though admitting that one touch of his head could make her foam at the mouth and start pulling his clothes off.

'Sure.' She went in search of scissors, reminding herself it was just like trimming a horse's feathers. She'd cut the hair of plenty of male riders in the past, and had yet to ravish one.

He sat at the end of the kitchen table. The laptop was tuned to streaming of the afternoon's dressage tests from Kentucky, one of which was Rory.

Tash climbed up on chairs redirecting every halogen light to shine on the work in hand so that Lough looked as though he was about to be beamed up by Scottie. It was luminously unromantic. He kept his eyes firmly on the computer, watching an American rider trot into the arena. The picture kept freezing as the live feed stalled.

Still playing for time, Tash drained her wine and went to pour herself another but the bottle appeared to be empty. She took a new one from the fridge and poured them both brimming glasses that splashed everywhere as she carried them over.

Then she took up position behind Lough. She was stupidly nervous, hands shaking so much that she was worried she'd cut off his ear.

His hair slithered through her fingers, heavy as lined satin curtains, as she set to work, running a comb through each section, slipping her fingers to either side of the lock of hair and feathering the scissors along the ends, snip-snip-snip.

He smelled shower-fresh, of warm skin and cool deodorant, toothpaste and shaving gel, but undercut with a masculine wood-smoke tang.

Tash leaned past him to reach for her wine, jumping as her breast rubbed against his arm. Even through a heavyweight jumper and thick wad of bra, her nipple fizzed disloyally. She dripped wine on him and set to work again, hands shaking even more.

Dark hair gathered underfoot as she worked, all too aware of the broad angles of his shoulders catching on her belly, his breath against her wrists as she cut that long forelock, the soft shell curls of his ears, the curve of his wide neck. She could see the edge of his tattoo poking out from his T-shirt neckline, matched with the wide inked bands visible on his arms.

On screen, the rider jerked forwards in stop-start images. Then they lost the pictures and the feed cut to the scoreboard and audio only. Neither Tash nor Lough noticed.

As if in a dream, her fingers fluttered closer and closer to the tattoo as she trimmed the fine hairs on the nape of his neck, perfecting the neat v-shape there.

But the tattoo was a decoy. It was the hollow at the base of his jaw that pulled her in, without warning, her left hand landing there lightly, as though just stilling his head to keep cutting his hair, if it weren't for the thumb, with a life of its own, sliding up under his ear.

In a flash, he'd lifted his arm and clamped a hand over hers.

They both stayed stock still for a moment, watching the pale screen of the computer lined with scores, and listening as a cheerful American commentator announced that it had just started raining heavily over Lexington.

At last Lough spoke, barely more than a whisper. 'You feel the same way.'

'You must go,' Tash said, her voice weird and unnatural in her head, almost drowned out by the pounding of her blood.

'You feel the same way.'

She tried to pull her hand away but he held tight.

'I can't think straight around you any more,' he said quietly. 'I can't breathe straight. I want to kiss you all the time.'

Tash certainly couldn't breathe now. All she could think about was kissing him.

'And into the stadium, in the pouring rain, comes a young Brit we've not seen here before, Rory Midwinter . . .' announced the disjointed voice on the laptop. 'Seems to be having a few problems getting the horse to the arena there, but backwards on two legs is fine as long as they get all the moves right when they've entered at A . . .'

Lough's hand warm on hers, frozen in time, they stayed silently rooted to the spot like statues, neither of them listening as the commentators talked through Rory's test. The voices droned on, talking about superb transitions and great showmanship. Tash barely took in a word, able to think of nothing but Lough's lips and hers finding each other.

When a distorted round of applause from the computer speaker heralded the end of the test, they both jumped with surprise.

'What a great effort from the young Brit after such a near-catastrophe at the start – and the worst weather of the day. The scores should be on the board any moment . . .' the commentator promised.

There seemed to be an interminable pause.

'He gets fifty or less, we kiss,' Lough breathed.

'I don't make bets like that,' she managed to croak, despite a crazy urge to agree. 'That's Hugo's weakness.'

'We have that in common, at least.'

Tash bit her lip, fighting to think straight. 'What is it you two bet on?'

'You, of course.' Lough's fingers had started to slide up her forearm.

Still resting against the hot skin of his neck, Tash's hand trembled. She snatched it away and stepped back.

Turning to face her, he stood up, his chair tipping over with a clatter against the flagstones, sending the dogs scuttling away. His eyes burned into hers.

On the live feed, the voice suddenly announced that Rory's final penalty tally was just over forty points, putting him in second place for the day, 'well in advance of any of the rest of the Brits to have gone, but with more to names including Olympic gold medallist Hugo Beauchamp to come tomorrow . . .'

The kiss was without warning or ceremony – a hot brand straight on to her lips, a hand on her neck and a body against hers. She felt her weight go for a moment, her feet struggle to stay under her, the pit of her belly pulled out like a drawer only to be filled with lit fireworks and slammed back in.

But all the time her heart was beginning to panic, desperate to run away and hide. She held up a hand. He gripped it, fingers lacing with hers, pulling her tighter, his lips opening against hers now, a muscular tongue tasting the first soft millimetres of flesh on the inside of her lips.

Just for a split-second, Tash abandoned herself. She yielded, welcomed his body hard against hers, his tongue in her mouth, his fingers on her skin, and welcomed her craving to drag him between her legs. But even as this strangeness, this newness of kissing Lough overwhelmed her, the wave of lust was already retreating, her hand had starting to struggle against his, pushing him away, her heart hurting in her chest.

Then the phone rang and the remaining lust cut off instantly, like a switch.

Lough gripped on to her. 'Ignore it.'

'It'll be Hugo.'

'Ignore it,' he urged, his lips still touching hers.

But the moment had gone. Her whole body felt scalded by disgrace and self-loathing.

She pushed him away.

Lough was a strong, athletic man and no lightweight, but he was caught off-balance; Tash rode up to eight horses a day and had arm muscles as strong as a rower's these days. She didn't know her own strength, and her thrust could probably have pushed over three muggers simultaneously.

She watched in horror as he stumbled backwards into the fallen chair, throwing an arm behind him in a futile attempt to grab the table edge. He crashed down against the flagstones, and his head made contact with the floor with a loud crack.

Tash screamed, her hands over her mouth, tears instantly rising in fear and panic.

Lough groaned and rolled over, blinking up at the ceiling, his huge, dark eyes flicking quickly across to Tash, clearly checking that she wasn't standing over him with a cosh waiting to finish him off. Then he slowly sat up. There was blood dripping from his newly shorn hair.

'Oh Christ, I'm so sorry!' She stooped down to him.

'Leave it!' He hauled himself up, clutching his skull. A moment later, and he'd disappeared out into the night, slamming the door behind him.

The phone was still ringing, echoing around the house.

Unable to think straight, Tash picked up the call.

It was Hugo, now breathlessly running from the dressage arena to the stables alongside Rory.

'Did you see it? He rode an absolute blinder,' he enthused. 'The horse was really far too hot, but all that work we've been doing paid off. He stayed focused and kept going forward, didn't get defensive and fight him. It was bloody superb to watch. Darling little Faith sobbed her heart out. Rory's about to go and do the press conference now, and absolutely loving all this American razzmatazz. God, I wish you were here.'

'I wish I was there too,' she said with all her shame-soaked heart.

Later, Tash crept out to do night-check like an SAS commando, dressed in dark colours, her eyes darting left and right in case Lough jumped out and demanded to know what the hell she was doing, playing mind games with him. But she needn't have worried. A low light was glowing in the lodge cottage and Lough showed no sign of coming out. His own horses had already been rugged, hayed and watered.

At the crack of dawn the next day, he and Lemon loaded his two up-and-coming advanced horses as planned and set off for Belton Park in Lincolnshire. Tash waited in the house like a coward until they were gone. She was entered on River, but had called the organisers to withdraw, claiming that she couldn't leave the yard so short-staffed that close to Badminton. The truth was that she was still far too frightened of riding around a track at that level to tackle it, and of being anywhere close to Lough.

In the kitchen Veruschka was squawking in Czech, having discovered last night's chicken still in the top oven of the Aga, and now charred to a crisp. Acrid smoke billowed around the room.

Donning oven gloves, Tash carried the smouldering remains outside, where she wandered around uselessly, wondering where she could put it to cool that was out of the way of the dogs.

Beccy trailed across from the yard to see why she was wafting about, carrying the smoking pan like a religious censer. 'Is that a Heston Blumenthal recipe?'

'Yes, cremated chicken,' Tash said through gritted teeth. 'It's all the rage at the Fat Duck.'

'Did you and Lough have an argument last night?' She watched as Tash finally dumped the roasting tray on the flat tiled roof of the old coal house.

'Not exactly.' Tash looked cagey.

Beccy was feeling both lost and strangely liberated without Lemon, who would be away for three days. They'd shared a disappointing meal the night before, which she'd ended up paying for, and which gave her indigestion because she'd eaten so well at Haydown the previous evenings. She barely got in a word at the Olive Branch as Lemon, who claimed to have forgotten his wallet, ran down British event riders non-stop, talking with his mouth full and snapping his fingers at Angelo for more wine every ten minutes. At first she'd been relieved to get away from the Lough and Tash dynamic, but she was secretly annoyed that she hadn't got to cut that luscious black hair, and doubly annoyed that Lemon had spent so much of their evening saying how much he hoped his boss screwed up Hugo's marriage. Afterwards, she'd had a stitch throughout their lovemaking, and Lemon had wanted to enhance the action by watching porn on the computer, which made her feel like a bit of a sideline rather than the main event. When Tash had first suggested that Lemon might not be ideal boyfriend material, Beccy had been livid, but now she was starting to see her point.

'Lem treats me like a child, sometimes,' she said, making a falteringly start at opening up to her stepsister, 'like I don't understand what's going on in the real world.'

'Nothing is going on,' Tash said quickly.

But Beccy was concentrating too hard on her own heart to notice how defensiveTash was being. 'He likes making trouble – it excites him – but at the same time he wants to protect me and keep me in my doll's house. I know I'm a bit of a daydreamer, but I'm wise enough to see that what's happening's not right.'

'It's really all perfectly innocent,' Tash blustered again.

'It's not, though, is it?' Beccy sighed, still thinking about the porn. 'It's so obvious he's only really in it for the sex.'

'You think so?' Tash bleated.

'That and the home cooking,' she nodded, 'and wanting to get one over on Hugo.'

'Oh God.' Tash covered her mouth.

'I want a boyfriend who looks after me,' Beccy went on, 'and who I can truly love, but he can be so selfish sometimes. He'd rather check his email than watch me undressing. This week, I even caught him sending a text when I was giving him a blowjob.'

Tash squinted at her in confusion. 'Beccy, are we talking about Lem here?'

'Of course, who else would it be?'

'Nothing – my mistake.' She shook her head. She looked as though she hadn't slept all night, Beccy realised.

'How do I make men love me?' she asked in a small voice.

'Oh Beccy, I only wish I knew.' Tash stretched out a hand to cup her face, although Beccy predictably ducked away.

'You hardly have that problem,' she muttered. 'You have two men in love with you. What's your big secret?'

To Beccy's surprise, Tash looked as though she was going to cry. Shot through with an unfamiliar compassion that for once blotted out jealousy, she reached out and clutched her stepsister's arm. 'You're not going to leave Hugo, are you?'

'No!' Tash gasped in horror. 'Of course not. Everything will be fine.'

'Good.' Beccy smiled, surprised by how relieved the news made her. For all her fantasies that Hugo would one day fall in love with her, she had never really believed that the Beauchamps' marriage could crumble. Now that cracks were snaking up the walls and plaster raining down, she suddenly found herself wanting to rush around erecting scaffolding.

Arm in arm, they walked back to the stable yard.

'Why haven't you taken River to Belton today?' Beccy asked casually. 'Is it because of what's happening with Lough?'

'Not at all,' Tash answered too quickly. 'And nothing's happening, I told you. She's just not ready. Besides, I can follow progress in Kentucky better from here.'

'Who d'you think'll win?'

'Hugo.'

'Honestly?'

Suddenly uncertain exactly what she was being asked, Tash looked across at that innocent china doll face. 'Hugo will win.'

Chapter 60

Hugo's dressage test, just after the lunch break on Friday on the reliable if rather short-paced Oil Tanker, awarded him fractionally more penalties than Rory on Rio. They were second and third on the leaderboard going into cross-country, with the American veteran Stella Herchz in the lead. Both men had walked the course three times, but they still set out at first light on Saturday to go over it one last time, companionably striding out distances together, yet lost in their own thoughts as they walked their meticulously planned lines again, and made sure they had a plan B and sometimes C for the tough combinations where the slightest error could require quick thinking. Kentucky was a big, testing four-star course, particularly in the second half.

The weather had finally come good after two days of intermittent downpours, the sun melting away a milky dawn mist to bounce sparkles from the white Horse-Park rails like the gleaming teeth of an advertising smile.

Record crowds soon gathered around the most thrilling fences, particularly the famous Head of the Lake water complex: the vast grandstand to one side of it was soon packed with faces eager to see a splash.

Rio was a bold cross-country horse with a great mile-eating gallop, but he also needed to be ridden with great accuracy and commitment to keep his line into fences. As he and Rory set out from the start box to eager whoops from the British supporters, Faith rushed away to position herself by the video screen, knowing that the next eleven minutes would be lived with her soul split in two, half riding with Rory every inch of the way, half waiting in for his return with iced water and the biggest, proudest welcoming smile at her disposal.

That welcoming smile was bigger than even she could have imagined when he thundered through the finish, tears in his eyes.

He whooped as he slithered off, as usual forgetting to unbuckle the release cord of his inflatable body protector so that it puffed up, almost crushing his ribs. Not caring, he unzipped it, and gathered Faith into a hug and planted a big kiss on her mouth. 'That was better than sex!' he gasped afterwards.

For a heady moment, Faith thought he meant the kiss, which had certainly done it for her, but then she realised he meant the ride. A second later, a cloud of Rive Gauche almost asphyxiated her.

'Zen you 'aven't 'ad enough good sex lately, *non*?' purred a smooth voice as MC stepped forward to congratulate him. 'Zat was beautifully ridden. I am sorry we 'ave not spoken more zis week. You are a clever boy.'

Scowling, Faith unsaddled Rio and started to work at bringing his temperature down, sluicing him with cold water repeatedly in a procedure known as 'aggressive cooling', yet keeping him on the move to avoid cramped muscles or stiffened joints.

When Rory eventually joined her, reeking of Rive Gauche, she was too jealous and angry to speak.

'He was fantastic!' Rory raved, not noticing her set face. 'Just so smooth – the line through the lake was a dream, and he made mincemeat of the log cabins and the steps, like they were prelim stuff. I was sure we'd get our knickers in a twist at the offset brushes, but he stayed absolutely straight.' His ego had always been very quick to swell, along with that other reliable part of him that MC so adored.

'Bravo.'

'What a horse. I don't mind saying, I rode him bloody well. Did you hear MC back there? She thinks I rock. She even whispered in my ear that she thinks I'm the best she's ever met. In fact if I play my cards right, I—ugh!' He leaped back as a great splash of cold water slopped against his groin. 'What d'you think you're doing?'

'Aggressive cooling,' Faith hissed, leading Rio back towards the event stabling, to walk him in hand for another twenty minutes before bathing and rugging him, spending the next few hours checking his legs and wind for any signs of the big cross-country test having taken an undue toll.

She managed to get away for long enough to join the rest of the British supporters, including the Earl and Countess of Malvern, to see Hugo and Oil Tanker streak around the course, with just one wobbly moment tripping in the sunken road, when they didn't look as though they had the space or momentum to get out. But Hugo never wavered and Oil Tanker was a clever self-preservationist who never looked as though he was making a great effort and never gave any fence more than a fraction of an inch to spare, yet got round so efficiently and with minimum time-wasting that he beat the clock by almost five seconds despite his limited gallop.

That evening, with Hugo away having supper with the Earl and Countess of Malvern, and Rory sneaking off, presumably for a tryst with MC, Faith kept up the regular checks on Rio and commiserated with the Johanssens, who had suffered less fortunate rounds. Stefan had taken a nasty fall at the big Normandy bank when his horse turned over, leaving them both bruised and battered. He had been forced to withdraw his second ride. And Kirsty's horse had run out twice, dropping her right to the back of the field.

The atmosphere around the Vegas encampment was therefore subdued. Faith was pleased that Hugo had left her with the golf buggy to save legwork back and forth to the stables, and found herself giving lifts to several other grooms, all Americans, whose positivity and upfront sassiness she appreciated.

'I'm loving your breast augmentation,' one girl said as they bounced along Nina Bonnie Boulevard for the third time. 'Your Brit surgeons are the best.'

'They're chicken fillets,' she confessed. 'They come out at night.'

'Like *ugh*,' the girl was horror-struck. 'That must be so unhygienic.'

About to explain that they weren't made of real chicken, Faith changed her mind and said, 'They *are* organic.'

It was the little things that cheered her up right now.

Later that evening, Rio trotted up sound and very pleased with himself, and Faith settled him down for the night with cool clay wraps on his legs and his magnetic blanket to draw out any last vestiges of heat and pain.

To her surprise, Rory was already tucked up in the trailer-nose bed when she got back.

'Got to get a good night's sleep,' he said sheepishly, peering up from the covers as she fumbled about for her night things. 'Thanks for looking after Rio so brilliantly.'

'He's my horse.'

'Of course he is. I do appreciate him, you know. And you.'

Suddenly cheered, she dived into the privacy of the little loo cubicle to put on her pyjamas, keeping on her bra and her chicken fillets and cleaning her teeth until her gums hummed.

Rory was asleep on his platform mattress, snuffling contentedly, when she emerged. Still feeling euphoric, Faith got into her cramped bench bed and lay awake for hours, listening to his breathing and wondering what it would be like to hear it every night while curled up right beside him.

At the final vet's inspection, the crowds groaned and cat-called as the long-time leader, Stella Herchz, had her horse held back to be re-examined by the ground jury and veterinary delegate. The horse was undoubtedly stiff, its paces slightly irregular, but whether it was actually lame was debateable and the jury went into a little huddle.

Eventually, after much deliberation – and a lot of head-shaking from Marie-Clair Tucson in particular – the hands went down and the crowd wailed in horror as their greatest hope of victory shuffled back to the stable yard. A couple of days later, an x-ray would reveal a very small chip on one fetlock that could have seriously compromised the horse had he jumped. It was a decision that had almost certainly saved his career.

Rory and Hugo now faced an agonising wait as competitors jumped in reverse order from lunchtime. At least Hugo was briefly diverted by an Olympic medal-winners' parade. Rory had no such distraction or camaraderie, and paced around the stables restlessly, driving Faith mad as she packed up Rio's tack trunks, ready for a swift departure.

'Oh, go and shag MC.'

'Shh! Keep your voice down. Besides, she's far too demanding.'

Faith didn't want to know, but jittery, nerve-racked Rory needed to talk just to keep sane. 'She says I have all sorts of bad habits and have never been taught properly, like a badly schooled horse, so she's rebroken me.'

'Good for her.'

'It's a real eye-opener. I never realised how incredibly sensitive certain parts of the female body are, and quite different from men.'

'That a fact?' She threw boots and bandages into a trunk.

'I need someone like her. I've been too bloody selfish with women.'

'You surprise me.'

'I think I'm a much better lover now. In fact, I'd go as far as to say I'm bloody good in bed.' He watched her closely for a reaction.

'Speaking on behalf of the female population, we're thrilled,' she replied tersely.

'I just need to find the right girl, settle down.'

She dropped the brushes that she was sorting through and looked up at him sharply. 'Are you feeling okay?'

'See!' He laughed, pointing at her. 'I knew that'd get your attention. God, I need a shag right now.'

'Hmmph.' She picked up the brushes again.

'Are you up for a quick knee-trembler in one of the empty stalls?'

Hiding her reddening face in the grooming box, she told him to get lost. 'You'll definitely have to win the Grand Slam before *that* happens.'

'Oh, I know. That's why I plan to win it.'

Again she looked up in surprise, but he was gone.

Three hours later, after what felt like the longest wait of his life, Rory was the last rider to enter the huge open-air stadium. As with the dressage, Rio took exception to the arena, rearing and crabbing, trying to whip round when he saw the huge crowds and vast expanse of space jewelled with brightly coloured fences.

The sun was still out, but the wind was howling at near gale force, buffeting the flower arrangements around the jump wings and even dislodging the odd pole. The flags along the grandstand roof snapped and cracked furiously.

After the hooter blew, Rory remembered little of the following sixty seconds. He had less than a jump in hand over Hugo, who had put in a clear round on the economical Oil Tanker, rattling almost every pole but leaving them all up.

Rio had no such intention. His nerves fraying and attention wandering, he ballooned the first three fences.

Watching between her fingers from the collecting-ring funnel, Faith held her breath. Then she felt a strong arm around her shoulder and she realised that Hugo had jumped off Tank and was propping her up. That arm didn't move until the moment that Rory sailed over the last fence and punched the air in victory, his first-ever four-star win secure.

Faith let out a scream of sheer, unbridled elation and Hugo pulled her into a hug, even as pats of commiseration rained down on his back.

'Congratulations,' he said proudly as they were jostled about. 'You got him here. That's one hell of a horse.'

'He won!' she shrieked.

'And you have just become a very wealthy young woman.'

'What?' She couldn't take much in.

'The owner wins over sixty thousand dollars.'

'I do?'

Hugo laughed in delight. 'You really had no idea, did you?'

Faith shook her head, not really caring. She was crying too much to speak. As she clung tightly to Hugo and watched the love of her life gallop Rio around that amazing arena, waving his hat in the air, her heart was burning bright. But, curiously, all she found in her head was an echo of Rory's voice, repeating over and over again, 'I'm bloody good in bed.'

Chapter 61

When Faith returned to Lime Tree Farm she received few congratulations for owning the winning horse at Kentucky, although Gus did ask to borrow some money: 'I've got my eye on a fabulous five-year-old if you fancy investing. You won't want to work here now you're loaded. Typical! Badminton week and I lose my best member of staff.'

Penny swept her quickly to one side. 'Take no notice – he always gets like this before Badminton. We need you more than ever.' Her berry eyes were bright with good humour, but also anxious. 'You're not going to leave us, are you? Gus is right: you're our best worker.'

Faith shook her head hastily. She could never leave while Rory was so close by, or forfeit being at Badminton to support him. For all her disappointment in Kentucky that he was so smitten with MC, she would never forget his face when he won. It had been pure joy. The cockiness and thoughtlessness was just an affectation, she was certain, an act to cover up the big part of him that thought he didn't deserve success, just as she knew aggression was her cloak to cover so many inadequacies.

So she forgave Rory returning to England with a head as big as the ten-gallon hat he had bought as a souvenir. He needed that confidence to take him through Badminton. He also needed unswerving support from his owners. She called Dillon.

'What now?' he answered. 'I paid my horses' bills like you asked. Is there a problem?' Faith had never heard him so curt. She almost hung up, but the need to petition for Rory made her stick with it.

'You are going to be there for Rory this week, aren't you?'

'Not you too,' he complained. 'Sylva's on my case about this.'

Faith felt her lip curl at the thought of Sylva sniffing around Rory again, despite being grudgingly impressed that the nation's favourite single mum had Badminton in her sights. Most glamour-girl celebrities favoured the safe allure of dressage or the quick fix of show-jumping; at least Sylva had stuck with the thrills and spills of the horse world's greatest challenge.

'Are you two really getting married?' she couldn't resist asking.

'So the papers say,' he hedged.

'She's very beautiful,' she said politely, more because she wanted to be positive than because she rated her higher than any other pretty celebrity, although Faith had no doubt of her charms, and she sometimes still wondered if life would be better had she allowed Farouk Ali Khan to give her replica Sylva Frost boobs after all. The public clearly worshipped her, as did at least two of the loveliest men Faith knew. 'Congratulations. I'm sure you'll have a really . . . amazing life together.' Her natural honesty made the tribute tough going.

The long, rather mournful sigh at the other end of the phone surprised her. 'Faith, is there anything else? Only I'm in the studio right now with a bunch of session musicians and engineers waiting on our every word.'

'No. That's it. Hopefully see you at Badminton,' she squeaked, her own world suddenly feeling very muddy and insignificant.

Then she remembered that he had taken her call within three rings, despite all those engineers and musicians around him, and the thought made her feel somewhat better. She sent him a text. *Best of luck with the new tracks.*

He texted right back: *You are beautiful. Thanks.*

Faith stared at the words for a long time, wondering whether he'd got his recipients muddled up, then decided not. If Dillon saw the beauty within, who was she to argue? On a high, she texted Rory *how's it going?* hoping his return to West Berkshire had been a bit more celebratory than hers, although she'd already overheard the

Moncrieffs gossiping about the shaky state of the Beauchamps' marriage.

Rory's reply bore this out. *Hugo demanding regular yard handkerchief checks, like Verdi's Otello. Only wish the music was as good. New head groom has b awful taste in radio stations.*

What's she like? Faith demanded jealously, not interested in the main tragedy.

Amazing body. Into bondage. Great at plaiting.

Rory had a way to go before he saw the beauty within, she reflected sadly.

At Haydown, Tash and Lough may not have spoken since Belton, but the yard kept functioning regardless, and Badminton preparations were well underway by the time Hugo and Rory returned. The horses the two men had entered had been brought to peak fitness in their absence and were raring to go, along with two campaigners for Lough, one of them a scratch ride that had come through an old New Zealand teammate sidelined by injury.

The ride was Koura, a horse that, years ago, Hugo had produced from nothing, but he had lost the ride when a petty disagreement with the owners had escalated. This still rankled with Hugo, because he'd rated the horse as world-class. Along with Lough's complete indifference to the yard's Kentucky glory, this was guaranteed to wind up Hugo to snapping point within hours of arriving home.

His disappointment at missing out on victory by such a narrow margin was hidden from all but those closest to him, and that meant Tash bearing the brunt. A win in the States would have put him well in advance of Lough in the sponsorship race. Meanwhile, Lough had won both his sections at the trials in Lincolnshire, and Hugo couldn't understand why Tash had withdrawn when she needed the completion to qualify Deep River for four-stars again.

'You were winning everything in sight while I was in Florida. Why stop now?'

'Those were mostly just pre-season warm ups. I'm not ready for the big tracks yet,' she told him, earning an irritated look.

'No point warming up if you're going to go cold again,' he pointed out, although he was secretly relieved that she'd not been sharing a horsebox with the Kiwis at Belton.

His suspicions would not go away, however cavernous the

apparent chasm between her and Lough now. The way they edged around one another, always aware where the other was, one leaving a room as soon as the other entered, never on the yard at the same time, was incredibly telling. There was no customary welcome-home celebration with every chair filled around the kitchen table, no big Team Haydown pre-Badminton gathering on the Monday night as would usually happen, Hugo noticed.

When Gus made a flying visit to scrounge Haydown's spare car passes, he was one of the few people brave enough to raise the subject of Lough. 'He was in a stinking mood at Belton, with that black eye and the bloody great cut on his head. Did Tash beat him up while you were away?'

'I hope so,' Hugo said darkly.

Lough's injuries were a cause of much speculation, but nobody seemed to know how it had happened. When Hugo interrogated Beccy on the subject, she went red, then explained, 'Tash gave him a haircut.'

'With what kind of blunt instrument?'

Constantly running around with armfuls of tack, or children, or both, Tash was determinedly avoiding confrontation. Hugo knew they needed time alone together, but there was no window of opportunity. It was all smoke and mirrors and the darkened glass of the horsebox as it was rapidly loaded with supplies for another four-star event.

The turnaround between the two international three day events held within a week of one another at opposite sides of the Atlantic was always frantic, and never more so than this year with Haydown fielding so many entries and yet being so chronically short-staffed.

The arrival of Hugo's former head girl Franny should have been a cause for nostalgic celebration, but her long-held mistrust of Tash only added to the tension. Brought in to look after the yard while the team was away and await the return of Oil Tanker and Rio from America midweek, straight-talking Franny was very quick to pick up on the appalling atmosphere at the yard.

'I won't come back and work here if it stays like this,' she told Jenny on Monday night as they shared a pizza in Jenny's little estate cottage, which Franny was occupying for the duration of her stay.

'It won't,' Jenny assured her. 'Something's got to give.'

'Like what? Tash's knicker elastic? She and that Lough are obviously shagging like stoats.'

'They have been very close,' Jenny admitted. 'He helped her overcome her nerves and get back in the saddle.'

'There you go. Leg up, leg over. Seen it a million times before. Look at me.'

Franny's on-off boyfriend Ted, a former event rider turned dealer, had recently booted her out of the static caravan they'd shared on his yard near Bristol to move in a younger model, leaving Franny homeless and on the job and singles markets simultaneously.

'Does Hugo know what his wife's up to when his back's turned?' Franny asked slyly.

'Don't you dare say a thing!' Jenny ordered. She'd known her since agricultural college, where the tiny, black-haired siren with the Betty Boop body had stirred up trouble.

But Franny didn't need to say a thing. The atmosphere between Hugo and Lough was already so strained that it threatened to explode on the penultimate day before Badminton, especially when Hugo took a bad fall from a young horse on the road after a motorbike came flying past – and he was certain Lough was riding it.

'Bloody idiot!' he raged as Tash patched up bloody grazes on his face, hands and elbow.

'He hasn't left the yard all morning,' she pointed out gently. 'He's been washing down his horsebox and loading it up ready to go.'

'Very Maori warrior,' he sneered and then winced as she daubed his bloodied chin with Dettol.

Watching with great interest from the floor near by, where she had gathered an emergency ward of fluffy toys, Cora giggled, 'Daddy cry.'

'Daddy is not crying,' Hugo snapped. 'He's just fed up that Mummy keeps siding with the Kiwi.'

'I am *not* siding with him. There are no sides.'

'Could have fooled me,' he grumbled. 'Somebody is out to get us, and I'm sure he's in on it. There's more shit on the internet this week, saying we bribed the ground jury to spin Stella's horse at Kentucky. And there's a piece about the Mogo sponsorship race, suggesting that I'm so scared Lough will beat me I've offered him bribes.'

'What bribes?'

'Cash, sex, the usual.'

'Not sure you're really Lough's type.'

'The sex would be with you.'

'Marry me, Franny, and I'll give you beautiful babies!'

It wasn't a line many women would want their boyfriend to shout to another woman within an hour of meeting them.

Lemon wasn't a particularly great boyfriend, Beccy had decided. He still flirted with everybody and anybody, and risqué, rubber-wearing vamp Franny was his new target; they adored one another.

Beccy felt rejected. She longed for a romantic gesture, a sign that he cared for her more than just as a convenient way of getting regular sex and the housework done. The novelty was wearing off for both of them. He shared less of his body and his secrets each day, and his loyalty was extremely questionable. Being with him had smoothed none of the sharp edges of Beccy's painful love-hate crush on Hugo, or her regret that she had muddled with Lough's mind. Lemon was devoted to his boss, and Beccy was a poor runner-up, as she was about to find out.

The night before travelling to Badminton, she cooked his supper in their little kitchenette while he packed his bag next door in his room, which he refused to let Beccy turn into a living area even though he always slept in her bedroom. He was listening to loud techno music, its bass turned up to max making the floorboards vibrate.

Beccy had just endured a teeth-grinding drink in the Olive Branch, during which Lemon had flirted so outrageously with Franny that landlord Angelo had twice been forced to ask if they could tone it down. Now his music was going right through her, and she'd had as much as she could take. She was going to demand some changes.

She marched in, and he looked up furtively from his knapsack. 'How many *times*?' he shouted over the din. 'Don't walk in on me like that!'

But Beccy didn't care what he was doing. She turned off the music. 'You need to shape up your act.'

'What?'

'You need to take better care of me.' She launched straight into her rant, voice climbing scales. 'I cook for you, I clean this place, I do your washing and muck out your horses when you want a lie-in. I pay for everything. I give you a massage every night. And what do you do for me, Lem? What do you do for me?'

He looked astonished, and more than a bit pissed off. 'Lay off, Beccy.'

'Lay off?'

'I don't need this right now. Save it, okay?'

The red mist in front of her eyes thickened. She'd expected anger perhaps, self-justification and a bit of much-needed contrition, but not irritation. He was waving her away like a wasp that was trying to land on his lolly.

Beccy might be twenty-seven, but her experience with boyfriend-girlfriend relationships dated back to her teens and she had no reference points beyond that. Negotiation wasn't in her repertoire.

'In that case, it's over!' she wailed.

Lemon shrugged, buckling up his knapsack. 'Fine by me.'

It was her turn to look astonished. 'You don't mean that?'

He nodded, glancing up at her coldly. 'I need to stay focused for Lough, especially this week. Maybe it's best we call it a day. Let's quit while we're ahead, yeah? Stay mates.'

Beccy opened and closed her mouth, the words forming yet unable to get past her tongue. She wanted to scream and shout. He had to care for her more than that, surely? She needed him, his security and support. Admittedly, they lacked romance, but he was her friend and confidante. Without him, she was lost. She couldn't possibly 'stay mates' with someone who was willing to hurt her this much.

'How long till we eat?' he asked now, as though she had merely popped in to offer him a choice of vegetables.

Saying nothing, her throat full of razor blades, Beccy walked straight out of the flat, leaving supper to burn on the hob. She wandered through the yard, uncertain where to go. She wanted to call her mother, but Henrietta and James were away playing golf; Em was with her family in the Dorset cottage for the week. She briefly thought about running to Tash, but it would be too humiliating to bear her ruptured heart in front of the woman who had everything Beccy wanted, and the thought of Hugo being a party to any of it mortified her. She'd already tried to talk to Tash about Lemon, after all, and that had got her nowhere. She knew she could call Faith, who was so loyal and fair, but what did Faith know about relationships, when she had never had one? Beccy had nobody to turn to. Up until five minutes ago, Lemon had been her closest ally.

Tears streamed down her face. Was this how men worked, she wondered. They could just switch off and walk away without a backward glance. What little experience she had seemed to confirm it. She reached the two horseboxes parked side by side beyond the stables arch, ramps down, ready to be loaded with horses in the morning, Hugo's huge Oakley HGV and Lough's smaller Ketterer. She knew she couldn't go back to the flat, but there were mattresses inside the lorries, if she could only get in. The outside doors of both were locked, but when she stepped up the ramp of the bigger box and through the horse area, she found the groom's door unlocked and slipped inside, curling up in the dark in one corner of the seating to let the tears roll. She jumped with alarm when there was a great scraping and moaning at the door, but it was just Karma who had followed her mistress. She let her in and hugged her tight, weeping into the soft, curly fur.

Almost an hour later, tears running dry and self-pity dissipating, she realised she would have to go back to the flat. She hadn't packed her own stuff, she was filthy and tired, and had a pounding headache. She wanted to crawl into bed and pull the duvet over her head.

But as she was about to creep out of the lorry, the yard work lights flashed on outside. Perhaps Lemon had come to find her after all?

She heard footsteps coming up the ramp and through the box towards her, and clutched Karma's collar, her heart crashing in anticipation.

But it wasn't Lemon that stepped inside. It was his boss.

Lough started back to find her there in the dark. He clicked on the light and saw her puffy eyes and red nose, but said nothing.

'Just checking we packed enough bedding,' she sniffed, wondering why he was coming into Hugo's box when his own was next door. She guessed he must have heard her moving about.

'Easier with the light on,' he pointed out.

'I'd just finished.' She pushed past him.

'You okay Beccy?' He looked over his shoulder.

She paused at the top of the ramp, not looking back. The temptation to tell someone, anyone, what had just happened and how unhappy she was threatened to overwhelm her, but she managed to grip on to it. Telling Lough would be ten times more humiliating than telling even Tash.

'I'm fine, thanks,' she managed to croak past welling tears.

She heard him step behind her, his voice low and kind, that lovely sound she so seldom heard because he spoke so rarely. 'You're not fine. I can tell.'

'It's nothing!'

He laid a hand on shoulder, but she didn't dare look up. 'Is it Lem?'

'Lem?' she repeated in confusion, trying to join the dots through the misery of losing her first and only boyfriend by her own stupidity. But she had never really loved Lemon. And all you need is love, after all.

Eyes shining with tears, she suddenly jerked back her chin and stared at Lough through the darkness. 'Why are you trying to wreck Tash's marriage?'

'Is that what you think?'

'Yes. I d-don't understand why you would want to stay on here and do this, when it wasn't her you came to . . . it wasn't why you . . .' She still couldn't bring herself to admit to their text life out loud. 'We both know what happened before you came.'

'That wasn't why I stayed,' he said quietly.

Beccy knew she'd asked for that. Winded with pain, she wanted to run and flee, but he still had hold of her shoulder. 'I could ask you the same question. Why do you stay?'

She hung her head. 'I feel safe here. It's the first time I've felt safe in so long. I thought that was down to Lem, but I was wrong. It's the whole yard family, with Tash as mummy and Hugo as daddy. I love it here.'

'Strikes me as a pretty abusive family.'

'Then you know nothing.'

'I have first-hand experience,' he corrected.

'Tash is lovely.' She admitted it for the first time, and it made her cry even harder as she remembered how jealous she'd always been, how she'd dismissed her stepsister as just plain lucky and undeserving of Hugo. 'She was the only one of the Frenches who wrote to me in jail,' she sobbed. 'She sent me drawings of Cora and the horses. But I was so ungrateful because I just wanted a picture of Hugo. I swapped them for tobacco. I've never felt lonelier in my life than I did there.'

'I have first-hand experience of that too.' Lough looked up at the navy blue sky, where a few dim stars were blinking between the high shadows of clouds.

'How did you cope?'

'I thought about . . .' He stopped, clearly about to say 'her'. But he knew that wasn't really right. Instead he said 'coming here.'

'I wish I'd known I was coming here,' she sighed. 'I just thought about growing old in there. I read books – that's all visitors are allowed to bring prisoners. For twenty hours a day, I shared a cell with twelve women, with just straw mats to sleep on. I didn't think I'd get out until I was almost pensionable.'

'How come you ended up there in the first place?'

'I have bad taste in men.'

He waited for more, knowing it would come.

'I'd been living in an ashram in Tamil Nadu for a few years, but it was closed down and I went back to Thailand to look up some of the people I'd met there, the ones who worked stalls and bars on the islands, taught diving or yoga. Most had moved on, of course, but there was a Dutch guy who ran a surf hire shop in Phuket who remembered me and introduced me to some new friends. One of them was called Angel.' She pronounced it 'ann-hel'.

'Angel?'

She nodded. 'He couldn't have been less angelic, but he was so funny and charming I adored him. He came from Chile and had this fantastic accent, like a bandit in a movie, you know?'

Lough nodded, wondering how on earth she ever survived all those years on the road without being gang-raped or murdered.

'About five of us travelled through Cambodia and Malaysia together. It was a great time.'

'And you and Angel got it together?' He sat down on the ramp, patting the matting beside him.

She shook her head, settling down too. 'He flirted with everyone, but to be honest I don't think he really fancied me like I did him. But he was very kind. I got seriously freaked out when we got to Singapore – I hadn't been back since we lived there and my dad died – and Angel was fantastic. He looked after me through it and talked to me lots. He loved horses too, and I think he'd done some race riding in Argentina when he was younger.'

Lough smiled. He was starting to see the pattern forming.

'He had this dream of owning a little finca in Spain and breeding horses to sell back to South America – he said they paid huge money for them there. His uncle's family had invited him to live with them in Jerez and find him work with local breeding studs until he set himself up. He asked me if I'd like to be a part of it. I was so happy.

'Of course it was all pipe-dreams. Neither of us had a bean. I knew I could probably get a bit of money from my mother and James – they were desperate to get me home by then – but it would never be enough.'

'So you decided to raise the cash for a farm by smuggling drugs?' Lough was staggered by her gall. His own underhand methods of raising capital had been nothing compared to Beccy's, it seemed.

'Of course not.' She rubbed her face with shaking hands, having gone through the events that led up to her arrest a thousand times. 'I had no idea what was going on, but of course that counted for nothing with the authorities there.

'I had just enough money to get us both back to Europe. I found flights direct to Madrid, but Angel wanted to go via Schiphol, saying he had an errand to run for our friend at the surf shop, so I went along with it. It meant catching different flights because we were on stand-by, but that was cool. He went on ahead, saying he'd meet me there.'

Lough closed his eyes, the scenario easy to imagine. Poor, besotted Beccy happy to check in bags for her great friend Angel, only to find one of them jam-packed with Class As. He couldn't believe she'd been so naive.

'What were you carrying?'

'Khmer royal gold.'

'*Not* drugs?'

'God, no! They'd have executed me for that. The press over here often reported it wrong: it was jewellery. Rings mostly, just a few pieces, but incredibly old and rare so worth a lot of money. Angel must have got hold of it while we were travelling through Cambodia.'

'Did you ever hear from him again?'

She shook her head.

Lough looked across at the stars again, brighter now the clouds were blowing over. He could see Ursa Major lifting its saucepan high in the sky. 'You must have been so terrified.'

'My mother and stepfather flew over straight away and worked with the British consul, pleading for clemency. James put the best legal team together while I was on remand. When I was found guilty I was told I was lucky not to get the death sentence, but James insisted on an appeal and I was eventually freed on a technicality, something to do with the source of artefacts being untraceable.'

'He sounds amazing.'

'He's certainly pretty stubborn,' she said stiffly.

'Must be where Tash gets it from.'

Beccy fell silent, also looking up at the night sky. 'I used to gaze at the Great Bear from Changi and remind myself it would follow me home if I ever got here.'

'I did the same from my cell in Auckland.'

He turned to her, but Beccy's mind was still crossing its own continents. 'In India, they call it Saptarshi and each star is a sage. Some say they're the sons of Brahma,' she tilted her head up higher, 'but I secretly always preferred the story I learned in Classics at school, that Hera turned one of Zeus's lovers into a bear in a jealous rage, so he put that bear up in the sky to stop it being hunted.'

'That's more romantic, certainly.' His deep voice had a sardonic undertone.

Hugging herself for warmth, Beccy noticed the light was still on in the stables flat. She hadn't thought about Lemon at all for the past half-hour, she realised. The moment she did, a sob rose in her throat. 'Lem isn't at all romantic. I sometimes think he's quite nasty.'

'He's great with horses.'

'Just not women.'

'He doesn't know how.'

'He's like Lignère,' she said quietly, referring to the character from *Cyrano de Bergerac*, handsome Christian's offensive friend.

When Lough said nothing she stood up, rubbing her numb backside and fighting another onslaught of tears as she realised how pitiful her relationship with Lemon had been, and how shallow he was compared to Lough's unfathomable depths. 'Thanks for listening.' She started to walk down the ramp. 'You must be dying to get to bed.'

He stood up too, catching hold of her arm. 'Beccy, I must ask you . . .'

'Yes?' she froze, hardly daring to hope that he might at last start to see past Tash's leggy sweetness.

'Has she said anything to you?'

Beccy chewed her lip, her chest concave with the blunt pain of being less than second best, not caring if she was quoting out of context. 'Just that she wants Hugo to win.'

He drew a sharp breath.

Beccy turned back to him, savage with disappointment. 'I used to think that if I rode well enough Hugo would fall madly in love with me, but it doesn't work like that. We all want to win for ourselves. We do it because the adrenalin and the high of beating the field is the closest thing there is to that first punch-drunk moment of love. I stopped being competitive for a long time, but you know what? Now I want another chance.'

'To win what?' He stepped back, alarmed by her fervour. 'Not Hugo, surely?'

She shook her head. 'Respect, Lough. I want to win respect.'

'Sounds like a good plan.' His eyes glittered. 'Perhaps one day, if I ride fast enough and well enough, I'll shake the devil off my back too.'

'He who dares wins.' She smiled sadly. 'Tash has no idea how lucky she is to have you. Then again, she's the only one round here who's stopped wanting to win.' With that, she shook off the hand on her arm and hurtled down the ramp, running back to the flat.

The music was still booming from Lem's room; the hob had been turned off, but the pan remained in place, its contents reduced to a solid, blackened mess.

Wearily, Beccy went to clean her teeth before locking herself in her own room and plugging in her iPod. The first song lined up on her playlist was 'All You Need is Love'. She wept herself hoarse, but whether she was crying for Lemon, for her wasted crush on Hugo or even for Lough, perhaps the greatest missed opportunity of her life, she couldn't tell.

There's nothing you can do that can't be done, she reminded herself firmly, knowing she had to get through the next few days without being a weeping wreck. Lough was right, Lemon had no idea how to handle women, although knowing that didn't stop the feeling of loss that now ripped at her throat; she had just as little idea how to handle men, after all. She thought back over that recent, amazing conversation and suddenly yelped in alarm as it occurred to her what she'd said. *He who dares wins.*

Chapter 62

Eager to boost her profile, Sylva was determined to get Dillon to Badminton to watch his horse compete, but he had dug his heels in. Buried in a London studio most days, laying down the tracks of a new album, Dillon was uncommunicative and exhausted, only returning to the Cotswolds for brief periods to snatch sleep and check progress on the farm, or to entertain his daughters when they visited. He looked terrible, and was piling on weight from snacking through the long working hours, permanently unshaven and wearing the same ancient cut-offs and Gay Pride T-shirt everywhere because he claimed none of his other clothes fitted.

Based in Le Petit Château with Mama and the family, and working her own long hours promoting her books, beauty lines, perfume and lingerie, Sylva felt powerless. Their relationship didn't amount to very much at all, apart from press excitement and a couple of quick sexual encounters, the most recent of which had involved flying to the States for an unpleasantly rushed dinner at Nobu Malibu, which had left her with indigestion and carpet burns from the upholstery in her hire car. They'd had far more play-dates with all the children, Hana, Mama and Indigo than hot dates together. She now hated coming back to the Lodes Valley, finding its picture-postcard perfection too sugary and limited, its gardens already bursting with lupins and foxgloves, clematis and roses like sweets displayed in the window of the honey-stone shop to one side of the West Oddford Organics flagship store in Morrell on the Moor. She longed for something grander and wilder. She needed adrenalin and crowds and a man at her side.

Badminton Horse Trials with Dillon was her ticket to a little much-needed attention, public and private, and she wasn't going to relinquish it easily. Every obstacle he threw up, she overcame. The girls would be coming over: not a problem, they'd take them along with Hana and Zuzi – the more the merrier. He was needed in the recording studio all day Friday: not a problem, his driver could bring him straight to the hotel afterwards.

At Mama's insistence, Sylva had block-booked rooms at Calcot Manor Spa for the entire run of the competition. The luxurious surroundings, pampering and five-star food were exactly what they needed, Mama maintained, and it would finally kick-start the romance that was destined to lead to love and marriage, and the seven-figure exclusive wedding features that she and Sylva's management team were currently negotiating with *Cheers!*.

But a phone call to Dillon on the Wednesday of Badminton week yet again threatened her well-laid plans.

'We're just about to leave, darlink,' she told him as she stood on the drive outside Le Petit Château, kicking at the gravel with a pointed suede toe and watching nannies and drivers loading up her convoy.

Her camera team were filming her from behind a tubbed bay tree. She zipped up her little red suede jacket and turned away from them so that they couldn't see her face. She was already wearing big dark glasses and a baseball cap, picking up vibes from Dillon who loathed Rodney's presence and refused to let his team film him or his children.

'Leave where?' He sounded distracted, music and conversation in the background.

'For Calcot Manor. I'll see you there on Friday, yes?'

'Not sure I'll make it.'

'You have to!'

'There's so much to do here. We've all agreed to push on through the weekend if we need to.'

'But Pom and Berry are coming!'

'Their mother's flying over with them and she'll be in the London house, so I might as well stay there. It's easier for me to see them that way.'

She shuffled further away from her documentary team, lowering her voice. 'Zuzi will be devastated. She has been so desperately looking forward to seeing your girls. She always mentions Pom and Berry in her prayers each night.'

That hit him where it hurt.

'She has had such a traumatic little life,' she went on in a heartfelt whisper. 'Her father in Slovakia has just forsaken Hana for another woman. They are trying to keep it from Zuzi, but children have an instinct about these things.'

That would surely score another body blow, Sylva decided, with Dillon unable to avoid painful parallels with his daughters' suffering when his own long-distance marriage crumbled.

'Is Hana okay?'

'Hana?' Sylva struggled for a moment to register what he was talking about. 'Oh, fine. They did not love each other for many years. She is better here with me and Mama.'

'Your family mean everything to you, don't they?'

'They must come first.'

'I'll be there on Sunday with the girls.'

'You will join me at the hotel on Saturday night?'

'No. I can't leave London. We'll meet at Badminton.'

Sylva felt that, in the circumstances, it was as good as she could hope for – another play-date, this one played out in public at least.

At Calcot Spa, Sylva and Mama enjoyed massages, facials, manicures, body wraps and polishes on the first day, while Hana and the nannies entertained the children in the crèche and took them for adventures in the grounds. On Friday, Sylva worked out in the gym and swam hundreds of lengths in the pool, Mama had an eyelash tint, fake tan and cellulite treatment, and a protesting Hana was frog-marched to the spa for a facial and hot-stone massage.

By Friday night, when they tucked into veal sweetbreads in the Conservatory restaurant, there was a curious unity between the mother and daughters. Then Hana made a comment that shattered the family truce.

'Why do you want to marry a man who does not want to marry you?' she asked her younger sister calmly over vanilla-poached peaches.

Mama's squawks of protest were interrupted by a text message arriving from Dillon.

Will be in studio all tomorrow day & night. Can't make Badminton.

Sylva narrowed her eyes murderously. She might have guessed he'd wimp out. She already had a contingency plan, and so she immediately texted Indigo, suggesting a family outing that weekend.

D stuck in recording studio, but I know you and P can talk him round.

Her thumb criss-crossed her phone's touch screen, its long acrylic nail scratching against the glass. *Would be so lovely to spend more time with all my new family, and D needs a treat. Can you help?*

It was a bold move, Indigo could easily call her bluff and checkmate, but Sylva doubted she would deny herself the opportunity to cash in on her recent mother-in-law gamesmanship. It was Indigo who had started the engagement rumour, after all. She liked to play as much as Sylva. If she wanted to see it through, she knew how important it was to make sure that Sylva and Dillon were seen together in public, and soon.

She replied in seconds: *Wicked stepmother on case.*

Sylva giggled, earning curious looks from Mama and Hana. Indigo rarely betrayed a sense of humour, laughter being the enemy of smooth skin, but when she did Sylva found her almost human.

Not pausing for a beat, she put an urgent call through to her personal hair stylist.

'Gary will come here tomorrow,' she told Mama afterwards. 'I am going blonde again.'

Mama's face lit up, having thought the brunette very drab. Sylva was a good girl, and professional to a fault. If she couldn't guarantee the top-ranking headlines that she ideally wanted to come next week, from an appearance with 'fiancé Dillon Rafferty' at Britain's biggest equestrian event, then she could at least try to avoid slipping BKK by eliciting the media's interest with a new hair colour. Now *that* was dedication.

Chapter 63

The atmosphere – and weather – at Badminton had already tested the Haydown team to the limit. Both dressage days were marked by unseasonably chilly temperatures and gusty showers, making the horses crabby and disobedient.

Hugo performed his first test in a hailstorm and came out with a cricket score on Sir Galahad. Twenty minutes later, in sideways rain, Lough and his scratch ride, Koura, picked up an equally unimpressive clutch of penalties by rearing after the rein back and fly-bucking through the flying changes. Both men were so hellbent on beating one another that they over-focused and over-pressurised their mounts.

Early on the second day, The Fox gave Rory an easier ride than his stablemate, despite a hailstorm during his canter work, and the pair raised the stalwart dressage crowd's spirits with an electric test, only marred by the rider's over-cocky bows and winks to the judges, like Liberace flirting over a piano.

Left to his own devices away from the Hugo-Lough grudge match, Rory was on a roll and loving the attention his Kentucky win brought. To his delight, Marie-Clair had flown in to catch some four-star action en route to her stud in France, supporting one of her coaching protégés, a young French rider called Kevin, and checking in with her British interest.

They watched the other Haydown contenders from the stands. Hugo scraped into the top ten on a volatile The Cub and Lough raised his game too, riding Olympic horse Rangitoto with iron will to end the day in seventh, but neither competitor was happy, and MC was quick to proclaim why.

'Zey ride wiz zeir cocks. It is always a mistake – like driving wiz your nose, huh?'

Rory flashed a smile, not entirely certain what she meant. She was frighteningly like Eric Cantona at times.

'And your cock?' she demanded, earning some shocked looks from near by seats.

'Entirely at your service,' he told her in an undertone, spoken into his collar like a spy.

'Good. I book a hotel for tonight.' She stood up. 'You lie fourth, I sink.'

'You mean there are three others sharing your bed before me?' Rory gulped, unhappy with the idea of queuing up for his French mistress, however irresistible he found her lessons.

'On the leaderboard, Rory,' she laughed throatily, blowing him a kiss. 'You are fourth after ze dressage, but always first in my heart, as I am in yours, *non*?'

'Of course.' Rory blew a kiss in return before setting off to the temporary stables to feed Fox a roll of Polos and give him a thank-you pat. Crossing back through the park, he half hoped he would bump into Faith and be able to share the news of his top-five slot with her, but she was nowhere to be seen as he returned to the Beauchamps' horsebox to pack his things.

Paranoid that their trysts would be discovered by the scandal-loving British eventing crowd, MC had booked a B&B several miles away using a false name. Rory loved that the guesthouse's owner called him Monsieur Nom de Plume without apparent irony.

'Zey will talk about us still, of course,' MC predicted minutes later as she undressed Rory with consummate skill, fingers as deft with buttons as a catwalk stylist changing a male model. 'Now you are winning, you weel be on everybody's lips.'

'Do you really think so?' he asked, hoping nothing bad was being said about him in the Lime Tree Farm lorry, parked in the prime Badminton pitch it had occupied for over a decade, like the central tepee in a Native American encampment. The Moncrieffs were notorious gossips, so their lorry was a campfire for all-comers.

'*Absolutement.*' MC removed his trousers faster than a casualty nurse treating a minor burn. Then she dropped to her knees. 'But tonight, you are only on my lips, *chéri.*'

Rory closed his eyes ecstatically, deciding on balance that he didn't mind being talked about if it involved lip service like this.

But talk in the lorry park that week was not about Rory and MC. Nor was it still debating the identity of Lucy Field's married lover, a topic that had kept the scandalmongers speculating for two seasons now. It was all about the Tash-Hugo-Lough love triangle. Rumours were running riot, with claims that Lough and Tash had been spot-ted kissing in the ha-ha at Hyam Hall, canoodling behind the bushes at Larkhill and fornicating against the orangery at Belton.

'It's all such rubbish – Tash didn't even go to Belton,' Penny Moncrieff complained to Gus. 'Where on earth do they get it from?'

Gus coughed uncomfortably, but said nothing.

By the Friday night, Tash and Hugo, sharing a rented cottage on the edge of the estate with the children and au pairs, were feeling so much tension from the obvious scrutiny that they were under, that they were barely speaking.

On Saturday, the weather flipped sides and was unexpectedly hot, throwing cross-country preparations into disarray as the going changed from soft to sticky. Riders grumbled about the stamina-sapping ground, the risk of injury and slippages. Everybody knew that the toughest course in the world would take no prisoners in ideal conditions, let alone in punishing heat and with claggy going.

'They'll come home exhausted, if at all,' Julia Ditton, commentating for the BBC, predicted darkly. The first two horses on the course bore this out by retiring early.

Next out was Hugo's first horse, Sir Galahad. The duo seemed set to defy the pessimists, streaking round in Hugo's inimitable, quick-witted style. But disaster struck when the horse tripped badly on a loose leg boot in the middle of the bounce into the lake and chested the second element, propelling Hugo out over the jump and into the water.

'Now there's a sight you don't see very often!' Mike Tucker chortled delightedly on the live commentary as Hugo waded out to catch his horse. 'Beauchamp taking a swim!'

'Hot day. Nice to cool off,' Hugo managed to joke through gritted teeth when Julia Ditton dashed up to him with a microphone at the end of his round.

There was no laughter back at the stables when Jenny examined the cause of the fall. The straps of the boot had been cut.

'I put them on myself, and taped them before you warmed up,' she said. 'They were fine.'

'Could anybody else have got at them before the start?' Hugo demanded.

'No – I mean, we were all there checking everything and putting on the leg grease, me, Beccy – and Lem was there for Lough, helping out.'

'Was Lough near by at the time?'

Jenny nodded. 'We should complain to the stewards.'

He waved the idea away. 'Waste of time – we can't prove anything. Just looks like sour grapes.'

Jenny cleared her throat awkwardly. 'Beccy has been . . . very strange all this week.'

It was true that Beccy couldn't stop crying, and wouldn't tell anybody why. She kept locking herself in the loo of the horsebox and refused to come out.

'Okay. Say nothing, but don't let her near Cub from now on. I'm going to get out of these wet things.'

Tash, who'd seen the fall on the screen in the supporters' tent and had been running around trying to find Hugo ever since, was handicapped by Cora who had become very clingy lately and refused to leave her mother's side, but weighed a ton to carry and was far too slow and unsteady to walk any distance. She finally tracked him down at the horsebox, changing into dry clothes.

'Are you okay?' she gasped breathlessly, Cora dangling round her neck.

'Never fucking better,' he hissed as he pulled a T-shirt over his head.

For once not telling him off for not wearing a Mogo top – or pulling him up about swearing in front of Cora – Tash let the wriggling toddler slither to the floor. 'I've just seen Jenny. She says it was deliberate.'

'Looks like it.'

'I think you should withdraw Cub. It's too dangerous.'

He held up his hand to quieten her as the distant cross-country commentary announced that Lough Strachan had cleared the first fence and was away. 'Lover boy's on course if you want to watch.'

'Please don't say that,' Tash said, not noticing that Cora had appropriated her father's spare cross-country helmet and was filling it with food from the fridge as a make-believe picnic basket.

They walked back towards the supporters' tent in silence. Hugo had several hours before he needed to start warming up Cub, and wanted to face the commiserations of his fellow riders straight away to get it over with. He also secretly hoped to watch Lough suffer a similar fate on the big screen.

But Lough gave an exemplary performance, piloting the unfamiliar ride around his first-ever Badminton as though they'd been a partnership for years, taking all the direct routes, picking out the most brilliant, economic lines and the best of the ground to preserve the horse's legs. They galloped through the finish inside the time to be greeted by enormous cheers of support, particularly from the female spectators. Lemon bounced up and down like a rubber ball as he took over the horse to cool him down and loosen off while Lough was hailed from all sides by the excited owners and fellow New Zealanders.

It had been a breathtaking bit of riding. His was the first penalty-free clear round of the day; to go inside the time had been thought impossible until now. Anybody who had not yet realised that Lough

Strachan had arrived in the UK and was a force to be reckoned with, was now left in no doubt that the Devil on Horseback was here.

Swept away by the hysteria of the supporters' tent, Tash felt jubilant. Seeing the man she'd been training with finally start to get the recognition he deserved, she urged Hugo to come with her and the children to congratulate him too: 'Let's bury the hatchet, show a united front. We can get past all this nonsense.'

'Since when was trying to steal another man's wife nonsense?' He stood up and marched out.

By the time she'd gathered Cora in her toddler reins, Amery in the buggy and all their paraphernalia to follow him, he'd disappeared from sight.

Spotting Veruschka and Vasilly at a burger van, she apologetically handed over her children and dashed straight to the stables. But Hugo wasn't there, only Jenny, plaiting up Cub.

Nor was he in the lorry park, although she found his phone in the horsebox. Shame-faced, she checked the many unread good luck and commiseration messages cluttering the inbox. Two stuck out horribly, both listed as from Shadowfax. She recognised the name with a jolt.

Sent five minutes before his start time: *Pride comes before a fall.*

Then, sent just a minute after his crash into the water: *Told you so.*

Heart slamming, she held the phone like an unexploded bomb when a message suddenly came through from V. *Where r u? Thought we said meet in the Allen Grove at one? Can't be spotted by you-know-who! Xxx*

A lime pit of corrosive, angry indignation stripped her skin. How dare he! How *dare* he march around full of aggrandised hurt when he was the one being unfaithful. He had been unfaithful with V for months and months. Jealousy pulled the artery from her throat and starved her mind of oxygen as she hurled the phone at the wall.

She looked at her watch. Five past one.

Bursting out of the horsebox, she crashed straight into Lough.

'Is Hugo around?' He looked furious. 'People are saying I sabotaged his ride. This has gone far enough.'

Angry tears were suddenly falling from her eyes. She knew she looked half-mad. Sitting outside a nearby horsebox on folding chairs eating their lunch in the sunshine, several riders and their teams were watching with interest. One discreetly reached for a mobile phone and turned on the camera.

'What is it?' Lough took her hands in his, like ropes tethering her rocking ship to a harbour wall.

'I can't – I must –' She fought the tears but they were coming hard and fast now.

'What, Tash?'

'It's such a mess. Such a bloody mess. I can't take it any more,' she sobbed.

His eyes lifted to her face, full of hope.

She tried to pull away from him, but the harbour ropes were harnessing her now.

She felt his body against hers, hard and solid and still hot from riding across country.

'You don't have to take it, Tash.'

'Tell that to Hugo!' she raged through the tears.

'You have no idea how much pleasure that would give me.' He laughed suddenly, that rare laugh that she'd grown so fond of, despite its rarity, like a nightjar's call.

Tash leant back and stared up at him, taking several frantic heartbeats to take in what he was saying.

And she knew that it was unmistakeably there, a gong struck in her chest, an inability to catch her breath, focus or see past him without the urge to fall into his arms. She wanted to throw herself against his heat and love, to blot out what was happening.

But she shook her head violently. 'Please let me go. I don't want that.'

He dropped his hands, his eyes so lost in hers that it was a while before she realised she was free to leave.

Then she ran as fast as she could.

In the Beauchamps' lorry a beeping from Hugo's phone announced a new photo-message.

Allen Grove was a wood at the far end of the estate's park, just beyond the limit of the cross-country course, and out of bounds to the public, although those who remembered the long-format competition, which had involved miles of roads and tracks plus a steeplechase before horses set out on the cross-country, knew it well. Tash ran all the way there.

Chest burning, legs heavy with lactic acid, she climbed over the first gate she could find and ran blindly on into the woods. But it was a huge, dense area. All she could hear were birds calling overhead, her steps crunching, her breath gasping and the distant Tannoy.

She would never find them here. It was a perfect adulterer's lair.

She sagged back against a tree trunk and closed her eyes, grateful for the cool and privacy of the woods. But a moment's silence gave her a hundred intense flashbacks to Lough touching her, holding her, to her excitement and shame and now, far more dangerous, her competitive streak.

It was better to keep running.

She could hear the commentary about Rory now and felt a cramp of disgrace that she had neglected him, as had they all. She turned to leave the woods the way she'd come in. Then she realised that a couple were having sex up against a tree, just a few metres away.

The woman was facing Tash, and she recognised her with immediate horror. Lucy Field, minxy blonde eventer notorious for trotting up her horses in the shortest of skirts and highest of heels at every veterinary inspection, for appearing in every nude horsy charity calendar and for sleeping her away round most of the horseboxes in the lorry park before she settled down with nice-but-dim Jamie Stanton, middle son of a great eventing dynasty.

It was Lucy, she realised, feeling faint. Hugo was screwing Lucy.

But even as she thought it she heard the man grunting and groaning out of sight and she realised he wasn't Hugo. And when he started to speak, she knew exactly who he was.

'Yes! Don't stop. Bloody Jesus. Don't stop!'

That voice had shouted at her a hundred times and more.

It was Gus. Eventing's lovely vintage teddy bear who'd lost his stuffing. Penny's Gus. Lime Tree's Gus. Everybody's Gus.

'OHMYGOD! We've been seen!' Lucy shouted suddenly.

But Tash hardly registered it. Her mind was bubbling over now, totally incapable of finding its balance. If Gus was at it and Hugo was at it, was everybody at it? Rory was forever at it . . . the Cole Porter song sprang into her head, rattling ludicrously with its cheery suggestion that *birds do it, bees do it, even educated fleas do it . . .*

She shook her head violently to make the song disappear.

Keep running she reminded herself. Keep moving.

Turning away as Gus and Lucy dived for cover, she sprinted back towards the safety of the horsebox, but found her stepsister had beaten her to it and was sitting on the ramp, tears streaming down her face.

'What on earth is it, Beccy?'

'I'm having the w-w-worse time of m-my *life* here!' she announced theatrically, snuffling madly. 'And now I c-can't get in the h-h-horsebox because it's l-locked.'

'Is this about Lem?' Tash had noticed they were keeping well apart.

Beccy nodded, then shook her head, then burst into tears again. Tash hugged her tightly and waited for the tears to ebb, fishing the horsebox keys from her pocket and holding them up. 'Now you can get in and get whatever it is you need.'

Beccy shrugged and shuddered with abating tears. 'I was going to lock myself in the loo.'

'Ah. So was I, but we won't both fit in there so we'll have to take turns and I'll make you a cup of tea.' Tash steered her to the front of the big Oakley.

Beccy rubbed her eyes and studied Tash closely. 'Are you going to leave Hugo for Lough?' she asked hopefully.

'Christ, where did you get that from?'

'Everybody's saying it. They say that's what the grudge match between them is all about.'

'Well everybody's wrong.'

Beccy sat at the table in the horsebox and began fiddling with the mobile phone that had been abandoned there. She turned to Tash. 'So why is there a photo-message on here of you and Lough in a clinch?'

It was only after Beccy had eaten half a packet of biscuits and told Tash the gritty details of her split from Lemon that she remembered she was supposed to be grooming for Rory.

Faith hadn't forgotten Rory, and made up for Beccy's last-minute absence, watching him on the big screen in the arena as he flew around, trusting The Fox who had been round clear the previous year and knew what it was all about. Less headstrong than his brother, who Hugo would ride later, he was nevertheless so agile and fleet of foot that he devoured the track. And he clearly revelled in Rory's light, skilful handling, the partnership having cemented itself more and more with each outing.

She welcomed them home as heroes. She was so proud that she even forgave MC for swooping in at the finish again and claiming Rory. '*Formidable!* I must introduce you to some very interested owners, *chéri.*'

Faith scowled, but Rory's departing look lifted her heart a little as his eyes sparkled into hers and he blew her a kiss.

She knew MC's powerful contacts could be a lifeline for Rory, who had so few real supporters, especially now she had probably scuppered his future with Dillon by being over-demanding. Her chest compressed uncomfortably at the thought.

Once Fox's heart rate and temperature had stabilised she led him back to his stable to wash him, rug him up and and apply leg-cooling clay before dashing across the old stable yard to check on Gus's ride, By Dickens, who had been round earlier, glancing off the corner in Huntman's Close to scupper their chances in an otherwise foot-perfect performance.

'Rory went clear,' she told Penny breathlessly. 'He was quite brilliant given the ground is so churned up now. His fuel tank started to empty after the Quarry. Rory nursed him home with just a couple of time faults. Have you seen Lem? He borrowed my penknife and I need it back for the corkscrew.' She held up a bottle of Sauvignon Blanc.

'Rory's on the wagon,' Penny reminded her, emerging from By Dickens's stall where she'd been wrapping his legs in her own customised injury-avoider of chilled supermarket cool bags cut down and encased in bandaging.

'It's not for Rory. It's for us.' Faith waggled it at her.

'You are fabulous! So like your father.' Penny laughed, not noticing Faith's shocked face because she'd spotted Tash arriving with a tearstained Beccy.

'Did you see my man go, Tash?' she called out, her berry eyes alight. 'Bloody brilliant. He'll be back in a minute, he's just gone to change. You've got ages before Hugo goes. Have a glass of wine.'

Certain that an image of Gus and Lucy Field in the woods was flashing up on her eyeballs like a cinema trailer, Tash looked hastily away. 'Where is Hugo?' Their area was deserted apart from Sir Galahad pulling at a haynet and looking very chilled out despite his earlier dunking. 'I thought he'd be here.'

'Taken Cub out in the park.'

He was probably in Allen Grove, meeting V, she realised wretchedly.

Then she saw Lough step from Rangitoto's stable and, grabbing Beccy, went violently in reverse.

To cheer Beccy up, Tash took her to the retail village and bought her the eventing must-have, a pair of Dubarry boots, which she knew her stepsister had always lusted after. Just as she was paying for them, she felt a tap on her shoulder.

'Good to see you, Tash. Hope you're well – your little fellow must be almost one now?' A tall, thin figure with iron grey hair pecked at her cheeks like a blackbird plucking a worm before leaning closer and whispering through a fixed smile, 'Make a fool of Hugo and the whole eventing world will turn against you.'

'Who was that?' Beccy asked as the woman stalked away.

'Gin Seaton,' Tash said in a frozen voice. 'Used to have a horse with us until her husband pulled the plug, saying it was too expensive.'

She had to battle to stop herself running after lovely, kind-hearted, upright Gin and scream, 'He's having an affair. It's not me, it's *him*!' But the trade-stand assistant was holding out a keypad and asking for her pin number. As she paid for Beccy's boots she decided to make a determined effort to be a good wife, however difficult Hugo was trying to make things.

She had never felt so wretched about her marriage and so certain that it was on the rocks.

They headed to the arena to watch Hugo set off, reuniting with the au pairs and the children who were in roaring sprits. But when she tried to get close to Hugo in the collecting ring, Tash was almost mown down by a rival's horse and he snapped that she should rejoin the children beyond the fence and stop distracting him. Already standing well back, Jenny gave Tash a sympathetic look. Then her eyes flashed with warning and Tash saw Lough riding in from the warm-up area, followed by Lemon who was carrying buckets full of equipment and spares, his Mohawk dyed black in a gesture of Kiwi patriotism. She fled behind the barriers before Hugo could start picking fights.

As soon as Tash had sweet-talked the officials into letting her little posse watch Hugo's round in the competitors' tent, Alicia lurched up to join them, positively flying after a very merry lunch with her cronies.

'Just heard you've taken that lovely Kiwi boy as a lover,' she slurred in a stage whisper as she claimed the chair beside Tash. 'Bravo! The first time I got Henry to sit up and take notice again after the boys were born was when Dickie Bingley-Bowers and I were caught in flagrante. Told you the secret is to get them to see you as a desirable woman again. Got a light? Is that Hugo?'

Tash wasn't listening as Hugo streaked off through the start to the usual whoops of applause, The Cub battling for his head, giraffing up his neck in front of the first fence, chestnut ears pricked.

From the very beginning it was a round marked with the stroke of brilliance that wins Badminton. The horse was fresh and bravely over-jumping, despite all the work Jenny and Hugo had put in to take the edge off him before the start, yet Hugo stayed with him, worked with him and settled him into rhythm without ever fighting him. Like his father Snob, the only horse in history to have won Badminton three times in a row, Cub was fearless, clever and very, very bold. He was just Hugo's sort, rider and horse ideally matched in mercurial brilliance.

Then they got to the spine of the course, the testing Vicarage Fields run where big fence after big fence, coming in quick succession, required horse and rider to cross and re-cross the huge, gaping ditch. The television camera mounted on a quad bike loomed up alongside Hugo.

From the first leap at the Countryside Turn, crossing the ditch and banking up to an angled brush, it was obvious something had gone wrong. The Cub pecked on landing and Hugo's weight seemed to shift sideways, throwing him out of balance so that he reached forwards to grab at the chestnut neck and right himself, looking down.

'What's wrong?' Tash yelped, covering her mouth in terror.

Such was his ability, Hugo turned without hesitating for the accuracy-demanding hexagons that spanned the ditch once more and kicked on. The horse committed to the stride and flew over the first. Again Hugo jolted sideways on landing, but recovered and turned to ride for the second element with equal flair. It was only when he came closer to the bike camera once more that Tash – and the rest of the tent – realised what had happened.

'His girth's broken!' someone gasped. 'The bloody girth's broken!'

The girth was flapping loose beneath The Fox's belly, slapping his legs as he galloped.

'He'll pull up,' they all agreed.

He didn't.

Like most eventers, Hugo always rode with an over-girth around the saddle for safety, but it was little more than an elastic belt to stop the saddle slipping; it was never intended to hold it in place and certainly not over the most taxing fences in the world with his earlier nemesis, the Lake, still to come.

Hearing what was going on, riders and their crews had started pouring into the tent to watch on the big screen.

'The stewards will red flag him in a minute!'

They didn't.

Having cleared the Colt Pond and, miraculously, the sweeping corners at the Farmyard complex, Hugo reached down to unbuckle the loose girth and throw it aside.

He'd managed to find his balance on the shifting sands of the saddle, riding with a forward seat like a jump jockey, letting his knees do the work, his lower leg staying absolutely firm to balance his long upper body over the fences.

'They'll stop him on course,' Alicia predicted grumpily. 'Not allowed to ride heroically these days. Health and safety and all that. All bloody cowards now.'

But while the officials frantically leafed through the Rulebook to see whether they should stop him, Hugo rode on, thrilling the crowds and the BBC commentary team, who couldn't find enough superlatives to describe what they were seeing.

'Not since Toddy rode Bertie Blunt around this course with one stirrup have we seen horsemanship of this magnitude,' Mike Tucker told red-button viewers.

'You are seeing history in the making, my friends!' Matt Ryan agreed excitedly.

Julia Ditton was more pragmatic: 'That must hurt. He's taking all his weight through his knees. Most of us would have pulled up by now.'

In and out of the Sunken Road they hopped, taking the perfect line despite the fact that the saddle was very obviously moving backwards now, straining against the breastplate. As they flew the Barn Table the saddle went back almost to the horse's loins before shifting forwards again. The Cub was getting stronger and stronger, recognising that, for once, he had the chance to dictate the pace.

'It must be like sitting on a see-saw,' a rider exclaimed. 'He'll never get through the Lake.'

'Oh God.' Tash covered her eyes as Hugo and The Cub, chins up, determined but starting to fight each other, hurtled towards the Mitsubishi pick-ups in front of the famous Badminton Lake.

'Going too fast!' Alicia groaned.

Tash cowered as she heard gasps and groans and then whoops. When she opened her eyes Hugo was through the lake and galloping out across the park.

'Oh God, I missed it,' she howled.

''s all right. You'll see it again,' Alicia assured her. She was right; it would be played again and again in sporting hero moments for years to come, as would his incredible ride through Hunstman's Close, finding the angle that so many had missed with all their tack firmly in place; then on to the Quarry, where the huge drop on the way in moved his saddle right up the horse's neck, but Hugo clung on, up and out into the final gallop home, even checking his stopwatch to the crowd's delight. And to their even greater delight, he was on target.

Within sight of the finish, the Rolex Turn almost claimed him. Flying through the keyhole cut in a giant brush and angling left for a skinny, the saddle slipped so far that Hugo couldn't centre it again before the next element and The Cub made an almighty cat-leap, knocking the flag from the fence as he twisted in mid-air. Yet somehow Hugo stayed on, nobody quite knew how, and they galloped into the arena with the saddle hanging off to one side, Hugo riding bareback.

Afterwards he admitted that he had planned to call it a day at that point. The situation was too dangerous and the horse too valuable to risk. But he had always been an adrenalin junkie, as had little Cub, whose heart was as big as his famous father's, and hearing the roar of the crowd, who had followed their progress around the course with mounting excitement, realised they couldn't possibly pull up so close to home.

They scrambled over the Mitsubishi Garden, dangling stirrups pulling up flowers, and raced through the finish. They were, to the crowd's raucous approval, exactly on the optimum time.

Jenny grabbed The Cub as soon as Hugo jumped off, pulling off the dangling saddle and leading him to the vet to be checked over while she and Lemon, there with Lough once again, started to cool him down as quickly as they could, knowing the extra exertion would have put incredible pressure on his body.

Julia Ditton had already come up to Hugo with a microphone: 'That was some round!'

Hugo rarely ran out of puff: he was one of those annoyingly fit people who could eat and drink and smoke as much as he liked, yet still run ten miles without getting out of breath. But that round had knocked all the wind from him. All he could do was nod. He nodded like a dog on a parcel shelf for an interminable amount of time before he finally managed to splutter, 'Tash.'

She was already almost there, running across the arena towards him, face alight with fear and pride as, barely pausing for thought, she engaged her Meg Ryan leap. Spotting his wife sailing through the air towards him, Hugo's expression changed from breathless joy to total astonishment. The moment that Tash jumped into his arms was remembered for years as unbelievably romantic, not least because Hugo literally fell over backwards, leaving the two of them lying in the hoof-marked turf.

Riding past as he headed towards the start box, Lough didn't even glance down.

Hugo looked at Tash. 'Let's draw a line,' he breathed, reaching up to cup her face. The adrenalin rush hadn't left him. He looked as high as a kite.

'Where?' she asked fearfully, not understanding the insinuation. Lines meant crossing out, putting an end to things and saying no more.

'A line under all this,' he explained. 'Let's draw a line under all this.'

She nodded with tearful relief, looking into his blue eyes, determined not to think about V.

As they stood up, Lough was being counted down in the start box.

His huge, dark-rimmed eyes didn't move as he stared out between his horse's grey ears, waiting to hear 'Go.'

Hugo's hand tightened around hers. 'May the best man win.'

Tash prickled all over with discomfort.

'. . . three . . . two . . . one . . . go! Good luck!' The bowler hat was raised and Lough thundered away.

Hugo turned to Tash. 'Let's go back to the horsebox and make whoopee.'

She couldn't possibly tell him how much she wanted to watch Lough's round. 'But we have to help Jenny with Cub. And you need physio, or you'll stiffen up.'

'That's what I'm hoping,' he grinned.

The lorry-park gossips were even more animated when the Beauchampions appeared arm in arm and locked themselves in their lorry. Moments later the curtains were drawn in the pop-out pod. They didn't emerge for over an hour, by which time multiple texts had been sent and tweets posted, and the leaderboard chalked up. Rory was lying second behind Sonja Runiker, Germany's top woman rider, with Hugo back in fifth. Lough was still in contention with Koura, but he had slipped right down with Rangitoto, having trashed his second round. Those still spectating commented that watching him ride his own top horse so badly, compared to the borrowed horse he had piloted so brilliantly that morning, was like watching two completely different men.

Chapter 64

When a helicopter landed in the Calcot Manor grounds in a haze of scattering blossom, Sylva joined the onlookers gathering by the windows and was delighted to see Dillon Rafferty jump out and run towards the house. It was a pure Milk-Tray moment, only slightly marred by his bad temper and the Gay Pride T-shirt.

'Dad kidnapped me,' he grumbled as she hurriedly shrugged on her jacket.

'Pete's here?' Sylva tried to stay calm.

'He's piloting the chopper.' He yawned tiredly, having stayed up most of the previous night working in the studio.

He didn't even notice the newly white-blonde hair snaking over Sylva's tweeded shoulders, or the outfit that had been hand-picked to ignite his lust faster than a match in a jerry can. At first glance she looked like a standard-issue Badminton spectator, but the plunging cleavage of her crisp shirt revealed a transparent baby blue basque from which her magnificent breasts rose like a double sunset over a lake, and the skinniest of skinny designer Japanese bikini jeans that exposed her glossy, toned hips. Dillon hardly gave her a second glance as he headed back to the helicopter.

Nonetheless determined to make the most of this coup, Sylva kissed Mama excitedly. 'You and the children will follow on in cars. Tell Zuzi that Pom will be there.'

'Here.' Mama had reached into her cavernous bag and pulled out a velvet drawstring bag that she now thrust into her daughter's palm. 'You must use these, before it is too late.' She sounded like one of the Kaiser's men briefing Mata Hari.

With an obedient nod, Sylva pocketed the bag and raced after Dillon.

On board the helicopter, Indigo was sitting blank-faced and beautiful beside Pete, who liked nothing more than taking the controls of his little Robinson Raven on a family day trip.

'Hello Trouble.' His predatory smile flashed from beneath the darkest of aviator sunglasses as Sylva climbed into the cramped space behind them. 'Almost didn't recognise you with that barnet. Thought Dillon had got himself a new bird and the wedding was off for a minute.'

Clambering in behind Sylva and struggling to buckle his safety harness because of the weight he'd put on, Dillon shot his father a filthy look.

Glancing over her shoulder, Indigo gave Sylva a ghost of a wink.

The final day of Badminton was another scorcher, and the weathermen were confidently predicting the start of a mini heatwave.

Having been up to check on the horses first thing, the Haydown team encountered mixed fortunes. The Fox was springing off the ground so freshly he might never have galloped four miles the previous day, but his brother was as stiff as an old man, the slipping saddle having taken its toll. Despite a treatment from the Beauchamps' equine physio, Cub was too uncomfortable to be put up for presentation at the veterinary inspection and so Hugo was forced to withdraw his one remaining ride. It was the first time in five years that he hadn't posted a top-ten finish, and the first time in a decade that he had failed to complete the event. His only consolation, on the sponsorship front at least, was that his great rival looked equally unlikely to feature at the prize-giving. Both of Lough's rides lay outside the top ten, giving him little chance of making an impression at his first big event in the Northern Hemisphere.

Then, in the late-morning sunshine, the New Zealander piloted his great ally Rangitoto around a show-jumping track that was plagued with bogey fences and a very tight time limit for one of the only clear rounds. Again and again pairs crashed through the planks going away from the collecting ring, the treble combination on an awkward stride, or the narrow stile that had to be taken at an angle so as not to lose too much time. By the lunch break Lough had risen from thirty-fifth to twenty-first on Toto, with his second ride still to come in the top twenty combinations that would jump after lunch.

Great excitement greeted the arrival of a helicopter bearing The Fox's famous owner and his equally famous consort. To the crowd's delight, they were accompanied by the Rockfather himself, with Indigo at his side. The press went berserk, especially as Dillon and Sylva were sporting ostentatious matching rings.

'Just love tokens,' Sylva flicked her extensions and waved away any talk of engagement rings as the little group were hastily escorted to VIP quarters in a sponsor's marquee to watch the jumping.

Dillon, whose ring had stuck fast when Sylva crammed it on to his ring finger during the flight 'just for fun, to see how it looks', said nothing. His finger, now an alarming shade of blue, throbbed painfully.

'Where can I lay a bet?' Pete asked, lighting a fat cigar and reaching for a pair of field glasses.

'Dad, I don't think this is the—'

'Who would you like to lay sir?' An artful member of the catering staff asked smoothly as he delivered free champagne.

'Sylva.' Pete smiled at him, pulling a wad of fifties from his breast pocket. 'Can that be arranged?'

Sitting close enough to hear, Sylva smirked delightedly.

'I'm sure it can.' The waiter melted away, but was back again within five minutes. 'I'm afraid there's no horse in the trials called Silver,' he reported. 'There is a Koura, which I'm reliably informed is Maori for gold. That's as close as I can find.'

'What are the odds?'

'Twenty-five to one.'

'Can we go each way?' He shot a brief sideways look at Sylva who sent a lingering look back.

'I'm sure we can.' The waiter slipped away again just as the band display finally finished and the parade of competitors began.

'I suppose we should really have bet on Dillon's horse,' Sylva mused, settling back to admire Rory on his flashy chestnut – quite the most handsome horseman in the field in the absence of Hugo. She couldn't see what all the fuss was about Lough, whose thick-set features and glowering menace she found quite off-putting, plus his tattoos, which hardly fitted in with the upper-class eventing scene. Dillon also had rather a lot of tattoos, which kept changing shape as he gained weight. There was a little deer on his inner thigh – logic told her that it had got to be a homage to Fawn, but ego told her that it was just a love of the countryside thing – that kept shedding its antlers back to stubby buds and then growing them again.

He so obviously didn't want to be there with her today. His fingers, legs and jaw muscles twitched out a constant rhythm, and his eyes danced around, avoiding hers yet unable to settle.

The only thing that seemed to earth him was the children, arriving with Hana, Mama and Dong half an hour later, allowing him to get down on his knees in their hospitality tent and pretend to be a show-jump while Pom, Berry, Zuzi and even Hana and Dong jumped over him in fits of giggles. Left with the boys and a clutch of small adoptees to guard, Mama sent out distress signals to Sylva who smoothly ignored them and turned to Indigo, beautifully placed between herself and Pete, like a striking statue between two cocktail-party flirts on a balcony.

Indigo flashed her cool, threatening smile.

Sylva smiled back warmly, her eyes drifting to Pete who was mouthing 'I want to fuck you' behind his wife's back. Coming from anybody else, it would be revolting. From Pete Rafferty, it was a rite of passage, yet Sylva couldn't help looking into Indigo's ice-chip eyes, their tinted contact lenses the same colour as her made-up name.

Smile dropping, she turned to watch the jumping, which was about to restart, reminding herself that she was here today with Dillon – wearing their rings and getting photographed from every angle – because of Indigo. The woman had come up trumps and Sylva rewarded her by lusting after husband. It had to stop.

'I tried to buy one of these horses a few months ago, but they wouldn't sell it to me,' she told the collective Raffertys.

'Which one'd you try to buy, love?' Pete asked casually.

'He's not here, I think.' Sylva was looking at the programme, then glanced up as Lough rode into the ring. 'But I like this one. It's a very pretty colour. I asked Tash for a palomino!'

The New Zealand horse was in fact the palest sorrel chestnut, but in the bright sunlight with his flaxen mane and tail gleaming like spun gold, it resembled a fairytale steed, its rider the noblest of avenging knights.

'This is Koura – the one you bet on.' Indigo was consulting the programme too.

Taking a deep drag on his cigar, Pete smiled to himself as Lough jumped his second clear round of the day.

By the time the top ten jumped, Lough's two rounds were the only clears. With other riders averaging double-figure penalties around the trappy course, he was breathing down the neck of those still to go, both of his horses now miraculously well placed to rival the leaders.

In the arena, the top ten crumbled one by one. Poles fell as willingly as pine needles from an ageing Christmas tree, planks were brushed off their shallow cups and time penalties clocked up. Lough rose up the leaderboard, past Lucy Field who knocked out the narrow stile, past veteran Australian Mick James, and young British hopes Colly Trewin and Miranda Hayter. Soon, to everyone's amazement, and especially his own, only two rounds lay between him and victory.

Then a handsome figure rode into the arena like Young Lochinvar, mounted on a world-famous horse. All the confidence from a four-star win a week earlier and an easy passage to Badminton's top three lifted him and the crowd to mutual devotion. Rory was the exciting young British hope, tipped for a place on the team for the European Championships later in the year, handsome and heroic, up in the top ten while valiant also-ran Hugo wasn't even going to finish this year. The crowd had a new favourite.

His confidence – hyped up to the point of cocky indifference and gratified by MC's devotion – paid dividends, but only just. To the delight of his connections, Rory and The Fox jumped clear. The more knowledgeable watching could see that he took ludicrous risks and showed off appallingly, and had his horse been stiffer and flatter from the previous day's cross-country he would have paid the price.

But he scraped his clear and punched the air, rather unsportingly pointing at Sonja Ricker as she cantered in to jump for victory and calling out 'Beat that!' The partisan crowd turned a blind eye and carried on cheering him all the way out.

Having watched from the sidelines, Faith rushed forwards as Rory jumped off Cub, eager to cheer his clear, but then she stopped short as MC swooped in to clasp him in her talons and join his entourage in watching the final round, carefully keeping out of camera shot as the collecting-ring television crew focused tightly on his excited face. Disheartened, Faith took the horse and patted him heartily before discreetly taking up position behind them. There was a slow puncture starting to deflate her hopes and her love.

When Sonja knocked down the penultimate fence, assuring victory for Rory, the patriotic crowd went wild. The ringside television cameras caught every moment of the young British champion celebrating with red-blooded gusto, kissing all the girls – and women, most particularly veteran French Olympian Marie-Clair and long-suffering Julia Ditton, who yet again braced herself for a quick interview that involved Rory saying nothing but 'Bloody brilliant!' over and over again. Thankfully the television audience were compensated by the arrival of owner Dillon Rafferty at his jockey's side. Despite the scraggy beard and Gay Pride T-shirt which had been covered up by a vast on-screen strapline showing his name, his smile worked its magic and Rory's victory was sprinkled with the fairy dust of celebrity. When Sylva Frost appeared at Dillon's side and held his hand, subtly lifting his garish ring into view, the cameras went into overdrive.

'Is it true that we have a celebrity wedding to look forward to?' Julia asked reluctantly, prompted by screaming demands in her earpiece.

Sylva blushed and said nothing, but her look to camera melted hearts in sitting rooms around the country. The nation's favourite single mum had got her dream man, a modest rock star and farmer who would surely make her happy at last.

Chapter 65

The traditional post-Badminton party at Haydown, shared with the Moncrieffs, was not as joyous as in previous years. Wrought with undercurrents from the start, all eyes were on Hugo and Lough as the tension between them threatened to combust within just an hour.

Wholly overlooked despite his epic victory, Rory appropriated a bottle of champagne and jumped gleefully and victoriously from the wagon for the night. MC had already flown back to France, leaving him in quandary. Eager for a little partisan company, he located Faith in the garden talking to Gus and Alicia.

Her companions were both puffing away on Rothmans. All three were having a heated debate about the state of eventing in Britain, voices raised and hackles up, even though they were all essentially on the same side.

'It's being dumbed down!' Gus stormed. 'When I was Faith's age we rode everything by the seat of out pants.'

'Exactly!' Alicia raised her hipflask of gin. 'Young things like Faith here need to feel the danger.'

'There is no danger if you ride well enough,' Faith said, turning to watch Rory stumble through the rose bushes towards her, champagne bottle in hand. He was tilting sideways, but the fact that he had sought her out at all made her heart soar.

He joined them and immediately bummed a cigarette from Alicia.

'You don't smoke!' Faith protested.

'Feel the danger,' he whispered in her ear, elbowing her cheerfully. 'All this passive smoking is white-knuckle stuff.'

'Actually, I'm a passive-aggressive smoker. If you light that near me, I'll hit you. '

It was too smart-arse for Rory, but he did at least toss the cigarette away.

He was leaning quite heavily against her, offering a swig from his champagne bottle.

Oh, the bliss of drinking from the cool glass his lips had just encircled.

'Let's take a walk among the lavender borders,' he suggested, lurching off.

The lavender borders smelled intoxicatingly heady.

Rory was already intoxicated enough. He was slurring so much that only one in three words was distinguishable as he rambled again about his victory, and achieving two of the three Rolex Grand Slam legs.

'I'll win it for you, Faith my darling!' He tripped over a step. 'I am the best! *We* are the best! Spent your winnings yet?'

'No.'

'Pleash don't have any more plashtic surgery. Itsh shuch a waste.'

Faith felt bleak. He obviously meant that surgery was wasted on her, as such a lost cause. Her flat chest shrank back from her biggest chicken fillets and she felt so stung that it didn't even register with her that he still thought she'd had her full boob and body makeover.

They had reached the raised seating at the far end of the rose garden, which had been constructed to take advantage of the view out across the parkland to the west. The last streaks of sunset bleached an otherwise inky sky ahead of them, the distant woods rasping with roosting rooks.

'I need your help, Faith – here.' He handed the bottle to her again because he needed both hands to help steady his way to sitting down on a bench. 'Faith-full,' he went on, struggling over the pun. 'My old faithful, young faithful. My mate. Too talented to waste her life as some working pupil with old war-dogs like the Moncrieffs.'

'I'm happy there.'

'But you're rich now. You don't have to work for them.'

She said nothing, her defences rising because she suddenly feared that he was only interested in her money. When he took the ride on Rio, they had never made a formal deal. She had never been able to afford to pay livery, but at the time he'd taken the horse on he'd never dreamed of the league Rio would now be competing in. And now he had four horses at that level, perhaps he was after his cut of the winnings?

He had taken her hand in his and was swinging it companionably against his cheek, a strange, unnatural gesture because he was being brotherly but she wanted to lift his hand to her lips and kiss his every calloused knuckle.

'Time to take a leap of Faith.' He sounded as though he was talking to himself.

'Meaning?'

'Marie-Clair has asked me to go to France and compete on the Continental circuit. She thinks I need to be away from Haydown while the shit hits the fan.'

'What?' She froze.

Rory shook his head. 'Hugo's a shit and Lough's not his greatest fan. Thing is, I need your help here, Faith.'

He didn't need to elaborate. She immediately guessed what the deal was. He needed her money – and horse – in Europe. Long accustomed to unrequited love, to battling to keep close to him, the thought of him leaving her again was almost too much to bear.

'Marie-Clair is very demanding,' he sighed.

'Do you love her?' She snatched her hand away, causing him to sway sideways.

But he didn't appear to be listening. 'She says I still have a long way to go, but she thinks I have potential. She says my cock is compact and powerful, like a Norman Cob.'

Faith bristled. 'So she wants you to ride around Europe with your Norman Cob on stand-by for when her husband's away on business?'

'Something like that.' He sighed again, reaching up to remove a leaf from the top of her head, his eyes crossing so he inadvertently pulled out a few strands of Faith's hair, which really hurt.

She jerked her head away, appalled by how much she wanted to beg him not to go away again. She couldn't stop thinking about his Norman Cob now. She stood up nervously and turned to face him. 'And you need *me* why, exactly?'

Rory looked up at her. It was his golden opportunity, his moment to put into words those unfamiliar feelings which had been pulling hidden pockets of his soul inside out since Kentucky, probably longer. For the first time that night, Rory wished he was sober.

He'd spent much of this evening psyching himself up for this, and imbibed so much Dutch courage that he struggled to speak at all. Marie-Clair's offer was once-in-a-lifetime stuff, but it meant nothing without Faith on side. He wasn't sure he wanted to go to France at all. MC terrified him. She had him by the balls, but Faith had his heart and he had no idea if she wanted it.

'Faith, I—'

'Yes?'

Rory faltered, knowing he had to get this right. It was a pretty shabby heart, he felt, covered with so many dents and cracks after years of rough riding that he now kept it protected as he did his spine, plating both in protective armour to stop them feeling any pain when he took more knocks. Yet he was prepared to lay it open tonight. He'd go down on one knee if necessary.

He patted the bench beside him.

Faith perched on it again, as far away from him as she could, the whites of her eyes flashing mistrustfully.

He swivelled to face her, slid an arm behind her to rest it on the back of the bench and – realising too late that the bench had no backrest – fell backwards into the rose border, his legs in the air.

Faith looked down at him, only mildly concerned. She'd seen him drunk enough times to be immune to his clumsiness. 'Why do you need me?'

There were roses to the left of him, roses to the right. In his mind, he plucked one and held it up to her, saying something killingly romantic.

In reality, he lay with his mouth open for a stupidly long time, staring up at her, then said, 'Face it, Faith, we're stuck together.'

He knew exactly what he meant, and the devotion it implied.

Faith didn't.

'Are you asking me to come to France as your groom?' For a moment she was quite excited at the thought, but then the reality of letting down the Moncrieffs and enduring Rory and MC together quickly arrested her enthusiasm.

'No! MC has grooms laid on,' Rory was saying, drunkenly starting to ramble to make up for the fact he'd just literally fallen head over heels protesting undying love, or so he believed, and was hugely embarrassed. He tugged at his signet ring, trying to wrench it off his little finger. 'Her yard there is amazing, the highest spec. It's a world apart from you and me working together with just the basics at Overlodes, a world apart . . .' He let out a nostalgic sigh.

Faith took this to mean he couldn't wait to get to the high-tech yard in France. She stood up, unwilling to hear more in case it hurt too much.

'I was thinking more of me being the groom!' He struggled upright, lacerating his arms and hands on thorns.

Oh God, he was going to *marry* MC, Faith realised. She'd divorce her husband, get a seven-figure settlement and marry Rory. He would finally have his dream come true with a Sophia Loren looka-like that could ride, and she'd have a dream work jockey.

'We've never talked anything through.' He was clambering over the bench now. 'Never laid any ground rules about . . . Rio . . . us . . . what you wanted to happen when you gave me the ride . . .'

If he married MC he would want to keep Rio in France. *Her* horse, who she had given to him along with her heart and everything else.

'I need to know what you want, Faith.' He managed to settle on the bench again, still tugging at his signet ring. 'What you really want.'

Faith was standing back in the shadows. I love you, I love you, I love you, she thought desperately. But please stop hurting me.

'You can have the Kentucky prize money,' she said quietly.

It took Rory a moment to register what she was talking about. 'I don't want your money.'

'You don't?' She hugged herself tightly.

'I want to win the best prize of them all, Faith.' He suddenly slipped off the bench and knelt in the shrubbery. Then looked down in horror. 'Fuck – I've dropped it.'

Faith didn't care what he'd dropped, apart from clangers. She knew what he was trying to say in his drunken, roundabout way. He'd just won Kentucky and Badminton. He had the best back-up team in Europe waiting for him and the best horses to take there, including hers. He deserved this break. She couldn't stand in his way.

'Go to France,' she whispered.

Rory gave up scrabbling in the undergrowth for his signet ring and straightened up, pressing one fist to his chest as he peered into her shadowy lair.

'Are you still there?' He squinted into the darkness.

'Win the Grand Slam.' She took another step back. 'You're two-thirds of the way there,' she said as she prepared to turn and flee.

Rory wished his surroundings weren't spinning quite so quickly as he needed to concentrate. He closed his eyes, determined to say his piece, ring or no ring. 'Did I ever tell you Dillon told me to win the Grand Slam when he first bought me horses, and he knows fuck-all about eventing? But he knew you were a good thing from the start. He told me you'd step from the shadows one day, and he was right. You are my shining light, Faith. I'll win the Grand Slam for you, but you are the prize I want most of all.'

When he opened his eyes again the shadows were still, apart from a few rose petals still drifting to the ground.

She had already gone.

Rory groped his way back onto the seat behind him.

'Oh fuckety fuck.' He pressed his hands to his face and slumped back in despair, forgetting yet again that there was no back to the bench so he landed with a thud among the familiar thorns and stared up at the sky, where stars crowded to watch his fall from grace.

The same stars would be looking down on him from France, he realised groggily. At least there he had someone backing him all the way. Nobody here seemed to care.

As soon as Lough arrived at the party Tash was aware of him, like a hot rash that moved around her body as he moved around the room. Huge amounts of lovemaking with Hugo in the past forty-eight hours had done nothing to stop her wretched, disloyal heart beating with giddy-making irregularity whenever Lough was near. All her erogenous zones, freshly heightened, throbbed for the thrill of that new, unfamiliar touch. Any rapprochement with Hugo was far from done and dusted while she still had no idea who V was.

She drifted through the party in a daze, talking to friends without really taking in what was being said, eyes drawn to Hugo to check if he was flirting but her heart disloyally beating a drum call for Lough. She couldn't stop it hammering out louder and harder whenever he came close, like a Geiger counter sensing radioactivity.

As the evening wore on it was inevitable they'd knock together, like two boats roped to a harbour wall in a rising squall. When it happened, however, the encounter was more *Upstairs, Downstairs* than *Titanic*. Tash was bearing a half-empty tray of sausage rolls back towards the kitchen along the narrow rear lobby when he emerged around the corner, carrying fresh supplies of wine.

Don't look him in the eye, she told herself. Don't look him in the eye, don't look him in the—

She looked him in the eye.

Her stomach seemed to drop six inches towards her pelvis and then, like loose electricity cables, set it alight.

He was equally frozen to the spot, dark eyes eating hers.

'Step aside, Lough,' a voice spoke quietly behind Tash.

Lifting his chin, Lough glared at Hugo and didn't move.

Tash's tray wobbled so much that three sausage rolls toppled off. Appearing from nowhere, the Bitches of Eastwick devoured them.

Still Lough stood firm, his eyes not leaving Tash's face, although she was feigning interest in one of the lobby's portraits. The hall was the traditional hanging-place for Hugo's uglier relatives, and this one – a great-great-aunt with a face like a walrus's – was particularly hideous, she noted, hoping Cora hadn't inherited any of those Beauchamp genes.

Realising that this was ludicrous – she and Lough facing one another bearing trays and wine like a couple of inefficient banqueting waiters while Hugo the butler sniped at them – Tash marched forwards and managed to squeeze past Lough and into the kitchen.

Busying herself by assembling a cheese board, she heard raised voices echoing along the lobby.

Wearily, she set aside a slab of cheddar and waded back in.

They were going hammer and tongs, arguing about Badminton.

'Someone took a knife to Gal's boot-straps and Cub's girths yesterday,' Hugo was raging.

'What exactly are you saying, Hugo?'

'You know damned well what went on.'

'I had *nothing* to do with it.'

'Like hell!'

Tash could see both men's knuckles whitening as they edged closer, veins rising on wrists and necks.

'Stop this!' she shouted now.

'Shut up, darling,' Hugo snapped.

'Don't tell her to shut up,' Lough rounded on him.

'She's my wife.'

'She's nobody's property.'

'Which is why you think you have a right to try to get in her knickers, I suppose?'

'Stop this!' Tash pleaded.

They ignored her.

'Don't fucking lower this to biology, Hugo.'

'You've been trying to slip her one every time my back's turned, Lough!'

'Please stop it!'

'I love her!' Lough raged.

For a moment both Hugo and Tash were silenced, rocked back on their heels by the reality of what was happening.

Then Lough's huge, coal-furnace eyes fixed on Hugo. 'You told me to take her, remember? You said I was "welcome to her".'

'What are you talking about?' Tash bleated, looking from one to the other.

Without another word, Hugo marched along the corridor, straight past Lough and Tash, so that for a crazy moment she thought he was going to walk out of the house for good. She glanced across at Lough and was hopelessly lost in his eyes for a second, before ripping her gaze away.

He stepped towards her, but she bolted back, taking cover in the shadow of the kitchen door.

Her voice sounded horribly strangled when she spoke. 'What d'you mean, Hugo said "you're welcome to her"? Was he talking about me?'

Before he could answer, footsteps marched back across the kitchen and Tash turned to see Hugo returning with a shotgun. She screamed.

Lifting the barrels to point at Lough, he asked him very politely to leave his property straight away.

Equally civil, Lough nodded and, his eyes not leaving Tash's face as he walked along the corridor towards her, he paused briefly at her side.

'Come with me.'

Tash turned away from him, her heart bursting from her chest with shame and pity. 'I can't, Lough. I can't leave my children. Hugo. My life.'

Nodding courteously, he left without another word.

Emotions churning through her, Tash was distraught.

To make matters worse, Hugo took his gun back to lock it in the cabinet, fetched a bottle of scotch and proceeded to get blind drink, which meant she couldn't get a straight answer out of him.

She was too angry and humiliated by Hugo's actions to know if she ever wanted to talk to him again. Any rapprochement seemed totally undermined by his lack of trust and his utter hypocrisy.

Having gathered at the far end of the lobby to witness the high drama, the majority of the Beauchamps' guests agreed that this was the most entertaining post-Badminton party they'd ever been to.

Chapter 66

For the next twenty-four hours, the atmosphere at Haydown remained volatile, with Lough's horses still in situ, like unwitting hostages annexed by a civil war. Lemon arrived to muck out before dawn, pointedly ignoring early-bird Beccy; Lough kept his distance; Hugo's brooding silence made everyone on the yard cower as he passed.

Gradually, however, as his hangover lifted, so did his mood. He remained snappish and sarcastic but there was no doubt that Lough's departure had reset the clock on the time bomb – although nobody knew how long it could last.

'They'll have to sort something out soon,' Franny said to Jenny. 'Lough can't sleep in his horsebox indefinitely.'

It was the Moncrieffs, so stoic and practical, who came up with a solution. Lough and Lem could relocate to Lime Tree Farm for the short term. There was enough room, and they badly needed the money. Lough's rent, riding skills and increasing appeal to sponsors and owners was a life-saver for the perennially cash-strapped yard, and it would relieve the impossible situation at Haydown.

'He's far too good a rider to lose,' Penny told Tash when she rang to broach the idea. 'We know he's been terribly impetuous, and we adore you and Hugo of course, but Lough deserves a chance to get on with the job for the rest of the season, don't you think?'

Tash tracked Hugo down to the tack room after Penny had rung off.

'They'll only go ahead if we're absolutely okay about it,' she told him anxiously.

'Lime Tree's hardly out of bloody earshot. Can't anybody else take him?' Hugo snapped, making Lough sound like a delinquent in need of foster care. He stalked past her and out on to the yard.

'Keep your friends close but your enemies closer,' came a voice. Tash jumped, realising that Beccy was quietly cleaning tack in a corner.

With a worried look, she raced after Hugo.

Beccy was miserable at the thought of losing Lough. She was happy to see the back of Lemon, who had hijacked her body and whose hatred of Hugo had poisoned her mind for so long. She was relieved he'd soon be gone, but Lough was an inspiration. He rode as though the horse was a part of him, like a centaur. He was one of her best-ever daydreams, and losing him refocused her heart painfully and exclusively on Hugo once more.

In all of the recent high drama, nobody had thought to tell Beccy what was going on. When Rory had suddenly loaded four horses into his lorry and driven off that morning, she'd found herself wondering if he was having an affair with Tash, too. It was Jenny who explained that Rory was spending six weeks on the Continent, teaming up with Marie-Clair Tucson's young protégé, Kevin, to compete at Saumur and Dijon before heading to Germany. It seemed everybody in top-level eventing was aiming for Germany that June, with Kreuth and Luhmühlen three day events running on successive weekends, the European Championships in Aachen straight after that, and Jenny's wedding to popular German rider Dolf Bauer sandwiched between.

Beccy was dreading Jenny's departure. The Beauchamps' jolly headgirl had already begun to hand over her duties to irascible replacement Franny, whose new job had been gifted her more by luck than design since Hugo and Tash hadn't found time to look for anyone else, and Franny's dire straits made her the obvious choice because her horse dealer ex had given her marching orders and she had no family to fall back on. Her dedication to Hugo was unquestionable, and her work rate was fearsome. She made even Faith look unproductive.

This left Beccy's nose thoroughly out of joint. Jenny rarely trusted the capricious Haydown team member with anything much more demanding than a water bucket, which suited Beccy just fine. But Franny gave her tasks of great responsibility and cajoled, bullied, huffed and puffed when she failed to come up to scratch.

With no Lough and with Rory's easygoing good humour absent too, it seemed the life force was draining from Haydown. And with the summer season really kicking in, and competitions coming in quick succession, the yard would be left with skeleton staff.

Beccy had started to contemplate going AWOL again, this time on a more permanent basis.

But then Tash reappeared in the tack room looking much more buoyant.

'How would you like to start competing?' She sat down and steepled her fingers over her nose, her mismatched eyes watching Beccy's face hopefully.

'You're more than ready,' she went on. 'I know how much your riding's improved. We need another work rider now we've lost Lough and Rory's away, so what d'you think?'

For a moment, ten years of Beccy's life dropped away and she was an eager seventeen-year-old desperate to break into the sport where her hopes and heart lay.

'What does Hugo say?' she asked cautiously.

'He's willing to give you a trial run at Haddenhill. They know us really well there, so we can swing it with the organisers to let you ride one of ours *hors concours*.'

'But that's tomorrow!' Beccy bleated.

'Please say yes.' Tash chewed her lip. 'I'm not sure I'd be able to talk Hugo into giving it a go another time.'

Suddenly Beccy found herself smiling so much it hurt. This was her chance to prove herself. There was no way she was going to refuse. Perhaps Lough departing had its compensations after all.

The following morning, after the Haydown HGV had departed, Lough moved his horses to Lime Tree Farm, overseen by Franny.

'She's like a bloody Rottweiler,' Lemon complained as Franny frisked his tack boxes to make sure he wasn't trying to make off with anything of Hugo's.

Lough said nothing. Looking around the beautiful strawberry-pink yards one last time, he went to say goodbye to Dove's foal. Tash had named him Liberty, but today didn't feel like any sort of liberation.

Beccy's first competition in ten years was at a busy weekday trials just across the Wiltshire border.

Tash put her on a very safe and very classy homebred novice that Beccy knew well and got on with. Their dressage was unremarkable, but Beccy was simply relieved that she didn't forget her test which she'd learned overnight. An hour later, she just about remembered the show-jumping course to make it round with just one pole on the ground.

'Point and shoot,' Hugo remarked ungenerously, knowing the horse was a four-star prospect and had been expected to win hands down with Tash on board.

Beccy gritted her teeth.

She'd always lacked the finesse of her stepsister, but she rode across country with absolute determination and her adrenalin so high that she knew no fear. The fierce, competitive streak that she'd believed she had cast off during her travels was back with vengeance. Working alongside top riders had given her great insight into the drive and skills required to win, and she focused completely on the challenge. The horse didn't put a foot wrong, and neither did Beccy. They would have came a creditable sixth in their section had they not competed *hors concours*.

Tash was over the moon. She seemed far more pleased with Beccy's modest placing than the three wins she and Hugo clocked up between them, although Beccy was convinced that she was being condescending.

Nonetheless, Hugo was impressed enough to support her inclusion in the Haydown competition team.

'Okay, you've got the gig.' He fixed Beccy with that direct stare that turned her belly to molten lava. 'You'd better not let us down.'

'I won't.' She turned predictably red. 'I'll ride for my life.'

Hugo had just been through a week he never wanted to repeat and was permanently in a foul mood as a result, but for the first time in days he laughed. 'Spoken like a true eventer. Welcome to the squad.' He stooped to give her a congratulatory kiss on the cheek and when he straightened up Beccy thought she might lift up like a balloon attached to his lips by static.

As the Haddenhill trials were local, they got home early for once, coming back just before the children's bedtime. Tash rushed into the house to take over, leaving Hugo and Beccy to unload the lorry.

All Lough's horses had gone, Beccy realised sadly. It made her feel horribly hollow. The thought of going up to the empty stables flat without Lemon there was equally daunting. They hadn't spoken for over a week and she guessed life would get better with him gone, but she'd got used to knowing there was somebody else close by. She took a long time to rug up the horses, putting off the moment she'd have to go up.

'Come and have supper with us.' Hugo leant over the stable door. 'We can plan the next few weeks.'

Looking up, Beccy couldn't remember the last time she had seen him smile like that, his eyes creasing deliciously. Now the New Zealanders had gone, it was as though tens of tiny splinters had been removed from his face, allowing it to animate again.

Beccy beamed back at him, realising she was being invited in from the cold at last. She'd won her first stripe and it was time to start earning respect, just as she'd promised Lough she would. Riding and winning was everything now.

Twenty minutes later, standing in the kitchen and staring blankly into the fridge, Tash wished Hugo had offered to fetch a takeaway, but he'd taken a second scotch up to the bath and the local Indian didn't deliver so far away from civilisation. She was shattered and they only had a few eggs, Cora's processed cheese strings and some ancient salami. She hadn't had time to go food shopping since before Badminton.

She heard his step behind her.

'What do you want to eat?'

'You.'

He kissed the back of her neck. It felt delicious. She could smell the soap on his skin. The next moment, his hand was undoing the buttons on the front of her shirt.

'We mustn't! Beccy's coming to supper.'

'I told her to give us an hour.' He reached into her bra and teased out an eager nipple.

Still mud-splattered and sweat-stained from her day in the saddle, compared to Hugo's freshly-showered cleanliness, Tash experienced a strange role reversal from the many times last season that she'd spruced up to welcome him back from a competition still wearing grass-stained breeches. He stripped her bare, laid her back on the kitchen table and tasted every piece of delicious, dirty, aching skin until it quivered and jumped with desire.

'Beccy will be here any minute!' She tried to wriggle away, shame-faced.

'I've locked the back door.' He held her down until she came with such a delicious burst of pleasure that she swept a huge pile of paperwork to the floor and kicked over a chair.

'You're mine' – he looked down at her now – 'and don't forget it. Now go and change while I cook.'

In their bathroom a few minutes later, she looked at her reflection in the mirror above the basin, uncertain if she'd been forgiven or indeed if there was anything to forgive. Was temptation as much of a betrayal as true infidelity?

When Beccy wandered into the main house to find Hugo cooking a vast omelette her heart flipped over in sympathy with the sizzling contents of his pan.

'Tash is just upstairs – open a bottle of wine and we'll get planning.'

It was suddenly like her daydreams in the early days. Beccy allowed herself a quick fantasy that she was Haydown's top rider, and that this was their usual debrief after competitions.

'You look lovely,' Tash said when she appeared, having managed just a quick flannel wash before changing into jeans, the hot water in the house having been used up by the children's baths and then by Hugo.

Beccy flushed happily. She'd scrubbed from head to toe, anointed herself with scented oil and dressed in her favourite tie-dye dress. She now had a stake in the yard's future, and was determined to impress.

'Right, let's get started.' Hugo dished up great wedges of omelette on to cold plates. 'I'll just open a window – smells like a fire in a joss stick factory in here.'

'It's the burnt food,' Tash told Beccy quickly, seeing her crushed face. The pong of patchouli oil was admittedly rather overpowering, but Tash preferred it to her own horsy reek.

She worried that Beccy would be as flaky as ever, but instead she seemed shot through with a positive energy that infected them all.

Like a depleted but undefeated army, the new Haydown competition squad discussed their strategy late into the evening, consulting the big year planner and event schedules and agreeing that, with Lough gone and no Rory in play for the coming weeks, Tash would need to ride alongside Hugo at some of the bigger events as well as orchestrating the young horses at the smaller competitions with Beccy as her co-pilot.

'Now you'll be riding full time, I've asked Franny to put the word out among her cronies to bring in more hands on the yard,' Hugo told Beccy. 'But you'll still act as travelling groom at the big trials and I'll need you to groom for me in Germany.' He consulted the planner, which had a line through most of June that indicated he would be away.

'Of course,' Beccy agreed, although she kept herself firmly in check. Not long ago the prospect three weeks on the road with Hugo would have had her dreaming night and day, imagining the nights they would share living in the horse box, fantasising that they'd find what they'd lost at New Year, this time with no hurry and nobody to interrupt. She knew she mustn't risk blowing an opportunity to experience the excitement of the big European events by letting her crush run riot.

But Hugo was eyeing the planner more closely now, spotting all the events still pencilled in it for Lough during the Germany run. 'On second thoughts, Tash should come instead.'

Both women looked at him in horror.

'I'm needed here,' Tash protested. 'I'll fly out for Jenny's wedding and stay on to support you at Aachen if you're selected. That's what we always agreed.'

'Someone needs to compete the horses here,' Beccy pointed out.

'You can do that. Franny will be in charge. We've plenty of time to get you up to speed before we go.'

'Absolutely not.' Tash shook her head, clearly thinking he'd gone mad. 'Beccy can't ride above novice, for a start, and—'

'We'll give the higher-level horses a break.'

'In the middle of the season?'

'Why not?'

'What will the owners think?'

'I don't give a fuck. You're coming with me to Germany.'

'I am not!'

Beccy was mortified to be witnessing the Beauchampions at one another's throats, the thin veneer on their marriage cracking. Lough had charged between them like a cavalryman.

'I'm not leaving you here with that bloody Kiwi nearby,' Hugo raged.

'For Christ's sake, Hugo. We've been through this!'

Beccy observed the exchange with mounting panic. It seemed only a matter of time before Tash and Hugo blew apart, just as her own life was finally starting to make sense. She couldn't let it happen.

Hugo's face gave nothing away, but his voice was infused with the acid of suspicion. 'He'll be over here as soon as my back is turned.'

'Of course he won't!'

'Please stop this!' Beccy interrupted with a shriek. 'I'll do whatever you tell me to.' She demanded their attention, knowing her face was turned up to maximum red yet again, but not caring. 'Just tell me what to do.'

They stopped arguing and turned to stare at her as though they'd forgotten she was there.

Hugo spoke first. 'Go and get some rest: it's been a long day. I think you should go to bed.' Clearing his throat, he stood up and chivalrously walked her to the door, his voice softening. 'Take no notice of us, darling. We'll sort this out. Well ridden today.'

Nodding mutely, Beccy retreated to the stables flat to replay the day in her head, one of the best she could ever remember despite the row and the final brush-off. She hadn't let herself down. She'd shown she could compete against the best in her class. She'd felt a part of the team and the family. And then Hugo had sent her to bed, sounding just like her late father. But he had only wanted to protect her; they both did. All was forgiven.

Climbing into bed, she lay awake, reliving every second of her cross-country round, determined to make them proud of her.

As the Beauchamps got ready for bed the argument rattled on, Radio Four droning unheeded in the bathroom while Tash finally ran her longed-for bath.

'I just don't see how we'll get any time with the children,' she pointed out. She'd studied the planner again before going upstairs, taking in the punishing schedule ahead, its dawn starts, dusk home-comings and nights spent away from home.

'You won't.' Hugo marched in from the bedroom to clean his teeth. 'My mother and Verruca can look after them.'

'Or perhaps we can bring them along?' she suggested, appalled at the idea of seeing them so little.

'Impossible on this schedule. We're hardly going to see each other as it is.' He plunged his toothbrush into his mouth and gave her an angry look in the mirror, marking an end to the debate.

Tash understood why Hugo was being so controlling. All of Lough's target events were still written on the year planner they'd pored over, mapped out long before everything changed, and the new schedule was carefully structured to avoid Lough and Tash competing at the same trials unless Hugo was present. The only exception was while Hugo was away in Germany. He didn't trust her.

Leaving the taps running and heading into the bedroom to fetch a towel, she spotted his mobile phone lying on the bed and felt a snagged nail of resentment scratching at her.

She had no idea whether Hugo could be trusted either, camped out in the lorry parks two or three nights a week with carousing event riders, then heading to mainland Europe for almost a month with just Beccy as abstracted chaperone. What if V joined him there?

She paused and picked up the phone. Given a window of oppor-tunity to check the evidence at last, and by now such a whiz with technology, she was scrolling his messages in seconds. Everything from V had been deleted.

The phone suddenly leapt to life in her hands, playing Mozart's Horn Concerto Number Four, the ringtone assigned to British chef d'equipe Brian Sedgewick. He must be calling with the news of the shortlist for the European Championships team, straight after that evening's selectors' meeting.

Tash panicked as she realised Hugo would be out of the bath-room in seconds. Thrusting the phone hastily into his jeans pocket she sprang away from the bed.

At the same moment, he appeared through the door in just his boxer shorts.

'Where is the bloody thing? I left it right here.' The phone stopped ringing. He started rooting through his clothes.

'I'll just jump in that bath while it's still hot!' Tash belted off, face flaming.

Two minutes later she let out a yelp of alarm as Hugo lifted her clean out of the water. The look on his face told her that he definitely wasn't about to accuse her of snooping at his texts.

'I take it you're on the shortlist?' She laughed breathlessly.

'Am I?' He kissed from her throat to the rise of her breasts. 'It's gone clean out of my mind. I'll have to call Brian back to check.'

Shortlisted for the British team, Hugo's riding and sex drive immediately lifted a few notches, as it always did when he was presented with an opportunity to defend national honour.

Two days later at the Chatsworth trials, baking in the ongoing heatwave, they celebrated top-ten dressage scores with a moonlight flit from the lorry park to the centre of the famous maze, where Hugo drenched her in champagne and drank from every hollow before they rode one another home with breathtaking speed. Mistrust still raged between them and they couldn't yet get close to opening their hearts, but their bodies were another matter.

Tash understood that he was laying claim to her in the only way he knew how. She longed to talk through it more, to share the sense of it, but while the sensation was so good she didn't dare break the spell.

First out on the course and galloping into the dazzling morning sunlight the following day, Hugo saw a long stride at a new fence to the competition that year, a suspended tree trunk over a fast-running stream. Backing off, unable to see exactly what he was being asked to jump, Oil Tanker put in a half stride that left his front legs on the wrong side of the big log. His body rolled sideways over it and crashed down on to Hugo as they were both pitched into the stream.

Moments later, the horse trotted away unscathed. Hugo didn't get up.

That he escaped with just cracked ribs was a small miracle, but it didn't stop him being in a furiously bad mood about it all when he was finally discharged from Chesterfield's accident and emergency unit. First, because he would be laid off until a week before he departed to Germany, meaning he'd miss the final training session with the British squad and put any team place in doubt until he could prove himself fit to run. Second, because Tash had withdrawn from the competition to rush to the hospital.

'You need the mileage,' he complained.

'You could have died!'

'Falls like this come with the job.'

'Remind me to look for a new job,' muttered Tash, who had seen exactly how bad the accident looked on the CCTV screen in the rider's tent.

He turned and fixed her with a steadfast gaze. 'On the contrary, you've just been promoted.'

'What?'

'You'll need to take over my rides while I'm laid off, of course.'

In an instant Tash was back in the big league.

The following week's Tilton International Three Day Event in Suffolk was Tash's biggest challenge since returning to competitive riding. Run over a notoriously twisty course, it was the qualifying ride she needed to get back to four-star competitions, postponed after her withdrawal from Belton Park and failure to complete at Chatsworth – and now she was competing not one but two horses in the advanced class. Hugo wasn't allowed to drive for three weeks and could earn more money coaching at home but he insisted on coming along, partly because he knew Tash would need moral support, and partly because Lough would be at Tilton.

From the moment they arrived Hugo guarded her closely. Having not seen Lough since he'd left Haydown, Tash kept her distance, terrified what bumping into him might trigger. She daren't gaze into that wishing well of thought and hope, however much she longed to just see that he was okay. At the competitors' briefing they sat on opposite sides of the marquee and didn't look at each other once, but Tash was so acutely aware of his presence it was as though they were locked in a wardrobe together.

She knew she had to concentrate on her riding. Her nerves were back in force, and having Hugo around was a mixed blessing. He offered endless support, but he always advised her as though he was riding the horse himself, and because he was a far stronger, more attacking rider, his tactics were at odds with what she felt she could handle. At the top of her form, she had always thrived on Hugo's positivity and drive, that unrelenting competitive streak, but while her nerves remained so frayed, she responded better to a quiet, easy-going voice.

Dressage was always her strong suit, and she was well placed after the first day on both Vixen and her own favourite mare, River. But battling her terror demons as best she could in the cross-country, she rode too defensively, mistrusting poor Vixen and hauling her around several alternatives when she could have easily tackled the faster direct routes and kept her rhythm. The mare ran out twice, both times entirely down to pilot error.

'For God's sake take the handbrake off. You're much better than this, Tash,' Hugo snapped afterwards. He was trying to help, and Tash knew her riding was embarrassingly below par, but his exasperation just added to her fear.

She fared slightly better on River, but her anxiety still meant that she took too many pulls and clocked up expensive time faults that slipped her down the order and earned her another telling off from Hugo as Beccy led the horse away to wash off. 'Your sister here rides with more conviction.'

Heading back to the stable lines, Beccy glanced up to see Lough in his customary black cross-country colours chatting to the Australian Mick James. Just for a second Lough caught her eye, and Beccy felt the blush rush up through her as instantly as litmus paper dipped in sulphuric acid.

Beccy hated staying overnight in the horsebox with Tash and Hugo; it made her feel like a cross between a gooseberry and a referee. They had strange, stilted conversations charged with sexual static. Beccy hardly slept at all, clutching Karma to her side in her narrow bunk and listening to the occasional calls of nocturnal wildlife and misbehaving event riders outside.

She felt incredibly sorry for Lough, who'd been walking around looking absolutely miserable, although he was riding better than ever and leading two of the three sections. Beccy longed to say something to him, even if it was just to wish him good luck, but was too embarrassed, and too wary of bumping into Lemon.

She knew from Faith, who was at the trials grooming for Gus, that Lough was already transforming Lime Tree Farm's fortunes, with new owners and potential buyers calling all the time, and that he and Gus worked surprisingly well together when they were at home. But Faith also said that it was like having an unexploded bomb on site, and one that never stood still long enough to disarm. Some days he rode from five in the morning until seven at night, only pausing briefly to change horses.

Lying awake in her bunk in the early hours of show-jumping day, she switched on her phone and read through the texts Lough had sent all those months ago when he'd thought she was Tash and she'd been too swept away by her *Cyrano de Bergerac* fantasies to care.

Are we still talking? she messaged now.

Later that day, Tash took River clear around the show-jumping track. She was too far off the pace to finish in the prize money, but was relieved to get their four-star qualification back, and a pat on the back from Hugo that felt like a benediction.

Lough won all his classes. He didn't reply to Beccy's text.

On the long drag from Suffolk back to Haydown, Hugo sat between Beccy and Tash, his feet up on the dashboard, trying very hard not to tell his wife how to drive the lorry, which she was handling as nervously as her cross-country rides. He knew he'd over-egged the pep talks and needed to rein in his enthusiasm to get her back to top form, but he believed that he had quite the best apologetic gesture up his sleeve.

'Now that you can ride at four-star again, you can tackle Luhmühlen.'

'I've told you, I'm not coming to Germany before Jenny's wedding.'

'It's only an extra week if you fly out for the event.'

Beccy had discreetly unplugged her earphones in order to listen in, noticing that her stepsister's eyes were flashing their whites with fear.

'Forget it. You saw how much I froze yesterday.'

'So *un*freeze.' Hugo's tone remained upbeat, but there was impatience underlying his words.

'I'm going to Bramham that weekend. We agreed.'

Aware that Lough was entered for Bramham, Beccy braced herself for more sparring, but Hugo sprang a surprise.

'I'm taking you on holiday after Luhmühlen.'

'Holiday?' The word was alien to Tash at this time of year, but it still made a smile spring to her face.

'You missed out on France last autumn.' He kept his tone light, but his eyes practically burnt two holes in the windscreen. 'There are a few days to kill before the wedding. We'll hire a car to drive down to the Black Forest, pick out a couple of good hotels to stay in.'

Tash reached across to touch his leg, her face alight. 'Are you really serious?'

'Of course I'm bloody serious.' Hugo covered her hand with his, fighting not to point out that she was driving across two lanes. 'I've already spoken to the Moncrieffs,' he went on. 'They're happy to take Beccy and a couple of horses to competitions when they have space – Penny's getting Faith out competing their lower level horses a fair bit now, and you two are mates, aren't you, Beccy? You could have fun.'

Beccy nodded, blushing as she realised what she was being entrusted with. It scared her a great deal more than she dared admit. In fact, it terrified her, like being told to leave home before she was ready. She hurriedly put her earphones back in and closed her eyes, listening to Dillon Rafferty, imagining herself competing for glory and winning admiring glances, especially from Lough. Daydreaming was the only comfort at times like this.

Tash glanced at her worriedly, equally uncertain that Beccy was ready for this level of responsibility. 'So who will groom in Germany?' she asked Hugo.

'I'm working on that,' he assured her, taking his indestructible phone out of his pocket. 'I'll phone Luhmühlen now and tell the organisers there'll be a rider change for Cub.'

Tash felt like somebody was giving her an emergency tracheotomy. 'I can't do it.' She stared fixedly at the road, fighting tears of self-loathing at her stupid, paralysing nerves. There was a long pause. Hugo slowly put his phone away.

'My heart lies in this sport,' his said quietly. 'Don't keep kicking it because, believe me, it'll stop beating.'

They drove back in silence.

At home, both children awoke when Tash crept into their rooms to kiss them goodnight. Thrilled and tearful to see them after just two nights away, she hugged their soft, clinging warmth to her chest. She didn't want to leave them to compete far from home, and yet she knew Hugo was making the ultimate gesture of sacrifice. For him to give up a four-star ride really meant something, especially in the midst of a sponsorship race and team selection, and he was trying terribly hard to show how much he cared. Cub was just like his sire, which meant Tash would never hold him – she had battled for years with Snob, losing all strength in her arms half way round every cross-country course, unable to apply the brakes. It had been a terrifying education in control and the reason why she had ultimately handed the ride over to Hugo.

Yet as she held their children tight the thought of a holiday with Hugo, a real chance to patch up their differences, made it almost worth the risk. She knew she had to conquer her fears to survive, and Luhmühlen was a very user-friendly four-star. With time off afterwards to relax with Hugo, she could at last admit how vulnerable she felt when he was away, how much she missed him, and they could talk about how to help their growing family stay together around the eventing calendar. Given time, she might even pluck up the courage to finally tackle the issue of V.

With Cora and Amery tucked in her arms, both sleepily demanding attention, she headed out on to the landing to intercept Hugo as he came upstairs. 'I'll go to Germany.'

Wreathed in smiles, he kissed her then took Cora and carried her back to her bed, telling her a story about a magical unicorn that made her giggle as he punctuated it with goodnight kisses. Within moments, she was asleep.

Joining Tash in Amery's room, Hugo continued the story for his son as they both tucked him back beneath his cot blankets, although he was far too young to understand a word. But Tash did.

'. . . and the magical unicorn flew all over the world with children on his back, taking news from kingdom to kingdom, passing on stories and folklore, spreading happiness. Some children were too frightened to ride him, but as soon as they did they realised what they had been missing as they soared above the clouds, higher and faster . . .'

'. . . over trekhaners . . .' Tash injected softly, giving him a knowing look.

He smiled back, knowing he'd been rumbled '. . . and drop fences . . .'

'. . . skinnies . . .'

'. . . ditches . . .'

'. . . bit of a wobble at the Sunken Road, but got away with it.' She started to imitate an eventing commentator.

Hugo followed suit: 'Jolly positive riding there. Letting the magical unicorn get into a rhythm. Kick on.'

Eyes glittering, Tash quoted a late, lamented commentator whose inadvertent gaffes had always left them howling with joy: 'Almost went down on her there, but she pulled him off and gave him head instead.'

Hugo put a hand on his strapped-up chest.

'Please don't make me laugh,' he begged.

They'd neither of them had a lot to laugh about in recent weeks, but set that challenge Tash hammed up a few more legendary one-liners, suddenly finding irrepressible mirth joining a rare moment of family unity. It was a heady mix, and the thought of a holiday, of make or break, set them both alight with laughter and hope. Every time they looked at one another they doubled up. No amount of mutual shushing and pointing at Amery as he finally nodded off, comfort blanket in mouth, could stop them. Hugo clutched his chest in pain and fought valiantly for control, but somehow the release was too great. It was like a high, their senses feverish from the all recent emotion.

Speechless with laughter, they backed away from their sleeping son and crept out of the room before landing in a heap on the landing, tears pouring down their faces.

Later they made love very carefully, trying not to aggravate Hugo's already-aching ribs. Taking it steady lent a sensuality Tash had almost forgotten amid the high-energy performances Hugo had been putting in lately. It was heavenly, and afterwards she curled up beneath his arm like an ammonite within its rock, feeling truly safe again.

That night it seemed that this closeness, this skin against skin, could heal everything.

Chapter 67

With Hugo sidelined for a further ten days, the year planner was revised yet again. Beccy was immediately called upon for extra competition duty to double check that she was up to the job if left alone. In a busy week of three back-to-back trials, Tash took on all the trickier and more senior rides while Beccy had the most straightforward youngsters at lower levels. She coped easily, her determination to succeed almost feverish, especially across country where she rode with such grit that the lorry-park pundits were already describing her as Hugo's new protégée. She kept her focus at all times, and she was in fact a great deal calmer than Tash, who was suffering from nerves more killingly than ever.

Beccy had no intention of letting this chance slip. Her dream was being realised, and she was becoming a fully fledged event rider. A decade later than planned, perhaps, but it still ticked an empty box inside her, made all the more empty since Lough had departed Haydown.

She missed his dry one-liners, his quick brilliance in sussing out horses, his tireless, endless hours in the saddle. She missed watching him ride. Right now, competing was the only way of seeing him on or off a horse, and she wanted him to notice her. She kept finding herself thinking about that night just before Badminton, sitting on the lorry ramp, looking up at the stars and telling him that winning was like falling in love.

A week later, that same ramp was lifted on a full complement of horses as it made its final UK competition run of the month before heading to Germany. On this last team trip, at Brigstock trials in Northamptonshire, Beccy won her first class.

That evening in the lorry park, she found herself lying awake after midnight yet again. Tash had three rides the next day and Hugo – back in the saddle – had two, but Beccy had none, being deemed too inexperienced for the bigger classes, which annoyed her a lot more than she let on. She'd had almost half a bottle of wine over the celebration supper that Tash had cooked in her honour on the horsebox's little hob, her favourite vegetarian Thai curry followed by banana fritters, but it wasn't much of a celebration. Tash had been almost mute with tiredness and nerves, and Hugo was yet again in a foul mood because Lough was at the event.

By fate, his lorry was parked just two away from theirs.

The knowledge that Lough was sleeping so close by kept Beccy awake into the early hours. Listening carefully to make sure that Tash and Hugo were conked out behind the curtains over the Luton cab, she crept out with Karma at her heels and stood outside Lough's box.

She had received no reply to her *Are we still talking?* message.

She stood beside the shiny Ketterer so long that the first silver threads of dawn were fusing on the horizon when she finally slipped away.

The next day, Beccy was a zombie, making endless mistakes like forgetting to check tack, put in studs or cool horses down properly, to the point that Tash asked her if she was deliberately trying to sabotage her chances. Tash's nerves were ragged. Riding too defensively, she piled up penalties across country. Yawning as she watched, Beccy thought she could have done better herself, sleep or no sleep.

Then, as they cooled off her last horse together, Tash put an arm around Beccy and told her to take a break. 'I'll groom for Hugo in the advanced. God knows I need to take my mind off that round, and you look done in, you poor thing. Sorry I was so snappy earlier. My fault.'

Beccy sloped away, humbled by her stepsister's kindness. But then, trailing back from a crêpe stand with a sugar fix, she saw something that ignited her anger.

Having waved Hugo off on his cross-country round, Tash kept an ear on the commentary as she sorted through the kit she'd need when she met him at the finish. She now had his phone in her pocket and the urge to nose through his messages was making her almost giddy. But as she reached for it, a hand touched her arm, making her jump out of her skin.

'Don't turn round.' Lough's deep voice made that skin as highly charged as cat's fur brushed the wrong way.

Tash gripped the phone so tightly in her pocket that it started to beep.

'I have to talk to you.'

'Not here.' There were tens of eyes on them.

'I might not get another chance. I know you're going to Luhmühlen.'

'Yes,' she croaked, fear gripping her.

'It's going to be tricky.'

'I know,' she whispered, suddenly overwhelmed with the need to confide in him. Of course Lough would understand how big a deal this was going to be for her. He understood her nerves better than anyone.

'Thing is, I'll be—' His voice was drowned out by the commentary on the speaker overhead, raving about Hugo's exemplary ride through the tricky water complex. '. . . is that okay?' he finished.

Tash nodded, tears choking her. She didn't need to hear the words to know that he'd be with her in spirit. Her heart felt like an inflated balloon in her chest as gratitude and shame took her breath away.

'I'll be there for you,' he said quietly.

'I know.' She reached back and let her fingers brush against his, just for moment.

Seconds later he was gone. She hadn't even looked at him.

When Hugo rode through the finish beaming from ear to ear with the best clear of the day, Tash's left arm was still numb from Lough's fingertips.

Watching from behind the cross-country course ropes, Beccy felt wretched. Her first win meant nothing in the wake of Lough's single-minded desire for Tash. Winning wasn't like falling in love at all, she realised. It was the consolation prize.

As if to illustrate her point, Hugo won one of his two sections, proving his fitness for the European Championships, although in private afterwards it was obvious how much discomfort his cracked ribs were giving him. He was knocking back painkillers like Smarties. Tash insisted on driving home.

As they headed for West Berkshire, Tash as tense as ever at the wheel, Beccy got a reply from Lough.

Let's talk was all it said.

Suddenly she had no fear of being left alone while the Beauchamps were in Germany. She hugged the phone to her chest, thinking back to their starlit conversation, and of Lough's assertion that one day they might both ride the devils off their backs.

It wasn't the winning that counted, she realised, it was having the ride of your life.

At the wheel of the lorry, Tash ran her tongue backwards and forwards over her teeth so many times it started to develop a raw groove.

Lough stepping up to her side earlier that day had short-circuited her thinking. He could see how close she was to cracking up, even if nobody else could. She was running on nervous energy.

When would it go away, she thought wretchedly as, without noticing, she let the lorry drift across the M40. When would she shake this urge to leap wildly into the run-through-me green grass on the other side of the fence, even though her own grass was so green it blinded her at times? It made her sick with guilt and longing in equal measure.

One touch of their hands had seemed to scoop her up and lift her so high the air had thinned. Now she had been dropped back down to ground zero, her head pounding and her body aching from competing three horses that day with her heart beating in her throat.

Beside her, Beccy and Hugo were texting like mad. She wished her support team could be more supportive sometimes.

'Anything worth knowing?' She turned to Hugo, hoping he wasn't exchanging hot SMSs with V.

'I've just found us a groom for Germany.' He tossed his phone on the dashboard victoriously.

'Who's that?' Tash asked suspiciously, not liking the way his face was blanketed in smiles.

'India Goldsmith.'

She laughed in disbelief. 'Penny's niece?'

As a horse-mad teenager growing up at Lime Tree Farm, where her mother Zoe had taken refuge after the break-up of her marriage, India had groomed at the top level, and ridden in junior and young rider classes before pursuing a media career. Now in her twenties and working in London, it seemed impossible that Hugo could have bagged her for a small tour of Germany.

But he was nodding. 'Franny's sorted it. They've stayed close since their old Lime Tree days. India's freelancing and has nothing lined up, so is dying for an excuse to get out of London. I've just had a text from her. God, Franny's wonderful.'

'Thank heavens for Franny,' Tash agreed hollowly. She had always adored India, who was six feet tall, looked like a model, had an encyclopaedic veterinary knowledge and could plait a horse in ten minutes. She knew she should be thrilled, but she suddenly felt very jumpy indeed, especially when she recalled that at Lime Tree Farm India had been known as Vindaloo, a nickname given to her by Gus's lusty eventing cronies because the curry-loving student was too hot to handle. Was she V?

And Hugo was looking very pleased with himself. Too pleased, Tash decided.

Later that night, the alacrity and enthusiasm with which he undressed her and mounted her from behind then sideways, then above, then below, worried her even more. He was insatiable.

Is he thinking about lovely, long-limbed India, she found herself questioning as she lay at the end of the bed, legs hooked over Hugo's shoulders as he slid in and out of her. He took one of her ankles and pushed the leg back, deepening his thrusts, his balls banging against her. Is he thinking about India like I'm thinking about . . .

Reactive ripples started to course through her.

Stop thinking about Lough, she told herself firmly. Stop it, stop it.

She thought about Lough. She thought about him approaching her earlier that day, the first time since his departure, since his declaration of love. She thought about his eyes on hers, so full of understanding, his hand on his shoulder that had made her feel like he'd shot her with a stun gun.

Hugo pulled the other ankle off his shoulder and turned her sideways so that she lay on one side of the bed, his thrusts deeper than ever.

She thought about her one kiss with Lough. That kiss all those weeks ago in the kitchen, after she'd cut his hair. Just one stolen kiss. His body against hers. His hands on her skin. His cock inside her. Oh, God, stop it, Tash . . . stop . . . stop . . .

'Don't stop!'

The orgasm was ripping through her now, sending molten showers from crotch to toe to fingertips to nose. It was everywhere, and it was so full of shameful pictures of Lough that, afterwards, she wanted to cry.

India arrived the next day, as overwhelmingly pretty and tall as Tash had remembered her, but with one critical difference. She was now at least a size eighteen, entirely in proportion but positively plus size. And it was immediately obvious that Hugo hadn't seen her in as long as Tash.

'Are you sure she's up to the job?' he asked in an alarmed undertone as India rushed off to hug Franny. 'If I ask her to warm up a horse it could die.'

'Don't be so mean,' Tash hushed, knowing that she had been a similar size straight after giving birth to Amery and Hugo had regularly tried to leg her up on to a horse – and get his leg over – without complaining.

Yet she couldn't deny the sight of India cheered her enormously. She was just as she remembered her: bright, joyful, open, enthusiastic and the absolute antithesis of Beccy. She'd be great to have on side in Germany, and her gorgeous curves helped Tash keep the jealousy demons, and closely related Lough fantasies, at bay. V was still out there, but at least she wouldn't be bunked up with Hugo in the horsebox on the Continent with India sharing close quarters.

Hugo and Tash spent the evening double-checking arrangements. Hugo had been passed fit to get back in the saddle a week ago, and they had been riding together all day, making the most of a final exchange of ideas. In a bullish mood, he talked tactics throughout supper and a shared bath, still reminding her of what she would need to do in coming days as they headed into the bedroom knowing they would make love. Then, just as easily as he'd been dictating terms all evening, Hugo said, 'Let me blindfold you.'

Tash looked at him doubtfully, but she couldn't face a fight the night before he left. And a part of her was excited at the thought. He'd asked if he could bind her before and she'd always refused, frightened of relinquishing control and, perhaps worse, him losing interest and abandoning her blindfolded and tied to the bedposts as had happened to one comely event rider she knew, whose lover had stepped outside to take a call from his wife on his mobile then rushed straight home to a crisis, leaving his mistress lashed to her brass bed for three days until her cleaning lady found her.

This time he talked her round, plying her with wine and a massage and whispered sweet nothings that left her so horny she could barely see for lust, love and dancing dots in front of her eyes. As he gathered a stray scarf from the arm of the button-back chair, she quivered with anticipation, admiring the tight curve of his buttocks. Then, realising which scarf he had in his hands, she shook her head. 'Not that one.'

'What?' he stalled.

'That was my grandmother's. It's Férier. We can't use that one. It doesn't seem right.'

He fetched another, but Tash shook her head again. 'Mummy gave me that.' The next one was similarly rejected. 'I can't stand that colour.' Then 'too scratchy', and 'Hugo, that's a pair of tights.'

Soon Hugo was whipping scarves from drawers and wardrobes like a magician pulling handkerchiefs from a hat. One by one each was dismissed. Ardour and enthusiasm flagging, he eventually stood facing her, a chiffon scarf in each hand like a belly dancer. 'What *would* be acceptable?'

'A hunting stock would be okay.'

'Right!' He headed to his tallboy, but all the stocks were out on competition duty or in the laundry. 'Shit! Hang on.' Still naked, he headed off in search of one.

Tash stifled a yawn and snuggled back in bed, not really feeling the moment any more. There were scarves everywhere, she noticed, wearily guessing she'd be the one to pick them all up in the morning.

Hugo must have had to search far and wide, because by the time he returned she'd nodded off and was having an alarmingly sexy dream about performing the dance of the seven veils in a tented palace for an exotic, black-haired king of Judea.

A silk stock was slipped around her eyes. Still half asleep, she rolled over and he snaked a scarf around her wrists and anchored her beneath him.

'Imagine I've gone away,' he whispered as she lay enveloped in darkness. 'Imagine you're all on your own here.'

His fingers worked around her nipples, his breath between her legs. 'Imagine I'm another man, coming in here, finding you tied up like this.'

She really didn't like where this was going, especially the way her nipples and clitoris had hardened to bullets, along with the shortened breath and hot flush creeping down her chest.

'Imagine I start to taste you,' – his hot breath traced her labia – 'start to claim this beautiful body for myself.'

'Untie me!' she demanded, knowing she'd climax at any moment if he didn't.

'Not before you come.'

'Untie me, Hugo!'

'Shh. You'll wake the kids.'

'Then you'd better do as I say.'

He untied her wrists and she ripped off the blindfold to find herself looking straight into his accusing eyes, mistrust etched in every line of his face. It wasn't a look Tash cared to dwell on. Barely pausing to think, she blindfolded him.

'Imagine you're all on your own . . .' she started, fighting not to giggle nervously.

'I am,' he drawled. 'Often.'

'Me too,' she pointed out.

'Then we should *both* be blindfold.'

'Fine by me.' She reached for the scarf he'd used to bind her arms and covered her eyes again, knotting it behind her head. The giggles instantly died in her throat.

The moment she did it, the mood in the room changed. It was a trust game, and they were too fiercely competitive to do anything but play along with total commitment. Nothing would entice them to pull off their masks and cheat, short of a fire or a screaming child.

Tash felt his hands on her, claiming, greedy, unseeing, so familiar and yet so deliciously new. And she reached out in the darkness for him.

It was the most emotionally connected lovemaking they'd had in months. It was deeply intimate and physical. At times the vigour between them became so concentrated that it seemed impossible to keep up the intensity, but they stayed there, trusting and believing. When Tash came, she'd never climaxed like it. As he drummed the tip of his cock against her cervix, her orgasm was like a pumping heart trying to pull him further and further inside her. The rush seemed to go on for ever, peaking and peaking, shooting so much pleasure into her that she knew her body would be hijacked by it for days afterwards.

'Let's have another child,' he breathed into her ear, so deep inside that she felt he was a part of her.

Tash said nothing. She still couldn't speak for the shocks and swords of pleasure running through her.

Afterwards they slept in their blindfolds. Whether they were too ashamed to show their faces to one another or too exhausted to care, neither really knew.

Chapter 68

Unable to sleep, Beccy took Karma into Flat Pad and stood in front of Snob's grave, remembering the sheer power and lion-hearted bravery of Tash's famous stallion. He remained the most inspirational horse Beccy had ever encountered.

Hugo would leave for Germany in just a few hours; Tash flew out in less than a week. Soon Beccy would be at greater liberty to shake the devil from her back. The way forward was increasingly clear to her. Riding was her only escape from all the tension and blame at Haydown; competing made her forget about what was happening, what Franny referred to as 'the fall of the house of the usher' because bets were being taken on the circuit whether Hugo's marriage would last until the big wedding in three weeks' time. It was common knowledge that the Germany trip was a make or break for the couple.

After years of ambivalence, Beccy now found herself desperate for them to stay together and willed the glue to stick, determined to hold up her end of the bargain and do the yard proud while they were away. That included renewing her text life with Lough.

Let's talk had started badly, with Beccy texting back *Are you in love with my sister?* And Lough replying *Yes.* She knew she'd walked into that one – and God, he was honest – but it wasn't great for the ego, making her angrily text straight back: *If let's talk means let's talk about Tash, I'd rather stay silent.* To her surprise, his reply had been just as quick: *How's Heart?*

When living at Haydown, Lough had always had time for the eye-catching bay who demanded attention from all around him as he recovered from his injury. Bolshy, bargy and bored from his long box rest, Heart was incredibly tricky to handle, and now that he was allowed to walk out for twenty minutes a day, he was flattening the staff on a regular basis as he mowed them down in his enthusiasm to get to the horse walker. Beccy was happy to report that news, at least. They'd exchanged more messages over the past two days, mostly routine stuff about horses and competition plans, but Beccy cherished the contact. She saw them as two *Titanic* survivors talking about life back home as they bobbed around on a life-raft awaiting rescue, knowing that they were in this together, and that talking took their mind off the perilous sea around them.

But then, earlier that evening, Lough had rocked that boat again by asking after Tash, wanting to know how long she'd be staying on in England before leaving for Germany. He obviously planned to try to see her. Beccy had yet to reply, determined not to be cast as go-between. She'd already done enough damage as *Cyrano de Bergerac*, and blamed herself for sowing the seed that had sprouted into a tree of temptation in this idyllic garden.

Turning to look at Haydown, a beautiful doll's house pearlised in the moonlight, her self-hatred hardened.

Please leave Tash alone she texted Lough now.

She sat on the damp grass until the early hours. There was no reply.

The next day, the big Haydown horsebox and three other event team lorries companionably hooked up in convoy on the M20 to travel together to the ferry port, where they were forced to wait for a crossing. Storms were blowing in, making for long delays.

At a terminal cafe, Hugo found himself nursing a revoltingly chemical-tasting coffee beside Lucy Field and staring glumly out at the rain-lashed windows while she texted non-stop, no doubt communicating with her 'mysterious married lover', whose identity was now such an open secret that nobody would be surprised if they got his and hers tattoos that season. The incessant beep-beep-beeping of her key strokes set his teeth on edge.

'Why don't you just call him?' he snapped. 'His wife's away in Shropshire today.'

'This is sexier.'

'Do you text each other while you're shagging, too?'

'C'mon, Hugo. We all do it. You'll text Tash all the time from Germany.'

'Tash doesn't do texts. My wife prefers to talk like a grown-up.'

Lucy bridled at his sanctimonious tone. 'So all those texts Lough's been seen sending aren't to her?' she asked bitchily.

'What?' he turned to glare at her.

'He was at it non-stop at Stoke Heath yesterday. Everybody noticed.'

'Let's hope he was booking his flights home,' Hugo said coolly, pushing away his coffee and heading off to check his horses as the wind buffeted the lorries from all sides.

Chased by the storms, Tash and Beccy drove to the Welsh borders in the ancient hunting box for the two-day trials near Bishop's Castle, arriving as the sky blackened with approaching rain and thunder. They would ride a horse each in the entry-level class, after which they would camp overnight, ready to compete two more in the bigger classes the next day.

Going first on the batty Lor, Tash knew it wasn't the weather for heroics. They posted a diabolical dressage score and later flattened most of the show-jumps by approaching them sideways, or even backwards.

Determined to beat her stepsister, Beccy rode her best dressage test to date on her more stolid entry, then secured a rare clear round on a day when most horses had the wind up their tails and poles were flying.

As she rode back to the box to change, she took her phone from her pocket and switched it on. Lough had replied to her previous night's text at last.

I just need to know that Tash is okay, was all he'd written. Reading it with a heavy heart, Beccy knew how hard he must have found it to ask, how much pride he was losing by confiding in her, his adoring spy.

She is very okay, she punched each letter of her reply angrily. Beccy felt like a schoolgirl cast as the nurse in *Romeo and Juliet*, when she'd only ever auditioned for the title role.

A dramatic electrical storm was blowing in by the time Tash set off across country. As she nursed Lor around, taking time to settle her into a quiet rhythm and riding all the longest, safest lines, she was only grateful Hugo wasn't around to witness her wimpiness. But at least they arrived at the finish intact and relieved.

By contrast, Beccy flew out of the start box as though she was on the turf at Epsom. Spurs niggling at her horse's side, she stoked him out of his natural rhythm into a full-pelt charge.

Walking Lor around higher up the hill in the park to cool her off, Tash was appalled to see Beccy riding so carelessly. Lightning crackled through the air as she belted through the water faster than a medieval herald warning of an approaching enemy. The young horse was looking increasingly ragged and unhappy. Just two fences from home they parted company as he sensibly ducked out of a combination they'd approached far too fast, and Beccy carried on alone, landing neatly on top of the jump.

She was surprisingly unruffled afterwards, blaming the weather. 'They're all misbehaving today.'

'You were the one out of control, not the horse,' Tash pointed out.

Beccy's pale eyes didn't blink. 'I knew precisely what I was doing.'

'So you were *deliberately* trying to kill yourself?'

She shrugged mulishly, looking away.

Tash sighed. 'Beccy, you have a touch of brilliance, but you'll wreck it if you ride like that. It's as though you didn't care whether you lived or died out there.'

Beccy refused to speak to her for the rest of the day.

Her erratic behaviour concerned Tash, and she suspected Beccy was far more hurt by the break-up of her relationship with Lemon than any of them realised. She'd been too wrapped up in her own worries to tackle it, but her stepsister's mood swings and insomnia hadn't gone unnoticed.

Thunder still rolled angrily in the distance as they bedded down for the night. The atmosphere inside the box wasn't any better.

'I'm sorry I had a go at you.' Tash tried to mend the rift as they both fidgeted around on bench beds as hard as prison bunks, seeking comfort. Having drawn the short straw with the sleeping bags, she was zipped into an old relic that probably dated back to Hugo's teens and mummified her completely. 'You really could be very good, you know. We just have to harness all that talent.'

Beccy was reluctant to accept praise from a woman who had

approached most of today's jumps with her eyes shut. 'Hugo says you have to ride to win at all times.'

'Not if winning endangers you and the horse.'

'This sport *is* dangerous, Tash. We all know that. And I like danger.'

Tash peered across at her from the depths of her hooded sleeping bag. 'You're amazing, you know, Beccy. You seem so timid, yet you have the heart of a lion. When you learn to control that, you'll be unbeatable.'

Beccy accepted this a little more gratefully, but she was fighting too many demons in her head to believe the advice.

'People are starting to talk about how good you are, you know,' Tash told her now.

'Nobody that counts.'

'Well it takes a bit of time to catch all the right eyes for—'

'Nobody gives a stuff if I do well.'

'Of course they do. I care. Hugo cares. Your mum and Daddy – I mean James – are going to be so proud of you when they see you compete.'

'They won't want to see me ride.'

'Of course they will.'

'My real dad will never see me ride, though.'

'He'd have been very proud of you.'

'Whatever.'

Tash sighed, realising she wasn't making much headway. Beccy was impenetrable. Yet competing together threw a line between them that neither could escape. Beccy might want to cut it straight through, but Tash wanted to death-slide along it.

'You're probably very like him, you know,' she tried again. 'Your father must have been such a wonderful man. I bet he's the one you get your fearlessness from.'

'He was more of a man than James, that's for sure.'

Tash bit her lip and decided to give up. She was just making things worse. They fell silent and she thought Beccy was conking out, but then she heard a quiet sobbing, just audible above the wind and thunder outside.

When she tried to stand up and go to console her, Tash found that the zip of her sleeping bag was stuck fast. With only her face poking out, she was a useless wriggling caterpillar. Thrashing around until she made it off the bench, she stood upright, hopped about, fell over and ricocheted against the sides of the box until, eventually, she raised her arms enough to catch the end of the zip and lower it, Houdini-style, bursting out to comfort Beccy in the dark on the sleeping bench opposite.

'Beccy, you poor thing. What's wrong?' She automatically reached out to hug her stepsister.

The arm came out of the dark like a flail, missing Tash's face by inches but catching her on the shoulder with enough force to push her away. 'L-leave me alone!'

Tash stood in the shadows for a moment, unable to bear the sound of sobbing wracking through Beccy.

Cautiously, she crouched down by her head. 'Please tell me, Beccy. I want to help.'

'I g-get so unhappy sometimes. I can't b-bear it.'

'Shhh. It's okay. I'm here. It's okay.'

This time, when Tash reached out her hand to touch her shaking shoulder, Beccy let it rest there. A moment later, she'd scrabbled into Tash's arms, clinging on tight as her whole body was overwhelmed by weeping.

For minutes on end, Tash just held her tight, astonished by the sobs that shook Beccy like the thunder raking the landscape. It was like holding Cora after a bad dream or a fall, a child with no comprehension that these feelings weren't the end of the world.

Beccy needed to be held. She hadn't been hugged tight in so long, she hardly dare try to work back through her memory to remember when. Lemon had never been into hugging, or kissing, or comfort to any great degree. Beccy craved comfort. That she was in the arms of her nemesis no longer mattered. It was a long time since she'd felt this low.

Tash stroked her hair and kissed the top of her head, grateful when the tidal wave of tears finally began to retreat. She felt Beccy's muscles relax into the hug, just like Cora getting sleepy. A heavy head rested against Tash's shoulder, her slow, warm breathing regulated against her collarbone.

'I was seven when my dad died,' she mumbled unexpectedly, just as Tash thought she was dropping off to sleep.

'I know.'

'And you're right, he *was* wonderful.' She tilted her head back and looked at Tash, wet eyes gleaming. 'He was the most civil of civil engineers, the bridge builder in every sense. Nobody had a bad word to say about him. He's our lost hero, me and Em and Mum. Your father could never live up to that.'

'I know.' Tash held her tighter. 'He knows.'

'But that's all lies.'

'No. Beccy, don't say—'

Beccy buried her face again. 'Do you know how he died?'

'He fell from a bridge,' Tash replied cautiously.

She felt Beccy's facial muscles tighten against her shoulder. 'He killed himself.'

Tash took in a sharp breath, not knowing how to react. 'It was an accident, surely?'

'I saw him jump.'

'You were so little—'

'I saw him jump, Tash. And I still have his suicide note.'

'But . . .'

She pulled away. 'He fucking abandoned us!' Her eyes were luminous in the half light. 'I hate him.'

'Beccy, you don't know—'

'I saw him. I was there that day,' she sobbed. 'Tash, nobody knows this. *Nobody*.'

'Tell me.'

There was a long pause. Beccy sniffed and hiccupped, fighting back another rush of tears. Then she said in a small voice, 'If I tell you, will you *swear* not to tell anybody else?' She sounded terribly young and frightened.

'I swear.'

'On your life?'

'On my life.'

The story, as it came out in stops and starts, in coughs and gulps, told Tash so much about the Beccy she had never understood, about this secretive, manipulative, childlike woman whom nobody in the family could ever get close to. It was no wonder she'd run away to the other side of the world and had never wanted to come back.

She knew much of the background already. Married young to dashing and talented Andrew, Henrietta had followed her civil engineer husband around the world as he designed and built bridges. The couple had two adorable blonde daughters, enjoyed expat life and seemed to have an enviable marriage until, ten years into marriage and thirty-five years into his life, Andrew Sergeant had fallen from a semi-constructed suspension bridge in Singapore.

Grief-stricken, Henrietta had returned to England with the children and struggled to rebuild her life, supported at first by his company's life insurance, but that had soon run out. She got her rusty typing back up to speed, signed on with an agency and got a job as secretary to venture capitalist James French. Andrew was rarely mentioned, but when he was, he was portrayed as a noble, heroic figure and his death seen as the untimely loss of a great husband and father with everything to live for.

Outside the horsebox, the storm moved in overhead, buffeting their little tin confessional so that it groaned and rocked like a ship at sea, but Beccy didn't seem to notice.

'Mum has no idea what really happened, but she knows a lot she never lets on about. Dad was bipolar – manic depressive. It took me a long time to get that out of her, but it made a lot of sense. He was the best father in the world one month – just such fun. Then the next he flipped a switch, turned off and withdrew himself. He didn't want to know us. It was so confusing. Em remembers more, but she edits it like Mum. Keeps the best bits and remember his death as heartbreakingly valiant.

'They weren't even at home that day; they were away checking out a new international school. It was just me. Dad had been off work for days in one of his moods, sitting alone on the veranda just staring into space. I was being looked after by our nanny, but I kept going to find him because I wanted him to read to me. He told me to go away. When he said he had to go out I begged him and begged him to take me with him.

'I don't think he knew where he was going or what he was going to do. He'd never have taken me with him if he had. We sat on the banks of Singapore River near the bridge he'd been designing and he cried a lot. I had a book with me – a pony book from England. He made me give it to him and he wrote all over it. I was so angry. Then he handed it back to me and cried again. I said I wanted to go home, but he wouldn't take me. He said he was going to climb his bridge and asked me if I wanted to come up with him. I was afraid of heights even then and I was still angry about the book, so I said no, I'd wait for him there. I think that saved my life.'

She started to cry again – not the all-consuming sobs of earlier, but the quiet, desperate gasps of truth escaping after decades bottled up.

'I didn't really watch him climbing, to be honest. I was trying to read what he'd written in my book, but his handwriting was all spidery and I wasn't very good at reading then.

'Then I looked up and he was at the top, waving at me. At least I thought he was waving at me. The sun was so bright in my eyes. I remember shading them. And I waved back. But the next moment he was falling. My dad. Just falling . . .'

Tash held her as tight as she could as the tears shuddered through her.

It was a long time before she could speak again.

'Somebody from the site took me home. I don't remember anything about that. Mum said it was an accident and I believed her. For years I believed her, even though I had the writing in my book, which I was too frightened to read.

'It was only when Mum married James that I read it. I was so unhappy I figured it couldn't make me feel any worse. I wanted to be close to him, to my own dad, not yours.'

'Oh Beccy.' Tash pressed her face to Beccy's hair. 'My poor Beccy.'

'There it was. My father admitting he couldn't go on. Saying he was a bad person. And, forgive me, Tash, but I blamed you all at the time. I blamed all the fucking Frenches for killing my dad, because I knew it was my fault really, and I j-just couldn't admit it. As soon as Mum married into your family all my memories turned bad. I didn't want James, I wanted my own father back. The father I'd allowed to die. The father I could have stopped d-doing that t-to himself.'

Tash kissed her head and stroked her arms. 'I can't believe you never told anybody this. That's such a weight to bear.'

'I've told you now.' She carefully removed Tash's hand from her arm and made to push it away, but then she felt the battered little hoop on her third finger and gripped on.

'Why d'you wear your wedding ring to compete?'

Tash was so thrown by the sudden change of subject, it took a moment to realise what she was asking. 'I always have done.'

'Most riders take them off to stop them getting damaged, don't they?'

'Well I've never bothered. Beccy, about your father—'

'I don't want to talk about it any more.'

'You should tell your mother.'

She gripped Tash's hand like a vice. 'You swore you wouldn't say anything!'

'And I won't, Beccy, but you must please think about sharing this, maybe getting some professional help, there are bereavement counsellors or—'

'No way!'

'Okay,' Tash sighed. 'We'll put it aside for now. But I cannot forget about it, Beccy. You've shared this with me, and that can't be forgotten.'

'I just figured I owed you an explanation. Why I fuck up. Maybe you're right – I'm just like my dad. You have to be pretty fearless to jump off a bridge, after all.' She let go of Tash's hand and pushed it aside.

Rubbing her sore fingers to restore the circulation, Tash guessed how much talking about this must have taken out of Beccy.

'I've always known that there had to be something you weren't telling us. Something very big. Nobody disappears for almost a decade without a lot of demons at their heels.'

'Oh, I'm not that unique. I met a lot of lost souls on my travels.'

'I'm sure.'

'I still do. Look at Lough. He's run half way around the world and I don't think he'll be going back to New Zealand for a long time yet, do you?'

Tash looked up at her, surprised by Beccy's insight.

'Perhaps not,' she said quietly, not wanting to think about Lough.

But Beccy wouldn't let it go that easily. There was more she needed to confess that night. 'I met him on my travels.'

'Lough?'

She nodded. 'Small world, huh? We met in Melbourne six years ago. In June.'

'I was in Melbourne then,' Tash realised in astonishment.

'I know. You met Lough there too.'

Tash shook her head, bewildered.

'When I left Britain to go travelling you'd just announced your engagement. I hoped I'd never see you again.' Beccy's voice shook as she stared down at Tash's wedding ring, a simple gold band battered and misshaped from so much riding. It must still have been quite shiny in Melbourne, she guessed.

'But then a couple of years later I ended up in Melbourne. I was in a really bad place then. I didn't know what I'd hoped to change by travelling – to find something of Dad, I guess. I planned to visit the place he died in Singapore but I kept flunking it. I was so scared I'd find just bad spirits there to haunt me. Turns out I did, and got arrested for it, but that's another story. In Melbourne, I was crazy miserable. I started to think I must be like him, you know, bipolar? I still wonder sometimes.'

Tash nodded, appalled that she might have been struggling with the disorder for years without treatment. 'We can find you help, Beccy.'

Beccy didn't appear to be listening. 'I've never been as low as I was in Melbourne. I just wanted to die. When I picked up a newspaper in a coffee shop and read that you were there with Hugo, luxuriating in an all-expenses-paid hotel, something just clicked in my mind.'

'It wasn't that glamorous,' Tash assured her. 'We stayed in a motel near the racecourse and I was in hospital for the last few days.'

'I know you lost a baby out there.' Beccy stared at the window, dry-eyed now. The storm had passed and dawn was beginning to break. 'It made me want to die too.'

'Oh Beccy. I wish I'd known you were there, seen you.'

'You did.'

Before Tash could react, Beccy swung back from the window to stare at her. 'Were you terribly upset about the baby?'

Tash sighed, thinking back to those awful weeks that had followed the Australian tour. 'For a while, yes. I blamed myself. I'd only just found out I was pregnant before the trip. Hugo wanted to cancel it but I insisted I'd be fine. There was no medical reason not to go, but perhaps I shouldn't have carried working so hard. I didn't feel pregnant, you see. I now know that I never do, apart from morning sickness, but back then it was my first experience so I had no idea what I should feel like, and any nausea I put down to jet lag and competition nerves. When I miscarried I thought it was my fault for not taking it a bit easier, but the doctors assured me that it could have happened at any time.'

'But the accident caused it, surely?'

'What accident?'

'In the cross-country at the three day event, someone ran in front of you.'

'God, that.' It was a memory she had kept packed away for many years now, along with everything else about that terrible day. 'I don't think that made—'

'I didn't plan it!' Beccy blurted.

Tash stared at her for a long time.

'It was *you*?'

Beccy nodded. 'It happened so quickly. One minute this image formed in my head of showing you how much you'd ruined my life. The next, there were hooves and metal shoes everywhere. Then somebody was dragging me away and you'd gone, galloping away without a backward glance.'

Tash looked at her, unable to speak. She'd received a lot of criticism for riding away from the incident that day, the sense knocked from her head. Now that she knew it had been Beccy, she couldn't bear to think what might have happened.

'You think I abandoned you too?' she whispered eventually.

Beccy shook her head. 'You've always ridden all over me Tash, but I am entirely responsible for ruining my own life, I know that.'

'You're only twenty-eight,' Tash protested. 'There's a lot more life to lead out there.'

Beccy chewed at her lower lip, staring at the window again. A bright, low sun was fighting through early morning mist. Occasional figures were moving about outside as fellow competitors started to emerge from horseboxes.

'What happened on the course had nothing to do with my losing the baby,' Tash assured her quietly. 'It was just a horrible coincidence. And I had no idea it was you. Like you say, it all happened so fast. A girl then a man – I didn't see the faces at all, just—'

'It was Lough.'

'Lough?'

'He was the one who grabbed me.'

Tash lapsed into silence again, staring at Beccy's profile by the window, searching her face for signs of make-believe, but that innocent china doll expression gave nothing away. She looked almost serene.

'Are you sure it was Lough?'

She nodded.

Tash rubbed her eyes tiredly, the lack of sleep and too much high emotion making her increasingly lightheaded. 'Why has he never said anything about it?'

'It's the day he fell in love with you.'

'That's rubbish.'

'I've been trying to figure it out,' Beccy went on, almost cheerfully. 'I guess it's like the Florence Nightingale effect, only instead of a carer forming a slow, romantic attachment to his patient, this was a hero forming an instant fixation with his damsel in distress. What's that, d'you suppose? Fireman complex?'

'Stop this, Beccy,' Tash pleaded, 'it doesn't help.'

'He came to see you afterwards, to reveal himself as your valiant knight.'

'He didn't.' She shook her head, again wondering how much of all this was some sort of fantasy Beccy had invented.

'But you were really ill and he couldn't save you a second time. He's never got over that. Lancelot trapped in a crowd at court, watching Guinevere suffer.'

'That's enough!' Tash held up her hands, the pain all too tangible again.

Beccy slumped back in her bench bed and turned to the wall.

'We have to set aside this conversation for now,' Tash said, pulling herself together. 'We must check on the horses.'

'Forgotten but not forgiven,' Beccy muttered.

'Not forgotten.' Tash reached out and touched her shoulder. 'And there's nothing to forgive.'

'You can't mean that?'

'I will never abandon you again, Beccy, I promise.'

Slowly and tentatively, Beccy's hand closed over hers.

They held hands for a long time, two women in a tatty horsebox in a field, sharing family secrets that had lain buried for years.

Then they got dressed, mucked out four horses in temporary wooden stables and rode so incredibly badly they both retired after the show-jumping and went back to the horsebox to get some sleep before the long drive home.

'It was you who wrote to me from the Solomon Islands after I lost the baby, wasn't it?' Tash asked Beccy as they settled back on their benches, trying to blot out the sound of voices, horses and commentary outside. 'The letter meant a lot. I've kept it.'

'Not me,' Beccy said sleepily. 'I've never been to the Solomon Islands.'

'Then who wrote it?'

'It must have been Lough.' She yawned and fell asleep.

Tash felt beaten up with tiredness, yet couldn't switch off enough to rest, her head whirring through her adolescence, her stepsister arriving in her life, that shy blonde shadow who blushed so easily and found making friends hard, storing up that terrible secret for so many years.

And then she was back in Melbourne, reliving the near miss and the terrible day that followed. She couldn't picture Lough there at all, but knowing that he had been there knitted him even more tightly into the fabric of her life, cloaking all her restless thoughts in confusion as she lay staring at the horsebox ceiling.

On the opposite side of the cramped living space, Beccy slept like a baby, so many of her secrets released that now she felt as light as a feather, her dreams sweet.

As soon as they got back to Haydown Tash shut herself quietly in the study and phoned Hugo. He was driving through France, speaking on the hands-free and having to shout over the engine rumble.

The final line-up for the European Championships had just been announced, he reported cheerfully, and he was once again on the British team. It made what she was about to say even more difficult.

'I can't come to Germany after all,' she told him. 'I have to stay with Beccy.'

'She's had a fall?'

'No, nothing like that. But I can't leave her.'

'Why not?'

Tash knew she couldn't betray that confidence right now, their fragile bond after all these years of family angst, not even to Hugo. Beccy's wellbeing was too important. This could make or break her future happiness.

'I can't explain just now – but I will soon, I promise.'

'You have to come.' His tone was icily uncompromising. 'Bring Beccy with you if necessary.'

'No. She couldn't cope with that.' Her stubbornness fuelled Hugo's anger.

'You expect me to believe this is about Beccy when we both know who's five minutes' drive away?' he stormed eventually.

Tash tried to stay calm. 'This has nothing to do with him.'

'Like hell it doesn't. I bet he's constantly scratching at the back door. Well, you have to choose between us.'

'This is about Beccy, not Lough!' she howled.

'No, Tash. This is about *us*. Stay away and this marriage might as well be over.'

'You're not seriously suggesting we separate?'

'If you don't come to Germany, I want you out of the house by the time I get back.'

She was too shocked to speak, listening to the rumbling engine his end, the horn-beeps and traffic, imagining Hugo driving furiously along the autoroute, his ultimatum hanging in the air on both sides of the Channel. However recklessly spoken, it was too late to take it back now.

As her mind raced she suddenly realised she could hear a woman's voice purring directions to Hugo, deep and seductive, nothing like that of his official travelling companion India. Jealousy ran its knife through Tash's already hammered heart. It had to be V.

'You hypocrite!' she screamed. 'You bloody, bloody hypocrite!'

It was only after she had hung up and finally calmed down a little that she realised the voice had been one she'd heard a thousand times before. It was the horsebox's sat nav.

Still reeling, too frightened of Hugo's anger to risk another call, she went in search of her much-neglected BlackBerry and hurriedly composed a badly typed text. *Pls lets forget that conbersation eve hapened. i love you zzz.*

He called her half an hour later, his voice intimate and apologetic as hands-free was abandoned in favour of a quiet corner of a roadside café. 'It's forgotten.'

She laughed with tearful relief. 'We so need this holiday. Just us. Time to relax.'

'No more texts?' he said quietly.

'No more texts,' she agreed, not quite understanding. 'Better to say things out loud.'

'Quite,' he coughed tersely. 'One doesn't text a bolting horse to ask him to slow down.'

Bolting horses were something Tash didn't want to picture right now. Having put Luhmühlen to the back of her mind, she felt sick as she contemplated riding the strongest horse on the yard around one of the toughest tracks in continental Europe in just a few days' time.

'Cub will look after you,' Hugo assured her. 'So will I. Just be there.'

Chapter 69

Tash didn't want to leave Beccy behind on her own. She was terrified she'd run away, or worse. She knew it was illogical to suddenly start panicking, having trusted Beccy to her own devices for so long now, but her instability made so much sense in the light of recent revelations and it frightened her that she'd done nothing to help.

Beccy was adamant that she was fine: 'I really feel so much better for talking. I just want to ride. I've got Franny to look out for me, and the Moncrieffs. You must go. Hugo would never forgive me for wrecking his plans.'

She did seem remarkably controlled and sensible about it, and Tash knew she couldn't let Hugo down. Their marriage was on a far too wobbly tightrope to change direction, and she'd been plagued with terrible nightmares since Beccy's confession, involving Hugo and the children falling from bridges and under horses. The more her stepsister had offloaded her angst, the more Tash seemed to acquire her own. She was so jittery and forgetful she put Beetroot and the Rat Pack in the back of the car to drive to the airport, only realising her mistake once she was on the M4, and necessitating a hasty turnaround. She missed her flight and had to wait several hours for the next available seat.

When she called Hugo to explain he was unsympathetic, 'You were already cutting it fine. Now you'll barely have a chance to sit on this horse before the competition. He's way too fresh.'

She'd barely give her first four-star ride in years a thought. She knew she should try to blank her mind of everything going on at home and focus on the competition, but instead she waded through a very heavy volume about depression on the flight to Hamburg. By the time she arrived at the venue for the Luhmühlen three day event her head was throbbing with details of hypomania, cyclothymia, melatonin activity and cognitive functioning.

Concerned that she was so late, Hugo barely pecked her on the cheek before legging her up into the saddle.

Her first ride on The Cub showed up her distraction as he took off with her across a schooling ring, dumping her unceremoniously at the foot of the arena rails. Later, after the competitors' briefing, the first official course walk came as a shock. Luhmühlen was traditionally less challenging than its British four-star counterparts, but this year the cross-country course left many of the competitors scratching their heads over its technical complexity. It wouldn't suit a big galloping horse, they all agreed. Cub was a very strong, galloping horse.

'I think you should have the ride back,' Tash told Hugo. He ignored her.

After the course walk, she rode again. Hand-galloping Cub along one of the tracks at the outskirts of the equestrian centre, she decided to test his brakes so kicked him on for a short pipe-opener then tried to pull up and failed. Instead, they careered back to the stables at breakneck speed, much to the delight of her fellow countrymen.

The large British contingent was in party spirits, seeing the event as a prolonged hen and stag party for Dolf and Jenny. A fancy-dress barbecue in the lorry park was planned for that evening, after the first horse inspection, and some of the jokers among the Brits even trotted up their horses wearing their costumes, much to the disapproval of the more humourless members of the ground jury. Rory, dressed as a guardsman complete with bearskin, cut a very dashing figure as he clanked alongside Humpty.

'He looks like the Hamley's logo,' Tash laughed.

'Entirely appropriate, given that he's been like a kid let loose in a toyshop since he's been based with MC,' Hugo reflected as the toy soldier quick-marched past.

'More like a knight on a crusade from what I hear,' said Tash.

Rory had taken the European circuit by storm since teaming up with MC and Kevin. He had posted wins in France, Belgium and Germany in the past month. His place in the British team at the European Championships was now assured. In contrast, Tash could barcly remember what it was like to earn her first cap; it seemed a lifetime ago.

Her nerves took another pounding as Cub gave her a black eye when he knocked her flying during his trot up, bouncing sideways in high spirits and propelling her into a flower arrangement. Only just hanging on to the reins, she scrambled out with geranium petals in her hair, her nose and cheekbone throbbing where she'd banged them against the ornamental urn. To the crowd's amusement, one of the Brits called out, 'Coming to the party as Ophelia, Tash?'

Cub passed the inspection with flying colours and a colourfully floral handler, whose deep purple bruise was already taking shape around her hazel eye, making the mismatch with its green counterpart all the more striking. Tash felt horribly self-conscious, and Hugo's reaction hardly reassured her that her eye looked any less than grotesque: 'It's okay, your costume has a mask.'

'Can we skip the fancy dress?' she asked as they headed back to the lorry afterwards. 'I really need to go through the dressage test a few more times. I'm not sure I can take a party.'

'You've forgotten what four-star eventing is about,' he insisted, determined to evoke past years when they'd whooped it up on the circuit every weekend. 'It's not just the winning, it's taking the parties. India's chosen a Batman theme for the Haydown team.'

But Tash was far from gracious about the choice of fancy dress costume, hired from a local shop.

'What *is* this?' she exclaimed in horror when she opened the bag and saw a lot of orange fake fur.

'Batman for me, Catwoman for you.'

'Catwoman?'

'There was a bit of a mix-up at the hire shop,' he said cheerfully.

When she pulled it out there was no mistaking the face on the vast fluffy head, with its half-closed eyes and laconic grin. 'Hugo, this is a Garfield costume.'

'I know.' He smiled unapologetically as she held the bodysuit in front of her, its fat, padded belly dangling above what appeared to be furry orange tights. It was hideous.

He picked up two huge paws. 'It's too late to take it back. You'd better try it on.'

She clambered into the hideous suit, which was as hot and uncomfortable as it was unflattering, covering her from fingertips to toes in orange fluff. The tail, stiffened inside with some sort of wire netting, jutted out like a caveman's club, clouting everything within range as she turned. The feet were bigger than diving fins and kept falling off. With the head on she was over six feet tall and could barely see a thing through the little mesh peephole in the pale pink nose.

'Jesus!' Hugo, wearing nothing but his boxers, abandoned attempts to figure out his Batman suit and stared at her in wonder. 'That is terrifying.'

She pulled off the head, hair statically charged so that it stood on end. Her blackening eye was stinging like mad. 'It's far too hot.'

'You'll have to wear less underneath it then.' He grinned, looking increasingly pleased about the accidental costume selection.

Tash scowled, shrugging off the fat suit to strip off her T-shirt and leggings.

'Here, let me help.' Hugo moved behind her, pulling her top over her head, his breath on the back of her neck. 'You know, I think this bra looks far too hot.'

'You think so?'

'Definitely.' He started to unfasten the clasp. 'Best not wear it.'

With India still at the stables, they had the horsebox to themselves.

Perhaps fancy dress wasn't such a bad antidote to stress and tension, Tash decided as Hugo turned her to face him and raised one of her legs so that her foot rested on the chair beside him. Then her naked superhero almost lifted her off her feet.

Knowing that his wife was wearing nothing but a lacy black g-string beneath the monstrous orange suit, Hugo guarded her ferociously from all the hot-blooded event riders that evening, Batman cape flapping. He needn't have worried, however, as the six-foot Garfield attracted no lascivious looks whatsoever, although speculation was still raging around the lorry park about the state of the Beauchamps' marriage, and Lough's involvement. India, dressed as Robin, refused to be drawn when she was cornered by Lucy Field in a very pink fairy queen outfit.

'I don't think Tash is even in there.' Lucy eyed the fat orange cat with suspicion as it tripped over its own feet by the drinks table. 'I bet she's already running back home, saying her nerves are bad again.'

'You're just frightened she'll steal your crown.' Having heard the rumours about Lucy's involvement with Gus, India disliked eventing's leading lady rider intensely.

'A cat may look at a queen,' Lucy smirked, 'but that doesn't put it in line for succession. Even if' – she dropped her voice to an intimate whisper – 'she's bonking the Prince of Darkness.'

'She's married to the king,' India reminded her crossly.

There was a crash from the drinks table and they both looked up to see Garfield causing havoc among the beer bottles with his huge, padded tail.

Tash had been a very well-known face on the circuit for many years, but hadn't competed internationally for quite a long time, instead being associated in more recent years with being pregnant or carrying a baby in a papoose and supporting her husband from the sidelines. Her reappearance as a four-star contender and unabashed comedy turn delighted many, particularly the younger riders who'd grown up with her as their idol.

'You're quite the most cheering sight I've seen all year,' Rory told her when he raced up to give her a hug, 'and that includes the Lexington and Badminton trophies with my name engraved on them.'

'Thanks,' she said in a muffled voice.

'How can you eat or drink with that thing on your head?'

'I can't,' Tash admitted, uncomfortably hot and dehydrated in the baking evening sun. 'Hugo's gone to find me a straw. I hear you're doing brilliantly. Well done.'

But Rory surprised her by announcing how homesick he was. 'God, I miss you all – and the Lime Tree mob! How is everyone? Beccy? Faith?'

'Oh, all fine,' Tash said vaguely. She didn't want to think about Beccy right now. 'You're doing really well, I hear.'

'Not sure how much longer I can stick it,' Rory confided in an undertone. 'MC is a slave driver – even worse than Hugo, although at least Hugo doesn't expect me to shag him after riding six horses across country. That's your job, ha ha.' He certainly looked tired, with dark rings beneath his sleepy almond-shaped eyes.

As gossipy as ever, Rory was keen to swap stories and recounted a couple of scandals: 'Have you heard the rumour that Lucy Field's married lover is, in fact, a *woman*? . . . Did you know when Hugo turned up here with India – who's lovely, by the way – everybody assumed that you'd finally run off with Lough and that this was his new squeeze. Isn't that a hoot?'

Tash forced a jolly little laugh. Rory continued, now complaining about his celebrity owner: 'Honestly, I've left enough messages for Dillon, letting him know what's going on, but I never hear a thing. The Fox is representing Great Britain in the Europeans in less than a fortnight, and this is Humpty's first four-star. You think he'd at least send a text, wouldn't you? Faith is brilliant at keeping in touch about Rio. Really professional.' He sighed rather forlornly. 'She always seems incredibly busy.'

'The Moncrieffs work her pretty hard,' Tash said distractedly as she caught sight of Hugo bearing down on them. 'She's doing well on your grey, though. Got a double clear at Brigstock last week.'

Hugo clearly wanted to spirit Tash away, but Rory was hungry for more gossip. 'Is it true Lough's competing here?'

'He's at Bramham,' Hugo snapped.

'Not what I heard.' Rory pushed back the bearskin that was falling over his eyes. 'The Kiwis say he's been offered the ride on Arondight.'

'Laura McRae's Olympic horse?' Tash remembered the hotly tipped New Zealand team horse that had fallen badly at the Games and was now only just coming back to form.

'Poor Laura broke her leg at Bialy Bor a couple of weeks ago,' Rory explained. 'Rumour has it she'll be off for the rest of the year, so the owners have offered the horse to Lough if he gets his arse over here on time. Might not be true, of course.'

'He wasn't at the trot-up,' Hugo snarled. 'He can't possibly declare this late in the day. I'll complain to the ground jury if he does.'

Suddenly Tash realised what Lough had been trying to say to her that day in Northamptonshire. He'd been warning her that he might be competing in Germany too. Sweating in her cat suit, she felt sick and faint, uncertain how she – and Hugo – would handle it if he did. It was one thing seeing him at a crowded event at home, quite another in the confined crucible of a foreign three day event.

Hugo was still muttering angrily about Lough breaking the rules.

Desperate to change the subject, Tash turned to Rory, inadvertently clouting Hugo in the groin with her tail, which at least silenced him. 'Where's MC this week?'

'Husband,' Rory muttered, rolling his eyes. 'They're at a very serious dinner party. No bad thing because, between you and me, the sex is *exhausting*. You older women are insatiable.'

'Let's get some food,' Hugo suggested irritably as, this time, he dodged his wife's swinging tail.

'Yes, let's,' agreed Rory, sidestepping to avoid a whack on the bottom. 'I need to talk to you about coming back to Haydown, if you'll have me.'

'Of course we'll have you. We need you back.' Hugo nodded, suddenly cheering up. The two men started to walk away and he beckoned for Tash to follow.

But she shook her big orange head, her appetite gone as she thought again about the impossibility of controlling The Cub. She had to cool off and concentrate on tomorrow's dressage test. The smell of the barbecue was making her feel nauseous so she pulled off her big paws and grinning head and went for a walk in the shade of the pine woods behind the lorries, ripping open the long Velcro seam up the back of the sweltering fur suit to let in some air. She started to run the dressage test through in her head. It was a new test to her, with endless changes of tracks and a very complicated canter mid-section involving multi-looped serpentines up and down the arena. She'd watched it many times, but riding it was another matter.

Unconsciously, she started to make her way through the test's shapes in the thick, springy grass of a shady clearing, striking off with canter left and criss-crossing the imaginary arena with flying changes at X, her tail swinging jauntily.

It was a while before she realised that she was being watched.

Lough was leaning against a tree, unsmiling even though he had just stumbled upon her riding an imaginary dressage test in a fat-bellied Garfield suit.

Tash halted suddenly, not at all four square. 'You *are* here.'

'I'm here.'

'When did you arrive?'

'A couple of hours ago.'

'Why aren't you at the party?' Her voice sounded ridiculously sing-song, her small talk rattling artificially from her mouth while her heart crashed around in her throat.

'Needed to sit on a horse and walk a course.' He played idly with the rhyme. 'Besides, I don't really know Dolf.'

'You know Jenny.'

'I'm not in a party mood.'

'Me neither,' she admitted, stooping to reclaim her cartoon head, which was face down in a patch of bracken.

'How'd you get the black eye?'

'Silly accident.' She scuttled past him to pick up Garfield's paws, which she'd thrown down near his tree. Her hands were shaking so much they wobbled like fluffy orange jellies.

'You don't have to be frightened of me, Tash,' he said softly. 'I'm quite safe.'

'I'm not frightened of you.'

'You look terrified.'

'I am terrified, just not of you.'

'Hugo?'

'Partly.' She felt disloyal saying it, and quickly added: 'It's the horse really.'

He'd seen her grapple with pre-competition nerves often enough to realise there was truth in that, at least, but this was a great deal worse than anything he'd helped her work through in the past. Tash knew her face was slick with sweat from wearing the head, her wet hair was plastered to her head, the ugly black eye swollen and closing, her skin grey from nausea and worry. Yet Lough was regarding her with that amazing, intense expression she knew so well, as though she was the most precious and beautiful creature in the world.

'I'm here if you need me.'

She nodded, feeling incredibly sick again. She longed to offload her worries that she wouldn't be able to hold the horse across country, but she knew he was absolutely the wrong person to be talking to. She started to turn away. 'Hey, it'll be fine. I'd better get back; Hugo will be wondering where I've got to.'

'You're pretty easy to spot in that outfit.'

'I think that was the general idea.'

'Perhaps you should do up the back first.'

There was nothing suggestive in his tone, that flat, dry New Zealand drawl that gave so little away. Yet every hair on her body felt as though it had a pair of tweezers plucking at it. She could feel the cool breeze against her naked spine now, and remembered the way Hugo had removed her bra earlier that evening, his lips on her neck, sparks in her belly. The open seam went from neck to tail, revealing a long stripe of bare skin and buttocks, with just a wisp of black lace framing them. Tash spun back to face Lough and hide her nakedness, her tail crashing through the bracken. As soon as she looked in to his eyes she was lost.

What was happening to her? She wondered. She was a nymphomaniac despite being sick with nerves and possessing a marriage laden with secrets and lies, held together only by increasingly competitive lovemaking. And here she was, panting over Lough again.

Taking another step back, she found her eyes couldn't leave his. She was tumbling in, faster and faster, dizzyingly and lustily falling.

'Jesus!' Lough leapt forwards to catch her a fraction too late as she blacked out.

The next thing Tash knew, she was looking up at tiny pinpricks of fading, red-streaked sky flickering through tree branches.

'What happened?'

'You fainted,' Lough told her as his face appeared between her and the pinpricks. He smiled anxiously.

'I'm so hot.' She reached up to wipe her sweaty face with the paw gloves that were stitched to the costume.

'Hardly surprising in that creation.' He touched her forehead. 'Christ, you're burning up. Here – ' He tugged at the fluffy hands to help her free them.

Elbows pinned fast against the orange fur to cover her modesty, Tash let him tie the costume arms around her back. Now the monstrous garb looked even sillier, like a fat-bellied furry boob-tube, but at least her temperature began to drop and her head to clear.

Lough crouched beside her, feeling her forehead once more. 'That's better. No wonder you fainted. You're supposed to go weak at the knees *when* we kiss, not before.'

'Did we kiss?' she asked groggily, looking at him in alarm.

His eyes trapped hers again, so intense and sensual, drinking her in.

'I think we were about to.' He reached down to brush a couple of pine needles from her face, making her draw in such an anxious gulp of breath that it loosened the knot on the furry sleeves around her back. Then his mouth moved closer to hers and she felt faint again. 'No, Lough, I don't—'

'I'd like to hear you both talk your way out of this one,' demanded a familiar voice behind them.

They turned in horror to see Hugo framed among the trees.

'What's the matter?' His face was mocking, but his blue eyes blazed with fury. 'Cat got your tongue?'

Late that night, lying next to the impenetrable wall of Hugo's turned back, Tash stared up at the dark ceiling, her eyes as wide as a bush baby's, reliving every dreadful second of turning to see Hugo standing there.

Looking back, she guessed there were few more compromising positions than the one Hugo had found her in, topless and wanton on the forest bed with Lough crouching over her, lips puckered. Every time she thought about it she groaned aloud, her body curling into the foetal position.

Unfortunately, for the next two days she could think about nothing else, even when she was riding her first four-star test in three years and made such a fudge of it, including two errors of course, that she was lucky not to be eliminated.

The encounter had the opposite effect on Hugo, who rode like a man possessed. Sir Galahad was at the top of the leaderboard on Friday, with Lough's chance ride hot on his heels, just two penalties adrift, and Dolf in third.

Hugo refused to talk about what he had seen. Icily civil to her in public, silent in private, he still shared her bed in the lorry and they ate agonisingly silent meals. He offered Tash no opportunity to make her peace, nor the support she so desperately needed. Yet the night before the cross-country, his hands drifted over her thighs and breasts and she took what comfort she could from it as they made soundless, humourless love in the pitch dark, her insatiable body craving the relief that the quick, heady seizures of orgasm gave so fleetingly.

On cross-country morning Tash was so sick with nerves and unhappiness that she vomited behind every third fence of her final course walk. She took Cub for a short hack, her hands shaking so much that she had to brace her reins and hold on to the saddle like a beginner. She didn't dare go any faster than a trot in case she vomited again.

Hugo had, predictably, disappeared on a long run – typical behaviour for him on cross-country day. The four-star competitors didn't start until after lunch, the smaller three-star phase in the morning. Tash sat with some of the British riders to watch, feeling increasingly distanced and unwell. She went to lie down in the lorry and found three voicemail messages from Penny, saying that when they had turned up at Haydown that morning to fetch Beccy for the Great Tew trials they found she'd gone AWOL, her bed unslept in.

Groaning, Tash rang Beccy's phone continually until she picked up.

'Where are you?'

'Somewhere near Sheffield.'

'Sheffield?'

'I thought I'd take a drive. It's all right, I'm going home now.'

Which didn't really put her mind at rest, although at least she could call Penny and reassure her that Beccy was safe, if not necessarily very well.

'Good luck today!' Penny said cheerfully. 'It's like old times, eh? You and Hugo going head to head. You'll feel like you're back on Snob again.'

Ringing off, Tash realised she couldn't go through with it. She couldn't ride across country on such a strong horse with her head all over the place.

Hands shaking, she dialled Hugo's mobile to tell him that she was going to withdraw, but it rang inside his coat lying beside her on the seat.

Angrily, she wrenched it out of the pocket and scrolled through his messages. There were three texts from V: *So disappointed I can't be there with you x . . . Thinking of you x . . . Remember your secret 'other half' is rooting for you xxx*

Hurling the phone across the living area, Tash stood up shakily and changed into her familiar red cross-country kit. Now her sense of indignation was revving at full throttle, she was determined to conquer her fear and go head to head if it killed her. Yet the adrenalin high did nothing to assuage the nerves attacking her ability to function, and by the time she'd walked to the stables she was drenched in a cold sweat, almost hyperventilating and her vision closing.

Holding Cub and waiting to leg her up, India looked at her in shock. 'You look awful.'

'I'm s-sick,' she told her.

'You'll have to withdraw'

'No way – it's just n-nerves.'

'Stay there,' India insisted, thrusting Cub's reins at her. 'I'll fetch help.'

There were tens of people around, and Tash huddled in Cub's stall wishing them all gone, along with the noise and the fuss and the excitement. She wanted to be back home with her children.

Thinking about Cora and Amery made her cry. She had deliberately put them to the back of her mind, but now she'd conjured up their faces she couldn't make them go away. How could she ride a horse she couldn't control with two such small children relying upon her? What if they were left motherless?

A warm hand closed reassuringly on her shoulder. She knew who was standing behind her even before he spoke.

'Calm down, Tash.' Lough's voice was as deep and soothing as a mountain lake. 'Just breathe slowly. Concentrate on breathing, nothing else. In. Out. In and out. Deep breaths. That's right.'

If Hugo saw them he'd freak, Tash realised, letting out a hysterical laugh.

'Just breathe, otherwise you'll faint again. In and out. Slow breaths.'

She did as she was told and oxygen finally started to make it to her addled head.

'In and out. In and out. In and out. That's right. Good girl. In and out.'

Oh God, she was thinking about sex again, she realised and started to laugh once more.

'Calm down, you're losing it again,' he said levelly.

Within five minutes she was breathing regularly, her heart slowing and the cold sweat receding as Lough got her to focus entirely on her cross-country ride ahead, making her visualise the task in front of her, break it down into manageable sections to realise it was well within her capabilities.

'Okay, jumps one through four – how will you do them? How will it feel to clear them and kick away afterwards?'

She told him, repeating the exercise throughout the course.

'And you gallop through the finish. How does that feel?'

'Fantastic,' she replied, feeling as though she'd already done it.

'Okay, let me check Lum's got my horse ready and we'll go through that again while you warm up.'

Many an elbow nudged another at the sight of Tash and Lough warming up at the edge of the woods, cantering circles side by side, trotting on a loose rein, popping over the practice fence, talking all the time.

'He says more to her than he's said to the rest of us in three years on the New Zealand squad,' one of his team-mates complained.

'Certainly more than her husband's saying to her right now,' another observed. 'Looks like the rumours are true. Mrs Beauchamp might be riding for the Kiwis soon.'

Tash didn't notice the scandal-mongering or care, her determination to ride well now eclipsing all other thoughts. Without Lough, she probably wouldn't have started out on the course at all, and she certainly wouldn't have finished.

But it was Hugo who saw her off, turning up in the nick of time to take over from India, checking her girth, patting her thigh and wishing her luck. 'You look nice and relaxed.'

'I *am* relaxed,' she realised with surprise, glancing momentarily across the warm-up area to see Lough chatting to fellow New Zealanders in the distance, his big dark eyes meeting hers across a hundred yards and giving her courage.

By the time she was being counted down in the start box, Tash was looking forward to it. She could hear Lough's voice in her head: 'Okay, fence one – how do you ride it? How does it feel?'

Letting Cub surge under her, harnessing his power, she flew the first as she'd intended and it felt even better than she could ever have imagined.

She rode the course for a safe finish without heroics, taking the straightest lines to maintain her rhythm without getting into any battles with Cub, knowing that her lousy dressage had put her too far out of contention to be competitive. This was about self-preservation. She needed to contain and channel Cub's strength, not fight it. Her confidence soared as they progressed, checking her timing markers, clearing the fences with barely a touch and left in no doubt of Cub's scope and self-assurance. As Lough had predicted, when she galloped through the finish she felt fantastic, all the more so to see him there, on the other side of the ropes waiting to start, dropping his reins and clapping his hands over his head in delight as she rode past giving him a thumbs-up and looking deliriously happy. It was the first time anybody had seen him smile in weeks.

Hugo was waiting at the finish with a conciliatory hug, his own smile guarded and his attention already being pulled away from her because he'd stopped warming up his horse to watch her and had to remount. But his respect for how she had ridden was totally heartfelt, burning a brief hole through any wariness between them. 'That was magnificent. You looked just like your old self out there.'

Tash couldn't stop smiling.

There were no smiles in the Beauchamps lorry that evening, however, despite two clear rounds. Word had got back to Hugo of his wife's last-minute coaching session with Lough, yet he said nothing, his handsome face more shuttered than ever. Nor did he make any comment when he discovered his phone lying in one of India's boots.

The atmosphere between them was corrosive, a row brewing like an over-inflated dinghy waiting to burst, yet neither of them yet willing to dig in the first needle. Tash wanted to tackle him about V, to round on him about his hypocrisy, but she was too exhausted to move. Two nights of insomnia followed by an epic battle with her nerves had drained her. She couldn't eat a thing and it took all her energy to clean her teeth and crawl up to her bed.

If Hugo's hand stole across her body that night, she had no idea. She was dead to the world. She didn't even know if he came to bed at all. By the time she woke up at six-thirty, her head pounding, he was already out running, his phone with him.

Lough didn't smile again that weekend, not even when he claimed victory at Luhmühlen in a last-minute reprieve when Hugo's horse kicked out the penultimate show jump, dropping them just behind the New Zealander and gifting Lough top slot. His first four-star win in the northern hemisphere was no triumph compared to forfeiting Tash, who Hugo had policed closely all day.

At the ceremony, just for a brief moment as the two men lined up side by side to collect their laurels in a reversal of fortune from their famous Olympic meeting, Lough turned to Hugo. 'Can I have her now?'

Hugo didn't take his eyes from Sir Galahad's twitching ears. 'You haven't yet won the bet, Lough.'

'Watch me. I'm on one hell of a winning streak.' Lough rode forward to receive his trophy, the crowd applauding and whooping appreciatively for the great battle they had witnessed between the year's most talked-about rivals.

Chapter 70

With India not qualified to drive the big HGV lorry, Hugo and Tash were due to share the long haul down to Düsseldorf and then across the Dutch border to a big equestrian centre near Maastricht where the British horses were all to be stabled prior to the European Championships in Aachen.

Hugo had arranged for them to pick up a hire car and drive south to Switzerland after that, before crossing back over the border into Germany and into the Black Forest to the little village in which Jenny and Dolf were holding their wedding celebrations. It was to be the closest thing to a romantic break he and Tash had enjoyed since Amery was born, and although it seemed almost laughable in current circumstances, Tash clung to the idea of a holiday, knowing it was their only chance to be alone and try to mend the rapidly widening cracks.

But they had barely got out of Luhmühlen, heading west past Bremen before she felt monumentally car-sick. Wedged beside India and Hugo in the cab, she battled nausea all the way to Düsseldorf. She'd always suffered travel sickness on and off, particularly when over-tired, and today was as bad as it got. She couldn't drive at all.

Propped up by coffee and energy drinks as he stayed at the wheel, Hugo was chillingly unsympathetic and increasingly wired on caffeine.

'Are you pining for something?' he baited. 'Or is that a guilty conscience?'

The row had been simmering quietly for hours, mostly consisting of sniping from Hugo as Tash felt too lousy to fight her side properly, and was acutely aware that poor India had found herself the sturdy tree trunk around which cat and dog were running, snapping and hissing.

'Let's not get into this now, Hugo,' she pleaded.

It was after eleven o'clock at night. They were roaring along the near-empty Autobahn, eating endless miles of tarmac, the occasional sports car flying past them at full pelt. The radio was playing dreary Euro-pop.

Hugo couldn't let it go. He was furious: furious with himself for yet again missing out on a victory; furious that Tash should have done so much better on a horse that would have won with Hugo on top; most of all he was furious because he had caught Lough Strachan on top of his wife.

'You can't even be bothered to lie about it any more,' he hissed.

'There's nothing to lie about,' she said wearily. 'I fainted. I was practising my dressage test. He happened to be there.'

'And you *happened* to be topless.'

'I'd passed out because I was so hot!' She felt nausea rising. 'It was ninety degrees in the shade. That furry cat thing was *your* choice!'

'Rather fitting given that you've been shagging like a feral cat all week.'

'Only you.'

'Too much information!' India held up her hands.

Hugo ignored her.

'Yesterday, Lough was practically in the saddle with you.'

'I was spaced out with nerves. You were nowhere to be seen.'

'You could have rung my mobile.'

'I did.' Bile was rising so high Tash struggled to speak and she tasted the acid in her mouth. 'It was in your coat. In fact—'

'The man is in love with you, Tash!'

India held up her hands again. 'If you're going to argue like this, would you mind not dribbling and spitting on me so much?'

They lapsed into silence, and Tash suddenly realised she was going to throw up again.

'I can't possibly stop yet,' Hugo told her when she made distress signals. 'We're on the Autobahn. You'll have to go in the back.'

She managed to scrabble into the living area via the cab's cut-through and rushed to throw up into the chemical loo, the smell of vomit and waste making her retch all the more. She then lurched back towards the cab wondering whether she should try to lie down. She felt faint again.

'I think you should see a doctor.' India had swivelled around in her seat to peer at her through the cut-through. 'You look grim.'

But Tash shook her head. 'I always get travel sick.' Seeking medical attention late on a Sunday night in a foreign country with four horses on board a seventeen-tonne lorry wasn't really an option unless she was dying.

'Well, you're both certainly going to need that holiday,' India pointed out brightly, determined to lift spirits. 'Although I'm not sure a road trip would be my first choice if I suffered from travel sickness,' she joked, turning to Hugo to recommend a hotel she knew in Strasbourg.

Poor India, Tash thought wretchedly. She had looked after the horses well, groomed superbly and been tremendously cheerful and diplomatic, but she must be wishing she had stayed in London.

Tash sat down on a sofa seat in the swaying living area for a moment before she fell down. The thought of a road trip appalled her. India was right, what had she been *thinking*? A mountain driving holiday was her worst nightmare, especially given how fast Hugo always drove.

A holiday meant time to talk. A holiday meant time to sleep. A holiday without the children, however selfish, meant time to try to patch things up, to talk about the Lough situation and – if she dared – to tackle the V texts. The word 'holiday' had deafened her to all else until now, as she contemplated the very real prospect of chucking up at every bend in the road.

Jenny had told her that the hotel in the Black Forest where all the wedding guests were staying was incredibly romantic, part grand ski lodge, part schloss and part cuckoo clock, surrounded by wooded mountains. Battling down the motion sickness, she lurched back to the cut-through. Hugo's temper wasn't improved when she accidentally kicked him twice clambering back into the cab, then knocked his Minstrels everywhere, but she still pitched her idea, stomach churning.

'Let's fly straight to Stuttgart once we've dropped off the horses,' she said as she settled back into her seat, sweets crunching beneath her. 'I'm sure there are flights.'

But Hugo seemed determined to re-enact the opening credits of *The Italian Job*. 'I want to drive there.'

'Flying's so much more relaxed,' she pleaded.

'I've planned the bloody route.'

'I want to fly!'

They were passing the eastern outskirts of Düsseldorf now, the city stretching out in a bright urban glow.

Hugo indicated to turn off at the next slip-road.

India studied the glowing little rectangular screen on the dash that indicated they drive straight on. 'Natalie Sav hasn't said anything about coming off here.'

'But Mrs Beauchamp has,' he said acidly as they left the Autobahn.

India looked to Tash who shook her head, feeling too ill to worry about it. She didn't care where they were stopping as long as she could get some fresh air.

As Hugo navigated roundabouts and more anonymous highways, it became increasingly obvious where they were heading. They were following signs featuring a little aeroplane and closing in fast on Düsseldorf airport.

'Hugo, you can't take a horsebox into an airport.' Tash realised what was going on with a yelp of alarm. 'What are you doing?'

'Dropping you off darling,' he hissed. 'You want to fly. This is an airport. Domestic or international?'

'Hugo, don't be silly!' This facetious side of him appalled her. She hadn't seen him behave like this for years.

They were already within the airport's perimeter, following the bus and coach routes to avoid any height restrictions. It was almost midnight and very few people were about. Nobody stopped them or even gave then a second glance as Hugo drove the big shiny horsebox emblazoned with Team Beauchamp Event Horses right up to the terminal, pulling up in a coach stop.

'Get out!' he ordered.

'Hugo, please don't do this!'

'Yes, stop it, Hugo,' India agreed, close to tears. 'This is awful.'

He was glaring out of the windscreen, knuckles white on the wheel. 'You fly on ahead, Tash darling,' he drawled. 'Can't have you puking all the way through the lowlands. Now push off. These horses need to get to their beds.'

'You can't just throw me out.'

'You want to have your Black Forest gateau and eat it, that's fine by me. Why not give Lough a call and see if he can meet you there? An All Black in the Forest.'

'Stop it!' Tash covered her ears.

An airport security guard had started to take an interest in them now, talking into his two-way radio and fingering his gun as he approached the horsebox.

With horror, Tash realised she was going to be sick again. She clutched her mouth and, groaning, wrenched open the door. The blast of heat and diesel fumes in her face, mixed with cigarette smoke from the smokers by the door made her reel. She only just leaped down and across to a discreet gutter in time.

'Better ask for extra sick bags on the flight,' Hugo called after her before turning to talk to the security guard who had appeared at his door and was starting to complain vociferously.

When India jumped out of the cab carrying Tash's bag, into which she'd crammed some essentials, along with her own duffel bag, she said, 'You're ill. I'm staying to look after you.'

But Tash shook her head, wiping her mouth. 'You have to stay with Hugo.'

'No way. He's gone barking mad.'

'The horses need you there. Please, India!'

'Then come with us. He'll calm down.'

Now she was out of the lorry, Tash had no intention of getting back in. She'd never felt so sick, or known Hugo so angry or cruel.

'You talk to him, Ind,' she begged. 'Try to get some sense out of him. I just can't get through. He really thinks I'm having an affair with Lough.'

India looked at her incredulously. 'But you *are* having an affair with Lough.'

'I'm not!'

'Everybody says so, even Rory. It's been going on for ages, since Hugo was away in America.'

'We're truly not!' she bleated, but it was obvious India didn't believe her.

Hugo had placated the security guard. He called out to India that they had to go and started the engine before shouting something at Tash that she couldn't hear.

India looked at her uncertainly.

'Go,' Tash insisted. 'Tell Hugo I'll go straight to the hotel. It's the

Hotel Ballenberg – the details are in the horsebox. Tell him he must come, India.'

'And if he doesn't?'

'Then it's over, isn't it?' She looked up at Hugo in the cab, that beautiful profile fixed straight ahead, that ludicrous, fierce pride unable to see the truth. 'If he believes everyone else rather than me, then it's over.'

Giving her a hug, India grabbed her own bag and jumped back on board just as Hugo released the air brakes with a deafening hiss. Tash could hear the horses kicking in the back as the big lorry slid away. She felt as though she was taking blows straight to her chest. Watching the tail lights fade and the Mogo logo disappear into the distance, she slumped down against the wall of the terminal building and sobbed.

The security guard, who was by now thoroughly fed up of these English idiots, marched up to her. 'You cannot do that there. This is Düsseldorf Airport and we have rules, *ja*?'

'Is there a designated weeping area, then?' Tash asked, picking up her bag and wandering inside.

Chapter 71

Tash lay across two seats on a near-empty Air Berlin shuttle, wishing that she had booked herself on a Heathrow flight instead. The temptation just to go home had, for a while, been so strong that she had shut herself in an airport loo and cried, reminding herself that if Hugo followed and found out, she would look even guiltier. Lough would be back in West Berkshire. She was safer in Germany, fighting for her marriage.

By the time she reached Hotel Ballenberg she had been in transit for over sixteen hours and was dead on her feet. She would have happily slept in the foyer but they gave her a third-floor room with wooden walls, dark carved furniture and a beautiful view down across sweeping pine forests to a gorge. She stared at it from the little balcony where she took up position after a restless sleep and sat for hours on end, feeling sick, waiting for Hugo to call and tell her when he was arriving.

He didn't call, or reply to the messages she left when his phone always went straight through to voicemail. She was convinced that he must have run straight into V's loving arms.

In a daze, she phoned Haydown.

'How are the Swiss Alps?' Franny asked cheerfully.

'Very like the Black Forest.' Tash looked out across the undulating treetops and realised that Hugo couldn't have let her know what had happened. He must still be on his way. 'How's Beccy?'

Franny reported that, having reappeared cheerful and unrepentant after her drive to Sheffield, Beccy had gone with Penny and Faith to the West Wilts trials that day: 'I know it's not my place to say this, but I think she's pushing the horses – and herself – too far, taking too many risks. She knows no fear.'

When Tash called her mobile later, however, Beccy excitedly reported that she had just 'ridden a blinder' and won her class. It was hard to argue with results like that, particularly in the light of Tash's own crippling nerves, which she was certain had blighted Haydown's winning reputation all year, along with all the rumours about the Beauchampions' rocky marriage. Thinking about Hugo made her well up so she hurriedly cut the call to Beccy with vague congratulations and reminders to 'stay safe'.

It took several attempts to get through to Alicia. 'The Krauts are marvellous,' she reported. 'They do everything. I'm thinking of getting a pair of my own for the Dower House. The children are happy as sand boys, and I don't have to lift a finger. How are you and Hugo?'

Tash wavered, unable to tell her mother-in-law that she thought their marriage was over. Alicia had been the very first to suggest Hugo had a mistress, all those months ago when Tash was heavily pregnant with Amery. She hadn't taken her seriously at the time.

Alone in the Black Forest, sitting high on her balcony, she tried to contact her own mother, but there was no answer on her mobile, so she was doubtless in some remote corner of the globe. In desperation and in need of an honest ally she called Penny.

'Your sister is frankly dangerous.' Penny started speaking before Tash could say more than 'hello'. 'She doesn't listen to a word of advice and rides far too fast. Now, tell me what happened at Luhmühlen? Lough's come back looking as though he's just had his best horse shot, not won a four-star—'

'I think Hugo might have left me for someone else,' she whispered, saying it out loud for the first time with such a stab of pain that she couldn't speak again for several minutes.

But Penny's cynical reaction shocked her. 'Oh, he'll be back. Welcome to the Eventer's Wives Club.' She sounded almost cheerful to have a new recruit. 'One starts out with such throat-cut shock, thinking you won't see the week out, and then a year later they're still shagging their way around the circuit like a dog pack and it no longer feels so dreadful. I hesitate to say it's normal – I want to cut Gus's balls off some days – but we rub along pretty well, and get the job done. We still make each other laugh, and at least the pressure for non-stop nookie is off, although he's been dropping heavy hints about me wearing stockings this coming weekend. I suppose I could oblige; I've dug out an old linen dress suit for the big day that's very serviceable and shows off the pins. Gotta keep these bad boys of ours aware of what they're forsaking. What are you wearing to the wedding?'

As soon as the call ended, Tash crawled into bed and the foetal position, her worst suspicions seemingly confirmed by Penny's lack of surprise. As with his great friend and ally Gus, Hugo's infidelity must be an open secret on the circuit, kept as gently and kindly as possible from the ears of their wives.

To her total amazement she slept for fifteen hours straight through, waking up just in time for the hotel's buffet *Frühstück*, which of course involved lashings of cold meats, cheeses and *Brötchen*. Ravenous, Tash helped herself to thirds, popped a few rolls and pastries in her bag for later and retired to her room to compose another text to Hugo, but she only got as far as *I know you are having an affair* . . . before she had to rush to the bathroom to be sick. The reality of the situation wiped her out.

He'd made her promise 'no more texts', but she was left with no choice. It was this or carrier pigeon.

Back on her balcony, she drafted her message long-hand on hotel writing paper. It was three pages long, tearstained and very heartfelt. But when she came to transcribe it into her BlackBerry, her huge breakfast still giving her terrible heartburn, she gave up and edited it down to a few lines:

When I tell you that nothing has happened between Lough and me, I expect you to trust my word, Hugo. And when I hear that you are having an affair, I don't believe it. Or am I just a fool?

She sent it, not realising that by editing all the love and tenderness from her words she had stripped it to an aggressive, challenging minimum. Heartburn twinging, she went to have a shower. She had already run out of clean clothes; India had only crammed a few essentials into her bag. She had nothing suitable for going outside for a walk, let alone a wedding. Without Hugo she had no desire to hear the marriage vows out loud. She knew she hadn't broken hers, but she strongly suspected he was smashing all of his right now.

Her phone beeped while she was in the bathroom, hand-washing her underwear. She raced through to read the message.

It was from Hugo.

Will be at the wedding.

That was it. No explanation, no apology, as succinct as a text to the feed merchant announcing he was on his way to pick up an extra bag of barley rings.

Hugo was good to his word. He was at the wedding but went directly there without stopping at Hotel Ballenberg. His hire car, thick with dust and dead flies from the journey, sported several alarming dents from a lengthy and recklessly fast mountain detour.

The marriage ceremony was taking place in a beautiful painted church in a medieval hamlet deep in the forest. It was pure Brothers Grimm. Had word come down from the hills that the giant ogre from the nearby schloss was looking for a virgin in exchange for three golden eggs and a handful of magic beans, nobody would have been surprised.

Hugo was outside the church doors in his morning suit, handing out service sheets with Gus Moncrieff when Tash arrived on one of the coaches ferrying the guests from the hotel. She was wearing a borrowed dress that was far too short, and an awful hat Penny had brought as 'a spare', and which looked like a dead pheasant.

'Bride or groom?' He looked up as she approached, those blue eyes like laser pointers.

'Wife,' she said, battling to stop her voice shaking. 'I'm your wife, and I won't let our marriage fall to pieces like this.'

'Not now, Tash.'

Unable to say more because the lump in her throat was threatening to garrotte her, Tash rushed into the church and deliberately sat among some German-speaking riders, who all looked at her –

and her hat – in alarm. She tipped the feathery brim down over her eyes and cried throughout the ceremony for all the wrong reasons.

Jenny looked stunning in a huge meringue complete with embroidered horses on her train and a tiara as tall as a top hat. Dolf wept as he said his vows. They rode away after the ceremony on his favourite event horse.

Hugo travelled back to the hotel in a different coach from Tash and, thanks to Jenny's super-efficient and partisan seating plan, spent the next three hours at the roof garden reception sitting between an influential, busty German sponsor and a willowy Belgian dressage coach, while Tash sat between Brian Sedgewick and Mick James, both of whom had heard how bad things were between her and Hugo and offered a shoulder to cry on in best eventing tradition:

'Always fancied you,' Mick said matter-of-factly, 'so if you need a bit of comfort . . .'

'Hugo's a difficult man,' Brian said more cautiously. 'His breed need constant stimulation and yet no distractions. You are very stimulating, but also far too distracting, Tash. I have a lovely little cottage in the Lakes if you need some time away to think . . .'

Tash tuned them out, just as she did the speeches, continually finding her eyes drawn to Hugo.

His eyes, surprisingly, seemed equally drawn to her, although his expression was unreadable. He was downing champagne horribly quickly, she noticed.

By contrast, she couldn't even drink her way to oblivion. Alcohol was making her ill.

When the tables were pushed back for dancing she fled gratefully for the lifts.

Just as the doors were closing a hand reached in to pull them back and Hugo stepped in.

'Going down? Or do you just do that for Lough?'

Tash closed her eyes despairingly for a moment. 'What do I have to do to stop this?'

'Divorcing me would stop it pretty effectively.'

She felt faint with dread. 'I don't want that.'

'Don't you?'

The lift shuddered to a sudden halt and a fat German in swimming trunks stepped in, heading for the basement pool. He nodded at Hugo and stared lustily at Tash's short dress.

When their hour came at last they stepped out. Tash slotted in the key card, but Hugo made no move to follow her into the room.

'I guess this is it,' he said quietly.

'Is it?' she croaked, turning to look at him.

He nodded, his face quilted with tightly knotted muscles.

Tash felt the long corridor walls tilt in as her vision tunnelled for a moment. She gripped on to the door handle, worried she might faint. 'I don't know how to make you believe me that nothing happened with Lough. Nothing. I don't care if I never set eyes on him again in my life, just so long as I don't lose you.'

His eyes darted towards the lifts, as though longing to step in to one and avoid the topic.

'You have to trust me, Hugo.'

'I don't see how.'

'We have children together.' Her voice broke with emotion. 'We have built so much, our family life, our livelihood, our love' – she battled back sobs – 'and we've built trust, even if some of that has been lost. It's all about trust. We can build it up again. We just have to talk.'

He let out a long sigh. 'You really think that can mend this?'

'Surely it's worth a try?' She held open the door, heart punching up into her throat with such hope and fear that it felt as though it would dislocate her jaw.

He walked inside.

Shaking with relief as she followed behind, Tash closed the door and leant against it. 'I love you so much. It's been such a hellish year. We have to lay our hearts on the table here about – everything.' Her voice shook as she thought about the V texts.

But Hugo was not a man brought up to talk, let alone lay his heart or any other part of his anatomy on a table. He'd heard enough for now. Turning to look at her in a storm of silent, misunderstood confusion, he did the only thing he knew to work.

Moments later the borrowed dress slid to the floor and Tash's well-spring of eternal optimism bubbled up again as Hugo scooped her up and carried her to the bed.

The Beauchamps missed the wedding celebrations that night.

Up in their wooden, bedtime-story room, with its twisty hand-carved furniture and shutters, Tash and Hugo celebrated togetherness in body if not in mind.

It had been less than a week, but Hugo could already feel more bone jutting through his wife's skin, which had previously yielded softly to his touch, and she had a new listlessness that concerned him. He was amazed by how deeply she slept afterwards and worried that she was ill, but at least her unconscious state meant he could go on to the balcony to smoke and plot ways of murdering Lough.

Sitting outside, he found Tash's draft text to him paper-weighted by a potted alpine on the table. He read it in the half-light, eyebrows raised.

Then he set light to it and watched its ashes flutter away towards the treetops.

Reaching for his phone, he texted V. *Not over yet.*

Be brave, darling one, she replied with gratifying speed, as always.

The following morning Tash skipped the big gossipy breakfast and enjoyed a long soak while Hugo laid siege to the buffet downstairs, his appetite predictably enormous.

After her bath, she wrapped herself in a towelling robe and peered at her reflection. The black eye that Cub had given her at the first trot-up in Luhmühlen had now faded to a patchy yellow, lending her face an unflatteringly jaundiced tinge, but there was no denying the way in which the hollows beneath her cheeks heightened her bone structure and made her eyes look huge. Her face bore little resemblence to that of the plump-cheeked, happy wife who beamed out from so many photograph frames at Haydown, hugging Hugo and their children. This morning, she let herself hope that happiness was within reach again; they were both turning over new leaves as eagerly as two gardeners preparing their Chelsea stand.

Then she wandered out onto the balcony to breathe in the Black Forest air and found Hugo's phone on the table.

'Don't look at it,' she told herself firmly, turning away.

She turned back. For a few moments, Tash turned to and fro on the high ledge like a figure on the Trumpton clock before she gave into temptation and grabbed it.

Soon the little rubber-armoured mobile was flying through the air, high over the pine trees, where its manufacturer's indestructibility guarantee would be tested to the limit.

Still swathed in her robe and her wet hair up in a turban, she marched downstairs, tracking Hugo down to a table of very hungover eventers, including the Moncrieffs.

'Who is V?'

He stared at her blankly for a moment.

'Is she your mistress?'

The restaurant had fallen eerily silent, apart from the odd scrape of a chair being moved back to allow a better view of the confrontation.

'Ah, V.' He slowly set down his coffee cup on its saucer, adjusting the spoon to sit neatly in the rim. 'V means no more to me than Lough does to you. Trust me.' His eyes met hers challengingly. 'It's all about trust.'

At that moment the newlyweds walked in to a raucous round of applause. Jenny made a beeline for Tash and Hugo.

'I'm so glad you two have made up your differences.' She hugged them both happily. 'It's a double celebration now. I told you this place is wildly romantic. Good to see you've been using the spa, Tash. Now promise me you'll both come on the forest walk today? We're going to have a huge picnic and play volleyball.'

Tash couldn't look at Hugo. She hoped they might find his phone out there somewhere, even if trust was still far out of reach.

Chapter 72

'No!' A universal cry of horror went up in the Moncrieffs' tatty sitting room as Hugo and Oil Tanker ran out at a straightforward corner on the Aachen cross-country course. Only Lough remained silent, his face giving nothing away as he stood apart, arms crossed in front of him, at the back of the room.

The Lime Tree Farm mob had gathered on the threadbare sofas and chairs with dogs on their laps and mugs of tea in their hands. All were wearing breeches, having 'just popped in for five minutes' tea break' to look in on the European Championships action. Now, with the British trail-blazer in trouble, they couldn't drag themselves away.

'That was so unlucky,' said Penny.

'Oh, c'mon, he's riding like a dork,' Lemon pointed out cheerfully as Hugo turned a circle and took the alternative before kicking on away from the fence while dispirited Union flags were waved by a couple of eager Brits in the crowd. 'He's probably been up all night with his pretty new groom. Leopards never change their spots.'

Perched on a footstool by the bookcases, Faith shot a warning look across to the armchair in which the little Kiwi was sprawled, keeping up his constant critical commentary. His barbed and personal remarks kept edging dangerously close to revealing Hugo's drunken New Year's Eve tryst, a secret he'd sworn to keep for Beccy's sake, as Faith had. She was certain the Moncrieffs would pick up on the insinuation that Hugo was bedding Penny's niece, but they were totally absorbed by the on-screen action.

The British team were expected to win at Aachen, and led by a big margin after the dressage. They had the strongest team in years – Olympic gold medallist Hugo, defending European champion Lucy Field, world championship runner-up Colly Trewin and the Kentucky and Badminton winner Rory. How could they lose? But now their pathfinder, who had already failed to show his usual panache in the dressage, was clocking up penalty points faster than a speeding Ferrari on the M25. Chef d'Equipe Brian Sedgewick had deliberately changed tactics this year, thinking his team so invincible that it would pay to rattle the opposition from the start. Thus Hugo had found himself cast as trailblazer. Accustomed to anchoring Britain's hopes as last team member on the course, riding first was a novelty that he was not enjoying. He'd been expected to post a lightning-fast clear to throw down the gauntlet to the other European teams. Instead, he seemed to be riding in mittens.

To more groans in West Berkshire they overshot another corner in the main stadium. Hugo's face was ashen, knowing he'd let down his country.

'Oh Hugo!' Penny covered her eyes.

'His mind's not on the job!' barked Gus, who was still smarting that he hadn't been selected for the team.

Penny peeked at him through her fingers. 'I told you at Jenny and Dolf's wedding this would happen. He's all over the place.'

'Man shouldn't let the shaky state of his marriage affect his riding,' Gus grumbled.

'Well you certainly never do,' his wife sniped back.

Faith and Lemon exchanged a look. Behind them, Lough didn't blink as Hugo cantered dispiritedly through the finish, where Tash was waiting.

'She looks dreadful,' Penny sighed. Tash was deathly pale and looked painfully thin. The cameras panned from Hugo jumping off and running up his stirrups, barely acknowledging his wife's presence, to their children in the arms of the Czech au pairs behind the near by barriers, all loyally wearing Team Mogo polo shirts. It made for a photogenic tableau, but to insiders like the Moncrieffs it was clear that the Beauchampions were barely on speaking terms and that their marriage was hanging together by a thread.

Lough headed to the door, calling for Lemon to follow. 'We have horses to work.'

'But I want to stay and watch,' Lemon whined. 'Surely you can't leave now?'

'I've seen all I want to see,' Lough muttered, stalking out. Sighing, Lem tipped a dog off his lap and trotted after his boss.

'Are you *sure* Lough and Tash were all over each other at Luhmühlen?' Penny whispered to Gus after they'd gone.

'So everyone says.'

'India didn't seem to think so.'

'Believe me, they were rolling in the hay every time Hugo's back was turned,' Gus assured her, his hypocrisy escaping him. 'He was bloody brave to keep going.'

'I know that feeling,' Penny snarled.

In the corner of the room, Faith tried to blend into the bookshelves.

The Moncrieffs' marriage might be stitched together with somewhat better thread than the Beauchamps', but it was still looking as frayed as their soft furnishings.

The second British team member out on course was Lucy Field. Her horses had been plagued with injury all season so that she was piloting her third string but the public favourite, the little coloured gelding Love To Bits, who was owned by a royal and so meant the added burden of publicity.

Faith noticed the eager way in which Gus leaned forwards as she set out, his breath shortening, making low encouraging noises over each fence and his eyes gleaming with pride. So did Penny, who gripped Dolly the collie's collar so tightly she yelped.

When Lucy tipped up over the second part of the Camel Humps and parted company with the diminutive skewbald, Gus howled in anguish. His stricken face gave him away; it was a complete over-reaction. Lucy's fall was enviably elegant – she landed almost balletically on her feet, keeping a hold of her reins, but it still meant automatic elimination and put British hopes under incredible strain. Penny's hopes strained even more.

'I'm just so disappointed for the team,' Gus blustered when she glared at him.

'I'll put out the lunchtime feeds,' she spat, stomping out. Gus lingered briefly, watching in silence as Lucy remounted to hack home, her pretty face desolate. Then he, too, wandered out of the room.

Moments later, Faith could hear the beep-beeps of him writing a text in the corridor.

She stayed glued to the screen, knowing that the last two riders had to make their rounds stick.

Third to go Colly Trewin managed after a fashion, but her big Irish Sport Horse, Mighty Mouse, found it hard to cope in the heat and ran out of steam three-quarters of the way round, racking up expensive time penalties as a result.

It would be left to Rory to defend team honour.

Faith rested her elbows on her knees and chewed her thumbnails, as nervous as she would be if she were riding the course herself. She quickly pulled her phone from her pocket to text him good luck, but the battery was dead.

About to head up to her attic room to find the charger, she realised Stefan was setting out across country representing Sweden, and sat back down to watch him.

Riding out on the sun-baked downs, Beccy was in a black mood because she'd wanted to stay in the Haydown tack room watching the European Championships on the old portable all day, but Franny had insisted that she must ride her allotted horses that afternoon instead of putting them in the automatic walker.

Now Beccy was cantering rather too fast along one of the chalk tracks on top of the downs, eager to get back in time to watch Rory's round. As she cut across the pasture and took a short cut to drop back down the hill towards the village, she realised too late that she'd chosen a slope that was far too steep and was travelling far too fast to pull up. Her only choice was to lean right back and pray as the horse put his hindlegs right under him and almost slid down on his bottom as though tackling the Derby bank at Hickstead.

A lone rider was trotting along the track directly below and had to stop sharply as Beccy's horse almost landed on top of him. 'What the hell . . .?'

'Sorry about that,' she said cheerfully as she brushed dust from her knee and gathered up the reins, beaming with relief that she hadn't fallen off. Then, to her horror, she realised the other rider was Lough.

Blushing with customary ferocity, she kicked her startled horse in the ribs and began to trot in the opposite direction, grateful that it was pointing her towards home.

'Wait!' he called, turning his own horse around.

Beccy checked back to a walk and gazed down at her hands, tight on the reins. As Lough drew alongside she couldn't look him in the face, but in her peripheral vision she saw his long legs and dusty black riding boots three feet away.

They rode side by side in silence, Beccy nervously pushing into a trot again, out on to the village road, hooves striking as rhythmically as her hammer-on-anvil-heart.

They were almost at the fork where Maccombe's single-track lane peeled away from the bigger Fosbourne one when Lough eventually spoke, his deep voice sending the hammer into overdrive.

'Thank you for the texts.'

She could melt the tarmac with her face now. 'Yes – hum – sorry. I've stopped doing that.'

They dropped back to a walk, the turning just yards ahead of them.

'Please don't. I miss them.'

'You do?' She looked across at him. His huge, mocha eyes were so intense, she had to look away again. 'I've been focusing everything I have on riding better.'

'It's paying off.'

She shook her head, staring fixedly at her horse's ears. 'I was disqualified for taking the wrong course at Stonar yesterday.'

'Happens to us all, especially if we ride as fast and strong as you do.'

She felt as though her saddle was inflating and she was riding high, thrilled by the compliment; Franny just yelled at her non-stop for being slapdash.

'I watched you at Milton Keynes last week,' he told her as they reached the fork. 'You're good. Very good. Keep it up.' With a nod, he trotted on.

No mention of Tash whatsoever, Beccy realised, heading up on to the wide verge to canter up the hill to Haydown like a balloon floating on an almighty high.

She was so happy when she got back to the yard that she quite forgot about Rory in Germany, anchoring the shaky team and chasing his first individual medal. An astonished Franny watched as Beccy marched straight past the live coverage to swap saddles, saying that she was going to school all her horses until dusk.

Rory was in total disarray. His love affair with Marie-Clair was over, as of three days ago, when he'd caught her in bed with fellow rider, Kevin.

In many ways, it was a relief. For the first time in his life, he had fallen completely out of love. Easy come, easy go Rory had a terrible reputation with women, but in fact he had never ended a relationship until now. In his early twenties he'd lurched between crushing rejections as he gave his heart away too freely. Since then, one-night stands and convenient short affairs, mostly with older, married women like MC, had filled the gaps, but he didn't really trust love as an emotion and was frightened of his over-zealous heart. He was no good at romance. He was better at riding, and it was the one relationship he had stuck with, increasingly successfully this year as he cut out the drinking that had always blotted out the lost love.

He knew that MC had never pretended to be anything other than a passing trainer, in sex and horses, but of course he had loved her in his impetuous, imperfect way and to lose that love left him more homesick than ever. She'd taught him that if he was prepared to raise his game and give more he would get so much back. Over recent weeks, he'd repaid her instruction by riding better than ever and making love like never before, but he was increasingly pining for what he had left behind.

In his heart, he knew that his tempestuous French siren, who was so dominating and certain and driven, was just an echo of what he really needed. What he needed had been there all along. There was a love that had been bowled at him too often to be ignored, but which he was now almost too frightened of hitting straight into another's hands to begin to walk to the crease to strike it. He had to earn it first.

At Aachen Rory was determined to prove himself worthy as he prepared to ride across country. He knew she'd be watching. His dressage had been superb. He was the young pretender in pole position for the Championship gold, with his nation's pride riding on his big white shoulder protectors and his horse's gleaming chestnut back. He wanted to return home a hero and sweep her off her feet.

He'd texted Faith an hour before his start time. *Wish me luck. Can I buy you supper if I win?*

He was still waiting for a reply when he was finally forced to hand his phone down to his groom as the starter counted him down.

On the tight, twisting course, the fences came up thick and fast with not much thinking time in between. It was not a course for a man with his mind elsewhere.

All alone in the Lime Tree Farm sitting room, Faith pulled a cushion on to her lap and chewed its rim as Rory started. One of the host country's individual riders was on the course and the patriotic German production team kept cutting away to show him just as Rory was approaching a fence, making her moan with frustration.

Then the German finished and the television cameras focused on Rory, who was by now half way round the course. He was clear so far and on target for time, riding more determinedly than Faith had ever seen. Fox looked magnificent, his chestnut coat like hot toffee, his ears flicking backwards and forwards, listening to his rider and assessing the task as he prepared for each fence. They were a true partnership now, Faith realised. Being with Marie-Clair these past weeks had really improved Rory's technique; he was calmer and more accurate, less cocky and devil-may-care.

But then, as they approached the Sunken Road, it all went wrong. It was as though Rory lost all concentration. Coming in too fast, he gave Fox no time to find a stride on his way out and the horse tripped up the step. He lurched towards the jump and made an almighty, honest leap to try to clear it, twisting as he hit it with his stifle before crashing down on top of Rory.

'No.' Faith felt terror scour her skin. 'No, no, no, no!'

The Fox scrabbled upright, his hooves inches from his rider's body. Rory didn't move.

'No,' Faith breathed, her throat cramping. 'Please be all right. Please be all right.'

Penny was in the doorway, having rushed in from the office to watch. 'It's okay – look. He's getting up.'

Faith let out a gasp of relief as Rory slowly knelt, before being helped to his feet by a steward. Paramedics were rushing towards him but he waved them away. Smiling ruefully, he reclaimed his horse and patted him apologetically, hooking the reins back over Fox's neck and stooping down to check his legs. Moments later, Rory collapsed. This time he didn't get up again. The television cameras cut away to some picturesque shots of the showground.

Pressing her hands to her temples, Faith let out a scream of such terrifying dismay all the dogs around her scrabbled from the room in a panic and Gus rushed in from the yard thinking somebody was being murdered.

Rory would often thank his lucky stars for the superb Teutonic efficiency that had him in a bright yellow ambulance hurtling towards a specialist injury unit within minutes of falling.

At the time he knew nothing; he was unconscious for almost two days. His brain had started to swell badly, he was told afterwards, and he had been put in an induced coma to control it.

'Good job it washn't that big in the firsht place,' he joked when he finally regained consciousness.

His speech had been affected by the fall, which the doctors assured him was probably only short-term. He now sounded permanently drunk, which frustrated him enormously as he struggled to be understood. The irony was not lost on him.

'I ushed to shound like this all the time when I hit the shcotch,' he complained. 'Now I don't drink and I shtill shodding well shound plastered.'

But he was left in no doubt how close to death he had come, and he was continually told that he was very lucky not to be embarking upon a long battle to learn to walk again. Sounding like Sylvester the Cat for a few weeks was a small price to pay; in all other ways he was remarkably unscathed.

He was in hospital in Germany for almost a week before being deemed stable enough for transfer to Oxford, where his family and friends could visit him more easily.

Faith was among the first to arrive at his bedside, loaded with eventing DVDs and digital photos of his horses.

'Oh Faith, I do love you.' He patted her hand and fell asleep.

'Common side-effect of a head injury,' one of the nurses told Faith calmly when she pressed the panic button, certain that he had slipped into a coma again.

'Declaring love or falling asleep?' Faith asked.

'Both,' the nurse said, pretending not to notice that Rory had one eye open and was watching Faith closely.

'Your horses are fine,' she told him and the eye snapped shut as she turned to look at him and take his hand, chattering away as she'd been told to by the nurses. 'I check them every day after work, and Franny is looking after them fantastically. Tash is riding them like you wanted – just ticking over to let them recover from all that hammering you did on the Continent. She's such a brilliant horsewoman, although they definitely miss you in the saddle,' she added quickly. 'But everybody says you'll be back for Burghley and the Grand Slam chance, even though you might miss out on the British Open this year. You're still top of the FEI Classics race, you know, with Lough snapping at your heels. God, he's a pain in the arse to work with. He drives me mad.'

She loved the way he smiled in his sleep.

'You're lucky to be away from it all,' she went on. 'The atmosphere at Haydown is really weird and Hugo's always so bad tempered. Beccy says he and Tash are trying to patch things up, so I hope it improves. Not that it's much better at Lime Tree Farm. It's so obvious Gus is shagging Lucy Field, but nobody is saying anything and they just carry on like nothing is happening, which is just mad. If I was Penny I'd castrate him. Men are such bastards sometimes.'

Rory stopped smiling in his sleep.

As she left, she took advantage of his unconscious state to drop a small kiss on his lips, trying not to dwell on the fact that the only times she had ever kissed him seemed to be was when he was comatose.

'You are awful,' a nurse told him afterwards when he sprang up out of bed to find a power point for the portable DVD player that Faith had thoughtfully brought in. 'You're not even supposed to be in bed at this time. Why d'you pretend to sleep?'

'Becaush I'm madly in love with her,' – he looked up at her through his long, sooty lashes – 'and that meansh I get completely tongue-tied when she'sh around. My brain starts shwelling up all over again whenever I shee her.'

'Ah!' All the nurses were very fond of him, and that news would go down better than a box of chocolates in the staff room.

'And other parts of me shwell up,' he added, still smiling sweetly.

The nurse decided to save that comment for the pub after work.

Later that day Lough loped into Rory's hospital room carrying a cactus and bag of sugared almonds.

'One's a prickly sod like me, the other's a hard nut like you,' he explained, settling in to a chair.

Rory's pewter eyes regarded Lough as he looked around the room and out towards the corridor. 'You misshed her by about half an hour.'

'Who?' He tried to look baffled.

'Tash. But you wouldn't have wanted to be here – the big, bad wolf was with her.'

Lough ducked his head. 'Sorry mate. I did come to see you, honest . . .'

'Forget it.' Rory grinned, helping himself to an almond.

He was in fact delighted, if rather surprised, to see Lough, who could give him the low down on what Faith had been up to while he was on the Continent. 'All she ever shaid in her texts was that she was riding non-shtop.'

'That's about it,' Lough confirmed. 'Especially now, with things so tense at the farm. Gus keeps buggering off without explanation, so Faith's doing twice the work.'

'Poor lamb.' Rory sagged back in his chair, looking suddenly washed out and reminding Lough of just how severe a blow he'd taken.

'Hey she's tough,' he reassured him. 'She bosses us all about. She told me to come and see you for a start. I'm glad I did; I thought you'd be a lot worse than this – she said you were in and out of con-sciousness when she visited.'

'Yeah, miraculoush recovery, huh?' Rory yawned. 'They say I can go home next week. I'll be riding by the end of the month, I reckon.'

'Surely you need the rest of the season off?'

'No way – if I'm allowed to compete I'll be back in the hunt. The doctorsh here aren't keen, but I think I can talk them round. Beshides, Hugo and Tash need me at Haydown.'

Lough's eyes flashed. 'You sure you want to go there?'

'You think there might be fireworks?'

'Who knows.'

'Lough, it's not for me to take shides or make judgements.' Rory looked at him wearily. 'Christ knows, I've slept on the wrong side of shomeone else's marital bed enough times and I like to think I've cheered up a few very unhappy wives. But the Beauchamps have stuck by me. They're a team, and Hugo's a good friend.'

'He's a lousy husband,' Lough replied with feeling.

Rory closed his eyes, and Lough thought he'd nodded off. But just as he reached the door, he heard him mutter: 'Back another horse, Lough.'

It was a sociable day for Rory; no sooner had Lough departed than there was a commotion in the car park as the biggest celebrity couple of the moment made their first public appearance in over a month.

Trailing a pack of semi-feral paparazzi in cars and on motorbikes, Dillon and Sylva had just stepped from the dark-windowed cool of their chauffeur-driven car wearing his and hers dark glasses and scowls. Not pausing to acknowledge the shouted questions and pleas to pose, they ran through the hospital entrance while their small army of PAs batted away the chasing cameras.

Rory didn't think he'd ever seen them so miserable. Dillon was generally quite a grumpy character, but even Sylva's customary cat that got the cream smile was missing; she looked more like one that had just been wormed against its will.

'We hate ze paps,' she complained, sliding her glasses up into her hair as she bent down to kiss Rory's cheek. 'We came as soon as we could, darlink. Here – we brought you some goodies. The hamper is from Dillon's farm shop.' She plonked it unceremoniously on Rory's bed, along with a new Nintendo DS, a big bouquet of flowers and some magazines, perching herself beside them. 'You look better than I expected. We heard you were practically a wegetable.'

'I'm sho chuffed you came.' He scrambled to sit up, noticing that several nurses were peeking around the door to see if the rumours were true that Britain's most famous engaged couple were in the building.

'It's just a flying visit,' Dillon muttered, chewing at a thumb nail as he sat down in the chair beside Rory's bed, his eyes already on the clock. He was at least a stone heavier than the last time Rory had seen him, with a bushy beard and the huge rings beneath his eyes darker than the sunglasses he'd been wearing. 'I'm en route for Birmingham airport. How are you feeling?'

'Okay,' he said, suddenly feeling very tired. 'Who told you I was that bad?'

'Faith texted me.'

'I didn't know you two were closhe.' Rory didn't like the thought of Faith having a text life with other men, especially if it involved comparing him to a vegetable.

'We're not especially.' Dillon sprang up again, unable to settle, and walked to the window. 'Jesus, there must be fifty of them out there. I said we shouldn't have come here together.' He turned accusingly to Sylva.

'We'll go out the back way – I'm sure one of the nurses will volunteer to wrap you in bandages if you want a disguise,' she said smoothly, smiling at Rory and patting his hand. 'I had to see my darlink riding instructor for myself and make sure he's going to pull through.'

'Oh, I'll never shtop pulling, trusht me,' he joked weakly, noticing that one of the porters had put his arm round the door frame and was discreetly trying to take a photograph with his mobile phone. 'Ish it like thish every time you two go out together?'

'We don't go out.' Dillon had also noticed the camera, and went to close the door.

'Staying in is the new going out,' Sylva said brightly. 'We like to spend as much time as possible with our children, which is why Dillon is now heading to Malibu to see his girls – again.' The last word had such weight that Rory almost heard it land. 'And I am going home to have a lovely naked swim. I use the pool at the Abbey,' she told him in an undertone, stroking his arm as though he was a comforting lap dog. 'Indigo is very generous now I am family.'

'She musht be.' Rory yawned, amazed that Sylva was let loose within reach of a legendary lothario like the Rockfather, let alone encouraged to go skinny-dipping in his pool. No wonder Dillon was looking so stressed out and hang dog. He shot him a sympathetic look.

But Dillon was too busy munching Rory's sugared almonds and flicking through the photographs Faith had printed to notice. 'Which of these horses is mine?'

'Most of them.' Rory stifled another yawn, now struggling to stay awake.

'Where's the one with the heart-shaped star? I liked that one.'

'He'sh not competing again yet. He'sh only supposed walk out for an hour a day, but every time Hugo getsh on Heart takes off for the hills like a rocket. He's been held back sho long that all he wantsh now is to run as fasht as he can, like the Gingerbread Man.'

'I know the feeling,' Dillon muttered, glancing at his watch. 'We must go.'

Sylva kissed Rory again, this time on the lips, her naughty smile reappearing at last. 'It has been *so* lovely to see you, darlink, looking so handsome and brave. I will think of you as I swim. Pass my kisses on to Tash and to handsome Hugo, too.'

'I think the kiss of life might be more appropriate right now.' Rory closed his eyes and waved them off. Wiped out from talking so much to so many people, he fell asleep within seconds and was so shattered that he barely stirred when Faith called by just before visiting time was over to bring him the latest issue of *Horse & Hound*.

'Beccy's thrilled because there's a bit in it about her winning her section at Tythercombe, calling her Hugo's new protégée,' she told him.

'I'm Hugoshpottygee,' he mumbled, eyes closed.

'You've graduated now,' she assured him, helping herself to a sugared almond. 'And you were far easier to pottygee train than Beccy. She drives them mad, always riding against orders.' She admired the huge Oddford Organics hamper taking up most of his bedside table. 'So it's true Dillon and Sylva visited you earlier. The nurses are all banging on about it.'

'Youknowitshtrue.' His voice was more slurred than ever, and barely audible because he was drifting off again: 'And why'dyou-callmeavegetable?'

'I did no such thing.' She looked indignant. 'I just said you were in a bad way.'

But Rory had fallen asleep again.

'I rest my case.' Faith sighed, planting a farewell kiss on his cheek. 'Lettuce pray for a swift recovery.'

Chapter 73

Less than a week after the Beauchamps returned from Germany, Tash took Beccy to an unaffiliated local trials where they entered two newly purchased ex-racehorses in pairs competitions with an older schoolmaster, a classic Hugo trick for schooling inexperienced horses across country. Leading the way on Mickey Rourke, Beccy took off far too fast both times leaving Tash totally out of control as her little ex point-to-pointers bolted along behind thinking they were racing between the flags again.

'What d'you think you're playing at?' Tash gasped as she pulled up after the second round. 'I said slower this time.'

'I was practically trotting.' Beccy glared at her. 'Any slower and the spectators would have overtaken us.'

Tash found Beccy even more impenetrable now that she'd been let loose at a few more competitions as a member of the team. She thought she knew it all.

'Her head grew way too big while you guys were away,' Franny told Tash in confidence once they'd unloaded the horses that after-noon. 'I've kept her in check as best I can. She's a talented rider, I'll grant you that, but she's way too random.'

Tash was impressed with Franny. She was running a tight ship, had galvanised the army of local helpers into a much more struc-tured shape to run the yard and was getting Beccy, at long last, to work reliable hours.

'Don't get me wrong, she works hard,' Franny said, being already very fond of Beccy. 'But she hasn't got any sense of routine.'

'It gets results,' Beccy replied airily when confronted about her lack of discipline. 'I'm riding on air. I love competing, Tash.'

Tash couldn't deny that her stepsister seemed happier than she had seen her in weeks, but her mood swings were alarming and she never followed team orders.

The next day, they fared equally badly at an entry-level affiliated event near Cirencester, held in the pouring rain. Having schooled a six-year-old round, Tash came back to warn Beccy that the going was very slippery and she must go slowly, only to watch her belting along like a lunatic and almost paying the price as the horse skidded into the bottom of a ditch. By some miracle of honesty and distant pack-pony heritage, it climbed out and scrabbled over the roll-top fence beyond it to get home inside the time and finish third in its section.

When Tash told her off Beccy was unrepentant: 'Look how well the horse did!'

'He's a baby. He needs confidence, not scary near-misses like that. We're trying to nurture careers here, not get quick glory.'

Beccy sulked all the way home, where Hugo was waiting, his mood equally blackened by spending all afternoon with wealthy prospective owners who had treated their visit to Haydown like a National Trust house and garden tour and had bought nothing.

'The only one they were remotely interested in was Heart,' he complained as he helped them unload. 'He's only just back in ridden work – and still technically leased out.'

'That ends soon, though,' Tash pointed out. They hadn't heard from Nell Cottrell in months, although Dillon still picked up the horse's bills.

Hearing this, Beccy perked up a little. She adored Heart, who was by far the best looking horse at Haydown and whose caged fury from months of box rest she fully understood. He shared her wanderlust. Now that he was being ridden again she longed to know what it felt like to sit astride all that beauty and power.

'Perhaps I should persuade James to buy him for me,' she wondered aloud. She'd recently begun petitioning her stepfather to honour his promise to buy her a horse again.

Hugo didn't dignify this with a response, but Tash stopped beside her in horror, her arms full of tack. 'No way. We can find you something much more suitable when you're ready.'

'That's my decision.' Beccy smarted, feeling hurt again.

'Well, if Daddy's paying, it should really be his decision,' Tash pointed out carefully as Beccy's eyes stabbed into her face, the subject of her stepfather as tricky to navigate as ever. 'You'll need a horse that will really look after you. But right now you need to learn more control.'

Beccy resented being talked to like a child in need of a safe first pony. 'Lough says I'm brilliant,' she boasted. 'I'm getting better and better, he says.'

'Was he there today?' Hugo demanded.

'No!' Tash shook her head, looking cornered.

'I'm allowed to have my own friends, you know.' Beccy eyed them both for reaction, like a rebellious teenager with her warring parents.

Hugo glared at her for a moment and then, to her surprise, his expression relaxed and he laughed. 'Of course you are. You're a grown woman, Beccy. Just don't bring him home with you. As for horses, let's see how you do at Barbury. If you impress us as much as you have Lough, we'll have a word with James about getting you something of your own to compete.'

'Heart?' she asked hopefully, knowing the horse would be cheap now he carried a history of injury.

'Don't push your luck.'

Tash said nothing, but her look of horror registered with Beccy, who realised that the Beauchamps would now go away and have an argument about it.

That night she lay awake, regretting her hypersensitivity and desperation to impress. She'd overridden and then overreacted when Tash criticised her. If that wasn't enough, she'd bragged about Lough, which was like throwing a petrol bomb through a window these days. There was a time when Hugo simply saying 'you're a grown woman, Beccy' would have made her feel sexy and empowered, but now it just made her aware of her wasted life. She knew that her crush on Hugo was in its death throes. The thought of him and Tash splitting up frightened her more than ever, especially if Lough was involved.

She pulled a pillow over her head and tried hard to blot out the memory of Lough saying that he loved Tash after Badminton.

The jealousy that gnawed at her bones had changed too. At the peak of her crush on Hugo envy and hate had been inseparable.

710

Now a strange metamorphosis had taken place. Telling Tash about her father had spun her on her axis, the centrifugal force so strong that all those mixed emotions had separated out: the resentment and enmity, the years of secrets and lies. Since that day a quite new emotion had settled on the surface of Beccy's consciousness, one that she was reluctant to embrace, yet which stubbornly refused to go.

Like a rare fruit tree finally coming into bloom after years of lying dormant, she now felt a deep, grateful love for her stepsister bursting out of her. It was a heart-openingly invigorating sensation that she could no longer deny. Tash cared for her and shared her passions more than anybody else in the French family, and Beccy loved her for it. The only problem was, everybody else loved Tash too. That felt wrong, very wrong, especially when one of them was Lough.

Insomnia gripping her as it did so often, she fired up her laptop and headed for her favourite horsy internet sites. On the biggest eventing forum she read a long thread puporting to be about the British team's Aachen disaster, but was clearly a thinly disguised excuse to speculate about the state of the Beauchamps' marriage. Within the sport, they remained for ever Burton and Taylor.

'Same old, same old,' Beccy muttered miserably to Karma. She was about to click on to another of her favourites when she spotted the post from someone with the username Shadowfax: *Hugo's notorious. You should hear what he got up to in the hayloft at Penny and Gus Moncrieff's New Year's Eve party. Now *that* would get Tash phoning a divorce attorney faster than Zsa Zsa Gabor.*

Face flaming, Beccy sent Shadowfax a private message, using her forum name Beauch-Babe: *Who are you?*

He was online and sent a message straight back. *A friend.*

Not of mine, she replied, terror mounting.

He deserves it.

Please, please stop this. Cold sweat beading her brow, Beccy reached for her phone with a shaking hand to text Lemon for the first time since they'd split up.

Is it you? She pressed send.

He didn't reply, but seconds later Shadowfax logged off.

Why? She texted again.

No reply.

Wide awake, Beccy made herself a cup of green tea and texted

Lough, with whom she'd had no contact since they'd bumped into one another out hacking. She'd made tens of false starts since then, but this time she didn't hesitate: *Can't ride the devil off my back, however fast I go.*

His response wasn't exactly reassuring, but it nevertheless made her feel better. It just said *Touché.*

The following week, the Beauchamps' big lorry headed for the wide open spaces and stunning views of Barbury Castle trials, high on the Marlborough Downs.

A firm favourite with the Beauchamps, the trials boasted some of the most beautifully built and presented fences in eventing, and incredible spectator viewing because it was possible to see more or less the whole course from any one point.

Beccy was hopelessly excited. With classes ranging from novice to three-star, all the famous faces from the eventing world were going to be there, including Lough, who had hit a winning streak and was competing half a dozen new rides, deputising for injured riders or satisfying fickle owners who wanted to try him out mid season.

The Beauchamps had taken a big risk in entering Beccy for the novice section which, far from what its name suggested, was a big step up from the entry-level classes she had been competing in. As they walked the cross-country course in early morning sunshine Tash gave her guidance at every fence, and repeatedly reminded her that this was a serious challenge requiring her to stay focused and keep her exuberance in check, that there was no leeway for wild riding.

Beccy knew Tash meant well, but she wished she'd shut up and let her get on with it. She was only relieved her mother wasn't there to add to the pressure. Tash had tried to persuade Henrietta and James to come along, pointing out the great views and proximity to Benedict, but they were yet again golfing in Portugal.

'These galloping fillers still take a bit of jumping,' Tash was saying as they walked up to an inviting brush fence.

Beccy didn't even look at it because she'd spotted Lough walking the course ahead of them with a bunch of fellow New Zealand riders. Behind them, Hugo had spotted it too and called Tash back to talk to the Moncrieffs.

Beccy rubbed her sweating palms on her breeches and swallowed fur balls of fear. She was going to show Lough and the rest of them just how good she was.

From the start, it was obvious that Beccy was overfaced, even though she refused to admit it.

Her horse, the admirably straightforward Crikey O'Riley, was in his third competitive season and, although he was never going to set the world alight, was a super-safe conveyance whom the Beauchamps planned to get to advanced level and sell as a schoolmaster, or to even encourage James to buy for his stepdaughter.

'We should pull her out,' Tash said after Beccy had tried too hard and over-ridden both the dressage and the show-jumping, winding up the usually brain-dead Riley.

'She'll be fine,' Hugo dismissed vaguely, with half an eye on Lough. It seemed there was no way Hugo could possibly catch him in the league tables now, but he certainly wasn't going to let him near his wife.

Tash was happy to steer clear. She had too much on her mind to crowd it with Lough. As well as worrying about Beccy and her own rides she'd noticed that Hugo had been texting furtively all morning. She couldn't get near his phone as he kept it stashed in his pocket at all times these days.

'Gus is just the same.' Penny, standing alongside Tash, sighed as she watched Hugo pull up in the far corner of the warm-up arena and begin messaging surreptitiously, using his black jacket to shadow the screen. 'He's permanently attached to that bloody phone of his, panting like a schoolboy every time his mistress fondles his inbox. They think we don't know.'

Tash turned to her anxiously, wondering what she had heard, but at that moment Penny spotted a familiar face nearby and leaped towards it. 'Gin! Haven't seen you and Tony for bloody ages! You got a horse running here?'

Tall, iron-haired Gin Seaton jumped, looking as though she'd just been caught shoplifting. 'Oh, no we – er – have no horses these days. We like to come to Barbury. Such a super event.'

Beside her, her big lantern-jawed husband Tony, who was upholstered from head to foot in tweeds like Mr Toad, was eyeing Tash appreciatively. 'You've lost weight, Mrs Beauchamp.' He then sidled up to her and whispered, 'Hear you've taken a lover; always good for the figure, eh?' He'd always been odious.

Tash would have liked to catch up with Gin, who'd been a good friend over the years and who had been so odd with her at Badminton, but Hugo had pocketed his phone now and was riding up to her wanting Sir Galahad's bandages removed.

'Who was that you were texting?' she asked.

'What?' He was in no mood for an inquisition, glaring at Lough as he rode out of the dressage arena to enthusiastic applause and jumped off to hand his horse to Lemon. A pair of teenagers then came up to him, giggling furiously, and asked for his autograph. Hugo narrowed his eyes. 'He thinks he's a bloody rock star.'

As soon as Hugo was in the dressage arena performing his three star-test on Sir Galahad, Lough brushed past Tash, muttering 'Talk to me now.'

She ignored him, her pulse electrified.

He did an about turn and brushed past her again. 'I have to talk to you. I have news.'

There was no privacy at Barbury. Everything was just too visible.

In the end she followed him at a safe distance to one of the only secluded spots on the course: up the ramp in the back of his lorry, tucked out of sight behind one of the partitions that separated the horses in transit.

'My father's turned up in Auckland.'

'Alive?' She gasped before she could think what she was saying.

'Of course alive,' he said crossly. 'Turns out he took the money I bunged him that night and blew the lot on a holiday of a lifetime on the Gold Coast. Won a small fortune on the tables the first night there, then went out celebrating with a croupier called Darlene before taking her on a road trip around Oz for six months. Now the money's run out, they've both just turned up in Auckland announcing they're expecting a baby.'

'That's great,' Tash nodded. 'You must be so relieved.'

He looked at her oddly.

'You didn't kill him after all,' she said encouragingly.

'Are you okay?'

'I'm fine.' Tash, desperate to get away, couldn't look at him; she was terrified of drowning in his sympathetic eyes again. Married life might be hell, but extra-marital life would be a whole lot worse.

His deep voice was hoarse with emotion. 'I want to help, Tash.'

'Well you can't.'

'Anything.'

'Okay.' She laughed hollowly. 'Find out who Hugo's having an affair with.'

There was a long pause, and Tash risked looking up at him. 'You already know, don't you?'

His eyes were molten.

Look away now. Don't drown. Don't drown.

She started to drown.

He shook his head and it was his turn to look away and break the spell, his cheek muscles quilting with tension. 'I heard something.'

'What?'

'It's nothing. Just a rumour.'

'*What?*'

'Something that happened on New Year's Eve – at the party we went to.'

Tash took a sharp breath, frantically thinking back and feeling a stab of terror as she remembered who had singled Hugo out for attention there. It was the evening she'd cried on Zoe's shoulder in the Lime Tree Farm larder, her marriage already fractured. And Sylva Frost had been all over Hugo. She'd dropped Tash as a friend almost immediately afterwards.

'What happened, Lough? Tell me!'

He shook his head again and turned away. 'It's not for me to say.'

'You have to!'

They both looked round in shock as Lemon appeared on the ramp behind them, breathless from running.

'Accident!' he panted, clutching his knees with his hands and looking up at them through the pain of a stitch. 'There's been an accident!'

'Oh no, not Hugo!' Tash cried, rushing out past him.

'No – Beccy,' he gasped, but she had already gone. He straightened up and looked at Lough. They could both hear the air ambulance overhead.

As Lough made for the ramp Lemon stepped forward to bar his way.

'She leaving Hugo or not?'

'Not now, Lem!'

'But you were telling her about Hugo and Beccy, right?'

Lough looked away, kicked with remorse. He should have said nothing; he knew the messenger always got shot. Now poor Beccy was in God knows what state. He shook his head, pushing Lemon aside.

'Hey, don't mind me! I'm only the groom,' Lemon recovered his balance and kicked the ramp angrily. 'I just get to do your dirty work for you.'

Over the Tannoy, the commentator announced an indefinite hold on the course.

Beccy had been showing off for Lough when she fell, unaware that he was far from sight.

Unwatched, unmarked and kicking on for all she was worth because she was frightened and fear always made her want to run faster like the horses she loved, she and Riley had hurtled at one of the most straightforward fences on the course on a complete loser of a stride. There was simply never going to be a take-off point, but such was their velocity there was no stopping point either. A pair of big-hearted, galloping optimists, they prayed right up until the last few metres when Riley took off far too early and paddled down into the fence, falling backwards on to Beccy.

Her lower body took the full force of his haunches crashing down, a hock jammed against her hip. The horse scrambled to his feet, but she couldn't move her legs at all.

Having just finished his dressage test, Hugo galloped directly from the arena to Beccy, leaving his horse with a bemused steward while he stepped into help, trying not to get in the paramedics' way. Beccy wouldn't stop screaming, which at least reassured them that she was fully conscious.

'Where the fuck have you been?' he demanded when Tash made it to the scene.

Saying nothing, she spoke briefly to the paramedics and then climbed into the helicopter.

Tash paced around the hospital corridors for hours, still in her riding boots and spurs, which made her footfalls sound like a clanking ghost. Eventually the nursing staff had to ask her to stay put in the relatives' room.

The diagnosis, when it finally came, was better than worst fears, but still bleak. Beccy had badly fractured her pelvis. There was no internal bleeding, but it was a complicated and very painful injury that would take many weeks to mend and then an even longer rehabilitation.

It was past eleven that night by the time Hugo arrived at the hospital to collect Tash. He found her reading a battered old copy of *Cheers!* magazine, the cover of which boasted an exclusive interview with Sylva Frost about her engagement to Dillon Rafferty.

'You don't want to believe a word of that manufactured pap,' he told her.

'You know that personally, do you?' she muttered, throwing it down.

Hugo stepped back in surprise, but Tash was too exhausted to pick fights.

'Let me just say goodbye to Beccy.' She rubbed the back of her stiff neck and stood up. 'She was awake last time I looked. Come with me. She'll appreciate that. She's pretty out of it on painkillers but your name crops up quite a lot.'

'Probably wants to sue me.'

'It was my fault,' Tash said shakily. 'I should have made her withdraw after the show-jumping.'

'It was nobody's fault,' he insisted. 'It was an accident. Is her mother flying back?'

'They're at the airport trying to get cancelled seats. Em's driving down from London first thing.'

Beccy had a single room, which was in near darkness with just the lights from her various remote-controlled drips, drivers and monitors like fireflies around her.

She swivelled her head as Tash and Hugo came in, her eyes softened by analgesia.

'Bad luck, Beccy,' Hugo said a little too glibly as he stooped down to kiss her cheek. 'Hear you've smashed your pelvis. Ruins your sex life for a bit, but you'll make up for it when you're winning Badminton.'

The eyes focussed briefly, tears welling.

'I wish I still fancied you,' she told him groggily, the drugs robbing her of any self control. 'You are so handsome.'

'Thanks.' He cleared his throat awkwardly and glanced at Tash, who looked curiously compassionate, having suspected her stepsister's crush for years.

Beccy had closed her eyes, smiling now. 'I'm glad we had our moment. I'll treasure that.'

'What moment?' Tash asked in a small voice.

But Beccy turned her head away. 'I think I might sleep now. Thanks for looking after me. I love you so much.' It wasn't clear who she was addressing, but she fell asleep with a very contented sigh, like Cora after her favourite bedtime story.

'I have *no* idea what she's talking about,' Hugo insisted as he marched around a deserted multi-story car park trying to find where he'd left his car, Tash hot on his heels. 'You know what a fantasist she is. She's totally spaced out. It could mean anything.'

'Okay, okay, let's leave it for now,' Tash pacified him as they finally found the Land Rover tucked behind a pillar. She didn't trust him to drive safely if they were arguing. He could kill them both in this mood, and bad luck happened in threes. First Rory, now Beccy. She didn't want to risk Cora and Amery being orphaned tonight.

They drove out of Swindon in stony silence, boy racers revving past them on the bypass in souped-up Corsas with tinted windows, vast spoilers and booming stereos. She was reminded of that awful night in Germany when he'd dumped her at Düsseldorf airport. Every time a bubble of anger shot up her throat demanding to be popped with questions about what happened with Sylva on New Year's Eve, what Beccy was talking about, who he'd been texting all day, she fought it back down. Hugo was already well over the speed limit.

'How's Riley?' she asked eventually.

'Dead.'

'What?'

'Massive crack in his stifle. Had to be destroyed.'

'Oh God.' Tash put her face in her hands. 'Poor Riley. Beccy will be devastated.'

They travelled ten more miles in stony silence before it occurred to Tash to ask after Hugo's main ride of the day.

'I won the Barbury Plate,' he reported matter-of-factly.

But neither of them was in the mood to take any pleasure from the victory.

When they arrived home the big lorry was already packed up on the arrivals yard ready to travel to Upton horse trials the following morning, where the Beauchamps had six horses to run over two days.

'I'll stay behind,' Tash volunteered. 'Beccy needs me.'

But Hugo insisted she must still come. 'She's got the rest of the family rallying round. If you scratch now we have to pull out all the horses. This is our livelihood.'

With nobody else to help on the ground Tash reluctantly conceded the point, phoning the older of her two stepsisters to explain that she'd be away for a few days.

'Well, I suppose you have to do what you think best,' Em said archly; she was sounding more and more like Henrietta these days. 'Mummy and I will look after her. She needs her family around her now, after all.' The implication was clear, and Tash felt as though she was letting Beccy down more than ever.

When Em arrived at the hospital, she found a visitor already at her sister's bedside, and quickly identified the yellow Mohican from Beccy's descriptions. She was surprised to see him there, having also been told that the split was far from amicable.

But Lemon was the picture of concerned friend, fresh flowers on his lap, a hand covering Beccy's limp one, his face tight with worry. He smelled strongly of horses and there was straw in his yellow hair, so he'd clearly come straight from mucking out on his yard.

Beccy, eyes closed, looked incredibly pretty, a cloud of blonde hair framing her pale face like spun gold around a pearl. Having not seen her since Christmas, Em was struck by how much healthier she was looking, her face rounder, her hair longer, her complexion clear and skin dusted with light freckles. Ironic, given she was lying in a hospital bed.

'She's asleep.' Lemon pointed out the obvious. 'They're pumping her full of opiates, lucky girl. Let's have a coffee and I'll fill you in, yeah? I spotted a canteen earlier.'

Em wasn't sure she wanted to be 'filled in' by her sister's ex, but Lemon was already bounding along the corridor like Willy Wonka giving a guided tour of the Chocolate Factory, telling Em all about the horrors of the accident, the ambulance landing at Barbury, the on-course rumour that Beccy was dead.

'Lough's competing at Upton today, but he's only got one on the lorry and doesn't need me, yeah. I had to catch three buses to get to this place, can you believe?'

'Beccy must be grateful you made the effort,' Em said stiffly as they found a snack bar. She found him incredibly grating.

'Black two sugars, thanks.' Lemon hung back. 'And I'd love a couple of Snickers bars, yeah? I skipped breakfast to come here.'

Em paid for their coffees and the chocolate and started back along the corridor towards Beccy's room, hoping he'd leave them alone for a bit.

But he was right behind her. 'This is all Hugo's fault. He over-horsed her.'

'You think so?' Em slowed down.

'Defo.' He drew alongside. 'She should never have ridden that class, yeah, but she'd do anything for Hugo.'

'Probably true,' Em sighed.

'Lying for him about New Year was bad enough, but getting killed for him . . . woah.'

'Lying for him?'

He shook his head, looking away. 'That bastard thinks he can do what he likes. I told her to go to the police, but she refused.'

'*Police?*'

He stared into his plastic cup. 'I wish I'd pushed it more now. She and I aren't too matey these days, yeah, but I still care about her and I can't stand back and watch while Hugo gets away with this too. She should sue him for making her ride that horse. He'll hardly want to contest given what she knows about him. She could take him for a lot of money.'

'And where do you fit in to this?'

He turned to gaze at the health information posters lining the corridor walls, small eyes narrowing. 'I came to offer my support.'

Em regarded him warily, uncertain how to take him, yet guessing he knew more about Beccy's recent past than any of her immediate family. 'What exactly did she lie about for Hugo?'

'I can't betray a confidence. Now if you'll excuse me, I'm going outside for a smoke. Trust me, what Hugo did to your sister was bad. Really bad.' As he headed for the exit he reached out and tapped a poster on the wall, offering a helpline for victims of sexual assault and rape.

*

At Upton, Tash called for updates on Beccy as often as possible, speaking first to Em and then later Henrietta, who finally made it back to the UK with James the following evening after an interminable wait in Portugal for available seats. She was very spaced-out, they reported cautiously. Henrietta in particular sounded guarded and reluctant to pass on news, and Tash worried that there were complications they weren't telling her about.

'I'm heading straight to Somerset to compete after we've finished here, but I'll visit her as soon as I'm back,' she promised, dreading the prospect of breaking the news about Riley.

That evening, Tash was appalled to find Gus and Lucy Field canoodling quite openly when they joined her and Hugo for a drink in the lorry. Penny wasn't there, having stayed behind at Lime Tree Farm. She would be taking her four-legged babies to Stockland Lovell later in the week, where Tash was also aiming next, while Hugo and Gus headed to advanced trials in Sussex along with Lucy. Tash dreaded to think what they'd all get up to there. It was the peak of the season, with riders on the road for weeks on end – traditionally the prime time for affairs to hot up.

'I can't believe you just stood back and let that happen,' she told Hugo after Gus and Lucy had left.

'What am I supposed to do? Throw a bucket of cold water over them?'

'Penny is an old friend.'

'Affairs happen in this sport; we all just have to get on with it. The Moncrieffs have been giving house room to your Kiwi admirer for weeks and I haven't kicked up a fuss, have I?'

'Don't start that again, Hugo.' Tash sighed, grateful that Lough had returned to Berkshire as soon as he'd completed his class and wasn't staying in the lorry park. 'We agreed to put it behind us. We have to trust each other.'

'Trust none, for oaths are straws,' he glowered out of the window, 'men's faiths are wafer-cakes.'

'Henry the Fifth.' Tash recognised, studying him curiously; she couldn't remember him ever quoting Shakespeare before.

He looked sheepish. 'I played Pistol in a school production.'

'Does that make me Mistress Quickly?' Tash anxiously recalled a downtrodden Judi Dench in unflattering sackcloth in the movie version she'd seen.

'You always knew more about literature than me.' He shrugged. 'I just remember it was hell wearing tights, and I kept forgetting my lines. Pistol talks far too much for a minor character.'

'Men of few words are the best men.' Tash reached out to touch his arm. Secretly she wished he would open up more, but his face was its familiar, handsome mask again, and she knew better than to cry havoc and let slip the dogs of war half way through a competition.

In her hospital room, Beccy was doing a lot of talking, but not all of it made sense. She was trying to explain about her father, but kept muddling him up with Hugo, past and present becoming hopelessly jumbled as she fought though a mental maze and physical pain.

'I loved him so much, even though he hurt me. Tash says I mustn't blame myself, but it was my fault, wasn't it? She only said that to make me feel better.'

'Tash knows?' Em gaped at her.

But Beccy wasn't listening. 'It's why I'm the way I am, why I can't ever have normal relationships. Lem really hates Hugo, so he called it sexual assault, but it wasn't like that. It was *my* fault. I'm the reason Tash and Hugo's marriage is in trouble. I led Lough on, just like I led on Hugo, just like I rode too fast and did this to myself. I deserved it all, Em. I'm to blame for everything.' She talked herself in circles, remorseful and wretched, never fully making sense, drifting in and out of tears and sleep, her fantasy world and her secrets unravelling simultaneously.

As soon as their mother had arrived from Portugal, tearful and contrite with a sullen James in tow, Em left them all together and went outside to phone Lemon, whose number she'd found on her sister's phone. Using her steeliest charms honed from years working in media high finance, Em demanded facts, and fast. False loyalty swept aside by such practised coercion, Lemon was a great deal more forthcoming, soon sparing no detail of the sordid, drunken encounter that had gone too far and left Beccy reeling. 'I'm only telling you all this because he mustn't get away with it, yeah?'

Tash was dumbfounded when her father and Henrietta appeared across the gravel car park at Stockland Lovell shortly after she arrived, looking out of place in their golfing casuals amid the scruffy polo shirts and breeches of the professional mid-week event riders.

One look at her father's face told her to be afraid. His usually ruddy cheeks were streaked with grey, and he couldn't look her in the eye.

'What is it?' Tash asked, knowing that if they hadn't driven all this way just to cheer her on.

'Let's sit in the box.' Henrietta couldn't look her in the eye.

'There's no luxury living in this thing,' Tash apologised as they clambered into a little groom's living area that was no bigger than a broom cupboard and sweltering hot, but there was a tiny table and two benches.

She was certainly glad to be sitting down when Henrietta finally confessed why they were there.

Tash couldn't take it in at first.

'Beccy is saying Hugo tried to rape her on New Years' Eve?' she clarified, so shocked that she almost wanted to laugh.

'Rape's a very emotive word, but what went on was certainly not entirely consensual.'

'Well that's rape, then,' Tash gasped, her head spinning. 'Christ. Oh bloody Christ. Why would she say such a thing?'

'Because it happened.' Henrietta was too angry to show any compassion. 'Those painkilling drugs that she's on are terribly powerful. Apparently all sorts of things come out when people are on them.'

'Is she sure it was Hugo? It must be pretty dark in that loft above the stables at Lime Tree Farm.'

'She's totally sure. They spoke. He said his name.'

Tash felt panic and bile rising.

'One of Beccy's friends alerted us,' Henrietta went on. 'In strictest confidence, of course. Beccy confided in those closest to her as soon as it happened. She was terribly upset at the time, apparently – I'm surprised you didn't notice.' She eyed Tash critically. 'Her friend wanted her to report it to the police, but she was adamant that she didn't want to get Hugo into trouble. She's very muddled about her feelings, you see. She still thinks she might have led him on.'

Tash was too horrified to speak. Her father, struck equally dumb with embarrassment, couldn't bring himself to look at her at all.

'We gather that Hugo has a bit of a . . . reputation,' Henrietta said delicately, while James cleared his throat.

'Says who?' Tash bleated.

'I think it's best not to reveal any names in case . . .' Henrietta looked down at her hands.

'In case what? The "friend" appears as a prosecution witness?' Tash laughed disbelievingly. 'Do you think I'm going to hire some heavies and have them frightened off for turning supergrass?' She pressed her face into her hands and fought to control her breathing. She knew she could hardly defend Hugo's reputation by pointing out that he'd been flirting with Sylva Frost for a lot of New Year's Eve. And then there was the Debbie Double-G fiasco, and of course V.

To make matters worse, when Hugo finally returned Tash's increasingly frantic calls he refused to take it at all seriously. He was at the Brightling Park trials and leading one section already. 'I'm riding two horses tomorrow. I'm not packing up early because of some nonsense Beccy's made up.'

'And what will you do if the police turn up and arrest you for rape in the start box?'

'It won't come to that.'

'It will if Henrietta has her way.'

Tash went to the hospital while Hugo was driving back from Sussex. She was still wearing riding gear, her cream breeches immaculate because she hadn't even got on a horse. This time, the trainers on her feet squeaked through the corridors as she raced to Beccy. They'd just moved her on to a ward, which made it difficult to talk, especially when the elderly woman in the next bed lent over chattily and admired Tash's mismatched knee-length stripy socks, which were pulled up over her breeches. 'Is that the fashion these days, dear?'

Tash smiled politely and drew the curtains around Beccy's bed.

'Please tell me this is some sort of terrible mistake?' she whispered.

But Beccy shook her head, her china doll face crumpling as tears gushed up. 'It's no mistake, Tash.'

'He tried to' – the word caught in her throat – 'to rape you?'

'No! It wasn't like that. We were both very drunk and got carried away, then I was upset and he just walked away and left me there.'

Deathly pale, obviously in a great deal of pain despite the drugs, Beccy looked utterly pathetic. Tash had known Beccy to cry wolf on many occasions, but this time she sensed she was telling the truth. It was just too terrible a thing to lie about. She patted her arm abstractedly, too anguished by the facts to feel sympathy or comfort. She was just furiously angry at them both, at Hugo and at Beccy.

'Did you encourage him?' she asked bluntly.

Beccy chewed her lips. 'I might have said something.'

'Said what?'

'A line I'd heard. I thought it was funny.'

'What line?'

Beccy was volcano-core red. 'I said something about taking the weight off his feet and t-thrusting it into—'

'Ok, I get the picture.' Tash held up her hand. Icy fingers gripped at her temples and throat. She'd heard that line before. Hugo had used it. She felt faint.

'What's going to happen?' Beccy asked.

'I don't know,' Tash said honestly.

Beccy turned her cheek to the pillow, her skin almost grey. Her forehead was glistening waxily because the searing pain made her perspire and there were deep black circles around her eyes. She looked truly ghastly. 'I wish Em and Mummy had left well alone. I didn't mean to say anything. I just want to forget about it.'

'These things don't get forgotten though, do they?' Tash sighed. 'The things that change our lives for ever, like what happened with your father.'

Beccy let out a bleat and closed her eyes. 'I've been talking about him too, you know, but Em blanks it out every time, like she just doesn't want to hear. I guess that's half the reason she and Mummy are kicking up such a stink about the other thing. They're happy to sacrifice Hugo's honour to preserve the memory of my father.'

Tash said nothing, thinking that Hugo's honour looked pretty shabby right now.

'I *did* lead him on,' Beccy whispered, desperate for atonement. 'There wasn't anything remotely romantic about it, I promise, and afterwards he just acted like it had never happened. I could have been anyone, really. He said he was excited by—' She stopped herself.

Tash looked up sharply. 'Excited by what?'

Beccy bit her lower lip, eyes opening and peering warily at Tash. 'Sylva Frost. I'd seen them flirting outside, you see. I set off a car alarm by mistake and Sylva went inside again, or was it the other way around?' Her eyelids were drooping again. She looked beaten up with pain and tiredness. 'Then Hugo followed me to the stables loft.'

Tash ran her tongue along her top teeth and nodded.

'I have to go.' She started to pull back the curtains.

But as she reached for her bag Beccy grabbed her sleeve. 'What happened to Riley? Is he okay? Mum and Em won't tell me.'

Just for a moment, Tash wanted to yell it in her face: he's dead, Beccy, he's dead like my marriage is dead, and it's all your fault.

But she couldn't do it to her.

She perched on the edge of the bed, keeping her voice low. 'He had an injury that meant he would never have competed again. It was kindest to let him go. He was in a lot of pain.'

Beccy shrank away, her eyes going strangely blank. 'I know how he felt.'

'Would you like me to call a nurse for more painkillers?'

'It's not my pelvis hurting, it's here.' She prodded angry fingers at her chest. 'Everyone hates me. *I* hate me.'

Tash took her hand. It was shaking. The nails had been bitten down so much they'd been bleeding. 'I don't hate you.'

'Even though Hugo wanted me to give him a blowjob, and I didn't say no?'

Tash winced. Put that way, hate was burning up every vein. Mumbling that she really had to go, she turned and walked out before she broke down in front of everyone on the ward.

The woman in the bed beside Beccy leaned over again, 'Next time, tell that friend of yours the stripy socks and cream leggings do nothing for her. Pretty girl, but doesn't make the most of herself, does she? Not surprised her husband had a crack at you.'

At Brightling Park the scandalmongers were on full alert, speculating why Hugo had left the event in such a hurry while he'd been topping the leaderboard on day one. Penny had already phoned Gus to alert him and it took all his powers of self-control not to share such momentous news, even with his mistress. But this was too dangerous a rumour. Hugo was an old friend and such a slur could ruin his reputation, even if there was absolutely no truth in it as Gus didn't doubt for a moment there was.

Lemon had no such compunction and was happy to let the story slip among the more gossipy grooms. Soon, word was out: Hugo Beauchamp had not only been caught with his trousers down, but with his wife's sister, and he'd taken it too far.

Focussing totally on the competition, ignoring course talk as always, Lough had no idea what was being said, although Hugo's prompt departure hadn't gone unnoticed. That evening, avoiding the lorry-park parties as usual, making tom yum soup on the little gas hob of his horsebox, the punch of the lemon grass and ginger in his nostrils reminded him of the night he'd cooked it for Tash.

He picked up his phone, but stopped himself just in time. Instead he texted Beccy to ask how she was doing, the first contact he'd made since her accident. He knew she'd smashed her pelvis; it was a big blow.

It was typically the early hours of the morning before she replied, his phone beeping in the dark. Thinking it was his alarm, he half woke, reaching for it. Blinking sleep from his eyes, he read the message.

'Lem!' he bellowed, causing his little groom to fall off his bunk in the opposite corner of the box. 'What in hell is going on?'

That night, Tash couldn't sleep. Hugo denied the accusation, treating it with total contempt, but she didn't know who to believe any more.

Looking back, she found herself wondering whether she had noticed a change in him since that night. Her mind threw trick images and lights across her restless eyes as she lay awake into the early hours, thinking about recent weeks, the way Hugo had seemingly revelled in treating her like a sexual object and had wanted to control her more and more. He must think so little of her to drunkenly force himself on her stepsister. How many other women had he been cavorting with? There was the mystery V and possibly a host of others in England and America. All the time he'd been beating his chest fiercely and haranguing her about Lough, he'd carried on taking his own pleasure wherever he found it, at home and away.

As dawn broke she stole out of bed and pulled on the first clothes she could find, going commando in Hugo's jeans and an ancient shrunken T-shirt, creeping through the house and out into the yard.

She saddled up a surprised Mickey Rourke and rode out through sleeping Maccombe to the downs, flying along the ridge with tears streaking back into her hair.

She needed her mother more than ever, she realised with hopeless sobs. She was as frightened as she'd ever been.

As she rode back she saw a familiar sight weaving along the narrow lane from the Fosbournes, glossy and black. It was Lough's horsebox.

Just as he started to swing in through the Haydown gates, Lough looked out of his side window and spotted her. He abandoned his box right there, cutting the engine and blocking the drive as he jumped from the cab and sprinted across the lane, hurdling a low hedge and running up the track towards her.

When he drew level she pulled up and he looked up at her, dark eyes cavernous with concern, black hair on end. It needed cutting again, Tash found herself thinking.

'Oh Jesus, Tash, I never wanted this to be true.'

'It's *not* true!' She caught her breath. 'Just how many people knew about it? Was it in *Horse & Hound* or something? Did I miss the press release?'

'Get off the horse,' he begged.

'No.' She shook her head as Mickey strained to be home for his breakfast.

'Why not?'

'Because I won't,' she replied mulishly, knowing that to be on his level would to be lost, because he would touch her and comfort her and she so badly needed to be hugged and reassured, but if that happened she didn't trust herself.

'I want you to come back with me.'

'Back with you where? To the Moncrieffs?'

'We'll find somewhere. We'll live in the horsebox. I don't care. I love you. I need to look after you.'

'I have two children.'

'They're part of this,' he agreed. 'They come too.'

For just a moment, just a split second, the salvation that he offered was almost tempting, the run-away escape, the blot-it-out craziness of eloping.

But she was already shaking her head. 'No Lough. No. You rescued me once before. That's enough.'

'What?'

'Melbourne.' She reached down to him and he took her hand and pressed it to his lips, electricity shooting through them both. 'Thank you. But I can go it alone now. We both can.'

Straightening up, she looked out across the valley steeped in misty early-morning sunshine, to her beautiful strawberry house with its courtyards of stables, the ultimate happily ever after any pony-mad girl might dream. And inside that house was Hugo, more exciting and magnetic than any fantasy she'd conjured up when pop stars and heart-throb actors had eventually usurped ponies. When she had met him for the first time, in her teens, she really had believed that all her dreams would come true if only he loved her. Now it was a living nightmare.

Kicking a more than eager Mickey, she cantered down the hill, jumped the little hedge Lough had hurdled and clattered across the road, almost causing the post van to drive into the ditch as the big grey spooked at the horsebox.

The postman, pale from his near-miss and now hounded by the barking Roadies, thrust a big pile of mail straight at Tash through the window of his van.

Dismounting on the yard, she let Mickey wander to the water trough for a drink as she picked up the postcard from the top of the pile, her heart lifting as she recognised the uniform of the Cadre Noir at Saumur, a handsome cavalryman directing his horse in the expressive capriole in hand. It had to be from her mother, probably posted from a desert island. A set of postage stamps featuring a despotic-looking ruler and an unfamiliar alphabet obscured part of the horse's head. Alexandra always took a clutch of French postcards with her on holiday, an eccentricity her family had never understood, although she claimed it stemmed homesickness, in the same way that she regularly sent 'Greetings from Rural England' postcards from the Loire.

And when Tash read the reverse, she let out a grateful sob: *Home next week! So many traveller's tales to tell. Speak very soon. xxxx*

His chin in his hands and his heart like lead, Lough sat on the hill for a long time as the morning mist cleared, affording an incredible view over Haydown from so high above it.

He saw Tash running across the yard to the main house, then various grooms coming and going. A string of horses from a nearby training yard trotted along the village lane, their riders pointing out Lough's horsebox parked across Haydown's entrance. Then suddenly Tash reappeared with Amery in her arms and Cora at her knee.

Lough's heart lifted as she loaded them into a car, followed by a suitcase.

Stumbling and falling in his haste to run down the hill to meet her, certain that she had changed her mind, he saw Hugo coming out of the house dressed in nothing but an old pair of cut-off jeans, waving his arms around and pleading with her. Tash's ancient shortsighted dog was cowering at his heels, trying to press her greying muzzle anxiously to his leg. Tripping over her, Hugo shouted even more.

White-faced, Tash got in the car and started the engine. Hugo pressed his palms to his head and watched her reverse and swing around, the wheels spitting gravel.

Lough had reached the hedge, and it was not so easy to hurdle a second time. It caught his ankle and turned him over, causing him to crash down into a dry ditch.

He stood up just in time to see Tash driving through the gates. Misjudging the amount of space needed to get her wide off-roader past his horsebox, she forced her way through the gap with a terrible graunching noise as she scraped all the paint off one side and ripped a skirt-locker door clean off, leaving a gaping hole. It was a hole that matched the slash in Lough's heart when she drove straight past him and hurtled away through the village.

'The Wheels on the Bus' was booming through the open windows.

Lough stood in the lane for a long time, staring after her, heart bursting.

When he turned back to his lorry he realised that Hugo was in his gateway, dogs at his heels, studying the wrecked paintwork.

'She did a good job on that,' he pointed out.

Lough ignored him, walking towards the cab. His horses were still on board, kicking and snorting impatiently.

'I suppose you're behind this ridiculous accusation too,' Hugo hissed.

Lough stopped, one foot on the cab step.

'Well, you got what you wanted,' Hugo continued, running a

hand through his hair. 'Well done. Shame she doesn't want you either. All bets are off.'

Lough said nothing as he climbed into his lorry and reversed into the lane. Standing sentry beside the pack leader, her small body still shaking with anxiety, old Beetroot's barks were drowned out by the furious roar of the truck engine.

As the horsebox drove away Hugo turned to walk back through his gates, but then stopped, stooping down to pick up the twisted metal locker door that had been ripped off in Tash's getaway and hurling it furiously at one gatepost. His aim was surprisingly accurate as one ancient, lichened lion rampant toppled from its pedestal.

Chapter 74

Sylva had recently let her friendship with Indigo cool to almost nothing, although it was her one fragile link with Dillon beyond the media circus. Dong infuriated her and Pete had been away in Ireland all summer while his young wife prowled around the Abbey, adding yet more ethnic furnishings and children.

Their girls' lunches were now a rarity, but Sylva still regularly used the Raffertys' underground gym and pool, and sometimes borrowed a horse for an hour. Pete and Indigo had much flashier horses than Jules: Andalusian stallions in every available colour.

Today she texted Indigo to ask if she could take a dip and was relieved to receive the reply: *Be my guest. Running with Dong. Help yourself to whatever you like. It's all yours for the taking. Ix.* Sylva always preferred going to the Abbey when they were out.

She decided to take her new Lambretta for a run, noticing as she zipped out of Le Petit Château's electric gates that there were quite a few more paps than usual, and even a couple of grubby journalist types stepping from cars, but she didn't hang about to talk to them, giving her snappers their action shot of the day by accelerating past them with a wave and racing off along the sun-dappled village lane before cutting through an alley far too narrow for them to follow, loving the throaty little gurgle of the vintage engine. Dillon's management had good taste.

Being Dillon Rafferty's girlfriend was a very profitable affair and great for her public profile. Sylva now had almost as many Twitter followers as Stephen Fry, more hits on her website than a laughing baby on YouTube and her Facebook wall was plastered with more comments than graffiti on a New York subway. Ratings for *Sylva's Shadow* were up twenty per cent and she was in constant demand for photo shoots and exclusives, including renewing her contract with *Cheers!* for a seven-figure sum. Business was looking good: her named range of products were selling better than ever and she was adding more and more income streams, including soft furnishings and children's riding clothes. Her latest book had been a *Sunday Times* top-ten bestseller for eight weeks now, although she hadn't yet got around to reading it.

She seemed to spend her life in the back of cars, on planes and in hotels, but the only reading she had done lately was a very enlightening biography of legendary rock group Mask, and a more detailed biography of its lead singer and sole surviving member Pete Rafferty, more famous now of course for his subsequent solo career which had led him to be known simply as the Rockfather.

Her own ghostwritten books were of no interest, and more recently she had started to forsake her own press too. For the first time in her career she had no interest in following what was being written about her and whether or not she was IFOP. She was always IFOP now that she and Dillon were 'engaged', but reading about it depressed her – she preferred non-fiction. She was accustomed to her own publicity machine exaggerating facts and creating newsworthy angles to otherwise apparently mundane activities and events, but this had gone into overdrive as the Sylva and Dillon myth was created. A snap of the couple together had become one of the most valuable commodities on the open market. She currently had photographers following her day and night, knowing that one shot could pay their mortgage for a year.

Their respective management teams were boxing clever, reluctant to be the first to pull the plug because it could reflect so badly on two such popular celebrity figures who had both been through a bad time, and the fickle public could go either way if they split.

Sylva's team, spearheaded by Mama, played closer to the flames, and to *The Sun,* with leaked wedding plan stories galore, but they could afford to because she was seen as a more sympathetic figure than her husband-to-be. Dillon's team had retaliated with the strange tactic of romantic gifts that had been arriving on a regular basis at Le Petit Château all summer, delivery of which were joyously snapped by her paparazzi gatekeepers: first it was a diamond-encrusted gold pendant in the shape of a horse, then a huge abstract painting, statues for the garden, the baby-blue scooter she was riding now, miniature Ferraris for the boys, a little palomino pony for Zuzi, and endless bunches of flowers, all just signed 'Rafferty'. Dillon denied all knowledge, but Sylva knew positive PR when she saw it. The public lapped up these expensive scraps.

Dillon had been in the States for over a month, much of it sequestered in his ex in-laws' Malibu guest lodge. He was due to fly back with his daughters tomorrow, and they would spend a week of their summer vacation at West Oddford before going to Scotland to stay with their maternal great aunt while Dillon and Sylva finally put a stop to the press speculation.

The obvious thing was to aim for an amicable split, with nobody else involved, citing too many differences and busy lifestyles pulling in opposite directions, but the fact that the children were involved, as they had been from the start, made that a delicate process.

The parties had only just begun to negotiate. A holiday in Dillon's favourite St Croix hideaway, far from their young families, was being discussed as a stage-managed 'make or break', allowing them both to top up their tans and ensure that they were looking their best for the break.

Sylva had no great desire for a week alone with Dillon's nerviness and earnest organic food talk while awaiting the go-ahead to split up. It was hurricane season in the Caribbean, after all. If there was already a media storm raging at home, she would rather maximise impact by staying put and going for the big, explosive break-up, with the army of nannies protecting the kids. But the growing attachment between Pom and Zuzi was a sticking point.

When they were apart the girls sent endless emails and instant messages to each other with the help of their mothers, full of bad spellings and smiley faces and even photo attachments. Hana put the children first at all times, backed up by a surprise ally in Fawn, who Sylva was certain was only using her sister as a spy to find out what her ex-husband was up to when he was in the UK.

Sylva resented the way in which Hana was becoming increasingly interfering. She wanted their secret to be made public, and had even talked to Zuzi about it, preparing the little girl for a short burst of media interest. This infuriated Sylva; the press were already digging very deeply right now and she had no desire to bring any more of her own private scandal into the cat-and-mouse PR game she and Dillon were playing. Mama backed her completely and Hana was clearly livid at being overridden in any decisions about Zuzi's life. Only that morning Sylva had caught her sneakily texting Dillon with the aid of an English–Slovak dictionary to arrange for Zuzi and Pom to play together while his girls were at West Oddford. When Sylva rounded on her, she was unapologetic. 'The girls have a real relationship, unlike their parents.'

Sylva needed to escape for a few hours before she and her sister truly crossed swords – never a good thing for two former pentathletes. She opened the throttle on the little scooter and it growled up the hill.

She always loved the moment when she crested the ridge above the valley and Fox Oddfield Abbey loomed into view, the big iced cake of a Regency house ideal for a wedding. Not that there would be a wedding, but the fantasy was nice to spin out. As she swung her new baby-blue scooter into the drive her phone vibrated in her pocket. Under the shade of a tree, she cut the engine and pulled off her helmet to take the call.

'Sylva, Gaz Pratt – *News on Sunday*,' came a sneering, mosquito whine of a voice. 'Just want to let you know about a story we're running tomorrow concerning your daughter Zuzi, who we believe was adopted at birth in Slovakia by your older sister, Hana.'

Sylva went icy cold with fear.

'No comment!' She hung up and rang straight through to Clive Maxwell's private line. He was at the Cartier polo tournament. She could hear chatter and commentary behind him.

'I'm heading out to the Cotswolds later, as it happens. Don't leave the house until I get there.'

'I already have. I'm at Fox Oddfield Abbey.' She suddenly wondered how on earth she would get home and what would be waiting for her there. She'd made herself so vulnerable by bringing the scooter, with no driver to threaten to drive over photographers to protect her, nor did she have the blackened windows of the car to shield her. Her visor wasn't even tinted.

'Pete Rafferty's place?' Clive sounded gobsmacked.

'He's never here. I know his wife.'

Clive cleared his throat. 'Then you'll know you're about three days too late for a catch-up. Now get someone to come out there and pick you up. Warn your family what's happening. Where are Hana and Zuzi?'

'At home with Mama and the boys,' she said, a sudden suspicion starting to form.

'Do they know Zuzi's their sister?'

'No, they're too young to understand, but Zuzi knows.' Hana has done this, she thought. She's gone ahead and told the press anyway.

'Good, then you have already made this situation a lot, lot easier for her. Dillon?'

'He has no idea about any of it. He's flying back from the States today.'

'Can you contact him?'

She looked at her watch, counting back eight hours. 'Only his management until he lands.'

'Do it,' Clive said darkly. 'We're all aware that the only thing the public will really want to know about this story right now is how you react to this as a couple. Now let's get off this line so we can both make some calls. I'll see you later and we'll put a statement together.'

As she rang off she heard an engine approaching and, to her horror, recognised the distinctive green livery of the Cotswolds Celebrity Tours minibus heading towards her along the tiny, wooded lane that ran in front of Fox Oddfield Abbey, packed with eager tourists and their cameras fresh from checking out Liz Hurley's pad and Pete Doherty's den, now dying for a gawp at the Rockfather's base.

She pulled on her helmet and scrabbled with the Lambretta's ignition, but in her panic she over-choked it and it wouldn't start.

The big gates in front of her were closed, but she knew the key code and punched it in. To her relief, the gates started to crank open just as the minibus drew level and Sylva pushed the scooter through the gap as soon as it was wide enough.

'That will be a member of Pete's huge army of staff,' she heard a thick Gloucestershire accent announce as she hurriedly pushed the little bike along the tree-lined drive so that it was out of the line of view from the road. She propped it on its stand behind a big cedar and called Mama, wandering distractedly along the shaded outskirts of the parkland in front of the house. Glancing through the trees she noticed to her surprise that the helicopter was on its pad. Her heart lurched with unexpected force.

Mama was close to hysterics, convinced that it would blow everything, and shouting at Hana in Slovakian that she would pay for this. But Sylva felt curiously calm as she soothed her: 'It's a story about a very special, very loved little girl, Mama. We will deal with it.'

Having placated her mother and arranged for her to organise cars and decoys, she made another call, walking a little closer to the house. The Ferraris were gleaming in a neat red line around the gravel sweep like overpriced ornamental boulders. They only came out of their climate-controlled garages when Pete was in residence.

As she waited for Dillon's answering service to kick in she drew level with the first Ferrari. Just as the voicemail beep rang in her ear to start recording her message, she felt a click underfoot as she stepped on some sort of pressure pad, and suddenly a siren started to wail. Moments later a figure appeared beneath the portico.

'Oi!' a voice shouted and then, without any further warning, a gunshot rang out.

With a shriek Sylva turned and ran, dropping her phone, the line still open to Dillon's voicemail as it recorded the encounter in full.

She almost made it as far as her scooter when she heard a huge, growling engine behind her. She was no match for its speed as it overtook her, swinging perpendicular in a cloud of burning tyres to stop right in front of her, cutting off her exit route.

Sitting aboard a massive Harley-Davidson, cowboy boots on the pegs, was Pete Rafferty. He was laughing his head off, his battered leather face creased with delight, his very white teeth and very blue eyes sparkling like roulette chips.

He cut the throbbing engine.

'I said,' he rasped in his trademark voice, 'oi!'

'I'm sorry.' She held up her hands, sounding more like a Bond girl than ever. 'I will leave straight away.'

'Do that, Trouble, and I might be forced to use this again.' He picked up the gun that he'd wedged behind him.

She held her hands higher, making him laugh even more. 'You are the sweetest thing. Come in for a drink. You liked the scooter then?' He shouldered the gun and indicated the Lambretta with a jerk of his head.

Sylva was too frightened to do more than nod, but things were starting to add up rather thrillingly.

'Race you,' he laughed, stretching down to pick up her abandoned helmet and hand it to her.

'That's not a fair match,' she managed to squeak. 'Your bike is bigger.'

He swung his leg off the Harley and stepped back, bowing to her as he indicated its leather seat. 'All yours, Trouble. I'll take the little Italian.' And he straddled the Lambretta. He was no giant – maybe five ten and wiry rather than muscular – but he still looked like a Highland chieftain on a Shetland pony.

Sylva cautiously swung her leg over the Harley, loving the sensation of warm leather against her groin. She was only wearing a tiny slip dress and the flimsiest of bikini briefs ready for a swim.

She'd posed on Harleys several times in her career; it was a classic glamour-model cliché. And she wasn't the sort of girl to let opportunities like that slip by without taking one for a run on several occasions. As Pete started the little scooter and raced ahead whooping, she kicked the hog back into life and roared after him. His expression of surprise as she raced past was one she would treasure. She slid the big bike to an angled halt in front of his house and wriggled back on the seat to make space for him.

'You show me how to really ride this thing!'

Grinning, he ditched the scooter in a flash and climbed aboard, trying not to show the wince of pain at his stiff hips.

For a heady twenty minutes, the Rockfather was in his element, the wind in his long hair as he took her on a whistle-stop tour of the freshly tarmaced private roads on his estate, beautiful black stripes snaking through an immaculate green playpen with its pollarded and fenced trees, shady walks and follies, the ultimate park for a latter-day rake, his thousands of acres kept show-stoppingly pristine for his very few visits each year.

Which could not be said of the house when they finally spilled inside, sun-drenched and wind-swept, weaving their way from one of the back entrances through a labyrinth of corridors.

'Brace yourself,' Pete warned her as they passed endless domestic offices with panelled, half-glazed walls. 'It's worse than you remember it. Indigo's wreaked havoc,' he moaned. 'She trashed the place before she walked out. It'll take years to put right.'

Sylva suddenly realised what he was saying.

'She's left?'

'A couple of days ago. Run off with her shrink – in every sense of the word. The man's a midget. Dong. Have you met him?'

They'd arrived in a basement kitchen as big as a squash court, which had been decorated to resemble a rainforest, with floor-to-ceiling ipé cabinets and an extraordinary chandelier of green glass mouldings like a tree canopy suspended over a central island that had a waterfall running through it and eight little breakfast-bar settings still laid around it.

'Took the kids.' Pete sighed deeply. 'Says I'm no father to them, which is probably right, but she kept getting more of the little bleeders. How was I supposed to remember all their names?' He opened a fridge as big as a garage. 'Krug or Cristal?'

'Whatever you prefer.'

'I'm teetotal,' he said ruefully, popping the cork on a vintage Cristal rosé. 'I still miss boozing. It just doesn't feel the same emptying a bottle of Perrier water over a groupie in a hotel room.'

He handed her a brimming flute and they headed up in to the main house.

It looked immaculate, the minimalist rooms with their wicker and carpet panelling, tribal masks and shields on the walls, earthy Budda Bags, central fires, prayer mats and exotic musical instruments all as strange and staged as Sylva remembered.

'I thought you said Indigo trashed this place when she left?'

'Not *when* she left,' he said, following her carrying a can of Coke. 'Before she left, when she lived here. Look at it! It's like living in a fucking African village.'

'It's where she came from,' she reminded him. 'It's how she felt at home.'

'She came from Bishops Stortford. Her dad's a postman. She made up all that Somali stuff to further her career.'

'You're kidding?' Sylva was agog.

'Bloody hell, it's over!' He let out a whoop, kicking a sag bag into orbit. 'She has been a living nightmare these last couple of years, collecting another orphan every time we had a row or I had a quick roll in the hay. At least the first Mrs Rafferty only collected dogs, cats and the odd horse. Indigo was out of control.'

'It really is over?' Sylva checked.

'It really is over,' he confirmed, settling on a huge floor cushion with a low groan as his hips gave another twinge. 'She's been banging on about divorce all year. She just needed an excuse.' He fixed her with his wicked gaze. 'I reckon they brought you in to test my mettle.'

'Me?'

'Indigo knows our pre-nup pays out double if I get caught with my pants down, so they brought in bait to tempt me – a gorgeous blonde who just happens to be my son's new bird. Bad old Pete would have had you upside down and pulling your pants off with his teeth within five minutes.' He chuckled fondly at the memory.

'So why didn't you?' Sylva thought it sounded great fun.

Pete gave her a look that made her bikini hot up against her skin. 'Believe me, I was tempted. But I've mellowed. My son's a good lad and I want him back in my life.'

Sylva looked away, irritated by the direction of the conversation and his shift from groupie shagger to indulgent father.

'So Indigo won't double her money after all.' Pete heaved himself upright with another groan of effort. 'And she won't get her Abbey Ever After either.' He walked up to a floor-to-ceiling window that looked out over his immaculate parkland. 'But she will get a father for her kids, and now she's found Ding-Dong, she doesn't need the Rockfather any more. She even reckons they're in love, which is quite cute really, 'cos she scares me shitless.' He cackled, turning back to look around the room again. 'I reckon I could like it here without the bongos and raffia. Time to get the decorators in.' He turned to her, wicked smile dancing. 'I'll get some of your new bedding, I reckon. Saw an ad in the Sunday papers last week and thought, that looks like something I want spread out on my bed every night.'

Sylva flushed excitedly. She knew the advert he meant, featuring her obviously naked and slithering luxuriously beneath sheets from her Sylva at Home bedding range that claimed to be Egyptian cotton but had a lower thread count than a fishnet stocking.

'Glad you're following my career,' she smirked, checking her phone which had just beeped with a text announcing that her driver was at the back gates.

'Stay for another glass.' He took her empty flute.

'I can't. I've got to get home and sort something out. I have a crisis meeting with Clive Maxwell later.'

'Me too.' He laughed uproariously, loving the happenstance. 'You know what mine's about. What's your situation? Don't tell me Dillon's been messing you about? He's far too strait-laced.'

She shook her head, suddenly feeling panicky again. 'It's something I did many years ago.'

'Another teenage lesbian affair?'

He'd read her cuttings, she realised.

'A love child.'

'Oh, I know all about those,' he reassured her, leathery face sympathetic. 'Got several myself.'

'It was years ago. In Slovakia. I was very young – still in my teens. I was on the Slovak pentathlon team then, and Zuzi's father was on the men's team. It's a big sport in my country. All I cared about was going to the Olympics. When I found out I was pregnant, I thought my dream was over. I wanted to get rid of the baby but Mama convinced me that would be a sin. We had enough time for me to train again afterwards and win gold for my country, she said.'

He whistled. 'That's dedicated.'

She shook her head. 'My sporting career was over: I had disgraced my team and was not welcome back. I was heartbroken. Mama found me a manager to promote my singing instead. My sister looked after the baby as her own. She is eight years older than me and her marriage was childless; they had been told there was no hope of children. We are a close family. We kept Zuzi a secret – that is my little girl. Hana's little girl, you have met them both.'

'And the press have got hold of the story?'

She nodded. 'Tomorrow's headlines. I must get home to deal with it. My driver is waiting outside.'

'Don't go just yet.' He reached out his hand and took hers, kissing it. It was a curiously old-fashioned gesture.

'You're not wearing your engagement ring.'

'Too much fake about me already,' she said carelessly.

Pete's gaze trapped hers. They both felt it again, that instinctive attraction so strong that it seemed to pull the walls in around them.

'Nothing fake about this,' he breathed.

'Nothing.' Her bikini felt as though it was on fire now.

'You're not really going to marry my son, are you?' The blue eyes, twice as intense as Dillon's at close range, seared into her face.

Sylva shook her head.

'Good.' He lifted the hand to his lips and kissed each finger. 'Because I'm going to buy a ring for every one of these pretty little things, with diamonds as big as wing nuts on them.' He bit her little finger quite hard, making her squeal deliciously.

The plug was pulled on her self-control and great whirlpools of lust eddied through her.

'I have wanted you since the moment I set eyes on you. You have no idea of the restraint I've had to show staying away from here these past few weeks.' He moved closer, his lips on her neck.

'Dillon's been nowhere near me. It's all for the papers.'

'That's not like Dillon. He hates being in the papers.' He slid the straps of her dress from her shoulders.

'It's what *I* do for a living.'

'We've all got to earn a living.' He stepped back, letting her dress slip down. 'And what a piece of living art you are!' He whistled, admiring the bodywork from all angles. He'd always liked custom-made cars and he was the same with women. This one could have been made to his exact specifications. She even had piercings to match his so they'd jingle when they screwed face to face.

'Get upstairs now,' he growled, narrowing his eyes.

'We can do it here.' She was already undoing his flies.

There was a time when Pete would have shagged Sylva up against the ornate panelling, only pausing to inhale a line of coke from her collarbone. Now he eyed the floor cushions doubtfully. He didn't think he could make it down there again easily and he needed to get to his drugs.

'Upstairs now,' he ordered. 'Or you're in trouble, Trouble.'

Sylva shuddered, thrilling at his arrogance. He was totally rock 'n' roll.

Following stiffly behind her in every sense of the word, Pete hoped the mighty Fender fretboard would stay true, but by the time his creaking hips and painful knees had made it up the majestic Abbey stairs he was shrunken to a ukulele and out of puff.

'Not in there!' He managed to wheeze to redirect Sylva who was heading for the master suite, another mud hut homage. He waved her towards one of the few rooms he had designed himself.

'Check out my sin bin.'

Meanwhile he dived into the adjacent bathroom to catch his breath and take an ibuprofen and a Viagra, the only drugs he used to enhance his sex life these days.

When he emerged through the interconnecting door Sylva was lying on a very battered old leather sofa, gazing around her at walls covered with photographs and platinum disks. She had expected a bondage chair, leather walls and chains, a few whips and cuffs, not a framed picture of Pete with Nelson Mandela and an old twelve-string propped up against the sofa.

'Why do you call this the sin bin?'

'Force of habit. All the Mask boys had a sin bin once we could afford a decent gaff – an inner sanctum, if you like. It's where I come to think.'

She smiled deliciously, sliding a finger beneath the jewelled clip on one side of her bikini briefs. 'And what are you thinking about now?' Her eyes widened as the legendary Fender came back into play, all twenty-two frets ready to be fingered.

'I'm thinking how much fun it'll be to get in to Trouble.'

Ping! One clip snapped open. '*You* sent me all those gifts, didn't you? The flowers and the jewellery and the presents for the children?'

He nodded, dropping his leather trousers and stepping out of them with practised skill, like a snake shedding its skin. 'Force of habit. If I see something I like I have to buy it. If I see a woman I like, I have to buy her presents. Two pleasures combined.'

Ping! The other side of her bikini G-string popped apart. 'I guess I should thank you.'

'I guess you should.' He stepped forwards and she sat up to sample a rock legend.

When Clive Maxwell arrived at Fox Oddfield Abbey later for the crisis meeting, he showed no surprise at the sight of Sylva lounging seductively on an ethnic sag bag dressed in nothing but a vintage Mask T-shirt and a pair of boxer shorts. Instead, he got straight down to business:

'You want to nick your son's fiancée and come up smelling of roses?' he asked Pete.

'In a nutshell.'

'You want public sympathy for giving away your first born as a teenager,' he checked with Sylva, 'and then later dumping the world's favourite sad ballad singer and organic farmer (who adores your children) in favour of his dad?'

She nodded.

Clive had handled plenty of relationship break-ups on the celebrity scene in his twenty years as a PR guru, but this was a complicated situation, even by his standards.

'Leave it with me,' he reassured them. 'Just don't say a thing to anybody for now. And *don't* get caught together.'

Chapter 75

Rory was determined to be discharged from hospital so that he could get back to his horses. The consultants were reluctant to let him go, but he lied that he had no immediate plans to ride and that his mother was taking him for a relaxation and meditation holiday in the New Forest, and they reluctantly acquiesced. He then begged a lift from Faith, who brought along Twitch for an ecstatic reunion, the little dog lean and fit after a month as chief Lime Tree Farm rat-catcher. 'MC had him transported to the Beauchamps along with your horses, but the Rat Pack kept chasing him away so Tash sent him to us.'

As they crawled south on the A34 in endless holiday traffic she filled him in with the latest Haydown news: 'The official line is that Tash has taken the kids for a holiday, but Gus is pretty convinced that she's left him. Hugo won't talk about it, apparently.'

'Ish Beccy really preshing chargesh?'

'Of course not! She never claimed it was more than a drunken mistake, but it's been blown out of all proportion by the jungle drums. Who told you about it?'

'Firsht I heard was a couple of texts from the usual shuspects. Then Lough came to see me the day Tash left and shaid much the same as you. Poor shod; I think he jusht wanted to lie low for a few hours. He doesn't give a lot away, but he wash pretty dejected.'

Faith hid a smile; Rory was sounding more like Sean Connery as his voice gradually improved. 'Not half as dejected as Hugo.'

'What wash he doing with *Beccy*, of all people?'

'She's very pretty,' Faith defended her friend.

'Hugo must be mad. If he was going to play around you'd think he's at leasht do it with shomeone hot like Venetia, not a hippy girl groom who alsho happens to be a member of his extended family.'

'You'd think he'd be faithful in the first place,' she snapped, unpleasantly aware that she herself was a mere girl groom and could technically be counted a member of Rory's extended family by dint of her grandfather's long-standing affair with his mother.

'Yesh, yesh!' he agreed, back-pedalling fast. 'If I had the woman of my dreamsh, there's no way I'd do anything like that. I'd be totally faithful for life. Hugo's an idiot. But he hash my horses right now, so I think it best not to mention my opinion on the matter. He needsh my help.'

She shook her head. 'You're the one who needs looking after right now, Rory.'

'I'm fine,' he insisted, rather more forcefully than he intended. He was tired of being seen as an invalid, particularly by Faith who had once looked up to him as such a hero. He wanted to get back to form as quickly as possible, to recapture the old Rory who could win the grand slam and the girl. 'I jusht need to get on with my job away from dishtractions,' he explained. 'I musht get to Burghley. That meansh more to me than anything.'

Faith went very quiet after this, dropping him at the Haydown gates and explaining that she couldn't stay because she was already on borrowed time. 'Gus will dock my wages – at least he would if he ever paid me. Don't overdo it. Good luck with Hugo. I'll call later.'

Knowing that Hugo was desperately short-handed and needed him back even if he was too proud to admit it, Rory hadn't phoned ahead. The yard was deserted, although the horseboxes were both parked up, meaning no one was away competing. Finding the key to the lodge cottage hidden beneath the usual plant pot, Rory let himself in to drop off his bags. It was obvious that nobody had been in since he and Lough left straight after Badminton; there was dust and mess everywhere.

He headed back to the yard, the sun directly overhead making him feel headachy already – he'd barely stepped outside in a fort-night. His horses were all back at Haydown, transported while he was in hospital, no doubt organised by MC. She'd sent him a very sweet card and flowers after his accident, saying there were no regrets.

He walked around his boys, breathing in their familiar smell and strength, loving the peace and fresh air of yard life after the sterile bustle of hospital.

Heart was missing, he realised, looking into the empty box where the big horse usually stood guard, bobbing his head for attention.

Glancing at his watch, Rory went back to feed Rio the rest of his packet of mints. 'You have to win Burghley for me and your mistress,' he whispered. 'Help me prove I can do this and win the woman of my dreamsh. Then I'll be very faithful indeed.'

The sound of a car coming through the arch took him outside again. It was Franny in a faded Team Mogo polo shirt and hot pants, weighed down with Lidl bags. 'Boy, do we need you!' she greeted him. 'I bet Hugo even cracked a smile now you're back.'

'Where ish he?'

'I thought he was here.' She dropped the bags outside the office and pushed at the door, but it was locked. 'I just ran into Basborough for supplies – there's not so much as a teabag in here or the house and Hugo has no food in whatsoever. How long have you been here?'

'About forty minutes.'

'That's odd.' She pulled out her mobile and tried Hugo's number, but there was no answer. 'He was just putting Heart on the walker when I left.'

They both turned to look at the horse walker. It was empty.

'He not in his stable.' Rory remembered.

'Oh shit. I bet he's bloody taken off again. He's impossible to keep hold of right now.'

The quad bike was also missing.

'Hugo must have gone after him.' Franny rushed back to her car. 'I'll start going round the lanes. You get up on the downs.'

'How?' Rory had no car, and his head was throbbing hotly now.

But Franny was already starting the engine.

Rory headed for the tractor and found to his relief that the keys were still in it. With a great diesel roar he reversed it away from the muck heap and set off along the beech-wood track towards the Haydown downland above Maccombe village. At the highest point, he cut the engine and climbed up on to its roof. Two red kites were circling overhead, eyeing him curiously as he cupped his hands together and shouted. One of the birds angled its forked tail to swoop closer, calling back with its long, meowing whistle. Nothing else answered.

Scanning the landscape around him for signs of movement, Rory took out his phone to call Franny for an update, but there was no signal.

Then, just as he was about to climb down, he spotted the familiar shape of the quad bike at the base of the scarp, where there was a rocky stretch of land known as the Glacier Pasture. Sliding down though the chalky grass to investigate, Rory could just make out Hugo in the shadow of the oak wood at its far corner. The horse was nowhere to be seen. He sprinted across the bumpy field.

'Oh Christ!' He gaped in horror when he saw what had happened to Heart.

A stream ran the length of the woods, creating a natural boundary where chalk soil gave way to heavy clay, its steep banks creating a narrow gorge of fast-moving water six feet deep in parts.

The horse had turned over in the narrowest gully, his neck trapped under an old fallen tree trunk and his head half-submerged in the stream. The water around him was red with blood. Huge gashes in one bank showed where he must have slipped on landing, the soft ground giving way beneath him and tipping him back into the trench.

Up to his waist in the stream as he battled to keep the horse's head above the water, Hugo was drenched and covered in blood and mud.

'He's still alive,' he told Rory, teeth gritted with effort, 'but I'm not sure for how long. He was panicking like stink when I found him which is why his neck's stuck like this. It's my fault he took off. I was leading him when my phone rang, lost concentration for a second and, woomph, he was up on his hind legs and away. There's no mobile signal here, not even SOS, and I can't let go because he'll go under water if I do.'

'I'll get help.'

'Take the quad. Phone Jack Fotheringham – you'll get reception on the far side of the wood. Tell him the horse has severed an artery near his off hind hock. Then fetch ratchet straps and tarps, and a wood saw. And any spare bodies you can to help.'

Rory ran for the quad bike, ignoring the screaming pains in his head. The woods seemed never-ending, the tracks riddled with pot-holes, boulders and deep, muddy puddles. At last he broke into sunlight again and raced up the familiar slope of the field known as Thirty Acres.

Ten minutes later, Gus took a call from Rory.

'I donnowhatodo!' his words were slurring even more than usual because he was panicking. 'Jack Fotheringhamshata sheminar in Newmarket; the clinic can't getanothervet here foranhour.'

Promising to be straight over, Gus rushed off to find Penny, but Lough was alone on the yard, washing off Toto. 'She and the others all hacked out about half an hour ago.'

'I'll have to go without her.' Gus started throwing shovels in the back of his Toyota. 'Hugo can't keep the tourniquet on the hind leg while he's holding the horse's head up. I don't think there's much chance of getting him out alive, frankly.'

'I'm coming too,' Lough said before he quickly led Toto back to his stable.

'Do you think that's wise?'

He re-emerged, squinting in the sunlight, deep voice gritty with determination. 'The horse will bleed to death without veterinary treatment. I'll just fetch my kit.'

Hugo had been struggling to keep Heart's head up for a long time. At first the horse had fought for all he was worth to escape, thrash-ing and kicking, sending water and mud and blood flying. But he had already galloped his legs off by the time he slipped into the ditch in the first place and the adrenalin had quickly dissipated. Now he was lethargic and resigned to his fate, his handsome head heavy in Hugo's arms, the heart-shaped star hard to discern amid the dirt and blood. He'd gashed his eye and poll, but that was nothing to the thick red stream still pumping from his hind leg. Hugo was literally stand-ing in a river of blood, his arms riddled with cramps, his body so cold that his teeth chattered now that the sun had dropped lower behind the oak wood and cast him in deeper shadow. He'd stopped being able to feel his feet half an hour ago.

At last Rory buzzed back on the quad bike with straps, chains and a heavy canvas tarpaulin ready to lift the horse out.

'Is the vet coming?' Hugo called, his voice cramped with cold.

Unable to trust his slurred voice, Rory just gave a thumbs-up as he passed and rocketed up the steep slope to fetch the abandoned tractor.

A moment later Gus's pick-up truck appeared, weaving through the boulders like he was in *Wacky Races*, and Hugo felt weak with relief. He gripped Heart's head tighter, kissing him on his cold, drenched muzzle. 'We'll get you out of here. Just hang on in there. Gus! Thank God. Apply some pressure to that hock will you?'

Then Lough Strachan stepped from the pick-up.

'What's he doing here?'

'He's a vet. You need a vet.'

'He's not coming anywhere near my horse!' Hugo hissed through chattering teeth.

Gus stooped down to his head level, dropping his voice. 'Right now, you have a choice: give this animal a fighting chance by pulling together for its sake, or carry on throwing blows until you're flogging a dead horse.

Hugo glared up at him. 'Did you give Lough that little pep talk too?'

'I didn't need to. He volunteered.'

Lough didn't look at Hugo as he got to work, putting a clamp on the artery to stop it bleeding and then giving a small dose of sedative and painkiller combined: 'He's pretty exhausted, but he'll start fighting again once we try moving him so it's best to keep him calm. A bit of dope will do him no harm.'

'Not the first time you've said that, I'll bet,' Hugo muttered, but Lough ignored him as the others began to slip the wide straps beneath the horse.

It took the four men almost an hour to get Heart out of the ditch, but eventually he was lifted out in a makeshift sling attached to the tractor's front loader as easily as moving a bag of fertiliser. Muddied, exhausted and bedraggled, they formed a bizarre cavalcade as they drove back to the yard, the tractor in the lead bearing the sedated horse in a tarpaulin sling like an oversized stork's bill, followed by the quad and the pick-up truck. All rolled under the arch and into the yard to be greeted by a loudly-cheering Franny, who'd prepared a bed in one of the open-fronted stalls.

As soon as the horse had been lowered to the ground, Lough worked quickly and quietly to sterilise and close the wound. The internal stitching was incredibly delicate and he was horribly out of practice, not wanting to let the others see how much his hands were shaking. It took him twice as long as it once would have to put in twenty external sutures, working slowly and meticulously, determined to leave as minimal a scar as possible.

'He's lost a lot of blood,' he told his audience, 'but not enough to need a transfusion and there should be no ill effects from lack of supply. There's no reason he won't be a hundred per cent sound on this leg again as long as he's given time to recover and the old injury hasn't flared up after his run, of course.'

'He got away from me,' Hugo said. 'Jumped clean over the yard gates and all the post and rails between here and Thirty Acres.'

Rory whistled. 'He's got shome scope.'

'Most exciting horse I know,' Hugo agreed, stooping to scratch Heart's neck and withers, putting him on a level with Lough, who was applying a dressing. He turned to him briefly. 'Thank you.'

Lough nodded, saying nothing.

The tension between them was monumental, but nobody could doubt Hugo's integrity or Lough's skill.

Eager to lighten the mood, Rory gave a jolly laugh that somewhat misfired, coming out as more of a Kenneth Williams sneer, his speech bad because he was wiped out. 'Teach youneverto anshwer your mobile when leading a horsh,' he told Hugo.

'I didn't get a chance to take the call.'

'Letsh hope it washn't important.'

'It was Tash.'

There was an awkward pause.

Gus appeared from behind the pick-up where he'd been smoking a cigarette, then thought better of it and went back to light up another.

At last Lough stood up from bandaging the leg. 'All done.'

'Good.' Hugo turned back to the house. 'If you'll all excuse me, I have a call to make. There's brandy and hot drinks in the tack room. Franny can look after you. Welcome back, Rory. Come for supper later if you're not too bushed.' He walked out of earshot, dogs at his heels.

'That's as close as you and I will get to a personal thank you.' Gus wandered back to Rory's side at the stable door, fag dangling from his mouth. 'Good to see you out and about again.'

Rory nodded wanly.

'Have you got analgesics?' Lough asked as he put his equipment back in the pick-up.

Rory shook his head. 'I left them behind at the hospital.'

Lough pressed a foil blister pack of tablets into Rory's hand. 'Take two every four hours dissolved in water.'

'What is it?' he eyed the pills suspiciously.

'Soluble Disprin.' He smiled. 'Strictly for human consumption.'

Rory waved them off and left Franny finishing off the yard.

He wanted to crawl straight into bed, but he managed to shower and change in to clean clothes before heading through the walled garden to call on Hugo, who was charring some sausages in his honour. The familiar comforts of the huge, warm kitchen were lost without Tash at its helm. Like the rest of the house, it was a tip.

'Silly and Verruca buggered off back to Czechoslovakia – sorry, the Czech Republic – last week,' Hugo explained. 'They seem to think that Tash has left me, so they decided to follow suit.'

Rory crammed his mouth with sausages because he didn't know quite what to say, and didn't trust his tired head to say it without slurring too badly to be understood. His own experience of broken marriages was limited, largely based as it was upon his mother, who was a notorious bolter. But when Truffle had left a husband she'd always had another lined up. Tash had run away from Lough as well as Hugo. That had to bode well.

'I'msureshe'llbebackshoon,' he said encouragingly, but it came out so jumbled and sibilant that Hugo clearly didn't take in a word. He just looked sad as he stared into his empty wine glass.

On the table between them, Rory's phone rang out with 'Jessica's Theme' from *The Man from Snowy River*, a photograph of Faith on Whitey lighting up on its screen. Cheeks instantly streaking deep red like sunset clouds, he politely apologised. 'I'll ring her back.'

'Take the call.' Hugo stood up. 'Trust me, you might not get another chance.'

Head throbbing more intensely than ever, Rory grabbed his phone.

'How are you?' she demanded anxiously.

'Great!' he feigned gusto. Hugo was still well within earshot, opening another bottle of wine.

'Really?' she sounded doubtful.

'Marvelloush!'

'And Hugo?'

'Edgy!'

'I heard there was high drama earlier.'

'All shorted!'

'Are you honestly feeling okay? You sound odd.'

'Not odd at all! Marvelloush!'

'You're with Hugo,' she finally twigged.

'Absholutrely!' He stood up and headed into the rear lobby for some privacy, leaning against a wall because he was suddenly very light-headed.

'And you're shattered, aren't you?'

'Rather!' His exclamations were losing some of their pizzazz.

'Go to bed. You are recovering from a serious head injury. I repeat, a *serious* head injury.'

'Understood!'

'I'll come and muck out your horses first thing tomorrow.'

'Not on your nelly! I repeat, *not* on your nelly!' He hung up, feeling faint.

Hugo found him squatting by the gun-room door, his head between his knees.

He patted him on the shoulder. 'Thank you for your company tonight. You need rest – go to bed. We'll muck out your horses in the morning.'

'Thanks.' Rory was feeling too ill now to protest.

Chapter 76

In the heat-baked Loire Valley the sunflowers were turning their heads from east to west through the day without the shadow of a cloud crossing their faces. Alongside these slowly shifting yellow acres, the fields of solar panels followed their movement. It was a landscape of paradox, modernity living cheek by jowl with age-old customs: nuclear power stations loomed over fields of ancient vines tended by hand; modern metalled roads skirted magnificent old estates with fairytale châteaux luxuriating in their lush park-land.

Le Manoir Champegny, nestled on the side of a hill overlooking the river just east of Saumur, was among the Loire's prettiest country residences, a full-scale doll's house with turreted towers built from creamy local tuffeau stone. Its broad, leafy flanks were patterned with shuttered casement windows fringed by scented climbers, and pretty circular dormers peeking from the grey slate roof. It was wildly romantic, with Juliet balconies and hidden court-yards, terraces on a multitude of levels shaded by vine-laden pergolas and vast, sculptural pots of topiary and fragrant shrubs. Beneath it lay a garden full of secret glades and paths, fruit orchards and a mosaic swimming pool that glittered like a big square sapphire tempting the house's occupants to cool off. It was in this impossibly seductive, romantic setting that Hugo had first fallen for Tash with that fierce, proud passion that had now apparently burned itself out.

She had wonderful memories of summers at Champegny: the entire family gathered around the pool, bickering and laughing and debating; the amazing feasts that seemed to last all night with gallons of wine from the manoir's own little vineyard; the days on the river with picnics and dinghies; trips to watch the Cadre Noir and visit the museum of the horse in Saumur, to hear al fresco recitals in Tours, or wander around glorious châteaux.

This trip had no such lustre of ripe grapes and sweet orchard fruit. Mildew had wrecked the harvest, rotten apples and sour grapes haunted her, and decay was running through the roots of her haven in the Garden of France.

When she arrived in the blazing midday heat she didn't imme-diately see the changes at Le Manoir, the way the garden had overgrown, the house had begun to crumble and corrode, the air of neglect and decrepitude. She was too wrapped up in her own agony, in the stress of driving two tots through France with tears continu-ally welling up, pain in her heart and unspoken pleas to Hugo running through her head and across her lips. Arriving was her single goal, and she had achieved it. All looked comfortingly famil-iar at that moment, down to the chickens pecking in the courtyard and the spaniels surging in a skewbald stream from the house; she hadn't thought beyond this arrival, apart from the reunion with her mother and the hug that she so desperately needed.

Appearing at last in the doorway, Alexandra looked quite extraordinary in an orange and purple kaftan, her skin tanned deep walnut and her neat, shiny bob now pure white. She was slimmer than ever.

'Caught dysentery in India. Great for the figure,' she explained, rushing forward to embrace her daughter. 'Tash, sweetheart, you feel like you've had a bout of it too – there's nothing to you.' She stooped to gather up her grandchildren. 'My lovely Cora – and Amery! We meet at last. My goodness, you are so handsome! *Just* like your father.'

Tash burst into tears.

Striding out of the house behind his wife, Pascal had been about to bear down on his favourite stepdaughter with kisses and Gallic bonhomie, but faced with a vision of wailing heartache he abruptly diverted his welcome towards the children, whom Alexandra swiftly handed into his care. The ultimate double act, they communicated with just a brief exchange of nods so that Pascal swept the disoriented toddlers away with promises of chickens, geese and ponies to admire, while Alexandra ushered Tash into the house for a strong drink and more hugs.

'What is it, my darling?'

As the enormity of her messy marriage struck her afresh, Tash found she couldn't even begin to explain. Instead, she hid behind cliché. 'I'm just tired,' she said lamely. 'You're even harder to pin down in France than you are when you were globe-trotting.'

It had been a nightmarish journey, with the car breaking down just outside Caen, forcing her to book into a hotel for two nights while the mechanic ordered parts. There, she found she'd left her BlackBerry at home with her address book stored on it and so couldn't ring around her mother's many numbers to find out whether they had arrived back in France and if so where they were, and her calls to Hugo seemed destined to be answered by a machine. When she'd finally got hold of somebody in Pascal's office who knew the d'Eblouirs' whereabouts, she was told that they were in Paris, Marsailles *and* the Loire, which hardly helped.

'Polly wanted to stay on in Paris after we landed, but I was desperate to see this place again,' Alexandra explained, hugging her again. 'Darling Pascal had to fly down to the coast to see his mother – she's almost a hundred now, you know. But he's back now and you found us, so we must celebrate being together.' Alexandra filled two small sherry glasses with clear liquid from an unmarked brown bottle. 'Jean's *eau de vie*. You remember him?'

Tash nodded; nobody could forget Le Manoir's ancient retainer, now widowed and living in the village with his large family, most of whom still worked for the d'Eblouirs. The drink was pure fire, but at least it scorched some much-needed colour into her cheeks and warmed her belly.

They settled in the Blue Room at the back of the house, which years ago Tash had helped decorate as an impoverished art school student, with little *trompe l'oeil* streaks of cirrus crossing the cerulean plaster ceilings. Now she had no such blue-sky thinking she wanted to grab a stepladder to add thunderclouds and the odd flash of lightning.

'Will Hugo be joining us this week?' Alexandra settled beside her as she gazed into space.

Tash said nothing, listening to the spaniels snuffling around underfoot and the lone cockerel patrolling on the highest terrace crowing outside the windows. Pascal had taken the children into the garden below now and little chatters and giggles indicated an *entente cordiale*. Hearing them, she started to cry again.

'Oh sweetheart.' Alexandra drew her daughter's head beneath her chin and stroked her hair. 'I shouldn't have gone away so long. I might have guessed you'd get in a terrible pickle.'

'I must c-call h-him.' Tash straightened up eventually. 'W-would you and Pascal mind looking after the children for just a little bit longer?'

'Of course.' Alexandra patted her knee. 'We'll talk later. Come and find us in the garden when you're ready.'

Tash went next door to Pascal's book-lined study and dialled Hugo's mobile, her heart ratcheting its way up into her mouth when she heard him answer.

'We're here,' she managed to croak. 'Are you okay?'

'Fine.'

The silence between them stretched on. She could hear music in the background and someone complaining loudly that the bridle numbers were missing before apologising when he realised Hugo was on the phone.

'Is that Rory?'

'He's lending a hand. We're at Knotton Manor.'

Tash chewed her lip. A year earlier the big Leicestershire trials had been the British Olympic team's final run. Heavily pregnant with Amery, Tash and Cora had gone to cheer Hugo on. They'd all camped in the horsebox, a supportive, happy little unit. Twelve months on, she could hardly believe they were the same family. 'How's it going?'

'Not great,' he admitted.

Another voice was talking in the background now, a booming female tenor, demanding to know whether the call was from Tash. 'Give the phone to me *now*, Hugo.'

There were several tussling, thudding sounds and then, to her horror, Tash found herself on the end of the line to her mother-in-law, who spared no time or rod in waging an attack. 'I thought better of you, Natasha. D'you know how selfish it is swanning orff on holiday at a time like this? We need you. I had to cancel a bridge evening to come here.' She ignored Hugo's protests that he hadn't even asked her along. 'You must come home *at once*. D'you know how bad this looks for Hugo? All he did was fondle a pretty girl at a party. Now you've gorn it looks so much worse. Show some bloody backbone and stand by your man. If you can't toughen up, God help you when you find out about any others.'

At this point Hugo managed to wrench the phone from his mother and there was a lot of background movement as Rory escorted Alicia out of the horsebox for some fresh air. When he came back on the line, he was obviously alone. 'Sorry about that.'

Tash ran her fingers along the carved scrollwork of Pascal's desk. 'What does she mean by "others"?'

'I have no idea. She's gone quite mad since you left. When are you coming home?'

'Not yet.'

'Call me when you are.' He rang off.

It was hardly the conversation Tash had hoped for, but she supposed it was better than the screaming row they risked if they'd continued any longer. He had a competition to win, and she had children to feed. She was too weary to fight.

As soon as she'd fed, bathed and settled Cora and Amery in the little tower rooms that her nephews and nieces had traditionally occupied during family holidays, Tash fell straight into bed in the Salle Orchidée, one of the prettiest rooms in Le Manoir, nervous exhaustion pitching her into the blackest of deep sleep.

Far beneath her, Alexandra and Pascal debriefed in the kitchens, sharing a candlelit supper of globe artichokes and garlic butter washed down with a bottle of local rosé. Pascal loved to cook; food was his great passion after wine and love.

'She would not eat,' he complained in French, always highly offended if somebody spurned his fabulous fare. 'She said she was too tired.'

'She is, *chéri* – it's exhausting travelling alone with children of that age, but I am glad she came. We should not have been away so long. Of all my children, I could have guessed Tash would be first to welcome me home.'

'I think there is more to it than that.' Pascal had seen Tash's haunted face that day. 'I think she is running away.'

'Oh, I'm sure of it,' Alexandra agreed.

Tash had always been notoriously difficult to open up, bottling things up for months and sometimes years. It was a family trait. There had been secrets stuffed in the cupboards and swept under the carpets of Benedict, her childhood home, since she was born, so it was hardly surprising she'd picked up on the habit. Sometimes Alexandra wished that she'd been more open with her children, had been a stronger character and a better mother, but she had little hope of redressing that now – apart from to do everything in her power to prevent the same legacy befalling Cora and Amery. She had a plan.

'Tomorrow we will all relax together,' she told Pascal. 'Then you must go travelling again, my darling.'

'But I have only just unpacked my walking boots and my Deet.'

'Oh, you won't need those, *chéri*. Just a raincoat and an umbrella. You're going to England.'

At Knotton Manor, Rory and Alicia took shelter in the Moncrieffs' horsebox and gratefully accepted cups of tea.

'Hugo's pretty explosive this evening,' Rory apologised, grimacing as he slurred his words. 'He needs to shimmer down for a bit.'

'Just like his father.' Alicia looked wistful. 'I've told him to go and fetch Tash back, but he's got Henry's stubborn bloody pride, too. When we were first married, and living in Kenya, I once wandered into the bush alone and was trapped there for three nights before he came looking for me because he thought I'd gone orff to sulk, whereas in fact I'd got caught in a poacher's trap. I was lucky to survive, quite frankly. I loved Kenya – such wonderful years.'

'Has Tash got in contact?' Penny settled down beside them at the cramped table with a box of fresh cream éclairs, berry eyes eager for news.

Rory nodded. 'She's in France, apparently.'

'Poor Tash.' Penny looked worried. 'She must be in such a state.'

Alicia let out a deep sigh and stroked Beefeater, who was curled up on her lap. 'Always was a lightweight, although I'm frightfully fond of the gel. What did Hugo think he was doing, groping a groom? His father didn't start doing things like that until his sixties.'

Penny and Rory exchanged glances. Alicia was in fact a lot more upset by recent events than she let on, hence her recent haranguing Tash on the phone. She'd insisted on coming along to Knotton Manor because she hated being left alone at Haydown with her family so shattered. But she'd had rather too many toots from her hipflask that evening, making her unpredictable and malicious. Now she fixed Penny with a beady look. 'Where's your chap?'

'Checking the horses.'

Alicia's faded blue eyes softened amid their heavy veils of creased skin. 'You're lucky there. He's got a bit of class. Told Hugo as much: "At least Gus Moncrieff is shafting the daughter of an ambassador – any wife would turn a blind eye to that".' She fed Beefy a piece of her éclair and beamed across at her.

Penny carefully set her cup of tea back down on the table. With great effort she returned Alicia's smile and turned to Rory, who was staring fixedly at the old calendar pinned to the wall, cheeks colouring.

'Four weeksh to go until Burghley!' he said brightly.

'Who exactly knows?' she breathed in an undertone so low that Alicia, who was going deaf, couldn't possibly hear.

'Everyone,' he whispered back, mortified for her.

But Penny was made of sterner stuff. When Gus finally joined them, looking flustered and shifty, his hair on end and his shirt buttons done up the wrong way, she offered him an éclair. Then she picked up a knife.

'Imagine this is your cock,' she hissed, slicing the pastry neatly into two lengthways, and then making three more divisions widthways. 'If you go anywhere near Lucy Field again, it *will* be your cock.'

Turning pale, Gus didn't touch his éclair. Alicia was only too happy to snaffle it up.

'Delicious! I must get Tash to put these on my grocery order when she gets back. Lord, I hope she gets back soon. I'll run out of fags, and who else is going to put on my bets for me? I was thinking of getting an au pair, but apparently most of them don't speak fluent English, which is such a bore.'

'I hear the Ladbrokes website is very good,' Penny told her brightly, laying the knife back down. 'And Ocado deliver whenever you like. You just need a laptop and you're away.'

'Marvellous.' Alicia wiped choux pastry from her lips. 'Can one hire in staff to work one's laptop?'

Chapter 77

Dillon loved the drive up to Scotland with Pom and Berry. It felt so normal and fatherly to sing songs in the car, play I-Spy and number-plate snap, although he was less keen on the service stations with their uniform bad food and over-priced shops. Getting recognised was always a pain, the camera phones angled towards him, the elbow-nudging conversations about him as though he was still on a television screen and unable to hear them.

Not that he was recognised much on this trip, not even when he forgetfully signed himself in with his real name to the rather bleak Northumberland guest house they stayed in overnight to break up the journey. Now tipping the scales at two hundred and twenty pounds with long hair and beard, his kids had nicknamed him Hobo. Certainly his ex-wife's aunt, a strict Presbyterian who thought her niece's acting life debauched, couldn't wait to get him off her front step and away, gathering in the little girls like evacuees from a war zone.

The return journey was not enjoyable at all. Dillon hadn't wanted to let them go for a week in Scotland in the first place, but Fawn insisted that they must stick to their routine, and his management were still eager to send him to St Croix with Sylva.

The situation was like a bad joke, and one he stewed over for many motorway miles. He hadn't seen her once during his week in the Cotswolds, despite various texts promising she'd 'pop by for a chat'. He'd seen her children – all three of them, it now transpired – arriving to play with Pom and Berry. They had been accompanied by the quiet, stern Hana, who maintained so much dignity despite the tabloid revelations in recent days, with her ex-husband appearing out of the woodwork to claim that Sylva had paid them to raise her daughter and that this cuckoo child had wrecked their marriage. Dillon didn't believe it for a moment. One only had to see Hana with Zuzi to realise that the two were utterly and unconditionally bonded by love, and Zuzi was certainly one of the best-adjusted kids he'd ever come across. 'My mother says that honesty is always best,' she'd told him this week. 'She says a good conscience makes a soft pillow.'

Dillon wondered how Sylva was sleeping at night. He certainly wasn't; even West Oddford had failed to bring him its usual solace. Now that he had no children around, no fun chatter to accompany him everywhere and no chance of any more playdates with Zuzi and Hana, he was reluctant to rush back to the farm. It was harvest, usually his favourite time, but his heart was restless and, instead of heading towards Birmingham to pick up the M40 he stayed on the M1 to the London Orbital, tempted to head for Notting Hill to see his sister Kat, who always cheered him up. He stopped at London Gateway services to refuel and call ahead, but when she answered her mobile Kat told him she was in Ibiza.

'Have you heard Dad and Indigo have split?' she asked. 'He sent me a text saying *Easy come, Indi go*. Good old dad. Sensitive family man, still.'

Dillon checked his phone and realised his father hadn't even bothered to text him at all. So much for the rapprochement. But he was relieved Indigo had gone. She'd never seemed to make Pete happy.

There were no messages from Sylva. He couldn't face a confrontation, so he texted her: *Let's be sensible and forget all the PRs. We'll call it an amicable split.*

She texted straight back: *You must take the blame.*

Whatever's easiest. He no longer cared what his management said; he wanted out.

You'd better get laid then. Maybe lose the beard and have a bath first.

Intensely irritated, he deleted her number to cheer himself up.

Looking through his other messages, he saw several from Rory, who he'd only visited in hospital once on that dreadful day with Sylva in tow. He knew that he was back at Haydown again now. It was many months since Dillon had been there. It was a beautiful place. He suddenly decided to go and visit his horses.

But when he called Rory he was also away at a trials in Leicestershire, and staying there overnight. 'Even Hugo's mother's here. Nobody at home but scary Franny,' he apologised. 'She won't mind showing you the horses, though – most of yoursh will be in.'

Dillon didn't like the sound of scary Franny. Scrolling through his phone book he found Faith's number and called her. 'Hello stranger.'

'God, I'm being called by a rock star,' she said dryly. 'Quick, let me sit down.' Even after months of no communication her reaction to him was always refreshingly the same.

He explained that he'd wanted to call in on Haydown.

'Yes, they're all at Knotton Manor. I wanted to take Whitey but there was no space on any of the lorries. We've completed two three-stars this year, you know. That rocks.'

'Great!' It meant nothing to Dillon. 'Do I own him?'

'No, he's Rory's old horse.'

'What are you doing this afternoon?'

'Working, duh! Some of us do, although for how much longer I have no idea.'

'How d'you mean?'

'Gus can't afford to pay my wages any more. I've been living off Rio's Kentucky winnings. They don't really need me with Lough and Lem here, but now Tash and Hugo have split up there might be some extra work going at Haydown.'

'Tash and Hugo have *what*?' he spluttered, then added: 'No, don't answer that. I'm coming to take you out to supper.'

Angelo at the Olive Branch was beside himself at finding a pop star dining in his restaurant. He had already whipped out his digital camera from behind the bar and plonked himself down between Dillon and the scruffy girl from the Moncrieff's yard to pose with his arms around them, beaming proprietorially while Denise took a snap for the wall to be framed alongside the pictures of a beaming Angelo with Niall O'Shaughnessy, John Francome and 'that bloke off Holby City' as he was known, because nobody could remember his name.

'You look terrible' was the first thing Faith had said to Dillon.

Dillon thought exactly the same thing about her, but he was too polite to say it aloud.

'God, I'm knackered.' She rubbed her face in her hands and slumped back in her chair.

From all Dillon had heard through very occasional texts from Faith and more regular contact with her brother Magnus, she should have been thriving. She was loving the life, learning lots, competing regularly and practically within touching distance of her great love, Rory. Yet she looked drained and ill, the sunburn on her nose, cheeks and forearms emphasising the translucency of the pale skin on her thin upper arms and bony chest.

'So take a holiday. You said yourself you're not getting paid.'

'It's the middle of the season,' she yawned. 'Besides, I get bored on holiday.'

'You're too thin.'

'You sound like my mother.' She laughed, eyeing him with that clever gaze. 'There's never enough time to go shopping or cook or even eat. All the Moncrieffs are the same. You should see Gus – he's a bag of bones. They live off catering-van bacon butties at events and beans on toast at home and I'm forced to do the same. I'm not anorexic or anything.'

Certainly the greedy relish with which she raced through her spaghetti carbonara seemed to back up her claim. And she had two puddings.

Talking with her mouth full, she told him about Tash leaving Hugo.

'Franny saw it all from her cottage,' she explained. 'Lough turned up and begged Tash to run away with him. Then she tried to ram his horsebox. High drama.'

'Jesus,' Dillon whistled. 'And I thought my life was melodramatic.'

'How is "the nation's favourite single mum"?' She was trying very hard to modulate her voice to hide any sarcasm.

He gave her a withering look. 'Popular.'

'Is it true you're getting married in a mountain-top Slovakian castle? Carly read it in *Cheers!* It said the fireworks alone are costing over a million.'

He changed the subject: 'Rory's back riding, I hear?'

As ever her face lit up at the mention of his name. 'Yeah – the doctors gave him the all clear, although I'm not sure he's right.'

'How is he?'

'Weird.' She started to eat his neglected pudding across the table. 'He's being really nice to me.'

'Well that's good, isn't it?'

'Yeah, I guess. But it's like he's embarrassed to talk to me, although he is tricky to understand with the slurred speech. And he won't look at me.'

'Maybe he's shy around you?'

'This *is* Rory we're talking about!' she scoffed. 'I've offered to work at Haydown for a bit. They really need the help. I did the same last year, but Rory won't hear of it. Told me I'd put him off, like some irritating schoolgirl that hangs around. I never hang around. I work my *butt* off.'

'I'm sure you do.'

'Not that I can keep up with Rory any more. He's obsessed with getting fit again for Burghley. He and Hugo run ten miles a day as well as riding a dozen horses between them.'

'Isn't that good?'

She shook her head. 'Rory shouldn't really compete so soon after an injury like that, certainly not at four-star level. British Eventing wanted to refuse his Burghley entry but he appealed to the inter-national body and Marie-Clair backed him.' She let out a small sneer. 'He's in with a real shout of the grand slam, so it would be horribly controversial to ban him, but what if he gets hurt?' Her eyes went suddenly teary.

'I challenged him to that in the first place,' Dillon groaned. 'I should stop him.'

She shook her head. 'Ask any event rider in his position what they'd do and they'd say "go for it". It's the Holy Grail. Rory wants it more than anything else in the world and he won't let anything stand in his way – even the things that are trying to help him.' She sighed, picking hay off her jumper, then looked up brightly as a thought struck her. 'If he does win it I'm going to give him the biggest kiss of his life, whether he likes it or not.'

Dillon smiled, watching her animated face, and realising that she was so fantastically focused in life, she had none of his angst and vacillation. He longed to have some of that drive. She had a really handsome and unusual face, he decided, like a young Meryl Streep.

'Everything to your satisfaction, Mr Raggety?' Angelo shimmied up with a tray of coffee.

'Rafferty. Yes, thanks.'

Beaming, Angelo clicked his heels, re-laid his napkin over his arm, executed a half pirouette and shimmied away.

'Why can't he see me as a *woman* not a child?' Faith was moaning, helping herself to sugar lumps.

'Well you could try sitting up straight, putting your napkin on your lap rather than tucked in your collar, and not eating the sugar lumps.'

'Huh?'

Dillon raised his eyebrows at her in return.

'Rory. I'm talking about Rory,' she clarified.

'Ah, of course you are.' He dropped a slice of lemon peel in his espresso. 'That might take rather more work.'

'Like what? Cosmetic surgery?'

'No! God, no. Perhaps if you played the field a bit more, got a bit more experience . . .'

Faith huffed. 'There's no way I can ever try to compete with sex vixens like MC or Sylva—' She covered her mouth as she realised what she'd just let slip.

'Sylva?' he beetled his brows at her. 'And Rory?'

'It was all in your ex girlfriend's kiss and tell,' she pointed out.

'I never read that, funnily enough.'

'She bigged it up *far* too much. It was nothing. Just a fling. Before Sylva's gay fling. And her you fling – not that it's a fling, what with getting married and all that.'

He rubbed his face in his hands. 'God what a mess.'

A flash suddenly went off at the window and he looked up sharply. 'Fuck.'

'What is it?'

'Paparazzi. Somebody must have tipped them off that I'm here.' He glared at Angelo as he sidled past at a leisurely pace to draw the curtains beside their table, hoping they'd get some nice shots of the exterior while they were here.

Faith giggled at the novelty of it all. 'I can see the headlines: *Sylva Love Rival – heartthrob pop star spotted with scruffy-looking teen in pub clinch*. Pucker up and we'll draw back those curtains again and give them a show.' She closed her eyes and pursed her lips theatrically.

He was about to throw a sugar lump at her, but he suddenly leaned forward and stared at her intently. 'You know, you might have a point.'

She laughed. 'It's okay, I think we're safe. Nobody is seriously going to believe I'm a rival to Sylva Frost.'

'If they did, it would make Rory sit up and take notice of you, wouldn't it?'

'True.' She was still laughing, not taking him seriously.

'You say you wouldn't be missed if you didn't work for a week?'

She shrugged. 'I have Whitey to look after.'

'And if I paid for him to be looked after?'

She stopped laughing. 'Why would you do that?'

'Come on holiday to the Caribbean.'

She gaped at him. 'This is a joke, right?'

'You need a holiday. I *definitely* need a holiday.' He nodded towards the curtained window, behind which the shadow of the photographer was still loitering. 'Let's give them something to talk about.'

'No funny business?'

'I'll phone your mother personally and assure her of my strong moral fibre.' He smiled the killer Rafferty smile which, despite his beard and double chin, rocked Faith back on her chair.

'There's no need for that. I am almost nineteen and I do know you're practically married. Will Sylva be there?' She didn't relish any close comparisons with Sylva's petite perfection while sunbathing.

'She's not invited.' He shook his head. 'Are you okay with that?'

'Absolutely!' She grinned. 'Won't that upset Sylva, though?'

'So I'm hoping.' He regarded her cautiously, suddenly realising how young she was and worrying what he was letting her in for. But she was tough, fun company and madly in love with someone else. That made her a perfect holiday guest. 'Have you got your passport with you?'

'It's in my room.'

'Good. Because that's all you're going to need.'

Within four hours of paying the bill and leaving the Olive Branch by the back door to avoid any more pictures, Dillon and Faith were on a private jet heading west. He refused to let her pack more than a toothbrush: 'Your clothes are awful. We'll buy it all there. My treat.'

It wasn't until they were airborne, her ears popping, that Faith finally took Dillon seriously and realised she was on her way to the Caribbean.

Chapter 78

Spending time at Le Manoir was good for Tash, who could feel the tension draining out of her even after just twenty-four hours, like a beach drying out after a monsoon, as she baked in the Loire sun and listened to Alexandra and Pascal talking of their adventures.

The globetrotting pensioners were clearly thrilled to be home, however much they'd adored their grand tour. Champegny was their haven. They were amazingly close and loving, more so than Tash had seen them for years. Barely more than a few metres apart throughout the day, they were never short of conversation, debate and shared humour. Often they would render one another speechless with laughter, bent double and tears falling from their eyes. Their pace of life had changed since Tash's last visit. They sat for longer over breakfast, then moved on to a terrace in the sun to read the papers, parasols angled strategically while Alexandra sported a floppy sunhat and Pascal donned huge Roy Orbison dark glasses, later walking steadily in the garden arm in arm, dead-heading, weeding and lopping as they passed.

They were living at retirement pace, Tash realised. They had slowed right down and suddenly looked old. It came as a total shock to her as she studied them with a fresh perspective. They were both grey now; her mother's once nut brown bob had been infused with palest silver for many years before turning white but Pascal's thick, Byronic black tresses had only recently become pewter, highlighting his darkly tanned skin and dramatic beetling brows, still raven black and now far thicker than before, with hairs that seemed to grow upward to sweeping peaks like a forest blackened by fire. He was ten years Alexandra's junior, yet early retirement and travelling had killed off his competitive streak and he was happy to focus on the woman he loved, his country retreat, his vineyard and his food.

Food was the centre of life, an axis around which the day solely revolved. The couple slowly prepared and then lingered with leisurely delight over lunch before taking a long siesta and rising just in time to start cooking and drinking and eating again. Meals at Le Manoir had always been lengthy affairs, but they now took for ever – far too long for Cora and Amery, who fidgeted and wailed after just half an hour. Trying to keep them entertained, aware that her mother and Pascal were nose to nose whispering sweet nothings, Tash was reminded all to vividly of the closeness that she and Hugo had shared before children, of the symbiotic life they had led working and competing together, talking all the time, supporting and sharing and becoming mutually exclusive.

She sat in the bath after putting the children to bed and cried herself silly, her eyes so puffy afterwards that she had to wear her spectacles at dinner.

'When one cries oneself blind,' Alexandra told her daughter over sautéed lambs' kidneys with tarragon and wine, 'one learns to see with one's heart so much more.'

Tash took this in thoughtfully.

'Pascal must go away for a few days,' she went on in a falsely cheery tone as she set the ball rolling. 'Can you stay and keep me company? Having you here is so divine.'

Tash wasn't sure that was true. So far, all she had done was run around manically after the children and blub whenever she was alone.

The following morning Pascal set out, somewhat huffily, for Tours airport, his suitcase crammed with a waxed coat, gaiters, thick jumpers and rain hats.

It was soon almost ninety degrees on the sun-soaked terraces. Tash let her mother entertain the children in the shade of the pergola while she took a long swim in the pool, closing her eyes and diving low into the cool water, trying to see with her heart. But she just got chlorine up her nose and even puffier eyes. She was forced back into her spectacles, this time with unflattering clip-on shades that Alexandra had lent her, which dated from the seventies and made her look like she was trying out for a *Cagney and Lacey* remake.

The moment the children had settled down for an afternoon nap, Alexandra fetched a fresh bottle of *eau de vie* and took aim with her biggest cannon. 'Tash, sweetheart, I think it's time to talk.'

Of course she knew that this was guaranteed to make her daughter clam up faster than a slammed freezer door.

'I don't really want to talk,' Tash replied, looking trapped.

'No, not you, darling – me. *I* want to talk.' Alexandra smiled at Tash's baffled expression. She knew her daughter's weak spot of old: Tash was impossibly polite, having been brought up to be totally fair-handed, a point that had probably been over-laboured by her bullish father. Combined with her natural generosity, it made her charitable to a fault. If invited to dinner, however ghastly the company, Tash would feel obliged to play hostess in return. She replied to every fan letter she, Hugo and the horses received, however vacuous or even malicious. If paid a compliment, she gave one back. If someone opened their heart to her, she opened hers.

Settling down for the first stage of what she knew would be a long and delicate operation, Alexandra opened the bottle and poured out two glasses.

At close to midnight, Alexandra phoned her husband from bed, speaking in French. '*Chéri*, how is my lovely England?'

'Wet,' Pascal grumbled. He hated England in August, or indeed at any time of the year, with its terrible food and transport system, full of angry bald idiots driving on the wrong side of the road.

'Tash has told me what's happening. Prepare yourself, *chéri*, it is rather worse than we feared.'

When he heard the details, Pascal was astonished. 'Hugo tried to force himself upon the girl?'

'So it seems. I need you to go straight to Haydown and find out Hugo's version of events, like Hercule Poirot.'

'He was Belgian,' Pascal reminded her, bristling.

'I'm sure there has to be another explanation for this,' Alexandra rushed on, ignoring his protests. 'It just sounds so unlike Hugo. You must find out the truth, Maigret.'

Pascal cleared his throat. 'He is not a man who opens his heart easily, I think – and my English is so rusty.'

'You'll be fine,' she assured him. 'And please stop off at a supermarket while you are there and – have you got a pen, *chéri*? Yes? Buy

Marmite, Birds Eye custard, Angel Delight (any flavour except raspberry), Spam, apple chutney, Colman's mint sauce and Typhoo tea bags.'

'How did you get Tash to talk?' Pascal asked just before they said goodnight, hoping to get some tips for getting Hugo to spill the beans.

'I told her about my marriage to her father and what went wrong.'

'I can hardly do that with Hugo,' he sighed.

'Of course you can,' she said brightly. 'You have four marriages to choose from. Now get some sleep. *Je t'adore.*'

Chapter 79

In Fox Oddfield Abbey, Pete gave an exclusive interview to the *Sunday Times* about the end of his stormy six-year marriage to Indigo, overseen by the ever-professional Clive Maxwell, who was orchestrating the careful release of the story to the media.

'Indigo says I have a madonna–whore complex,' he told celebrity profiler Christy d'Isle. 'But,' he continued, laughing at his pun, 'I told her there was never anything in the rumours – I like the woman, don't get me wrong, and she's played a blinder with the Sticky and Sweet tour, but she's not my type. Plus she's a mate of my daughter, so I wouldn't go there.'

'Strike that,' Clive said smoothly, giving Pete a sharp look to remind him that he was currently 'going there' with his son's fiancée.

'So there's nobody else involved?' Christy checked.

He flashed the Rafferty smile with such force her chair almost flew back against the wall. 'There's always somebody else involved, darling. The question is, are they sweet enough to stick?'

Clive closed his eyes in despair.

'Are you going to be a sugar daddy again then?'

Pete winked at her. They went back a long way and he liked her style. 'I'm the Rockfather, baby,' he laughed. 'And a stick of rock is very hard candy, remember.'

*

'How did it go?' Sylva asked him later when they met in the hermitage on the Abbey's estate, their temporary love nest hidden deep within woodland. To be extra sure of privacy, Sylva had sent out three of her fleet of cars that evening, hiding in one in the hope that the paparazzi would follow one of the dummies while hers crept through one of the many back gateways to the Abbey. In fact, the paparazzi hadn't followed any of them, believing Sylva to be hiding at home, weeping tears of despair that her pop star fiancé had gone to the Caribbean without her.

They seldom bothered following her when it was raining this heavily. For the past three days of intermittent downpours, Sylva's loyal gatekeepers had got drenched every time they clambered from their cars to snap their quarry doing something truly newsworthy like collecting her post. Now they preferred to stay parked up until the weather front passed.

The rain was still pounding down on the hermitage roof as she and Pete stripped in their little hidden pleasure palace, at such a peak of mutual attraction that they thought about making love together night and day. In the short snatches of time they did have together, they had to have sex before they could talk, while they talked, before they said goodbye and then again afterwards. Pete was knocking back his little blue pills like Smints, along with an increasing numbers of painkillers as his knees gave him more and more trouble, but he was far too besotted to complain about it.

As Sylva propped herself up on the table, lifted one slim ankle to his shoulder and swung out her other leg to reveal a pussy as sweetly pink and glistening as an orchid after a rainstorm, Pete growled with happy laughter and slid in, telling her about his interview. 'I just wanted to shout "I'm in love with Trouble!" I want to tell the world how beautiful you are inside and out, how glad I am to have found you, my little Sylva loving cup.'

Those wise, naughty blue eyes that had seen the inside of more hotel rooms and groupies than they'd seen sunsets watched her lovely face colour and her pupils dilate as her eyes lost focus and she came with a series of delicious grunts and squeals, like a comely Eastern European tennis pro serving a clutch of aces in quick succession.

Then, letting him slip out for a moment, she turned around and bent over the table, two perfect buttocks rising up to him with a pretty little oyster pink starfish joining the orchid as options.

'You are such a naughty girl.' He slapped one of her buttocks playfully. 'God, I love you.'

Laying her cheek on the scrubbed pine, she looked back at him over her shoulder and smiled.

During his difficult marriage with Indigo, Pete had suffered long bouts of depression and low self-esteem. Despite being an unreformed serial shagger, he relied upon a steady family life, something that his beloved first wife had understood, turning a blind eye to his infidelities so long as home was sacred and Dillon and Kat loved and protected. But ambitious Indigo, who had provided a crèche, prison and therapy centre, had no such blind spot when it came to his tour pussy and just tried to control him with increasingly rigid demands and threats. He was relieved to be finally free, although he needed the reassurance of a back-up plan. Like his son to whom he had bequeathed the same tendencies, Pete was reluctant to leave the warm, safe establishment of a long-term relationship unless he had a car waiting with its engine revving.

Sylva's engine was revving very loudly indeed, but he needed to check it was a truly personal limousine service, not just a card held up at the arrivals gate with the name Rafferty hand-written on it.

'My son's a fool to let you slip through his fingers,' he said as he spread that silken juice from orchid to starfish, dipping in finger and thumb to hold her like a bowling ball.

'I'm the one slippery in your fingers,' she gasped.

'He'll never forgive us for this,' he said, with surprising satisfaction. Having not had a top-ten hit in almost five years, Pete secretly couldn't help wanting to show the little upstart he was still boss, his good intentions forgotten in the wake of scoring the most satisfying paternal victory of his life. 'He knows I'll break your heart.'

'I'd rather have my heart broken by you than frozen by him.'

He smiled, reaching down to steer his eager cock into position. 'I'm never faithful.'

'I know!' she gasped deliciously as his electric eel slipped into the starfish.

'I like young blondes, threesomes and high-class hookers.'

'So do I,' she groaned deliriously as his fingers slithered in and out of the orchid's mouth.

'Tell me I'm a better lover than Dillon.'

'You're a better lover,' she said without hesitation. 'You're the real deal, Pete. He did nothing for me.'

'Nothing?' He drove faster.

'Nothing!'

He laughed, thrusting ever more eagerly, although he privately thought his son was much more of a chip off the old block than she realised. After all, he was currently entertaining a very young strawberry blonde on his father's private island, and Sylva clearly had no idea . . .

Chapter 80

With paparazzi buzzing around his St Croix villa like mosquitoes, Dillon had been left with no choice but to phone his father and ask if he could use his private Caribbean retreat, the jewel-like Golden Hinde Island, one of the smallest and prettiest of the British Virgin Islands (a fact that always amused Pete who called the island Goldie and liked to boast that he had taken many British virgins there, but never brought one back). Dillon felt rather like a goofy teenager asking his dad if he could borrow the car to go on a date, but Pete had been surprisingly easygoing about it: 'No worries, son – it'll keep the staff on their toes. Just take care of her.'

'I'm alone,' he said, not very convincingly.

'I was talking about Goldie. Don't forget to put the cat out, yeah?'

'I really appreciate this. I'll return the favour some time.'

'You already have, son,' Pete cackled. 'You already have!'

Dillon had no idea what his father meant, but was wholly relieved when they set off by helicopter later that day for the half-hour hop from St Croix to Golden Hind Island. He had increasingly cold feet about the press getting their hands on this story, or at least on Faith's identity, fearing that exposure of that magnitude could make her life hell for a very long time. She was his friend and she might talk tough and punch low, but she was still very young and innocent.

Faith was restless. She had read all her books, and the additional two that Dillon had bought her on the day he went out shopping and brought her back a complete wardrobe of parrot-bright sarongs, bikinis, flip-flops and pretty bangles ('You're in the Caribbean, what more do you need?' he'd pointed out, to which she'd replied 'An umbrella?' when a tropical storm broke overhead).

It was the hurricane season, but none were forecast for their stay, just the occasional refreshing cloudburst which she needed to cool her excess energy and hot head from time to time.

Accustomed to working twelve-hour days, with six of those spent in the saddle, to the thrills of competing and the spills of being shouted at by Gus Moncrieff, Faith found the pace of the tropics as stifling as the temperatures. Dillon hadn't even allowed her out of the gated villa on St Croix. At least here she was allowed to explore an entire island, although he told her not to go near the beaches, cliffs or coastline because the paps were still bobbing around at a distance, the canniest old hands knowing full well that he was trying to close their apertures to one of the biggest picture stories since a Texan sucked the Duchess of York's toes.

But when Faith went for a run inland, fighting her way along an overgrown path that ran up the spine of the old volcano at the island's centre, she found the mosquitoes and heat too oppressive, started feeling unpleasantly like a character in *Lost* running from the black smoke, and so returned to pace around the opulent main house, a ridiculous surfeit of luxury that obviously embarrassed Dillon, who kept apologising for it, from the twelve bedroom suites as big as penthouse flats to the full recording studio, cinema complex, gym and no less than four swimming pools.

'Dad likes to take a dip in to cool water between dipping in to hot women,' he had explained, scuffing around awkwardly, hands deep in his pockets and thoughts deep in his head.

Faith knew most girls would die to be in a place like this. Carly would probably never speak to her again if she knew where her friend was, but that was no great change because they hadn't spoken properly for months as it was, the friendship waning yet again in the light of a new boyfriend called Ryan who she claimed was as good as signed to the Premier League.

But Faith was going stir-crazy and longed to know what Rory was up to. She checked the internet constantly for updates from Gatcombe, where he was competing in the British Open Championships on Humpty. He was fifth after dressage overnight, which was reassuring and even gave her cause for a small celebratory drink with Dillon while they lounged on plantation chairs beside the infinity pool, watching the setting sun turn the sea from bright blue to gold like a cooling flame, and waiting while a lavish seafood banquet was whipped up by the team of three chefs.

He was on orange juice as usual, but she decided to counter her edginess with one of the rum cocktails that the butler Orlando was always boasting were the best in the Caribbean.

She chose a piña colada, thinking that, because she had heard of it, it must be safe. It was far from safe. Faith had no head for alcohol, and was steaming after just half a glass.

'I don't think Rory will ever love me,' she sighed.

Dillon, who felt like he had taken Rory from every angle in the past few days and could take no more, closed one eye and tilted his head at her, trying out a line his father would have been proud of. 'Do you know how beautiful you look tonight?'

'What?' She flared a nostril and curled her lip, which admittedly didn't add a great deal to the overall look, but it wasn't Faith's face Dillon was referring to. Her features had always been handsome and unique, like a Modigliani, although veneers had modernised the classical façade. Her body, however, had taken to the Caribbean like a ripening papaya and transformed spectacularly. She might claim to be a fish out of water, or a muddy pike thrown into a tropical tank, but her scales were glistening. With a real sun-kissed glow to her foxglove skin, her hair sun-bleached blonde and heavy with oils that turned the customary frizz to Pre-Raphaelite corkscrews, and her lean, fit body softened by five-star cooking, she was utterly stunning.

Like Faith, Dillon wished Rory was there to appreciate it. But she would have to make do with him, which was no bad thing given her lack of guile.

'You are a beautiful woman,' he assured her.

'Getoutahere.' She threw the straw from her piña colada at him and turned to look at the sun again as it winked its last red rays over the horizon.

'You know the key to sexual awareness is self love,' he said lazily.

She curled her lips. 'You sound like Beccy reciting her chakra crap.'

'D'you ever touch yourself?'

'Now you're getting creepy.' She reached for her drink and took a big gulp. Not a great move. It was like shooting the high grade rum into a vein.

'Okay. What I'm asking is, how well you know what you actually want?'

'I want Rory.'

'Let's take that as a given. What do you want Rory to *do*?'

'Kiss me.'

'And then?'

'We'd kiss for a long time.'

'Okay. You kiss for a long time. *Then?*'

'Make love, of course.' She went pink beneath her tan, her blushes mercifully spared by the arrival of a troop of waiters laying out their seafood on a nearby table, lighting candles and braziers and then melting away again as efficiently and quickly as scene-changing staff in a theatre.

'So you make love.' Dillon settled at the table, opposite her, and cracked open a lobster tail. 'What do you do?'

Faith picked up a fat prawn, dipped it in spicy mayo and looked at it. Then she looked at him, prawn aloft like the grim reaper's scythe. She narrowed her eyes. 'You tell me.'

'How can I say?' He popped a sliver of sea urchin in his mouth. 'I've never made love to Rory.'

'Nor have I.'

'But you love him, which gives you a head start in the fantasy stakes.'

Faith thrust out her chin rebelliously, but it was just to dart out a very pink tongue on which she landed her fat prawn, like a mahi-mahi on a jetty, sucking it back in and looking at him quizzically.

Somebody had filled up a champagne glass beside her. She politely took advantage of it to wash down the delicious mouthful, her mind rather disturbingly awash with Rory.

'You need to shave off your beard,' she told Dillon.

He laughed. 'You can shave it off if you like.'

'I will.' She reached for a conch fritter.

'Do you like shaving?' He was teasing her now, eyes crinkling at the corners with amusement.

'Now you're getting creepy again.' She spoke with her mouth full. 'I like clipping horses, although it can be a bit itchy when the cuttings get down the back of your neck. But I hate shaving my legs. So boring.'

'I can tell.'

Faith reached for her glass, amazingly refilled once more. 'You look at my legs?'

'I look at all of you, Faith. I'm a man.'

She started digging into a crab. 'You're just sex-starved.'

'Quite probably.' He delicately fingered a mussel, loosening it from its shell before slipping it into his mouth.

'I'm not sex-starved.' She had another swig of champagne. 'One has to assume a degree of satiation before starvation, after all.'

'Say again?'

She looked at him over her glass. 'My entire sexual experience amounts to a drunken snog with Flipper Cottrell and one de-cherrying with a gay friend.'

He raised his eyebrow.

She tilted her head from left to right as she weighed up this sum total. 'To be honest, the snog was sexier, but I can hardly remember how to do it now.'

'Didn't your gay friend oblige?'

'He doesn't like kissing much.'

'That's a shame.'

'I don't think he really likes having sex with women either, so I didn't pick up a lot of expert tips.' She let out a wistful sigh of breath. 'All of which makes my Rory kissing plan a bit hit and miss, I know – let alone the making love bit.'

'It could be tricky,' Dillon agreed, chewing spicy-mayo-drenched crabmeat.

'And he is *so* experienced, it terrifies me.' She reached for the champagne glass again, wondering how it kept refilling when she couldn't see a bottle or indeed any staff around. 'You know this MC he's been shagging?'

'Rory's been shagging an emcee?'

'No, Marie-Clair Tucson – they call her MC Hummer on the circuit because she's tough, off-road and driven by big dicks.'

Dillon laughed.

Faith didn't. 'Rory told me that she has taught him so much about sex that he, I quote "now knows how to pleasure women every which way but up".'

'Twat.' Dillon laughed then, seeing her thunderous face, held up his hands. 'Sorry. Knowledgeable twat. Knowledgeable *of* twat. Go on . . .'

'I have no idea how to pleasure a man.' Faith laced her fingers together and pressed her hands to her mouth, clever, drunken eyes on his, questioning and anxious.

Very slowly, Dillon laid down the langouste he was holding and regarded her thoughtfully. 'We're very simple.'

Faith dared herself, double dared herself and triple dared herself before she lifted her hands from her mouth for a second and blurted, 'Will *you* show me?'

'You're very drunk.'

She lowered her hands carefully to her lap and leaned back in her chair. 'If I can walk in a straight line along a given trajectory, will you do it?'

He grimaced. 'I'm not so hot myself, Faith.'

'You've had hundreds of lovers!'

'Drop a zero from that.'

'Still ten times more than me.'

He blew out through his lips, shaking his head. 'I thought I was pretty hot until I met Sylva Frost, but she had me beat.' He laughed in amazement that he had admitted it out loud. 'She scared the balls off me.' He looked up at Faith. 'The woman knows more about sex than I know about cheese. And I thought I was an aficionado of love and cheese.'

'You *are*. Nobody sings about love as cheesily as you.'

'Thanks for that.'

Faith propped a flip-flopped foot on the table edge and tilted her chair back. 'Rory says that MC feels it's her duty, as an amazing lover, to pass on tips to every man she beds so that the greater female populace benefits from her experience.'

'Very noble.' Dillon made a mental note to Google MC Hummer later and commit her face to memory for self-protection.

'I think you should feel the same duty,' Faith challenged him.

It was gradually dawning on Dillon that he was being propositioned although, being Faith, she was issuing it as a challenge.

'Darling Faith.' He laid down his fork and looked at her seriously. 'At one point in my life nothing would have given me greater pleasure, believe me. But I am older and wiser and know what it's like to live with the consequences of these things.'

'I'm cool with the consequences.'

'Well I'm not. I absolutely adore you, but I am much too old.'

'You're not much older than Rory.'

'I have an old soul, unlike Rory, or indeed my dad. The Rockfather might think groupie-shagging in the Virgin Islands rejuvenates the spirit, but this son begs to differ.'

'I'm no groupie!' she pointed out hotly, her chair tipping forwards again. 'I'm your friend. I don't particularly like your music.'

'A contradiction I'm now familiar with.'

'And I'm glad you're not like your dad,' she went on furiously. 'I wouldn't shag Pete Rafferty in a million years, even if he's much better at it than you.'

To Dillon, this was a come-on beyond any coy flirtation, but he refused to take the bait. 'They fuck you up, your mum and dad . . .'

'Meaning?' Faith tipped her chair back again and he clearly saw her neat, sculpted inner thighs, curving enticingly towards a picturesque hollow through which her bikini flew its triangular bright turquoise sail. Matching turquoise eyes watched him keenly from between her knees.

'Just Larkin about.'

'My mum's Danish.' She swapped feet on the table edge as her chair rocked back and forth. 'She thinks fucking is a very good thing. Healthy, like saunas and massage.'

'And your dad?'

'I don't know my real dad.'

'Perhaps it's time you did.'

The chair swung forwards eagerly. 'D'you think that's the key to Rory?'

'No, I think that's the key to you. Sex is cheating, like picking the lock.'

'In that case, I want to cheat.' Faith regarded him between her tanned knees, turquoise sail tacking left then right as both flip-flops paced against the table edge, rocking her chair to its absolute apex. 'I want to cheat with you.' With a wide, sexy smile she lost balance and tipped back into a potted palm, feet in the air.

Dillon stood up and, in gentlemanly fashion, set her upright again before dropping a kiss on her head and whispering, 'If you still want this when sober in the morning, we'll talk again. For now, sleep.'

Then he went to his suite for a very cold shower.

The next morning, there was a knock at his door just after seven.

Thinking it was his breakfast, Dillon groggily called them in.

'Aggh!' he screamed like a girl when Faith straddled him with a razor and a can of shaving foam.

His morning glory, however, rose in a manly salute to lift her off her feet.

'Ohmygod.' She looked down in delight. 'Either Lem was really, really small, or you're really, *really* huge.' She started to explore hitherto unchartered territory with her fingertips.

How could a man resist? She wanted to learn and, like the ambitious young rider she was, she insisted on learning from the best.

'When you touch a man's balls,' he gasped as her hands slid everywhere, 'you must be gentle.'

'Sorry.' She paused in her exploration.

'Don't stop. Actually, stop!' He lifted himself up on to his elbows to look at her. 'Are you sure about this?'

'Absolutely.' She nodded excitedly. 'I've been thinking about it all night and you're right, I do *love* Rory, which means making love with him should be easy. But I don't know how to make out, so I think you're the best person to teach me because you're my friend and you're handsome and talented and you've shagged hundreds – sorry, tens – of women, and you're ready.' She looked down. 'Or is that an illusion?'

He looked down too. 'It's not an illusion.'

'It's *so* big,' Faith gasped, wondering how all that would fit into her.

Dillon found it growing all the bigger for that. She was the perfect antidote to Sylva, he realised.

'*Milujem t'a.*' He rolled her over to start on some basics.

'What does that mean?'

'Slovak for "trust me".' He bent his head to start kissing his way around her body.

She sucked her lip guiltily. 'Did Sylva teach you that?'

'No – but she did teach me this . . .'

'Ohmygod*stop*it!' she shrieked, wriggling away. 'If you are going to do that then I'm definitely shaving your beard first . . .'

Chapter 81

Pascal arrived in Maccombe to find the weather as wet as Alexandra had predicted it to be, Haydown House and its downland setting as ridiculously beautiful as he remembered them, and to find Hugo stretched to the limit.

He'd just returned empty-handed from the British Open Championships, where gossip was rife and some spectators had even booed at him as he galloped past. Chinese whispers about the end of his marriage, and the reasons for it, had spread through the sport like swine flu. Infidelity had become sexual assault and then had become rape in just a few short, shocked exchanges at the ringside. His reputation and career were in peril. Several owners had already called to say they were taking horses away, and a key sponsor had that day announced they were pulling out of supporting the Haydown team, without explaining their reasons.

At Gatcombe a great many close friends had vouched for Hugo and supported him, yet an equal number of enemies had cold-shouldered and damned him. He was at a very low ebb and felt like jacking in the rest of the season and going back to America to teach.

Still, he welcomed his French father-in-law with typical good manners, digging out cognac and fresh coffee, sharing cigarettes and asking after the shipping business in his polite, upper-crust way.

'Dead in ze water, as you say, *mon brave.*' Pascal sighed with regret, realising as he watched him that Hugo was nowhere near as together as he made out.

'Vines well?' Hugo moved on, blue eyes darting from window to door, his unconscious trying to escape the interrogation he guessed was coming.

'Mildew,' Pascal lamented, rolling his eyes and reaching for his cognac.

'Alexandra and Polly?'

Pascal puffed out his cheeks for dramatic emphasis as he reported good-naturedly. 'My beautiful, demanding *femme et fille*, so alike nowadays. I am ze hero for one and euros for the ozer, but I love them, *oui*?'

'Marvellous.' Hugo lit one cigarette from another, barely listening. 'And the harvest?'

'You asked me about that already, *mon brave*.'

Hugo nodded, not looking at him. There was a pause. Eventually he asked: 'Are they all right?'

Pascal immediately understood. 'They are well. Your children are so beautiful. Xandra is so proud of her grandson.'

He nodded, his tongue running around one cheek, so much pain in his eyes that Pascal felt scalded by it.

'Tash, she bearing up as you say.'

'Good for Tash.'

'She is more beautiful than ever, *non?*'

'Isn't she just?'

'You two are in a mess, 'ugo.'

'You could say that.'

But however much Pascal tried to get him to open up, it was hopeless. Hugo was, as always, civil and just menacing enough to back him off.

There was a long pause. Pascal was too much of a good cop to push him, and too much of a scaredy-cat to ask anything challenging about any alleged sexual assault. Instead he decided to try his wife's trusty tactic.

'I have a little advice for you, *mon brave*. When my first marriage ended—'

'My marriage hasn't ended,' Hugo interrupted.

'*Bien sûr.*' Pascal cleared his throat and brushed imaginary fluff from his cashmere sweater. 'Let me give you another example. I was having a very difficile time with my third wife Lucille, who thought that I was having an affair with my secretary – in fact I *was* having an affair with my secretary.' He thought back fondly. 'Anyway, that is not important. Lucille, she say to me, "*Pascal, mon bélier*" – that is French for ram, which was her nickname for me because—'

'Pascal, is this going anywhere?' Hugo snapped.

Pascal looked hurt.

'Because, with respect, I have a lot of horses to feed out there and time is money.'

They went out into the summer rain, the grey sky over the downs arced through with a rainbow. As Hugo turned to shake Pascal's hand farewell, the Frenchman turned in the direction of the rose walks, his dark eyebrows aloft. 'Do you usually let your horses loose in ze garden?'

'What?' Hugo swung round just in time to see a distinctive heart-shaped star disappear behind a Cardinal de Richelieu in full bloom. 'Bloody hell, he's got out again. Franny!'

Pascal joined the team that circled the beautiful bright bay gelding and finally caught him by a pretty Rosa Mundi.

As they led him back, Franny was contrite in front of an apoplectic Hugo: 'I had the grille up. He must have jumped through the window at the back. I think Fudge left it open.'

'Cretinous girl.' He eyed the horse's heavily bandaged legs for signs of damage. 'She's even worse than Beccy.'

'Give her longer,' begged Franny, who had persuaded him to take on her cousin as a working pupil in the first place. 'It's only her first week.'

'*Le cheval* is fine, 'ugo,' Pascal agreed, admiring the huge horse, his coat grubby from rolling in garden bark chips, so that it was dusted like a young Grolleau Gris in his own vineyards. 'He is just bored and lonely, *non?*'

Having satisfied himself that Heart was unscathed by this adventure, Hugo let Franny lead him away as he turned to thank Pascal with the postponed farewell handshake.

'A lonely fellow needs camaraderie, *mon ami.* A lady to make him feel loved. *Une amoureuse.* If you have nussink here, you must buy one.'

Hugo looked at him curiously, obviously concerned that his father-in-law, who had purportedly come as a marriage peacemaker, was suddenly acting like a pimp.

Pascal suddenly guffawed, realising the misunderstanding. 'I was talking about ze horse. He needs a companion. My best race horse in France, he is just the same. He has a leetle girlfriend called Poupée.'

'"Doll"?' Hugo translated.

'*Non*, we name her Poupée because she poops a lot.'

As he joined in the laughter, the break in Hugo's tension was like the sun suddenly beaming through the rain overhead.

'Are you sure you won't stay?' He walked Pascal to his hire car.

He shook his head. 'Thank you, *mais non.* I am a terrible house guest. I prefer 'otels where I pay for the privilege of being able to complain as much as I like. *À bientôt.*'

Waving him off to drive to Fosbourne Ducis and the Olive

Branch, where he would no doubt complain at Angelo a great deal, Hugo turned back to the yard to find Fudge cowering by Heart's stable, an apology on her lips.

She tearfully watched Hugo pull a curl of cash from a rear pocket and peel off several fifties, certain that he was about to pay her notice and tell her to pack her bags. But instead he handed her both the cash and the keys to the hunting box. 'There's a miniature-Shetland stud just outside Marlbury, on the Basborough road. I want you to go there and buy a small, friendly one.'

Delighted, Fudge raced off and unwittingly acquired the fattest and meanest pony anybody had ever seen, thirty inches of fluffy white malevolence. All afternoon, speculation at Haydown was rife that Hugo was going to send this pretty, wall-eyed purchase to France as a love token to lure back his wife. Instead, rather to the staff's disappointment – and trepidation – he was re-christened Soul and given to the yard's escapologist as a stable companion.

'Heart and Soul,' Fudge sighed, admiring the grumpy little beast fighting his way to Heart's haynet. 'That's *so* sweet.'

'No, it's "Sole" as in Arsehole,' Franny explained, also watching as the already-besotted bay gelding stretched out to nuzzle his new playmate, who squealed furiously and chased him away. 'Treat 'em mean, keep 'em keen, eh Soul man? I like your style.'

The following morning, after a full English breakfast which he pretended not to enjoy, Pascal picked his way along the pock-marked drive to Lime Tree Farm, hopping between puddles to protect his suede loafers and linen chinos, a cotton sweater knotted around his neck and Lacroix sunglasses propped hopefully in his gunmetal hair despite the equally grey clouds amassing on the horizon.

An incredibly attractive man in tight green breeches was mounting a dancing black horse with four white legs on the main yard. With their matching black hair and wild, white-rimmed eyes, Pascal sensed horse and rider wouldn't hang around for long enough to be quizzed.

'*Je m'excuse*! I am looking for a man zey call The Lemon.' Pascal consulted the piece of paper from his pocket. 'And a girl who calls herself Faith.'

The man looked down at him distrustfully, horse still dancing, making Pascal step back.

'Are you police?'

'*Non, je t'assure*! I am Pascal d'Eblouir.' He squared his shoulders and looked up.

The man looked singularly unimpressed, but he jerked his head towards a large metal barn. 'Lem's in there.'

As horse and rider trotted away along the pot-holed driveway, Pascal ducked out of the beginning of another rain shower into a big, open-faced barn full of straw and shavings bales. Somebody was humming Abba's 'Gimme Gimme Gimme' to themselves just out of sight.

He cleared his throat. 'Are you The Lemon?'

'Depends who's asking.' Lemon peered suspiciously over a bale, Kiwi cockatoo to French rooster.

It took just a handful of twenty pound notes to convince him to sit alongside Pascal on a straw bale and tell his new Gallic friend anything he wanted to know.

'Hugo thinks Lough's been trying to scupper his career,' he told him, 'but Lough's gone soft since coming here: he's lost the balls to do stuff like that. He's just in love with Tash, which is his bad luck . . .'

Pascal puffed out his cheeks, eyebrows shooting up as he asked about the New Year's Eve party.

'Yeah, Beccy told me what happened the next day. Hugo's a red-blooded guy and he got a come-on there, no mistake, but he pushed his luck too far. It was one degree from brute force, yeah? She was terrified. If someone hadn't come along, I reckon he'd have taken her whether she wanted it or not. Tash has no idea what a bastard he is.'

When Lough rode back into the yard, Pascal was long gone.

'What did Inspector Clouseau want?' he demanded as Lemon appeared to take the horse.

'Nothing much,' the little groom shrugged. 'Talk about Beccy.'

'Beccy?' Lough kicked his feet from the stirrups, his horse backing up and both their eyes flashing.

'Just the New Year thing – Hugo forcing his dick into her mouth.'

'What did he want to know about that for?'

'Inspector Clouseau is Tash's stepfather.'

Lough hurriedly put his feet back in the pedals. 'Which way did he go?'

'I think he said something about staying with Ange and Den,' Lemon said vaguely as Lough turned the horse and clattered back along the drive.

At the Olive Branch, Angelo sensed a story. 'Signor d'Eblouir checked out half an hour ago.'

'Did he leave a number?' demanded Lough.

Angelo quickly found it for him. 'He is going to somewhere near Windsor today, he said.'

But Lough had already started to ride away. He punched the number on his mobile as he trotted back along the lane.

'Where is she?' he demanded as soon as his call was picked up, hooves ringing out beneath his words.

'Who is this?'

'Lough Strachan. I must get in contact with Tash.'

'Tash is not available.'

'Fuck you.'

Back at Lime Tree Farm, Lough washed off his horse before marching in to the house to find a vaguely familiar and very statuesque blonde making coffee in the kitchen.

'Hi Lough.' She beamed at him with such warmth he paused for a beat. She held up the coffee pot. 'It's best Arabica, bought from Borough Market this morning.'

He nodded, and she poured him a cup.

'India,' she reminded him of her name as she handed it over. 'Penny's niece. I groomed for Tash and Hugo in Germany.'

He nodded again, noticing that her face was incredibly pretty, her eyes as wide and blue as Matauri Bay.

'Have you seen my aunt at all?'

'Hartpury,' he muttered, referring to the venue where Gus and Penny were competing that week.

'I've been ringing her mobile all day,' she groaned. 'I must talk to her.'

He took a swig of coffee, as deliciously bitter as his heart. 'They'll be back tonight.'

India sat on the kitchen table, hugging herself. 'I'm flying out of Heathrow at six. I can't wait.' She pulled out her mobile and tried Penny's number and then Gus's.

'They're competing six horses back to back. They won't return any calls until they're home.'

She clicked her tongue on the top of her mouth and looked at him with her big, sea-blue eyes. 'If I write Pen a note, will you promise to give it to her as soon as she gets home?'

He nodded.

She disappeared into Gus and Penny's bombsite of an office while he helped himself to more coffee and some stale biscuits from the tin, his first food in twenty-four hours.

It was almost twenty minutes before India reappeared, reluctantly handing him an envelope. 'Tell Penny I'll call her about this from Mum's – as soon as I reach LA. And I'll visit her as soon as I'm back.' She glanced around the room, smiling to herself. 'I miss this place. I might just force them to let me work here again.'

'You do that.'

As conversations went, India had got more out of Lough than most, although she would never guess it. He even waved her off – or at least stood outside, shouldering the doorframe and finishing off the coffee and biscuits while she reversed her car and then drove away in the pouring rain.

By the time he had ridden two more horses, he'd completely forgotten about the note in his pocket.

That evening, Lough met Rory in the Olive Branch. In recent weeks, the two men had struck up a friendship that showed all the signs of sinking roots deep beneath them. Rory, like the Moncrieffs, saw no reason not to be friends with both Lough and Hugo. And he was a remarkably good friend: discreet when it mattered, salacious and very funny when it didn't, always upbeat and entertaining. Tonight Lough needed entertaining, his mood sullied by his encounter with Tash's stepfather. He just wanted to know that she was okay.

Rory was late as usual, hair wet from the shower and Twitch at his heels.

'God what a day!' he grumbled good-naturedly as they settled at the bar. 'We took a lorry full to Hartpury. Hugo had fielded this imposhible number of entries, thinking Tash would be riding too, and instead of withdrawing any he inshisted we could cover it and had written out this military timetable to stick to, but it was madness. We were like trick riders hopping on and off with Franny shouting at us. Boy she's scary.' His voice, improving all the time, was now far easier to understand.

'Tell me about it.' Lough had found himself on the wrong side of the Haydown head groom's tongue more than once. She was like a bull terrier, lying in wait for him out hacking.

'She thinks I'm incredibly dishloyal, meeting you for a drink. If she had her way we'd erect a barbed wire barricade on all the bridle paths between here and Maccombe to stop you getting close.'

'What does she think I'm going to do? Challenge Hugo to a duel?'

'Might clear the air. Faith back yet?'

Lough shook his head and Rory swilled the mineral water in his glass, wishing it had some scotch in it. The Moncrieffs were being incredibly vague about where Faith had gone, muttering about a family holiday, but Rory, who had spoken to an equally vague Anke just that week suspected it was no such thing. He just hoped to God she wasn't having more plastic surgery. The thought made him sick with worry. He drained his water and ordered another.

Landlady Denise took this as a cue to join her new favourite barflies to discuss the hottest local gossip.

'Seen who your best owner's canoodling with in all the papers today?' she asked Rory. 'Talk about two "souls lost in one moment" . . .' she sang a line from the previous year's number-one hit, her voice a surprisingly sweet and tuneful alto.

'I've not seen a paper all day,' Rory admitted with a yawn. 'Anyway, as she's always reminding me, Faith's my best owner, not Dillon Rafferty.'

'That's what I'm saying.' Denise slid a copy of the *Daily News* across to them. 'Take a look at this, boys.'

The red tops had all gone wild that morning with photographic proof that Dillon Rafferty had been cheating on poor Sylva Frost – super-mum, super-WAG, super-woman. Bleary photos of Dillon kissing a mysterious, slim blonde in a sun-soaked Caribbean swimming pool had been syndicated everywhere. Nobody knew who she was, the rags claimed, but there was no mistaking the red-hot passion between her and the rock star in the blue water.

'Bloody hell – it *is* her!' Rory's jaw dropped.

'Naughty old Dillon.' Lough whistled, tilting his head this way and that to try to make sense of the picture.

'Taken from a hot-air balloon,' Den explained. 'These are her legs around him here, you see, and they're both looking up so you can clearly see their faces, even though the features are a bit fuzzy. Looks much sexier without a beard, don't you think?'

'Faith or Dillon?' Lough lost interest as his mobile beeped a text alert.

Rory was too poleaxed to notice the way Lough's face lit up as he read it. Taking his drink, the New Zealander headed outside to write a reply.

'You all right, Rory love?' Denise asked worriedly. The young man's face had drained totally of colour.

'Think I need something stronger in this,' he mumbled, sliding his glass forward.

'You sure?' Denise turned to hold it up to the whisky optic, eager to confirm it was the Moncrieffs' groom and find out the girl's surname so she could call the *Sun* news desk and claim the reward on offer. 'So you're certain that's Faith with Dillon Rafferty?'

'Sure.' He stared down at the photo, swallowing hard.

'Only I thought she was – well – a little less attractive, shall we say?'

'Faith is fucking beautiful!' Rory howled, making the landlady step back.

'What's her second name again?' she asked casually.

'Beautiful,' Rory repeated, draining his first scotch since Boxing Day the previous year. It tasted like nectar on fire.

Half an hour later, Lough returned to find the bar unmanned and Rory with his head in his hands and the best malt bottle from the shelves on the table beside him.

'Beautiful,' he kept repeating. 'Shesh beautiful and I've losht her for ever.'

'Is this the slurring thing because of the accident or are you pissed?'

'Both, I guess.'

Half-supporting, half-dragging him to a quiet window seat, Lough placed himself squarely between Rory and the bar.

After almost three teetotal months, Rory was an instant drunk these days.

'Oh fuck, oh fuck, oh fuck,' he sighed quietly, pressing his face to his palms.

'Definitely a fuck-up,' Lough conceded. 'Blew your chance there.'

Rory felt anger flare. 'What the hell do you know? You're in love with Tash Beauchamp, and that's the mother and father of all lost causes.'

'Say again?' The voice had a chill factor that could frostbite any accusing finger.

But Rory was too hurt to care. 'It just ain't gonna happen, Lough.'

'You really think not?' The chill hit bone-deep.

Rory raised his eyes to Lough's face and two war masks squared up over the quiet pub table. The Brit didn't really fancy a fight: Lough was seriously ripped. The muscles on his arms were a landscape of hilly sinew and power, the left one covered with those distinctive tribal tattoos. But tonight he was too beaten up by jealousy to care if he took a few extra punches. It needed saying. 'I think not.'

It was a decisive moment, a pebble spun down in to their new well of friendship to check its depth. It was a long, long time before an echo came back up to them.

'Back home, there's a mountain on the North Island called Taranaki,' Lough said eventually. 'Maori legend has it that it used to live with its friends Tongariro, Ruapehu and Ngauruhoe, but then it made the mistake of falling in love with Tongariro's pretty wife, Pihanga. When Tongariro found out a huge battle ensued and Taranaki ultimately lost. He uprooted and plunged west towards the setting sun, gouging out a deep, wide trench through the land as he went. The next day, a stream of clear water sprang from the side of his friend Tongariro, and it flowed down the deep scar that Taranaki had left on his journey to form the Whanganui River. There are those that say Taranaki is silently brooding and will one day return inland to fight Tongariro again. The Maori are scared of living between the mountains for that reason.'

Rory listened, his head on one side, the alcohol rush receding. 'It's a beautiful story. I'd like to go there one day.'

His companion didn't look up, the pain of the story having ripped out his throat.

'Are you saying property prices will suffer between here and Maccombe because people will fear living between you and Hugo?' Rory checked.

Lough smiled sadly, looking into his drink and shaking his head.

'Or are you saying that Hugo will cry such a stream of tears the Moncrieffs will need to sandbag Lime Tree Farm?'

'Nah,' he laughed, surprised at the strange liberation joking about it granted. He looked up at Rory. 'I'm saying you're right, Rory. Fuck it, you're right.'

Rory nodded, appreciating how hard that must be for him to admit. He was nowhere near that close to admitting it about himself and Faith yet, despite clear photographic evidence to show him it was another lost cause.

'We all climb the wrong mountains sometimes,' he sighed now, 'but that doesn't make it any easier when we fall off the side.'

Lough managed another rueful smile.

'I've never even got past base camp,' Rory admitted. Then he thought about Faith and his heart blew open. 'Faith's not a mountain.' His head went into his hands again. 'She's my Sherpa. She'd climb alongside me all the way. Oh fuck.'

Lough looked down as his phone beeped with a text message. It was just Penny, back late from Hartpury after a very long negotiation to sell a horse, asking whether the yard horses had been fed and whether he had a note for her?

'Shit!' He groped inside his coat pocket and fished out the note India had written hours earlier, two hand-written pages in a shredded envelope now crusted like papier maché after so many downpours had seeped through Lough's seams and into the jacket lining.

Before he could phone Penny to explain and apologise, Rory started prising the leaves apart. 'They'll never know – we'll dry it on the radiator and have it looking like new in no time . . . Hang on.' He started to read a few lines. 'Fuck*ing* hell. Listen to this . . .'

India had, it seemed, stumbled on the truth behind a career- and marriage-wrecking myth. She and her brother Rufus were very close to their cousins by marriage, both of whom had been at the New Year's Eve party. Young Huey Moncrieff, in particular, had reported having a fantastic time there, something he'd been boasting about at his boarding school ever since. His GCSE work had improved no end: he'd leaped up the grade forecasts and was predicted all As and Bs. But it wasn't until Rufus took his cousin out for an end-of-term drink before the boy flew home to South Africa that the full story came out, and had now started the slow process of filtering its way back through the family.

'*"He told Rufe that he got very intimate with a girl at the Lime Tree party"*,' Rory read aloud now. '*"It was in the dark in the hayloft and it definitely went past first base, but not a lot further because he bottled it when his mother appeared on the scene. He doesn't know who the girl was, just that she was older and very experienced. Rufe said nothing to him about what's happened, and we really don't want to get him into any trouble and he doesn't think he's done anything wrong"*. . .' It was obvious from the letter that she wanted to protect her cousin. It was equally clear that the man who'd got carried away with a drunken Beccy on New Year's Eve hadn't been Hugo Beauchamp, it had been Huey Moncrieff. And to the young Hugo's mind, the encounter had been a first sexual experience close to perfection.

Rory and Lough stared at one another in shock.

'And Beccy cried rape.' Rory whistled in disbelief as he read through the crumpled pages.

'She never said that,' Lough snapped. 'Lem said that.'

'She's a hysteric.' He handed the pages back. 'Everyone knows she's a coin short of operating normally.'

'Take that back!'

'She's sweet, but she's a fruitcake. You don't know her, Lough.'

Lough carefully placed the sodden letter on the table. 'Actually I do. We text a lot.'

Rory stared at him in amazement. 'And how long has this been going on?' he asked, sounding like an elderly aunt.

'On and off, about a year.'

'A *year*?'

'Since before I came here. That was her texting earlier. She's very low right now.'

'I'm not surprised. She's screwed up a few lives recently, not least her own.'

'Don't be so quick to judge her,' Lough said quietly. 'She's taken a lot of wrong turns in life, and I know all about that. But she's amazing underneath.' A smile touched his lips.

Rory's face brightened with a sudden realisation. 'You think you've got the loose change to make her add up, don't you?'

Lough glared at him with such force Rory thought his eyeballs would freeze. 'It's not like that.'

'Wake up and smell the blue mountain coffee, Lough,' Rory laughed. 'You're half way up the tallest peak already, but you've been too busy looking across at Pihanga's pretty rockface to notice you've climbed so high.'

Another pebble fell into the well. This time it span for so long Denise had time to take their empty glasses, wipe the table, double-check Faith's surname really was Beautiful and pick a couple of dead leaves off the carnations in the vase between them before it splashed into the water.

'Can I borrow your car?' Lough asked Rory urgently.

'Totalled it ages ago,' Rory apologised. 'I've got Hugo's quad bike here. Any use?'

'Not to get to Windsor.' His Yamaha was up on a stand in one of Gus's barns with its back wheel off because he hadn't got around to fitting a new drive chain. 'I'll have to take my horsebox.'

Rory shoved the battered note under his nose. 'Go back to Lime Tree Farm and show them this: they'll lend you a car. If not, just nick Gus's bike – he leaves the keys tucked in his helmet lining for a quick getaway these days in case Penny discovers Lucy's been in touch and starts waving the kitchen knives around.'

He was out of the door before Rory could ask him why on earth he wanted to go to Windsor. It seemed an odd time to start sight-seeing.

Chapter 82

In Benedict House, a fine-looking Georgian villa sitting in ten acres of meticulously landscaped grounds where Royal Berkshire met commuter-land Surrey, Pascal had, for several hours, been enjoying Henrietta's hospitality as both patiently awaited Beccy's awakening in the pretty bedroom above their heads with its Laura Ashley wallpaper festooned with crystals and dream catchers. According to her mother, she had been lying wide awake in there for days reading endless trashy novels, watching daytime TV and crying a lot. But that day, rather curiously, she had been largely comatose. It was now almost dark, and she was still asleep.

'Her painkillers are very powerful,' Henrietta apologised as she made yet more coffee.

Pascal's mobile phone rang out with a refrain from Debussy's Arabesque No. 1, making Henrietta jump.

He held up his hand apologetically as he took the call. ''allo?'

'This is Lough Strachan again. Please don't hang up.'

'Okay.' Pascal was magnanimous.

'I have to talk to with Beccy Sergeant.'

'*Oui, bien sûr, moi aussi.*'

'No, I'm not Aussie, I'm from New Zealand.'

There was a brief pause before Pascal confirmed: 'I am visiting Beccy now, but she sleeps.'

'I must speak with her.'

'*Porquoi?*'

The New Zealand boy was clearly not a great communicator, especially on the phone to a stranger who couldn't understand much of his accent, but he said enough to convince Pascal to give him the address for Benedict House and agree to wait for him to arrive.

After the call, he glanced at his watch impatiently. He had booked a room at the Great Fosters, where he was very much looking forward to sampling the restaurant. He'd had half a mind to tell Lough Strachan not to come, but he had a feeling this break could be his only way of getting to the bottom of this whole sorry riddle, and he owed it to his beautiful Xandra to find out the truth.

He'd never seen the home where his wife's first marriage had been thrown against the rocks, and felt as though he had walked on to the set of a Jane Austen costume drama; it was so pretty yet fusty and formal. He found it all the more strange and disconcerting to be so politely welcomed by the very blonde, very English Henrietta. She had even baked croissants in his honour. James was away in Scotland, playing in a golf tournament with other retired bankers, she'd apologised, to Pascal's great relief.

And while Beccy was childlike in her morbid distress and wouldn't talk to him at all, Henrietta proved as sensible and openminded as she was protective and concerned.

'It was my older daughter Em who Beccy really talked to about the . . . sexual encounter with Hugo,' she explained, turning as pink as the stargazer lilies bursting from pots in her conservatory, but equally open. 'She hasn't said a lot since. She is very embarrassed about it, and the riding accident has knocked so much of the stuffing out of her.'

'Is it possible,' Pascal spoke carefully now, not wanting his bad English to confuse his meaning, 'that Beccy may have mistaken someone else for Hugo?'

'Impossible. He said his name.'

'I say my name, Pascal, but I am not the only one *en France*,' he pointed out. 'At a party, there are many of us I think and in a darkened room a pretty girl could find 'erself confused, *non*?'

Henrietta shook her head. 'You are unique to those who love you – the way you smell and feel and touch.'

'Beccy, she loves Hugo?' He was starting to understand the situation better, although he wished it were otherwise.

'A crush,' Henrietta nodded, 'but a very long-lived one.'

'That is the effect Hugo has on women.' He puffed out his cheeks in bewilderment, utterly failing to see the attraction these arrogant, sporty upper-class Brits had when their passionate, wine-loving Gallic counterparts were so much more rewarding.

Glancing discreetly at his watch and again hoping Lough would arrive soon, Pascal tactfully changed the subject to her beautiful garden, and before he knew it they were having a warm and animated discussion on slug control for nasturtiums. Ten minutes later, she was giving him a torch-lit guided tour of her herbaceous borders.

Beccy could hear their voices outside her open bedroom windows, ghastly old-fogey droning about aphids. She wanted to hurl something out of the gaping sash, but the only things to hand were her iPhone and her laptop, both of which provided vital communication with the outside world. Not that she was communicating yet, but she was keeping tabs.

The pain was searing again. She longed to ring the emergency bell Henrietta had placed on her bedside table, but couldn't face her mother lecturing her on reducing her analgesia again, and anyway she was set on pretending to be asleep until the French detective went away. She'd stashed a few of the really potent knock-out pills under her pillow. She dug one out now, and tucked it under her tongue. There were now just three left so she must have taken a lot more than she was meant to.

She drifted off to sleep, but woke up with pain searing through her pelvis, her hips full of razorblades. She felt dry-mouthed and sick so drank water, taking two more pills but not caring. It hurt too much.

Beccy closed her eyes and gritted her teeth. There was a droning, snarling noise in her head now, like maddened insects.

She must have dropped off again because she had a dream that Lough was in her room, standing over her and saying her name.

'Beccy – Beccy, wake up.'

'Hi.' She smiled up at him groggily.

Those turbulent, dark eyes came in and out of focus. He had a strange red stripe across his forehead.

'Is that a Maori thing?'

'Huh?'

She had to say it several times to be understood, her words slurring horribly.

'No, I borrowed Gus's bike off the yard and the helmet's too tight,' he explained and then he started talking about something, but she couldn't keep up. He was spinning around her.

She tried to remember how many pills she had taken. More than ten? Surely not. Then again . . . She started to tip over the cliff into lovely blackness.

Her eyes snapped open. Lough had his fingers laced through hers. How bizarre. How beautifully bizarre.

'. . . cousin called Hugo,' he was saying '. . . admits it all . . . just fifteen . . . carried away . . . terrified he's done wrong . . . got to sort this out . . . both your sakes . . .'

She closed her eyes and listened to his Kiwi drawl. She remembered flirting with him on the phone all those months ago, the giddy sense of sexual attraction, a world away from sucking salty stale underpants in a stables loft in Berkshire.

These painkillers were the best.

'This was Tash's bedroom as a kid,' she told him. 'You love her, don't you? Just imagine her lying in this bed at fifteen, dreaming about getting carried away in a hay barn, writhing away right here where I am.'

'Shut up.'

She opened one eye but five Loughs were spinning around so she closed it again, and waited to tumble over the cliff edge. At least the pain had gone, even if the dreams were weird. How many pills had she swallowed today? Ten? Twelve? Maybe more . . .

She'd stolen rather a lot of the pills in recent days, several little foil trays sneaked away when her mother wasn't looking. Could it be as many as sixteen?

Now, suddenly, through the soup of analgesia, Beccy started to panic. But her body was so sluggish and her mind so muddled, she had no familiar adrenalin spike of fear and fight.

Lough was talking again, that lovely voice: 'Beccy, this is serious. The man you were with on New Year's Eve wasn't Hugo Beauchamp.'

She started to feel as though she was floating up above her own body.

He took her hand. It was clammy and cold. 'Hugo *Moncrieff* is Gus's nephew. He's fifteen. He was the one you were alone with that night.'

'What a coincidence,' she murmured, her voice sounding miles away in her head. 'Life is full of them, don't you find?'

'Do you understand what I'm say—'

'I went to the Melbourne Horse Trials once,' she said dreamily, cutting him off mid-flow. 'The three day event. You were there. So was Tash. That's a coincidence.'

'Beccy, we have to talk about—'

'I ran out in front of my stepsister's horse. You saved my life.'

Lough shut up abruptly, a flutter running through his regular heart beat.

'Crazy thing to do.' Her voice was increasingly distant, especially to her own ears. 'But I just wanted to be gone. And you kept me alive. You kept me safe for just a little bit . . .'

Lough looked at her pale face, trying to recognise something familiar in the features, in the wide cheeks, rosebud lips and little snub nose. He'd relived that moment again and again over the years.

'I'm scared, Lough.' Her gaze was unfocused now, her voice barely more than a whisper. 'The pain was just so bad, I wanted it to stop.' Her voice slurred and she closed her eyes.

'It was a long time ago.' He squeezed her hand, which was limp in his.

'No.' Her fingers twitched as she fought sleep. 'You don't understand. I never could count very well . . . taken too many . . . kill the pain . . . feel so scared. Please don't let me die, Lough.'

'I'm here,' he soothed distractedly, guessing she was overtired.

He glanced around the room, Tash's old room, dating back to a childhood he knew nothing about, a woman he knew nothing about and, if he admitted the truth, a fantasy built from one fateful day. There were framed photographs of Beccy on horses all over the walls now, little personal knick-knacks on the dressing table and windowsills, china horses and old trophies. It smelled deliciously of sweet peas, cocoa butter and clean hair. It smelled of Beccy.

It took over a minute for Lough to realise that she hadn't fallen asleep again. Her eyes had rolled back and her breathing was so shallow it was almost gone.

Then it seemed to stop entirely.

With a bellow for help, he pulled back the covers and checked her airways, breathing and pulse before starting to perform CPR.

'Call an ambulance – I think it's an overdose!' he shouted at Henrietta as soon as she ran into the room.

The heel of his hand in the middle of Beccy's chest, fingers interlaced with those of his other hand, he compressed at regular intervals, counting down from thirty.

Then he tipped back her chin and pinched her nose, closing his mouth around hers – oh what a first kiss – breathing until her lungs filled. Once. Twice.

He started compressing her chest again. 'Thirty, twenty-nine, twenty-eight . . .'

When Beccy began to splutter and cough, clearly about to vomit, he pulled her torso upright and supported her, careful not to put any more stress on her broken pelvis than he had to. He rubbed her back, soft and pale between her shoulder blades where her little camisole revealed skin tens of shades lighter than the outdoor glow around her neckline and arms. As he stroked her, his fingers crisscrossed a small tattoo on one pearl-white shoulder. A mermaid smiled up at him.

He could hear the Melbourne Tannoy in his ears, announcing that Tash was at the lake. He saw the girl climb the barriers in front of him, so close her bag caught on his elbow, pulling it clean off her arm like a thief. She hadn't even looked back. He remembered her fear, her eyes as wild as an animal's, her body all bones and baggy clothes. She'd smelled of stale digs and the city, a world away from anything that comforted him or inspired him. She had smelled of his childhood.

Now her warm skin was sweet and moreish; she smelled of life as she hiccupped and gasped and groaned, fighting her way back.

'I'm so sorry,' she mumbled. 'I didn't mean to do it. I'm so sorry.'

'Don't you go away,' he breathed in her ear, 'I know who you are. I've taken long time to find you.' And, holding her tight, he dropped his lips to kiss the mermaid, stunned by the electric shock that rocketed right through him.

Then Beccy vomited.

As moments go, it wasn't the most romantic, but in that moment Lough changed indelibly. Even as she was wrenched away from him, spirited off in an ambulance by paramedics who insisted she must go to hospital, he knew he'd bet his heart on the wrong horse a long time ago.

Stomach pumped and pain relief strictly controlled, Beccy was monitored overnight before undergoing a psychiatric assessment in the morning.

It took Lough over an hour to pluck up the courage to call her mobile that afternoon, intending to leave a message. He didn't imagine for a moment that she would answer it in person, but she did.

'You saved my life,' she breathed.

He couldn't think what to say.

'Again.' She laughed tearfully.

'How are you?' he managed to ask eventually.

'Under observation, apparently, although no longer a suicide risk, which is nice.' Her nerves were making her babble. 'They do at least see that I took too many painkillers to try to kill the pain, not myself, and now I'm on the most fantastic new stuff that means I'm not in constant agony. They've spent all day assessing me. It seems I'm not considered a threat to myself or others. They obviously haven't seen me ride across country.'

He smiled, amazed at how upbeat she sounded. 'So when do you get out?'

'Any time now. I might even be going to France tonight, if the hospital will discharge me. Pascal thinks I should talk to Tash in person.'

'Can't you just phone?'

'I need to tell her the truth face to face.'

'And what is the truth?' he asked carefully.

Beccy breathed in deeply, the truth of it still hurting a lot. 'I was horribly drunk. I never saw him properly – just heard the voice and smelled the aftershave. And I so *wanted* it to be my Hugo – Tash's Hugo – even though it was so awful. I've had this crazy hang-up about him for years, you see. I've been a bit obsessed really.'

'"Every woman needs a little madness in her life."'

She recognised the quote with a sharp intake of breath. *Cyrano de Bergerac*. 'Oh, God, don't! I'm so ashamed that I pretended to be Tash all those weeks just to talk to you.'

'I'm glad you did.' He let out that rare, hot-spring laugh. 'Are you really going to France tonight?'

'If the consultant agrees. James was absolutely livid when he got back from St Andrews. You should have heard him: "But she has a broken pelvis, for God's sake!"' she impersonated her stepfather's bark. 'And Pascal just stood his ground: "Tash, she has a broken heart. That is much more fragile to travel. I will hire a private ambulance and a nurse."' Her French accent was superb. Lough fought a crazy urge to ask her to keep talking in it, but she was speaking again:

'I'm being wheeled over the Channel to say my piece. D'you want me to bring you back some Rosé d'Anjou? Send your love to Tash?'

There was an awkward pause.

'Sorry. Unforgiveable.' She said in a small voice. 'One psychiatrist asked me today if I self harm, which I don't, but I forgot to point out to her that I've been cutting off my nose to spite my face all my life.'

Hearing her speak with that rushed, nervous humour reminded Lough of the calls they'd shared before. He still struggled to separate Beccy from Tash during those early weeks, yet the more he thought about it, the more clearly he could hear the real Beccy speaking, with her playful, restless mind and her quick-wittedness.

'I was thinking of coming to visit you,' he admitted. In fact, he'd spent all morning grappling with his motorbike to get it roadworthy, running through what he was going to say in his head, while Gus loudly complained that his horses were going unridden.

'You still can,' Beccy said now.

'But you're going to France.'

'I am – the Loire Valley. It's not Bergerac, I know, but it's less far for you to drive,' she teased. Then, when there was a stunned silence at the other end of the line, she hastily added, 'Forget it. Stupid idea. Total fantasy.'

Still Lough said nothing and Beccy winced at her end of the line, her face now so red it was threatening to melt the fascia of her iPhone.

'Maybe we're both fantasists,' he said eventually.

Beccy caught her breath. 'They should lock us up.'

'They did once, remember? You in a Singapore jail, and me in a cell in Auckland.'

Suddenly they both burst into laughter, a magical release that rendered them both breathless. It was like a first kiss.

'I'll see you in France then, shall I?' he asked, clearly still uncertain if she was joking.

Gripped by fright, Beccy found the fact Lough had called at all surreal, and a paranoid voice in her head still insisted that he was using her to get closer to Tash. Like a child with a box of matches, she couldn't resist sending up sparks.

'If Tash and Hugo really have separated, there's nothing to stop you now. You're bound to want to talk to her. Le Manoir's really romantic, from what I've heard. Don't worry, I won't stand in your way. Can't stand up right now anyway.'

There was another yawning silence and Beccy closed her eyes, knowing she'd just totally blown it, the matches catching the few fragile silk threads that tied her and Lough together and burning them clean away. Her thumb was already fingering the End Call button.

'Must go – just cut myself badly with my tongue again. Need to call for a nurse. See you some time.'

In truth, Beccy felt she didn't deserve Lough's attention any more than she did Tash's forgiveness. She'd never been as terrified as she was right now. The thought of travelling to France to face her stepsister felt more intimidating than stepping off the side of a cliff.

That evening, accompanied by her mother and Pascal, Beccy was taken by private ambulance to Biggin Hill where she was carefully loaded on to a chartered plane bound for France.

As a treat, her mother had bought her a great doorstep of newspapers and magazines. Beccy picked up a tabloid from the top of the pile. Suddenly she shrieked, causing Henrietta to almost knock herself out on an overhead shelf in her haste to check what was wrong.

'That's Faith!' Beccy pointed to the strawberry blonde photographed on the front page, leaving a private Caribbean island by speed boat.

Very late that night, in his quiet corner of County Mayo, horse dealer Fearghal Moore answered the persistent knocking on the front door of his tatty farmhouse to find a stunning sun-tanned girl standing there, her hair the colour of rose gold.

Blinking sleep from his eyes, he took in her tanned face, white smile and strangely familiar features in silent astonishment.

'I'm Faith,' she announced nervously. 'Your daughter. Mum said it was okay to come. I might need somewhere to hide for a bit, if that's all right . . .'

'Sure, child. We've been expecting you.' He held the door wide open. 'By God, you look just like your mother.'

Chapter 83

En route to Le Manoir, Beccy entertained visions of speaking with Tash in a gentle, *La Dame aux camélias* fashion, in an antique bed, a slender hand to her furrowed brow, consumptive cough ever-ready and pity all around her. The little room she was put in when she arrived was perfect. It was called the Salle Bienvenue because it was in a circular turret right at the front of the magical old house, overlooking the formal carriage drive nobody ever used, with narrow, arched windows and its own small balcony. Beccy had been put in there because it was the only bedroom that had no steps to it, making it possible to wheel her chair in and out along the narrow passageway that ran from the rear courtyard. It was after midnight by the time she arrived, and Tash was already in bed by then so she had plenty of time to perfect her pose and work through the scene in her head.

But her apology was never enacted in the Salle Bienvenue. Instead, she was pushed on to a sunny terrace in a very obstinate hired wheelchair the following morning and left there batting away wasps while Pascal whisked Henrietta off for a tour of the garden.

Tash eventually appeared, clearly prodded by some unseen hand –

the same hand that was looking after the children in the house.

She looked terrible, Beccy realised. The pink-cheeked, baby-fattened stepsister she had moved in with a year earlier was now gaunt and wasted, the suntan a thin patina that barely distracted from the dark smudges beneath her eyes and the veins of tension running up and down her long neck.

'It wasn't Hugo!' she blurted without preamble. 'It was another Hugo, a teenage one. I had no idea, Tash, really no idea.'

Those big, mismatched eyes blinked, not quite daring to believe her.

Beccy looked away, too ashamed to face the very real emotional wreckage she had caused for a moment longer.

Ahead of her, the valley smouldered in a heat haze, the distant poplars like little flames licking up into a scorching blue sky.

'I don't suppose you'll ever forgive me,' she whispered.

'Oh Beccy, of course I do.' A warm hand enveloped hers as Tash crouched down beside her. 'But will Hugo ever forgive me for not believing him?'

Beccy's moods and their extremes might be up for professional consideration, but her sense of right and wrong was still fully functioning.

'He didn't believe *you* either!' she wailed indignantly. 'He still doesn't.'

'Maybe he's right not to.' Tash stared out at the valley.

Beccy turned pale. 'So you did have an affair with Lough?'

'No,' she said, her voice barely more than a whisper. 'We kissed once – that was it. But I fancied him.' She pressed her hands to her hot cheeks. 'I really fancied him.'

'Oh, that's just normal,' Beccy assured her, sounding terribly relieved. 'You'd have to be mad not to fancy Lough. He's just *so* sexy. In fact,' she smiled, 'mad people probably fancy Lough, too. Everybody fancies him!'

Tash turned to look at her stepsister in surprise. Beccy's face was lit up like the landscape around them. So that was where her affection now lay.

'He's a difficult character,' she warned, suddenly anxious about Beccy's fragility.

'So am I,' she pointed out. Then, turning pink, added, 'So was he a good kisser?'

★

After an even longer lunch than usual, with Pascal, Alexandra and Henrietta in rip-roaring form, Tash could wait no longer to tackle another difficult character, the one she loved with all her bruised heart. Quickly plonking the children, wide awake, in their travel cots for an afternoon nap and thrusting the squawking monitor apologetically at Henrietta, who appeared to be the only other adult awake in the house, she hid herself in Pascal's study and used the phone there, dialling Hugo's mobile.

'It's me,' she said breathlessly when he answered, blood rushing loudly in her ears.

'Yes?' He was typically curt.

She told him the truth as she had just heard it, simply and without embellishment; that Beccy had been mistaken, that it had been someone else.

'Fine. So when are you coming home?'

There was the sound of a Tannoy in the background. He was at a competition, she realised.

'Soon – tomorrow or Thursday.'

'Fine.'

There was a long pause and the lump in Tash's throat grew so big, she felt like a snake that had swallowed a whole egg.

'Is that all?' he asked.

She could barely breathe for unhappiness.

'I'm sorry,' she whispered hoarsely.

'Thanks.' He hung up.

He hadn't even asked after the children. Tomorrow was Amery's birthday.

Tash rubbed her face, anger flaring.

She pressed redial.

'Okay – here's how it is,' she raged as soon as he picked up. 'I fancied Lough. I was lonely and you were away and he made no secret of his attraction for me and I fancied him. That's all! Nothing happened beyond flirtation and one kiss. There was no affair. I fancied him, but I have always fancied you more and loved only you. Is that such a CRIME?'

'Tash, poppet, this is Rory. Hugo's just ridden in for the prize-giving and I'm holding his phone.'

'Oh, right,' she gulped, mortified.

'He won his intermediate section,' he informed her jollily.

'Great.' She could hear clapping in the background.

'Have you seen the papers today?' Rory asked, sounding less bright.

'I'm in France.'

'Of course. Faith's in all the tabloids. She's been named as Dillon's Caribbean Queen.'

'His what?' Tash was nonplussed.

'Hang on – Hugo's coming out. Oh, he's ridden straight past.' He dropped his voice, 'He's unspeakable right now, Tash. He obviously mishes you like hell. You must come back.'

'I will,' she promised.

'It wasn't him with Beccy at all, you know – it was Gus's nephew.'

'Mmm, yes.' Tash cleared her throat awkwardly, wondering how on earth Rory knew. Was the hayloft doppelgänger an open secret on the eventing circuit now, too?

But before she could ask, he blurted: 'D'you think Faith and Dillon will lasht?' His voice was slurring again because he was upset.

'I – I have no idea.' She found it very hard to get her head around the idea, or really focus on it, and so said, without thinking, 'I was always under the impression that Faith was far too madly in love with you to look at anyone else.'

'Really?' he gulped.

'Really.'

'Thanks, Tash! God, I've bloody got to win the Grand Slam. You'd better not beat me at Burghley. Your horse is looking far too fit and well for my liking.'

'She is?' Tash hadn't sat on River in over a week.

'Hugo rides her first every day, before everything else. Shall I go and see if I can find him for you?'

'No, don't worry.' Her anger had totally vanished now, and she just felt weary and sad. She had to check the children were asleep, not terrorising Henrietta who had enough on her plate looking after Beccy. Pascal would be up and cooking again soon. The rhythm of life at Le Manoir never altered, whereas at home it was a constant game of pinball.

'Any message?' Rory asked awkwardly, clearly hoping that he didn't have to relay the bit about her fancying Lough.

'No,' she sighed. 'No message.'

★

Faith found meeting and spending time with her birth father a revelation, making sense of so much in her life.

Unlike her cool, self-controlled, magnanimous mother, Faith has always had a wild temper and a passionately fierce partisan streak. Fearghal was just the same, with his shock of frizzy red hair, his furious temper, glorious sense of humour and single-minded passion for horses.

Anke had always told Faith that she would like Fearghal, and reluctant as she always was to concur with her mother, she now knew that she had been absolutely right.

He was outspoken, bloody minded, zealous and dedicated. He was also wholly eccentric and suffered no fools gladly, but forgave friends and family willingly. To Faith's delighted relief his fierce loyalty extended to all his children, legitimate or not.

Married and widowed once, divorced twice ('Never unfaithful, though – you came between marriages, darling girl'), Fearghal was as lapsed as a Catholic can get and wholly unrepentant. His current wife, Roisin, was half his age and twice his girth and had borne him four more children to make his brood up to twelve, including Faith. All of them rode. All of them had reddish-blonde hair. And all welcomed her with open arms.

'I wasn't sure you'd want to know me.' She was astonished by such overwhelming warmth.

'I've always wanted to know you. We all have,' Fearghal told her. 'But you needed to find your way here in your own time.'

'My friend Dillon talked me into it, really,' she admitted, having been more-or-less nannied on to the Dublin flight by the Golden Hind staff as directed by her pop-star lover who had then stealthily hopped a private flight to LA to vanish behind his ex-wife's entourage. Since the press had discovered Faith's identity the story had been splashed over every paper and magazine and the race was on to pinpoint her whereabouts and secure an interview. But they had no idea to look for her in Ireland.

Dillon had been right, Faith realised; she needed the space to recover from her crash-course in lust and lovemaking while the media furore died down. Their brief seduction had been among the most fun she could remember; her ribs still ached from laughing so much and her throat from talking too much on that stolen day in the Caribbean. But as they'd both agreed when their lost week of sun and sin came to an end, staying friends was far more important than making love.

'This would be the Dillon who makes the popular records that all you girls get silly about?' Fearghal had been briefed by his wise children on the furore surrounding Faith, even if he'd not bothered to look at a paper, his only regular reading being the *Irish Field*, partaken in the loo.

'Yes.'

'Well if he told you to come here he can't be all bad, although his music's terrible, so it is. Tell me, are you in love with him?'

'No.' She blushed, thinking about all the things that she had learned during her week away and praying that Rory might one day benefit from them.

'That's a relief,' her father told her. 'It never does to lose your heart too young.'

'Oh, but I *am* in love,' she told him certainly.

He tutted. 'Are you now?'

'He's a brilliant event rider.'

'That's something, at least. You were born in the saddle like me, so you'll need to live and love in it too.'

When he saw Faith on a horse Fearghal wept with joy.

'Sure, you have your father's hands and your mother's body,' he wiped his eyes. 'Did you not say you had a horse qualified for Burghley?'

'Only on paper,' Faith laughed, cantering around on one of his young sales horses, amazed at the power and quality beneath her. 'We're nowhere near good enough.'

But, once an idea took told, Fearghal would not be dissuaded and he insisted that she must take her chance on White Lies, faxing her entry through from his kitchen three minutes before the deadline. Faith was certain it was far beyond her – and that she would be balloted out even if her qualifications made the grade – but such was the force of Fearghal's personality he made anything seem possible.

'Child of mine, he'll notice you far more if you win Burghley than if you swan about with rock stars,' he laughed.

'Who are you talking about?' She coloured.

'This man you say you love.' Her father gave her a sage wink. 'If I know anything about event riders, and I've known a few well now, mark my words, you could be lying underneath Bono, Brian Kennedy, Chris de Burgh *and* little Ronan Keating and your man there wouldn't bat an eye, but get a fast clear at Punchestown and he's yours for ever.'

She laughed, but her heart stayed circumspect. 'You think I should try to beat him then?'

'Ah now there's a thing. Men have terrible fragile egos, so they do, so perhaps not beat exactly . . . just *impress.*'

'I haven't a hope of beating him anyway. His horses are far better, and I wouldn't dream of getting in the way of his Grand Slam dreams. That's when I'm going to tell him I love him.'

Fearghal's fierce little eyes softened beneath their bushy red brows as they studied her closely. 'Child, are you saying this man still has no idea that you do *love* him?'

'Of course he knows – it's patently obvious.'

'But you've never actually said it, written it or indicated it in a . . . *non-verbal* way to him yourself.' He cleared his throat, a terrible prude when it came to discussing anything carnal.

'No.'

'Ah now there's a thing. Men are awful thick eejits as well as having these terrible fragile egos. You might just have to spell it out to him.'

'You think I should actually *tell* Rory that I love him?'

'Yes, you should tell him! But not before Burghley,' he added hastily, thinking of the fifty-euro bet he'd just laid on her horse at a hundred to one. 'You need to keep a clear head, and so does that man of yours. Take old Fearghal's advice and keep out of his way until then.'

She nodded, swallowing uncomfortably at the thought.

'He'd be a fool to miss out on you,' he told her, reaching out to take her hand and kiss it. 'You are quite the most spectacular girl; so like your mother. Don't tell young Roisin, but Anke was always the one that got away.'

'Oh, I wish I'd known you all my life,' Faith blurted, unable to contain her affection as she covered his face with kisses.

At this, Fearghal turned a surprising shade of beetroot and held on to her hand very tightly. 'You have.' He banged both their laced knuckles against her breastbone and then his. 'In here, we've never been apart.'

'Can I hide here for ever?'

'You can stay as long as you like,' he assured her, 'but there's no more hiding to be done. Sure, they're bored with you already. You can come and go as you please now.'

He was right. Faith had spent less than a week in Ireland, but the press had already moved on from Dillon Rafferty's mystery Caribbean blonde. There was a fully identifiable blonde on his father's arm that was much, much more newsworthy . . .

'Lord, what a trollop!' Fearghal goggled over the photographs of Sylva Frost and the Rockfather canoodling by the River Odd with a champagne picnic. 'Sure, he looks like that cockney fella who drinks in O'Flannagan's Bar sometimes. And he's old enough to be her father, so he is.'

At this, Roisin caught Faith's eye and winked.

As soon as the Pete and Sylva story broke, Faith knew she had to get back to England to start riding White Lies again. 'Dillon left him with Rory to work, but he's no idea we're headed for Burghley. I told him Blenheim was too much for us this year – we were begging a lift with the Beauchamps to Le Lion d'Angers before you came along and changed my plans.' Her eyes flashed with fear.

'Aim high and you hit less timber,' Fearghal told her. 'Now I have a couple of little keepsakes for your birthday, my darling lost daughter. Close your eyes . . .'

'Oh my Lord!' she shrieked a moment later, jumping up and down on the spot. 'How do I fit those in my Ryanair baggage allowance?'

'I'll send them over with Ken Gamble next week. Happy birthday, child of mine.'

How Faith was going to explain to the Moncrieffs about the pair of fabulous grey, home-bred thoroughbreds he had given her was beyond her imaginings, but she decided to cross that bridge when she came to it. As Fearghal said, aim high . . . and aiming for Rory was still so high the air went thin and she couldn't breathe when she thought about it.

The sun was still relentlessly bleaching the Loire from verdigris to almond as Tash pushed Beccy's wheelchair along the rose walk striped by the shady, arched arbours. Beccy had Amery on her knee, who was sporting a very dashing legionnaire sunhat, and Cora was running ahead dressed in nothing but a swimming nappy and checked flower-pot hat, picking up rose petals. Behind them, Henrietta and Alexandra were arm in arm, eulogising about David Austin Roses and weighing up the relative merits of full bloom versus single, old varieties versus new hybrids.

'They're in love,' Beccy observed cynically, but there was laughter in her voice.

'Daddy will be livid,' Tash sighed.

Beccy reached back and touched Tash's fingers, grateful to feel the pressure returned. It had been a hellish twenty-four hours, but she had finally come out the other side. She was appalled at the pain and damage she had caused, but they all knew that it was a mistake, a foolish, fumbling mistake. When she thought back to her awful, blundering attempts at seduction with what had transpired was a teenage boy, she wanted to curl up and die of shame, and she now couldn't believe how she had possibly thought it was Hugo. But half-truths and misconceptions and believing what one wanted to believe had a way of escalating horribly, as she now knew.

Telling her mother the truth about her father's death had been a much, much harder task and she'd almost flunked it, letting the pressure build up until Henrietta had been helping her into bed the previous evening. Tears of shame mounting all the time for the pain she was about to inflict, Beccy had let her mother fuss around her, fiddling with her pillows and sheets. Then, as she bent down to press a kiss to her forehead, Beccy blurted it out.

'Dad committed suicide.'

The kiss lingered over her head for a long time before it was breathed back into her mother's lips. Henrietta straightened up and perched on the side of her bed, taking her hand between hers.

Out it came, the story she had hidden away for years, a cruel truth to blast away all the myths. She expected anger, denial, accusations of lies and mania, blaming her moods and her fantasy life, or her painkillers again. Yet Henrietta gave her nothing but support and love, grasping an opportunity that she wished she had been given during those ten long years her daughter had wandered in search of answers. She wasn't about to let her go again. 'I was married to him, I know what he was like. Oh, my little girl, keeping this in your heart so long. You are so brave.'

They'd talked until close to dawn.

Now, drooping in the sun, they were totally exhausted. Tash was desperate to set off back to England for Haydown and Hugo, but it was Amery's birthday and Alexandra insisted she hold on a few more hours for Pascal to return from his vineyard so that she could host a picnic party by the river.

'I've not had much luck with birthday parties this year,' Tash said gloomily, looking at her watch.

'Oh, Sophia was talking about that on the phone just the other day!' Alexandra exclaimed. 'She says—'

'Alexandra!' Henrietta interrupted rather desperately. 'What is this wonderful scented shrub beside us here?'

'It's orange blossom, darling. Isn't it obvious?' She turned back to Tash. 'Sophia wants Pascal and I to come to England for your—'

'Alexandra!' Henrietta sounded even more desperate. 'Is there a *secret* to having good orange blossom?'

'What?'

'A *SECRET*?' she was breathless with teeth-gritting effort.

'Oh yes! Hmmm.' Alexandra was exploding with anticipation, making her quite forget that Sophia had sworn her to secrecy about her plans for a party to celebrate Tash and Hugo's eighth wedding anniversary in November, a rescheduling of the disastrous, cancelled fortieth birthday party. Sophia was going to extraordinary lengths to keep it hush-hush, and the family had even been summoned to Burghley to talk tactics in a way that wouldn't alert the couple's suspicions. But now Alexandra thought about it, there might not be much to celebrate. Tash still seemed terribly apprehensive.

'All this waiting is so depressing!' she announced suddenly. 'Pascal can join us later. Let's all go to the river for a birthday picnic!'

It was a glorious afternoon. Lounging in the shade of vast old chestnut trees, Henrietta and Amery fell asleep curled up together on a checked blanket with spaniels wedged around them; Cora and Tash waded in the water shrieking as they tried to catch minnows, and Alexandra sat on a folding picnic chair beside Beccy in her wheelchair.

'You're terribly pretty now, you know,' Alexandra told her. 'Quite exquisitely pretty.'

For a moment Beccy's heart swelled stupidly large, but then she realised Alexandra had her eyes shut.

'As I told Tash' – the older woman reached out and took her hand without hesitation, before finally opening her eyes – 'one sees best with one's heart.' She smiled at Beccy. 'Is there a man in your life?'

Beccy turned predictably red.

'Gosh, how lovely to be young and in love.' Alexandra sighed, tilting her head back as she heard Pascal finally huffing up to join them, wine bottles clanking. 'Almost as heavenly as being old and in love. *Chéri*! At last! Tash is so desperate to leave, we've had to hide her car keys. Don't you think Beccy here is terribly pretty?'

'*Bien sûr.*' Pascal bent over to kiss his wife's sun-warmed cheek, winking at Beccy as he did so. 'She is the perfect English rose.'

'Don't let Henrietta hear you say that,' Alexandra confided in a giggly whisper. 'We spent most of yesterday arguing about Anne Boleyn and Jacqueline du Pré.'

'Eh?' Pascal's cheeks puffed out in outrage. 'You are telling me that she sinks a six-fingered harlot or a mad cellist more beautiful than her own daughter?'

'They're rose varieties,' Beccy explained shyly, deciding she liked Pascal very much indeed, especially now as he quoted Shakespeare in that fantastic French accent.

'A rose by any other name would smell as sweet.' He smiled at her.

'Call me but love, and I'll be new baptiz'd,' she sighed, thinking of Lough and wishing that she had told him her real name the first time they had spoken.

Starting out on her long drive back that afternoon, desperate for Haydown and Hugo, Tash regretted that she could not enjoy her mother longer. She cheered her up like a rainbow bursting through dark clouds.

But she knew she had to hurry back to Hugo. She caught a late-night ferry across the Channel. The children, who had been fast asleep in the car, started mewling and bleating when they were dragged out in to the noise and bustle of the ship.

The drive from Portsmouth to home was shattering, the blip-blip-blip noise of driving over cat's eyes making her jump each time as she realised that her concentration and the car were drifting off course.

They finally arrived home in the early hours. The back door was unlocked, but the house was in steely, near-dawn darkness, the dog packs yawning squeakily, stretching and fussing around her as she carried the children inside, breathing in the smell of home like the first life-saving breath after nearly drowning. By the time she'd put them to bed it was light outside. She wandered in to her bedroom to find Hugo already getting up.

'Welcome back,' he said coolly, glancing over his shoulder as he pulled on a pair of jeans. 'You've caught the sun.'

With a passing kiss so perfunctory and swift it almost took her ear off, he walked out of the room.

On the fake-fur counterpane, Beetroot was milky-eyed and delirious with happiness to see her mistress again, rolling upside down with such spine-wriggling, tummy-proffering excitement that she fell off the bed.

Chapter 84

In France, as dawn started to break, Beccy heard a motorcycle engine approaching Le Manoir, drowning out the sound of the crickets that had kept her company as she drifted in and out of uneasy dreams, the pain still so acute that it was hard to sleep.

Lying in the Salle Bienvenue, staring out and up through her open balcony windows at a huge, round moon suspended in the cloud-streaked sky like a pearl on a blue-black satin cushion, she heard footsteps. Then a cough. She held her breath.

When a cockerel crowed almost directly underneath her balcony she almost fainted with shock. Whoever was outside obviously felt the same way as she heard a whispered oath and then the squawk of a rooster being chased away.

'This is bloody hopeless,' a voice muttered in the darkness.

Beccy would know that voice anywhere.

She was trapped in bed just inches from the open window, yet far too far to be seen and at least ten feet above ground level outside. The footsteps were starting to retreat.

'Talk to me!' she called out.

The footsteps stopped and then retraced their way to just beneath the balcony.

Beccy heard the pages of a book being flicked and then a voice spoke, a lovely, husky New Zealand accent, as deep as thunder over the North Island:

"*'And what is a kiss, specifically? A pledge properly sealed, a promise seasoned to taste, a vow stamped with the immediacy of a lip, a rosy circle drawn around the verb 'to love'. A kiss is a message too intimate for the ear, infinity captured in the bee's brief visit to a flower, secular communication with an aftertaste of heaven, the pulse rising from the heart to utter its name on a lover's lip: "Forever."'*"

She let out a little squeal of pleasure.

He went on, reading from a battered book he had kept with him all the way from Auckland to Berkshire eight months earlier, and then all the way from there to France this past night. '"*How obvious it is now – All those beautiful powerful words, they were you! . . . The voice from the shadows, that was you . . . You always loved me!*'"

Beccy was crying too much to speak.

There was a long pause. 'Beccy, are you there? It is you, isn't it?' He suddenly sounded worried.

She mopped the tears that were coursing down her cheeks. 'I'm up here. I can't come out – I've got a broken pelvis, remember?'

'I'm coming up. Don't go away.'

Laughter joined her tears as Beccy heard a crackling of leaves and breaking twigs, and curses and groans of effort before a long silhouette appeared over her balcony. He had ivy in his hair and was carrying a very battered bunch of sunflowers.

'Sorry I'm a bit late,' Lough apologised. 'But I said I'd visit.' His huge, turbulent eyes were positively luminous with love and triumph for having made it across the Channel and through northern France to find the house, and to find her, on nothing but a rusty Bandit bike without a sat nav.

Crouching down beside her bed he dropped a kiss on her lips that made her feel as though her mattress was spinning around with massive centrifugal force then whizzing up and down.

'Wow.' She looked up at him.

'Wow,' he agreed, kissing her again just to make sure it really was that magical.

It was.

Then, very slowly and carefully because he didn't want to damage her already broken body, he kissed his way down her torso to her shattered pelvis, his lips soothing the bruised skin, exciting long-neglected corners.

'Tell me I'm dreaming?' Beccy breathed in wonder.

'I flew into this continent so buzzed up with love I thought I'd die of it.' He kissed his way along her inner thighs and calves to her ankles, disappearing out of sight at the end of the bed. 'It was you. That girl I saved in Melbourne. This unhappy, beautiful creature who talked to me on the phone with a voice like a lover, sent me messages, excited the hell out of me. I believed it was Tash.'

'But it was me – oh!' Beccy gasped with delight as he kissed the soles of her feet.

'It was you,' he agreed. 'I thought I'd come to take up Hugo's challenge, win the bet.'

He kissed his way back up her ankles and calves so that she could see him again, and she was astounded that somebody so ludicrously handsome could be looking at her, a self-proclaimed nutter and a cripple, with so much unfaltering love – and dropping his head to kiss her mouth again.

What had he been saying about a bet? she wondered, and then lost interest as they kissed on into the early hours.

It was only much later that Beccy remembered to ask about the bet. By that point it was mid-morning, and Lough had been introduced to his hosts, who seemed not in the least fazed to find Beccy entertaining an admirer who had climbed in through her balcony, as though it happened all the time. Alexandra and Pascal offered him warm welcomes and fresh coffee. Even her strait-laced mother took it remarkably calmly, barely looking up from the gardening books she'd liberated from Pascal's study.

'Hi Lough – lovely you're here. Have a croissant, though I'm afraid there's no jam left.'

'It's okay.' Lough looked at Beccy. 'I never eat jam.'

'You're like Beccy then.'

'But I love stew.' Beccy smiled into his eyes, suddenly remembering their early texts.

'I love stew too,' he nodded.

Then, when Beccy and Lough were dipping pains au chocolat into bowls of café au lait, unable to stop looking at one another and

813

brimming up with love and happiness like optics refilling in a busy bar, she remembered the bet he'd mentioned the night before.

'Hugo got really drunk at Blenheim the day you were first supposed to arrive,' she recalled, 'and he said he'd "lost" Tash in a wager.'

He closed his eyes, the corner of his mouth curling up as she'd so often seen it do in the past when he was uncomfortable. 'Hugo took me out for a drink during the Olympics to try to persuade me to ride with him in the UK,' he told her, reaching for her hands, big eyes already seeking forgiveness. 'It was the day after the three day event final. I was pretty mean-spirited about losing out to his gold medal, and then when he started to warn me that the authorities were after me in New Zealand for doping racehorses, I thought he was just threatening to shop me. I had no idea he was actually trying to help me. So when we ran into a spot of bother I didn't behave as honourably as I should. Shit, Beccy, you don't want to hear this.'

'It's okay.' She squeezed his hand. 'You are talking to the queen of dishonour, remember.'

'We were in this godforsaken private club someone had recommended, full of businessmen, transvestites and pushers, with a high-class knocking shop upstairs. We must have stood out like sore thumbs. Somebody spiked our drinks – a low-life pimp, trying to get a little extortion on the go. I didn't drink mine, but Hugo was completely out of it, so I found him a bed out the back with nobody in it and a lock on the door to make sure he'd be safe to sleep it off. But when he woke up in a hooker's bed with a video camera blinking down on him he thought the worst, and I let him believe it, poor bastard. Tash was going into labour at the time, but he only found that out later. If the press had got hold of it he'd have been lambasted. The truth is, he was no use to anybody that night. The British lion was well and truly sleeping, but he didn't know that – the nation's hero, Team GB's first gold medallist of the games celebrating his victory with a transsexual hooker. Can you imagine? He'd already had a streaker all over him at the medal ceremony. Even Berlusconi couldn't look that sleazy after three terms in office, and Hugo had managed it in twenty-four hours in the spotlight.'

'And nobody ever found out?' Beccy gasped, knowing that if an event rider coughed in Cornwall it was broadcast in

Northumberland seconds later, especially when gossip concerned riders with fresh medals in their pockets.

He shook his head. 'That's one night I never mentioned to Lem, thank God. The pimps in the bar had no idea who we really were. I got us out of there with a bunch of lies and cash, and some smart talking. There aren't a lot of positives about growing up in the slums on the wrong side of the law, but that's one moment when I was blessed. And Hugo sure as hell appreciated it. He said I could have anything I wanted from home. He meant a horse, of course, but I knew exactly what I wanted . . . or I thought I did.'

'Tash?'

He nodded. 'I asked for a night with Tash.'

She jumped, scalded. 'Why?'

He reached out and took her hand. 'I admit I always quite fancied her from afar, but I really only said it because I knew it would piss off Hugo.'

'Christ. What did he say?'

'He'd already said that if I could persuade her, we were welcome to each other.'

'Ohmygod!' Beccy's eyes stretched wide. 'Does she know this?'

He shook his head. 'I've thought about telling her so often, but the more I think about what the man said, the more I realise how completely wrong I read it. I thought he was such a heartless bastard at first. I really thought he meant, "take her, old chap, you're welcome, I don't want her any more, be my guest" and all that polite British crap because he owed me big time: "You saved my sporting reputation, now have my wife as a gesture of thanks", you know?'

'And he didn't mean that?'

He shook his head. 'That's just what I wanted to hear. What he *really* meant was that he trusted her – she would never betray him, never go for it, never fall for me. But if she did, she wasn't the woman he thought she was and I could keep her.'

Beccy gasped. 'She almost strayed, didn't she?'

He shook his head. 'Not even close.'

She let out a huge breath of relief. Then she saw the look on his face.

'Try telling that to Hugo.' He shook his head despairingly. 'It's broken between them, and it's all my fucking fault.'

'Both our faults.' She took his hand.

Chapter 85

The final run-up to Burghley was fraught with difficulty for the Haydown team, despite the Indian summer that finally took over to dry out the tail end of a soggy August, blanching the grass on the downs from pea green to sage.

Tash couldn't sleep, and her attempts to talk to Hugo backfired horrendously, winding him up more and more until he moved into the spare bedroom. With Amery waking throughout the night as big molars stabbed their way through his little pink gums, she was like a zombie by day. She knew that she was riding badly and, although she trusted River more than any other horse, she was almost certain that they weren't yet ready to tackle a big four-star track again.

But at least River was fit to run. Hugo was down to one ride, Oil Tanker being the only sound horse in his top string as niggling injuries plagued the rest.

And the media spotlight was firmly on Haydown. The press were taking sudden interest in Rory because of the very real chance that he was going to scoop the Rolex Grand Slam for only the second time in history. The heroic angle that he was still recovering from a crashing fall which had put him in a coma earlier in the season had caught the imagination of even the most equestrian-phobic tabloids. His opportunity was front-page news.

Yet the lame-horse scenario was bleakest of all for Rory, with two of his three qualified rides dropping out of contention in the preceding fortnight. Competed hard on the continent in early summer, they were leg weary. Snake Charmer had aggravated his old check ligament injury; The Fox hadn't yet fully recovered from his Aachen fall. Rio was his only hope, but a shadow hung over him as he became increasingly footsore on the hardening ground.

'He has corns,' Rory lamented when he and Lough met for a final pre-competition drink in the Olive Branch before the big procession to Lincolnshire.

Lough pressed a hand to his shoulder, knowing how desperate he was to win the Grand Slam, not so much for the huge prize pot or even the kudos, but because he saw it as the way back in to Faith's heart.

'She legs it every time I get near,' Rory said now.

'She's running to get fit, taking a leaf out of your books.'

'Looks suspiciously like she's just running away from me from where I'm standing. I came through the ford at Fosbourne Abbott yesterday and she was jogging along towards me – the next moment, she's jumped over a barbed wire fence and scrambled through a hedge to spring off through a field of cows. Now tell me that's normal?'

At one time, Faith had sent him twenty texts for every one of his, but now the reverse was true; she was definitely avoiding him and he was certain it had to do with that bastard Dillon Rafferty, with his fast cars, fast living and slow-matured cheese. Rory had developed a jealous loathing for the man on whom his livelihood depended. His only solace was that Faith was still wrapping her legs around his old horse every day, if not its owner.

'I can't believe she's seriously planning on taking my knackered chap round Burghley.'

'You're taking hers round.'

'He's not past it. Whitey's eighteen now and hasn't competed at that level for over three years.'

'And Rio's got corns like an old biddy.'

'True.' Rory looked at him for a moment. 'Talking of all things corny, are you sure there's been no sign of Dillon Rafferty at Lime Tree Farm?'

'None.' Lough shook his head. 'She's been a good girl. In bed by nine every night. Penny says she watches the same old movie in her room every night – *Snowy Mountain*, or something. Oh, but two fantastic looking horses did turn up yesterday and she said they were "presents", so that might be her rock-star admirer. Penny and Gus were livid.'

'Fucking hell, he's giving her expensive horses now,' Rory groaned, putting his face in hands. 'What can I give her? Horse muck?'

'Your heart.'

'Wizened old bit of gristle.' He thumped his chest and coughed.

'Win the Grand Slam.'

He laughed. 'You won't be saying that when I'm breathing down your neck next Sunday and you have less than a fence in hand. You'll want to win at any cost. What's the latest on the Mogo race? You must be miles ahead.'

'I'm sure they'll sign Hugo again.' Lough shrugged, reaching for his pint of Guinness. 'They only got me involved to sharpen him up.'

'Yeah, he's so sharp right now you get your throat cut just to walk past him.'

'That bad?'

'Worse. He won't tolerate anything less than perfection. He keeps sacking Fudge – the working pupil – then has to reinstate her because Franny threatens to walk out if she goes. They're cousins. Poor Fudge *is* useless, but she's all we've got, apart from the au pair couple who arrived from Poland last week. Bronislaw and Bronislawa, so you can imagine what Hugo makes of that. They're already threatening to leave. Poor old Tash is run ragged trying to protect them.'

Rory noticed that Lough no longer flinched at the mention of her name, although his eyes darkened with concern.

'How's Beccy?' he asked casually.

His face lit up tellingly. 'On crutches now.'

'Like most of my Burghley horses,' Rory sighed.

Chapter 86

The atmosphere at Burghley was quite different from that at Badminton, somehow managing to be more relaxed despite the equally grand setting and severity of the test. It helped that the sun was shining from the start and forecast to stay for all four days. Coming so much later in the season, combinations had prepared for longer and knew how well they were going. In some cases this was a great benefit, in others a disaster as horses that had campaigned all season started to feel the strain.

'Rio's not a hundred per cent,' Rory reported on the Tuesday when he came back from hacking around estate to shake off any travelling stiffness.

Haydown's farrier had come out the previous week to refit his shoes with leather pads underneath to try to relieve the pressure from the corns, but Rory knew that the horse was not right.

'The course going is fantastic,' Hugo reassured him, 'so if he does run, he stands a good chance of completing without injury.'

The old turf had been irrigated, harrowed and aerated so that the cross-country course curled like a lush green snake through the increasingly parched parkland.

'I don't think he'll make it through the first inspection,' Rory said despondently, seeing all hope of his Grand Slam slipping further and further from his reach.

He'd only seen Faith briefly since arriving, sorting through her trunks outside the temporary stabling, but they'd barely exchanged hellos before she had dashed off on some vague pretext to speak to Gus.

That evening, Rory spurned the traditional first night party, always the most raucous of the lorry-park gatherings, and curtained himself away on the sleeping shelf of the Beauchamps' lorry with his iPod on, listening to jazz to try to calm his mounting panic that his most valued prize was about to be stolen from him. Dillon had left a text message earlier that day, saying that he was planning to come and watch on cross-country day. Rory had hastily fired back a reply pointing out that he wasn't even riding one of Dillon's horses, but that didn't seem to put him off. He was certain that the cheesy pop legend was only coming along to claim Faith.

Good luck texts had been arriving all week, to his continued surprise. He hadn't thought he was especially popular, but his phone was buzzing non-stop with messages, an alarming number of which said 'We'll be there to cheer!' His Aunt Isabel had organised a small army of Oddlode villagers to come and support him through every stage, his mother and sister among them, along with cousin Spurs and Ellen with new baby Biddy; his mate Flipper and girlfriend Trudy with their baby, Alice; Piers and Jemima Cottrell; Giles and Ophelia Horton; and even various members of the rival Wycks and Gates clans, including Castigates and Delegates and newlyweds Saul and Godspell Wyck. He didn't want to let them down.

The press had been chasing him around all day, eating up preparation time. Earlier, he'd filmed a piece for the BBC from the horsebox, which had taken ages because Twitch, posing cherubically on his lap at the time, had in fact been flashing his overexcited pink manhood throughout the interview. They had shot it all again,

Twitch relocated off camera and Rory's replies to veteran horse-trials commentator Julia Ditton getting more and more staccato.

'How can I do it when my only horse is so footsore?' he'd wanted to shout at lovely Julia, but he answered the questions humbly and politely as he did all the press that hounded him, charming old hacks and new with his self-deprecation and continual insistence that it didn't matter what happened as long as the horses were safe and happy.

Tucking Twitch under his arm and pulling a pillow over his head, he tried to blot out the whoops and screams coming from outside and think his way through the coming days. Cranking up the volume on a particularly frisky Dizzy Gillespie solo in 'No More Blues', he imagined himself galloping across the turf to victory.

In the Moncrieffs' box just twenty yards away, Faith was doing the same, her music bouncy Irish jigs and reels that made her think of her father and his eternal optimism. He had sent her a good-luck card with a little leprechaun on it that she'd stuck to Whitey's stable door, along with cards from Magnus and Dilly, her gayfathers and Carly. Her mother was travelling to Lincolnshire the following afternoon to give her some much-needed dressage coaching before her test on Friday morning.

Faith had already walked the course once that afternoon with Gus. 'Good, taxing four-star,' he'd proclaimed while Faith felt far too ill to speak. She really needed Penny's positive vibes, but the Moncrieffs were on a very sticky wicket and rarely seen in the same square acre this month, although Gus was trying hard to patch things up. As well as steering clear of Lucy Field, he'd booked a luxury bed and breakfast in Stamford, meaning that Faith had the horsebox to herself to rattle around in, freaking out about the cross-country course. To her, it was on a whole new scale to anything that she had ever tackled before and she wondered why on earth she had let her newest father persuade her into this. She longed to talk to Rory who would understand exactly what she was going through, but he was strictly off limits and for very good reason. Her father had been right; every time she thought about him she felt giddy. She *had* to concentrate. She badly needed her mother.

She'd already watched *The Man from Snowy River* on her portable DVD player. She was tempted to fire it up and watch it again for comfort, if only just the horseback kissing scenes between Jim and Jessica that Rory loved so much, along with the stampede over the mountain – but of course that would make her think of Rory and she must not think of him.

'Aim high and you'll hit less timber,' Fearghal's voice said in her head.

She concentrated on the Irish music, closing her eyes. *Bum diddly um diddly un diddly*, the beat rattled along in her ears, making her imagine little girls in black waistcoats and bright skirts dancing through the horsebox.

In the George Hotel in Stamford, Tash was regretting her request for a four-poster bed all those weeks ago when she'd booked a room in the famous old coaching inn, so popular with riders and their connections that Burghley week reservations needed to be made months ahead. She must have called them around the time that she and Hugo couldn't keep their hands off one another, she realised now, when she had been like a sex maniac, in a constant state of arousal and imagining that she would be hanging on to an oak corner post while he entered from behind. Instead, they slept like two strangers forced to bunk up in the last room in the inn, almost hanging off their respective sides of the mattress. Tash wanted to suggest that he might be happier going head to foot or pitching up on the chaise longue under the window. At home they hadn't shared a bed for the five days before they'd departed for Lincolnshire.

This was to be the first time that the couple would be competing head to head in a major British four-star for over three years, a fact that had not gone unnoticed by the sporting press. Nobody could mistake the fierce competitiveness between them, though the chilly enmity was put down to a return to top form for Tash. It was certainly a far cry from the loved-up Beauchampions days.

She had gone against her own maternal instincts this time, arranging for the children to stay away until Saturday when her family supporters were all arriving. Surprisingly, Ben and Sophia had offered to bring them and Alicia as a part of their cavalcade, thus providing the new Polish au pairs with a long weekend off and Tash with much-needed family back-up.

'It's the least we can do,' Sophia had announced breezily. 'We'll have Granny Bea and Lotty, who loves to babysit, with us, so it'll be absolutely no trouble. I'll pop down to Haydown and fetch them on Friday.'

Knowing Berkshire to be well adrift of any route between Worcestershire and Lincolnshire, Tash had a distinct sense that there was something afoot, but she was far too preoccupied to worry about it.

Even Alexandra and Pascal had announced that they were coming to England, coerced by Polly who didn't start college for another week. In their honour, Matty and Sally had made last-minute plans for a night in Stamford and not to be left out again, James and Henrietta had found a convenient golfing hotel with a ground-floor room for Beccy, who was keen to support them all, especially Lough.

Hugo was highly cynical about Beccy and Lough's union: 'Rory and Sylva Frost had a better chance of making it to the altar, quite frankly.'

Tash disagreed, and she clung on to the thought that at least he had released Lough from his missile lock, even if Sylva remained on the radar. She was still the prime suspect for 'V'.

That evening, to her alarm, she'd received a message from Sylva on her own BlackBerry, wishing her luck and suggesting that she and her new squeeze might pop along to the trials incognito and say hello which, given that they couldn't get within a few yards of any of Pete's eight houses without being noticed, seemed unlikely. Sylva said she was looking for a horse again, but Tash did not dare mention it to Hugo. There wasn't much that she felt she could mention to Hugo at all, in fact. He was so explosive, she felt she should send in a bomb-disposal robot before she spoke.

The next day, after the competitors' briefing and the first official course walk, Hugo was incandescent with rage to discover Oil Tanker's stable bandages wrapped too tightly around his battered brown legs. He told Franny she was fired.

'And what the fuck are you going to do without me, you dick-head?' she yelled back with twice his fury.

'There are plenty of others here this week would give their eye teeth to work for me.'

'Not with a temper like that. Anyway, I didn't put on the fucking bandages – I left them off after you rode him this morning like you said to.'

'Then who the bloody hell's been fiddling with them?' He raked a hand through his hair. 'Not this again. I thought we'd seen an end to this after Badminton!'

'Calm down,' Franny soothed. 'It was probably Fudge.'

'Tell Fudge not to touch my horse again,' Hugo spat. 'She can look after Rory's.'

'No point,' Rory declared, coming out of his own stall. 'I can't present him.'

'You must!' Franny was appalled. 'What about the Grand Slam?'

Rory shook his head. 'The horse is more important. You see if you don't agree.'

Gazing limpid-eyed at them over his stall door, black coat as glossy as melted liquorice, the stallion was a picture of health and it was hard to believe that something as mundane as a corn could wreck his rider's one shot at over a quarter of a million pounds. But when Hugo lifted his hoof and pressed on the leather pad the horse flinched dramatically, almost dropping to his knees.

'He's not lame, but he's very short in front,' Rory told him as he watched fearfully, his dreams literally in Hugo's hands.

Hugo took him to the back of the stable. 'Chances are the ground jury will pass him fit.'

'What would you do?'

'For me, there's too much pain there to risk it. He's young. He'll have his chance.'

'I might not get another chance.' Rory's heart was rupturing.

'So run him.'

Rory shook his head. 'He's not mine to risk.'

Hugo patted him on the back, nodding towards the opposite side of the long lines of temporary stabling. 'Have you spoken to the owner yet?'

Rory heaved a deep sigh. 'She'll probably run away from me.'

'She needs to make the final decision.'

He trailed across the wide avenue, his handsome head drooping as all around him horses were strapped and polished and show-sheened and hoof-oiled for the first veterinary inspection.

These days, the riders were also expected to put on a show as they ran alongside their mounts, the popular theory being that a striking outfit might distract the ground jury's eye from a slightly unlevel horse. This year, with an all-male ground jury at least one of whom was a well-known roué, the girls were all going to town.

When Rory looked around for Faith in the busy row of temporary stabling that housed Whitey's stall, he didn't immediately recognise her. There were a lot of leggy Swedes to one side, including Hugo's old friend Stefan, who had welcomed him like a lost brother earlier, but whom he couldn't face talking to right now amid his lofty, model-like compatriots. Then, beyond Gus's two rides and Lough's top horse Rangitoto, were a lot of small, sexy Italians in figure-hugging stretch tweed applying each other's mascara. Despite standing in front of a box with a card that definitely read 'White Lies', Rory even struggled to recognise his old campaigner, now as luminous as a pearl, his usually unprepossessingly scraggy neck neatened by immaculate plaits, his big black eyes glowing kindly with their rims emphasised by Vaseline, his ungainly flat black hooves like gleaming coal and his rather pathetic tail still plaited to its tip and protected by a stocking, awaiting a last-minute liberation to retain its waves. The big pink and grey scar on his chest where he'd been impaled on a fencing stake just a couple of years earlier was still a vivid reminder of how close they had come to losing him, a fact Rory knew was the result of his negligence because he had been drinking heavily that day. Now the horse looked magnificent and as fit as Rory had ever seen him. The deep, demanding whicker that he let out on seeing his old master lifted Rory's dejected heart a little.

One of the tall Swedes had come to talk to him now, wearing a very short skirt and knee-length brown leather boots with scarily high heels. She had fantastic legs, tanned the colour of a Werther's Original. Rory's eyes got stuck there for a long time.

'Come to wish us luck?' she asked in a strangled voice.

His gaze shot up to the face, working around the tan and the make-up and the professionally straightened and highlighted sheet of blonde hair. The big smile was as white and straight as a toothpaste ad, but nobody could mistake the dimples in the cheeks and the sparkle in the fiercely kind eyes.

'Faith.' He managed to croak her name, his heart and groin fluttering disturbingly.

'Rory,' she confirmed.

'You look . . . different.'

She pursed her lips in a smaller smile, dimples deepening, and she gave a quick nod to Whitey. 'Your boy's in great spirits.'

He rubbed the satiny white neck and the horse nickered again, nosing his pockets for mints. 'He looks amazing and it's all down to you. You've done the most fantastic job with him, getting him here again. I'd given up on him, thought his career was long gone, but you had faith.'

'It's my name,' she reminded him, her own voice tight with nerves. Rory knew the first vet's inspection struck fear into them all, however sound they believed their horses to be.

'He's done it all before,' he reminded her. 'He knows what it's all about. He'll look after you.'

She nodded, not looking at him. It was the most they'd spoken since she had reappeared from her 'holiday' and she was almost hyperventilating with tension and the need to say so much more and ask so much more. But they were starting to call the first horses for the inspection.

'Shouldn't you be getting Rio?' she asked.

'We can't run him, Faith. His feet are too sore. Even if they pass him now he'll be in agony later.'

Faith took the news silently, staring fixedly at his neck because she still couldn't look him in the eye. Under such close scrutiny, Rory's neck, which was already itchy from the photo ID hanging around it, reddened dramatically.

'You think I'm right?' he checked worriedly when she still hadn't said anything after another full minute, and the Tannoy was calling horses with numbers ever closer to hers.

'I'm sorry,' she was still staring at his neck. 'What did you say?'

'Is it okay not to present him?'

'What are you talking about?' She looked into his eyes at last, blinking all the more because she wasn't used to wearing mascara and it made her eyes run.

At that moment, he wanted to kiss her with all his heart. He felt his chest expand until he thought it was going to burst. His mouth even started to water. That had never happened to him before.

'Faith, you're on!' Lemon appeared, thrusting his Mohican between them as he elbowed Rory to one side and unlatched the stable door. 'Where's his bridle?'

Faith snapped out of her reverie. Handing Lemon the bridle from the hook at her side, she reached out and took Rory's hand, towing him back towards Rio's stall.

'He really isn't sound,' he started to protest.

'I believe you!' she replied urgently, reaching his big plastic tack crate and cranking it open, where the suit-carrier containing his best tweed jacket, shirt and tie was lying neatly on top.

Then she started pulling his T-shirt over his head.

'Steady on!' he gasped as there were a few titters and a couple of catcalls around him. 'What are you doing?'

For a moment she couldn't speak as she found herself tangled up with hot, sinewy Rory and warm, Rory-smelling T-shirt, but then she wrestled the shirt free, clutching it like a rescued kitten for a moment. 'Getting you ready for the inspection.'

'But we're withdrawing Rio. I have to notify the ground jury.'

She unzipped the suit carrier. 'Yes, yes, but first you have to present Whitey.'

'No – I can't poss—' He was forced to shut up as she pulled a Tattersall-checked shirt over his head.

As it slid down, warm Rory smells floated up through the open neck and she had to take a few moments to compose herself again before snapping at him to do his cuffs up.

'Where did you get these clothes?' she sneered as she almost garrotted him with a tie he'd got as a free gift when renewing his tractor insurance.

'The feed merchant mostly,' he admitted while she reached up to straighten his hair before making him hold out his arms like an aeroplane so that she could put on a beige suede waistcoat.

'It's so old fogey.' She buttoned him up and stepped back.

'Faith!' Lemon was shouting urgently. 'They need you to go to the arena now!'

'Go on then.' She gave Rory a push.

'But, I—'

'You take Whitey. I can't possibly run in these heels.'

'But you're riding him.'

'No I'm not. I'll talk to the stewards now and get the substitution sorted, along with Rio's withdrawal. You just make sure this horse trots up sound.' She turned as Lemon hurried Whitey across the grass towards them.

The Tannoy was shouting for Whitey now.

'Go, go, go – they'll eliminate us otherwise!'

Rory knew there was no time to argue. His loyal Whitey was soon trotting like a show hunter at Royal Windsor. There was no question that the horse was sound and full of running, dragging Rory all the way to the arena.

'You quite sure about this?' Lemon peered up at Faith, who was way over his head height, especially when she had her high heels on.

She nodded. 'He *has* to win the Grand Slam.'

She dashed after Rory, with Lemon panting behind.

'He won't do it on that old thing.'

'He can!' she defended hotly, wobbling in her spiked boots.

'I can help fix it for you,' Lemon panted beside her.

'Yeah,' she laughed, putting on a burst of speed as she heard Whitey announced in the arena, and sprinted the last twenty yards just in time to see her beloved pair trot up.

Lemon was left standing in her wake, already out of puff.

'I can fix it for you!' he repeated, but he was out of earshot.

A moment later he heard 'White Lies – pass!' and a smattering of applause.

'Fuck you then!' He turned back to get Lough's horse ready.

The rest of the Lime Tree Farm and Haydown horses sailed through the vet's inspection, along with Whitey.

To Rory's amazement, there was no objection to his last-minute substitution. Event riders were notorious complainers if protocol was breached or favours seen to be granted, and just getting it past the ground jury was a tall order. 'What did you tell the officials?' he asked Faith, awed by her powers of persuasion.

'That I'm expecting your baby and have high blood pressure,' she replied, before belting off to meet her mother.

Tash and Hugo rode their dressage tests on the Thursday within twenty minutes of one another. In his current combative state of mind, Hugo had wanted to complain about the running order, which had meant that Franny was run ragged trying to ensure that two horses and their riders had everything they needed to warm up almost simultaneously, but Tash talked him out of it, pointing out that it looked unsportsmanlike.

Traditionally, all the big players came late on in the order, even though it was supposed to be a random draw, but this time Tash and Hugo were aware that they had been relegated to the graveyard slot to do battle, the apparent snub reflecting their slipping popularity and rankings.

Oil Tanker picked up on the atmosphere and showed off to disastrous effect, believing that his airs above the ground were far more entertaining than all the boring technical stuff that he was being asked to do. No matter how carefully and sensitively Hugo rode him, theirs was always going to be a mediocre score and well below their best.

Tash was pulling on her tailcoat as he came out. 'Bad luck.'

For a moment his focused blue eyes met hers and she felt a spark of the old connection.

'You show them what we're capable of,' he muttered, taking off his topper and propping it under one elbow as he rode the horse away to cool off, certain he'd blown any real chance of victory.

It was a long time since Tash had trotted into an arena with grandstands and crowds on the scale of Burghley, and even on the first day of dressage, just before lunch, the crowd lit up to see a well-known name returning to the big time on her lovely, rangy liver chestnut mare whose ears practically met in the middle as they trotted around the perimeter of the white-boarded rectangle, waiting for the judge's signal.

It wasn't the most polished test that she had ever ridden, but given her long absence from this level, she acquitted herself well and the crowd clapped and cheered as though she was still anchor of the British team. She felt enormously grateful to them.

As she walked River out on a long rein, acknowledging them with a self-conscious wave, she realised just how much she had missed the buzz. She was amazed to find tears in her eyes.

She rode out into the park to cool the mare after her efforts in the arena cauldron, her tails slung over the pommel of her saddle.

Hugo and Oil Tanker appeared at her side. 'Well done.'

'Thanks.' She smiled across at him, on far too much of a high to care if he was foul-tempered or not.

They both knew that the running order had been carefully orchestrated to create maximum tension, pitching the shaky, gossiped-about husband and wife team against one another on the first day. Yet, far from adding to the strain between them, it brought them closer together. Out in the park they debriefed, sharing details of their tests and how their horses felt for the next day, slipping back into old, familiar habits as they slid forward a gear in communication without realising it. The emotional thaw was setting in at last.

Once their horses were back in Franny and Fudge's care they returned to the horsebox to change out of their tails. Rory was lying on the seating, fast asleep in front of the racing on the little flat-screen TV, Twitch on his lap. Sleep was his coping mechanism at times of great stress, and it always amazed his peers that he could nap during the day at a three day event. He'd been training with Anke all morning, an exhausting process in itself, but the added mind-warp of seeing Faith standing beside her mother had opened the tap on his adrenalin and drained it out of him. He didn't even stir when Tash realised he was lying on her change of clothes and pulled them out from under him.

Twitch watched Tash and Hugo with interest as they stripped out of their breeches and into jeans. They watched one another too, but warily, eyes stealing glances while the other thought they weren't looking.

They walked the cross-country course again, together this time, sharing their thoughts about lines of approach, optimum speed and take-off points, turns and strides and sight lines, talking in low voices.

'If you're clever, you can swing River out to try to make a stride here,' he told her at the Discovery Valley, a tricky combination deep in the parkland's undulating terrain. 'The bounce could be too tight for her.'

Tash, who had been planning to go for the bounce, knew he'd probably saved her a run-out.

It was familiar territory and they stayed rigidly focused and on topic. They hadn't pooled resources like this for such a long time that it felt liberating. They needed one another's judgement more than they needed to protect their personal pride.

While the couple were out on the course the lorry park gossip was ruthless.

'They are finished,' predicted Lucy Field.

After the last horse of the day had exited at A, the dressage tallies were totted up. The Beauchampions' dressage scores were much further down the order than they would have been in their heyday, just a few short years earlier.

Yet that night Tash and Hugo slept facing one another for the first time in weeks. They had finished on an identical score. There could be no argument about that.

The Burghley organisers had got what they had hoped. Tash and Hugo were the story of the night, making it on to the national newspapers' sports pages the next day, when the focus would shift to Rory and his Grand Slam dream.

Had Rory been riding Rio, his dressage would have been one of the last on the Friday afternoon, in among the cluster of elite riders to guarantee maximum attention for his Grand Slam bid. But, having substituted for Faith on White Lies, he rode into the arena in the relative cool and quiet of an early slot.

Dressage had never been Whitey's forte, and during his long partnership with Rory they had struggled to overcome nervy, cumbersome tests riddled with errors. But the old racehorse had been in training with Faith for almost a year now, a far more classical and precise rider, and he had reaped the benefits. Rory, meanwhile, had been in training with the best event riders in the world – Hugo, Janet Madsen and MC among them – plus he'd had a last-minute fuel injection from dressage Olympian Anke. He was still a rough diamond, but he could sparkle on his day. He was sitting on his comfort horse, his teddy bear that was as familiar as his bed at home. He had everything to prove and lose, yet he knew the horse owed him nothing and it was such a joy to ride him in front of a crowd again that he pushed for those extra moments and marks that Anke had been harrying him for all the previous day.

To his absolute delight, he came away with the best score of the morning session. It didn't matter that his spot at the top of the leader board was almost immediately usurped by Stefan on his great horse Thor, and then later pushed further down the order by Lough and Rangitoto, Sonja Runiker and another German rider, Kevin the French boy wonder and Gus on his second ride. Seventh after dressage at Burghley was a dream come true, even if it wasn't quite the Grand Slam fairytale lead the media longed for.

He walked the cross-country course a final time with Anke, which wasn't perhaps ideal because she saw each fence from a dressage perspective and gave him long technical lectures on line and approach when his instinct – and knowledge of the horse – just said 'keep straight and kick on'.

'I thought Faith was going to walk with us?' He managed to get a word in as they stood in front of the Lover's Leap, a big galloping ditch and hedge of such gapingly straightforward magnitude that Anke had no tips on approach or prowess whatsoever, other than saying something in Danish that Rory was certain was an oath.

'I would have liked that too.' She sighed, tilting her head from one oblique degree to the other as she studied the beautifully clipped birch. 'But she insists she must stay away from you.'

'Why?' he asked forlornly, hopping down into the ditch which was as deep as his shoulder and so wide a tractor could drive along it. 'Has she got something catching?'

'She's had something catching for many years,' Anke said as she walked backwards, her head still angled. 'But she is very infectious right now. Do you think it would help set the horse's quarters underneath him to make a half halt about three strides away here, *ja*?'

Still standing in the ditch, his head barely visible to Anke, Rory stared up at the yawning blue sky between take off and hedge. 'I think it would help more to give the horse a bloody big boot in the ribs three strides away, frankly.'

'Shame on you,' Anke tutted, but she secretly knew that she would personally be booting for Denmark, eyes tight closed. She hadn't walked a four-star course with a competitor before and it was a very humbling experience. She had never seen anything as terrifying in her life as these huge, unforgiving timber fences to be taken at galloping speed with lightning reactions from horse and rider required at all times. Close up, they took her breath away. She was terribly relieved that Faith was no longer going to try to jump them.

'I underestimated you,' she told Rory when they finally walked back in front of the spectacular Burghley House to re-evaluate the last two fences on the course.

'Oh yes?' he asked vaguely, hoping that Faith had got Whitey fit enough to get here with fuel still in his tank. He was descended from a long line of fantastic staying chasers and could count Desert

Orchid among his close cousins, but without the fittening work he was nothing.

'My daughter is a wilful girl,' Anke was saying. 'She sets her mind on something and she cannot let it go, you know?'

'Oh, I know.' He wondered whether she was with Dillon tonight, but the thought made him too miserable to ask.

'For a long time I thought she had set her mind on something very impractical and wasteful,' she half-laughed, 'something that would hurt her very deeply in the end.'

'Eventing is much safer these days,' Rory assured her. 'I know you would prefer that she did straight dressage and that's such a great talent in her that she may do it one day, but this sport is like nothing else.' He held up his arms to their spectacular surroundings. 'And I really do think Faith has what it takes to make a very good event rider.'

'Oh, I agree.' Anke nodded almost tearfully. 'She will make a very good event rider. But will he make her happy?'

But Rory had moved out of earshot as he strode up to the big, arched Land Rover fence at the end of the course and imagined the euphoria of sailing through it with just seconds to spare. Cutting things fine was one of his specialities.

Now sharing unlucky thirteenth spot on the overnight leaderboard, Tash and Hugo slept facing one another again, edging a little closer this time. She could feel his breath on her nose, an idle fingertip touching her.

In the darkness she lay wide awake, her eyes open, feeling his breath on her lips, her heart so swollen in her chest that it seemed to drop anchor through the bed, a near shipwreck of a marriage almost washed up on rocks yet still somehow floating.

'I love you,' she whispered.

It was a long time before she realised that his eyes were open as well.

'I love you too,' he breathed.

Soon they were asleep, two inverted commas curled around a shared sentiment.

Chapter 87

Cross-country day at Burghley provided near-perfect conditions, bright sunlight countered by a light breeze that cooled the competitors and drew record crowds to the magnificent park, its four-star track laid out through rolling turf like jewels set in the plushest green velvet.

It was only when one apparently insignificant fence on the course began to claim scalps that mutterings of dissent started spreading through the stabling and the competitors' tent. The new complex, ironically sponsored by a health insurance company, consisted of two big tables set at oblique angles. Some of the riders walking the course earlier in the week had complained about the awkward, curving four strides between the elements, with no provision to turn a circle, but it was generally agreed that the distance was probably fair if ridden well.

Then really good riders started falling off. There were stops on the course every half hour, with competitors held up while the victims and debris were picked up and patched up, all due to this one obstacle. Ambulances rattled back and forth to collect casualties.

When Gus, 'Mr Stick-on', came back with a bloodied nose and smashed front teeth, leading his first horse behind him, tension really grew among the rest of the entrants. Rider representatives were sent off to talk to the ground jury; several less experienced combinations withdrew.

Out in the park warming up, Tash and Hugo didn't fully appreciate the extent of the carnage taking place on course. Not speaking much, but catching one another's eyes with ridiculous regularity, they took their horses for a quick blast at gallop and then a slow cool-down to the perfect tick-over to get ready to concentrate on the big jumping questions as soon as they were out on the course.

In the collecting ring and at the start, however, talk was all of the controversial tables fence. The rider representatives were pushing hard for a turning circle to be allowed between the two elements to increase safety, but the debate was still raging as Hugo was counted down.

'I think I should ride it as planned.' He looked to Tash for confirmation.

They both knew the alternative route was incredibly long and absurdly time-wasting.

Oil Tanker and Deep River were both scopey, accurate and experienced horses that jumped in a free-flowing rhythm. Fences like the tables were bread and butter to them.

But something in Tash hesitated as Hugo was counted down from ten, his blue eyes still on her and not the first fence, where they should be.

She knew that their loved ones were out there in the crowd: their children, her mother and father and their families, her sister and brother and Hugo's disreputable mother propping up the Pimm's tent. She didn't want to let any of them down, but she didn't want to frighten them either.

'. . . three . . . two . . . one . . .'

'Take the long route!' she suddenly shouted as Hugo got the 'go' and streaked off towards the Burghley Overture fence with an appreciative set of whoops and claps from the gathered crowd.

He hadn't heard her.

'The combination in front of you has withdrawn,' an official told Tash, 'so you can either wait for your official start time or go a little sooner if you're ready – the Beeb are live streaming so they do appreciate as many horses on the course as we can manage. There have been a lot of hold-ups.'

It was always lethal to tell Tash that somebody was relying on her. She couldn't do enough for them.

'Of course I can start.' She smiled, looking around for her family. At last she spotted them, Ben holding Cora, dressed in her fairy wings, on his shoulders, while Amery was bounced in Sophia's arms wearing a hat shaped like a horse's head with mad eyes and ears at fantastically wonky angles.

So full of love she thought she would take off over the course like a helium balloon, Tash suddenly relished the idea of setting out straight after Hugo across country and chasing him down. The sooner she and River finished, the sooner they could all be together.

'Count me down whenever you're ready,' she told the starter, heading into the box.

The crowd cheered loyally as she set off. Cora waved her fairy wand.

For just a few minutes, she and Hugo were on the course together.

Tash flew the first few galloping fences before dropping down the huge step at the tricky Leaf Pit and over a skinny box into open country once more.

Then, just as River had put in a thrilling flyer at the trakehner, she saw an official on the course waving a flag at her.

She pulled up the mare, feeling suddenly icy with fear. 'Is it Hugo?'

'Not sure – I'll find out what's going on,' the steward started gabbling into his walkie talkie and then walked off to consult with his cohorts, glancing uneasily over his shoulder at Tash.

Heart hammering, keeping the mare moving as best she could to ensure her muscles stayed warm and relaxed and ready to start jumping again, Tash strained her ears for more information, but there was nothing. Then, before she had a chance to find out what was happening, she was re-started on the course.

She struggled to get River into a rhythm once more as the big questions came at them thick and fast in this section of the park, her mind one horse ahead on the course, wondering where Hugo was.

The mare was sharp and precise but they were increasingly disconnected. They separated a marker flag from a fence corner, corkscrewed sideways over a skinny and then tripped in the water at the Trout Hatchery, almost tipping under. Splashing back out to an encouraging cheer from the crowd, she kicked on up the hill.

Then it was the tables. She sighted her line as she had planned on her course-walks and had talked through with Hugo the night before.

'Go the long route,' a voice told her. 'Go the long route.'

But she hadn't walked it well enough. This route looked much more straightforward. There was nothing obvious to make it tricky, nothing apart from the huge gouged skid marks in the turn at the second element take-off revealing how many valuable mistakes had been made there.

As she came over the first table and swung the mare left, she sighted the tree that she was going to use to line up her take-off point. Where was her stride? Where *was* her stride? It was looking far too long.

One . . . two . . . three . . .

River couldn't possibly take off from the point Tash set her at, yet there wasn't enough room to put in another stride before the huge table. Clever, careful and eager to preserve her legs and her mistress, River had no choice but to stop, rising up as she cranked back her huge momentum, back legs sliding under her.

Tash would have stayed in the plate were it not for a small, yappy dog choosing that moment to burst out of the crowds and fly at the mare's fetlocks. Already off balance, River shied away and practically sat down on one haunch, pitching Tash out behind her and cramming her up against the solid side of the table for a brief, horrifying moment, her head twisted on to her shoulder, trapped between solid timber and horseflesh, her hips and legs pinned under her struggling horse's back end.

The directors in charge of the live streaming immediately cut away and a howl of terror and worry went up in both the competitors' tent and in front of the main video screens where huge crowds were gathered.

There was another long stop on the course, and as soon as the air ambulance landed from depositing one casualty in Peterborough, it was given another.

Afterwards, riders were told that they were allowed to circle between the tables.

Tash didn't want to go to hospital and protested vociferously when they strapped her to a stretcher for her first trip in an air ambulance as a patient. Clamped into a neck brace, she looked up at a sign that read 'DO NOT PANIC – YOU ARE IN A HELICOPTER' above her head, intended for patients who recover consciousness en route to the hospital.

Tash had not lost consciousness, nor indeed did she feel injured, although the air travel made her quite queasy. As she was wheeled through echoing hospital corridors, grateful to be away from the deafening helicopter blades, she told the paramedics that yes, she knew her name and what day it was, and no, she had no neck pain and could feel all her limbs, although she had some sharp pains in her lower abdomen.

She was initially examined by an Indian doctor in a private side room, prodded and questioned at length before her neck brace was removed and she was moved in to the main Accident and

Emergency unit to be left unattended in a cubicle, handed a small pot and asked to provide a urine sample when she felt able.

'Why?' She wondered if the FEI had brought in even more covert random drug testing.

'Dr Singh was most insistent,' the staff nurse told her, heading through the curtain to check on a neighbouring patient.

Shuffling off her examination couch, she went to find a loo, handing her sample back to a nurse when she returned. She sat back down on her allotted bed.

In the neighbouring cubicle a very familiar voice was complaining that he absolutely had to get discharged and get back to Burghley to check how his wife had done.

'Hugo?'

The curtain swept aside and there he was, lying on his side in a bed in nothing but a skimpy surgical gown as blue as his eyes.

'What are you wearing?'

'They cut me out of my breeches,' he explained. 'A rather over-zealous new nurse seemed to think I had a smashed pelvis like Beccy and might be bleeding internally, whereas in fact it appears to be a bruised coccyx and another ruddy cracked rib. You?'

'Suspected drug-taking, or maybe diabetes.' She held up her palms in confusion.

Hugo sat up, tapping his fingers impatiently on the metal frame of the bed, eager to leave.

'There are more riders in here than the competitors' tent,' Tash giggled. 'I spotted two on my way to the lavatory.'

'Christ.'

'We'll have to hire a minibus to get back to Burghley,' she pointed out cheerfully, suddenly shot through with the strange high that sometimes comes after a fall, when one realises how lucky one is and that it's all going to be okay.

Her joy was infectious, making Hugo laugh.

'Come here.' He shifted along the bed to make room.

She crossed through to his cubicle and perched on the bed beside him, taking his hand. 'I'd never have forgiven myself if something truly bad had happened to you just now and we hadn't made our peace.'

He ran his fingers along hers. 'I'm bloody tough.'

'We're all fallible, all make mistakes.'

He looked at her levelly, eyes still bearing tiny ice chips of mistrust. 'Are we talking about our riding here?'

'Nothing happened with Lough.' She gripped his hand tighter.

'I know,' he conceded, eyes softening at last. 'I was a bloody fool not to trust you. I thought he'd won you away from me.'

'It wasn't a competition, Hugo.'

He looked away, muscles tensing in his cheek. 'It was. You were the prize.'

'What are you talking about?'

'The night I asked him to ride for Haydown, Lough got me all wrong. Christ, Tash, you don't want to hear this.'

'I certainly do.' She looked at him, eyes wide. 'You not telling me about it has hardly helped, has it?'

He ran a hand through his hair, looking away remorsefully. 'I got in a spot of trouble in a bar, had my drink spiked, shot my mouth off. Lough thought I was a dick. I *was* a dick, quite frankly. I'd just won gold, my wife was having our first son any day and I felt invincible. I can hardly blame Lough for turning the screw. I was all over the place.'

'And you offered me as a prize? For what? Getting to the top of the FEI rankings?'

He shook his head violently, turning to look at her and take her hand, blue eyes fierce with regret. 'We made a bet that got totally out of proportion. He told me that I deserved to lose you. I said I'd like to see him try.'

'Oh God.' Tash covered her mouth with both their hands as the truth dawned. 'You think that's what he set out to do all along?'

Hugo brushed his thumb along her cheek. 'I didn't know what to think at first, quite honestly. But I was still glad he was arrested: I hoped they'd lock him up for good. Then he turned up just days before I had to leave for the States and I saw that he hadn't just come to teach me a lesson. He was a man on a mission, head and heart locked on target. I have no idea what had changed in him, but it was terrifying.'

'The Beccy texts,' Tash sighed.

Hugo looked at her curiously. 'I hated leaving you behind with him. I was already fed up with being away so much. Every time I came back I felt like more of a stranger.'

'Why didn't you tell me?'

'You were always so preoccupied.'

'I *am* always preoccupied,' she admitted, 'but a big part of that preoccupation is you – you are a full time preoccupation, Hugo.'

'Perhaps we need pre-occupational therapy?'

She stroked his thigh. 'We do need to make some changes.'

He nodded. 'I've decided to spend more time at home schooling and coaching from now on. There'll be no winter training in the States unless we go as a family. In fact, I'm not going to compete overseas any more unless you and the children are with me; the same in the UK. We'll make it work for all of us. Team Beauchamp. I'm miserable without you all by my side. We'll build a crèche in the bloody horsebox if we have to,' he laughed. 'It might catch on: enough eventers travel with their kids these days.'

'We'll be crèche test dummies.' She laughed too, leaning across to nuzzle his shoulder. 'I can see it now: ball pits in the tack lockers; nappy changing on the ramps; Shetlands tackling miniature cross-country jumps. We'll never have any privacy for nookie, of course.' She slid her hand higher up his thigh.

'We'll make damned sure we do.' He covered her hand with his, turning the battered wedding ring on her finger, looking at her seriously, blue eyes alight with hope. 'We can make life better, Tash.'

'We will make it better.' She stetched up to kiss him, sliding her hand higher so that it disappeared beneath the blue gown, 'Crikey, you're not wearing any pants.'

'They cut those off too.'

His blue gown had started to feature a prominent and exciting landmark as her hand sneaked further underneath, cupping his balls and letting her fingertips roll through the soft hair.

'I must say, I like your bedside manner.' He started to kiss her throat. 'You have lovely warm hands.'

'You know what they say.' She swung her legs up onto the bed and knelt over him, lifting up the gown. 'Warm hands . . .'

'. . . warm heart?'

'That too,' she started to kiss her way up his thigh. 'You know, I don't think there's much of an injury down here at all.'

'No?'

'No.' She wrapped her hand around his cock, now at full mast and ran her thumb along the taut flying buttress of sinew at the back of the shaft. 'It feels pretty intact to me.'

'Are you sure you're examining it with the right equipment?'

'Hmmm, perhaps I should take a closer look.'

'Ahh . . .' Hugo groaned happily a moment later. 'Warm hands, warm mouth.'

When the curtain swished back, it shook on its metal rings briefly before being swiftly closed again.

'In my twenty years of medical practice in hospitals all over the world,' a tense Dr Singh announced from the other side, 'I have seen people do some very strange things in hospital emergency wards, but I have never seen *that* before.'

To a mortified Tash's relief, he took it incredibly well, especially when he pointed out that the pregnant woman in the first trimester can have an unusually high sexual appetite.

'Really?' Hugo looked delighted.

'Did you say pregnant?' Tash squeaked.

They gaped at each other in shock.

By the close of cross-country day the bogey fence had claimed a significant proportion of the field, including both the German riders who had been in the top ten before the phase started. Now Lough was leading with Rory in second after a blistering round inside the time on White Lies, his old ally playing to his greatest strength which had always been fast galloping on big tracks.

'He's a lousy show-jumper,' he admitted quietly to Anke afterwards. 'We could really stuff it up tomorrow. I have only one fence in hand over Stefan and Kevin, and Lough has two over me.'

'You must think positively!' Anke insisted brusquely.

Rory tried to feel positive – it had been one of the most thrilling cross-country rides of his life, yet he only wanted to share it with one person and she was still lying low.

He even went along to the raucous grooms' party hoping that she would be there, but she wasn't and Franny, dressed in an extraordinary red rubber catsuit, decided it would be fun to get a gang of girlfriends to tie him up and cover him with show sheen, which didn't greatly improve his temper as he slithered back to the horsebox to slip about on his bed like an eel.

He jumped as a text came through on his phone, heart pounding crazily when he realised it was from Faith.

Just done evening check on Whitey. All well. Sound as a pound. Sleep well.

Thank you. You are an angel. Sleep well too, he texted back, adding lots of kisses and then cursing himself after he'd sent it because he must come across as a gormless berk, especially if, as he feared, she was with Dillon, possibly about to take a moonlit walk around the deer park and do nefarious rock 'n' roll things to one another among the trees.

He'd not seen much of his celebrity patron that afternoon, having been too focused on Whitey, but he knew from the chatter around him at the stables that the cheesy popster had arrived in a very big black car with several overexcited little girls in pink jodhpurs and a nanny in tow, all of them eschewing the VIP and members' areas and trooping around the course to watch the action at close hand, no doubt sharing hot clinches with Faith at every opportunity.

Well, they would both have to take notice of him tomorrow, he told himself, trying to let it sink in. He'd either triumph or crash and burn; there was no mid point.

I'm almost there, he realised, suddenly terrified.

The prospect of the next day overwhelmed him, the sheer pressure of the task ahead and the number of things that could go wrong. Even assuming Whitey passed the vet's inspection, which was no certainty given his age and history of injury, there was still Lough to beat, just as there were tens of very shallow plastic jump cups holding up the poles that stood between him, a quarter of a million pounds and the revelation of a truth he feared may already be lost.

Laughter and a hushed argument directly outside the horsebox made him reach for his iPod, guessing Franny was back and, as he had feared, she had company.

But he had barely slotted a tiny white headphone into one ear when somebody started knocking on the door.

'It's open,' he snapped, hoping Franny's companion was good at removing rubber outfits quietly.

Whispering at someone behind him to wait a moment, Dillon Rafferty walked in, looking more like a Greek farmer than a pop star, with a newly regrowing beard, mahogany tan and dusty clothes. But the big white teeth still flashed a thousand watts when he saw Rory.

'There you are! We'd given up on you.'

Rory eyed him warily over his own feet, which were encased in a bright blue sleeping bag.

'You're doing great.' Dillon gazed around him at the horsebox. 'Christ, it's just like being on a tour bus, only with mud.'

'This is what we do.'

'I like it.' Dillon sounded surprised.

Rory tried to sit up too fast, sliding around in his sleeping bag because he was still covered in show sheen.

'You can ask her in.' He managed to sit up again. 'I know she's out there.'

Dillon looked awkward. 'Sure?'

'Sure.' His heart cracked a little, and he reminded himself angrily that she had never been his to lose.

But the figure who stepped up into the lorry wasn't Faith. It was a blonde woman Rory had definitely seen before, fine and willowy with alabaster skin, hollow cheeks and huge, haunted eyes. Nodding hello, her hand instinctively slipped into Dillon's and he squeezed it tightly before lifting it to his lips.

Rory's eyes, wide as two pewter plates, gazed from her to Dillon as the colour mounted in his cheeks.

'This is Fawn,' Dillon introduced them.

Suddenly Rory recognised her. 'But I, but you, but . . .'

Even more high-cheeked than Rory, and flashing that graceful Hollywood smile immortalised on a thousand billboards, Fawn Johnston held out her hand to shake Rory's. 'Great to meet you, Rory. You're one hell of a rider.'

'I'm learning.' He cleared his throat.

'Fawn really wanted to meet you. We've rented a cottage on the estate and the girls are all in bed – Hana is watching them. She's going to nanny for us now we're . . . um—'

'Back together,' Fawn interjected smoothly, smiling widely. 'I'm gonna be based here in England more from now on,' she told Rory.

He nodded, but he wasn't taking much in as his mind finally, laboriously connected the wires: Dillon and Faith are not together, he realised. Dillon and Faith are not together. Dillon is still in love with this woman, his wife.

'I'm real passionate about horses,' Fawn was explaining. 'I rode horseback as a little girl and I still do it for movie roles. I love it that Dillon own horses with you. We were so excited to see you ride today.'

Dillon laughed, looking at his wife with total devotion. 'She made us all run around like idiots trying to see as much as possible while you rode White Tie.'

'White Lies,' Rory corrected, shuffling his sleeping bag to the lip of the Luton and smiling at Fawn, who he had suddenly decided he liked very, very much. 'I'm retiring him after this – he's been a great servant, but he needs a quieter life, hacking and hunting. He's so cool – you could put a baby on him one day and ride him round Aintree the next. You and Dillon should take him on.' He had no idea where that came from, but it suddenly made sense. 'You have him after he retires if you want.'

'You're kidding me? That would be so cool.' Fawn's pretty grey eyes widened.

'We must go.' Dillon had started to tow her back towards the door.

But Fawn tugged him back. '*Tell* him, honey. We agreed.'

'Oh yes, I almost forgot.' Dillon swung around, looking hugely embarrassed. 'Faith.'

Rory swallowed a cannonball. 'What about Faith?'

Dillon cleared his throat a few more times, clearly not knowing where to start.

Fawn hissed across at him, 'You gotta tell him *everything*, D. Like we agreed.'

'Okay.' Dillon coughed awkwardly. 'Fact is, Rory, Faith was the one who pushed me into it. I'd have never got involved otherwise.'

Rory eyed him with alarm from his slippery sleeping bag. 'I don't think I want to know this.'

'She sort of forced me into it.'

Rory closed his eyes, imagining his beloved Faith tying Dillon Rafferty to a bed in the Caribbean.

'But I love it now,' Dillon was saying, 'especially now I know Fawn wants to get involved. I understand why she's so passionate about it.'

'Eh?'

Fawn smiled her ice queen smile. 'What Dillon is *trying* to say is that Faith was the one who persuaded him to buy horses for you to run in the first place, Rory.'

Rory stared at her, not understanding.

'I knew Faith by sight from learning to ride with you, of course,' Dillon explained. 'But I hadn't been up to the yard since breaking my leg, and I was at a pretty low ebb when I bumped into her in Cottrell's sales room. We got talking and she said she'd been sent there by a friend to bid on Trudy Dew's piano. Then Trudy herself showed up and played "Two Souls". I wanted that song so badly it hurt, and I wanted the piano to go with it.'

'You outbid Faith?'

He shook his head. 'She'd made it pretty clear her friend would go as high as it took.'

'Of course, it was Flipper,' Rory remembered. 'It was the day of Whitey's accident. He desperately wanted to buy Trudy her Bechstein back, but was too busy saving my horse's life to go to the sale and bid himself.'

'Faith could see I'd pay a hell of a lot more than Flipper could afford. So she said that she would refrain from bidding if I promised to get you some decent horses.'

'She did?' Rory gaped at him in amazement.

He nodded. 'She's a pretty determined character, as you know. I think she'd have spent all afternoon out-bidding me if I hadn't said yes, cranking the price up to cost more than a stableful of top horses. And I always thought you were a great rider, so it made sense to shake hands on it. She was fantastically businesslike; she even got our agreement in writing. I've just adored her from that day on. If she thinks I'm letting you down as an owner, she's on my case like a shot.'

'I thought it was Nell who got you into it,' Rory laughed incredulously, eyes shining as the scales fell from them, 'but she's always preferred the bright lights to boggy fields. Darling Faith, my clever, gorgeous girl. I still can't believe she did that for me. She pretty much blackmailed you.'

'I prefer to think of it as collaborative negotiation.'

With an impatient tut, Fawn stepped forwards, increasingly uncomfortable with all this eulogising talk of Faith. 'Yes, they cut a deal in an auction room – hey, let's not go into any more details.' She waved her hand airily. 'All I know is, she's one heck of a girl. And the sooner you two get it together the better.' She narrowed her eyes, lowering the temperature in the horsebox by several degrees. 'Besides I want her occupied.' The smile warmed a degree. 'And you two guys would be *so* perfect together.' She gave him a sweet, albeit frosty, wave and headed outside, making Rory wish he hadn't offered her Whitey.

With a nervous nod, Dillon bolted after her.

'Wait!' Rory and his slippery sleeping bag tumbled from the Luton before hopping through the horsebox like a boy in a sack race. 'I need to know what happened with Faith in the Caribbean.'

Dillon regarded him over his shoulder. 'D'you remember what happened to Trudy Dew's Bechstein in the end?'

'You gave it back to her.'

'Exactly,' he nodded, stepping outside. 'It played its sweetest music for her. You must keep the Faith, Rory.'

'But you and she . . .' The sack race hopped after him.

His head reappeared around the doorframe. 'Forgive me. I never lost the Faith because she was never mine to keep. She's a one-man religion. You win this slam thing tomorrow and you'll find out just how much she cares.'

'I already know,' he croaked.

'Good.' Dillon smiled at him. 'Now go back to bed and don't forget to say your prayers.'

Chapter 88

As ever on the final evening of the three day event, all those with a horse still in the running were on full alert, even the hard-partying grooms, regularly heading back to the stables and checking for lumps and bumps and any unsoundness that might cause their charges to be spun at the following morning's final veterinary inspection.

When a groggy Lemon appeared from the grooms' party at close to eleven, Lough was in his horse's stall.

'Looks like I'll be going home early,' Lough told him, looking up from examining Toto's near hind leg which was already thick with swelling above the hoof, the horse reluctant to bear weight on it.

The shadow of a small round head and Mohican was silhouetted over the door in the moonlight. 'No way! You're *leading*. There's nothing wrong with him.'

'The fetlock's badly bruised, Lem. He's hopping lame.'

'I've been icing it all evening. It's just a bump.'

'I'm the fucking vet.'

'You got struck off!'

'I stopped practising,' Lough hushed him in a harsh whisper. 'It's different.'

They glared at one another. Their relationship, always volatile, had become increasingly tense in recent weeks, particularly since Lough had followed Beccy to France in a state of high agitation and then returned unable to stop smiling, his heart beyond Lemon's reach for ever.

'We'll see what he's like in the morning.' Lough straightened up, letting the horse's rugs drop back over his quarters. 'I won't present him at the trot up if I'm in any doubt. And it'll take a miracle if he's sound, quite frankly; he's way too sore.'

Lem's eyes flashed in the half light.

'We can dope him,' he breathed. 'We have before.'

Lough hissed through his teeth. 'Not my horses we don't.'

'You know the trick with the leg bandages,' Lemon rushed on eagerly. 'The painkiller's localised so it'll make him sound but won't get into his system enough to show up on blood test. We'll never get found out.'

'No way.' Lough's voice was a low threat.

'Is this 'cos of Rory and the Grand Slam?' Lemon sounded desperate. 'Because if it is, the man doesn't deserve any noble gestures from you. We *deserve* this victory. He's had everything handed to him like candy.'

'It makes no difference. He wouldn't be where he is if he didn't have the guts to win.'

'And a hell of a lot of people clearing a path in front of him,' Lemon sneered.

Lough shook his head, reaching out to open the door. 'We have to put the welfare of the horse first. Toto is injured.'

'Like fuck he is!' Lemon barred the way. 'You can lie to the ground jury but you can't lie to me, mate, and I'm not going to let this happen. I've worked too hard to get you here to stand back and watch you piss it away as a part of some fucking British upper-class conspiracy to own this sport.'

'Steady on, Lem.'

'I will *not*!' He was starting to crackle like static, the several tequilas and amyl nitrite rushes he had recently tooted mixing toxically with beer from the grooms' party and the pep pills he knocked back on a regular basis to stay awake.

'I risked so much to get you up here, to knock Hugo back down to size. *You* should have won that Olympic gold and he knows it.'

'How d'you figure that out?'

'You're the better rider. You're the better man. Hugo needed teaching a lesson.' He was starting to gibber. 'All those fucking years of effort. The best horse you've ever had and he swans up with all his money and class and glamour and grooms and steals gold from you. And you still bloody liked him! You even sent me over here to this godforsaken country and got yourself arrested so I was stuck here, unable to help you, camped with the *enemy*!' He started to cry.

'Oh shit.' Lough put a hand on his shaking shoulder, still unable to get through the stable door because Lemon's body weight was slumped against it, his head in his hands. 'I had no idea . . .'

'I love you!' he howled. 'I fucking love you!'

Further along the line a pair of tipsy grooms checking their horses by torchlight started to giggle, and Lough fought an urge to ask Lemon to keep his voice down.

'Hugo's like an upper-class rat – everything you throw at him, he survives: bad rumours, falls, brake failure, failed deals, lost sponsorship.'

Lough felt a cold scorpion trail of recognition scuttle up his spine and sting him behind the ear.

'*You* were behind that?'

Nodding, Lemon sniffed, wiping his nose on the back of his hand. 'He needed to suffer. I thought I'd die of unhappiness when I realised you were in love with Tash. It took me a while to figure that you chasing his wife would hurt Hugo more than anything I could throw at him, and I was right.'

'Christ alive,' Lough breathed. 'You could have *killed* him.'

'Nah. He has nine lives, like a cat. An aristo-cat.' He laughed that odd, whooping laugh of his, part hyena, part kookaburra.

Lough stood in the darkness, barely able to take it in. He'd always known Lemon was crooked, a shady little horse-handler who had longed to be a jockey and never made the grade, who knew every dirty trick in the book when it came to racing and had no compunction when it came to transferring them to horse trials.

He had been an intrinsic part of the mix that enabled Lough, the poor scholarship boy turned country vet, to succeed against all expectations in a sport where huge financial backing was essential. Lemon's racing contacts had provided an essential income – highly illegal, deeply regrettable but the only way they could ever cover their costs for long enough to break through to the big time.

To his shame, he had never thought to question why Lemon was so loyal to him, why this little renegade, an Artful Dodger with no close family and no ties, had stuck with him through thick and thin over so many years now. Love would have been one of the last reasons he'd have come up with if asked before now.

'Neither of us got what we wanted in this fucking country, did we?' Lemon was muttering bitterly.

'Maybe we just didn't know what we wanted when he came here,' Lough replied carefully, thinking of Beccy.

Lemon's anger stripped his voice to a croak. 'Well I've had enough, yeah? I'm not staying on after this season.'

'That's your choice.'

'I want to go travelling through Europe.'

'Sounds a good plan.'

He looked up, eyes still full of tears. 'You'll let me go just like that?' He snapped his fingers.

'If you want to go I'm not going to stand in your way, Lem. But you owe Hugo an explanation, an apology, before you go.'

'Fuck. Listen to you! You sound like one of them.'

'Tell Hugo what you did.'

'He could have me arrested!'

'Of course he won't.'

'I don't do all that fucking toadying like you – "I'm terribly sorry I tried get in your wife's knickers, old man."' He laid on his bad cut-glass English accent. '"But I tell you what, I'll take your mad, crippled sister-in-law off your hands and let's call it quits shall we?"'

'Take that back!' Lough snarled, making Toto jump to the back of his box, eyes boggling.

'I can understand Tash, yeah,' Lemon ranted on, 'she's a fit bird, and funny and a great cook, but *Beccy*? *My* cast offs? She's a spinner. C'mon, Lough, you can do better than that.'

The punch flew out from the black stable so fast Lemon didn't see it coming. The next thing, he was sprawled on the grass in the moonlight, literally seeing stars.

Letting himself out of the stall, Lough checked that he was conscious.

'You'd better pack your things and go tonight,' he told him. 'I'll send the rest of your stuff on later.'

'You can't sack me in the middle of Burghley!'

'I just have.' He reached down and took the photo ID from around Lemon's neck. 'You have an hour to leave the site.'

Standing up unsteadily, Lemon glared up at him. 'You'll regret this,'

'I don't think so.'

'Rory Midwinter won't win tomorrow, you know, even if you and half the rest of the field withdraws.'

'We'll see.'

Rolling his jaw, Lemon narrowed his eyes, aiming a huge bullet of spit at Lough's feet before walking away.

Sitting down outside Toto's stable, suddenly drained, Lough pulled his mobile from the pocket of his jeans and phoned Beccy, surprised to find the background noise almost drowning out anything he could hear of her.

'We've only just started pudding,' she explained. 'It's all been very exciting. Tash and Hugo have *the* most amazing news. Hang on – I'll put you on hands free so I can use my crutches to get away from the table.' There was a lot of crackling and rustling. 'That's better. God, I wish you were here.'

'I need to focus,' he reminded her, adding, 'and I'm hardly welcome at their table.'

'Oh, he's already over it. He's going to be a father again. Tash's pregnant!'

'Christ.' He felt a blade run through his side. Yet it hurt a lot less than he feared; it was barely even a flesh wound. 'But she had a bad fall today. Is she okay . . . the baby?' Terrible echoes were haunting him.

Despite the hubbub around her, Lough knew that Beccy understood. They'd haunted her too. 'Both are in great health. The hospital gave them a scan as soon as they found out what was going on. She's already almost fourteen weeks.'

'No kidding?' He tried not to think back to all the desperate, lovelorn lusting he had been doing over Tash while all the time a tiny new life was kicking off inside her.

'Are you okay about it?' Beccy asked nervously, having now clearly moved to a quieter spot, her laboured breaths revealing how much pain she was still in when she walked with her crutches.

'Yeah, I'm great,' He laughed and realised it really was true. 'You and me will have lots of babies one day.'

She laughed too, loving how easy he made it sound. 'You and me might even enjoy lots of sex one day,' she sighed regretfully. 'Hugo was right – breaking your pelvis wrecks your love life.'

'I don't know,' he said in a low voice. 'We can figure out ways.'

'We can,' she breathed. 'God, I wish you were here now. Please come.'

He looked at his watch. 'I can't really. Toto's hopping lame and Lem's gone.'

'Lem's gone?'

He explained the little groom's revelation that he had been behind the accidents surrounding Haydown and the smear campaign against Hugo. 'I thought Hugo was mad accusing me but he was closer to the truth than I realised.'

'Oh God.' Her voice dropped to barely more than a whisper. 'I knew Lem hated Hugo, but I thought it was all front. I never knew—' Encroaching tears and panic gagged her.

'Shh, Beccy. It's okay. I know you feel bad, but you couldn't have done anything to stop him, trust me.'

She was still incredibly fragile and he couldn't wait to embark upon the long, gentle task of helping build her back up again, restoring her confidence and sense of self, much of which had been destroyed all those years ago when she had witnessed a sight no child should ever see, far more extreme than any spectacle he had grown up with, even his drunken father's regular beatings of his mother. He saw Beccy as a nervous, neglected horse, like some of the wrecks he bought off the racetracks for a few dollars and whose lives had been a procession of different yards, owners, trainers and riders, sometimes crossing continents before they settled with him to be patiently given a second chance. He had a lifetime to give Beccy that chance, but he was sure it would take a lot less long than that. Emotionally neglected, over-bright, allowed to develop selfish and dysfunctional behaviour patterns, Beccy had a lot of bad habits and existed in an orbit so far removed from most of her family's everyday lives that she could be almost impossible to reach. But when someone did reach her she was a unique, bright-burning star of such intensity and radiance it was impossible to forget her. Lough had never met anyone like her in his life. He was almost blind with love. She lived in his mind's eye everywhere he went, but that was no substitute for the real thing, and being with her in person felt like waking up from a coma.

'I must see you tonight,' he realised. 'I'll walk over to Stamford once I've got Toto comfortable.'

'We're not staying here,' she reminded him. 'We're in a golf club hotel near Bourne. I can't remember its name.'

'I'll find it,' he promised.

Tash and Hugo's hopes of a quiet, romantic room-service meal eaten naked in bed that night while admiring one another's bruises had been completely scuppered by so many of their friends and family gathering in a private dining room of the George in Stamford, which Sophia, purportedly wearing her indulgent event horse owner hat, had booked weeks earlier and orchestrated so that the long table was set up like a wedding banquet, with place names hand-written on little cards shaped like cross-country jumps and even themed dishes such as Hurley Burghley Soup and a fish course of Trout Hatchery Mousse.

'Anyone would think we had won, not been eliminated the day before the show-jumping,' Tash whispered as her family toasted them and delighted in being gathered together under one roof, chattering and bickering and gossiping like mad.

'We have won,' Hugo pointed out, leaning across to press a kiss to her ear.

Tash shivered deliciously as his lips traced the curve of her ear-lobe.

'We survived the seven-year itch,' she giggled.

'Is that what it was?'

'Penny says that's why the seventh wedding anniversary is celebrated with wool, because it makes you itch.'

'Too right,' he whispered, his hand resting between her legs beneath the table cloth and starting to stroke her thigh, lifting her skirt to touch bare skin. 'I'm always itching for you. What's the next one?'

'Bronze,' she said distractedly as his fingers crept higher.

'Sounds good,' he breathed in an undertone. 'I am certainly as hard as—'

'Are you talking about your wedding anniversary?' Sophia demanded across the table.

'Mmm.' Tash managed a vague nod, reaching down to trap Hugo's hand before she started to make inappropriate pleasure-noises.

'Your wedding day was so wonderful,' Alexandra recalled happily, reaching for a wine glass brimming with Meursault. 'All those beautiful autumn colours, and *so* many people at the party. There must have been, what, two or three hundred?'

Henrietta was having terrible trouble keeping a straight face for some reason, Tash noticed.

'We could have a party this year,' she suddenly realised, thinking that was just what they all needed after a hellish few months, and it would make up for Hugo's cancelled fortieth.

But he seemed strangely unenthusiastic. 'I was thinking of something more intimate,' he insisted.

She was about to protest, but then his hand closed on hers and slid it from her lap to his, so that she could feel his early bronze anniversary present growing in readiness.

'I suppose I will be pretty pregnant by then,' she agreed. 'It might all be far too exhausting to organise.'

Opposite them, she caught her sister winking at Hugo in a most unSophia-like way and she frowned, wondering if she had somehow missed something. With the high dramas of helicopter and hospital, she had failed to witness Sophia's strange behaviour that day. She had not seen her sister running around the Burghley site like an overexcited girl guide, cornering event riders and owners, supporters, international regulars and British Eventing stalwarts to issue invitations, check that they knew what was planned and how exactly to spring the surprise of the year.

But Tash was far too excited by their own delicious surprise growing inside her to worry about Sophia's strange facial tics for long.

Using pregnancy tiredness as an excuse to go to bed early, she dragged an all-too-willing Hugo with her as they left the rest of the family to petit fours and coffee.

'The pregnant woman can have an unusually high sexual appetite in the first trimester,' she told him breathlessly as she closed the door behind them and leant against it, licking her lips. 'And the second, it seems . . .'

Hugo raised his brows and beckoned her towards him. She shook her head, slowly lifting her hands to her shoulders to edge off the straps of her tea dress. 'Take your clothes off.'

He shot her a bemused look but did as she urged. Off came the shirt, wrenched over his head, cufflinks falling randomly. Off slid the trousers, kicked aside along with the socks. His erection was already poking from his underpants like a welcoming arm raised through curtains before he tugged them down and let them fall.

Now was the perfect moment for her Meg Ryan *Top Gun* running jump, Tash realised. It was time to cast aside previous false starts and failures. Tonight it would be perfect.

Flexing up on to the balls of her feet like a gymnast eyeing the vaulting horse, she looked at his true blue eyes, then his beautiful body with its blackening bruises from the fall he had taken, then his amazing, vigorous cock waiting to thrill her.

And then she sprinted faster than a triple jumper, took an elegant bounce into launch position and leaped around him.

'Jesus!' Hugo laughed as they tipped back towards the bed, hands on her thighs, his hips clamped between them. Then they landed together and his expression changed from joy to pain.

'My coccyx!' he wailed.

'Oh God, have I hurt it?' Mishearing him, she looked down and felt his wilting erection with a cautious hand, her probing fingers having an extraordinary analgesic effect on the back pain and a restorative effect on his sexual enthusiasm. 'Feels incredibly well to me. Shall we test it out?'

'Better give it a ride just to check,' he agreed as she angled her hips and mounted.

She leaned down and kissed him, on and on and on, lips as soft as ripe cherry flesh, tongue in his mouth greeting his, hands on his face, hot body sliding closer around his in the most intimate welcome.

The four-poster bed more than earned its keep that night as Tash clung on to each newel post in turn, loving her increased sexual appetite.

★

Downstairs, Sophia gave a brief speech before her troops dispersed, making sure that they had all got their personalised instructions, checklists, guests lists and phone-tree numbers.

'This time, *nothing* will go wrong,' she announced dramatically.

Watching her from the opposite end of the table, Ben Meredith thrilled at the sight of his wife in full flow. His loins tightened hungrily and he made a mental note to fill out the breakfast in bed form as soon as they got to their room.

In a golf hotel near Bourne, Beccy limped to her door, her crutches thumping, to let in Lough. She pressed her finger to her lips and nodded towards a connecting door that led from her little room through to her mother and James. If one were to stay very quiet it was possible to hear James snoring.

They were indeed quiet, although inside their bodies firework noises raged. Kissing filled their heads with rushing blood, heartbeats in their ears, electric crackles in their groins.

Lough could only stay for half an hour, he explained in a whisper. He had borrowed an ancient scramble bike from a fellow rider, but he had to return it by midnight, like Cinderella's pumpkin, and check on Toto again.

He wanted to stay so much. He wanted to lie her down and kiss between her thighs again, to part her downy-soft pubic hair and drop kisses there, tease out those silken petals and taste the dew on them.

Instead, they kissed like teenagers on a doorstep, barely moving from the same spot as the room spun around them, the force of the vortex making minutes become blinks of time.

'Stay,' she begged, her broken body so alight with love and lust that she couldn't believe anything this heavenly could lead to pain.

He shook his head, drinking last kisses, backing reluctantly away and opening the door.

'We have a lifetime,' he reminded her in a whisper.

Then, unable to stop himself, he walked straight back into the room and shut the door again behind him. 'That lifetime starts right now.'

Lying alone in the Moncrieffs' ancient horsebox, Faith fought all her overwhelming urges to run barefoot across the lorry park to Rory's box and hurl herself on top of him. Instead she listened to Irish jigs on her iPod and started composing a text.

When the phone leaped in her hands, buzzing with a new message before hers was complete, it almost slipped from her grip like a fish and flew through the air.

But it was just Lough, asking her to check on Toto.

Rory knocked on the door of the Moncrieffs' old Bedford HGV, his heart hammering far harder than his knuckles. But there was no answer. It was in darkness. Faith must be asleep.

He headed to the stables to check on Whitey.

Faith had run all the way to the temporary stabling only to realise that she had left her ID pass behind so ran all the way back for it, detouring via the lorry park marquees where the last dregs of the grooms' party were still lurching around. She was grateful to see that Rory wasn't among the staying chasers, although Franny was attached to one of the injured German riders, her catsuit making squeaky noises as they kissed hungrily.

She dashed into the lorry to collect her ID, flicking on all the lights in her search until she tracked it down in the pocket of her sleeveless hoodie. Running yet again, breath sharp and fast in her chest now, she dashed to the stables security gate.

'Busy in here tonight,' the official yawned, having only just waved another one through a minute earlier.

Faith checked first Whitey, who whickered eagerly, still wide awake and fit to party, and smelling strangely of freshly crunched mints, then Rangitoto, who looked sleepy but comfortable despite keeping all his weight on three legs.

She hurtled back to the horsebox park, battling the urge to detour via the big, shiny Beauchamp box like a heat-seeking missile.

It was no good. She just needed to stand near him.

Creeping up to the Beauchamps' box, she propped herself up on the steps as silently as she could and peered in through the nearest window. It was almost dark inside; the little reading light was on above the Luton and the curtains open to reveal a crumpled sleeping bag, but nobody was occupying it.

When Rory wandered back past the Moncrieffs' old Bedford he was surprised to see all the lights on this time, the lorry glowing amid its darkened companions like a party boat in a sleeping harbour. But there was nobody aboard.

He turned away with a sigh, disappearing around the tail end of the lorry just as Faith appeared at the cab end, wearily sorting out the correct key to let herself back in.

She got straight back into bed and texted Lough that his horse was okay but sore.

Her DVD player was still on her bunk. She watched Jim and Jessica's kissing scene again, but the battery conked out half way through.

She remembered Fearghal's words: 'Of course you must tell him you love him. Just wait until after the trials.'

He was right, of course, she told herself as she switched off the light and closed her eyes tightly. It was just another fifteen hours until the outcome.

Her eyes snapped open.

What did Fearghal know, she thought hotly, sitting up and groping for her phone. He was just a dodgy horse dealer from County Mayo. Hadn't he said that her mother was the one that got away? That meant he had got it wrong all those years ago and had let Anke get away. Well, she couldn't risk that happening with Rory.

Whether you win or lose tomorrow, she typed out on her little phone, *I love you with all my heart and I always will.*

Closing her eyes and screwing up her face, she pressed Send. Then she hid under her duvet, groaning with shame.

Her phone beeped back within seconds.

I love you too.

Chapter 89

When Rory and White Lies trotted into the arena at Burghley as the last combination to jump, they had just one fence in hand as a safety margin against any mistakes that might rob them of the title and the Grand Slam.

856

The crowd, knowing how much was riding on this round, were absolutely silent.

In their midst, even Sylva Frost was holding her breath and jabbing Pete in the ribs to stop him signing autographs over the membership enclosure fence and start concentrating.

'That the butch bird you were shagging from the stables?' he asked vaguely as Rory trotted past, waiting for the bell.

'Darlink, this is a man called Rory,' Sylva told him, handing him his prescription sunglasses. 'He is a friend.'

'You want me to buy you this horse?' He checked as he put on his glasses and realised that what he had taken to be a big-boned woman riding a large white cow was in fact a pale-faced man riding an ugly grey horse.

'No,' she purred. 'I want the black mare Kevin the French boy was riding.'

'Righti-ho.' Pete yawned, grateful that wearing his dark glasses meant he could close his eyes without being rumbled. All the sex was exhausting. At least this was the last horse and they could get back in his chopper soon, although he feared his chopper might get another rotary action from Sylva's tongue. She was showing a great predilection for high-altitude sex, which made piloting tricky.

Sitting beside his father, Berry on his knee, Dillon ignored Pete's loud yawns and concentrated on Rory, Fawn's hand in his with her fore and middle fingers crossed as the unprepossessing grey horse lumbered towards the first fence.

Whitey had never respected coloured poles as much as he should, and in old age he had become increasingly arrogant and eccentric towards them.

He was as fit as he had ever been. He had bounded through the final inspection with such enthusiasm and spring that the ground jury had laughed as they passed him with a wave, unlike poor Rangitoto, who had not even tried his luck.

With the overnight leader withdrawn, the way was clear for Whitey to convey his rider to victory, but he was never going to make it easy for Rory or the breathless crowd.

He barely lifted off the ground for the first fence, crashing through it so belligerently that horse and rider almost stopped, disoriented. The crowd groaned, sensing a huge anticlimax in store with poles set to fly everywhere.

He hit the next three fences so hard that it was a miracle they didn't come down; the top pole of the fourth jumped clean out of its cups before landing neatly back down in them, then he rattled the next two.

It seemed he was almost enjoying the anxious gasps from the crowd every time he tapped those flat black feet down on the wooden poles. Later, some spectators swore that he winked a dark eye at them as he lumbered past the stands.

Yet they were soon half way around the course and everything apart from the first was still up.

In the collecting ring Stefan, lying in second, couldn't bear to watch.

Bang, rattle, bang, Whitey clouted the double of gates and the angled oxer. Thwack, clunk, rattle, he scraped over the stile, the triple bar and the wall. He then set the top plank swinging and muddled his stride up so much that he dipped a leg in and out of the big parallel, somehow leaving it untouched.

But as Rory rounded the far end of the arena to set up for the final line, a treble combination followed by an upright, something seemed to go wrong and he looked down in alarm, then leaned forwards to look at Whitey's head.

He was riding in a hackamore, a bitless bridle that gave control by exerting pressure on the horse's nose and thus relieving his mouth where the bit had left him a little desensitised after cross-country day. A hackamore required a greater degree of skill from the rider, but Rory had been using it with the horse for years and knew he was safe in it as long as the contact was light.

Now the contact was so light it was non-existent.

One rein had broken, severed just beside the metal arm of the bridle that applied pressure to the horse's nose.

Rory was racketing towards the final four fences on the course with no steering and limited brakes.

'Ohmygod!' In the grandstands beside her mother, Faith covered her eyes and wailed.

In the collecting ring, Hugo said a prayer and held on to Tash, who gripped his hand so tightly in return that his signet ring flew off and his fingers turned blue.

Standing closer to the arena entrance, Lough groaned aloud, suddenly remembering Lemon's warning: 'Rory Midwinter won't win tomorrow even if half the field withdraws.' It had seemed a hollow threat at the time but now, as the horrified crowd watched Rory lose control down the last line, he knew Lemon had cut the rein as a parting gesture.

'Just do it!' he breathed, willing Rory on. Beside him, leaning on her crutches, Beccy let out three little squeaks for each of the elements of the treble Whitey cleared. She had let out similar squeaks of pleasure last night, Lough remembered, only those had been far wilder and harder to conceal as they'd stifled all their sound effects in case they awoke Henrietta and James.

There was nothing stifled about the squeal that Beccy emitted when Whitey's soup-plate black hooves landed back down on the turf after that final upright without spilling a pole.

The crowd followed within a split-second, roaring and screaming and clapping and whooping as Rory thrust his hat in the air and hollered with glee, patting Whitey's grey neck and dropping a kiss on his plaits as the old horse thundered around the arena taking a victory lap, imagining himself back at Cheltenham, in the Foxhunter Chase.

Julia Ditton was waiting for the victors in the collecting ring, microphone aloft and running shoes on so that she could jog alongside Rory as soon as he came out, demanding an in-the-saddle quote live on BBC2.

But of course Rory had just one rein attached to a now-useless hackamore. And Whitey was enjoying himself far too much to slow down. He might be eighteen, but he was as fit as a fiddle and the crowd's cheering ringing in his ears was sweet music after so many years away from the limelight. He lapped it up, literally, bombing round and round, ears pricked, eyes shining.

Eventually, just as the arena officials were starting to mutter about trying to catch him – rather a humiliation, it was felt, for the Burghley victor and first winner of the Grand Slam in almost a decade to have to be cornered like a hard-to-catch pony in a field – Whitey slowed to a trot, blowing heavily but happily.

Then he came to a very decisive halt directly in front of the packed South Stand. Puffing excitedly, he let out a shrill whinny and bobbed his head.

There must have been a hundred faces staring back at Rory from just that one small section of seating, but he only had eyes for one.

The BBC producers, going mad that Julia was still waiting for her interview with this incredible triple crown winner and that the network coverage was now about to switch to the snooker, ordered her to run in to the arena to grab a word.

Julia and her cameraman were just yards away from Rory when he stood up in his stirrups and talked directly at the crowd.

'I love you, Faith Brakespear!' he called out. 'You are the best thing that has ever, ever happened to me. I want to make you happy and look after you for the rest of our lives!'

The BBC producer who had been ordering his control room to cut to the snooker anyway suddenly hissed, 'Stay with the horses! Stay *with* the horses!'

Faith had turned very, very red, from her hands to her cheeks, but her smile was just inescapable.

'Come here!' Rory called hoarsely, a medieval knight to his lady, farmhand to rancher's daughter, Jim to Jessica.

Faith turned to her mother, astounded to see tears pouring down Anke's usually impassive face.

'Hurry up, *kæreste*!' Anke told her, pressing a kiss to her fingertips and laying it on her daughter's hot cheek.

To claps and cheers from the crowd, Faith clambered through the seating, over the sponsor's banners and in to the ring, where Rory leaned down to kiss her just as Julia Ditton finally panted up with her microphone, eagerly telling the viewing public that Rory was about to reveal to them all who this very lovely girl was.

But as she thrust the microphone at him Rory slipped his hands under Faith's arms and hooked her up towards the saddle in front of him, where she sat side-saddle like a gypsy girl at a fair. It was their moment, the scene from his favourite movie enacted in front of thousands. He kissed her again and she felt her heart grand slam against her chest.

'Hang on tight,' he whispered in her ear, 'I have no steering.'

Acknowledging the delighted crowds with a wave, they galloped out of the arena.

A divot of earth now hanging in her immaculate blonde hair, Julia Ditton turned to her cameraman and said 'Bollocks!' live on air. A moment later the picture cut to Ronnie O'Sullivan potting a pink.

★

The paparazzi, who had yet again donned their green wellies to dodge horses, dogs and dung in their pursuit of the ongoing tabloid soap that was Sylva Frost and the Rafferty men's love lives, were getting increasingly confused. No sooner had an unknown girl groom called Faith Brakespear been revealed as Dillon's 'mystery Caribbean blonde' than she had jumped into a clinch with another man and galloped off into the sunset (well, into the main catering area to be accurate, where Whitey's lack of steering had caused havoc among those sitting around the Pimm's stand watching the action on the big screen). Then, minutes later, Dillon had been spotted loping up to congratulate his sporting protégé with his famous ex-wife on his arm and lots of overexcited children in tow, looking to all the world like a steady family man. At the same time, Pete had emerged from the retail village with Sylva and a small army of Slovakians carrying shopping bags and had joined the family tableau.

'Hang on—' One pap checked his notes against a rival. 'The horsy bloke's now with the Caribbean tart, Dillon's with the wife and Sylva has had the Rockfather, his son *and* the horsy bloke, but is definitely sticking with Pete. Am I close?'

'Something like that. They're sex mad, the horse set.'

Trotting happily from the trade stands with Ben, Sophia Meredith decided with a sad sigh that it had been a terribly dull Burghley – apart from the blonde boy from Hugo's yard winning the Rolex Grand Slam. The horse they part-owned had been eliminated cross-country, Zara Phillips wasn't there – nor any Royals of note – and the shopping had been very lacklustre. But at least she had managed to get secret RSVPs to almost all of her invitations to the surprise party next month. It looked like it was going to be a show-stopping night.

Much later, in the Beauchamps' state-of-the-art horsebox, Rory handed Faith his new Rolex watch and made her promise to check that he would be on time for every date that he planned to take her on in coming weeks and months.

'I am going to wine you and dine you to make up for lost time,' he promised.

She clipped the watch around her wrist, where it slipped right over her hand. 'We've got all the time in the world now.' She set it aside, stretching forwards to kiss him. 'Oh, I do love you, Rory.'

He kissed her back until it all started to get so electrifying and frantic that he lifted her up and staggered towards the steps up to the Luton mattress.

'I'm probably not as exciting a lover as Dillon,' he fretted anxiously as they started to pull off layers.

'He was just coaching me,' she assured him.

'Like MC was coaching me?' he realised, unwrapping her from her shirt with delight, hot stains of colour creeping into his cheeks.

'Exactly.' She reached down to pull his shirt from his breeches. 'We've both been coached by pros. Now we're ready to ride together.'

He may have been coached by a pro, but MC had never possessed a Wonderbra. Rory gave up wrestling with the fastening and settled for feeling the parcel through the wrapping.

'Wow,' he reached out and cupped one of her improbably globe-like breasts. 'I really shouldn't approve of these, but they feel amazing.'

It wobbled strangely under his touch. Then it capsized. Faith froze, panicking that he would no longer fancy her without boobs.

For a moment Rory looked terrified, thinking he'd hurt her. Realisation dawning, he peered at the chicken fillet. 'You didn't have cosmetic surgery?'

'Of course not. You told me not to.'

'But I thought you went ahead and did it anyway?'

Faith swallowed uncomfortably. 'You mean all these months and you haven't even *looked*?' It didn't say a lot for his devotion.

But Rory's pewter gaze was positively eating up her body. 'I've looked, Faith. Believe me, I've looked at this amazing woman I'm in love with, who is the most beautiful woman I know, who almost blinds me. But I thought I'd lost you, that you'd moved on. I wanted the real you back, the one who was always in my case about something, who was just as beautiful, just as amazing, just as gorgeous in every way.' His eyes brimmed with love.

Turning pink with pleasure, Faith let out a little squeak of happiness.

'You were always perfect. These are fun . . .' He pulled out the second chicken fillet, 'but I *love* these.' He dipped his head to kiss the treasure trove beneath.

Making love with Rory seemed the most natural thing in the

world to Faith. He was so familiar and so special, his lips and fingers on her body just burnt her love all the more indelibly. It *was* making love, she realised as he shuddered to a climax inside her and her heart seemed to fill up the rest of her shaking, tingling body. She loved him now more than ever. And they could make more and more and more of it for as long as they lived, like a never-ending love-making factory.

As they sank back on the mattress, sweaty and sated, they heard feet clattering up the lorry steps.

Rory just had time to reach out to pull the curtain across when Tash walked into the living area carrying two bottles of champagne, Beetroot at her heels, followed by Hugo with Cora dangling around his neck and Amery on his hip.

'Oh, they must have popped out,' she realised. 'Go and check the stables, will you? They might be helping Franny pack up the trunks.'

Grumbling, Hugo clanked out again, still with Amery. Behind the curtain, Rory rested his cheek on Faith's hot, naked chest and listened to her heartbeat hammering in his ear. In the living area they could hear Tash clattering about packing up the lorry living, while Cora sang 'Nick Nack Paddywack' and clambered all over the seats.

'Watch!' she announced, holding up the dropped Rolex.

'That's odd.' Tash took it from her and placed it carefully back in its box on the table.

As she washed up all the plastic plates and cups and put them back in their storage boxes for travelling in the cupboards, Cora – who was very in to climbing – ascended the ladder steps to the Luton and peered around the curtain.

'Hello Rory!' she greeted him brightly.

'Hi,' he smiled back.

'Hello Face!'

'Hi,' Faith waved politely.

At this, Tash let out a bleat and Cora was hastily removed. 'Ohmygod I'm sorry!'

But at that moment Hugo thumped back in. 'No sign of them, but look who I *did* find.'

'Hi.' It was Lough's dry, Kiwi voice, sounding distinctly awkward.

In contrast, Hugo was unusually conciliatory. 'I've insisted he joins us for a drink.'

'That's lovely,' Tash blustered. 'But can we all go outside?'

Hugo didn't appear to be listening. 'He's just told me who was behind the smear campaign, and you are not going to *believe* how bloody thick we all were not to see it under our noses, Lough here being stupidest of all.'

'Thanks.' Lough let out his gruff, embarrassed laugh.

'We're practically brothers-in-law.' Hugo popped a champagne cork. 'Being stupid is a prerequisite – look at Ben here.' He welcomed the third man into the box.

'Just popped in to congratulate the Midwinter boy,' he hawed. 'He not here?'

Tash tried again. 'Hi Ben, do you think you could just turn around and lead the – oh.'

Then there was another voice with a distinctive Swedish accent that Rory knew straight away. 'Tash, my darling! I hear you have champagne.'

'Yes, Stefan.' Tash was getting more and more flustered. 'The thing is – congratulations on your second place by the way – the thing is, oh hi there, Kirsty.'

'You're having another baby!' Kirsty whooped. 'That's great news.'

'Budge up!' ordered a familiar bark as Gus Moncrieff joined the fray. 'Getting a bit crowded around this doorway.'

'Perhaps we should all go outside, then?' Tash suggested hopelessly.

'Don't be daft, it's starting to rain.' Penny's distinctive laugh rang out as another champagne cork popped. 'Have you heard the gossip? Pete Rafferty has made Marie-Clair an offer she simply cannot refuse for that lovely black mare Kevin rides . . . rumour is Sylva Frost is going to compete it . . .'

'No!' Stefan gasped.

'I heard he was going to take it to America . . .'

'Is it true Lem's run off to join a Cossack stunt-riding troupe, Lough?'

'Did he really try to kill Hugo at Badminton? It's all round the lorry park.'

'I thought they'd all be far more interested in talking about Rory's romantic stunt.'

'Oh, wasn't that gorgeous?'

Behind the curtain, Rory started to kiss Faith again. Ardour quickly revitalised, he quietly shifted himself on top of her, reaching down to lift her leg.

She raised her eyebrows.

He said nothing, but she knew exactly what he was thinking. In the gypsy life of three day eventers, where everybody was crammed cheek-by-jowl in tiny horsebox living quarters in lorry parks in muddy fields, they would soon get very accustomed to this. They might as well start practising straight away.

'Don't Rory and Faith make a lovely couple?' Kirsty was saying.

Making love just a few feet away, Rory and Faith couldn't agree more.

Chapter 90

November that year

'SURPRISE!'

Friends appeared out of cupboards and from under tables; they came down from upstairs and up from the cellars; they burst out of side rooms, emerged from behind the curtains and flooded in from the yard. There were more waiting in a marquee discreetly erected at the back of the house, yet more on the lawn and even a few early drunks hiding in the pool, teeth chattering. Cars soon started flooding in as the second wave of guests arrived, cramming every available parking space. A hired coach full of event riders who had block-booked a local hotel dispatched its load in the village lane before turning round to go and fetch more. The more enterprising had brought their horseboxes to stay in overnight, so that one of the Beauchamp's turn-out paddocks now resembled a horse trials lorry park.

'Did you know about this?' Tash asked Hugo in total astonishment.

'Only that your sister was going to arrange a small get-together for our anniversary.'

'But there are more people here than came to our wedding party. And why are so many of them wearing cowboy hats?'

Sophia had pulled out all the stops for what had become known as the Haydown Hooley to all its many co-conspirators. It was a huge, barn-storming party that had succeeded in taking Tash completely unawares and even caught Hugo broadside because Sophia and Ben had led him to believe that this would be a modest anniversary surprise. Instead, the party was also a belated fortieth birthday celebration for Hugo on an epic scale. He hadn't for a moment expected to return from the short break he and Tash had taken at Le Manoir after Pau trials to find three hundred people waiting for them at Haydown.

Lots of familiar faces were there, scores of event riders congregating from all over the country along with many events organisers, sponsors and owners old and new including Dillon and Fawn Rafferty, Venetia Gundry, the Bucklands and the Seatons. Many had flown in from overseas or delayed their return home at the end of the season. Marie-Clair was there along with Janet Madsen, Stefan, Kirsty and the Florida gang; Jenny and Dolf had come from Germany; Australian and New Zealand friends chattered and joked about the forthcoming long hauls home to see families over Christmas; and the O'Shaughnessys had flown in from LA.

All of Tash's disparate family were in on the act: her mother and Pascal with Polly, who had been keeping them unwitting captives in the Loire while Sophia was setting the scene; James and Henrietta; Matty and Sally; aunts and uncles and nieces and nephews galore. Hugo's tribe was smaller, but none the less conspicuous: Alicia had got the family diamonds out of the bank to sparkle brighter than anyone, and Hugo's brother Charles had brought his family along from London for a rare visit to his childhood home. Em and Tim had also made the voyage along the M4, along with India and Rufus, and a host of Tash's old college friends who she hadn't seen for years.

Hugo stood back for a moment to watch his wife shrieking and jumping up and down as she was reunited with a gaggle of equally happy, tearful, squealing women. He was incredibly humbled to realise that they had so many people whom they could count as friends and that so many of them had made a gargantuan effort to be there. Some had travelled thousands of miles. Others had merely walked up the road or across the courtyard, like the Bells and the Carolls, the Maccombe and Fosbourne villagers, Rory and Faith and the Moncrieffs, but for them it had been one of the toughest journeys of all. Their marriage had been in injury time since the exposure of Gus's affair with Lucy Field, but it was finally looking as though they might make it through too.

Gus was among the first to congratulate his surprised host.

'Can't believe they've pulled it off. You should have seen this place yesterday – marquee in the wrong place, catering vans stuck in the mud, portaloos facing the wrong way. Every time I hacked past your sister-in-law was standing in the same place in the garden shouting into a mobile phone. It was only the third time I came through the village that I realised her heels had sunk and she couldn't budge. Fourth time past, just the shoes were left, like she'd combusted.'

'Sophia's amazing,' Hugo laughed.

'Dread to think what it's costing you.'

'Rory's paying for it as a thank-you.'

'He can certainly afford to,' Gus pointed out as he spotted the Grand Slam victor being fêted from all sides. Rory, whose second place in Pau the previous week had now secured the top spot in the FEI Classics ranking and a handsome prize pot to add to his many other accolades, was currently the biggest star of eventing, with the fattest annual prize-money cache on record. 'I'm surprised the path from his cottage isn't paved with gold.'

'We all have purple patches,' Hugo told him.

'Penny would say I just have cross patches.' Gus grabbed more champagne from a passing waiter and raised the glass in his friend's honour. 'But to cast aside my customary malaise for a moment, congratulations on eight years with that super wife of yours, and on your ever-expanding brood of little Beauchampions. I gather you're planning to bring them all on the road next season?'

Hugo grinned, raising his own glass. 'Best to start them young, we feel.'

'Well one's jumped clear around Blenheim already,' Gus pointed out, referring to Tash's recent win while four months pregnant. He looked around at all the decorations and props that had been used to dress up the beautiful old house and hired marquee to make it look like a Wild West ranch, from bunting to swinging saloon doors, sawdust and straw bales; there were even gigantic cacti dotted about and the odd strategically placed tumbleweed ball. 'It's like walking into an episode of *Bonanza*.'

'You wait till you see the automatic rodeo bull. Brian Sedgewick's already pulled a groin muscle and is threatening to sue, I hear.'

'The Milky Bar Kid can pay for that, too,' Gus sniffed, finding it a lot harder than Hugo to forgive Rory his current success.

But Hugo didn't resent his protégé enjoying his good fortune, because he'd more than proven his loyalty and worth lately. Despite the well publicised ride-off between Hugo and Lough, it was Rory who had been offered the lucrative Mogo deal. In an extraordinarily unwise but very loyal show of solidarity, all three men had told the company in a collective letter to get stuffed.

Hugo missed the income – and clothes – but not the constant pressure and fear that came with having so many eggs in one basket. He had been working hard on replacing them and already had the makings of a good spread of sponsorship between four or five companies for next year that looked set to match the Mogo fund. And eventing's biggest new owner – who now had horses in training with Hugo, Lough *and* Rory – was about to drop in on the party.

Making a show-stopping arrival in the Rockfather's private helicopter, Sylva Frost couldn't wait to show off a diamond as big as a hazelnut on her ring finger, her engagement having been announced via a sixteen-page *Cheers!* exclusive just that week. Her craggy-faced fiancé beamed proudly at her side.

'I have told my darling Pete that he must now buy me a horse called Diamond to go with the others,' she told Hugo and Tash amid lots of air kissing. All her new horses were named after precious metals and stones: Sylva's Gold was with Lough, Sylva's Sapphire with Rory and, most recently, Sylva's Ruby and Sylva's Platinum with Tash and Hugo.

'I want a new horse called Sylva's Diamond. Can you fix that for me, Hugo, darlink?'

'I've got one that's just come back from an injury and looks bloody good,' he suggested. 'It was leased last season, but that's lapsed and the owner wants to sell.'

'Is it grey?'

He shook his head. 'Bay with a heart-shaped star.' Heart was confounding expectations and his long unlucky streak by staying sound and sane, and looking set to take the world by storm the following season. Devoted to small, evil companion Soul, he no longer tried to escape from stables and fields at all, and had relaxed in his work too. He still had that touch of brilliance which would always make him a sharp ride, but it was easier to control now that he was mellowed by love.

But Sylva wasn't interested. 'I want a grey one.'

Hugo had a lot of demanding, eccentric female owners, but few had such strange buying criteria as Sylva, who chose the colour first. Not that he minded. Having resisted her determination to buy herself in to the sport for so long, he was amazed to find her a very supportive and loyal owner, and gratifyingly hands-off.

'The bay's stablemate is grey,' he pointed out cheerfully.

'Pure white?'

'Indeed, but I warn you he's rather on the small side and very bad tempered.'

'No matter. He sounds perfect, darlink.' Her eyes scanned the room, locking on to a high-grade celebrity target with pinpoint accuracy. 'Who are Dillon and Fawn talking to?'

'Rory and Faith.'

'No, the other couple.'

Hugo vaguely recognised the tall, dark-haired girl, but her red-haired companion had his back to them. 'No idea.'

'I'm sure that's Prince Harry. We must say hello!' She whisked Pete off in the direction of his famous son and daughter-in-law, while Tash gathered Hugo to greet more old friends.

Left unmarked, Gus let out a melancholy sigh. 'I used to have a horse called Diamond Geezer,' he told nobody in particular with a heartfelt sigh as he remembered the good old days. 'Best horse I ever had.'

Penny stepped in beside him. 'The best wife you ever had would like to dance.'

His sad, bloodhound eyes looked to hers, seeking forgiveness. 'Really?'

The Moncrieffs made up a set with the O'Shaughnessys and Matty and Sally French. Protesting loudly, Niall and his old friend Matty tried their hardest to get out of the Kentucky Reel, but their wives had a very firm grip. Only Gus obediently walked straight on to the floor to take his place opposite Penny, knowing that there was no point in putting up a fight.

'Sophia's excelled herself again,' Matty grumbled good-naturedly as they waited for the caller to start shouting. 'Even the ceiling's gingham.'

'Why a barn dance hooley?' asked Niall, flashing his big, charming smile at his wife, who was clapping her hands in time to the music and looking eager.

'I guess they're celebrating eight years of hooley matrimony,' Matty suggested as the caller coughed into the mic in a fake Southern accent:

'Grab your dogs and grab your gun, let's start to dance and have some fun!'

Two minutes later, all three couples were weeping with laughter as they twirled and whirled and do-si-doed. Proving remarkably talented, Matty whipped a delighted Sally under his arm and around his back, flipping her this way and that like Patrick Swayze in his prime, and reminding her of their student days at May balls. Niall, a great Irish wolfhound let loose amid obedient collies, was less skilled but added greatly to the hilarity. And Gus and Penny astounded everybody by locking eyes, lifting chins and dancing with the elegant skill of a pair of dressage riders performing a pas de deux as they trotted this way and that, performing airs above the ground and only letting out the occasional naughty buck, all those hours spent schooling together paying off.

Long after the other four had all retired exhausted to a table for champagne, the Moncrieffs were still out there like young Elizabeth and Robert Dudley at court, flirting deliciously with their eyes, trust starting to rebuild in the most unexpected setting.

Dillon was grateful that his father's loud complaints about his sciatica meant their current group forfeited the dancefloor. Forming a set in which he had slept with all four of the women would be far too awkward, and Fawn was still marking him very closely.

Not that she had any reason to be suspicious. All those ex-lovers were deeply in love, not least Faith who radiated so much happiness it was like standing next to a glowing chiminea. With Rory blazing at her side, they were warmer than any Caribbean sunset. Despite his recent unbeatable form, Rory was far more boastful of Faith's success than his own, and was her greatest supporter as she continued to climb the eventing ladder. As he towed her off to introduce her to Janet Madsen, Dillon found himself engulfed in a cloud of Sylva's latest signature fragrance.

'Is that *Prince Harry* with Nell?' she whispered excitedly, her false eyelashes tickling his ear.

Dillon had been surprised but none the less pleased to see Nell at the party, along with her very dashing red-haired companion, whom she'd introduced simply as Harry. She looked fabulous and seemed genuinely happy. The way they held hands non-stop was very sweet.

Now he laughed, shaking his head as he turned to Sylva. 'He's something in the City, apparently, and likes eventing at weekends. Nell was going out with his father Piers for a bit, but I gather the son rose more often.'

The irony was not lost on Sylva, who let out a long, kittenish giggle and patted his cheek. She was not quite as bad a prospect as a stepmother as Dillon might have feared, and they got on surprisingly well on the occasions they met, although Fawn mistrusted her deeply. Even now, she hurriedly broke off from telling Nell that she'd encouraged the girls to embrace feminism from pre-school and drew him back to her side.

'I hear you and Pete plan to get married at the Abbey?' she asked Sylva coolly.

It was a question guaranteed to trigger the little Slovakian into a long and detailed description of her grand plans, as spearheaded by wedding-organiser extraordinaire, Mama, who made Sophia Malvern's party planning look small fry. With a good-natured groan, Pete headed outside to smoke a cigar, having heard it all before.

About to follow his father, Dillon found Nell's hand on his arm, her face defensive yet curious.

'You look well,' she told him stiffly.

'I was thinking the same about you,' he smiled.

At her side, handsome Harry cast an indulgent look at the love of his life. It was what she'd wanted all along, Dillon realised. The hotel room fetish, non-stop tantrums and desperate demands for commitment were just the glass casket she'd been sealed in to and tried to break by hurling stones. She had just wanted to be saved by the dashing prince with unconditional love.

'How's Gigi?'

'Great.' Her voice softened. 'She and Harry adore one another. Your girls?'

He nodded. 'They're fabulous.'

Despite this outward politeness, her sea-green eyes were drawing layers off his face as the tide of hurt finally retreated. Their relationship may have ended badly, but neither could deny they were in a better place now.

Nell dropped her voice to a breath, glancing across at Fawn. 'I knew you two would get back together one day.'

'You did?'

'You're a one-woman man, Dillon. All the best ones are. Look at Hugo.'

They turned to look just as Hugo was cornered by Venetia Gundry in a plunging checked shirt and figure-hugging leather chaps, which was unfortunate timing. Wrapping her arms around him, she pinned him up against a stack of straw bales and branded his cheeks with red lipstick.

Dillon felt Fawn's hand slip in to his, and was immensely grateful to know that she'd be straight in with a pitchfork if any woman tried that on him.

They wandered outside to find Pete standing back, admiring the house which had been floodlit for the occasion, the flint panels amid its mellow strawberry bricks gleaming like silverwork.

'Nice gaff, this.' He chewed the end of his cigar. 'I might buy it. Make a good wedding gift for Sylva, doncha think?'

Laughing, Dillon shook his head. 'I knew you'd say that if you came here. I think you've got more chance of buying Balmoral.'

'Fair dos,' he cackled. 'In that case, I'll stick to Plan A and get a big Slovakian castle that the mother-in-law can live in.'

Still inside the marquee, Sylva was eyeing Nell Cottrell's boyfriend suspiciously. 'You know you really are the spitting image of Prince Harry, darlink.'

He gave her the ghost of a wink.

Butterflying around the party as she had been all night, bump to the fore, Tash stopped at her brother Matty's table to catch up and watch the action on the dancefloor. It looked huge fun.

'I must get Hugo to come and give me a spin.'

'Are you sure that's wise in your condition?' Matty asked piously, sounding like their father.

'It *is* my third,' she countered. 'And I'm only five months gone. I'm still riding.'

'You're *not*?' Matty looked appalled.

'Ignore him – he was like this every time I was pregnant,' Sally told her. 'Keep it reel – you dance if you want to.'

'Why wait for Hugo?' Niall stood up and took her arm graciously, not noticing that behind his back Zoe and Sally were issuing frantic hand signals for Tash to watch her feet.

Tash was certainly reeling from all the friends and family who greeted her with such affection everywhere she went, never more so than on the dancefloor where she was so elated and dizzy that she hardly noticed Niall stamping all over her flat pumps as she spun between them all, tears of happiness in her eyes.

Then she suddenly found herself standing opposite Hugo, and the lights dimmed as the band struck up a beautiful, mournful bluegrass number.

Tash sank into his arms, breathing in his perfect smell. She rested her cheek in the hollow crook beneath his chin as they started to sway. She was so giddy with euphoria that she didn't immediately pick up on his tension.

'Oh that's so romantic – look at them.' Henrietta sighed tearfully from the table she was sharing with Alexandra and Pascal, a rather uptight James, Hugo's mother Alicia and a lovely couple called the Seatons.

'Hugo and Tash are still so terribly in love, aren't they?' Gin Seaton agreed wistfully, glancing at her husband of almost five decades who hadn't danced with her since their youngest daughter had got married fifteen years earlier.

'Oh what are they doing?' Alexandra demanded, unable to see past one of the alarming six-foot cacti that Sophia had posted around the room.

'Having a bop, obviously,' James muttered stiffly, wishing Henrietta hadn't insisted they all stick around together like this. He found sitting with his current wife and ex-wife incredibly awkward.

But Henrietta and Alexandra felt no such embarrassment. Increasingly close these days, they had been chattering away all night; about Lough and Beccy who were currently in New Zealand but due back any day and planning to move in together at the little yard he was renting near Salisbury ('Beccy said she met his father yesterday, which came as rather a shock because I'm sure Tash told me he was dead'); about Polly, who was scandalising her fashion college ('She's so lazy, she stuck two bits of gaffer tape on a model's nipples for her first design show and was called a genius by someone who'd worked with Gaultier'); about Em's return to work and Sophia's plans to start up a three day event at Holdham to follow on the heels of her successful music festival. Most of all, they enthused about Tash and Hugo, and how blissfully happy they were after such a shaky year.

They both took as proof of total marital perfection the fact that the couple had secretly commissioned almost identical anniversary presents for one another – from Hugo a bronze sculpture of Tash's beloved late stallion Snob, now proudly leaping a brick and flint plinth on the rear lawn, and from Tash a bronze of Hugo's late, great horse Bodybuilder standing by the gate of Flat Pad where the two horses were buried.

'How could they afford it?'

'They each sold a horse to pay for them. Rather ironic, when you think about it.'

'Oh, what are they doing now?' Alexandra craned round the cactus.

'Tash has her arms around his neck,' Henrietta told her. 'And he's muttering sweet nothings in her ear.'

'How wonderful,' she sighed.

Tash's bubble of happiness deflated slightly as a very irritated Hugo told her in a fierce undertone that he didn't like her dancing with Niall, 'especially not when you're pregnant. He's always had a perverted thing about pregnant women, especially you.'

'He hasn't,' she scoffed as they swayed romantically in the centre of the dance floor.

'You two practically had phone sex when you were pregnant with Amery,' he hissed. The deep jealousy about Tash's ex was hardwired through him.

But he wasn't the only one who still harboured long-held, badly buried suspicions.

Cocooned by her pregnancy since Burghley, Tash had sat on her fears like a hen on a nest of eggs. In the hectic end of season mêlée, she'd found no more evidence of Hugo's adultery, but she remained mistrustful. There may have been no incriminating messages stored on his phone when she'd sneaked a look, and there had been no obvious floristry purchases: she'd started shopping in Waitrose again, and the chatty manageress sympathised that romance must have faded a little now that Hugo had stopped buying her flowers each week. Yet Tash couldn't shake the dread that snaked around her throat late at night, especially when Hugo was away. And tonight it was asphyxiating her. It burst out from nowhere, ransacking her unconscious and charging like a bull from the back of her mind.

'You can talk,' she muttered into his chest.

'I can talk?' He steered her through the bodies canoodling on the dancefloor.

'Who exactly is V for a start?'

'V?'

'Yes, bloody V,' she wailed, leaning back to look him in the eye. 'The V who texts you. The one you meet for secret trysts on cross-country courses all over England.'

One or two couples nearby were starting to look across at them worriedly.

Hugo's eyes darted. He looked cornered.

'Is she the one you used to buy flowers for at Waitrose every week?' Tash demanded, suddenly fighting tears.

'What the fuck are you talking about?' He had stopped dancing.

'You were spotted!' she accused, voice rising. 'The manager told me you were in there most weeks buying flowers.'

'When was this?'

'Last year.'

'Last *year*?'

She nodded. 'Just before the Olympics.'

Nobody around them could ignore the fact that they were arguing. The band tried to play louder, but the happy couple were very clearly having a screaming match on the dancefloor.

'I have no idea what you're talking about.'

Dancing into range, the Moncrieffs paused nearby and Gus stepped forward, prodded by Penny. 'Couldn't help overhearing. Might be able to help you out on that one.'

Tash and Hugo both turned in surprise, one with tears in her eyes, the other daggers in his.

Gus cleared his throat awkwardly. 'I was the one buying the flowers in Waitrose.'

'*You* were?' Tash and Hugo spoke at once.

'Yes.' He hung his head with an apologetic glance at his wife. 'Manageress there recognised that I was an event rider once – she'd seen something about me in the paper – and started asking a few questions. Put me on the spot. When she asked my name, I said it was Hugo Beauchamp.'

Tash gaped at him. 'Why?'

He stared at the floor, swallowing unhappily.

Penny took Gus's hand in hers. 'The flowers weren't for me, Tash.'

With a mournful groan Gus pulled his wife to his chest and they slowly danced away, lost in their world of slow-release absolution.

Tash's eyes flooded further as she watched them retreat. Then Hugo suddenly put a firm arm around her shoulder. 'Walk this way.'

'What are they doing now?' Alexandra demanded across the room, while trying to manhandle the cactus out of the way.

'Walking towards our table,' Henrietta whispered, agog.

Hugo was as mannerly and charming as always, apologising for the interruption.

'Gin darling, would you mind if we had a quiet word?' he asked their table companion.

With a baffled look to the circle around her, Gin Seaton patted bullfrog husband Tony on the knee and followed the Beauchamps out of the marquee into a very chilly starlit night, the light of the near-full moon gleaming off the bronze quarters of the new statue of Tash's famous stallion on the main stretch of lawn.

Virginia Seaton stood tall between the couple, an elegant sighthound between two snarling gundogs.

'This,' Hugo raised an open palm to her, 'is "V".'

'*You*'re V?' Tash had known Gin for over a decade as one of her husband's stalwart supporters and owners, a great, old-fashioned fan of eventing who continued to champion and rally for Hugo even though the Seatons no longer had any horses competing.

'My husband doesn't know I'm still involved,' she admitted. 'I bought a half share in Sir Galahad using a legacy my late aunt left me, and then a couple of other legs including Oil Tanker, but he mustn't know.'

'Why didn't you tell me?' Tash looked from one to the other.

'I swore Hugo to secrecy,' Gin apologised. 'Your sister and Ben own the other half of Gal plus an equal share in Tank, and I'm terrified this will get back to Tony. I had no idea you would think our text messages were in any way naughty, although I confess I got a bit nosy when I knew things were bad between you. Hugo has become such a chum, and I adore you both. Gosh, I can't believe you thought we were having an affair. How thrilling! That really has cheered me up.'

Over seventy, with a body as gangly as a scarecrow's, hair like a teased-out Brillo Pad and thread veins running through her cheeks and across her chest, she was no great temptress, but when she headed back to the marquee she had a skip and a wiggle in her step as never before.

In the marquee the bluegrass music played on, a dolefully pretty song about a soldier returning from war to find his wife with another man.

Hugo lent back against the bronze horse and eyed Tash warily, uncertain if he'd been forgiven.

'Why are you so secretive?' she asked him.

'I'm not.'

'Women throw themselves at you.'

'Quite painful if they land on me at speed.' His true-blue gaze almost wiped her out with the force of its love. 'I could never desire another woman as I desire you. Never. I was designed to adore one woman for life, and to my eternal gratitude that's you, Tash.'

She let out a whimper of delight and, throwing caution to the wind, joined the masses in jumping on him.

She was perfecting her Meg Ryan leap, but it still wasn't quite there yet, especially when five months pregnant.

He let out a low groan of pain and toppled over backwards, as he usually did when she tried the move. Wife wrapped around him, he landed with a thud on the grass beneath his recently commissioned bronze. Pinned beneath the shadow of the only other arrogant bugger ever to threaten his primacy in Tash's life, Hugo willingly acquiesced as Tash covered him with kisses.

★

'What are they doing now?' Alexandra demanded from inside the marquee, where she was now tethered to the saguaro cactus by her piano shawl, which was caught on a hundred tiny needles. Beside her Henrietta was carefully trying to unpick it without damaging the antique silk.

'They appear to be copulating on the lawn,' her ex-husband told her, afforded a clear view through the plastic windows to the flood-lit gardens.

'Oh how lovely,' she smiled. 'Do you remember when we used to do that, James?'

There was a loud ripping sound as a silk piano shawl was torn from a giant cactus.

Party organiser Sophia broke the tension by sweeping in along the tented link from the main house and stopping urgently at their table. 'Has anybody seen Tash and Hugo? Only the caterers are ready to bring the cake through.'

'I'd tell them to leave it five minutes,' James said, clearing his throat.

'Apparently they're making love outside,' Alexandra said brightly.

'They're just spooning,' Gin Seaton pointed out, having better eyesight.

'Bloody typical! We now have to extinguish eight sparklers and forty candles. And what on earth are you doing to that cactus, Mummy? It's on loan from Kew.' Sophia swept away again, thriving on the drama.

'Faith, would you do me the honour . . .'

In the lodge cottage, where they had escaped from the party for an hour alone, Rory proposed: a full-on, traditional, down-on-one-knee, ring-in-a-box cliché of a proposal that made Faith laugh, cry and nod her head frantically all at the same time.

'Is that a yes?' he asked worriedly, still on one knee.

'It's a yes!' she sobbed.

After a great deal of kissing, more sobbing and more laughter, Rory reminded her that, being an old-fashioned sort, he would need to ask her father's permission.

'Which one?' she laughed.

'I thought it was only fair to ask all of them.' He kissed her again and then leant back, tracing her jawline wonderingly as he looked at her face. 'You're the most beautiful girl in the world.'

For the first time in her life Faith didn't deny it. Right now, she felt more beautiful than she had ever imagined possible.

'Where are we going to live?' she asked later, after they had made love in front of the open fire, only suffering one small burn from a leaping coal and a minor bite when they rolled on top of Twitch, who had been roasting himself on the hearthrug.

'Ah.' He looked down at her anxiously. 'I've been thinking about that. Would you mind very much *not* moving back to the Lodes Valley? Jules has made an offer for the business, and with my Grand Slam money I think we might just about be able to afford a proper yard of our own.'

'Where were you thinking?'

'Well I was talking to Stefan and Kirsty earlier and they said they could definitely help us out finding a set-up like theirs, so I was rather thinking—'

'America?!' she shrieked.

'Is that such a bad idea?' He looked anxious again, but from the way she was pulling him back down on top of her and hooking a long leg around his haunches, drawing him into the most rapturous of long, breathless kisses, he guessed it wasn't such a bad idea after all.

Just audible from the lodge cottage, the band in the marquee struck up 'Take Me Home, Country Roads'.

For a moment, Faith stopped kissing him and tilted her head. 'Oh my God, listen!'

'Yeah,' he laughed quietly, 'that's pretty appropriate.'

'No – not that, listen to who's singing.'

Nobody could mistake that trademark gravelly voice ripping every male hormone from the song and punching it out to the audience, instantly turning a John Denver classic into a rock anthem. Harmonising with that, his voice as uniquely melodic and heart-breakingly emotional as his father's was whisky and smoke, came a lilting descant, another aural curveball that sounded mesmerising.

On stage in a party marquee on the Berkshire downs, for the first time ever, rock legend Pete Rafferty was dueting with his son Dillon, accompanied by a lot of very drunken, crooning event riders.

'We could ask them to sing that at our wedding.' Rory smiled down at her, lips diving in.

They kissed through three verses, rapturous applause and an encore.

When the Denver hit had reached its culmination with another huge, explosive cheer from the marquee, the piano struck up with Dillon still at its keys and his father at the microphone, a song so suited to his sexy timbre that all the hairs in their already goosebumped bodies stood on end. This time, he was joined in the duet by a female voice of immense, spell-binding power, possibly even more ravaged and sexual than the Rockfather himself.

It was so good that even Faith and Rory had to stop kissing to listen.

'*Who the* . . .?' Faith laughed in wonder as the woman, her tone so sultry and lived-in that Janis Joplin could have come back to life for one night, told her audience all about making whoopee.

'Who cares?' Rory's lips traced her throat again. 'You heard the song . . .'

Watching the couple grouchily from his budged-up spot alongside the warm fender, a stars and stripes handkerchief around his neck as his master's concession to the hoedown, Twitch crossed his paws in front of him and rested his chin on top of them, unaware that before very much longer he would be swapping the rats and squirrels of West Berkshire for the opossums, raccoons and chipmunks of West Virginia while his master made whoopee a lot.

Hugo and Tash had wandered out of the light spilling from the marquee to the shadows of the gardens, stopping behind every tree to kiss and ending up against the metal rails alongside Flat Pad, where they stopped by the second bronze horse.

'I think your mother's singing on stage,' Tash said, inclining her head to listen to the distant duet.

Not caring, Hugo kissed her again until her ears were muffled by heartbeats. When she resurfaced, the band was playing 'Wonderful Tonight'.

Slipping his hands to her waist, Hugo lifted his wife aboard the bronze horse, and then hoisted himself up behind her.

'Want to ride against me?' he breathed in her ear.

She swivelled around until she was facing him. 'I'd rather ride with you.'

Epilogue

Pau Three Day Event, a year later

The bay gelding was a notoriously difficult ride, particularly show-jumping. He charged into fences as though he wanted to break through them rather than leap over them, then at the last minute crouched and sprang like a big-cat attack. It was nerve-racking stuff for spectators and jockey alike, particularly with so much riding on it.

Charge, crouch, ping. Charge, crouch, whoof!

He rattled poles and made the crowds in the stands gasp.

They were the last combination to jump, the overnight leaders with less than a fence in hand to secure victory. The FEI Classics series had gone right to the wire too, and everything was riding on this round. If they went clear they would win the series after the closely contended battle that had been running throughout the season between the two best known rivals in eventing.

Charge, crouch, spring.

They turned for the final fence, the whites of the horse's eyes gleaming, nostrils two red furnaces set in that smoky muzzle, his distinctive heart-shaped star lifting higher as his head shot up and he locked on to the striped poles and charged, pulling the reins from his rider's hands and taking off almost a stride too early.

The surge of power was spectacular, the muscles in his gleaming haunches shifting beneath the copper skin like polished pennies pouring from a slot machine. But it still seemed an impossible leap.

Tash closed her eyes and waited for the sound of thudding poles. Instead she heard cheering.

'He's won?' She opened her eyes again. 'He's won!'

Despite having a baby in a papoose and a toddler to each side of her, she started to run round in excited circles, cheering gleefully. Then she rushed forwards to kiss the winner as he exited the arena after a lap of honour and jumped from the horse to claim her.

Julia Ditton was on hand with her microphone, now reporting for Eurosport after a rather ignoble departure from the BBC following the now infamous Burghley Bollocks incident.

She tried to get a word with the man who had just won the biggest eventing prize of the year, but couldn't get past the mass of supporters, well-wishers, family and connections crowding round him, not least his wife, who appeared to have leaped aboard him like Meg Ryan in *Top Gun*, baby papoose and all, both laughing and kissing delightedly.

Giving up, she turned to the runner-up who was standing near by, waiting to add his congratulations, and she thrust the microphone at him. 'You won the Olympic silver to Hugo's gold, and now you've just lost out here at Pau,' she pointed out rather ungraciously. 'So tell us, Lough, how does it feel to be the bridesmaid but never the bride?'

Lough rarely laughed, especially in public, but today a delicious, deep rumble of noise bubbled up like a hot spring and he gave Julia and the camera the benefit of his rare and delectable smile. 'Actually, I'm marrying the groom next week . . .' He glanced over his shoulder.

Leading his horse around behind him the groom in question blew him a kiss.

When Beccy Sergeant and Lough Strachan married in All Saints Church in Ascot it was a quiet family affair. Lough's mother and sister travelled from New Zealand; James gave his stepdaughter away with tremendous pride; Henrietta, Em and Tash cried happily non-stop; the Beauchamps' new baby Winifred – known to all as Whoopee – cried for five minutes before being removed by a doting Hugo. And Sophia, sharing quiet asides with her mother throughout the ceremony, was so swept away by the simplicity and romance of the occasion that she didn't make one bitchy comment.

Afterwards, they had a wedding party at Benedict, mostly close eventing friends, the Haydown and Lime Tree crowds, Lough's New Zealand team-mates and new friends from their Salisbury base.

The couple delayed their honeymoon by a week because they wanted to spend time with Lough's visiting family, and because they had another wedding to go to . . .

*

A week later, Faith and Rory married in the chapel at Fox Oddfield Abbey, which had been granted a special licence when Pete and Sylva had married there earlier in the year, in an extravaganza that had lasted for three days, three *Cheers!* spreads and three episodes of *Sylva's Shadow*.

A hundred guests crammed in for the ceremony. Rory's mother and sister wore rival hats of such magnificent proportions that nobody on the groom's side could see past them; Faith was given away by all four of her fathers; Anke and Tash cried happily throughout; baby Whoopee cried unhappily for five minutes before being removed by a doting Hugo.

Afterwards, they held a reception with two hundred additional guests in the main house. It was a joyful, raucous, debauched party typical of the eventing crowd, the highlight of which was a one-night-only repeat performance by the Rockfather and his son.

As the first bars of 'Take Me Home, Country Roads' struck up, the newly married couple took to the dancefloor.

'I'm home.' Rory buried his face in his wife's sweet-smelling neck.

Faith threaded her fingers through her husband's hair and felt her heartstrings knot ever tighter to his. 'And dry.'

They swayed deliciously to the beat, Rory's hipflask jabbing into her ribs through his morning suit. She pulled it out and unscrewed the top.

Rory's cheeks coloured. 'I'll always be a badly behaved event rider . . .'

'Me too.' She lifted the flask to her lips, a smile breaking there as she tasted nothing but lemon barley water.